DESTINIES & RESOLUTIONS

An utterly gripping page-turner

FAITH MARTIN

writing as

MAXINE BARRY

Revised edition 2022
Joffe Books, London
www.joffebooks.com

First published in Great Britain in 1997

This paperback edition was first published
in Great Britain in 2022

Cover art by Dee Dee Book Covers

ISBN: 978-1-80405-573-1

PART I: DESTINIES

CHAPTER 1

Germany, 1939

The schloss belonged in a fairy tale — a castle of dreams. Its steepled and turreted towers stood tall and proud in the midnight sky as they looked down over lush, meadowed moonlit valleys. But its dungeons were full of prisoners, some dying, some dead already, while others sobbed in the darkness, heard only by the Gestapo officers who were their interrogators. A castle of nightmares, then, rather than dreams.

But on this night, Friday, 13 October 1939, the schloss was also playing host to a social extravaganza. For the guests, the only battle tonight was to be the best dressed, to have the most stunning *coiffure*, to dazzle with the best jewels. For the men, the arena was to be fought in front of Hitler's elite — to have the ear of Goebbels, to be watched with favour by Göring or even any of their leech-like underlings. And for this battle, the castle had been transformed. Floodlights lit up the moat, where swans swam under the windows, ready to pounce gracefully on any scraps thrown their way; brightly coloured paper lanterns hung from the portcullis, while music (Mozart, naturally) filled the night air.

Inside the flower-bedecked rooms, the clink of expensive crystal goblets, full of the best wines, fought for supremacy with the bright and brittle laughter of women. Instead of gunpowder smoke, the scent of imported Cuban cigars and finely mixed French cigarettes dissipated in the carefully perfumed air.

Outside, flirting with the mountain breeze, a huge red flag rippled in the crisp October night. Against its stark white centre, a huge black swastika was proudly visible, proclaiming the doctrine of the Third Reich to any and all who might have business on the lonely mountainside, high above sea level.

Wolfgang Helmut Mueller stepped out of the big black car that had transported him and his wife from their Berlin mansion and surveyed the scene with a brief and coldly satisfied smile, before turning to help his five-months-pregnant wife from the back of the car.

'Trust Olga to hold her party here,' Marlene Mueller commented bitchily. She took out a compact and checked her makeup. It was, as usual, flawless.

'The Goebbels will be here,' Wolfgang commented with suave satisfaction. 'She'll be desperate for her little soiree to outshine the Press Ball.'

'Of course. But I shall be the belle of *this* ball.' And Wolfgang didn't doubt it. His wife was stunningly beautiful, with white-blonde hair, and eyes truly a cornflower blue. Her skin, now thirty-six years old, was still flawless and wrinkle-free. Her one regret was that her pregnancy was beginning to show, spoiling the line of her usually svelte and slender figure.

Accompanying her husband into the schloss, she sighed deeply. The Führer was keen on German womanhood adding to the blonde, blue-eyed populace, and Wolfgang had insisted on another son. If only Helmut had been more to his father's liking, Marlene thought bitterly, she might have been spared this . . . this . . . inconvenience, for a second time. She thought briefly of her four-year-old son, waiting for them back in Berlin. He'd cried again when he'd heard that she and Wolfgang would be going out. Maybe, she thought, Wolfgang was right. The boy was a pitiful disappointment...

Her head came up and her smile raced into place as they stepped into the hall, the sound of the orchestra filtering sweetly through from the ballroom. By her side, Wolfgang stood tall and straight. At six feet two, with blond hair and blue eyes every bit as natural and remarkable as those of his wife, he knew that they were considered to be the racial ideal, in this, the sixth year of Hitler's reign.

Wolfgang was an aristocrat and, like most of his class, secretly despised the lower-class, ranting little tyrant, but even he had been forced to admit that Hitler had restored Germany's strength and pride in a remarkably short time. Now, his fatherland would have another chance to show the world that Germany was the true master of Europe.

They were announced at the top of a pink-marbled flight of stairs and envious eyes watched their triumphant descent. In the uniform of a Luftwaffe major, Wolfgang looked like a conquering hero of old, his reputation not at all suffering from his sheer good luck in having met, and flown with the late Baron von Richthofen, the notorious and much-feared Red Baron of the Great War.

'Wolfgang! Over here.'

Wolfgang nodded briskly at the colonel who beckoned him, and murmured a brief word to his wife, who inclined her head graciously. Accepting a glass of champagne from a circling waiter, she selected a lesser wife on which to sharpen her claws, and moved into the crowd, smiling like a shark.

Joseph Goebbels, Hitler's Minister for Public Enlightenment and Propaganda, lost no time in seeking out Wolfgang, who was a walking propaganda dream. With no Red Baron this time around, Germany needed another aerial ace to worship and adore, and Goebbels had selected Mueller for the job. With a beautiful wife and a blond-haired, blue-eyed son as the ultimate accessories, he was a rousing example of German manhood.

4

Wolfgang stiffened as Goebbels homed in on him. He would never be foolish enough to forget that, just as Goebbels had 'made' him, he could as easily break him again.

'Wolfgang, glad to see you could make it,' Goebbels greeted him, imperiously clicking his fingers to a passing waiter and selecting a fresh glass of a superior Rhine wine. 'I wasn't sure your wife was feeling up to it.'

'She wouldn't have missed it, Herr Goebbels, for all the world.' It was, both men suspected, something of an understatement. Marlene heartily approved of her husband's growing fame and power, and would do anything to ensure it continued.

Goebbels smiled. 'You are hoping for a girl this time?' he asked, nodding towards Marlene.

'No, I want another son,' Wolfgang said shortly.

'Oh?' Goebbels said, eyes narrowing. 'You named your firstborn . . . ?'

'Helmut, Herr Goebbels,' Wolfgang supplied reluctantly.

'He is not . . . satisfactory?' Goebbels went on, his voice as mild as milk, which immediately set off a klaxon in Wolfgang's brain.

'It's not that, Herr Goebbels. He is a fine boy, tall for his age, and already he can read and write. It's just that . . . I suppose I am slightly old-fashioned. I still believe a man cannot have too many sons.'

Goebbels laughed, well pleased with the reply. A son who was not healthy and perfect in every way had no place being born to one of the 'chosen' few. He began to talk of Poland.

Wolfgang felt an immediate sense of relief. It was not that he had lied about his son — his tutor was already raving about his intelligence. In fact, if he'd been asked to pinpoint the exact reasons for his disappointment in the boy, Wolfgang wouldn't have been able to do so. There was just something in the boy's eyes, the way he looked at you . . . He only knew he would be happier once Marlene had presented him with another son. He had the name all picked out — Hans, after his father.

'It appears that Finland is going to oppose Moscow,' Wolfgang said, steering the conversation firmly away from the subject of his family.

Goebbels nodded solemnly. 'Indeed, yes . . . ah, Wagner. I must confess to a weakness for Wagner,' he sighed, as the orchestra began to play a stirring piece. 'Come, meet your commander-in-chief,' Goebbels then ordered and, under Marlene's approving eye, her husband was led away to talk over important matters with some of the country's highest leaders.

She turned her thoughts back to dominating the party and approached the buffet table. Several dashing young SS officers waylaid her there, offering her the tastiest of delicacies arranged on the finest Dresden china. She accepted a little of the more prestigious offerings but declined the delicious desserts.

Shaking off her fawning audience, she walked through the spacious rooms to the interior balcony that overlooked the ballroom. Everywhere there was the flash of jewels and the swirl of sumptuous skirts. After surveying the scene for several minutes, Marlene was finally assured that her own necklace of sapphires and pink diamonds was the finest there.

Her eyes narrowed as they sought out her husband and found him dancing with Magda Goebbels. Good. Once Wolfgang was established as *the* darling of the Luftwaffe, she could begin to rest on her laurels. She laughed happily. Excitement was in the air tonight.

Germany was poised on the brink of a glorious and, this time, victorious war. She spied the leader of the *Bund Deutscher Mädel*, the League of German Girls, and graciously approached, preening under the young woman's almost worshipful gaze. Marlene was becoming as famous and powerful — in her own way — as her husband; again she laughed happily. A pleasant night of backbiting and compliments stretched ahead.

It was past midnight when Wolfgang excused himself from the presence of the Italian Minister for Popular Culture and trotted up a spiral staircase in search of a toilet. Opening the first door he came to, his eyes encountered only a dark room, decorated with Louis XVI bergères and an authentic Aubusson carpet. He was about to leave when a slight sound made him hesitate. A soft but unmistakable groan was quickly followed by a harsher one. There was a mirror on the far wall opposite him, reflecting a rounded settee and the couple lying on it.

The girl was no more than twenty, with long dark hair. The top of her dress was undone and, in the moonlight shining through the mullioned windows, Wolfgang could see that her nipples were shiny with saliva. The man on top of her was older and wearing the uniform of a naval officer. The girl's legs looked milky white as she hooked them around him, her bare heels drumming on his back.

Wolfgang's eyes narrowed. They were fools to do that here — if the wrong person happened to stumble on them, there'd be hell to pay.

The man fumbled with his trousers, and in the mirror, Wolfgang saw the man's penis, engorged and hard, spring free. Then, with a forward lunge, he plunged neatly between her spread legs. The girl convulsed, their bodies rising and falling with jerking rapidity. The girl's head flew back against the armrest, her face now full in the moonlight. Wolfgang felt his own loins tighten at the rapturous look on her face. Her mouth fell slightly open and she moaned in low, guttural delight.

Wolfgang left them to it. He was suddenly in a hurry to get home. He knew that Marlene was getting less and less amenable as her pregnancy wore on, but there was always the new maid.

People were already leaving as he stepped across the threshold; within seconds, Marlene appeared by his side. She was always perfectly in tune with his thoughts and wishes, and never publicly disagreed with anything he said. Together they graciously took their leave, of their hostess first, then of Goebbels and Göring. Wolfgang had, of course, made a favourable impression on the chief of the Luftwaffe.

* * *

From his upstairs window, the four-year-old boy watched the big black car pull inside the double, wrought-iron gates, his little heart beating harshly. He was supposed to be in bed; if he was caught looking out of the window, he knew he would be beaten. Quickly, he clambered back in, folding the bedclothes neatly around him, just in case his mother came in to say goodnight. She didn't come very often; when she did, she scolded him about the mess he made of his blankets. Every time he woke up they were in disarray, silent testimony to the restless nights he spent, plagued by bad dreams that he could never remember when he woke up.

Downstairs, in the salon, Marlene kicked off her shoes and quickly kissed her husband on the cheek, wishing him goodnight, before he had the chance to suggest something amorous.

In his bed, Helmut heard his mother's footsteps approaching and prayed for her to come to him. He loved the touch of her cold mouth on his forehead, and the way it always made him want to hug her. He never did, of course — he knew it wrinkled his mummy's clothes, and she hated him touching her pretty hair. But the footsteps went past his room without pausing, so there would be no kisses. Instead he felt the warm wet caress of his own tears sliding down his cheeks, and he quickly, furtively, wiped them away. It sent his father into a rage whenever he saw him cry, and Helmut would do anything to avoid being beaten.

The night settled back into its quiet desolation, but Helmut was restless. Perhaps Nanny would make him a hot drink of chocolate if he went to her and told her he couldn't sleep? Of course he'd have to be very quiet. If his father found out . . . Torn between fear of his father and the tortures of the night, he lay in agonized indecision for a few minutes. Then, spurred on by the thought of Nanny, plump soft warmth and soothing, sherry-fumed breath, he pushed the blankets aside. His little feet were bare as he set them upon the floor and walked over to cautiously open the door.

* * *

8

Wolfgang stood by the small casement window and watched the girl undress. She'd shown no sign of surprise on opening the door to his discreet tap and finding him on the other side.

She had the rosy-cheeked complexion that he expected from a country girl. At only eighteen, she was already big-breasted, with a triangle of curly golden hair below her belly. For a second or two he just looked at her, and then neatly stripped himself, revealing a well-muscled, slim body and well-endowed manhood. The girl gasped in pleasing admiration.

As she eagerly walked over to him, Wolfgang smiled. Falling to her knees, her hands went unerringly to his member, her fingers closing around it with surprising strength. Wolfgang closed his eyes, his fine, patrician nostrils quivering as he breathed in quickly. 'Ah . . .' — what was her name? Urma, was it? — 'Ah, Urma, you have good hands,' he muttered, his voice even more guttural than usual.

The maid smiled. If she pleased him enough, perhaps he would come to her regularly — at least while the Frau was pregnant. Leaning forward, she closed her eyes and opened her wide mouth, slowly circling her tongue around the length of his shaft, grazing her teeth around the thick stem with teasing, threatening nips. Wolfgang drew in his breath sharply, his hands resting on the top of her head to steady himself; his own head was thrown back, throat tendons taut with ecstasy.

Made bold by the favourable reaction, Urma pushed him back until he sprawled on the lumpy mattress. Positioning herself atop him, she skewered herself upon his shaft with a grunt of pleasure, and began to move up and down rhythmically. Wolfgang closed his eyes and pictured the more beautiful face of the girl from the schloss. Urma clenched her feminine muscles savagely, making him buck in helpless reaction. Stretching out his hands, he gripped the iron headboard, like a man stretched out on a torture rack. And torture it was — but of the exquisite kind. Sweat stood out on his forehead as his head began to thrash from side to side. He moaned, uncaring that the noise carried clearly to the other servants through the thin walls, unaware that the sound of his voice had transfixed his young son, who now slowly walked to the door and, goaded by curiosity, began to open it.

Sweat trickled down Wolfgang's chest as Urma began to quicken the rhythm, her strong knees on either side of his thighs holding him in a firm vice. He felt his heels dig into the mattress, as his climax pushed his seed to fountain deeply and triumphantly inside her.

Helmut stared at his father's face, a huge knot feeling hard in his chest. He couldn't understand all the heaving and groaning. Why should his father want to fight with Urma? Just then Wolfgang turned his head, his eyes piercing the gloom to transfix his son, who promptly began to shake.

'What the hell are you doing there?' Wolfgang roared. He felt ridiculously ashamed that the boy had been watching his performance.

'I c-c-couldn't sleep, Papa,' Helmut gulped, the hated stutter coming to plague him as he slowly backed away. He never stuttered, except in the presence of his father.

'You've been spying again,' Wolfgang accused him, pulling on his trousers and stalking across to the terrified boy. 'You're nothing but a prying brat!'

'N-no, P-papa. I just w-w-wanted a hot drink . . .'

Leaving the rest of his clothes behind, he hefted the boy under one arm; once back in his son's room, he flung the boy on to the floor, where he cowered under his father's shadow.

'Tears again!' Wolfgang spat, disgusted. 'How many times do I have to tell you, boy? Only girls and weaklings cry.'

Helmut sniffed, hoping to stem the tears, but even that small, pathetic sound served only to enrage his father more. Taking off his belt, Wolfgang roughly hauled the boy by the scruff of his neck and upended him over a chair. Yanking down the boy's pyjama bottoms, he brutally applied the belt to the naked skin. Helmut screamed, and quickly stifled the sound, knowing it would only earn him a longer beating. In the morning, Helmut knew, Nanny would apply home-made salve to the vicious red welts, but he'd still have to sit on a cushion for the next few days.

Eventually, Wolfgang's rage abated, and he turned and left the sobbing child without a word, slamming and locking the door behind him.

With every step pulling at his aching and bruised skin, the child climbed back into bed, pressing his hot cheeks against the cool pillows. Why had he been beaten? It had something to do with the strange thing his father had been doing with Urma. He began to cry again, soft, despairing sounds. But with a maturity that went far beyond his years, little Helmut Mueller finally admitted to himself that nothing he could do would ever make his father love him or be proud of him.

His father was glad that his mother was going to have another baby. But for Helmut it was sheer agony. It made him want to beat his fists against his mother's rounded belly, to shout and scream his outrage at the thought of someone taking his place. His mother barely noticed him now. If she had another baby to take care of . . . He'd hate the baby — he'd hate it. And he hated his father too. And he hated the whole wide world and everyone in it as well.

That Friday the 13th, little Helmut Mueller came of age.

CHAPTER 2

Kansas, USA: Four Years Later

The day was hot and arid, the kind that sucked you dry of both water and willpower. The sky stretched overhead, sun-baked to a hazy white, and only the merest whisper of a breeze rippled over the young green stems of corn. A rust-riddled beat-up truck spluttered and almost cut out as its driver turned from the highway onto the dirt track that led to the small ramshackle farming community called Burmanville.

Hank Harcourt cursed as the gears jarred. Ramming his foot down on the sponge-like clutch and using sheer brute force to ram the gearstick home, he cursed again. His face was that of a sixty-year-old, though he was not yet forty. His hat, of indiscriminate pedigree, was floppy and sweat-stained around the brim and he lifted it now, tossing it on to the torn passenger seat.

After several miles of rough road, he came to the outer-most buildings of the town — if one street, a few stores, and a number of scattered ranches could be a town. The place had a scorched, dusted look; all faded paintwork and warped wood. A big dun-coloured dog lay panting under a raised sidewalk. As he rattled his way through the potholes, Hank sketched a salute to his old friend Fred Galaway, who owned the only garage for miles.

At this time of day, there was hardly a soul to be seen. A rusty sign squeaked on its hinges, and Hank swatted some flies from his face, hardly noticing that he did so, the gesture having become automatic over the years.

A large van, battered and old, but new to the neighbourhood, had him slowing down. Like all those who lived in the vast cornfields of Kansas, where little ever happened, his curiosity was easily aroused. Hank watched as a stranger dragged a huge table into the general store. He was small in stature and wore a navy-blue suit that was already wrinkled, sweat-stained and dusty. Hank pulled the battered Buick alongside but did not cut the engine.

'Howdy,' he said, his washed-out brown eyes surveying the stranger with mild friendliness mixed with a touch of contempt. He had the look of a city slicker about him. Somewhere in his late forties, his round, shining face sported a neatly cut black moustache.

'Howdy,' the response came back readily enough, but sounded a little self-conscious, as if the new owner of the Burmanville Stores and Grain Merchants felt uneasy about uttering the laconic, all-American word.

Yep, Hank thought, definitely a city slicker. He reached out his hand, a huge red calloused paw, and introduced himself. 'Name's Hank Harcourt. I own the High Bluff, about ten miles up the road.'

The stranger's hand was white and soft. 'Oscar Smith.'

Hank nodded to the van. 'Just movin' in, then?'

'That's right. Mr Jennings was right when he said there was plenty of room.'

Hank grinned. Old Clyde Jennings would have said his store was sat on a goldmine if he thought it would help him sell it. He'd been saying he was gonna move out to Chicago and foist himself on his eldest daughter for years, surprising the whole town out of its collective breeches when he actually upped and did it. Hank surveyed the new man with a keen eye. He looked like the sort who'd charge you for the air you breathed, if he could figure out a way to do it. 'When d'you open?' he asked, thinking of the state of his stores. June was running low on flour and salt.

'Tomorrow,' Oscar Smith promised promptly.

Giving a laconic nod, Hank was about to go, and had actually slipped the truck back into gear, when a woman appeared from out of the store, dusting her hands free from years of accumulated dirt. 'Lord, Oscar, you should see the . . . Oh, I didn't know you had company.'

Hank found himself being assessed by a pair of bright green eyes as the woman drew level with the truck window. She looked to be in her mid-twenties; under the orange patterned headscarf she wore, just a few stray wisps of bright red hair clung to her damp forehead. Her face was lightly freckled, and her large mouth was pulled into a welcoming smile. But the fulsome image was misleading. Hank soon found himself squirming under her blatantly sexual appraisal.

'This is my wife, Magda. Magda, Mr . . . er . . . Harcourt.' Oscar Smith made the introductions with a reluctance so obvious it was comical.

'How do you do?' Magda asked, leaning forward to give Hank a glimpse of her impressive cleavage. Hank took her hand like he might take the tail end of a rattler, gave it a quick shake, and quickly dragged his paw back into the safety of the Buick. He was old enough to be her daddy! This one was gonna have the town in an uproar right from the word go, Hank surmised, half-amused, half-indifferent. Just wait until the women took her measure. He'd soon find all his drinking buddies operating under a strict curfew.

'Won't you come in for a drink, Mr Harcourt?' Magda offered, but Hank hastily refused. A simple man, born of simple farming folk, Hank was a one-woman man. He'd gone to school with June and, when both were seventeen, they had married. They'd had seven kids, and seemed to be holding at that, and his inclination to wander on to pastures new was completely zero.

'I have t'git goin',' Hank muttered. 'I'll probably call in t'morra for a few things, though.'

'You do that, Mr Harcourt,' Oscar said, his round little face lighting up at the thought. 'We'll be open from six a.m. to nine p.m. from now on in. Yes, sir.'

'Uh-huh,' Hank muttered, roughly coaxing the old Buick back into first, and pulling away. Once on the road again, he let out a sigh of relief. Just what Burmanville needed — a money-grabbing storekeeper with a maneater for a wife. Hank was glad there were younger men in town who'd be more-than-eager victims for the green-eyed Magda. Young Jimmy Banks for one . . . Suddenly Hank frowned. No. He was wrong. Soon all the youngsters would be off abroad, to France, and all them sort of places, fighting the Nazis and the Japs.

Hank had been too young for the First World War, and an injured knee from a farming accident five years ago would keep him out of this one. He felt sorry for them Londoners, having their homes blitzed, and their kids blown to bits. But it all seemed like a whole world away from Kansas and the corn. And he bitterly resented the thought of his own sons, and the sons of his lifelong friends, marching away and maybe never coming back.

As he slowed down to pass the town's simple wooden church, with its rickety, picket-fenced cemetery, his eyes strayed, as they always did, to the middle of a row of three, where a wooden cross stood, bleached white by the sun. His mouth went dry, and he swallowed hard as he lifted his huge hand from the steering wheel and gave a little wave towards the cemetery. 'Hello, Pammy,' he whispered, his eyes watering for a few moments.

A few more miles, and he was back on Harcourt land. Another mile, and he rattled his way past two tall gateposts. They had once had the name '*High Bluff Ranch*' painted in red on a squeaking board hung about them, but it had long since disappeared. The ranch house itself was made of wood and thick mud-brick. As he pulled up in front, he noticed Kier, his youngest son, sitting on the bottom step, industriously drawing something in the sand with a stick. Climbing stiffly out of the truck, he limped around to open the hood, letting the steam gush out before checking the valve, which was red hot. Walking to a water trough, he picked up an old tin can, kept there for just such a purpose, and gave the thirsty truck a good lick of water, careful to shut the hood again. The sun could boil his gasket within hours, if left unprotected.

'Hi, Pa,' Kier said, his face still creased in a frown of concentration. The boy was six, going on seven, and was tall for his age. His hair was the same earthy brown that Hank's had once been, and his brown eyes were still deep and dark, and undimmed by worry and gruelling hard labour. He had the fine looks of his mother — long thick lashes, a straight, manly forehead with thick eyebrows. Already Hank could see that when the boy had a few more years on him, he would be able to have the pick of the girls for miles around. Maybe even get himself a city gal from Kansas City.

'What you got there, son?'

'A storyboard, Pa.'

'A what?'

'A storyboard. Y'know — like in the movies. This picture is of a boy, sneakin' around the back of a shed. Inside is a dog — see? The dog's been stolen and . . .'

'Is that what it is?' Hank interrupted hastily, totally uninterested, and he watched, half-amused, half-exasperated, as the boy's chin jutted out. Kier had all the stubbornness of a mule. If only the boy would save all his determination for the farm, Hank thought uneasily. But all Kier could talk about was Hollywood, and all this talk of movies was beginning to worry him. It was all Jim Cleever's fault for starting up a picture house in the first place. Ever since the kid had first seen John Wayne's *Stagecoach*, Hank felt as if he'd lost him.

'Have you chopped the wood for your ma?'

'Yes, Pa.'

'Good. I suppose you'd better do your homework, or Miss Ritter will be complainin' again.'

'I already done it, Pa. She say's I'm doin' real good in English, and she's even gonna let me write a story for the school play. Can you believe it? Ain't that great, Pa?'

Hank shrugged off his doubts. The boy was not yet seven. At Kier's age, Hank had wanted to drive a locomotive from the Pacific to the Atlantic. But now, nearing his fortieth birthday, he had never even been out of the state. But . . .

'I don't want you writing no play. The school never did plays when I went there. When is it, anyway?'

Kier felt his stomach dip in disappointment. He looked down at the sand, his lower lip trembling. 'Don't know, Pa,' he lied. Miss Ritter had warned him that just because he could write the play, it didn't mean he could play the biggest lead. She had looked quite amused when he'd sombrely explained that he didn't want to be an actor, he just wanted to make sure the play went right. When Miss Ritter had jokingly said that it seemed they had a new Cecil B. DeMille in their midst, he'd heard, for the first time, the word 'director'.

'Hmm. Well, your mother'll know, I expec',' Hank said, limping past his son into the house. Walking on through, he found his wife hanging out the washing on the clothesline at the back, and Hank paused in the doorway to watch her. Like himself, she looked far older than her years. Her shoulders were stooped, and the hair that hung limply to her shoulders was already turning grey. Her belly protruded in mute testimony to all her years of childbearing, but it was in cruel contrast to the rest of her, which was so skinny and fleshless that she seemed to be a collection of sticks. Yet she was humming as she hung up the washing, and when she turned and saw him, her face broke out into a ready and still dazzling smile. Hank did not envy Oscar Smith his pretty, dissatisfied young wife.

But her smile couldn't hide the pain so obvious in her eyes. Ever since Doc John had told him she had cancer, that dreaded word that was never spoken of in polite company,

Hank had known both terror and despair. Doc John had gently told him that his June had only months left. Hank had no idea what he'd do without her. Even though he'd decided not to tell her, and even though she never talked about it, Hank knew that she knew. The gnawing pains in her belly had nothing to do with the 'change', as Doc John had maintained. The knowledge was there in her eyes, in the way she would stop to stare at her children, as if imprinting them on her memory. It was there in the way her hands would squeeze tightly around his as they lay in bed at night. He wasn't sure whether it was to give him comfort, or because, in the dark night-time hours, she felt more afraid than she did when the sun was shining and the song sparrows were singing.

'You look good,' Hank told the lie lovingly, characteristically clumsy in his compliments. June didn't mind. He meant them — every one, and that was all that mattered to her. She gave him another smile.

'Did you get the chicken wire?' she asked, picking up the empty wicker basket, which he quickly took away from her and carried into the house. She silently followed him, a soft smile on her lips. The basket weighed next to nothing, and she'd just spent hours on the hand-wash tub, then another hour painstakingly putting the clothes through the mangle. Not that she begrudged the hard work. She knew that her husband laboured all the hours of God's day, and would labour even harder now that Pete was goin'. . . Every day she prayed Pete would come back, but if he didn't, then at least she, Pammy and Pete would all be together. They could wait for Hank and the others together. She didn't have any clear idea of what Heaven would be like, but she'd been raised a solid Baptist all her life, so she knew, with a certainty that was as strong as rock, that it did exist, and that it waited for her and all her children.

'Pastor Shimmidy came by this mornin',' she said, putting the kettle over the fire that perpetually burned in the grate, and spooning coffee grains into a battered tin pot. 'He said Amy was a natural-born singer. Asked if we had thought about having her voice trained . . . y'know, professionally and everything.'

Hank grunted, but his eyes were fond. Amy, Kier's elder sister by three years, was the apple of his eye. 'Can't afford it,' he said heavily, and June nodded.

'I already told him that,' she said, then looked carefully away. 'Did Kier tell you his good news yet?'

'Good news?'

'About the school play.'

'Oh — that. It's a waste of time. I told the boy so.' June added raw sugar to the mugs, then gasped as pain savagely lanced through her body. She grabbed the worktop hard. In moments she felt his hands on the tops of her arms, aware that his tears were sliding down the back of her neck to run, hot and straight, down the ridges of her spine. She collapsed into a chair, taking deep, agonizing breaths. Wordlessly, despairingly, Hank straightened and poured out the coffee, unable to look at her in case his big heart burst on the spot. When the worst was over she took the cup he offered her with hands that would not stop shaking and took a sip.

When she'd collected herself, she leaned back in the chair. What she had to do next was too important to let a small thing like pain stop her. 'Kier is different from the rest, Hank,' she said quietly, knowing she must get a prom-ise from him before it was too late. For her, and for Kier. 'I've read the stories he keeps writing — you haven't.' Hank blushed. He was not that good a reader. 'He's not like Marty or Pete. He don't have the soil in his blood like you all do.'

Hank sighed. 'I reckon that's true enough.'

'We've got to give him room, Hank. You've got to let him have his dreams, and let him go after 'em, when the time comes. He's good at schoolin', and Miss Ritter says she's gonna steer him towards a scholarship. Maybe even Oxford . . . y'know, in England. Promise me, Hank?' June pleaded, her soft voice raw with the pain that still ate at her.

Hank could see it in her eyes, and he quickly nodded his big craggy head. He'd do anything for his June. 'All right,

19

darlin'. I promise.' His hand groped blindly for hers on the table top, his fingers engulfing them.

Outside, Kier Harcourt began to draw a new scene for his play. He was still too young to know what tragedy meant. But he'd learn, soon enough.

CHAPTER 3

Atlanta, Georgia — One Year Later

The mansion belonged in a scene from *Gone With the Wind*. Riveree, a fourteen-bedroomed, white-columned, gleaming and elegant edifice, stood on a gently sloping hill, looking out over the willow-draped expanse of the Chattahoochee River, flowing north of Atlanta. Moss-draped trees shaded it, while bougainvillea bled purple, scarlet and pink blooms from every flower bed. Clarissa Somerville opened the French windows at the east wing and stepped on to a terrace. Her hair was ivory blonde and pulled into an elegant chignon. Her eyes were slate-grey, and her skin, at thirty-two, was still as creamy and pink as the magnolia blossoms that lined the great driveway. Her figure was exquisite, and she fitted in at Riveree like a human extension of the house.

'I'll have the tea out here please, Billie,' she informed the maid in her usual lazy, southern drawl, and pulled out a wrought-iron garden chair as the maid left to do her bidding. Life should have been wonderful for Clarissa Somerville. She was rich, beautiful and the leading light of Atlanta society. But she was so vulnerable, she lived in a state of constant anxiety. For Clarissa Somerville was also in love. And not with her husband.

'Your tea, ma'am.' the maid said as she returned. 'Will the master be coming home soon, ma'am? Cook's worried about him over in them foreign parts.'

'No, Billie, he can't leave Switzerland for some time,' she explained patiently, yet again.

'Yes, ma'am,' Billie replied miserably, and left.

Clarissa continued to stare out over the beautiful gardens, her mind on other things. On a shabby cabin outside Burford, to be exact. Clarissa knew she'd have to go to him soon. She'd held out as long as she could, and now she was so restless it felt like a physical pain. She wandered into her husband's study, hoping to find something there to keep her mind distracted.

On the wall was a portrait of her mother- and father-in-law, ninth-generation Somervilles. Clarissa had been born a Charleston Gough, and everyone had agreed what a good match their families made. Duncan Somerville's mother had been urging him to marry and produce an heir for years, and Clarissa knew that she wouldn't find a better husband than the amenable Duncan. If it was actually Riveree that she had fallen in love with at first sight . . . well, one couldn't have everything. She'd settled down to become a good wife and hostess. The parties she'd thrown were all spectacular successes and written up reverently in the Atlanta press. She'd even produced the much-anticipated Somerville heir. True, the child had been a daughter, but a woman could inherit as easily as a boy. And again, everyone had been so pleased. After all, heiresses were very fashionable.

Thoughts of her precious daughter spurred Clarissa on to the upstairs nursery, where squeals of laughter greeted her.

Her five-year-old might be dressed in white lace and organdie, but she rode her rocking horse as if it were a bucking bronco. Old Jennie stood with hands either side of her, to catch her if she should fall. But Oriel would not fall. She was far too tenacious. Clarissa's child might have her ivory hair, grace and beauty, but she had a strength of indomitable will that couldn't have come from either Clarissa or her easy-going father. Her eyes were a lovely periwinkle blue, and Clarissa felt her heart swell as she watched her daughter play. She was so talented, wayward and brilliant. Clarissa had Oriel's future as carefully planned as one of her own parties. The best school, the Ladies' Academy in Charleston, followed by a year at a Swiss finishing school. Then home for a dazzling debutante season, and then marriage. To the richest, the best, the finest.

'Hello, my angel.' Clarissa kissed her daughter, her voice thick with emotion.

'Look!' Oriel gurgled, riding the horse with fierce abandon.

'Very nice, darling,' Clarissa murmured. 'Your daddy would be proud.' Oriel missed her father, and Clarissa faithfully read her his letters. Clarissa had made no demur when Duncan had joined the diplomatic service. It pleased her to see him happy.

'Whoa there, poppet. You'll wear poor Dobbin out,' Clarissa scolded mildly, ruffling her daughter's hair.

'Don't care!' Oriel said, chuckling with good humour as the room whizzed past her, her tummy doing funny somersaults that tickled.

'I'm going out for lunch today, Jennie. Make sure she eats her greens.'

'I will, Miss Clarry,' Jennie said, both women ignoring the child's woeful wails.

Downstairs, Clarissa paused in the high-ceilinged hall to check her reflection in the cheval glass. Her cheeks were flushed. She knew why, of course. She always looked that way when she was about to visit Kyle. It was ridiculous. The boy was practically a peasant, the youngest son of Burford's garage mechanic, and seemed perpetually dirty. Sometimes she'd make him shower. And then again, sometimes she wouldn't. It depended on how desperate she was for him. He was young, almost fiercely resentful of her wealth, and could be crude, ill-mannered and downright brutal. He was also the most spectacularly handsome young man she'd ever seen in her life. And she was viciously in love with him. It terrified her. If anyone found out, she'd be ruined. Her family would be scandalized. Her husband disgraced. But she was helpless. She could no more live without Kyle than she could without breath.

She got into her imported Bugatti sports car, her heart racing. She drove on autopilot through Atlanta's suburbs, giving way quickly to the dreaming countryside. She paid no attention to the beautifully blooming orchards of citrus fruit, and the ubiquitous cotton plants, in their neat rows, were so commonplace as to be beneath her notice. Her thighs trembled in delicious anticipation. She knew it was madness but put her foot down on the accelerator anyway. After an hour of steady driving she turned off onto the backroads and at last, the deserted cabin came into sight. She parked the car under the shade of an ancient oak, her stomach churning. As a lover, Duncan had been adequate, nothing more, but Kyle . . . With hands that shook, she opened the car door, and set her designer shoes onto the rutted dirt track. Kyle must never know the power he had over her. He must never know how much he obsessed her. If he did . . . she would be powerless. So it was that Clarissa Somerville acted the rich, tough bitch. In their relationship, she was the dominant one. The demanding one. And she played her role so well, she knew that Kyle hated her as much as he loved her.

She walked straight in without knocking and headed for his bedroom. It was his day off, but he wasn't expecting her. Kyle never knew when she'd suddenly show up, all but ravish him, then leave again, to go back to her fancy house and her fancy friends.

The room was dark, but her eyes were drawn like magnets to the young man sleeping on the bed. His shirt was off, showing a lightly muscled chest. His skin was tanned light brown, the nipples darker, and beckoning. His jeans were dusty and rumpled, his feet bare and dirty. Clarissa felt her heart begin to trip harder as she slowly walked to the bed.

She gazed down at his peacefully sleeping face, which was so handsome it made her breath catch. Although his hair was raven black, his complexion was surprisingly fair. His eyes, when they were open, were of the deepest navy blue that turned black when he was in throes of passion. And Clarissa loved to watch those eyes turn black . . . He was only nineteen and looked it. The difference in their ages terrified her. How long before he would think her old and ugly . . . She dragged her agonizing thoughts away from that road. Instead, she drank him in. His cheekbones were high and very finely shaped, his mouth sensitive. His tongue was long . . .

He murmured something, turning on the old-fashioned, king-sized bed. Clarissa slipped off her shoes and stockings. She hesitated only a moment before slipping off her panties too. Doing a slight gyration, she removed her bra without removing her dress, and felt her nipples press turgidly against the silk, yearning for the feel of his moist, hot tongue. But she remained silent, wanting to prolong the agony of waiting. His body had a tensile strength that she found thrilling. She stirred restlessly, feeling her thighs sliding together, made slippery by the juices that dripped from her own ivory triangle. Suddenly aware of a presence in his room, in an instant Kyle was up on his elbows, alert, his senses attuned to danger. His eyes focused on her immediately, and a smile, an almost ugly, reluctantly hungry smile, settled across his mouth.

Clarissa swallowed hard. She liked this game, even though it terrified her. 'Hello, boy,' she said softly, the term deliberately derogatory. Her use of it was purely defensive. She had to make him think he meant nothing more than that to her. She had to keep the upper hand. Her life — in a very real sense — depended on it.

'Hi, bitch,' Kyle said, slowly sitting up and swinging his legs to the floor. Clarissa quickly moved to stand in front of him before he could rise, looking down at him with a mocking, challenging smile. Kyle's lips pulled back into a sneer as their eyes met, clashed, and fought. Then the sneer vanished as he slowly looked at her bulging nipples, clearly visible through the creamy silk, now almost directly on eye level with him. Noticing how her lovely face had become tight and tense, he slowly leaned forward, his eyes never leaving hers until the last second before he fastened his mouth on one silk-covered breast.

Clarissa cried out, her whole body rippling in tiny shocks. She felt his arm come around her waist, and her knees buckled as she was pulled roughly onto the bed. 'Kyle,' she moaned as his dirty hand thrust into the clean, gardenia-scented freshness of her hair, and dragged it free of its elegant chignon. His fingers twisted in her hair as he jerked her head back, at the same time twisting his body over hers so that she was half-sitting and half-lying on the bed and he was leaning over her.

Her eyes, a stormy, sea-grey, opened with startled pain, and he stared at her for a long, agonizing second while they fought a silent, familiar battle. Then, after what seemed an age, he lowered his lips to her exposed throat. She gasped, then moaned, as he ripped her dress open, forcing her back against the mattress as he did so. She was breathing hard now as he stared down at her. Kyle watched her eyes, not his own hands, as he slowly caressed her breasts, brushing his thumb across her nipples, smiling grimly at the way she shuddered with every rough caress. He moaned softly, almost despairingly, as he acknowledged that he was as hooked as she was. They were like a mutual drug, each needing a fix, each denying it until it drove them crazy.

'Oh, Clarry,' he said despairingly, then, with infinite gentleness, he lowered his head and suckled on her breast, greedily pulling its peak deep into his mouth, his tongue pressed flat and hard against the nipple. Clarissa closed her eyes, her body quivering in reaction. 'I hate you,' Kyle said softly, leaving her breasts to kiss her stomach, slowing making his way to her navel.

'Why?' she groaned, her breath leaving her in a pained gasp as his tongue dipped into the indentation on her stomach and flickered against her flesh.

'Because you make me want you,' he muttered angrily, his voice thick and harsh. 'You're a bitch — a rich bitch, who looked, and wanted.'

Clarissa laughed, knowing by the way he paled that she had hurt him. Instinctively she went to touch him, then gasped as his hands suddenly jerked open her thighs. 'Want this, bitch?' he snarled, and dipped his head quickly, his fingers opening the womanly lips he found there, clearing the way for his tongue, which he thrust deep inside her. Clarissa arched convulsively in shock, but he was ready for her, his hands clasping her hips to hold her ruthlessly still.

'Oh, Kyle!' Clarissa screamed, her head jerking from side to side on the pillows as she writhed helplessly. Kyle's tongue was hot on her clitoris as he pleasured her without mercy. It was payback time.

If they met on the street, she looked through him like he was garbage, and then she came here, to his house, like a bitch on heat wanting . . . wanting this, he thought savagely, lifting his mouth from between her scented thighs and then delving two fingers deep inside her. He stretched alongside her as he did so, taking her chin in his hand to stare into her glazed eyes as he stroked her with erotic, savage skill. She stretched her legs, helplessly clamping her thighs together, but he was too strong for her. Panting, with their faces only an inch away, he found her clitoris once more and began to stroke it in a circular motion that drove her wild.

'You bastard,' she moaned, her legs jerking helplessly as he ruthlessly pushed her to a climax. She jerked, moaned and then lay panting, breathing in great gulps of air. While she lay, reclaiming her breath, Kyle took off his jeans.

'That Bugatti of yours needs tunin'. Bring it in to Dad's garage tomorrow.'

'All right.' She watched the jeans come off, and then he turned to face her, showing her the bulge in the square white briefs. 'Come here,' she demanded, her arms out.

'I need a new car,' Kyle said flatly. As revenge, it wasn't much, but it was the best he could think of.

'I'll buy you one,' she promised feverishly. 'Just come here!' She sat up as he came to the bed and stood beside her. Greedily, her hands reached for the briefs and dragged them down over his thighs. She gasped, as she always did, at the size of his manhood, and her hand closed greedily around it. It felt on fire — hard as iron, and smooth as velvet.

'I'm gonna own that garage one day,' he said. 'That and dozens like it, all over the south.'

Clarissa smiled. 'You're a greedy little boy, Kyle. A lower-class, dirty, greedy . . .' Her words broke off as he pounced on her with a snarl, coming down on top of her, roughly grasping her wrists and pinning them above her head. Without entering her, he slowly gyrated his body, rubbing his penis against the side of her thigh. She whimpered. He smiled. 'Kyle! Oh, Kyle . . .'

He felt the power of the moment, like an aphrodisiac, bite deep into him, but he wasn't fooled. His power was only of the moment, whereas hers was total. If she should withdraw her custom from the garage, he'd be out of a job. A word from her in the Sheriff's ear would have him thrown in jail, on any charge she cared to make. And she knew it. He hated her. And wanted her. Oh yes, he wanted her. Slowly he positioned himself at the very edge of her opening, and with a slow push began to enter her, only to stop and withdraw, and then enter her again. Clarissa moaned and thrust her hips up, but he was too quick and drew away. He began again, tormenting her, tormenting himself. Sweat broke out on his forehead, but though she pleaded, cursed, threatened, begged, he did not thrust fully into her.

Only when they were both on the verge of insanity did he suddenly bury himself deep inside her, and her scream, pure and high, reverberated around the tiny cabin. Her nails dug into his back, drawing blood, but he hardly noticed. His mates at the garage had become used to the scratches on his back whenever he stripped off his shirt. He fielded their coarse suggestions and ribald teasing with satisfied goodwill.

If he were to tell them who had put them there, they'd die of envy. But Kyle was not stupid.

He plunged into her with sure strokes that buried the entire length of him in her. The southern princess was skewered to a lumpy mattress, staring at a dirty, flaking ceiling, and ecstatically enjoying every moment of it. She moaned, her heels making indents in his buttocks as she clamped him savagely. But he took his own time, slowly building the rhythm, forcing her to one climax after another until they all seemed to roll into one long, torturous moment of ecstasy.

'Kyle!' she screamed, her face contorted with pleasure, her lips bitten free of lipstick, her lithe, willowy body bathed in his sweat and her own, smeared here and there with oil and dirt. 'Kyle! Ohhhhh . . .' she shuddered, bucking so hard they almost fell to the floor.

He felt his own climax coming, and convulsed, the warning alerting her just in time. Quickly her hands went to his face, holding him still. 'Look at me,' she commanded, her elegant southern drawl harsh and demanding. 'Look at me, you bastard,' she screamed, driven beyond endurance. 'I want to watch. I want to see it in your eyes. I want to see the exact moment when your mind blows out of your head.'

Kyle snarled and tried to shake his head free, but it was too late. His body was exploding, his climax destroying him. He groaned deeply, his eyes turning obsidian, his young, flushed face suddenly innocent again, but racked with the pain of his explosive orgasm. 'Clarissa,' he moaned helplessly, shuddering his seed into her.

Clarissa laughed, her hands holding his face as she claimed her prize. Oh, how she loved him. 'Poor Kyle,' she said tenderly as his strong, dominating body collapsed weakly atop her, all his wonderful strength spent inside her.

Kyle's head dropped onto her shoulder as he took deep shuddering breaths. He was almost crying as her hands stroked his damp scalp in tender semi-circles. After a few minutes she rolled him onto his back. His arms lay limp beside him, his body drained.

'You can check the oil in my car before I go,' she ordered.

Kyle closed his eyes briefly, then opened them again. 'One of these days,' he said, his voice totally devoid of all emotion, 'I'm going to kill you, Clarissa.'

Clarissa looked down at him, then smiled. 'Not if I kill you first,' she said. And ran her hand up his thigh. He frowned, a helpless, totally stunned look flashing across his eyes as his body leapt at her touch.

Clarissa watched him, outwardly triumphant but secretly beaten. For she couldn't help but touch him any more than he could help but respond to her. 'Poor Kyle,' she said again, lowering her lips to within a millimetre of his but not kissing him, her hand busily at work, her hawk-like eyes feeding on every fleeting expression in his darkening eyes. He moaned again, his back arching off the bed.

'Poor, poor, Kyle.'

And poor Clarissa.

CHAPTER 4

Germany, April 1945

Wolfgang Mueller's armoured car paused momentarily at the gates of the Koblenz concentration camp as two privates scurried to raise the barrier. He was leaving the hellhole for the last time — though no one, as yet, knew it. The rats were deserting the Nazi ship with a speed that had set the top brass reeling. The defection of Hess in the early years had been little more than a propaganda defeat, but now not even Goebbels' expert media manipulation could hide the galling truth. The war was all but over. And Wolfgang Mueller was about to disappear. He'd planned long and hard to secure his own future — now, all he needed was some final insurance. Which was why he was headed for Berlin, instead of south, to Lake Constance and the charming town of Meersburg, where his wife and sons waited for him.

Wolfgang could admit to himself that he was scared. He'd sent his adjutant, Lieutenant Heinlich, ahead, with specific orders to retrieve all files relating to Wolfgang that were currently being kept in SS files. These were dangerous times . . .

As the car began to approach the suburbs of Berlin, Wolfgang knew what must inevitably follow, and he planned to be long gone when it did. He had had all his cash turned into precious gems, and through his contacts, had already shipped most of his more valuable heirlooms onto a neutral South American steamship that was currently on its way to the Mediterranean, where Monte Carlo awaited. Wolfgang was going to be very rich, very shortly, but he needed insurance badly. There was going to be a first class witch-hunt by the surviving Jews and Wolfgang, as Commandant of Koblenz, knew himself to be a prime target. If only he hadn't been wounded so badly that he'd had to stop flying. He'd hated the boredom that had been his life at the camp, and the loss of kudos had been hard to bear.

The car turned into Kantstrasse and quickly accelerated. Everywhere the streets seemed ominously deserted. He made a quick stop on Perlebergerstrasse to say a tearful farewell to his mistress, then was once again back in the car, turning on to Leipzigerstrasse where the secret records office of the SS were hidden underground. Wolfgang strode confidently into the building, his rings, forged orders and his naturally commanding bearing easily allowing him to dispense with the fanatical SS guards.

The underground bunker was a poorly lit rabbit warren, full of bustling, sharp-eyed but pale women. Wolfgang made his way immediately to the office of his old friend Karl Zimmelmann.

'Wolf, my friend. I didn't know you were due in town.'

'I'm not,' Wolfgang said, quickly coming to the point. 'I want to see the records for Koblenz.'

Karl said nothing for several seconds, simply looking into his friend's eyes with a long, level stare. 'You want to destroy them?' he asked softly, and Wolfgang paused, then nodded. If Karl would not help him, he'd kill him here and now. He had planned on pointing the finger of blame for the missing records on Heinlich anyway. A murder, added to treason, would hardly make any difference.

'Of course,' Karl said, not the slightest trace of censure in his voice. 'Follow me.'

As he followed him even further into the labyrinth, Wolfgang wondered if Karl's own escape route was as safe as his own. 'Here. You've got ten minutes.' Karl opened a thick steel door to reveal rows and rows of filing cabinets.

Wolfgang nodded. 'Thanks. Are you all right . . . financially?'

'Of course. This is for old times' sake.'

Wolfgang clapped him on the back. '*Ja*, old friend.'

The moment the door closed he set to work, burning all the Koblenz records in a big tin waste bin. Wolfgang watched the evidence disappear in smoke, and his handsome lips curved up in a whimsical smile. Behind him the door opened, and Karl coughed. 'A few more minutes,' Wolfgang said, not turning around. 'My man Heinlich is at the Tauentzienstrasse bunker. Can I borrow a couple of your police?'

Karl nodded. 'You have him in mind for a scapegoat?'

Wolfgang nodded. 'After I've recovered the documentation from him,' he confirmed. The SS were not so foolish as to keep all records in one place, and the other site held lesser, but still damning, proof of his Nazi involvement.

'I'll call the section supervisor and have Heinlich held.'

'Good.' Wolfgang paused, then held out his hand. 'Good luck, Karl.'

'You also, my friend.'

His car was parked neatly in front of the offices. The day was appropriately dank and a dismal grey rain began to fall. Once at the Tauentzienstrasse offices, he was met by Otto Von Schtrom, the section supervisor, with bad news. 'The traitor Heinlich has fled, Commandant. A record clerk showed him into the camp section, as per your written orders, but after the call from Herr Zimmelmann, we found he had disappeared.'

Wolfgang felt surprised rage explode in his head, and he swallowed hard, keeping his voice level with the greatest of effort. 'What is missing?'

The supervisor was obviously waiting for this question and checked a list, quickly reeling off information.

Again Wolfgang was surprised. The weasel had taken not only damning evidence against himself, but against other top-ranking officials. 'I see,' he said grimly, slipping back into the car. 'You have a search party out looking for him?'

'*Ja*, Commandant.'

Wolfgang nodded, but did not hold out much hope. He curtly answered the supervisor's salute, and gave the driver his instructions. 'The Hauptbahnhof — quickly.' The driver nodded, heading the car towards the main railway station with a knowing smile. In the back, Wolfgang seethed. He had underestimated Heinlich, a thing he very rarely did.

Wolfgang alighted at the train station and commandeered a seat on a goods train carrying coal. The countryside they travelled through was ravaged, the cities bombed and bleak. He was nervous, jumping every time the train stopped. But as the countryside began to become more mountainous as it neared the Swiss border, so Wolfgang began to smile. If only he knew where his treacherous adjutant was . . .

* * *

Frederich Heinlich stood on the Seestrasse in Meersburg, his eyes scanning the lake for the fishing boat that was going to take him across to Switzerland. He patted the briefcase he held to his chest with a small, smug smile, then quickly swivelled away as a tall blonde woman with two little boys turned his way. He was not out of the woods yet. If he'd known his superior was only hours away, and getting closer, he'd have been feeling a lot less sure of himself.

* * *

Marlene Mueller found a seat that overlooked the lake and sat down. 'Come here, Helmut,' she called impatiently as her eldest son wandered to the railings, next to the funny little man with the briefcase.

'Yes, Mama,' he said, but made no move to go to her.

Marlene sighed and pulled Hans onto the bench beside her.

Helmut picked up a stone and threw it. White water birds bobbed on the azure blue lake. He'd felt no great misery on leaving Berlin and looked forward to the adventure ahead.

Marlene would be glad when Wolfgang arrived. She felt nervous on her own, and prey to bitterness. Damn the Allies! She thought of all the things they'd had to leave behind — the paintings and grand piano that were worth a small fortune, the chandeliers and carpets, the beautiful Austrian furniture.

'What's Monte Carlo like, Mama?' Helmut asked, suddenly materializing at her side and making her jump.

'Stop sneaking up on people,' she snapped.

Helmut had grown even taller for his age, showing all the signs of the striking good looks that would shortly be his. His blonde hair was turning a light copper, and his face was square and firm-jawed.

Helmut shrugged and moved back to the railings, looking craftily at the man whose gaze was scouring the water with painful intensity. Helmut was sure he'd seen the man before. He had an almost photographic memory, and he never forgot a face. Helmut suspected that he was some SS officer on the way to Switzerland, like his own father. The way he hugged the briefcase, as if expecting someone to snatch it, gave him away as nothing else could. He's a fool, Helmut thought, with swingeing disapproval. Why didn't he sit down in a café, have a drink, look normal?

As if aware of the close scrutiny, Frederich looked around, but relaxed on seeing only the boy. Helmut almost snapped his fingers. Why it's Lt . . . Lt . . . Heinz? No, Heinlich, his father's adjutant. But why hadn't Father told them the man would be coming with them? He turned reluctantly when his mother called him, and silently followed her back to the hotel. Hans, his five-year-old brother, was busily sucking a lolly. Helmut had not been offered a lolly, and when Marlene wasn't looking, he quickly flicked his finger against his brother's hand. Hans wailed as the red ice slipped and fell to the pavement.

'You did that on purpose,' Hans accused, his little fists swinging in Helmut's direction.

'Did not,' he lied.

'Just because Mama didn't buy you one.'

For a moment Helmut felt tears sting his eyes, and he gritted his teeth. 'That's because I'm too old to have a lolly,' he said defensively. 'You're just a kid. I'm nearly a grown-up.'

Marlene turned, arms akimbo. 'Come on, you two, or I'll tell your father you've been bad.' At that dire threat, both boys hurried to catch up with her.

It was nearly two hours later when Wolfgang joined them. She expressed no joy at his safe arrival, nor did she kiss him. For his part, Wolfgang strode straight over to Hans and hoisted him into the air. Hans gurgled wildly. 'The boat's already in the harbour,' he said briefly, setting the boy back down. 'Are the things packed?' Marlene nodded.

The captain of the small, battered fishing boat was Swiss, of German descent, and nodded curtly to Wolfgang, who thanked him and immediately went to a small wheelhouse where he changed into civilian clothing. Heinlich, sat on the deck by some tarpaulin, froze at the sound of Mueller's voice. His face blanched white, and he dove under the tarpaulin on his belly, to lay there quivering. He'd paid the captain extra to keep quiet, and the fisherman had no idea of any connection between them, but would he mention to his illegal passenger the fact that he was not alone on this boat ride to freedom?

For the first time in his life, Frederich Heinlich began to pray . . .

Within moments the little fishing vessel was pulling out of the harbour. Helmut stood at the rails, watching the German coastline slowly disappear. Wolfgang emerged dressed in a sober black suit and walked over to Marlene, who stood weeping quietly a little further along the rails. Helmut moved a few steps closer the better to hear them. 'Be quiet,'

Wolfgang said, a thread of steel running through his voice. 'The crew will see.'

'I can't help it,' Marlene murmured.

Wolfgang swore under his breath. 'I know. But we'll soon get used to Monte Carlo. You'll see.'

Marlene wiped her eyes and sniffed. 'I still think we should go to Bolivia.'

'We're not living in that godforsaken backwater. Don't worry. Our new identities are iron-clad. We're Americans, of French descent. Even our children have American names now. It's rather ironic, don't you think?'

Marlene shrugged, in no mood to see the joke. Her own name was now Mary, a name that she thought sounded utterly ugly. Hans was now Henri and Helmut had chosen the name Wayne, mainly, she suspected, to offend his father, who had said grimly that it was just the kind of name he would have expected Helmut to choose. 'I hope our things will arrive on time,' she said querulously. 'What if the ship is sunk?'

'It won't be. The house is already rented, the papers are safely here . . .' He patted his breast pocket, where there were passports, insurance numbers, identity cards and every other certificate and documentation needed to start a new life. 'Before long, we'll be speaking French like natives, and English too. How are the boys' lessons progressing?'

Marlene shrugged. 'Helmut—'

'Wayne,' he corrected sharply.

'Wayne,' Marlene repeated dutifully, 'is almost word perfect already. His tutor says he has an excellent brain.'

'And Hans?'

'Henri—' Marlene took pleasure in correcting him '—is coming along.' Then she sighed wearily. 'I hate it that they have to lose their heritage, their . . .'

'I know. But it can't be helped. And it's more imperative now than ever that they adapt quickly. That bastard Heinlich has disappeared with the documents I sent him to collect.'

Marlene gasped, turning ashen. 'Wolf . . .'

'It's all right. No one will connect Marcus D'Arville and family of Monte Carlo with the Berlin Muellers, that I promise you. Besides, Heinlich will probably be shot as a traitor before he's gone a hundred miles.' Under the tarpaulin, Heinlich began to sweat. He must stay hidden until the Muellers had disembarked on the other side. The captain knew a way to dodge the Swiss patrol boats, and already they were headed for a little cove, miles from the nearest Swiss town or border post. Now, Heinlich froze as he saw that his tie was lying outside the tarpaulin. His hands shook crazily as he lifted the tarpaulin a bare inch and began to pull it in.

With his peripheral vision, Helmut saw the movement and turned, bending down on his knees a scant yard away from the sweating man. For a second, startled brown eyes stared into grave blue ones. Too late, Heinlich recognized his superior's son. Helmut smiled. Slowly Heinlich let the canvas cover him, his heart beating so hard he felt sick. He felt smothered, gagging. He was surely going to die. He waited for Wolfgang's brat to call out to his father. But a minute passed, and nothing happened. Then Mueller's voice was closer. 'Well, Wayne, we'll soon be in Switzerland. I hear you've progressed well with your language studies.'

'Yes, Papa.' Wolfgang did not praise him, and Helmut did not expect him to. 'Didn't Lieutenant Heinlich come to dinner once, Papa?' Helmut asked, knowing that Heinlich would be in a state of near hysteria by now, listening to every word they uttered.

'I think so. Why?'

'Wasn't he small, with beady rabbit-brown eyes and dark hair?' Helmut prompted, glorying in his knowledge, his first taste of power. It was so heady and sweet. He knew, in that instant, that he must have more of it — much more.

'That's right,' Wolfgang said sharply. 'Why?'

'Oh, nothing.' Helmut shrugged. 'I just heard you talking to Mother about him. Would you like to know where he is, Papa?' Under the tarpaulin, Heinlich stuffed his knuckled fist into his mouth and wet himself.

'Indeed I would,' Wolfgang said savagely. 'Have you seen him?'

Heinlich waited, his hot urine trickling down his leg, his raw knuckles bleeding equally warm blood over his wrist. Then, after what seemed an eternity, Helmut said softly, 'No, Papa.'

Wolfgang nodded, then turned to smile lovingly at Hans, playing on the deck. Wolfgang could finally relax. He was free and clear at last, and that was all that mattered.

Helmut watched his father walk away, then glanced at the tarpaulin. Slowly he began to smile. He had just discovered the joy of power, and life was suddenly very, very sweet.

CHAPTER 5

Kansas, Nine Years Later

The throng of youngsters running from the white-washed wooden building whooped with delight. School was out for the summer! Kier Harcourt walked slowly down the dusty drive, his face thoughtful as he swung his bundle of books, his mind going back to the exams. Had he passed them all or not?

'Hey, Harcourt — you on fer tonight?' Kier looked up as Billy Johnson's freckled face overtook him.

'Yeah, I'm on,' Kier said. 'And I don't want none of you clowns messin' with my play. It's supposed to be a modern tragedy, but you guys'd turn it into a farce, quick as lightnin'!'

Billy grinned. 'OK, Cecil,' he held up his hands placatingly. Ever since the Cecil B. De Mille incident at the school play all those years ago, the nickname had stuck, despite Kier's valiant efforts to shake it off. But over the years, Kier's plays had become the highlight of the church fund-raising, taking in more money than all the bring-and-buy stalls, home-baked cake stands and raffles put together. The club Kier had set up, however, kept a little bit of the money back to finance group outings to the cinema. A club had to live, after all.

Kier was seventeen and already turning female heads. At five feet ten, his hair was a rich earthy brown, thick and always glossy in the harsh Kansas sun. His eyes were widely spaced, with thick black lashes, and were the exact same shade as those belonging to a timber wolf. He walked like a wolf, too, with a loose-limbed stride that required the minimum of effort and gave the girls who constantly gazed at him the sensation of watching liquid movement. One girl called him 'poetry in motion', so now all the girls called him 'The Poet'. Kier chose to look on it as a reflection of his directing and playwriting abilities, rather than as a statement about his physical attributes.

At the end of the school road he retrieved a battered pushbike from under a scraggly tree and pedalled off, his mind still stubbornly on his exams. He'd worked like a demon for the past two years and, if he failed now, he just didn't know what he'd do. Of all the scholarship opportunities Miss Ritter had put his way, he'd selected the most ambitious, the most outrageous of them all. Oxford University, England — where no one from Burmanville had ever gone before.

With the bike still in motion, he hooked his leg over the handlebar like a trick-cyclist and drew to a well-controlled stop in front of the store, where he had a part-time job.

'Howdy, young Kier.' Oscar Smith looked up as he came through the door, then returned to his books, checking columns industriously, always paranoid that someone would somehow cheat him.

'Hey, Mr Smith. What d'ya want me to do first?'

'I've got some flour sacks from the cellar that need bringing up and put on the shelves in the back.'

'Yessir.' He opened the door to the cellar and walked down the rickety stairs. It was windowless, stale and muggy, and with a quick impatient movement he pulled his shirt, still buttoned, over his head. Reaching for a hefty sack, he began the laborious climb back up the steps. After half an hour he was bathed in sweat, and covered in a fine white film

41

of flour, but he was used to gruelling hard labour and barely noticed. At the rear of the shop he began stacking them on the shelves.

From her window, Magda Smith watched his progress and licked her lips. It was about time she gave herself a special treat. And special was a word that suited Kier Harcourt. And not just because of his looks either. There was an indefinable 'something' that clung to him — a kind of aura, a feeling that made her skin tingle. Every feminine intuition she had told her that here was a boy who was going places. She could feel it, taste it, smell it. Unlike Kier, she had no doubts that he'd passed his exams and would later be going on to Oxford and all that culture.

She came downstairs, her heart thumping. 'Oscar, can I borrow you for a few minutes?' she asked, as Jake Gordon, the town's odd-job man, walked in and started rummaging around in a big box of mismatched screws and nails.

'For what, dear?' Oscar kept an eagle eye on Jake.

'I need some furniture moved, hon.'

'What can I do for you, Jake?' Oscar asked, just as Kier came into the storeroom. He was sweating hard, and he rubbed his hand wearily across his forehead.

'Honey,' Magda wheedled, with perfect timing, 'I need someone to move the furniture.'

'You know I can't leave the store,' Oscar hissed impatiently, looking around and spying Kier. 'You finished with the flour, son?'

'Yessir.'

'Then help Mrs Smith move some furniture, huh?'

Kier nodded, following the exultant Magda up the stairs with all the innocence of a lamb going to the slaughter. Magda went first to the kitchen, turning around and watching the boy who stood nervously in the doorway. 'You must be thirsty after all the hard work, Kier,' she said softly, walking to the refrigerator and bringing out a pitcher of iced lemonade.

Kier gratefully accepted a glass, wiping the taste of flour from his mouth with three or four healthy gulps. Magda watched his strong Adam's apple bob in his throat, and took a long, slow breath. She had waited a long time for this and she was going to enjoy it to the full.

'So, you're the last one left at home now,' she said, slowly raising a hand to her throat and then fanning her face. 'My, isn't it hot?' She undid the first two buttons of her dress.

'Yes, ma'am.'

'I saw your pa the other day. He ain't lookin' too good.'

Kier shook his head. 'Amy was his favourite. Now she's moved to Wisconsin, he don't talk much. It's not the same without Ma. And he still misses Pammy. She died during the Depression. She got real sick, and we couldn't afford to pay the hospital.' Kier hadn't been born then, but he recited the facts grimly.

'Oh, that's an awful shame,' Magda said, her voice soft with genuine sympathy. 'Life's a bitch. Whether you enjoy it or not, it all boils down to money.' She looked at Kier, then smiled. 'You'll have money one day, Kier. I can tell.'

'Yeah?' he asked, his face coming suddenly alive. 'You really think so?'

'I do,' she said, perfectly seriously, and Kier felt himself flush with pleasure. 'And what'll you do with all that money, when you get it?'

Kier's eyes began to glow. 'First thing I'm gonna do is buy the mortgage back on the farm, and hire some hands for Pa.'

Magda reached out and rested her palm against his cheek. 'You're a sweet boy, Kier Harcourt.'

Kier blushed, very conscious of her hand on his cheek, making him shift nervously against the doorjamb. He wasn't sure whether he was glad or sorry when Magda moved away from him and walked onto the landing. His eyes fell to her rounded bottom, which swayed hypnotizingly as she walked and, try as he might, he couldn't tear his gaze away. Magda nodded to the spare bedroom. 'The furniture's in there.'

He gulped and nodded. 'Yes, ma'am.'

'Do you want to wash up a little first?' She walked into the tiny cubicle of the bathroom and ran some water into the basin. 'You must be feeling sticky.' She turned and walked to the door, her body brushing against his as she squeezed past. Kier walked to the sink, surprised to find that he was trembling. He drenched a flannel and wiped it over his chest. His nipples seemed bigger than usual, and rock-hard.

Through the crack of the door Magda watched, panting slightly. When he came back out, she had moved a few paces away. Quickly she led him to the spare bedroom. It was square, tiny, and crammed with useless junk.

'I'll soon have it all cleared, ma'am,' Kier promised.

He walked to a crate by the window and dragged it across the floor. 'Just put it out back, by the trash,' Magda called, deciding to let him do some work first, just in case Oscar asked what they'd been doing all afternoon. When he came back, Magda had taken off her dress. Spying him, she seemed to flush in embarrassment. 'Oh, Kier, don't mind me. It's just so hot, and I didn't want to make my dress all sweaty. 'Sides,' she smiled, 'this ol' petticoat covers as much of me as the dress did, doesn't it?'

'Yes, ma'am,' Kier said doubtfully. The petticoat was white and see-through and he could see the outline of her bra-less breasts perfectly. The palms of his hands began to itch.

'And if you don't tell anyone, nobody'll know.'

'No, ma'am.'

'This town talks because it has nothin' better to do.'

'Yes, ma'am,' Kier mumbled dutifully.

Magda quickly ran a dry cloth over the windows. She looked around for inspiration, spotted something and smiled to herself. Stretching up against the wall, she tried to dislodge a couple of leather bridles that were hung from two nails near the ceiling.

'Here, let me,' Kier offered, walking over to her. He reached up, his fingers clutching the leather, his bare chest brushing against the cold, white plaster of the wall. Then he froze. Magda's hand was on his back, her fingers tracing the indentation of his spine. 'You know, Kier,' she said softly 'you've grown a lot since you first started working here.'

'Yes, ma'am,' he gulped, his eyes staring at the wall not an inch away.

With insistent fingers she turned him around. 'Let me take a good look at you. Hmm . . .' Her fingers ran over his chest, slowly and idly circling one nipple, as if she was doing it absentmindedly and not really realizing what she was doing. Kier's eyes widened as they looked into cat-like green ones. Excitement began to inject adrenalin into his veins.

'You're gonna be a real heartbreaker, aren't you, Kier Harcourt?' Magda cooed, her hands reaching up to play with the leather straps that Kier still held above his head, the brass rings holding fast to the nails.

'I don't want to break no hearts,' he muttered, his own heart thumping so loudly in his chest he was sure she must hear it. He was a little bit scared but totally fascinated. It was going to happen. He wasn't quite sure what 'it' was, but he knew men laughed about 'it' in the saloon, and slapped each other's backs when talking about Maisie's brothel, over in Buffalo. Now it was going to happen to him.

'But you will break them,' Magda said, stepping closer to him. Her breasts brushed against his chest and her nipples felt like hard pebbles through the flimsy lace of her petticoat.

Kier swallowed hard. 'Mrs Smith,' he said, half a plea for mercy, half a demand for more.

'Hmm?' Magda purred and, leaning forward, kissed him full on the mouth. Kier felt her tongue dart against his teeth and his loins hardened, straining painfully against his jeans. He moaned, his eyes widening and then languorously closing as the kiss deepened. Magda slowly pulled away and then looked down at his erection.

'Kier Harcourt!' she said, her voice sounding shocked and scandalized. Kier went scarlet. He made an attempt at escape, but Magda was too quick.

'Oh no you don't.' She placed a hand against his chest. 'If my husband knew what you were doing he'd take a horse-whip to you.'

'Yes, ma'am,' Kier said humbly, all but hanging his head in shame.

In response, she stood on tiptoe and began to twine the bridle leather about his wrists in tight, complicated hoops. Dumbfounded, he remained passive. 'So we mustn't tell him. Must we?' she whispered, looking into his startled brown eyes and smiling.

He shook his head, totally confused. 'No, ma'am.'

With his hands held above him by the leather thongs, Magda ran her hands up his arms, and then suddenly dipped her head to kiss his armpit. Kier jerked, totally unprepared. 'You like that, my little poet?' Magda whispered, surprising him with her knowledge of his nickname. Wordlessly he nodded.

'You must say "yes, ma'am", Kier.'

'Yes, ma'am.'

Magda kissed his throat, moved on to the ridges of his collarbone, then slid down to fasten her mouth on the nipple above his thundering heart. Kier gasped, his hands pulling down automatically, but the leather reins held. Kier curled his fingers around the straps, his palms sweating, his fingers sliding against the dark leather, unable to get a firm grip.

'Did you like that, Kier?'

'Yes, ma'am,' he said hoarsely, running his tongue over painfully dry lips. Again she stood on tiptoe, this time so that her eyes could be on a level with his. Slowly she slid her hand down between their bodies. When her palm was resting flat against the hard bulge of his jeans she began to rub him — surprisingly hard. Kier closed his eyes and groaned, his legs growing weak. Magda was panting hard now. She loved virgins — their reactions were always so strong and pure. And Kier was the choicest she would ever have, she knew this instinctively. She watched his sensitive face twitch, exulting in the way small gasps feathered past his lips, smiling as his young, innocent body began to undulate against the wall in a helpless rhythm that she dictated.

'You like that, too — don't you, Kier?'

'Yes, ma'am,' he groaned.

She quickly dispatched with his jeans, all the time looking up at his face. He had become perfectly still.

Magda smiled. 'Oh, I'm not going to hurt you, my little poet,' she promised. 'I'm gonna teach you everythin' you need to know fer when you go to Oxford and meet all them fancy English girls.'

Slowly she kissed his sternum, then sank to her knees to kiss his stomach, her tongue darting into his navel. 'You like that, Kier?' she asked, then moved lower.

'Oh, yes, ma'am,' he moaned, his young, sweat-slicked body jerking helplessly as she sucked on him, her mouth a hot and wet implement of torture. He saw lights flash against his eyes, as his arms strained at his leather bonds. Kier moaned, his throat stretched taut as he leaned his head back against the wall.

Magda, her mouth full, nevertheless managed to smile. He might think it was all over, but she knew different. She'd untie him, and then start all over again. Only this time she wouldn't waste his erection. If he thought this was something — and the way he was moaning and carryin' on, he obviously did — just wait until she introduced him to her vagina. Her inner muscles would squash and mash him into a frenzy. She'd hold him clamped in her with her long, strong legs, and make him work like he'd never had to work before.

Kier, unaware of the afternoon that still lay ahead, began to jerk spasmodically . . .

* * *

Kier arrived late at the old barn, where rehearsals were halfway over, looking totally washed out.

'Hey — here's Cecil,' Johnny Carter greeted him cheerfully. 'Thought you'd show up then?'

'Yeah. Come on, you mugs, let's see how you've been spending your time.' And as he listened to Johnny go through the script, his professionalism began to take over. Under his eagle eye, the play started to take shape. He improvised, redirected and even rewrote where necessary. And as the summer drew on, the play became perfected. The three nights that it was to run came and went without incident, earning record money. In July he learned that he had passed all his exams and had won a Rhodes Scholarship to Waynflete College, Oxford, beginning in three years' time. Miss Ritter threatened to heap extra studies on him that would set his head to busting.

He worked on the farm, he worked at the store, he worked at his studies and he worked beneath, on top of, and by the side of, Mrs Smith.

And when the time came for Kier to go to Oxford, he was more than ready for 'all them fancy English girls'.

CHAPTER 6

Switzerland, Two Years Later

In the Bernese Oberland, Oriel Somerville watched a train approach, and meandered out of the railway station into the warm summer sun. A lone buzzard circled high on the thermals in the clear, azure sky. The station was spotlessly clean, and flowers hung from baskets, frothing scarlet geraniums, periwinkles and white, cascading bellflowers. The whole wooden structure was set against a backdrop of snow-capped mountains, liberally forested in rich, verdant green.

'We're terribly late, you know,' a glum voice said in her ear. Oriel smiled, and turned to look at her best friend, Betty Wooster, an English Right Hon.

'What's the matter? Worried old Scarecrow will have you served up for lunch? With the proper sauce, of course.'

Betty grinned. 'And all the appropriate cutlery and . . .' the two girls began to chorus together, in a high-pitched German-accented voice, 'the apprrrrroprrrriate linen, corrrrrectly folded.' They burst into laughter at the end of their imitation of the school's etiquette teacher, causing the station master to smile indulgently. Every year the young girls came to Johan's Finishing School for Young Ladies, and every year

49

they seemed the same. There were the English — in clothes that were too tight, too short or too ugly, with nasal voices that always bemoaned the lack of horses in Switzerland. Then there were the mixed Europeans, dressed in classic French clothes, with haircuts of sleek bobs, perfect makeup, precise French and a superior attitude that always offended the townspeople. Then there were the Americans, who were perpetually friendly, outspoken and good-naturedly boastful.

The little blonde American, who was asking for a ticket to Interlaken Ost, was the pick of this year's litter. At five feet five, she had long pale hair that most girls would kill for, wide-spaced blue eyes, an elfin chin and a heart-shaped face that had his grandsons moon-eyed and unworkable.

The girls boarded the train and settled on the surprisingly comfortable wooden seats. 'Oh, hell,' Betty grumbled. 'Why are we always late?'

Oriel grinned and shook her head. 'Beats me,' she said, her southern drawl reminding Betty of Scarlett O'Hara. Betty sighed. Her friend really was rather glamorous, unlike Betty, who had a short, unruly mop of nut-brown hair that curled around her head like out-of-control barbed wire. She was a brilliant mathematician, lousy language student, and was the school loser. It was a constant source of amazement that the school darling, Oriel Somerville, should have chosen the beleaguered Betty for a friend in the first place. Betty, at first, had suspected some cruel joke on Oriel's part. But, after a month, the two were inseparable, Oriel's daring exploits getting the blissfully happy Betty into more trouble in the space of a year than she'd ever been in for the whole of her life.

'I say,' Betty said. 'You will be coming home with me for the summer hols, won't you? Daddy will be in London — he practically lives in the House of Lords nowadays, and Mummy has already swanned off to the Bahamas. So we'll have the shack to ourselves.' The shack, as Oriel knew, was a seventy-three-roomed ancestral mansion deep in the heart of Bedfordshire.

'I expect so,' Oriel agreed. 'But I'll have to go home for a couple of weeks first.' As the train started to pull away from the station, Oriel gave the stooped old station master a cheerful wave and settled back against the seat.

As the train began to climb, they passed waterfalls that ranged from foot-wide torrents to mere inches of clear trickling water. Chalets lined the railway tracks with their deep roofs and brightly coloured walls. As they climbed even higher, lush meadowland began to stretch as far as the eye could see. Wild purple orchids became commonplace, as did pink and white campions, moon-daisies, buttercups and blue gentians.

'I love this country,' Oriel said, craning her neck as a small herd of cows came into view, all wearing monstrously outsized cow bells.

'What time is it, Or?' Betty asked nervously, and without looking at her watch Oriel gave an unconcerned shrug.

'Too late.'

'Wonderful,' Betty grumbled. 'I wish I had nerves of steel like you.'

'The trick is just to not give a shit,' Oriel told her, the crude word falling so gracefully from her friend's pretty pink lips that Betty laughed. Betty sounded like a horse with hiccoughs when she laughed, but Oriel didn't mind. She was so uncomplicated. Oriel's thoughts wandered to her mother, back home in Atlanta, and she began to frown. She was not looking forward to going home.

The train, after a hair-raising climb, pulled into their station. 'We're in for it, I expect,' Betty said glumly.

'Oh, I expect so,' Oriel confirmed, and took Betty's hand. 'The dastardly duo strikes again.'

'Awol,' Betty said. 'Worth at least five hundred lines. Thou shalt not sneak off during nature walks.'

Oriel nodded. 'And written in French, I reckon.'

'Oh no!' Betty wailed. 'Not French!'

The girls' feet began to drag the closer they came to the white-washed three-storey building that was school, home

51

and entertainment centre. They were instantly spotted by the headmistress who, with a hooked, imperious finger, beckoned them forward. The two girls looked at one another, sighed deeply and trudged forward.

Frau Reinhart watched them approach with a heart that was much warmer than either girl could ever have guessed. 'Miss Somerville. Miss Wooster. We've been expecting you.'

'We do our best,' Oriel said cheekily, and Betty bit her lip, keeping in her horse's laugh with a great deal of effort.

'I think, under the circumstances, Miss Somerville, you can leave the school a few weeks early.'

Oriel paled a little, but other than that made no sign that she was surprised. 'I don't suppose that will pose any undue difficulties, Miss Reinhart,' she mimicked the prim diction of the older woman with perfect precision.

Miss Reinhart nodded. 'Max will take you and your luggage to the train station. I've been speaking to your mother, and she expects you soon.' The headmistress dismissed and watched them go. It would take a good man to bring the southern belle under control. Miss Reinhart rather envied her.

'What a bummer,' Betty said, who had picked up the turn of phrase from her American friend and was using it now more than any other.

'Oh, I don't know. A girl should get expelled from at least one school during her lifetime, don't you think?' Oriel asked cheerfully as, once back in their room, she began to pack.

'I don't suppose I'll ever manage it, though. Unless I can get booted out of St Cat's,' Betty said miserably.

'What?'

'St Catherine's. It's a college at Oxford. I'm going to read Mathematics there. I told you that, didn't I?'

'Ah yes, that's right. I wish I could go to Oxford,' Oriel murmured thoughtfully. 'Daddy could easily afford to send me as a foreign student. Oh, I don't want to go home,' she finally admitted in a wail, holding a lambswool sweater in pastel pink under her chin.

Betty looked at her curiously. 'What's so bad about home?'

Oriel shrugged. 'Nothing really. It's just . . . stifling down there. If you've never been to Georgia, you can't understand. And, what's worse, Daddy will be away all summer.'

'On business, is he?' Betty asked, and Oriel grunted.

'The Somervilles of Atlanta don't do anything as gauche as business.' Then she sighed. 'But that's not fair. During the war, Daddy worked here as a diplomat. Now there's an international committee being set up to track down the Nazis, and Dad's on it. He just can't sit by, like everyone else, and leave it to others to tackle evil. He believes it's his duty to track down war criminals. He has the time and the money and nothing else to do with it. So . . .'

Betty sighed. Her father spent his time sleeping in the House of Lords.

'Which means there'll be just me and Mummy,' Oriel concluded gloomily. 'And every time I go home I get the feelin' that I can't breathe. There are coffee mornings, and cocktail evenings, parties and luncheon at Gwenny's. Always the same good ol' boys, the same conversations, over and over. Ugh' — she gave a theatrical shudder — 'the thought gives me the willies.'

Betty sighed again. Families!

'The thing is, I'm not like my mother,' Oriel went on. 'She leads a double life the way you or I would wear a blouse. It fits her somehow. I'll bet she can't wait till Daddy leaves for Europe so she can start seein' that long-time lover of hers again.'

She finished packing, unaware that Betty's mouth had fallen open. 'A lover?' Betty squawked. 'You mean . . . a real-life . . . lover? An actual man on the side? I can't imagine my mother actually doing . . . it . . . with a man. Any man!'

'Well, I can imagine my mother doing it all right with Kyle O'Sullivan, or O'Connor or . . . O something, anyway.'

'You mean you know who he is?' Betty squealed.

'Oh, yes,' Oriel confirmed airily. 'He runs a garage in Burford.'

'What's he look like?' Betty asked, fascinated. 'Is he all short and oily?'

Oriel snapped her suitcase catches, her face thoughtful. 'Well . . . much as I hate to say it,' she mused, 'he is rather gorgeous.' Her face twisted for a moment. 'Poor Daddy. Oh well, at least she didn't try to seduce our butler,' she added savagely.

Betty's eyes became round saucers, and Oriel could stand no more. She began to howl with laughter, ducking when her friend lobbed a pillow at her. The subsequent pillow fight ended when a knock on the door brought Max, telling her it was time to go to the station. The two girls looked at each other miserably, hugged, and promised to see each other soon, the minute Betty could arrange for Oriel to visit.

* * *

Oriel missed Switzerland the moment she got home. The south seemed to her like an overripe fruit; too soft, too hot, too . . . everything. Georgia hadn't changed much, she thought grimly. Nevertheless, as she set eyes on Riveree's white magnificence, she felt a reluctant sense of homecoming. She could see her mother's slender figure, straight and relaxed in the portico's massive frame. Oriel took a deep breath and paid off the taxi driver.

Oriel and Clarissa stood silently for a while, studying each other. Then Clarissa smiled and held out her arms, and Oriel ran into them. Held in the warm embrace she could smell the familiar Dior essence of her mother's perfume and felt the familiar sensation of cool silk under her cheek. Mother and daughter pulled away and looked deep into each other's eyes.

'Are you mad at me?' Oriel wanted to know, and Clarissa smiled ruefully.

'Not if you've learned how to be a proper lady.'

Oriel groaned and pulled away, walking into the hall. 'Don't worry, Mama. I'll never be able to burp or fart again.'

'Oriel!' Clarissa snapped, and her daughter stopped stomping across the hall and turned around, at least looking contrite.

'I'm sorry. I'll be good, I promise. I can arrange flowers, discuss a menu like I was a cordon bleu chef, and I know enough about makeup and clothes to start my own boutique. OK?'

Clarissa relaxed, noticing the natural elegance with which her daughter walked, and the classic, understated simplicity of the dress she was wearing. Her money had been well spent, after all. 'You must be totally exhausted. Why don't you pop upstairs, take a shower and then sleep until dinner, hmm?'

'Sounds blissful,' Oriel agreed, and headed for the stairs at a fast skip.

Clarissa watched her, full of pride and love. She was still so young, like a graceful filly.

She turned as a voice in the alcove behind her said, 'Was that Oriel I heard just now?'

'Yes, she's just this second arrived,' she told her husband. 'She'll be down for dinner. The poor girl was shattered. I didn't have the heart to scold her about her behaviour.'

Duncan looked up the deserted stairs and smiled. 'It's good to have her back,' was all he said, then turned and disappeared back into his study.

Sighing, Clarissa followed him in. 'We'll have to start preparing for her season,' she said. 'I know you'll be in Luxembourg for most of it, but that's no reason why she shouldn't be deb of the year.'

'As you say, my dear,' Duncan said, sitting down in an enormous black leather chair that seemed to swallow him up.

'What do you think of Billy Bob Walker? He'll be inheriting his daddy's diamond mines in South Africa soon. He'd make a fine husband for Oriel.'

Duncan opened his mouth, then closed it again. It would have been futile to point out that Oriel was only seventeen. 'Whatever you think best,' he said mildly, but a small frown tugged at his pale brows.

Clarissa nodded, not expecting any other kind of answer, and left the study. Her husband was immersed in his search for Wolfgang Mueller before his wife had even closed the door behind her.

Dinner was a relaxed affair, Oriel entertaining her father with tales of Switzerland. But after a while, Clarissa deftly turned the conversation to what she considered more relevant topics. 'There's a party tomorrow at the Randolf,' she named the most prestigious hotel in Atlanta. 'You will come?'

She looked across at her daughter, who nodded and said, 'I suppose so.'

'You don't sound very enthusiastic, kitten,' Duncan mused.

Oriel smiled, then shrugged. 'Well, I guess it'll be nice to see the old gang again. Oh, before I forget, the Right Honourable Elizabeth Endora Wooster has asked me over to the ancestral pile of bricks this summer. Can I go?'

'Of course,' Duncan said.

'I don't think so,' Clarissa said at the same time. Oriel looked across at her mother and reached forward for her wine glass.

'Why not, Mummy?' she asked, with misleading mildness.

'Well, there's so much to do this summer,' Clarissa said, a little nonplussed by the sudden hardness in her daughter's voice. 'I thought we'd spend some time in Charleston and look for a whole new summer wardrobe for you. Then there's the Gregson Ball in July, and the Yacht Club meet in August. We've got to visit Savannah for the hunt, and then . . .'

Oriel closed her eyes and sighed. 'Oh, hell,' she said so quietly that only her father, sat immediately on her right, heard her. Under the table he reached for her hand and squeezed it gently.

The following night, at one o'clock in the morning, Oriel burst into her father's study. She was wearing a beautiful lime-green evening dress, but her face was flushed and she was breathing hard. Duncan put down the papers he'd been studying. 'What's the matter?' he asked, instantly alarmed.

'That . . . that . . . bastard, Billy Bob Walker,' she spat. She wiped the back of her hand viciously across her mouth. Rage leapt into Duncan's eyes. His hands closed into fists.

'What did he do?'

'Got fresh, that's what,' Oriel snapped, then looked at her father with narrowed eyes. 'When I told him to get lost he asked me what was wrong. Didn't I know that he and I were practically engaged?' Oriel paused, her chest rising and falling with the effort of keeping her rage under control. 'Engaged!' she repeated, stating the word as if it were something ugly. 'Now where did he get an idea like that? Do you know?' She shot the question accusingly at her father, who sighed deeply and walked around from behind the huge desk.

'From your mother, I expect,' he said heavily. 'As usual, she's taken things too fast.'

'Mother? What's she done now?' Oriel asked, her shoulders slumping as her righteous anger began to wither. 'I thought that moron Billy Bob was acting too damn self-confident.'

'Your mother seems to think he's perfect matrimonial material,' Duncan admitted, pouring two small measures of the finest Napoleon brandy into huge, bulbous glasses.

'Oh no!' Oriel wailed. 'I don't believe it. Daddy, you've got to help me. I need an escape route!' She half-laughed, but in her eyes her father clearly saw a growing panic.

He nodded his head briskly. 'All right. Where do you want to escape to?'

The question took her by surprise for a moment, and then she began to smile. 'I want,' she said, clearly and slowly, 'to go to Oxford.'

'Oxford?' Duncan repeated, totally taken aback. He'd never heard her mention that university before.

'Oxford,' Oriel repeated firmly.

Duncan slowly began to smile, then raised his glass. Solemnly they clinked them together. 'To Oxford,' he said. 'And your mother can rant and rave as much as she likes.'

Clarissa did.

CHAPTER 7

Monte Carlo

The principality of Monte Carlo lay shimmering in the bright summer sun. In Port Hercule a flotilla of craft bobbed on the gentle swell of the Mediterranean, their white hulls echoing those of the seagulls' wings that soared overhead. Masts thrust into the air, sails neatly furled, brass adornments gleaming like gold. High up on the hill stood the Royal Palace. Rumours were rife concerning the possible marriage of Prince Rainier to the American film star Grace Kelly. Already the women were deluging the boutiques and salons for hair colourants of the exact same shade as that feted actress. The cool, elegant blonde look was in.

Wayne D'Arville walked slowly along the promenade, his azure blue eyes hardly noticing the lighthouse in the harbour, or the swaying of the exotic palm trees all around him. A tourist next to him turned to his wife and excitedly pointed out that they could actually see the Cap d'Antibes, and Wayne didn't bother to put him right. His lips curled into a superior sneer as the couple began to take photographs with a cheap Kodak. He hated Monte Carlo in the summer. The roads became chock-a-block and you couldn't move on the pavements. Ice-cream cones littered the enchanted streets, and the blue-canopied cafés became overrun. Still, it also meant that the casino trade became ever more frantic. He could just imagine the millions of francs now pouring into his father's place, the Droit de Seigneur Casino.

Wolfgang was excessively proud of it. It served the best wine and food, and did not pretend to be a country mansion, just the best casino in town, the famous Casino de Monte-Carlo, naturally, being exempted.

Wayne strode between the traffic with ease. Now, at the age of twenty, he was six feet four inches tall. His hair was the pale copper of autumn leaves. His eyes were big and blue, and his face had the square, intelligent look of his race. Girls stopped to look at him, their eyes speculative, and not just because of his spectacular looks. He walked quickly and with purpose, as if he were in a hurry to get somewhere, and he had the hard-eyed, firm-jawed look that told everybody that he'd get exactly what he wanted. But then, he'd known that the moment they had all moved into the house on the hill in La Turbie. He wanted everything his father had. It had been his constant goal in life and drove him to be the best. He'd studied so hard and so furiously that he'd earned a place at the Sorbonne. Not content to be only intellectually superior, Wayne had worked on his body, exercising it until it was a well-muscled machine. And yet, as he neared the casino, its familiar Gothic facade holding no beauty for him, he could feel a familiar weakness coming back. Unbelievably, he knew, he still felt the urge to try and please his father.

He could still remember the glow of satisfaction he'd felt when Wolfgang had looked proud of him for coming first in his baccalaureate exams. Even his mother, an older, still elegant version of the Berlin hostess, had pinched his cheek with her white-gloved hand and smiled proudly into his eyes. He'd felt capable of walking on air. Until the following day, when Hans had won the amateur local water-skiing competition. For Hans there had been a night out at the Belle Epoque at the Hermitage Hotel. For Hans there had been a reporter come to interview him for the local paper, the *Nice-Matin*, with his picture being spread across the centre pages. For Hans there had been champagne, although Wayne had not been allowed to drink it at his age. For Hans, Wayne thought as he pushed through the revolving doors that led into the lush interior of the casino, there was everything. At only fourteen, Hans ruled.

Wayne paused inside the casino and looked slowly around him, letting his bitterness settle back into its usual hidden place, lurking like a diseased rat in the corners of his mind.

The decor of the casino was overwhelmingly crimson. Overhead, chandeliers lit the green baize of the gaming tables, and deep mahogany furniture glowed in the artificial lighting. The rooms had no windows and no clocks. Most of the games were rigged, of course. But every now and then Wolfgang would allow someone to win big. It was marvellous publicity, and kept the steady stream of idiots coming in. With an ease born of long practice, Wayne began to scan the faces. He could spot local housewives, gambling the money for the Sunday roast on the hopes of earning enough to buy a Balmain original. Then there were the professionals, men dressed in rumpled suits, faces betraying nothing at all. And, of course, the tourists in T-shirts. The slogans varied from year to year. This year, '*Draft Beer — Not Students.*'

Slowly Wayne walked through the room, avoiding the tuxedo-clad waiters. The constant whirr of the fruit machines, relegated to the outer halls, provided the background music. The clacking spin of the roulette wheel, the roll of dice, the tap-tap of chips, all droned together to become one long, insignificant hum.

A waitress deliberately nudged him. 'Oh, pardon, monsieur,' the girl said, a slight blush staining her suntanned cheeks as her pert breasts rubbed against his arm. She liked everything about the casino owner's son, from the way he wore the Pierre Cardin grey silk trousers and matching shirt with perfect ease, to his pale-flame hair. She pouted at him playfully. Wayne smiled, his loins tightening momentarily before shrugging the lust away. He had other things on his mind at the moment. Giving her a cool smile, he left her and walked on through to the high-risk salon.

Here only the greatest of high-flyers and the richest of the rich were accommodated. Wayne barely paused. The spectacle of the casino was as commonplace to him as buses were to bus conductors. Walking through, he entered a private, narrow white corridor and entered the manager's office.

Edouard de Lepee glanced up, his narrow face tight and alert. On seeing Wayne he visibly relaxed and Wayne felt the familiar helpless rage assail him. Edouard de Lepee was his father's right-hand man, and he had not taken long to see the lie of the land. Hans, and not Wayne, was the unspoken heir to the D'Arville inheritance. Around Wolfgang, Edouard was fawning and sycophantic. Around Hans, he was careful, and avuncular. Around Wayne, he was nothing at all. Wayne felt his hands curl into impotent fists by his sides as Edouard finished some paperwork.

'Wayne,' he said curtly. 'What can I do for you?'

'I was looking for my brother,' Wayne said, none of his almost murderous thoughts showing on his face. One day, Wayne thought, he was going to take the greatest of pleasure in sacking this piffling little nobody and . . .

'Hans is on the beach. He's practising the high-dive for the school competition.'

Wayne nodded curtly, turned and left. One day, he thought savagely, I'll be master here. And Hans and all the rest will jump when I say. His teeth began to ache, and he realized he was biting down so hard that his gums were going numb. Once more on the street, he took several calming breaths. He hated the noise of the tourists. He hated the heat of the sun. He hated his brother, his father, and that dog De Lepee. He still hated the whole world.

He walked to a Maserati two-seater and opened the door. It was bottle-green in colour and sported custom-made wire wheels. He pulled the top down, able to breathe more easily once he was on the Rue Terrazzani and headed out of the city. Hans, he knew, would be further up the coast, diving from the cliffs at Saint Michel. High-diving was his younger brother's latest accomplishment. He drove fast but well along the serpentine road that hugged the coastline, called the Sentier du Littoral. He was not sure what he'd say to Hans when he found him. He was never sure what to say to Hans. The boy worshipped him, much to Wolfgang's displeasure, and Wayne was aware of a dangerous conflict of emotions at work within him concerning his younger brother, rival and enemy. He'd grown perversely fond of little Hans, and it worried him sometimes. He could not afford to get close to anyone.

He gunned the engine viciously as Saint Michel came into view. The rock was a good forty feet high and as he pulled the car onto the grass dunes by the silvery shore, he saw a bright red blob halfway up the cliff face, and recognized the scarlet trunks belonging to his brother. Without thinking, he tooted the car horn in a friendly, spontaneous gesture. Over the distance he saw a pale hand wave eagerly in the air. He didn't wave back. Still Hans kept waving with puppy-like determination, and slowly, almost reluctantly, Wayne felt compelled to lift his arm and wave back. Angry with himself, he took off his shirt and shoes and began to walk along the beach, slowly entering the shade underneath the rock face as Hans climbed higher, way above him. He could hear the chattering voices of Hans's entourage at the top of the cliff, ready to applaud their school hero's latest daring effort.

Wayne had never been popular at school. His sole ambition was to be the best, which made him a teacher's pet, but earned him the scorn of his peers. Angry and hurt by their scorn, he had become cold and superior. Boys stupid enough to pick a fight with him had ended up with broken noses and in one case, cracked ribs. He'd earned the reputation of school bully, although that was not totally fair. So long as they left him alone, he left them alone.

Wayne suddenly heard his brother's voice, high above. Out on the waves a single fishing boat cruised a hundred yards or so away, and Wayne watched the single fisherman with vague interest, his mind on other things.

Hans enjoyed being liked. He enjoyed running in the sun with his friends, he enjoyed kissing girls and playing chess with his father. In short, Hans simply loved life. As he perched on the rock face, looking down into the gentle swell of the blue sea he felt no fear. He thought of Wayne, tall, handsome, wonderful Wayne, waiting on the beach to watch him dive, and he grinned, his freckled face revealing a missing tooth. As he paused, his arms extended, Hans decided to do a backwards somersault. That would make Wayne proud of him. If all went well on Saturday, he'd have another cup to bring home for Papa to put in the darkened glass cabinet he'd had specially made for him.

Hans leapt, his heart strong, sure of himself and of his place in the world.

Below, in his peripheral vision, a plummeting body yanked Wayne's eyes from his casual interest in the fishing vessel. There was just an instant when he realized there was something horribly wrong; that there was something odd in the fall and angle of the body that was not right, causing Hans to hit the water with a harsh slap, instead of a clean glide. After a few, frozen seconds it became obvious Hans was not about to resurface with a laughing comment and a cheery wave, as he usually did. Wayne's heart jerked in his chest and his mouth went dry. He stepped two paces forward, his body tense and quivering, ready to plunge into the surf . . . and then he stopped. He stood for long seconds, watching the sea, then saw his brother's pale hands flap limply above the waves. Wayne felt his innards churn. The sand under his bare feet seemed to burn his soles, but his eyes stayed fixed on those white hands, slapping weakly against the water. They looked like pale butterfly wings, insignificant and irrelevant in the mighty blue sea. Wayne felt sunk in the sand and unable to move.

* * *

Claude Rissaud straightened on the deck of his boat, his youthful face creased into a frown. '*Merde*,' he muttered, dragging his faded blue T-shirt over his head and levering off his deck shoes. Claude was only seventeen but had been swimming since he could talk. Within moments his fit brown body hit the water like an arrow. Dimly Wayne heard the splash and dragged his eyes away from where his brother's hands had been. He could see another swimmer in the water now, pulling away from the rusty trawler with brisk overarm strokes.

Within a few minutes Claude had reached the inert body of Hans Mueller, also called Henri D'Arville. Water trickled from the small face, and the boy's chin felt cold and clammy when Claude cupped his hand under it and began to haul the body towards the shore where he'd noticed the copper head of the man who'd stood on the beach and watched the boy drown. Rage filled Claude as he found the shale under his feet and stood up, dragging the body onto the sand. He collapsed onto his knees and stared down at the boy's face. His eyes were open, but the boy's chest didn't move. Quickly, Claude administered the kiss of life, remembering how it was done from a book he'd once read in a dentist's waiting room.

Nothing. He began desperately to thump on the boy's chest, but again there was no reaction. Claude started to shake with shock. He had never encountered death so closely before. Those open blue eyes, the small, lifeless body . . . He felt tears smart in his eyes, and he took a deep shaking breath, rubbing the back of his hand against his nose.

A shadow fell over them, and Claude sat back on his heels, looking up into the man's face. He recognized him immediately, of course, just as he had instantly recognized the drowned boy as being the younger son of Marcus D'Arville. Claude gasped. The man who'd watched him drown had been the boy's own brother! For the first time doubt began to circulate in his mind. Had shock rendered Wayne D'Arville unable to go to his brother's aid? Was that why he had stood, frozen to the spot, when only yards away his own brother had lost his pitifully short life?

'Monsieur D'Arville . . . I'm so sorry,' Claude stuttered, rising shakily to his feet. He was horribly conscious of the older man's status and power, and felt dwarfed by Wayne's size. Would he blame him for not reaching Henri soon enough? 'I . . . I just couldn't get there in time,' Claude cried, his voice uneven and appalled. He began to shift uneasily under Wayne's steely blue gaze, and self-consciously rubbed the wet black hair from off his forehead. 'The dive went wrong, you see . . . I watched him. He couldn't straighten out and he hit the water on his back.' Claude gestured helplessly to the cliffs above them, and then stumbled into silence.

Wayne nodded. 'I couldn't see his dive from where I was.'

'No, of course not,' Claude murmured, ice beginning to creep into his blood. 'You probably didn't see it all go wrong.'

'No,' Wayne repeated with soft, chilling emphasis. 'I didn't.'

Claude nodded vigorously. He was suddenly terrified but was not sure why. There was something very still about the giant man standing in front of him — something menacing. 'It's a tragedy, monsieur,' he finally muttered, unable to stand the silence any longer.

Wayne looked down at Hans's face, and a small muscle began to beat at the side of his jaw. 'Yes,' he said, his voice dead. 'It was a tragedy. I wish . . . I wish I'd never seen it happen.' His voice began to crack.

Claude let out his breath in a relieved whoosh. He had been wrong, after all. For a few awful seconds he'd actually thought . . . 'In fact,' Wayne said, his voice suddenly hard and precise, 'there's no reason anyone should know I was even here. There's no point in upsetting my family even further.'

'Monsieur?' Claude said, puzzled.

'The kids on the cliff top did not see me arrive. And you did not see me here, either. Did you . . . Rissaud, isn't it?'

Claude went white. He knew he did, and he took a few steps back, as if Wayne were some poisonous cobra about to strike him. 'You did it on purpose,' he accused, his voice an appalled whisper. His young face wore a look of such disgusted horror that Wayne felt a white-hot fury erupt within him. In a flash his fist shot out and caught the young fisherman on the side of his face. Claude flew back in the air and landed in the surf. He lay there unmoving as Wayne walked a few more steps and stood towering over him.

'Your family owns a fishing boat, yes?'

Claude said nothing.

'I believe things have not been going too well recently,' Wayne continued grimly. 'Tourism is ruining the lobster beds, and the catches are getting smaller and smaller. That's so, isn't it, Rissaud?' Claude nodded. The waves felt like ice water around his elbows, and his heart was hammering so loud he felt sick. The way the man talked, the way he acted, no one would know that his younger brother lay dead at his feet.

'You don't want the bank to call in any outstanding loans, do you, Rissaud?' Wayne asked. 'Or for your boat to mysteriously catch fire one of these dark nights?'

Claude turned away and vomited into the sand. Tears streamed down his face. He'd never known that such ugliness could exist in the world.

Wayne looked around quickly. There were no other boats on the water, and Hans had had the wind knocked out of him, preventing him from calling out his brother's name. No one need know he had ever been there. But the kids would be down soon, crying and screaming. Wayne looked down at Hans, an odd pride overriding his cold logic. Yes, his little brother deserved screams and tears. No one, Wayne thought with a cold certainty, will cry for me when I die.

'Pick him up,' Wayne said coldly. 'Take him to the road and flag down a car. And, Rissaud,' Wayne said softly, 'unless you want to join him—' he glanced at his brother's lifeless body one last time '—keep your mouth shut.'

CHAPTER 8

Oxford

Kier sat in the lecture hall of St Bartholomew's, affectionately known as the Bull Pit, staring at a stage that was small but adequate. He could tell at a single glance that extra lighting would have to be set up.

'Well, will it do?' a laconic, bored voice inquired lazily. Kier's roommate, Vivian Miles Tarquin Crane, was the eldest son of the Earl of Dorminster. With his long legs hooked over the back of the seat in front of him he looked disreputable and hopelessly romantic, with dreaming looks and a wild streak. A bohemian at twenty, he was rich, precociously talented and had an aimless, directionless life that made Kier feel secretly sorry for him. They'd hit it off the moment Kier had walked into his room and found Viv already in residence, hung-over and begging for an aspirin.

'It'll have to, I suppose. It isn't exactly the Old Vic, though, is it?' Kier responded, thinking of Olivier, but also of the crop of English budding talent — Finlay and O'Toole. He longed to see *Look Back in Anger* by the new playwright, Osborne. The era of the 'angry young man' was upon them, and Oxford seemed a million miles away from it all.

'Bloody Yank,' Viv said affectionately. 'Why do I get the feeling this is going to be the best bloody play OU Drama has seen for years?'

'Because it probably will be,' Kier said, folding his arms and leaning back in the uncomfortable seat, a mock-arrogant scowl on his face.

'Bloody Yank,' Viv said again, then with a lazy grin charmingly changed tactics. 'What are you calling this shindig again?'

'Kate versus Pete,' Kier said, knowing Viv hadn't forgotten, but was merely trying to wind him up. Living in England, Kier was beginning to learn a whole new concept in humour. He was even starting to grasp the intricacies of irony.

'Ah, yes. Modernizing Shakespeare. You don't want to take on much, do you?' Viv said, his eyes twinkling.

'I'm a barbarian, remember? A marauding invader to these hallowed halls.'

'Bloody Yank.'

'Precisely. Why do you suppose all you drama cretins voted me as director, huh? A pipsqueak upstart Rhodes scholar whose only credentials were the annual Burmanville hoe-down.'

'Because we were mad,' Viv said, his beautiful face wearing a look of pitiful dejection. 'We were all half-drunk, and when you came up with the idea of butchering *The Taming of the Shrew*, we all thought it was hilarious. Especially since it put old Flakey's nose totally out of joint.'

'Malcolm Flakestone,' Kier said, deadpan, 'is a total moron. I may not have been here last year to see his production of *Faust*, but I'm still hearing about the reviews, most of which seem to have been written on the john walls.'

Viv began to laugh. 'My oh my, you should have been there to see it. Mass audience participation. They all threw up at the same time, right on cue.'

'Sounds great.'

'Oh it was. But I think you might top it. You're not really going to rename the play Kate versus Pete, are you?'

'I am.'

'Bloody Yank.'

'First, though, I need scenery painters, lighting technicians — you can pilfer them from the Engineering department — prompters, some dress designers and . . . what else?'

'Actors?' Viv asked archly, elongating the word and affecting it with a painfully upper-crust British accent that would have done Olivier proud. 'How now, good Kate. What goes on 'ere? Isn't that how it'll go?'

'Not quite. Mind you . . .' Kier scratched his ear, his face thoughtful. 'I could work it in.' For a second or two Viv stared at him, half-aghast, half-dumbfounded, and then caught the glitter in the American's eye.

Slowly he relaxed back against the chair. 'Bloody Yank.'

* * *

Two days later in Broad Street (known to everyone local as The Broad), the sun was shining on a cool October morning. Blackwell's, the biggest and most famous of all bookshops, presented its black and white, half-timbered facade to the street, looking misleadingly small and quaint. Betty tucked her hand through Oriel's arm and took a deep breath. 'Hmm. Oxford in autumn. Nothing like it.' The beech trees still clung modestly to several golden copper leaves, and the creepers that clung to Trinity and Balliol college walls were a deep golden-veined red. Above them the sky was that curious deep blue of autumn, which in the summer had been alive with swifts and swallows, who made their cupped nests under the ancient eaves of Oxford's thirty plus colleges.

'I never realized till I got here that there wasn't actually any place, any building I mean, that you could point to and say, "There — that's Oxford University."' Oriel looked at her friend, who grinned widely. 'It's just a collection of colleges.'

'That's us British for you. Never do anything the easy way.' Betty was delighted to have her old friend back again. Oriel would make Oxford fun, somehow, Betty just knew it.

'When are the matriculation photos' going to be ready?' Oriel asked, for about the fifth time in as many days.

'I already told you. Not till next month. What's the matter — you got a fetish for subfusc or something?' Betty asked archly.

'Sub what?'

Betty grinned. 'Subfusc, dear. You know that charming little uniform we had to wear for the photo? Black skirt, white blouse, bum-freezer and cap?'

Oriel laughed. 'I love it. I love all of this,' she looked around the ancient city, the mellow sandstone quads, the gothic towers, the domed majesty of the Sheldonian Theatre, the ornate clock faces and the quiet, academic ambiance that proliferated, even in the town centre. 'I'm so glad I came. Wait till Daddy gets the postcards I sent him.'

'Humph,' Betty said, hiding her pride in the beautiful city with typical modesty. 'Wait until you see the Bull Pit.'

'That's even older than New College, isn't it?' When Oriel had first discovered that New College had been around almost 600 years, she'd nearly flipped.

'Yeah — with plumbing to match, I bet,' Betty predicted gloomily. 'We're going to freeze our cute little . . . things . . . off. Providing we get hired of course. I hear the director's one of your lot.'

'We'll get hired,' Oriel said, her blue eyes sparkling with anticipation. 'You're the best scenery painter in the whole world.'

Betty looked across at her friend, the usual, unmalicious envy filling her at the sight of Oriel's carefree beauty. Today she was dressed in lilac velvet trousers and a fluffy pink cashmere sweater. Her blonde hair was loose and gleamed like sunlight. If only I looked like that, Betty thought with a wistful pang, then shrugged. 'Here it is,' she said, leading her friend into an ancient quad. 'Can you see any arrows?'

'Nope.'

'Great. They said the theatre would be marked.'

Inside the unmarked theatre it was chaos. Kier sat at the back, well out of the way, watching the engineering boffins set up an intricate display of lights. Hammering, followed by mixed curses, came from the boys nailing canvas over the wooden frames that would soon be painted for the outdoor scenes. 'It'll never be done for Christmas,' Kier muttered angrily to himself. 'Never in a million years. Hell, what have I gotten myself into?'

'We've got a queue of girls auditioning for Kate,' Charlie Griffin, the co-director and top Classics scholar, yelled from down front. 'Shall we start?'

'Why not?' Kier yelled back, picking up his copy of the play that he'd rewritten, its pages now forlornly dog-eared and coffee-stained. 'Cut out the hammering for a minute, will ya?' he called over to two Experimental Psychology students, who were only too happy to oblige. They left, muttering dire comments about Freud and masochism.

For weeks the production team had been immersed in the technicalities of the play — the widening of the stage, the runners on which the scenery would be wheeled in, hopefully without a squeak. They'd discussed paint, light, cues, makeup, costume — everything but the fun part: the acting. Now the seats began to fill up with interested spectators as Kier walked to the stage and cleared a spot in the centre. He was dressed in disreputable jeans with tears at the knees, and his shirt was stained with sweat and covered with sawdust. He pushed the hair wearily off his forehead as several girls came through the door and stood nervously but with chattering bravado by the wall. Kier looked them over with a jaundiced eye, his gaze widening incredulously on one girl who looked like an electrified poodle. Before he'd had time to think about what he was doing, he was walking over to her. 'Gal, I love your spirit,' Kier said to the startled Betty, 'but despite what you may have heard, this isn't gonna be a farce.'

'Huh?' Betty said, her eyes as wide as saucers.

'Look, we might be doing a Molière comedy next year. Why don't you come back then?'

'Huh?' Betty said again, totally numb in the face of so much masculine gorgeousness. He looked like a

71

heart-breaking rogue, and he had the brooding, sod-'em-all air of Marlon Brando. Betty was wild about Brando.

'He means,' an icy voice said beside her, 'that he thinks you are not fit to play his precious Kate.' The voice, as well as dripping venom, was so mellow, so outlandishly southern belle in accent, that Kier turned startled eyes to the girl by the electrified poodle's side, his mouth dropping open at the sight of her. He felt the barrage of antagonism coming from the blue gaze and quickly ran his eyes over her, taking in her small, slender frame, the heart-shaped face and peaches-and-cream complexion. She looked like a pink and lilac fairy, with spun gold hair and china blue eyes.

Betty went red. 'Oh no. I . . . uh . . . I'm not here to audition.'

'As you'd have known,' Oriel snapped, 'if you'd taken the time to ask, instead of just jumping to conclusions.'

Kier heard a ripple of laughter wind its way around the theatre and flushed dully. 'Oh, great,' he muttered, turning away to salvage what was left of his battered dignity. 'Just what we need.' He stalked a few yards away, then turned back. 'We're not doing *Gone with the Wind*, sweetheart,' he mocked, gratified to hear the laughter come more loudly this time.

Oriel dragged in her breath swiftly. 'I'm not surprised, suh,' she said, exaggerating her accent to farcical extremes. 'To do such an epic would require a director with some modicum of skill.'

Betty looked from one to the other like a spectator at a tennis match. Both had colour high on their cheeks, both were breathing hard and both looked ready to kill.

'To direct *Gone with the Wind*, Scarlett,' Kier snapped back with savage mockery, 'you'd need a director without a brain. That would be the only way to make use of such utter trash.'

'Here here,' a very British voice applauded from the sidelines, and Oriel glanced briefly to where an outrageously handsome man was lounging over some seats.

72

'And you can shut up too,' Oriel spat at Viv, who blinked and began to grin widely.

'Kier, old sport,' he said, straightening out his long, lean form and walking over to where the two antagonists stood, very much the centre of attention now. 'I do believe we have our Kate right here. Have you ever seen such fire?' Viv took Oriel's chin, which she angrily shook off. 'Have you ever seen such shrewishness?' he continued like a bored Noël Coward, the bit well and truly between his teeth. Viv loved trouble like some of his contemporaries loved sex.

'Oh shit,' Kier said helplessly, rubbing his hand wearily across his forehead. 'Alright,' he called out, deliberately turning his back on Oriel and his troublemaking friend. He'd have a word with Viv later. 'Let's get this show on the road.' Kier clapped his hands, attempting to restore some order out of the chaos, and reaffirm his own leadership.

'Oh my gawd, just listen to him.' That voice again, that soft-as-maple-syrup, Scarlett O'Hara voice. 'The king of cliches,' Oriel jibed. 'Somebody tell me he didn't write the script for this little ol' production.'

Kier jerked around, looking ready to flatten her, and the snickering laughter suddenly stopped. Oriel's pert little chin jutted up, ready to do battle. Kier took a long, deep breath, and then sighed ostentatiously. 'Do you mind, Scarlett, if we begin the auditions?' He asked it with such lavish humility that Oriel felt her lips twitch. Her heart was hammering. Underneath her sweater, she could feel her nipples tingling, burgeoning into hardened nubs. She was aware of fine sweat creeping all over her, as she began to radiate heat.

He was the most handsome man she'd ever seen. And she hated him with such a passion it was exquisite.

Aware that he was watching her like a hawk, just waiting for her response, she quickly pulled herself together.

'Not at all, suh,' she responded in kind, and, just as an afterthought, gave a brief but perfectly executed curtsy.

Looking at Betty, who was doing her best to hide a wide grin, she stalked off to the front row and sat down, crossing her arms over her breasts with vicious strength, flattening them and making her wince. Kier stood a few yards away, watching her performance, and then half-bowed himself. 'So kind,' he said, getting in the last word.

He wanted to throttle her at the same time as he wanted to throw her onto her back in the middle of the stage and make love to her. He'd soon wipe that wide-eyed look off her face then, alright. He could just imagine his hands curling around her breasts, his tongue licking those nipples he could see straining against the pink fluffy wool of her sweater into ever harder points of pleasure. Then they'd see who could keep up the wisecracks!

The whole theatre seemed to breathe a sigh of relief, and it snapped his mind back to the task at hand. He felt like spitting. Never had a woman, any woman, managed to distract him so much when he was trying to work. He'd always known directing was in his blood. Now, it seemed, this spitfire was trying to worm her way into it, as well.

'Now,' Kier took a deep breath, reached for several copies of a scene and handed one out to each of the girls still stood by the door. 'I want you to read this scene. Take five minutes, then we'll begin. Uh, Scarlett, would you like a copy, or are you a mind-reader as well as a theatre critic?'

Oriel's lips thinned ominously as she all but catapulted herself out of her seat. She stalked to him like a tigress, yanked a copy out of his hand, then stalked back. Kier's eyes were glued to the exaggerated swaying of her hips, and the angry jerking movement of her limbs. His throat went dry.

Viv began a slow handclap.

'Shut up, you,' Kier rounded on him viciously, jabbing a finger in his direction. 'I can always cast Mark Gregory as Pete.'

Viv paled, then fell to his knees. 'Oh no, boss,' he said, his mimicry of Al Jolson perfect. He held up his hands, palms forward. 'I begs yah, boss, don' do that tuh me.'

The makeshift audience began to clap uproariously, and Kier couldn't help but laugh. 'Get up, you clown.'

A few yards away, Oriel simmered as she listened to Kier giving out the orders. 'What a big-headed, no-good, show-off, no-talent . . .'

'Prat?' Betty, who'd followed her over, offered helpfully.

'Moron,' Oriel preferred, her heart like a trip-hammer in her chest. She felt like committing murder as she watched him. But he looked so tall and capable up there, so powerful and dangerous, that she quickly lowered her eyes to read the script, hoping against hope that it was utter drivel. There was something so magnetic about him. She could actually feel her eyes straining to look up from the paper, but she valiantly fought the need to feast her eyes on him.

She took a deep breath and noticed how badly her hands were shaking. She made a small, angry sound in the back of her throat.

This would never do!

She'd heard on the grapevine that the new director of the OU play had also adapted it, and she scanned the lines quickly. It's *The Taming of the Shrew*, she thought incredulously, and before she could stop herself, her eyes flew back to him on the stage.

'He's only rewritten Shakespeare!' she said, her voice so shocked it was almost a whisper. Betty craned her neck to read the page for herself and smiled.

'So he has. You've got to admire his guts.'

Oriel didn't have to do any such thing. And just at that moment, Kier turned and looked at her, and their eyes clashed. Oriel almost expected to hear the sound of sparking steel, the moment was so physical. For a second, time seemed to stand still. Her eyes widened, her breath caught. Her whole body seemed to leap, even as it froze.

Kier felt the power of her gaze and knew he would never be able to look away from her. She was so damned beautiful. No woman had a right to look that perfect. He wanted . . .

Kier just wanted.

Then somebody coughed, and the theatre came flooding back. Kier turned once more to check on something in the middle of the stage, which didn't need checking, but allowed him to turn his back on her. His face was flushed.

Oriel let out her breath at last in a wonderful sense of release. If he hadn't turned away, she was sure, she'd have gone on gawping at him like some damned lovesick teenager.

Angrily, she turned her attention back to his so-called play. But although the scene was set in modern times, and used modern language, she saw immediately that it was as pithy, funny, aggravating and every bit as clever as the original.

'Well, at least he can write,' Betty said, having finished reading the scene over her shoulder, then jerked away as Oriel turned her head savagely. 'OK, OK. It's awful,' she placated, but still her lips began to wobble.

'It is awful,' Oriel insisted. 'Messin' about with Shakespeare indeed,' she said loudly enough to be heard. 'Just who does he think he is?'

Sat three rows behind her now, Kier stared daggers at her silver head. She's going to be lousy, he thought hopefully. She was probably — no, almost certainly — going to stink. She thought she was such a bigshot. No doubt she came from some mansion someplace down south and had all the men falling at her feet. Her doting mama had probably sent her to one of those fancy finishing schools. Kier knew her kind. For all her spoilt and pampered life, she'd had everything she ever wanted handed to her on a plate. And now she thought she could just waltz into *his* play, and secure herself the lead, just because she thought she could twist him around her little finger, with her big blue eyes and lovely . . . lovely . . . breasts.

Hah!

He'd soon put her right.

The first girl to read the lines was a tall brunette who looked perfect but couldn't act to save her life. The second had a saucy, teasing quality that would have been great in a *femme fatale* role but was all wrong for man-hating Kate. Oriel watched them, her blood still boiling, all the time aware of his glowering presence behind her, burning two holes in her back. She shifted uncomfortably in her seat, ready to explode.

The mean-mannered, arrogant, insensitive, handsome sono-fabitch! She'd show him. Just wait and see.

Viv played opposite the girls with a swaggering bravado that was perfect, and Kier felt relieved. No one could accuse him of playing favourites after this performance. Viv might be his best friend, but anyone with an eye could see he was a born actor. If worse came to worst, he'd be able to carry the play alone. Viv, naturally, took the opportunity to flirt with all the girls outrageously, and the third try-out began to giggle helplessly. As did the fourth. And the fifth.

Kier slapped his hand to his face and ran his fingers down his eyes, nose, and off the end of his chin. Let this last one be good, he prayed. Please, Lord, don't let Scarlett get a look in.

The last girl *was* good. She was competent, she had already memorized her lines, and she looked right. Kier felt a sigh of relief ripple over him. Below, Oriel could almost feel the waves of his relief washing over her, and she felt her backbone stiffen.

She had planned to go up there and play Kate like Scarlett O'Hara, just to show him. But now, as she heard his hateful cowboy drawl asking her if she'd care to partici-pate, she suddenly felt her world dip dangerously around her. Because, suddenly, unbelievably, she wanted that part. She wanted it more than anything in the world. And she knew why, of course. It would mean being around him. It would mean seeing him every day. It would mean listening to his voice, and sneering at him, and feeling that wonderful heat that seemed to flood over her when he was near.

She was getting hooked on him. And it felt wonderful!

Slowly, trying to gather her thoughts and calm herself down, she walked onto the stage, her eyes blue fire. She had not been voted best drama student at both her Atlanta and Switzerland colleges for nothing!

Viv watched her approach and whistled under his breath, instinctively sensitive to the lovely lady's mood. Suddenly the theatre became still as Oriel took several deep breaths. Kier's eyes widened as her face slowly relaxed, then transformed itself into that of another woman. With her left eyebrow pushed up higher and her lips twisted into a parody of a smile, she looked just like he would have expected Kate to look when meeting Pete for the first time.

'So — you're the whizz-kid from Birmingham, are you?' she delivered her first line with a sneer that was perfect, and not a trace of her Scarlett O'Hara accent. He could hear the contempt vibrating in her voice.

Viv caught on in a flash. Walking closer, he allowed himself a smug smile, falling into the character of the swaggering Pete with hearty gusto. 'And you must be Kate. I've heard a lot about you from your *lovely*,' he stressed the word, 'sister.'

Oriel strutted around him, and slowly ran her eyes up and down Viv. For the first time, she realized what a very handsome man he was. Not in the director's class, of course, but . . .

Suddenly, she flicked a look across the theatre, her eyes instantly zeroing in on him. A strange smile flashed across her face and was gone.

Kier tensed. He was sure that smile was not a part of her performance. His lips twisted. What was she up to now?

On the stage, Oriel turned back to Viv. 'You're rather *lovely* yourself, kiddo,' she read the line with cringe-making sarcasm, but at the same time, a husky breathiness that caught Viv unawares. His eyes sharpened on her. And what a sexy piece she was.

Kier felt his body shiver under the sexy double whammy of her voice and gritted his teeth. 'If you'll read the script, Scarlett,' he gritted, 'you'll see I've asked for contempt, mixed with a touch of fear. If I'd wanted a vamp, I'd have said so.'

Oriel smiled. Good. She was getting to him.

Viv caught the smile and almost laughed out loud. He glanced across at his friend and envied him. What fun these two were going to have. 'Why, thank you, Kate,' Viv said. 'I'm so glad you noticed.'

Oriel, for a second, couldn't remember her next line, she was so busy trying to gauge Kier's reaction to her. She dragged her eyes back to Viv.

'Oh, I notice a lot of things, kiddo,' she drawled. 'I even notice flies on the wall, and snakes in the grass.' The last line she delivered with her head turned, looking straight at Kier. His eyes narrowed.

Oriel turned back to Viv, who was helplessly wondering what she'd do next. It was like acting with a stick of dynamite. A *lit* stick of dynamite!

'A twelve-stone man presents no problems for *me*,' she finished. She'd been meant, she knew, to say it with bravado and dismissal, but instead she had deliberately leaned her body towards Viv, slightly turning one shoulder his way, and again bringing a huskiness to her voice.

Viv felt his loins harden, even though he knew she had not played the scene for his benefit. But he just couldn't help it. It was the most sexy thing he'd ever seen.

Every male in the audience thought so too. You could cut the atmosphere with a knife.

Oriel smiled in satisfaction and turned to the director.

Kier was now on the edge of his seat. His hands were curled into fists. He wanted to go across and shake her and tell her to stop coming on to Viv, dammit! But, of course, that was just what she wanted.

He'd be damned if he'd play it her way.

'Not quite what I'm after, sweetheart,' Kier said dismissively, and watched her eyes widen in alarm. 'You started off well, but I think we'll have to go with Janice,' he named the last girl, the girl who'd been so good.

Janice beamed from her seat in the audience.

Viv did a double take. Was he mad? This girl was Kate, with a capital 'K'.

'Perhaps, if you make your directions clearer, I could do it again,' Oriel gritted, but there was a touch of very real fear in her voice. Kier heard it and grinned wolfishly.

Oriel's lips tightened. The bastard! She turned to Viv. 'Let's start again, shall we?' she said.

Kier reared up in his chair. 'Hey, Scarlett!' he yelled, his voice cutting through the now mouse-quiet theatre like a scythe. 'Remember me?'

'As if I could forget,' Oriel snarled back.

Kier ignored her. 'I'm the director, get it? I'm the one,' he ostentatiously pointed at his own chest with his thumb. 'I'm the one who gets to say whether you should start again. That's my job, see?'

Oriel ground her teeth so loudly that Viv could actually hear her. He coughed. 'Er, I think, old man, we really should try it, just one more time.' He looked at his friend, all his stirring and muck-raking instincts leaping to the fore. 'I do have to play Pete, you know,' he added. 'And I would like *some* say in my partner.'

He gave Oriel an outrageous wink.

Kier fumed. He needed Viv badly, and Viv knew it, damn him. 'Alright,' he snapped. 'We'll do it one more time. But,' he jabbed a finger in Oriel's direction, 'play it like it says.'

Oriel saw the savagery in his eyes and her heart leapt. He was jealous of Viv! Hah! Not so high and mighty now, are you, Mr Director?

She nodded graciously. 'I shall do my best,' she drawled, and did.

From the first word she uttered, with Viv's willing help, they became the Shrew and her determined lover.

Kier watched the rest of the scene with a sense of fatality. When they'd finished, the people around him erupted into spontaneous applause. They'd been great! A smash, and everyone knew it.

On the stage, Viv looked up and found Kier with his eyes, shrugging helplessly. 'What can I say, old sport?' He was once again the archetypal English gentleman. 'She's simply brilliant, what?'

Everyone looked at Kier, wondering what he was going to do.

What he did was rest his face in his hands and say with a heart-rending groan, 'Oh, *hell*.'

CHAPTER 9

Two weeks later, Betty stood in baggy blue overalls, her forearms splashed with green paint. The scenery was almost finished, and behind her she listened to the rehearsals with half an ear. They were not going well, and yet they were going brilliantly. About on a par with the previous ones, she thought, grinning as she daubed.

After their first explosive meeting, the cast and crew had expected things to die down between their director and leading lady. After all, everybody reasoned, that kind of grating, repressed sexual tension and electricity could not be kept up for long without burning itself out. But, boy, were they wrong, Betty thought with a wide grin, as she outlined the leaves of her canvas tree with precise artistic skill.

Oriel and Kier's first rehearsal had set the scene for the weeks that had followed.

'OK,' Kier said now, standing on stage with his two principal actors. 'This is where Pete is looking you over,' he glanced reluctantly at Oriel, 'and telling you that it's no wonder you've never had a boyfriend because you're always trying to wear the pants. That shouldn't be any trouble for you, I think?'

Kier hated looking at her, just because he loved it so much. All his concentration went out the window with the merest lift of one of her fair eyebrows, or a twitch of her eminently kissable mouth.

Oriel smiled sweetly, her eminently kissable mouth pouting now, and driving him secretly wild. 'Not for me,' she'd agreed through gritted teeth, then looked Kier over in such obvious and minute detail that everybody held their breath. 'Of course, I'm trusting your instincts on this,' she added. 'Because it's obvious you don't feel comfortable in pants.'

Viv yelped with laughter, then clamped a hand over his wide and mobile mouth as his friend shot daggers in his direction.

'Let's get one thing straight,' Kier began, sighing wearily, and Oriel smiled even more sweetly and interrupted him.

'That would be a nice change for you, I imagine.'

By now, everybody, naturally, had stopped to watch the spectacle. It was not often you got this calibre of entertainment for free. 'I'm the director of this production,' Kier carried on, ignoring her needling dig. His voice was low and dangerous as he walked closer to her, step by menacing step.

In spite of herself she felt her heart begin to pick up a beat, but she held her ground. It was like facing off a tiger. She could almost feel his claws on her, stroking, his nails raking gently across her breasts, and . . . She firmly clamped the thought off and forced herself to concentrate on what he was saying.

'I wrote these lines,' Kier tapped his copy of the script ferociously, 'and if you want to play the part, you do what I say, when I say, how I say.' He'd been steadily bearing down on her throughout these hissed ultimatums, and now he leaned over her, so close that their faces were barely inches away from each other. 'Got it?' he snarled.

Oriel sensed the raw power of him and swore she could feel the heat from his skin scorching her bare face. Nervously she flicked out her tongue to moisten her lips, and then wished she hadn't. His incredibly soft orange-brown eyes wavered and then dipped to watch the movement. Oriel gasped, but so softly that only Viv and Kier heard it.

'Got it,' she managed to grate out with a good facsimile of her usual venom. Viv watched them in silence, then rubbed his hands together. This was going to be a very interesting season. Very interesting indeed.

Oriel decided to change tactics, and for the rest of the session she kept a wary distance. Icy politeness and exaggerated co-operation became the order of the day, allowing the rehearsal to speed along satisfactorily. But since the opening night was fast approaching, everybody was getting tense.

Behind her, the play carried on.

'NO!' Even Betty jumped as Kier's roar suddenly echoed throughout the confined interior of the room. 'I told you before,' he stalked on stage to where Oriel waited, fidgeting nervously.

This was the biggest play she'd ever been in, and she was beginning to feel unsure of herself. Although she wouldn't have admitted it to anybody, she was scared that she'd let her temper get her into a situation that she simply couldn't handle, and Kier's antagonism didn't help. Neither did the way her stomach flipped whenever he was near. 'You don't think it's funny when he tells you to shut up and kiss his ass. It enrages you, it doesn't make you grin, goddammit.'

Oriel finally snapped. For weeks she had put up with his bullying and his rewriting and his nit-picking criticisms. She'd just about had enough. Her anxiety and sexual tension was at fever pitch.

'I can't help it,' she yelled back. 'It's the way you wrote it. It is funny, dammit. Isn't it?' she appealed to the usual odd-job men and part-time audience, who began to nod. Her beauty, her talent, her good humour and her lack of prima donna vanity had long since endeared her to everyone but Kier over the last couple of weeks. But Kier's sole facial expression around her was that of a perpetual scowl.

'Don't ask them,' he yelped now, goaded beyond endurance. 'What the hell do they know?'

Oriel slammed down her script onto the stage floor, then stood staring at him, her breasts rising and falling so agitatedly behind her sweater that Kier couldn't keep his eyes off them.

'Why don't you,' she said softly, 'douse yourself in petrol, and go straight to hell?'

'Because, Scarlett,' Kier snarled back, 'with you as my leading lady, I'm already there.'

'Why, you . . . you . . .' Oriel felt the rage that had been on the back boiler since the moment she'd set eyes on him suddenly erupt. With a yowl of pure, goaded fury, she swung her hand and hit him, full on the face.

It was not any kind of screen slap, but an effort that bore the brunt of her whole weight and fury. Kier staggered back, his face on fire. Viv covered his eyes and sorrowfully shook his head. As the slap echoed throughout the theatre with a sharp 'crack' the room fell totally silent. Everyone held their breath as they waited for Kier's reaction. Oriel felt an appalled fear wash over her, vying for first place with a self-satisfied desire to nod her head, brush her hands and add, 'So there,' just for good measure.

Kier slowly straightened and looked her. For a second, their eyes met in electrified silence. 'That,' he said clearly, 'is just what you should do to Pete, when he asks you to kiss his ass. Get it right this time. Viv, your mark.'

Oriel blinked, as did Viv, and then suddenly the room was filled with laughter and applause. 'Thataway, Director,' someone yelled from the back. 'You tell 'em.'

Kier rubbed his throbbing cheek ruefully and headed past her for the steps at stage right. Oriel was torn between the need to laugh along with everyone else and stamp her feet in temper. 'I hate you,' Oriel whispered as he went past her, and she could smell the fragrance of his cologne mingled with sweat, the scent that was totally Kier. She wanted to kiss him so viciously, so much, she felt herself actually swaying towards him.

'Naturally,' he whispered back, his tiger-eyes flashing like amber fire, 'you want me.'

And with that heart-stopping statement he left the stage, leaving Oriel open-mouthed and staring after him, her heart in her throat.

'Right, from the top again,' Kier called, sitting in his usual chair in the middle of the front row and leaning back, stretching his arms across the backs of the adjoining chairs, for all the world as if nothing had happened. He felt good. He felt so good he wanted to sing. He'd been dying to say that to her for weeks. And the shattered look in her eyes was so sweet, he could still feel the honey of it on his tongue.

On the stage, he watched her begin to shake with a mixture of rage, frustration and something else much more potent that he doubted even she could name it. It was a relief to know that he was not the only one so totally head-over-heels in love.

'Huh . . . Kate darling,' Viv prompted, and Oriel turned to look at him, her eyes confused and tear-bright. 'Don't deliver the slap with quite as much wallop this time, hmm? I have a date tonight, and I don't want my beloved to be offered damaged goods. OK?' Viv wore a hang-dog puppy look of such dramatic proportions that she began to laugh helplessly.

From his seat Kier watched, scowling.

After one more run-through, Viv had to go for a class. The rehearsals broke up, the troops filed out. There were student meets to go to, politics to be discussed and grass to be passed round and smoked into the early hours while they listened to the radio or piled into a common room. This was Oxford, after all — radical, forever young Oxford. As usual Kier was left to last, making notes in the margins of his copy, taking pleasure in the way he could make vague and nebulous thoughts take solid shape up on the stage.

'It's going to be a good play.'

His head jerked up at the soft words, his eyes focusing lovingly on the woman on the stage. Without her audience and the persona of Kate to hide behind, she suddenly looked vulnerable and lost. He felt his heart lurch, painfully.

'Thanks,' he said briefly, folding his notes back into place and shoving them into the battered briefcase that he'd bought second-hand at a flea market.

'Look . . . I . . . I want to apologize for hitting you. I shouldn't have lost my temper like that.'

Kier, his body leaning forward as he shoved the papers into the case on the floor, looked up at her through the fall of hair on his forehead, and then shrugged. 'Forget it,' he said shortly.

Oriel nodded glumly and began to walk across stage. He was not making it easy for her, but then why should he? For a moment she felt a sharp stab of regret wash over her that they should be such bitter enemies. Kier straightened and saw the slouch of her shoulders, her head hung low, and felt like a prize bastard. 'Hey, look. Why don't we bounce over to Browns and have something to eat, huh? After all this hard labour, I'm starved.'

Oriel turned hopefully at the sound of his suddenly softer and cajoling voice, and found an instantly answering smile leaping onto her face. Was she so starved for some kind words from him? It appeared so, she thought ruefully. 'OK. I'd like that. And since I'm the one throwing the punches, I'm even hungrier than you are,' she couldn't resist adding.

Kier laughed. 'You're a saucy minx, I'll say that for you.'

'Sexist pig,' Oriel shot back, not totally joking, and Kier grinned.

'It's the play,' Kier explained. 'It gets into my blood, too. I always take on the character of whatever production I'm doing. I once did A *Tale of Two Cities* in Kansas and turned nearly suicidal for the whole summer.'

'Kansas. Is that where you're from?' Oriel asked eagerly, hungry for any scrap of information about him.

'Yep.' Kier left her briefly in the quad to deposit the bag in his room and grab some change, then quickly rejoined her. Walking briskly in the cold November air, they passed the Ashmolean Museum, where the white Corinthian columns of reminded Oriel of home. Glancing up at it, she sighed with a touch of homesickness, then shrugged it off. Passing the St Giles war memorial, they made their way slowly towards Woodstock Road. 'Betty says this street is beautiful in spring,' she babbled, suddenly nervous now that they were not at loggerheads. 'She says all the cherry trees are out and in flower then.'

'Oh?' Kier looked at her oddly.

'Yeah, but Five Mile Drive is even prettier. She says.'

'Oh,' he said again.

Oriel rubbed her sweating palms on her jeans as they passed Little Clarendon Street. 'You ever been down there?' she nodded her head in the street's direction. 'It's got this great shop that sells all kinds of junk.'

'Junk, huh?'

'Oh, will you stop it?' She gave an aggrieved sigh. 'I'm trying to be nice.'

'I know,' Kier said, deadpan. 'That's what's making me so nervous.'

They were still laughing when they entered Browns. It instantly reminded Kier of Casablanca. The chairs were wicker, the arched backs gleaming with black walnut. Rattan screens separated the tables, and living greenery climbed throughout from big terracotta tubs. Overhead, big old-fashioned rotary fans hung from the ceiling. They selected a padded window seat, ordering tea while they perused the menu.

'When in Rome and all that,' Oriel said. 'I'll have the steak and kidney pie.'

Kier breathed a sigh of relief at her choice, half terrified she'd order lobster. He didn't fancy washing up for the rest of the night because he couldn't afford to pay the bill. 'I'll have the same. So, tell me about yourself, Scarlett,' he urged as the waiter left with their order. 'Is that accent for real?'

Oriel laughed and apologized. ''Fraid so. Born and raised in Georgia.'

'Ah, an Atlanta belle. I thought as much.'

'And you're a Kansas hick.'

'Touché.'

They began to talk, tentatively at first, and then with growing honesty and detail about their homes, their parents, their schools, their lives. It was as if, now that the barriers were down, they couldn't talk fast enough. For weeks they'd starved themselves of information about one another, denying the real reason for their antagonism. Now the floodgates burst and they began to explore one another with eager, youthful zeal. He could picture her life like a movie playing before his eyes as she talked — the loving hypocrisy of her mother, the weak-willed nature of her father. He could see why she had needed to run away from that kind of life, and why she found Betty so very good for her. Kier, too, had come to like and respect Betty enormously.

And Oriel, in turn, felt tears burn her eyes when he described the hard life that had been his father's, and the tragic death of his mother. And the reason for the death of his eldest sister appalled her. Being rich all her life, she had never realized that such things could and did happen all the time to those who had no money.

They drank a bottle of red wine between them, the restaurant crowded by the time they left. Walking back to the college, they passed two boys, dressed in shorts that came to just below the knee and grey, V-necked jumpers, who were carting a scarecrow about in a wheelbarrow. 'Penny for the Guy, sir?' the eldest one, about eleven, asked hopefully, holding out a white tin cup.

'The what?'

'The Guy.'

Kier glanced at Oriel, who shrugged.

'They're Yanks,' the younger one said scornfully as Oriel asked what a guy was. 'It's supposed to be Guy Fawkes,' he went on to explain, pointing his head to the straw-stuffed effigy in the barrow. 'The fifth is Guy Fawkes night.'

'What are you collecting the money for?' Oriel asked, reaching into her jeans pocket and coming out with a shilling.

'For fireworks, of course,' the urchin said scornfully.

'Of course,' Kier repeated drolly, adding a penny of his own. 'What did this Guy Fawkes do anyway?' he asked, expecting a long-winded tale of heroic exploits.

'He tried to blow up the Houses of Parliament,' the younger one said, with ghoulish relish. 'And King James the First . . . or Second. One of them anyway.'

'My dad says it's a pity he didn't succeed,' the elder one said solemnly and Oriel bit her lip. But her grin broke loose and then she was laughing.

'Thanks,' the older boy said, grinning like a Cheshire cat when Kier put another penny in the mug.

'The British,' Kier said. 'Don't you just love 'em?'

They were almost at the college now, which was poorly lit at night. 'Do you want to risk coming in for a cup of tea or something?' Kier asked awkwardly, glad that the darkness hid the rising colour in his cheeks, but even more glad that Viv wouldn't be staggering back in until the early hours. It was, of course, against the rules for boys to enter the girls' rooms, or vice versa, but plenty of travelling went on at night, and any student stupid enough to report breaches of this law to the Dean were soon debagged and consigned to Coventry for the rest of the term. And Oxford — forever young and liberal Oxford — chose to turn a blind eye, unless of course, students were actually caught *in flagrante delicto*, so to speak.

Oriel's breath fluttered nervously in her throat. She looked around guiltily, but seeing only moonlight and deserted quads she nodded quickly. 'OK.'

The room turned out to be quite like hers — small, square, with one window, flaking walls, two single beds, one large desk, and bookshelves overflowing with ponderous tomes. 'What are you reading anyway?' she asked, pushing a dirty shirt off the bed and sitting down, watching Kier carefully lock the door without comment, although her heartbeat picked up in a mixture of fear, excitement and longing.

'English. You?'

'Languages. When I read the prospectus I realized it was the only thing I'd be any good at.'

'French and German?'

'Uh-huh.'

He heaped two spoons of tea leaves into the teapot and waited for the kettle to boil. 'This place is a mess,' he muttered, picking up dirty laundry by the armful and shoving it under a bed. 'Living with Viv is like living with a ferret.'

Oriel blinked at this analogy, then nodded towards the kettle. 'It's boiling.'

Kier made the tea, handed her hers, then sat down on the opposite bed, leaning against the white plaster walls and looking at her closely.

'Now, isn't this better than screaming at each other?' she asked, sipping her cup, screwing up her face and demanding sugar. Kier spooned her in two, then retreated back to the far side of the room. He was aware of the dangers and meant to keep them minimal. Already his body was thinking thoughts it shouldn't.

'It's certainly less painful,' he agreed, rubbing his jaw.

'Oh, Kier, I am sorry about that,' she said softly, putting down her mug and kneeling beside him on the bed. 'Does it hurt?' she asked, gently fingering his jaw. She could feel the stubble, deeply embedded in his skin, under her fingertips, which began to tingle.

Kier shrugged, shifting awkwardly back against the wall. 'Not really. It's fine.' He looked at his watch ostentatiously, but it was only 8.30. He almost groaned.

'Kier,' Oriel said softly, chidingly. He glanced at her reluctantly, then shrugged.

'Sorry. For one mad moment I thought I might actually escape.'

'No chance,' she said softly, then leaned forward and bit his ear — hard. He moaned, cursed, and then grabbed a handful of her hair, twisting her around and onto the bed, in the same moment lowering his head. He kissed her hungrily, his whole body beginning to oil itself in passion's sweet sweat. His hands roamed over her breasts beneath the heavy wool of her jumper, brushing the iron-hard nub of her nipples with his thumbs.

Oriel whimpered, her vagina melting into a hot mess as she stretched out her legs, arching her back and pushing up her breasts into his palms in instinctive reaction. A pounding started up in his brain, and he dimly realized that it was his own hot blood, raging in torrents through his veins.

'For weeks I've been telling myself you're nothing but a spoilt brat,' he muttered, his hands tugging her sweater free of her waistband and then pulling it over her head. Childlike, she raised her arms to help him, and the static electricity in the wool made her hair feather out across the pillow like strands of gossamer. For the first time a man's hand unfastened her bra, and Oriel closed her eyes, an exquisite, pained expression on her face as he lowered his head to suck on her bare breasts. Her fingers ran over his scalp as she jerked in reaction, and Kier felt his body begin to burn.

He rose to his knees and impatiently yanked off his shirt. Oriel watched him with wide, observant eyes. His chest was muscular and darkly matted with hair, but his shoulders and arms were smooth. He looked like well-oiled teak, and her fingers went to his nipples, pulling playfully on the hairs that ringed them. Kier winced. 'You knew this was going to happen,' he accused her, his chest rising and falling rapidly as her tormenting caress robbed him of breath, and she laughed, a slow, southern chuckle.

'Of course I did, you bloody Yank,' she drawled, borrowing Viv's favourite phrase. 'I knew soon as I set eyes on you.' Her hands were now on his belt buckle.

Kier gave a rueful grin then moaned as she slipped her hand inside his jeans and caressed his shaft through the white cotton of his underwear. Slowly he lowered the zip, satisfied to see all the humour leave her face as he stripped first himself, and then her, totally naked, revealing the virgin triangle of golden hair at the conjunction of her thighs. Slowly he lifted her ankle, his fingers closing around it as he drew her foot to his mouth. He licked her instep, then suckled on her toes, an area of her body she'd never considered erotic before. Then her eyes widened into saucers as delicious tingles shot straight up her leg and lodged in her womb. She began to moan softly.

'You picked the wrong guy to play games with, Scarlett,' Kier said sadly, and kissed the back of her knees. Oriel jerked and began to tremble. 'You see—' he carried on kissing his way up her thighs '—I had this teacher, back home. Her name was Mrs Smith.'

'Smith?' Oriel repeated, her brain turning to jelly.

'Uh-huh,' Kier confirmed, gently holding her thighs apart. 'She was a good teacher too,' he told her, and slowly lowered his head. Oriel moaned, biting down hard on her lower lip as his tongue flickered between the folds of flesh at the centre of her being and then found the taut, throbbing nub of her clitoris. She thrashed so hard she almost came off the bed as Kier sucked her to her first orgasm.

When it was over, and she lay throbbing and shaking in the aftermath, he slowly kissed his way past her navel, to her breasts, up her sternum to her throat, and then took tiny, supping kisses from her lips. She could feel his manhood against her thigh, and then felt its head, hot and persistent, nudge against her opening. 'Kier,' she gasped urgently, suddenly nervous, opening her eyes to meet his burning brown gaze head on. 'There's something I gotta tell you.'

Kier gave a soft, warm smile that made her heart flip in her breast beneath his caressing hand. 'Sshhh,' he soothed her. 'I know, Scarlett.'

'You do?' she asked, her eyes widening as he began to slowly, gently push into her, entering her so tenderly, making her thighs tremble helplessly. His face was tight with concentration as he began to withdraw, then slowly surge forward again, gently taking her virginity. 'I've done nothing but watch you, breathe you, *live* you for weeks now,' he gritted, his body coiled tight as she began to moan and undulate her hips in time to his slow, thoughtful rhythm.

Oriel moaned and then thrashed as he began to slip in and out of her more forcefully, now that she had become used to accommodating him. The pain was gone and was replaced by a finer, more exquisite torture. His stroking shaft was now tormenting her, pushing her higher and higher, his hands on her breasts, his lips on her temples, her neck, her ears, all merging to have her screaming out her orgasm as he played her body like a virtuoso. When she had shuddered into a second shattering climax, she clutched his shoulders as he moaned, then lay still and quiet, Kier's head cushioned on her breast as their ragged breathing returned to normal.

It was chilly in the room, and Kier pulled the blankets around them.

'I'll let you have that round,' Oriel finally said, a secretive smile on her face. 'But from now on in, I'm gonna be learning fast.'

Kier grinned against her nipple and gave it a half-hearted nip, making her jump and clamp her legs warningly against his thigh.

'Scarlett,' he assured her drowsily, 'I wouldn't have it any other way.'

CHAPTER 10

Paris

The Jardin du Luxembourg could be found within the boulevard triangle of Raspail, Saint-Michel and Saint-Germain,
and was Wayne's favourite spot for sunbathing. Through
the trees behind him he could see the Gothic edifice of the
Pantheon, and his own university, the Sorbonne, but he
had long since become immune to the architectural beauties
of Paris. Walking across the grass, he took off his shirt and
crumpled the silk Armani creation for a pillow, then lay back
on the newly mown grass. The scent of the lime trees around
him wafted gently on the breeze, and in the distance he could
hear the bells of Notre-Dame.

Term would soon be over, and he'd be back in Monte
Carlo. Since the drowning of Hans, he'd been only too
glad to leave the gloom and almost frantic despair of the
villa and escape to Paris, where he enjoyed a rather ironic
kudos attached to the loss of his younger brother. Fellow
students treated him with a touching sympathy that Wayne
both enjoyed and found painfully repulsive. Guilt ate at his
innards, filling his nights with nightmares. He enjoyed the
pain like a masochist enjoys biting down on a bad tooth, and

the pity of his professors, who gave him the extra assignments he asked for with sad shakes of their Gallic heads, gave him a perverse sense of pride.

It was twelve-thirty, and his few minutes of unusual relaxation made him feel oddly uneasy. The sun through the dappled shade of the trees warmed him; the drone of bees in the lime trees almost lulled him to sleep. But he couldn't afford to fall asleep — it was one thing to wake up screaming and sweating in the middle of the night when no one else could see him, and quite another to do so in the middle of Paris on a busy day.

On a bench nearby, two teenage girls, no more than sixteen, watched him get to his feet, their eyes widening at his height. They had been watching him for some time now, making giggling whispered comments behind their hands. They fell into an awed silence as Wayne passed them, and he gave them a smile, glorying in their flushes and giggles. He left the Jardin and crossed the Saint-Michel, heading towards the Sorbonne.

Wayne had 'done' all the usual things in his first term at the famous university where he was studying English and Economics. He had visited Versailles in a thunderstorm, and toured the Louvre, wondering what art treasures had been ransacked by his father's cronies. He had eaten real onion soup in the oddly named Rue du Chat-qui-Pêche (Street of the Fishing Cat). He had eaten truffles and trout at the Bois de Boulogne and seen the chandeliers hanging from the chestnut trees by the Seine at the Pont Saint-Michel. He'd watched the famous can-can dancers in the haunts of Toulouse-Lautrec. Not always alone, but never accompanied by the same woman twice. He had no intentions of limiting his sexual favours, and he already had the reputation of 'user'. He wasn't always very tactful about his dismissals, either, as several of his fellow female students had come to realize. Not that it prevented the women from trying to change him, of course — each and every one sure that she would be able to tame the monster within.

Wayne mounted the ancient steps of the Sorbonne, and walked into the high-ceilinged hall, pausing by a notice board to peruse the music section. Jean-Paul Montage watched the tall copper-haired man from some arched shadows, his deep green eyes narrowed and angry.

'They tell me the Rachmaninov concert is going to be superb,' Jean-Paul said softly, a feral smile on his lips as he moved forward, balancing his weight carefully and ready to lunge. Wayne turned abruptly. It took him only a second to register the anger in the other man's eyes and the tenseness with which he moved. 'Too bad you'll have to miss it.'

Wayne shifted, suddenly aware of something dangerous. But Jean-Paul was nothing, hardly worth his notice. Then his mind suddenly clicked. Jean-Paul was the boyfriend of his latest bedpartner, Jacqueline de Palin. She'd told Wayne she'd finished with Jean-Paul, but obviously the bitch had been lying. Very carefully, Wayne took the older man's measure, and let his lips curl back in a sneer.

'And why should I miss it?' he asked coolly, but was prepared for the answer. A man who was psyched up was a man to watch out for. And who should know that better than himself, who was permanently psyched and ready?

'Because you'll be in hospital, bastarde. *Cochon*!' Jean-Paul spat the insults, breathing deeply. His face was flushed, his rage so intense that it consumed him. Quick as a flash, Wayne's fist slammed square into his stomach, knuckles sinking deep into Jean-Paul's unprepared flesh with devastating force. The Frenchman doubled over and, with an agonized scream, fell to one knee. Wayne looked down on the bowed black head, thought briefly of giving him a good right hook in the face, and decided against it. The last thing he needed was to get expelled.

'Mind your manners, you pathetic bastard,' he said softly, yanking Jean-Paul's head up by a fistful of black hair. The face was white and sweating, his eyes now black with pain. 'Because if you don't,' Wayne whispered, his voice almost cheerful, 'I'm going to kill you'. He shoved Jean-Paul away with the ease of a dog shaking off a rat and strode away, whistling an extract from Rachmaninov as he did so.

* * *

The next morning Wayne's Maserati headed out of Paris in the early dawn sun.

As he drove along the route nationale, a Patek Philippe watch on his wrist ticked away the minutes from home. Home, where there was no Hans. Home, where his mother would be out at some art exhibition, coffee morning, charity bazaar or bridge meet. Home, where Wolfgang would look like an old, bent man. Hans's death seemed to have halved his father, taking away half his strength, half his zest for life, half his arrogance. During those blissful two weeks after the funeral, when Wayne had been awash in guilt and euphoria, he had watched his father with hot, eager eyes, crowing silently over every meal he left uneaten, over every glass of whisky he had guzzled down.

But if his father had changed, Monte Carlo looked no different. As he approached the perched village of La Turbie, Wayne slowed the purring car to negotiate the serpentine narrow streets that led to the Villa Mimosa and turned in. It was a huge, sprawling bungalow, painted such a brilliant white that it almost hurt the eyes. As its name suggested, mimosa grew in great profusion in the large, landscaped gardens. He pulled the car under the eaves of the two-level garage and left his bags in the boot. A yucca grew in the middle of a perfect lawn, while in front of the house, two fountains sprayed water from stone lotus flowers. A pond full of flowering water lilies and golden koi carp were the highlights on the patio.

Juan, their Spanish major-domo, emerged from the house and took the bags from the car, greeting him subserviently.

'Where is everyone?' Wayne wondered idly.

Juan smiled briefly, more out of habit than out of any pleasure at seeing Wayne, and told him that his father was at the casino, his mother out lunching with friends. Wayne nodded curtly and abruptly went ahead, stripping as he walked into his bedroom, a vast expanse of white carpet, cream walls and hand-painted ceiling. His bed was a vast, king-sized four-poster, from which mosquito lace hung. Sliding doors of dark African wood revealed the locations of the built-in wardrobes, and green-painted shutters matched the green quilt of the bed and the cushions thrown onto a pair of dark leather armchairs. Orange orchids in a crystal vase stood on a dresser, and out on the balcony a shell wind chime created impromptu music conducted by the sea breeze. Blinded by familiarity to all the luxury, he showered and changed, deciding to pass the rest of the afternoon away playing squash at a prestigious sports club by the harbour, of which he was, naturally, a member.

The dining room was a round affair of cool white walls, highly polished naked floorboards and a Pembroke table that could be extended to seat thirty comfortably. It was set for three at the moment, with a pink linen tablecloth, Royal Worcester plates and silver cutlery. As a centrepiece, pink and white carnations and fern fronds added colour and life.

'Mother,' Wayne said emotionlessly, walking around to where she sat to give her proffered cheek a quick kiss. He nodded at his father, said 'Papa' equally emotionlessly, and sat down.

Wolfgang reached for his wine goblet, which Juan had just filled with the finest Bordeaux, and barked accusingly, 'You're back early.'

Wayne looked at his father steadily. 'I'm ahead with my studies.'

During the intervening months, some of the shock of his beloved son's death had begun to wear off. Wolfgang looked less grey and haggard, and as Wayne sipped his wine and waited for the first course to be served, he sensed something different, something new, in his father's gaze.

'The lessons are going well?'

'Very,' he replied without any pretence of warmth, sure that Wolfgang had a report of his grades on his desk somewhere in the casino.

'That's very good, Wayne,' Marlene said, speaking for the first time, and smiling at him absently. Wayne wondered if she was already drunk. She usually was but was so adept at hiding it that it was often hard to tell.

'You'd better keep it up,' was all Wolfgang said, but to Wayne the words suddenly made sense. Of course! His father had been forced to look on him the way a man looks upon his heir. His lips twisted in a parody of a smile as Rosita Alvarez, Juan's daughter, walked in with the first course of pear and blue cheese salad. Wayne barely glanced at her, then did a swift double take. Rosita had worked for them since she'd left school at sixteen, almost two years ago, and Wayne found himself noticing the luxuriant blackness of her long wavy hair, the depths of her dark eyes that she cast his way and then lowered modestly. She flushed shyly as he smiled at her, and Wayne was pleased to see that she obviously had a crush on him. Her hand trembled as she placed the cut-crystal half-moon dish in front of him, and when she straightened, Wayne looked deep into her eyes.

'Thank you, Rosita,' he murmured softly.

'*De nada.*' She left quickly, amid more blushes. Used to dealing with hardened bitches, Wayne was surprised to realize that her innocence touched him, making him long to destroy it. He picked up his spoon, glancing across the table as he did so, and met his father's ironic gaze head on. Into his mind flashed the picture of Urma on top of his father, pumping away like a demented piston. His hand tightened on the spoon, then with deliberate precision, he cut a segment off the pear and raised it to his mouth. His eyes, which never left his father, were as hard as blue diamonds. Wolfgang sighed almost imperceptibly and, with a small shrug, set about his own meal. Marlene's glass was empty and she reached for the chilled decanter and refilled it, hoping no one would notice.

For a while Wayne was content just to watch Rosita, enjoying the way she shied away from him whenever he flirted with her. Her father occasionally cast harried and angry looks in Wayne's direction, but Wayne ignored him. He waited until Saturday night, when Juan was out chauffeuring his parents to a nightclub opening being thrown in Cannes. He was sitting alone in the dining room, the buzz of the air conditioner a low drone in the background. As soon as she served him the pâté de foie gras, he could sense her fear mingled with little-girl excitement. Her breathing changed to agitated little gulps whenever she leant over him to serve, and he smiled like a shark.

'Why don't you join me, Rosita?'

'Join you?' she asked, puzzled, then shook her head, blushing furiously. 'Oh, no, *señor*, I am not permitted to sit at the same table as the patron.'

'How long have you worked here, Rosie?' he asked, shortening her name at the same time as he caught her hand and rubbed his thumb across her wrists.

'Over two years, *señor*.' Her voice trembled as she spoke, and her pulse fluttered wildly under his fingers as she looked around nervously.

'And you've never sat at this table for a meal?' Mutely she shook her head, and with one foot he hooked out the matching chair next to him. 'Then it's about time you did, hmm?' Slowly, reluctantly, she subsided into the chair, her hands nervously twisting over her white apron. 'Here — try this,' he urged, forking some of the pâté and then bringing it to her lips.

Obediently she opened her mouth and tasted it. Under the eagle eye of the French chef, Rosita had never been able to even sneak a taste of the gorgeous food she regularly served her employers, and her eyes widened as she sampled the delicacy of the flavourings. Her heart was pounding hard in her breast as they finished the course, and he insisted she try the roast pheasant, imported from England out of season, and then the lemon sorbet, which was so icy cold it made her cheeks numb. She said as much, laughing freely as she confessed to it, her eyes sparkling like black jet, amazed at how quickly the master's son had put her at her ease. He was, as she'd always suspected, wonderfully kind.

And this was easily the most exciting night of her life. She had secretly loved Wayne D'Arville ever since she first came to work here. While everyone else had fussed over poor little Henri, Rosita had looked longingly at the lonely and aloof figure of Wayne, who always seemed to be on the outside looking in. She'd always felt the urge to love him, to hold him tenderly in her arms, her generous heart going out to one who was so clearly unhappy. But she had never, ever, expected him to actually notice her. Now she sipped the potent wine, feeling strangely light-headed. She demurred as he refilled her glass, but because he insisted so graciously, she sipped that too. She was a good Catholic, raised in the ways of her church, and knew that it was wrong for them to be alone in the villa. She prayed briefly for forgiveness but could not summon up the strength to walk away from him. He was so beautiful, so interested in what she had to say. And surely, one night of shared food and wine and a few murmured secrets wasn't *that* sinful?

Wayne put on a slow Strauss waltz and asked her to dance. Immediately she was torn, feeling totally grown up and desirable, and yet at the same time, alarmed. But when he stood up, smiling that tender smile and opening his arms to her, she found herself unable to refuse him.

As they danced, Wayne nuzzled her hair, which was silky against his cheek. She smelt of roses and soap, and he told her so, his seduction so practised it was almost mechanical.

'You're truly beautiful, Rosita,' he whispered, and as she thrilled to the words she'd never heard any man say to her before, he slowly danced his way to the patio, where the French doors to his bedroom stood open. As he led her protesting into his bedroom, there was a heady excitement in his limbs, a sensation of heavy languorous desire bubbling just below the surface. Perhaps it was merely the eroticism of seducing a servant, as his father had seduced Urma all those years ago, but he suddenly found himself wanting Rosita with a savage intensity that was totally new.

'*Señor*,' she whispered, the protest barely audible above her tear-constricted throat as he began to undo her blouse. Despite her hands trying to slap his away, he quickly freed her breasts. They were full and uptilting, with very dark areolae. Gently he reached out and cupped them in his palms, their weight and the hot silky feel of them immediately arousing him. He ran a thumb over a nipple and Rosita moaned, half in fear, half in pleasure. Fuzzily, her brain told her that she must get away, that she must stop him. 'Please, *señor*. We . . . we mustn't.'

Wayne demurred softly, enjoying the sensation of power he felt at such times almost as much as the sexual act itself. He picked her up as if she weighed no more than a cushion, and laid her on his huge bed, his lips sucking at one breast as her hands flew to his head, her suntanned fingers dark and feverish in his copper hair as she tried to push him away.

Wayne, aware that the hardness in his trousers was becoming uncomfortable, reached down to the zipper. His hand brushed her thigh as he did so, and she suddenly tensed. With the cunning of a weasel sniffing out weaknesses, he curled his fingers around the hem of her skirt and lifted it higher, allowing him to run exploratory fingers up her long, smooth leg, curling around her inner thigh. Rosita closed her eyes. '*Por favor* . . . no, no,' she murmured, but her legs fell treacherously open and he lost no time in pulling down her girlish, plain white knickers. For a moment he stared in surprise at the startlingly large bush of dark hair on her mound. Then he touched her there and Rosita clamped her legs together in instinctive, frightened rejection. Things were going too fast, and she couldn't think. Unused to alcohol, her head felt as if it were stuffed with cotton wool, preventing her from defending herself. Impatiently, he pushed her thighs apart, eager to taste her red lips that were so different from his own anatomy, and when he brushed her clitoris with his tongue she moaned, a deep frown settling over her darkened brows. This was wrong . . . It felt so good, but it was wrong . . .

Wayne began to love her in earnest and her moans turned to cries, her head thrashing from side to side on the pillow. With her skirt bunched up around her stomach and one of her nipples tweaked between the thumb and forefinger of his other hand, she became aware of a wave of crashing ecstasy building up between her legs, and her neck arched helplessly.

'*Por favor,*' she gasped, her body beginning to jerk under his hands, '*como se ilama.*'

Wayne smiled triumphantly as her features contorted in her first orgasm. Being unprepared for such sensations, her untouched innocence cruelly aided him in his seduction, and he found it profoundly ironic. While she lay in a panting and moaning recovery, he stripped off his clothes with wordless efficiency, giving her no time to rally her scattered defences, and when she next looked at him, her eyes widened in a mixture of fear and desire. Standing by the bed, he seemed to tower over her, his shoulders wide and tapering to a flat stomach. But it was to his manhood that her eyes flew, her gaze taking on the sheen of panic as she suddenly comprehended her dangerous position. She had never seen a naked man before, and the upright strength of his shaft made her womb suddenly contract. She murmured a denial, a plea for understanding, telling him she was still a virgin and appealing to his sense of honour and decency. Wayne, who with his knack for languages had picked up quite a bit of Spanish from various sources, understood her perfectly, but feigned ignorance, mocking her by making her believe he thought that she was egging him on.

'You really want it, don't you, little Rosita? You're really hungry. Yes?' He knelt quickly over her, his strong knees bent either side of her slender hips as she made a quick, abortive attempt to roll off the bed, but he quickly subdued her, his immense strength making it pitifully easy. Holding her confused, dazed eyes with his own, Wayne slowly released her, and took her hand. Gently but firmly he guided it to his shaft, curling her fingers around him. Rosita froze, her heart pounding.

It's so hard, she thought incredulously, but also so soft. Like steel encased in velvet. Then she shook her head, shaking off the heady cloying temptations of sexual arousal. '*No, no!*'

Wayne snarled impatiently, tiring of the game, and, pushing her thighs wide apart, he guided his organ between her legs and thrust forward deeply, with no regard for her innocence and uncaring whether he gave her pleasure or not.

Rosita screamed as her hymen broke and blood trickled onto the sheets, the pain chasing away the magic of the moonlit night, the heady drugging of the fine wine, the will-sapping lies of his murmured compliments and cajolings. She realized, too late, what had happened, understanding at last that because of her naivety and weakness, she had been cheated and abused.

And then he began to thrust against her, withdrawing and then slamming into her time and time again, the nightmare escalating terrifyingly as she thrashed helplessly on the bed, unable to buck off his muscled weight. Tears cascaded from beneath her tightly closed lashes as Wayne began to moan, his face tight and ferocious as he chased his own pleasure. Rosita, whimpering under the onslaught, prayed that it would all soon be over.

Ten minutes later Wayne was in the shower. When he'd finished, he wrapped a towel around himself and walked back into the bedroom where Rosita still lay on her back, her undone blouse lying across her shoulders, her nipples wet with his saliva. The skirt was still bunched up under her buttocks and around her waist. The sheets were wet with sweat and blood and he felt disgust rise up in his throat, threatening to choke him. It was Urma all over again. Suddenly he felt unclean. 'Get out.'

Rosita's eyes snapped open at the harshness of his tone, and one look at his tight, angry face had her scurrying off the bed and running through the door. She ran through the large, empty house to the servants' quarters, a hand clapped over her mouth. She flung herself onto the narrow bed in her tiny room where a wooden crucifix was the only ornamentation and began to sob convulsively. She would surely go to hell for this thing she had done — the priests had warned her so. Just when she thought she could cry no more, she heard her father come home, and found that she could.

She dreaded facing Wayne the next day, but he ignored her totally, acting as if nothing had happened. Better still, during the next two months she hardly saw him.

Wayne had gone back to work at the casino, amused at the change in De Lepee, who was now sucking up to him like mad.

He went yachting with friends whom he'd deliberately cultivated, choosing only the richest and the most influential to invite back to the casino. He bought himself a small yacht with the money that Wolfgang had given him for his birthday and dined with the loveliest daughters of his mother's friends. He was hardly home, and when he was he couldn't bear to look at Rosita, whose hurt eyes constantly condemned him.

* * *

One day, at the beginning of September, Rosita went to his room very early, desperation making her bold. He would be leaving for Paris soon, and she had to tell him. She had waited for her period with fear and dread, all the tales of God punishing the wicked coming true when first one month, then two, and then three had gone by, and still no period. Three days ago she had been sick in the morning, and this morning she had been sick again. She could no longer fool herself or procrastinate. Now, as she stood looking down on his sleeping face, she felt a familiar sensation of shame and fear stir her, and she quickly crossed herself. Nevertheless, a baby was too important and too sacred to keep to herself, much as she might want to deny Wayne the joys of fatherhood.

Wayne began to moan then thrash around on the bed. Hans was swimming towards him, a grinning shark giving him a ride. No matter how fast Wayne swam, the shark and a grim-faced Hans gained on him. 'No!' he yelled, sitting up so fast that Rosita nearly screamed in shock. Slowly the nightmare faded and his eyes sharpened on her and a dull rage began to flush his skin. 'What the hell do you want?'

'I have to talk to you, *señor*. Please.'

Wayne swung his feet onto the floor and caught her greedy eyes on his groin.

'Please, I have to tell you . . . I . . . I . . .'

'Well? What is it? Will you just say it and get out before someone finds you here?' Anxious for her to be gone, he had a sudden premonition of history reversing itself, and could see in his mind's eye his father bursting in on him in an embarrassing situation. The thought had him leaping to his feet, his hands fastening hard around her shoulders as he dragged her to the door.

Frightened by the rough manhandling and scared he'd evict her before she had time to tell him what she knew she must, Rosita blurted out the truth.

Wayne stood stock still and stared at her, appalled. 'Pregnant?' he echoed, his voice little more than a stunned whisper. 'You're pregnant?'

'Si.' Rosita saw his stunned face and smiled tentatively. 'It is wonderful news, no? A little bambino of your own?' The sweet, hopeful voice seemed to dig into him like bullets, and he staggered back and collapsed onto the bed, utterly dumbfounded. He'd got a serving girl pregnant? He could hear the gossip now, the sniggering laughter, the pointing fingers undoing all the hard work he'd done that summer, destroying all the groundwork he'd been laying to set himself up as one of Monte Carlo's elite. He could hear his mother's wailing and accusing voice — 'How could you? I am a laughing stock.'

But most of all he could see his father's ironical, smug smile and he felt sick. Sick to his stomach. His brain began to work feverishly. A way out — there had to be a way out.

He had no doubts that the baby was his, but that was beside the point. He paced, realizing he had to get her out of the way — right out of the way — and fast. He stopped pacing and glanced at her. 'You're leaving this morning. I'll drive you to the airport. Where's your passport?'

The words snapped Rosita out of her subservience as nothing else could. The thought of going back to Spain, back to the poverty of the hills, the gruelling hard labour that was the lot of Spain's peasantry, was not even thinkable.

'No,' she said, shaking her head, backing away and cringing against the corner as he menacingly walked towards her. But she was strong — stronger than even she had realized — and born of sturdy stock. As danger leapt to its highest point she felt a great shift of maternal strength flooding into her, and she straightened up, standing tall, all fear leaving her face. Even Wayne hesitated. Rosita put a protective hand on her stomach, and then thrust out her chin.

'I will not leave,' she stated, her voice clear and strong. 'This is your bambino and he will have all the things that I never had. He will live in this fancy house,' she waved her hands around her, 'and will call you Papa.' She might fear him, but for her baby she had the courage of a tigress.

Wayne saw at once there was no dissuading her. He recognized zeal when he saw it and knew there was no reasoning with it. Immediately he abandoned the idea of giving her money, and instead held up his hands in a placating gesture. 'All right, have it your own way.' Seeing her suspicious look at his sudden about-face, he added grimly, 'But don't blame me if he's not accepted and is branded a bastard. Because I won't marry you,' he assured her, stabbing a viciously angry finger in her direction.

Rosita paled at the thought of the disgrace, and then forced herself to shrug, even though her heart was hammering painfully in her chest. She had no doubts left that he might actually care for her, but perhaps after the baby was born, when he held his son or daughter in his arms for the first time, surely then he would feel less resentful? Who knows, perhaps the baby might work some loving miracle and change his mind about marrying her and giving their child a legitimate name. She could but hope. More importantly, she could afford to wait.

She left to do the grocery shopping the next morning, happily searching the markets for the best buy, the freshest fish, the ripest fruit, feeling confident and much more at peace now that everything was settled. The sun was warm, reflecting her simple cotton dress of canary yellow, and as she walked back up the steep hill she felt young, strong, healthy and full of dreams. When she turned the corner and walked into the gardens, the police were waiting.

A search of her room revealed a pair of diamond and onyx cufflinks in a biscuit tin under her bed, along with Wayne's watch and silver cigarette lighter. She was given no chance to explain, no chance to call a lawyer, no chance even to pack her things or speak to her father, who was once again out chauffeuring Marlene.

She was numb with shock as they led her to the back of the police car, their hands hard and hurting as they shoved her onto the back seat. There she collapsed, hugging her slightly swollen stomach and sobbing uncontrollably.

From his bedroom window Wayne watched, his face expressionless. Looking around numbly, still too stunned to take it all in, Rosita saw him. Twisting around in the back seat as the car pulled away, she banged uselessly on the back of the window with her hands, her face agonized, tears streaming from her eyes, shouting in Spanish for mercy, beseeching him uselessly to save her.

The last he ever saw of her was when she was dragged away from the window and cuffed across the face by one of the policemen.

They took her not to the police station as she had expected, but to the airport, where they put her aboard the first flight back to Spain, after confiscating her passport. They told her that she must never come back. If she did, they assured her, she would be thrown into jail immediately.

Rosita believed it.

CHAPTER 11

Clarissa and Kyle's first glimpse of Oxford was a perfect one. Their plane had landed at Heathrow at 5 a.m., and as they approached Oxford in the hired chauffeur-driven car, the lemon-yellow sun was just rising. It was a clean December morning, with a crisp frost turning everything silver, and low-lying mist in the valleys. The famous dreaming spires of Oxford were mellow in the sun and glittering with frost. Bells began to chime in St Ebbe's; the streets were deserted.

'This place has even Charleston beat,' Kyle said, his eyes sweeping the vista with quick, appreciative eyes. The years had been more than kind to Kyle, turning him from a handsome, petulant boy to a handsome, desperate man. The desperation lent him an air that made him irresistible to women, and Clarissa in particular. Without the haunted look in his eyes, he'd have been *too* handsome, turning him, perversely, into a less attractive man.

'It surely does,' Clarissa agreed with him, leaning back in the seat and pulling on soft kid-leather gloves.

Perhaps she would take a few weeks and explore the old country in earnest once she had Oriel sorted out. She turned to glance at her lover of nearly fifteen years. She was the reason for his desperation, of course, and it thrilled her, even as it slowly destroyed her. She found his name on her lips, and quickly bit it back. He would only turn to her, his pain in his eyes, and what would she say then? She couldn't let him go.

'Where are you booked?' Kyle asked, unaware of her thoughts, as they headed into the heart of the ancient university city, and Clarissa smiled.

'The Randolph, would you believe? Classiest hotel in Oxford, or so I'm told.' She hugged his arm close to hers. She'd never said the words 'I love you' to this man, but then, he had never said them to her, either.

Kyle felt his lips twist into a parody of a smile. 'I didn't doubt it.' Where else would his southern belle stay but the best place in town? As Clarissa raised a perfectly plucked and dyed eyebrow he added grimly, 'And where am I booked?'

'You're booked in the second best, of course.' She reached forward to pat his smooth cheek with her hand, ignoring the way he gritted his teeth. 'Only the second best for you, lover,' she husked. She wanted to kiss him so badly it hurt her. Kyle was not the only one to wear a mysterious aura of pain. But Clarissa kept hers much more cleverly disguised. Today she was wearing Chanel — clothes and perfume — and her smile was pure pussycat. Kyle didn't even suspect the power he had over her, and she intended to keep it that way. The passing years had been kind to her, too, but now nearly fifty, she was even more inclined to panic than ever. If he should ever leave her now . . .

Kyle closed his eyes briefly, then snapped them open as the Bentley began to slow down. The classic black car, sharing the limelight with the famous Rolls-Royce as one of Britain's finest automobiles, had been something new for him. He now owned his own garage back home, and several others, but he still liked to keep his hands dirty, so to speak. Used to weighty American cars, the silent engine of this classic, with its walnut and mahogany interior and maroon leather seats, had been an eye-opener for him. Perhaps he should think about going into expensive foreign cars back home? His love of classic cars had not diminished, and not even Clarissa had succeeded in driving the car mechanic from his soul completely.

'Nobody will be up yet at this godforsaken hour,' Clarissa pointed out as the chauffeur parked the car in front of the hotel, and began to take her bags from the back, 'so we'll have a shower, freshen up, and then you can meet me for breakfast here around eight o'clock.'

'Fine.'

Clarissa walked across the parking lot, unaware of his hot and angry eyes following her. She was wearing a cape of cream velvet and a matching turban. Her figure was the same as ever — slender and elegant — and at her throat a huge antique cameo held the cape secure. Her handbag was black leather and Italian with a gold clasp, and her makeup, although heavier now to hide the approaching march of time, was still classically understated.

Kyle watched her go, hating and wanting her. Nothing had changed in well over a decade as her lover. No, that was not strictly true. Once, nearly five years ago, he'd been desperate enough to make a run for it. He'd got as far as Chicago when her private eyes had picked up his trail. Forced to leave out auto engineering from his list of jobs, (that would have been the first place they'd start looking), he'd been working as a bus driver. He'd almost begun to think he was free, when, one day, he'd gone back to his bedsit after his 5 a.m. shift had ended, a cramped one-room affair with damp walls and the suspicion of cockroaches. He'd opened the door in his crumpled, grey uniform, and there she was, dressed in white satin. Her perfume had staved off the smell of boiled cabbage and garlic that always emanated from the bedsits below, and her lush pink lips were pulled into that mocking, depleting smile that immediately went to work on his nerves, sapping his will and stiffening his groin.

She had stripped slowly, giving him a chance to bolt through the door, but of course he hadn't. He hadn't been able to. The moment he'd seen her, he'd felt the chains, those delicious, dangerous, hated silken chains, wrap around him, pinning him to the spot. Oh, he'd had girls since he'd been on the run, two of them, in fact. He satisfied them, but not himself. And he'd known, then, that only Clarissa could send him to those giddy heights. It had made him want to scream and beat his fists against a wall until his hands bled.

And then, in that dirty, squalid room, she had peeled off her clothes, showing him silk undergarments, smooth pampered skin that was so much older than himself, and a truth that was now irrefutable — he would never be free of her . . . never.

He remembered leaning against the door and closing his eyes briefly in pain, but then she had been on him, bearing down on him with the merciless timing of a hunter. Her hands had been everywhere, her lips likewise, and within minutes he'd been naked, buried deep inside her, and straining to an orgasm that had him screaming. All night they'd made love, fighting, cursing, then loving some more. She'd left him in the morning, bitten, scratched, and unable to move. For a while he'd been surprised that she had gone. But then, after a day or two, he understood.

He could not run again. She'd not left him with the energy or the ability. Wearily he had packed up his pitiful belongings — two second-hand suits, a shaving kit and a book of antique cars — and went home. Home, where the garage was waiting for him, like some obscene consolation prize. Bought, signed, sealed and delivered. All his. With her as a silent partner, of course. Since then he'd opened two new garages — one in Savannah, and one in Dalton. He'd moved into a detached house in Atlanta, and now his hands were manicured, all traces of grease gone from the fingernails. He wore suits and ties, talked properly and wittily, dined out at least once a week, and had a reputation as the Stud of Georgia. And every night he waited to see if she would come to his house. A house on the outskirts of town, that overlooked open fields and not nosy neighbours.

So things had not changed where it really mattered.

As the car pulled up in front of a modest building of red brick and white paintwork, Kyle got out and lugged his own case from the boot, nodding the driver away. The hotel had lace curtains, a large well-kept garden, and was situated in a small cul-de-sac of private houses. Kyle gave a half-laugh of pure despair. Nobody was likely to see him here; or at least no one that mattered — none of the legion of matrons, politicians' wives, artists or charity organizers that seemed to come out of Clarissa's woodwork wherever she went. As he walked up the path toward the double doors set with dark glass his lips were smiling, but his eyes were bleak.

* * *

Oriel awoke and discovered butterflies in her stomach. Of course — tonight was *it*. Opening night. Quickly she dressed and made her way to the dining hall. At High Table, dons drank tea and munched toast while discussing the theories of Plato and comparing the endeavours of Shakespeare and Langland. Oriel settled for coffee. Betty appeared beside her with a plate of bacon and eggs, and looked at her anxiously. 'How you doing?'

'I'm terrified.'

'Normal, then.'

Oriel watched her tuck into her food and smiled. 'You free this morning?'

'After a calculus lecture at Wadham. Why? Want to go through your lines again?'

Oriel shrugged. 'No point. I know I'll forget every one of them when I get on stage.'

'Rubbish. Hello, what does she want?' Oriel looked up just in time to see the Dean's secretary bear down on them.

'Miss Somerville?' At Oriel's nod, the woman informed her that her mother was here and would like to see her. Oriel found her mother waiting in her room. She got up, looking shockingly chic and exotic, and so totally out of place in the untidy room. Then Clarissa smiled and held out her arms.

'Mama!' Oriel went to her for a kiss and a hug. 'Why didn't you tell me you were coming? Oh, I'm so nervous.'

She led her mother to the bed. 'Sit down a minute. How's Daddy?'

Kier walked along the narrow corridor to her door, keeping a wary lookout for any monitors. He knew her nerves must be raw, but as he heard the feminine voices, he paused, wondering if he should interrupt.

'I didn't come just to watch the play, darling,' Clarissa said, and fiddled nervously with the ends of her cape.

'Oh? Nothing's wrong, is it, Mother?'

Outside Kier could hear the fear in Oriel's voice, and he moved closer, intending to knock and make his presence known.

'I'm not sure,' Clarissa said. 'I had a strange phone call about you and some young man. Margaret Swainton — you remember her? Her daughter Maybilene is studying at the Ruskin? She called me. She thought I should know.'

Oriel felt her heart suddenly trip, and a sick feeling settled in the pit of her stomach. She knew just what was coming next, and she didn't like it. Outside, Kier froze.

'Well, darling . . .' Clarissa looked miserably about her. She'd been dreading this confrontation, ever since Margaret's call. Through the open door Kier watched Oriel's face firm into stubborn lines. He let out a long, relieved breath, only then realizing how tense he had been. For an ugly moment, he'd wondered if Oriel would bow to the pressure her mother was certainly about to put on her, and he felt ashamed for ever doubting that she would come through for him.

'You see, she said there were rumours . . .' Clarissa began delicately, but Oriel was in no mood for games and came straight to the point.

'Rumours about what?'

Clarissa noticed the levelness of her daughter's gaze, the determined thrust of her chin, and recognized the signs. 'Now, darling . . . you know how things are,' she began worriedly. It would be just like her wayward daughter to let her hot head lead her into trouble. And Clarissa didn't think she could bear it if Oriel were to make a disaster of a marriage, the way she had. She had to stop her angel from making a mistake. 'I'm just concerned, that's all. There's been talk about you and the young man directing the play. Some . . . cowboy from Kansas,' she finished, hoping to make her see how ridiculous this misalliance was.

Oriel almost laughed. The snobbery was so unnecessary! 'Kier Harcourt is not a cowboy,' she said. 'His father owned a ranch in Kansas, but he's dead now.'

'Yes,' Clarissa said grimly. 'I know all about it. A few hundred acres in a hick town called Burmanville. Really, darling, I hope things aren't serious with this boy. You're too young to—'

'Things are serious!' Oriel interrupted, just a small tug of doubt yanking on the back of her mind as she spoke. Since that first night together over a month ago, she and Kier had been lovers. They had talked, kissed, explored Oxford and its surrounding countryside, all the while laughing and holding hands, even making love behind a barn, shivering in the cold and then burning as they came together in an explosion of passion. They knew every minute detail of each other's lives. She had told him she loved him, whispering it in the night and in the mellow afternoons, and he had whispered back the same. But this was first love, and she wondered if Kier felt the same commitment that she did. It was the one raincloud on an otherwise brilliant horizon, and it worried her.

'Oh, darling,' Clarissa said, her heart drooping in dismay. How could she make her daughter see that marriage affected the rest of your life and, if you got it wrong . . . She thought of Kyle and sighed deeply. If you got it wrong, you wrecked your own life and those of others.

Oriel looked at her mother helplessly, seeing the pain and the love in her eyes. But why couldn't she just leave them alone? 'You haven't even met Kier, Mama. You have no idea of the kind of man he really is, deep down, where it counts.'

Clarissa got up and walked to the window, looking down into the quad. 'What does this boy want to do when you've finished your studies here? Take you back to Kansas?'

'For pity's sake, Mother, Kier is a Rhodes Scholar — he's not some hick you can just dismiss like you do the bell-boys back home. He wrote the play, he's directing it, and everybody says it's going to be good . . .'

'So he's going to take you to Broadway, or Hollywood, is he?' Clarissa asked wearily, turning back from the window and looking at her daughter with frustrated eyes. 'Darling, please wait. You're in a new country, you think you're in love for the first time, but things can change so quickly—'

'I am in love. And Kier is in love with me. And nothing you can say is going to change it, Mother, so you might as well face facts,' Oriel interrupted hastily.

'I couldn't have put it better myself,' Kier commented softly, making both women jump and look towards the door. Clarissa found herself startled by her first glimpse of the man who could so easily break her daughter's heart. She had convinced herself he was a raw hick who'd seduced her daughter with savage sex and charm. But now, as he met her challenging eyes head on, she could sense instinctively that Kier had something . . . an aura of power, perhaps, of something unnamed that very few men actually possessed. He reminded her — heartbreakingly — of Kyle. It rendered null and void his lack of background and breeding, and made him seem taller, greater than he was. Even dressed in dirty jeans and a black sweater with a hole at the elbow, he was a giant. Young, barely started out, yet still a giant. One of those men who were destined to take the world by the throat and shake it. All of this she could see, and it scared her. Oriel needed someone to look after her, not take her on a rollercoaster ride that would scare her half to death. Oriel had been raised in a genteel environment. This man . . . was a savage by comparison! She could feel desperation rise in her like a suffocating wave as, for the first time, it began to occur to her that she might not be able to nip the romance in the bud so easily.

'You're Kier, I assume,' Clarissa commented, forcing her voice into ice as she fought to regain her composure.

'Do you always lurk in doorways, spying on people's private conversations?'

Kier grinned. 'Whenever I can,' he said softly.

Oriel felt a wide smile pull on her mouth, feeling relieved that he couldn't be snowballed by her mother's icy disdain.

Clarissa looked steadily at Kier. 'I want to talk to you. Alone.'

'Mother, I'm not . . .' Oriel interjected hotly, but it was Kier who held up his hand and said soothingly,

'It's alright. Don't worry.'

Reluctantly she got off the bed and walked past him, looking deep into his eyes. 'Be careful,' she whispered.

Kier cupped her face gently, and kissed her thoroughly, ignoring the hiss of outrage emanating from the other side of the room. 'It'll be OK,' he assured her softly. And, suddenly, Oriel knew it would be. Her mother was used to getting her way, but as she looked into the solid brown eyes of the man she had come to love with her heart and her soul, she realized that this time Clarissa would lose. She wondered what she'd done to be so lucky. To find a man like this, at first attempt, seemed almost greedy. She shot a triumphant look at her mother who stared stonily back at her, and then left, closing the door behind her.

Clarissa walked to her handbag and extracted a cigarette. 'She's obviously smitten with you,' she admitted shakily. 'But she's still young. Doubtless you are her first love.'

'And lover,' Kier clarified determinedly, but without spite. Much as he disliked her, he could admire Clarissa's control. Most mothers would have been ranting and raving.

'However,' she continued, as if he'd not spoken, 'these things are easily quashed. If I stop paying her tuition, she'll be forced to come home. We'll see what thousands of miles between you and months of separation can do.'

Kier smiled. 'I'll just quit college as well, and we'll both get a job.'

'A job?' Clarissa said incredulously. 'Oriel has never had to do a day's work in her life.'

Kier just looked at her, wondering how a girl's mother could know so little about her own daughter. 'She'll learn,' he said briefly. And the way he said it made Clarissa's heart lurch in fear. What did he intend to do? Live off Oriel?

'How much, you little Kansas hick?' she asked with soft but savage hatred. 'How much will it take for you to leave my daughter alone?'

Kier felt disbelief, then rage, then pity sweep over him in successive waves. 'Lady, you're pitiful,' he said, then turned and left her.

Oriel, who was waiting a little further down the corridor, straightened as he came out. 'What did she say?'

'The usual, I imagine.'

Oriel grimaced. 'What do we do now?'

'We find Jinksie. His father owns a private plane. He keeps it at Kidlington airport, a few miles away.'

'What do we want with a plane?'

'We're going to fly to Scotland.'

They were outside, in the courtyard now, and Clarissa looked down on their heads, a vague sick feeling in the pit of her stomach. She would have to stay on in England for longer than she'd planned. Oriel needed protecting, whether she knew it or not. Clarissa would not let that one take advantage of her baby! She glared at Kier's brown head with loathing.

'Scotland?' Oriel repeated, her voice barely above a whisper. 'Why would we want to go to Scotland? And what about the play tonight?'

'We'll be back in time for the play,' Kier assured her, hooking his arm around her shoulders. It felt heavy and warm and comforting, and Oriel fell into step beside him, suddenly so happy to be alive. 'What's in Scotland?' she asked after a few quiet moments, as they slowly walked towards the lodge gates, each filled with private thoughts.

'Gretna Green.'

'Who's that?'

'Where,' he corrected. 'It's a place where you can get married without parental consent.' They were past the lodge now, and Oriel stopped dead in her tracks to gape at him.

'Married?'

'Uh-huh. That woman back there—' he nodded his head toward the college 'won't leave us alone.'

'And you're scared she'll break us up,' Oriel finished for him, a sensation of disappointment sinking in her stomach.

Kier shook his head. 'She couldn't break us up in a million years,' he stated bluntly. 'But until we're married, she's going to hang around here making a real pain of herself. And I, for one, don't need the hassle. Do you?'

Oriel stared at him and then found herself laughing helplessly. Passers-by stared at them, smiles forming on their lips as the young couple suddenly hugged each other, Kier swinging her around and around.

They found Jinksie in the dining room, wolfing down porridge. He was delighted at the romance of the proposition, and readily agreed to take them. He could be witness and best man, Kier told him, and on the private plane, Jinksie actually found some champagne, with which they toasted themselves in advance.

By midday they were in Scotland. Jinksie loaned Oriel a tenner to buy a long white dress and Kier used up the change in his pockets to buy her some flowers, some seasonal Michaelmas daisies in pink and purple, and a single red rose. The registry office was small and sparse, but what did it matter? It was a cathedral to them. Jinksie's eyes were suspiciously bright as he listened to them take their vows, and afterwards insisted on flying them down to Edinburgh and treating them to a slap-up lunch, where they ordered beef Wellington and apple crumble. It was the best wedding feast Oriel could ever have imagined.

But the best moment of the day, as far as she was concerned, was just before the registrar called them in. Jinksie had slapped a hand to his forehead, looking appalled. 'A ring,' he moaned. 'We haven't got a ring.'

And then Kier had smiled and pulled a simple plain band from his pocket. And looking at the golden ring in that dark hall as they waited to become man and wife, she suddenly knew that he had intended to marry her all along, and that the visit by her mother had only speeded things up. She had cried then, and laughed, and kissed him, and was still kissing him when the registrar had called them in.

The plane had been refuelled when they got back from their lunch, and they took off straight away, landing back at Kidlington airport at just after six. Rushing like mad, they dashed back to college, Oriel to change and Kier to go to the theatre, where everyone was in a panic. Viv was the first to see him. 'Where the hell have you been?' he all but screamed, the rest of the cast and crew looking at Kier with mixed expressions of relief and annoyance.

'Sorry,' he apologized to the room in general. 'I had things to do.'

Viv stared at him, open-mouthed. 'Things to do,' he repeated incredulously, looking around at the others for support. Kier's best friend he might be, but even he had begun to wonder if his friend had chickened out when the day had worn on, curtain time drawing ominously close, and still no bloody Yank. Now his voice was hard but also playful as he recited a list of grievances. 'You should have been here this morning. One of the stage props got broken, a set of lights has failed, and Midge called in sick.'

'Is it all fixed?' Kier asked, yanking off his coat and rolling up his shirtsleeves.

Viv's mouth fell even further open. 'That's not the point. You're the director, you bloody Yank. Where've you been all day? You should have been here, holding our hands, protecting us from all this disaster. What have you been doing instead? That's what we'd all like to know.'

There was a general and still ill-humoured murmur of agreement and Kier glanced around at the hostile faces, then grinned, looking back at Viv before shrugging. 'I've been getting married,' he said simply. For a second there was total silence. 'In Gretna Green,' he added. More silence. 'To the Shrew,' he finished off, and suddenly everyone erupted into laughter, applause, ribald comments and wolf whistles as they realized he wasn't joking.

Viv walked up to him, then slowly shook his head. 'You bloody Yank,' he said softly, then thrust out his hand. Kier took it, a broad grin on his face. He was actually married. He had a wife. The world had a Mrs Kier Harcourt. Suddenly it began to sink in, and he sat down, feeling giddy, exultant, terrified.

'I've never had my leading lady snaffled right from under my nose with such panache before,' Viv wailed. 'How the hell did you get to Scotland and back in one day?'

Kier told them, the work grinding to a halt as he was forced to give them all the gory details. The only bit he left out was the arrival of Oriel's mother that morning. But no doubt that would soon get around. Especially since the lady herself would be present at curtain time in exactly . . . he glanced at his watch and yelped. 'We've got thirty minutes to go. Bloody hell!' At his horrified words and utter panic, everyone began to laugh.

'Welcome to the glorious world of showbiz, Yank,' Viv said heartily, and slapped him on the back.

* * *

By seven o'clock the lecture room was full. In the tiny room that had been set aside as 'backstage', Betty put the finishing touches of makeup on Oriel's face, because her own hands were shaking too much. She had just abjectly apologized for the seventh time for not taking Betty to Scotland with her, when the cue boy called for 'curtain up'.

'Oohhhhh nooooo!' Oriel stared at herself in the mirror. In the space of a day she'd probably lost a mother, gained a husband, and now she was due to step out on stage in front of a huge audience for the first time in her life. What a day!

In the front row, Clarissa sat between a Physics don and a famous visiting conductor of the London Philharmonic. Behind her was the cream of Oxford society, all gathered together for the student drama of the year. The curtain went up to reveal the drawing room of a suburban house. Clarissa frowned. Hadn't she heard that this was supposed to be The *Taming of the Shrew*?

For the next two hours she sat and stared. On the stage her daughter was barely recognizable — the accent was gone, all the charm and class were gone and in her place was a man-hating shrew, intent on bringing down Peter, her male antagonist. Through the first scene Clarissa prayed that the play would fall flat on its face — that the audience would boo and hiss, and denigrate the upstart who had dared rewrite Shakespeare so outlandishly and with such arrogant confidence. But by the interlude it was obvious the play was a smash. It was funny, aggravating, touching and almost unbelievably sexy. Viv, the leading man, was all potent power, and as she watched him with Oriel, Clarissa wondered if she couldn't ask Viv for help. Surely Oriel couldn't play opposite him like that without feeling some reaction to the man? She asked the don next to her who the male lead was and was told he was the son of an earl. Clarissa nodded, suddenly filled with hope. An English earl was by far a better prospect for her daughter. Oriel was born to be a lady of a great house. And a title too . . .

As the curtain folded on a now meek and mild Kate, lovingly putting slippers over Peter's hole-filled socks, the audience rose as one to start clapping. The minor characters took their bows first, then Viv, then Oriel. The applause for the two leads was stunning. Oriel looked out over the clapping crowd and felt breathless. She'd stepped out on stage a nervous wreck, her mind groping for her first line. Then she'd seen Viv and the look of encouragement in his eyes, and the next second her voice came out, loud and clear, just as she'd rehearsed it. Throughout the play Kier had watched closely from the sidelines, his presence a solid, comforting rock. By the third act she was enjoying herself immensely. The calls came now for author and director. When Kier hesitated, Oriel walked over to him and took his hand, leading him out onto the stage. The applause magnified as they all took their final bows.

* * *

Backstage, Kier sank down into a chair as Viv slapped him on the back. 'Well, you poor old married man you, you did it.'

Kier groaned. 'Never again. I'll never direct another play as long as I live.'

Everyone laughed, tension easing away in the aftermath of euphoria that came with a successful opening night.

'Did you see Flakey fuming in the back row?' somebody asked, to more helpless laughter. Then it went quiet as Viv suddenly raised his glass. It held cheap white wine, which was all the production could manage, but nobody minded.

'To Kate versus Pete,' he said. Unnoticed, Clarissa hesitated in the doorway, craning her neck to try and see Oriel. She intended to congratulate both her daughter and Kier Harcourt warmly. It *had* been a good play, after all.

'And to our leading lady and director. Congratulations on your marriage! Good health to you both, and may all your troubles be little ones. And if you ever decide to go off and elope to Scotland again, don't do it on the opening night of your next play!' Viv raised his glass again, and there was another toast. Kier and Oriel grinned and kissed. There was a lot to be done. They'd have to find an apartment together, for one thing. Then tell the Dean, get their names altered on the college registry . . . Kier held out his hand, and she took it, their eyes meeting and locking.

In the doorway Clarissa went white. Her eyes flew to the hand of her daughter and saw the glint of a golden ring. Wordlessly she turned and stumbled away. She walked like a robot up Broad Street and across St Giles, but by the time she had reached the hotel she was white-hot with pain-filled rage. Oh, Oriel, *what have you done?* Her mood swung wildly — she would disinherit her, leave her penniless. But of course, she couldn't do that. Oriel would never be able to cope. She'd force them to get divorced, somehow.

In her suite, Kyle stood beneath the shower. He heard the bathroom door open and through the frosted glass saw a shadowy figure walk to the bed and begin to undress. Suddenly the shower door opened, and he began to turn. He stumbled against the tiled wall as she launched herself at him, her hair darkening under the shower spray as she stepped beneath the spume. Her lips were hot and vicious on his, and he felt her sharp teeth nip his lower lip. Automatically his hands came out to her wet shoulders, his first thought being to shove her off. But, of course, the moment his fingers touched her skin he was lost, and he could only drag her closer. Her nipples were hard as iron against his chest, and his manhood leapt to attention, prodding impatiently against her thigh. Quickly her hand slipped down to clasp it, her fingers squeezing so tightly that he cried out, his whole body ricocheting with the sexual punch of her savagery.

Clarissa stared at his tight, handsome face, Kier and Oriel momentarily forgotten. Kyle was her life. As she caressed him, her own body began to tighten in sexual anticipation. Wordlessly she positioned herself in front of him, and holding on to his strong shoulders, leapt lithely off the ground. Kyle's arms automatically held her thighs as she hooked her legs behind his buttocks.

His eyes shot open as she took his shaft with her free hand and guided him into her. He moaned, then gasped as she began to slip up and down on him, his arms taking her weight easily. She worked hard and furiously, battering him against the wall, the shower water beating a warm and hard jet against her moving back. Her legs were locked like vicious scissors around his waist, making him gasp, opening his mouth to drag in air as she pumped frenziedly. She cried, shuddered, gasped for breath and then began all over again. Eventually even his great strength gave out, and he jerked hard, swinging around and pressing her against the wall. His face twisted and contorted in ecstasy, and he groaned as his seed burst forth in a red-hot torrent. Satisfied by the shattered look on his face, Clarissa lovingly pushed him away. Slowly he slid down the tiles and onto the shower mat.

'That bastard married her today,' Clarissa said, her still pert breasts rising and falling with every tortured breath she took. 'He flew her to Scotland and married her. How could she be so . . . weak? And how could I have been so stupid?'

As Kyle learned the reason for his assault, he wanted to smile, but didn't have the energy.

Then Clarissa looked down on him and smiled gently. Reaching for the soap, she began to lather her hands, intent on inflicting more sexual torment, her eyes pinning him to the floor. Kyle closed his eyes, glad that the shower spray hid the tears that squeezed past his tightly shut lids.

One day, she was going to push him too far.

CHAPTER 12

Paris

Opposite the Trocadéro, with the definitive view of the Eiffel Tower, stood the Hotel D'Concordia, with three storeys of mellow stone, arched and terraced windows, a centuries-old flag flapping in the Parisian breeze, and a clientele that could be read from a European book of *Who's Who*. It was towards this hotel that Wayne quickly walked, with a newly minted graduation document tucked in the inside of his jacket pocket. He had passed all the examinations in the top two per cent of the class, and only the formal ceremony was left, where parents could sip champagne, talk to lecturers and visiting dignitaries, and look on with satisfaction at the achievements of their embarrassed offspring.

But Wayne knew that neither Wolfgang nor Marlene would come to the official ceremony, and his steps were not as light or carefree as many of his fellow students who were now pouring into the Café Chat for a boisterous celebration. The Café Chat, with its smoky dark rooms, rustic red wine, sultry singer and dingy walls had never appealed to Wayne. But, in keeping with his decision to make it with the 'in' crowd, he frequently went there with a gang of five or more to discuss the French politics of the day, the latest new artist to make a splash, and, of course, the exploits of Alain Delon and Romy Schneider.

But this morning he had other fish to fry. Important fish.

The double arched doors of the Hotel D'Concordia were made of solid English oak, inlaid with windows over 200 years old. A doorman dressed in scarlet and gold livery opened the door for him, touching his cap respectfully as he did so. Royalty often visited the hotel and, in today's modern age, the doorman could not be sure that anyone passing between the hallowed portals, dressed in the most casual attire, was not actually a foreign prince or potentate. Wayne, dressed in a navy suit, walked like a prince. His eyes barely acknowledged the man who held open the door, and his advent into the loggia with the high domed hand-painted ceiling, where a walnut desk housed several receptionists, caused more than six female heads to turn his way.

A chandelier cast light in the circular hall, and beneath his feet the carpet was eighteenth-century oriental. Tall yucca plants stood in corners, and from hanging baskets orchids and flowering stock cast a sweet perfume into the air. An antique clock chimed the hour behind him as he walked briskly towards the reception desk, where a pretty blonde straightened her back and thrust out her breasts behind the pale blue uniform jacket she wore. But a few yards from the desk Wayne paused, his eye caught by the glimpse of gold in a telephone kiosk, discreetly tucked away in one corner. It was an old-fashioned booth, made entirely of teak, with just a single window, at about face height, to reveal whether or not the booth was occupied. Wayne changed direction, his gaze fixed on the woman inside. Her long, golden hair gleamed in a stray beam of sunlight, and she was laughing as she spoke into the receiver. She had a high forehead, aristocratically straight nose, and wore an unmistakable panache of class along with her red lipstick and Balmain summer frock. Without hesitation, he slid open the door of the kiosk, and stepped inside. Before she could turn around he closed the door behind him and took the telephone from her hand. A chattering female voice was suddenly cut off as he put down the receiver, and the blonde attempted to turn around. But the booth was too small and now infinitely too crowded with the two of them, and so Wayne's hands on her shoulders forced her to face the wall before he slid them down over her bare arms and brought them round, his fingers coming to rest momentarily on her curvaceous breasts before splaying over her flat stomach.

The blonde gasped, her head falling back onto his chest, her hair spilling over the navy jacket fitting snugly across his shoulders. Slowly he reached forward and kissed her ear. 'Toinette. How do you know I'm not some randy bellboy?' he whispered, his hands sliding down to hike her skirt further up her thighs, which were bare of tights in the hot weather. Slowly his fingers caressed the soft skin of her inner thighs with circular, teasing movements.

Antoinette Montigny, the eldest daughter of the Duc de Montigny, one of the oldest families from ancient Normandy stock, allowed herself a self-satisfied smile. 'I didn't,' she purred, her voice husky and breathless as his fingers found the elasticated band on her peach silk cami-knickers and began to caress her soft mound. 'The bellboys around here are all handsome, after all.'

Wayne smiled, but there was no humour in his eyes, and he bit her ear sharply. He had met Toinette at a party in Chateauvalliers, the residence of one of the richest couples in France. A murmured inquiry into a friend's ear had told him immediately the name of the gorgeous blonde flirting cruelly with the wine waiter. An heiress to millions, with a title and impeccable background, Toinette Montigny was ideal material for a wife.

His approach had been to watch her, hold her gaze when their eyes met, smile ironically and then turn away. He had not even approached her by the time the party had begun to wind down, though she had obviously expected him to, her cool dove-grey eyes mocking and knowing as she watched him dance with the second most attractive girl there, a Parisian model with an Italian count for a father. But Wayne had surprised her, not to mention totally rocked her complacency, by leaving with the Italian model, and not even Toinette a second glance. When they met for the second time, at the opening of an art gallery in Montmartre, Toinette had taken matters in hand and aggressively attached herself to him, dragging him into her car at the end of the evening and driving into a narrow, deserted street, where they had made cramped but very vigorous love.

The French, Wayne had learned very early on, were not quite the romantics they would have the rest of the world believe. Though Toinette had had more lovers than Wayne cared to think about, when it came to marriage, there were other considerations to take into account. The first time he met her father, at a hunting weekend in the Loire Valley, the Due had given him the third degree enough to make his head ache. He was left with the uneasy feeling that although he was presentable enough, and his family was rich enough, his pedigree left a lot to be desired. Of necessity the D'Arville family history was vague at best, and American immigrants, returned to Monte Carlo after the war, did not make for ideal in-laws. Which was why Wayne was working so hard to keep the insatiable Toinette happy. Hearing her gasp as his fingers found the sensitive nub they had been searching for, he began to stroke her hard. A man waiting to use the phone glanced in, his eyes widening, his mouth following suit. Smiling conspiratorially, he walked away to wait at another booth.

Rubbing her back against him as he caressed her into orgasm, Toinette closed her eyes. Her head reached just about to his shoulder, and that was in four-inch-high heels. She loved tall men, she loved handsome men and she especially loved men who knew how to please her. Naturally astute and unclouded by the fog called love that affected some of her more intelligent friends, she'd recognized immediately what Wayne wanted. Her title, her respectability and the security of marrying a de Montigny. At four years his senior, she knew full well that in order to keep getting the monthly cheques from her father, she would have to marry soon, and produce an heir. And Wayne, with his wonderful physique, his outlandish background and uncomplicated sexual expertise, was as good a proposition as any other. She enjoyed the novel and risqué idea of owning a casino and possessing a husband that any woman would want. And would probably get, once the marriage was safely secured. She was not foolish enough to expect fidelity, but there was a cold, calculating dangerous streak in Wayne that fascinated the rebel in Toinette and set him apart from the usual run-of-the-mill playboys that normally shared her bed and lifestyle.

Now, as her body shuddered convulsively in another orgasm, she smiled, sighed, and straightened her clothing. Within a minute her breathing was normal, her body heat back to where it had been only a few minutes ago. 'That was nice,' she murmured, turning at last to look up at him, her grey eyes mocking but warm. As she reached up and kissed him, he felt a stab of resentment ripple through him, and wondered sourly how many other men had heard her say those words.

They made their way to the Chevalliere restaurant, where Wayne drank and ate with little enthusiasm but was content that all his plans were going so well.

* * *

Hundreds of miles away, on the treacherous roads of Monte Carlo, a car hurtled against a wall and was thrown over the barriers down a thirty-foot drop, to roll to a mangled stop on the corniche below. Inside, Gillian and Pierre Rissaud, the parents of Claude Rissaud, died instantly.

* * *

After lunch Toinette and Wayne went back to the hotel, where they had a boisterous afternoon testing the bedsprings

130

of her Queen Anne bed, and afterwards she drove him to Orly Airport, where he caught the plane for the brief flight to Nice.

It was nearly dark by the time he picked up his Maserati from the airport car terminal and drove to the Villa Mimosa. The sun was going down as a ball of red fire behind him when he walked through the garden, the music of the fountains creating an atmosphere of tranquil peace in the velvet night.

Rosita's father had left their employ a few months after Rosita's disgrace, and now a new gardener, whose name escaped him, cut blooms from the flowerbeds that would later grace the dining table. Taking the key from his pocket, he opened the door, the smell of lavender polish and the lingering scent of his mother's Dior perfume giving him a rare sense of homecoming. The villa was in darkness, as he'd expected, and he walked briskly into the main salon, where a huge fireplace was laid with real logs. No fire burned during the hot summer nights, though, and he moved across to the open French windows, stopping at the mahogany bar *en route* to pour himself a snifter of Napoleon brandy.

His body felt pleasantly relaxed after today's session with the woman that he'd just become engaged to. He had popped the question when she was sucking on his hardened nipple, and she had lifted her head long enough to look up, take the expensive solitaire diamond ring he held out and slip it on her finger. Then her head dipped again, leaving Wayne to smile up at the ceiling, a pleasant picture of the chateau in Normandy flashing across his mind, with himself as the owner and occupier, once the old Due finally did the decent thing and died.

Now Wayne glanced at his watch and wondered what the reaction of his parents would be to the news of his marriage into one of the premier families in all of France. With his top Sorbonne qualifications, an eminently suitable wife, and heir to two fortunes, he was on top of the world. His first purchase after his marriage would be a bigger yacht. He could no longer live in Monte Carlo without a decent boat. A few thousand tonnes of two-storeyed boat, with every modern convenience, including a cinema room, a gym, several suites and games room, should do nicely for starters. Then, of course, to keep Toinette happy, a world cruise and a year off before taking up the reins of his new office: President of the House of Montigny.

His first act would be to tackle the American market. That was where the real money lay. Providing wine for the European elite was fine for prestige, but the serious money lay in middle-of-the-road wine for the American middle classes with their delusions of grandeur and enormous capacity to spend money. Marketing and promotion was the magic of the modern business world. The old Due might scream and rave, but Wayne was confident that he'd be in a position of power that would be unbeatable after a few years. Of course, he'd have to take things carefully . . .

He turned from the window and poured himself a second glass. He felt oddly restless and on edge. He wanted to see his father's face when he heard the news — he wanted to feel his power grow and come to life right before Wolfgang's eyes. He wanted revenge. Still. Only. Always revenge.

As he walked through the hall to his bedroom, he noticed a light on in his father's study, the narrow wedge of light winking out from under the closed door. He frowned, surprised, and slowly walked towards the room that had been off limits for as long as he could remember. His father's sanctuary, as he called it, it was his office at home, full of papers and files. Wayne wondered vaguely what could possibly have kept his father from the casino and, unable to resist giving him the news, he raised his hand and tapped briskly on the door, walking in without waiting for a reply.

His father was sitting behind the desk, a single lamp illuminating his face. There were no papers set out in front of him, but his hands clutched the front of the walnut desk, his knuckles tensely white in the glow from the lamp. An expensive cut-crystal paperweight and a silver-handed stiletto-type paper knife glinted in the same light, but Wayne barely noticed the trappings of wealth that littered his father's desk.

Instead his eyes were on Wolfgang's face. As he slowly closed the door behind him, his father's blue eyes watched him with an expressionless, reptilian intensity, and he sat unnaturally still as Wayne slowly approached the massive desk. 'Father,' Wayne said, 'I have some news for you.'

Wolfgang said nothing.

'I became engaged this afternoon. To Antoinette D'Montigny.'

Wolfgang blinked, once, twice, and then slowly let go of the desk. He had been sitting there all afternoon, and only now became aware that he had put on the lamp, and that outside it was dark. His first instinct, on being told that afternoon by Jacques that there was a fisherman waiting to see him, had been to laugh and send the boy away with a flea in his ear. But curiosity had got the better of him, and Claude Rissaud had been admitted. Hours ago, it must have been, but Wolfgang couldn't be sure. Time seemed to have no more meaning.

Wayne stood behind the black leather chair, resting his hands against the upholstery, watching his father with wary, puzzled eyes. Wolfgang looked at the elegant hands against the seat, then up into his murderous son's face and felt the numbness slowly begin to disperse. The fact that Wayne had killed meant nothing in itself, of course. But it was no Jew, or prisoner of war, or gypsy or other no-account rubbish that he had killed, but Hans; the best, the finest of them all. Hans. His Hans, his brightest, most beloved son.

'We thought we'd get married at Christmas time, and then take our honeymoon in St Moritz. Of course, the Due will make me his vice-president, so I'll probably not be spending much time here.'

Wolfgang felt his fingers close around the letter opener. What was he saying? He shook his head to clear it, and as he did so, Wayne's words fell like red-hot coals into his mind. While Hans lay dead in his grave, his murderer was talking about marrying, about holidaying in the richest playground in the world. While Hans would never know the joys of a woman's bed, or feel the sun on his face again, his murderer . . .

Wayne was totally unprepared when his father launched himself from the chair, his startled brain barely having time to register the flash of silver in the lamplight as the wicked blade of the stiletto plunged towards him. Only instinct had him turning in time and raising his hand to deflect the accurately aimed blade from his heart. The razor-sharp tip skidded across his chest, ripping through the fine wool of his suit and lodging in his shoulder. Wayne screamed, but his left fist was already coming up automatically to slam into his father's jaw.

Wolfgang grunted, the impetus of his forward movement cannoning him first into Wayne's fist, and then knocking him back against the desk. It had all happened so quickly that for a second, as Wayne stared at the old man half-sprawled against the desk, he was unsure of what exactly had happened. He grabbed the stiletto handle in his shoulder, wincing as a vicious pain ran down his arm as he gingerly pulled it out and stared at it incredulously, the blade stained red with his blood.

Wolfgang straightened, calling him a murdering bastard in guttural, hate-filled German, his hand curling around the base of the lamp, and not for the first time did he curse his advancing years. He hated being old. Once he could have taken his son in a straight fight and killed him with his bare hands, as he now longed to do; instead, infirmity dictated that he use a weapon.

Wayne had barely a second to realize that somehow his father had found out about Hans, and then the lamp was being hurtled towards his face, its heavy steel frame glinting dully in his father's wrinkled hand. Ducking, he charged forward, his head burying itself in Wolfgang's belly as the lamp crashed down on his back, shattering and cutting through his clothing into his skin as the bulb exploded. His own grunt of pain and that of his father's mixed as they crashed to the floor. Landing on top of him, Wayne began to punch his father with quick, vicious jabs to the face, chest and belly. Between the blows, Wolfgang managed to grab Wayne's throat, his old, bony fingers biting into his son's windpipe with remembered Gestapo skill. Wayne felt his eyes begin to bulge and black blotches flashed across his vision. His hands desperately circled his father's wrists, trying to prise them off, but Wolfgang was a man demented, and his fingers only dug deeper, threatening to shatter his son's larynx. Wayne's lungs were on fire now as he realized with mounting panic that he could not dislodge the throttling hands around his neck. Blindly, his hands groped toward his father's face, searching for a way to make him let loose. He could feel his senses beginning to fade, and just as he thought he was going to die, the soft orbs of Wolfgang's eyes rolled under his fingertips, and he dug in sharply, his fingers curving in and out with a ferocity born of panic. Wolfgang screamed, his hands losing their strength as the unbelievable pain penetrated even his hate-filled frenzy, allowing Wayne to pull away and stagger back, dragging painful breaths deep into his lungs as he stumbled to the leather chair and slumped down. There he dangled his hands limply between his legs as he leant forward, his head spinning, and his big body shaking all over. A few yards away, Wolfgang lay curled on the carpet, his hands clutching his eyes, moaning like an animal.

Slowly, Wayne became aware of a stickiness on his fingers. Looking down at them, he found them covered in blood, and a great wave of nausea engulfed him. Sprinting to the French windows, he opened them and was violently sick among the roses and hibiscus bushes. When he finally got up from his knees and walked back into the room he felt numb, his shoulder and back bleeding hard, staining his expensive suit beyond repair.

Wolfgang had crawled back behind his desk, his hands still covering his eyes. They felt on fire, and he could hardly breathe without moaning, but he daren't open his eyes, afraid of what he might see; or, more accurately, of what he might not see.

'I'll have you guillotined for this.' He had heard his son retching outside and heard him return, and his voice was a hiss of pure hatred. For a second, Wayne felt ice course through his veins as the spectre of capital punishment flittered horrifically across his brain. Then he laughed.

'No way, old man,' he said, his voice every bit as thick with hatred as Wolfgang's had been. 'You so much as call in the police and I'll notify the Nazi hunters as to your whereabouts. Remember the Heinzberg kidnapping, Papa?'

Wolfgang did. Vividly. Four years ago one of his contemporaries had been snatched from his home in Bolivia by the Israeli Secret Service and had been tried and executed in the new state of Israel. It had made Wolfgang paranoid to a point where security at the casino and at the villa had made life unbearable for a few months. Marlene had finally been able to persuade him that such fanatical security would only make him look suspicious. Now, as Wolfgang realized just how powerless he actually was, he began to curse in German, his words so full of bile and filth that even Wayne blanched.

Through the fingers held over his eyes, Wayne could see blood trickling over Wolfgang's hand, and he turned away, suddenly feeling ill. He had to get out of there — he just couldn't stand the sight of the old man a moment longer.

As he heard the door open, Wolfgang's hand tightened over the ruined mess of his eyes. 'I'll kill you,' he whispered, thinking of hired assassins, of men who would do the job slowly and painfully . . .

'You do,' Wayne said, standing in the doorway, leaning back against the wall weakly, 'and copies of your life story will be released automatically to both the press and the Israeli Secret Service. You'll stand trial for the killer you really are — in Israel, in view of the whole world.' Then, because he thought his father might be beyond caring what happened to him, he played a trump card that he knew would assure his own safety. 'Your precious Hans will be dug up from out of that cemetery and put in unhallowed ground. You don't think the French will want the son of a Nazi contaminating their graveyard, do you, Father dearest?'

Wolfgang slumped back in his chair, utterly defeated, as Wayne staggered from the room, stained with their blood, knowing he would never have to fear an assassin's bullet. He drove, with some difficulty, to the home of their family doctor, knowing he could not risk going to the hospital where one of the nurses might tip off the press. The scandal magazines were notorious for paying nurses well to spill the beans on any 'celebrities' that might come their way.

Dr Hulot gave him ten stitches and a tetanus shot, bandaging him up without asking a single question. Wayne was halfway out the door when he hesitated, in an agony of indecision. Then he sighed. 'You'd better get up to Villa Mimosa,' he said curtly, then turned and left.

He drove as far as Saint Jean de Luz, leaving Monte Carlo behind with a sigh of relief. He stayed at the Hôtel Le Petit Trianon, close to the beach. He needed to be somewhere clean and unpolluted. At first he felt blissfully numb, but soon he began to hurt, remembering back to his boyhood in Berlin and praying for his mother to come to his room. He wanted her now; he would have given anything to have her hand on his forehead, her voice telling him that everything would be all right. He felt ill, disoriented, afraid and totally alone. For the first time in his life, he knew that he actually needed someone, and a fierce craving for human contact hit him. Not for sex, but for something more lasting, more meaningful. Suddenly he needed a friend, something that he had never had. A man who understood him, who liked him. A man that he could talk to, play cards with, laugh with. A friend . . . The first acute wave of longing slowly faded, but its core remained hidden, only awaiting the right moment to flare savagely into existence again.

He stayed for five days. His shoulder ached, and his nights were feverish. He awoke in the mornings drenched with sweat, feelings of euphoria, horror, regret and guilt warring for supremacy. When he finally felt fit enough to drive, he motored north, to Normandy.

The Chateau Montigny was on the outskirts of a small provincial town, set in lush hay meadows, overlooking a fairy-tale river. The iron gates were kept locked, but a camera set on one stone pillar monitored arrivals. He sounded the horn and looked at the camera, waiting for someone to open the gates. Five minutes passed and he thumped the horn again, but still there was no reaction. He cut the engine and got out, a nasty feeling slowly creeping into his innards as he walked to the gate. When he touched them, an electric charge shot through his arm, making him yelp and leap back. Rubbing his hand, he cursed graphically in French. A few moments later, he heard the crunch of footsteps on gravel and waited warily as the Due walked towards him, a broken shotgun hung professionally over the crook of one arm.

He was a tall, thin man, with white hair and the enormous nose of a vintner. His eyes were steel grey and emotionless as he stopped on the other side of the gates and looked coolly at the man his daughter had chosen to marry.

Wayne looked back at him through the intricate iron-work of the seventeenth-century gates, his narrowed eyes following the movement of the Due's hand as he wordlessly reached into the top pocket of his tweed jacket and withdrew a small object which he tossed through the ironwork. It fell onto the ground with a soft 'ting'. Looking down, Wayne saw a diamond ring. He glanced at it but made no attempt to pick it up.

'I want to see Toinette.'

'She isn't here.'

Wayne met the unmoving eyes, his first instinct being to call him a liar. Then he realized that in all probability Toinette would have run away, her cowardice prompting her to avoid an embarrassing scene. It was just the kind of gutless reaction he'd come to expect from women and the world in general.

'Where is she?'

'America. She said to give you that.' The Duc nodded toward the ring, but Wayne didn't look down. Instead a helpless rage began to clog his brain, and his lips pulled back into a savage sneer.

'You never wanted me in your precious family in the first place, did you?'

'No,' the Duc admitted readily, without the least sign of unease.

'Don't think that this is over,' Wayne warned him, enraged by the man's careless dismissal. 'Toinette wants—'

'Toinette wants to live a life of luxury,' the Duc interrupted him. 'To indulge herself with everything life has to offer. She can't do that with a man who has nothing.'

'Nothing?' The word sounded foreign on Wayne's tongue, and for the first time the Duc de Montigny smiled.

'Your father phoned me yesterday to tell me he has disinherited you. He also told me that you cannot go back to Monte Carlo . . . at least, not if you want to live. He assures me that nobody in Monte Carlo will give you the time of day. In fact,' the Duc said, with so much smug satisfaction that Wayne felt like reaching through the ironwork, electrified or not, and grabbing him by the throat, 'you're not wanted in France at all.'

Wayne stiffened, for the first time fully comprehending that he was practically penniless. His future, which only days ago had been so promising, was now in ruins, and the enormity of his problems was suddenly overwhelming. He felt like shouting in rage and defiance, but none of his emotions showed on his face, except for a slight tightening of his jaw.

The Duc had taken an immediate dislike to the giant of a man Toinette had brought home just over three months ago, sensing that something dangerous lurked beneath his surface charm, manners and good looks; something that was dark and unstable. He had never been more relieved in his life than when Marcus D'Arville had called, telling him the news, and he'd been even more satisfied when, with a few tears of regret, Toinette had agreed to let him go. Even she had seen the futility of trying to salvage the situation. Now, as he watched the man in front of him straighten and stiffen, the eyes turning opaque and expressionless, the Due could not help but feel uneasy. Looking into his eyes was like looking into a diamond — there was nothing there that he could call human, and in his ears he could hear his own blood began to pound with a heavy, frightened beat.

Slowly Wayne stooped down and pocketed the ring, realizing that he'd need all the money he could get. The Due watched, the look of contempt on his face quickly fleeing under the ice-cold, level stare of the younger man. Uneasily, the Due took a step backwards, despite the electrified iron between them. Seeing it, Wayne felt his own power bite deep. It was something separate from money or position. It was in him, a vital and integral part of his very being. And suddenly he knew that he would be on the top again soon.

Somehow.

CHAPTER 13

San Francisco

The old lady had lived in San Francisco all her life, but for all the seventy-two years that she had trodden the same hills, she'd never managed to tread them any flatter. It was nearly 90 degrees, and her shopping basket, weighed down with tins of cat food, seemed to pull her arms from her sockets.

'Hello, Mrs Dobson. Bit warm, isn't it?' The voice was soft and kind, and made her stop in her tracks. As she turned into the sun she saw the halo of a young man, the bright daylight behind him turning his hair a deep red. She blinked, and the boy moved, his face coming into focus.

'Oh, it's young Sebastien, isn't it? I'm a bit puffed, I'm afraid.'

'Here, let me take that. I'm going your way.'

He wasn't, but her old and lined face was bathed in perspiration, and her little wisps of white hair were plastered to her pink scalp in damp waves. He looked down in surprise at the weight of the wicker basket, and then saw all the tins of cat food, and a great wave of compassion had him mentally abandoning all his afternoon plans to visit the rehabilitation centre.

'How's school nowadays?' Enid Dobson asked, reaching out to the wall to give her extra support as they turned down Pitman Street, a residential street of quiet, slightly decayed elegance. When she had been a girl, it had been the height of fashion to live in this area. Of course, in those days everyone had been talking about the great quake as if it had only just happened. Everyone had seemed to lose someone to that giant earthquake and even now it was remembered with horror. Ah, those were the days, Enid thought, looking up at the tall, three-storey houses with their canary-yellow paintwork and Florentine lace curtains.

'I've just graduated,' Sebastien interrupted her thoughts, hoicking the basket onto his other arm and taking her elbow in a courtly olde-worlde gesture that had the venerable Mrs Dobson blushing like a schoolgirl and looking at him coyly out of the corners of her rheumy blue eyes. Ah, such men were a rare breed nowadays! Sebastien was of medium height, but even so his five feet ten inches seemed to tower over the diminutive old woman, and she was briefly transported back to pre-war days, when they had danced waltzes instead of the awful modem gyrations young people went through nowadays, and when more men looked and acted just like this one. In those days, it was easy to tell the sexes apart.

'Just graduated, eh?' she repeated, shaking her head. 'I would have liked to have gone to college. But . . . well, in my day, young ladies never seemed to go to college. And then there was the war, and we all went to the factories . . .' Her voice was cracked with age, but full of strength of character, nostalgia and wistfulness.

Sebastien shook his head, his regret genuine at the thought of all that waste. To take her mind off bad days, and because he was genuinely interested, he prompted her with some gentle teasing. 'And what would you have liked to study, Mrs Dobson? Poetry, I bet. All those dashing exploits of the mad, bad and dangerous-to-know Lord Byron, for instance?'

Enid chuckled, her laughter surprisingly young and carefree, and several passers-by looked at them curiously.

They made an odd couple — the small, bent old woman and the young, handsome man, with hair the colour of English chestnuts.

'Ahh, now wouldn't that have been nice. Poor Lady Caroline Lamb. She died of a broken heart, you know. I don't suppose anybody does that nowadays. And Tennyson, of course — 'The Lady of Shalott' was always my favourite. You majored in English?'

Sebastien grinned and shook his head, revealing a row of perfect white teeth in his square-jawed, boyishly handsome face. 'Uh-uh. Psychology. I'm due to start my psychiatry internship at the General this fall.'

'Oh,' Enid said. She wasn't at all sure she trusted this new-fangled subject. It seemed to her that people should keep their problems to themselves, like they always had. Going around and revealing all your most intimate secrets to a perfect stranger filled her with horror. 'Oh. Well . . .' She struggled for something nice to say because she'd watched Sebastien Teale grow up from a kind-hearted and polite little boy, and she didn't want to be unkind to someone who had once rescued her Fluffy from beneath the wheels of a milk float. 'I'm sure you'll do very well indeed. I'll have to start calling you Doctor, then?'

Sebastien, reading her thoughts practically word for word, laughed. 'Not quite yet. I have five more years yet to do. At the same time I have to undergo three years' psycho-analysis myself.'

'You do? Aren't you the one who's going to be the doctor, then?'

'Uh-huh. But the medical board has got to be sure that I'm fit myself. After all, I can't go helping people if I'm a secret lunatic myself, now, can I?'

'Oh, you!' The little old woman tapped his arm play-fully, then sighed. 'Ah, at last. Here we are. I'm quite worn out.' Her own house was at the end of the road, and she was forced to pause to catch her breath by the five stone steps that led up to the front door. A black and white cat of enormous proportions, most of it fluffy fur, sashayed down the steps and wound a tail seductively around Sebastien's legs.

'Hello, Fluff. Still chasing milk floats, hmm?' The hand he ran over the cat was casual, but the cat went into immediate ecstasy. A loud, lawnmower purr vibrated from his soft underbelly, and the green eyes narrowed into blissful slits. Thus encouraged, Sebastien began to rub the cat's belly, and the lawnmower revved harder.

'Oh, that cat!' Enid said, her voice affectionately exasperated. 'He'll be the death of me.'

Sebastien had a way with animals that astonished many people. Vicious dogs, even some trained security animals, became putty in his hands the moment man and animal met. As a boy he had brought home an injured or stray animal of almost every species known to his native California — including a big old bullfrog whose hind leg had been mashed by a car. He'd called it Harry, and had kept it for six years, much to his mother's distress, before it had died of old age. He'd been the only boy in school who could catch bluebottles with his bare hands by the time Harry finally croaked.

But it was in his dealings with people that Sebastien's true talents lay. Always listening more than talking, he had been a keen observer of human nature from childhood. His own particularly sensitive nature had developed over the years into an uncanny, almost paranormal ability to see past the mask people habitually wore and discover what lurked beneath. As a boy, instead of getting embroiled in the usual childhood squabbles and coming home with a bloody nose or bruised shin, he would come home with a note from the teacher, congratulating his parents on his behaviour in mediating between troublemakers, preventing fights, and even, more often than not, bringing antagonistic boys together to become the best of friends.

A good all-rounder, his main interest from an early age had leant towards the humanities, much to his father's dismay. His studies in sociology, at the age of fourteen, had totally fascinated him, unlike many of his friends, who found the subject boring. He had, with a special dispensation from a delighted psychology teacher, started studying the subject a year early, and by the age of sixteen had passed with flying colours exams that eighteen-year-olds struggled to get through. But it was not academic brilliance, or his good looks, or his ready and funny wit or sense of humour that attracted people to him by the droves, earning him more friends than he seemed able to count. There was something very human — not to mention *humane* — about Sebastien Teale that people reacted to both consciously and subconsciously. It drew wounded spirits to him like a magnet. His soft voice, soft eyes, listening ear, keen intelligence and total lack of judgemental superiority made him a perfect, if incongruous, father confessor.

At fifteen, Arthur Wight had confided to him that he was hooked on whisky, knowing that Sebastien would not squeal or condemn him. His belief in his friend was fully justified. Without talking to his parents or teachers, Sebastien read up on the subject of alcohol addiction and worked out a drying-out routine for his friend to follow, sticking with him through the withdrawal symptoms, spending weekend after weekend at his house, ostensibly to study, but in reality to make sure he didn't slip. And there were many other incidents. Girls and boys came to him with any and every problem that agonized teenagers worldwide.

When she became pregnant, Sue Anne Haynes had turned to him, though in a higher year herself and hardly knowing him. He had gone with her to a family clinic, had held her hand as she talked with a doctor, had talked her through all the options, and had gone with her when she had told her parents.

In almost any other boy, such popularity would have inevitably led to jealousy, making for a painful backlash by some of the older boys. But not so with Sebastien. His level gaze, never judgemental but never weak, had seen him through several confrontations with older boys who were obviously insecure and afraid of him and his puzzling maturity, and bitterly envious of his status with girls, who found his good looks a delicious cherry on top of a very sweet cake.

Sometimes, as his mother had watched him grow, she wondered if he had ever really been a child. As a three-year-old, he'd watched her in the house with those warm sherry eyes, a ready smile always on his cherubic face, but the intelligence had been evident right from the start. An IQ test at twelve had placed him potentially in the Mensa bracket and had opened the whole academic world to him. But he had stayed at home, studying at the local high and then college, doing in two years what others did in four, but without vanity.

Now, as the cat's soft paws clung to his hand in trusting adoration, he straightened, lifting the cat into his arms, and carrying the basket up the steps.

'You will have some lemonade, won't you?' Enid asked, hoping her voice did not sound as pitifully eager as she felt. Since her husband had died in the war, she had been so alone that sometimes she talked to her cat. She felt like a silly old woman, but Fluffy never seemed to mind.

Hearing the plea for company as if she had spoken it out loud, he smiled and nodded. 'I'd love to,' he said, and knowing the old woman wouldn't appreciate pity, added cleverly, 'This sun sure works up a giant thirst.'

Inside, the house was full of bric-a-brac, cheap crockery, chain-store pictures of autumns in New England, and faded chintz-covered sofas. She lived only on the first floor, the stairs being too much for her. Chattering happily, she led the way into the kitchen, a square room of yellow Formica and white furniture, where he began to unpack the groceries for her. As she poured icy lemonade into a glass, he sat down, looking around at the things that needed doing. He'd be here for at least three hours, he gauged, eyeing the flaking paint on the window-sills and the grime on the windows keeping out the sunlight and making the place look dim and dingy. He'd cook her a meal, too — something light and simple. Most old folk that lived alone didn't bother to eat properly — this he knew from his work with Age Concern.

'Why don't you rent out the top two floors, Mrs D?' he asked, watching as she looked first startled, and then alarmed.

'Oh, no. No, I couldn't do that. I mean . . . well, it's such a mess up there.'

Sebastien took a sip, knowing he had to tread carefully now. She was picturing young couples having midnight parties, shuddering in humiliation at the notion of neighbours complaining, of dogs killing her Fluffy, of children making too much noise, and she was afraid. She'd lived alone so long, the thought of company all day, every day, scared her.

'I was thinking that you might want to rent out to retired couples. Take Mr and Mrs Pettit, for example. He worked for Growers Home and Garden for forty-six years in one of their company houses. The rent was only twenty-five dollars a month, but after having six children, who've all flown the nest now, they don't have any money left to buy a place of their own. Now that he's retired, they're living in a one-roomed bedsit at the shelter, just because landlords don't want to rent to old people.'

Enid, whose face had become more and more angry as he'd told the story, suddenly slammed down her glass. 'That's terrible. Really terrible. I don't know what this country is coming to. The Spanish . . . now they know how to look after their old folk. Poor dears. One room, you say?'

Sebastien nodded. 'All they want is a place of their own. I happen to know they can pay forty dollars a month at a stretch . . .'

'That's far too much!' Enid erupted, her flushed face indignant, her old eyes flashing sparks. 'Why, I don't even use those rooms upstairs.'

'And of course, Mrs Pettit, poor old thing, gets lonely with no one to talk to when her husband goes out during the day to work in the shelter. He's a proud man, and the Reverend needs all the help he can get. And you have such a big place here — plenty of room for poor old Mr Crocket too. He's a widower, you know . . .'

Five hours later, he left the little house with its brown faded pictures of a handsome man in an Air Force uniform, its big black and white cat and its yellow kitchen, now with sparkling windows and freshly painted sills, feeling pleasantly pleased with himself. The shelter would soon be minus three old people, leaving room for someone else. Mrs Dobson would have slightly younger hands to help her with her shopping and plenty of people to talk to.

The sun was getting low, sinking towards Fisherman's Wharf, the delight of every tourist that flocked to the city during the summer months. As he walked, Sebastien wondered if he felt like risking Ghirardelli Square, then decided he wasn't in the mood for a crowd. He felt tired and listless and was angry with himself — and he knew why. He'd spent years getting to know himself, his every reaction subjected to intense scrutiny. If something annoyed him, he couldn't rest until he'd found out the exact root of it and corrected it. He knew all his faults and kept a wary eye on them, being harder with himself than he would ever dream of being on anybody else. And so he knew that it was time, once and for all, to try and make his father understand that he was not going to change his mind about his career, no matter how much he was bribed, threatened or emotionally blackmailed.

Nob Hill, in all its gleaming white wealthy beauty, was spread out before him, but he didn't want to go home just yet, to that sprawling bungalow, filled with the fine art that was currently all the rave in the executive set. He needed time before running the gauntlet of his father's disappointment and his mother's silent condemnation.

He turned blind eyes to the oft-photographed Golden Gate Bridge, instead concentrating on the gloomy island that housed the famous Alcatraz prison, in a strange way the root of all his troubles. For he was determined to work in the field of criminal rehabilitation. Not for him a discreet clientele from Nob Hill of which his parents could approve and mention in polite company. He simply wasn't interested in petty problems that caused patients mere annoyance or social embarrassment. He wanted to *help* people. He wanted to tackle pain head on and defeat it. And as he looked on at Alcatraz, he knew that his goals were legitimate ones. Inside that grim fortress there lurked real pain and despair. And if there was one thing Sebastien truly hated, it was watching human beings suffer.

When he got home, about an hour of hard thinking later, he noticed that there were several lights on, and he glanced at his watch, puzzled. Usually his parents were out every night, ruthlessly climbing the social ladder. He shrugged, then dug into his jeans pocket for the house key and let himself in, coming face to face with an ugly iron sculpture, his mother's most recent purchase. Throw rugs were currently all the rage, so the hall was littered with Mexican rugs of deep red, white and black. Next month it would be something else.

He walked into the living room, which was redolent of pipe tobacco, and found both his parents sitting on the settee, dressed to go out. So, they had been waiting for him. He sighed slightly, then shut the door behind him, watching silently as his father uncrossed his legs and slowly got up. 'Hello, Sebastien. Do you want a drink?'

'No, thanks. I think I'll turn in.'

His mother, who had been sitting in a high-backed rattan chair imported from Japan, suddenly stood up, her movements uncharacteristically jerky and nervous. 'Can you wait a moment? Your father and I want to talk to you.' Sebastien knew that tone well, and for a second felt a moment of pain, mixed with dread, snake down his back. Then he nodded and shrugged, knowing that this moment had been inevitable, and that putting off an emotional scene was never a good idea.

'OK. I think I will have that drink after all.' He poured himself a small gin and tonic, more tonic than gin, and walked to the small settee, embroidered with Spanish sequins.

His father cleared his throat while Sebastien looked at him, feeling a great well of love and pity choke him. At forty-five, Donald Teale looked the epitome of the middle-aged, upper-class American. His hair was neat and grey, his moustache equally so. His body was just beginning to run to fat around the middle, but the extra weight, so far, suited him. He had a healthy tan, flat brown eyes, and on his hand was a single black signet ring. 'We wondered . . . that is . . . your mother and I . . . we had hoped—'

'Why don't you just spit it out, Pop? It's a lot easier that way,' Sebastien said gently.

'Very well. Do you still intend to—' he coughed delicately 'work in the . . . er . . . penal community?'

For a moment Sebastien met his father's hopeful, dread-filled look, and felt tempted to lie. Sebastien hated pain — he hated it with a ferocious vengeance that some people reserved for politics or religion. He hated it as if it were a personal enemy, and his instinct was to avoid inflicting it at any cost. Then common sense took over. Sometimes it was unavoidable, and the only option left was to keep it to an absolute minimum. So he took a deep breath and answered honestly. 'Yes, I do.'

'I see.' Donald looked at Jayne, his most satisfactory wife of twenty-one years, and shrugged helplessly.

'Sebastien,' Jayne said, elongating his name thoughtfully, a habit that indicated she was about to give an order, but trying to make it sound like a suggestion. 'Have you ever thought about Europe?'

Sebastien blinked. 'Europe?'

'Hmm. I mean, you're young, single, and you must want to travel, to see something of the world?' She stood up as she talked and paced restlessly about the room, her Italian shoes leaving tiny indentations in the carpet, her Chanel perfume battling against the aroma of her husband's expensive tobacco. Silk swished at her calves as she moved, but she carefully avoided eye contact with her only child.

'I would leave if I could,' Sebastien said, still not sure where all this was leading. 'But I have my training to do. And nothing, but nothing, is going to interfere with that,' he finished determinedly. And Sebastien, as his mother knew, was a very determined young man. Sometimes, surprisingly so.

Jayne turned to him, her eyes moist but resolute. He'd always been a good boy. Even as a baby he'd been obedient and hardly ever naughty. But still, this . . . this . . . obsession of his was just so, well . . . embarrassing!

'We understand that,' Douglas cut in tersely. 'But I've just been on the phone to Julius Remus. You remember, I told you about him? We met during the war, when I was in England.'

'I remember.'

'Sir Julius is the finest psychiatrist England has to offer. He studied with Jung in Switzerland, I believe. He and I became close during the war. Let me tell you, liaising with a man of that calibre . . . well, I need hardly point out what a fine career move it would be. He is a very fine man. Retired now, of course, but when I told him about you, about the way you've already got your doctorate . . . he said he'd be delighted to have you over there. He's still, technically, the chairman of St Edmund's in London.'

'*The* St Edmund's? The psychiatric home for the criminally insane?' Sebastien asked eagerly.

Douglas winced at the description, but nodded coolly. 'The same. He says he can get you onto the staff there. In a junior capacity, of course. He also very kindly offered to be your . . . er . . . psychoanalyst.'

'I see. England is so wonderfully far away, isn't it?' Sebastien tried to laugh, but it did little to hide his hurt. 'And Sir Julius is a wonderful name to be able to drop when explaining away my absence to all your friends,' he added sadly.

Jayne gasped, tears coming to her eyes, excuses to her lips. 'Sebastien, please.'

She needn't have bothered with the latter. He was defeated the moment she began to cry.

'All right, Mother,' he said quickly, going to her side, and taking her gently in his arms. 'England sounds wonderful.'

* * *

151

The lake was cold but deserted, and Kyle began to strip eagerly, looking forward to its cold caress. Beside him, Clarissa laid out a large beach towel on the grass and began to rub sun lotion onto her bare arms. She glanced up at her lover with gentle eyes, quickly looking away when he glanced down at her.

Kyle smiled wryly. Clarissa had no reason to be so coy. She still had the figure of a twenty-year-old and knew it. But then, he thought grimly, would it make any difference to him if she looked her age? He jerked his shirt over his head and flung it viciously onto the ground. Of course not. He'd be just as much her slave if she looked like a crone.

'Be careful, darlin',' Clarissa drawled, her sweet southern voice so slow and lazy it rippled over his skin like melted honey. 'The water's cold.'

Kyle stepped out of his trousers, to reveal black swimming trunks that clung lovingly to his muscled body. He heeled his shoes off and dipped in a toe. He shuddered in pleasant, slightly masochistic anticipation.

Clarissa watched him wade into the lapping water and glanced around her. But there was no one in sight. Talman's Lake was set well away from the nearest town, and they'd discovered it quite by accident, a year or so ago. Now they came here often, to swim and make love.

'Are you coming in?' Kyle asked, turning to look at her. She was dressed in a one-piece peach-coloured costume that did wonders for her hair and skin.

'Not just yet, darlin'. You know I like to watch you.'

Kyle's lips twisted grimly. 'It's a pity your husband doesn't want to watch *you* more,' he muttered gruffly under his breath, but she heard him nevertheless. If only her husband kept tighter reins on her, she wouldn't be able to keep snaring Kyle like this, keeping him trapped in this torturous game.

Clarissa laughed gaily and wagged a finger at him. 'Now, now. You know Duncan doesn't mind about you. I told you — neither of us married for love. Duncan even has his own mistress over in Charleston. Did I tell you about her?'

Kyle sighed heavily. On the one hand, it was very nice to know he wasn't breaking up a marriage or causing Duncan Somerville any pain. On the other hand, it was depressing to know that they had her husband's blessing.

'No, you didn't,' he said shortly, and neatly duck dived beneath the clear but startlingly cold water. He came up, the breath knocked out of him and gasping for air, a few yards further out, Clarissa's mocking laughter ringing in his ears.

Kyle began a slow, lazy crawl. The coldness of the water brought out the goosebumps on his arms, but he ignored the draining effect it had on his limbs. Instead, he let his mind roam to other things.

And, as always, the 'other things' meant Clarissa. What malicious twist of fate had made their paths cross all those years ago? And why hadn't he outgrown his teenage fascination with her? He was in his thirties now, he thought angrily, turning over onto his back and staring up at the sky. And yet . . . he thought he would die if she stopped coming to him. Just curl up and wither away if she told him she was bored with him. He'd want to kill her if she told him she'd found another, younger lover to take his place. It was . . .

Love, he thought savagely. He might as well face it. He loved the manipulating, scathing, lying . . . wonderful . . . bitch.

Kyle felt a sudden sharp pain in his calf at the same instant that he felt himself begin to sink. He had time to give one startled yelp of surprise, before his head sunk under the cold water. The nasty taste of lake water filled his mouth. Cramp, he thought coolly, and without a hint of panic. Great. Just what he needed. He relaxed and let his body come vertical in the water, so that, with his unaffected leg and arms, he could thrust back to the surface.

On the shore, Clarissa had been watching him with all her usual covetous longing, and had heard his sudden cry and seen him disappear. She'd realized what it was, even before he had, and without a thought she had plunged into the water. Now her heart raced with fear so sharp, it tasted like bile in her throat. Where was he? He hadn't come to the surface yet. Panic lent her slim body an amazing strength, and within moments she'd swum out to him.

As his dark head suddenly appeared on the surface, she gave a loud sob of relief, unaware that she'd been sobbing near-hysterically ever since hitting the water.

Kyle felt her presence beside him and turned startled eyes towards her. Clarissa didn't give him a chance to speak. With surprisingly strong hands, she cupped his chin, and began to head for shore. Her legs kicked strongly, towing them both to the grassy bank. After a surprised instant, Kyle shrugged and let her get on with it. If she wanted to play lifeguard, why spoil her fun?

Once at the bank, Kyle managed to drag himself on to the grass, his chest heaving with the effort.

Clarissa, still half-sobbing, bent over him, her hands hard on his shoulders. 'Are you all right?' she all but screamed at him.

Kyle stared at her blankly. Her face was an image of fear, pain and relief. Her hair hung in wet, lank strands on her shoulders, and her lips were washed free of all her expensive lipstick. She looked haggard, he realized incredulously. He'd never seen the elegant Clarissa Somerville look anything other than well-groomed and superior before.

Clarissa's hands were all over him — touching his face, his chest, his arms. But, for once, her touch was gentle, almost reverent. Her eyes were enormous, her face as pale as milk. She was trembling like an aspen.

Her eyes went to his calf, still twisted and contorted with cramp. Still unaware of it, she was sobbing as she breathed. 'Oh, Kyle. Oh, Kyle,' she said his name over and over again, like a talisman. 'I thought you were going to die.' Her hands went to his leg, her strong fingers kneading, taking away the sickening pain.

But Kyle barely noticed.

Instead, he was staring at her, his own eyes wide and enormous, his mouth slack with shock at his astounding discovery.

Clarissa was terrified. She was sure he'd been about to drown. She—

'You love me,' he said, his voice accusing.

Clarissa's hands froze on his leg. Her shoulders stiffened as her heart leapt up into her throat. For a moment, she was unable to comprehend it. Then it crashed against her like a hurricane. Her secret was out. He *knew*. Now . . . now she had no power over him. He'd laugh at her. The power that had kept him by her side for all these years was gone.

He'd leave her.

Slowly, inch by dreadful inch, she turned to look at him.

His face was pale with shock, his lovely navy-blue eyes almost black with surprise. 'You love me,' he said again, his voice strong and furiously angry. 'All these years . . . *all these years* . . .' Kyle heard his voice crack.

Clarissa's eyes filled with tears. To his utter astonishment, his beloved tormentor began to cry.

And not pretty little tears, either, but soul-wrenching, body-shuddering tears that tore at his heart as none of her cruel barbs had ever been able to do.

For a long moment, Kyle just stared at her. In the space of a second, his whole world had turned about-face on its axis.

He said again, for a third time, his voice wondering, husky, and full of disbelieving astonishment, 'You *love* me.'

CHAPTER 14

Hollywood

It was a golden spring in Hollywood, filled with golden stars, golden movies, golden screen goddesses and golden lives. James Dean had shocked the world a few years back by dying on the road to Salinas while driving the silver Porsche he fondly called 'little bastard'. He'd tasted the fame that *East of Eden* had given him, but had not lived to see *Rebel Without a Cause*, or his just-completed epic, *Giant*, hit the silver screen. America was in a fervour of thanks directed at Jonas Salk, who had cured the country of the terror of polio and saved the public baths from extinction as children flocked back. Ike and Mamie were still in the White House, and Oriel and Kier had left behind Harold Macmillan at Number 10 Downing Street.

'From Oxford to Hollywood,' Oriel said whimsically, sitting beside her husband of two years as he drove the second-hand Oldsmobile down Lexington Road, heading out of town to the less elitist part of Beverly Hills, that up-and-coming showplace attracting more and more of Hollywood's top stars. 'Can you imagine a greater culture shock than this?' she asked, looking around wide-eyed at the desert that was still the dominating factor of the fledgling city.

'Nope,' Kier admitted, coaxing the ancient car into third gear. They had left behind an Oxford of mellow buildings, dripping with centuries of history, and landed in Hollywood just two months ago, where the desert sun was fierce. Two months to become immunized to the gossip of Hedda Hopper, the glory of stars like Victor Mature, Tony Curtis, the up-and-coming Kim Novak and, of course, Grace Kelly.

'It's like a dream,' Oriel whispered, still overawed with the city, and craned her neck as a Cadillac cruised by. 'Wasn't that Audrey Hepburn in the back of there? Did you see?' Her excited voice made him smile, and he looked in the mirror to see the taillights of the luxury car fast disappearing.

'Could be.'

Oriel swatted him playfully. 'You don't fool me, Kier Harcourt,' she warned him. 'You're as gobsmacked as I am.'

'Gobsmacked? My, my, Scarlett, you do have such an interesting vocabulary.' He rendered up the voice of the much-loved W.C. Fields at the same time as he tweaked an imaginary cigar, making Oriel burst into delighted laughter.

The last two years at Oxford had been idyllic. They'd moved out of college and found a small apartment in Magpie Lane, right in the centre of town. It was actually a converted attic in a tall narrow house, and had rickety plumbing, uncertain drains, and was definitely home to a fair number of mice. Kier had taken on a job as a waiter in one of the swankiest eateries in town, while Oriel completed her course. She'd also taken some small parts in the Oxford Playhouse, doing minor roles that nevertheless paid for half the rent. She liked it well enough but had no desire to be an actress. She never enjoyed stage fright and found performing the same role night after night boring and repetitive. Besides, Kier gave her all the limelight she needed. They studied like maniacs, Kier working as much on making contacts with the English film industry as on his own postgraduate studies, and Oriel had graduated with a First Class degree. They had explored England in the holidays, and by visiting the homes of friends from college, sponging off them shamelessly, they had just about managed to keep body and soul together.

Now, the only cloud on Oriel's horizon was the break with her family. She missed her father pitifully and had spoken to him several times on the telephone. She knew Duncan called her from his office so that Clarissa wouldn't be upset. At first, Oriel had been afraid that her father would be disappointed in her, but the first thing he had asked her was if she loved her husband.

Since Kier had been standing right beside her at the time, his hand splayed across her waist in silent love and support, her answer had been easy, and filled with a conviction that had satisfied Duncan Somerville all those thousands of miles away. Now both Kier and Oriel had calls from him regularly, and she had gradually grown to accept the situation. Of her mother, they heard nothing. Oriel's allowance had been stopped immediately, of course, but they had expected it, and for the first few months Kier had been anxious, wondering how his new bride, used to every pampered luxury life had to offer, would take to a life of relative poverty. He need not have feared. She complained seldom, and only when she'd had a really bad day, and they laughed more than they cried. Their arguments had been few and far between, but had been humdingers, reminding them of the early days and the play when they had been so much at each other's throats. Vigorous and satisfying love-making followed every argument though, curled up in their creaky bed where they shivered in winter, because there was no proper heating, and sweltered in summer, because heat always rose to the top of the house. But they loved it, and the crooked, oddly named road where they lived.

They'd almost been reluctant to leave. Almost, but not quite. Hollywood was where Kier's dream was, and Oriel was fast learning that all that guff about a wife being by her husband's side through thick and thin was not guff at all.

'Do you suppose we got anywhere this morning?' Kier asked, interrupting her wonderful thoughts, and she frowned, thinking over the interview with Howard Shoesmith, the director of Cougar Studios.

'I'm not sure,' she said truthfully. 'I think he was interested, but . . .'

'But?' He took his eyes off the road for a scant second to look at her as they took a left into their street.

'Well. There are hundreds of guys in this damned town who want to direct. All of them probably have at least as much experience as you do, honey. I think he liked you, but I wonder if anybody can be as hearty and friendly as he is, and still run a studio successfully? Know what I mean?'

Kier did. Howard Shoesmith was a small-town boy made good. Cougar Studios was small, but independent, and made modest but solid profits every year. Howard Shoesmith couldn't have got as far as he had at the age of forty and actually be the good ol' boy that he tried so hard to appear. It had taken them twelve days to wangle an interview with the man, fighting through a barrage of secretaries, assistants, receptionists and a seemingly endless line of middlemen. Then, yesterday afternoon, when Kier had been out trying to sell a screenplay he had written, a secretary had phoned with the appointment. Hearing his wife answer, and knowing her employer very well, she had quickly informed her that the interview was for both of them, which had momentarily left Oriel speechless. Then she had quickly agreed. What did it matter, after all? A successful man in Hollywood was allowed his eccentricities.

Kier had worn his only suit, Oriel her best dress, one of the few she had packed to take to Oxford, so although it was years old, it was still a classic of hyacinth blue in pure silk. With her hair up in an elegant chignon, and a pair of pearl-drop earrings in her lobes, she looked like a movie star herself.

Kier had held open the door of the Olds for her, aware that the car wasn't fit for her. Then and there he vowed that one day he'd bring her a limousine to ride in, with a chauffeur to match.

One day.

The studios were on the outskirts of town to avoid the city noise, and they'd had to drive through false-fronted western towns where Ronald Reagan might have ridden up on a horse for a shoot-out with Gabby Hayes. The air of unreality and falsity made Oriel wince, but Kier was fascinated. He was so close now, discovering things that he had only read about, and to him the city was already home.

Determined to make a good impression, they had arrived early and had to wait half an hour before being shown into the hallowed office. It was a strange room, a mix of expensive imported furniture and the smell of cheap cigars. On the wall were posters of films that Cougar had made, mostly B-pictures, with B-stars. But most of those B-stars had gone on to become big box-office draws, and Cougar had a reputation that was not to be sneezed at.

Howard Shoesmith, like the room, was a mix of class and common man. His suit was expensive but rumpled, and cigar ash lay on his lapel. He was a small man with black hair and fierce black eyes and looked as if he came from Italian stock, but his voice, when he spoke, was straight out of Wyoming. He greeted Kier first, but his eyes were on Oriel. His first words set the tone for the meeting. 'I thought you were here to discuss being a director, son. But I see you have a star lined up already.'

Oriel, perversely, felt insulted and was not sure why; being told by a man who had created big-name stars that she herself was star material should have flattered her, but somehow it didn't. It was not even that his gaze was more open than it should have been, for she was used to men looking at her just as this one did now. There was just something about Howard Shoesmith that she didn't trust.

'My wife, Oriel,' Kier introduced her, his voice just a touch chilly.

'And I'm not an actress, I'm afraid. Nor do I want to be,' she added quickly, but with a smile to take the edge off her words.

Howard was surprised and looked it. He was used to beautiful women with the Hollywood bug conning their way into his office. He was used to making his conquests on the casting couch and enjoyed his unique sense of power. Anywhere else in the world, a man like him would be a nothing and a nobody. But here he had some real power and a constant tap to the most beautiful women the country had to offer. It was not very often that he came across a beautiful woman who was not willing, and it intrigued him.

'Well now, sit yourselves down and take the weight off. Cigar?'

Kier declined, not trusting the bonhomie. This man might talk like a cowboy, but he looked like a shark, and he had the sensation of treading through a minefield as the interview progressed. For the next half hour they talked about the three plays he had produced in Oxford, Shoesmith reading the excellent review clippings with obvious interest. He listened to Kier's ideas, nodding his head, smiling, agreeing, his eyes occasionally flicking to Oriel. Then he talked of Cougar, of the films they'd made in the past, finally finishing with a rough sketch of the latest studio idea for a film. 'You see, son,' Howard said in that aggravatingly condescending tone that Oriel was sure he used on purpose, 'I heard from a friend of mine in the know that all the big studios are making these new science-fiction things. They're cheap, give the audience a thrill, and are perfect for a studio like ours. They're effective in black and white and don't need big stars.'

Kier nodded, understanding immediately the budgeting advantages of this type of genre which would appeal to a man of Howard's money-pinching type. 'And if this new film *The Blob* makes it, your picture will have a ready-made audience.'

Howard nodded, obviously pleased with the answer, and acknowledging Kier's observation. In fact, he looked pleased about a lot of things, but not especially so. Kids like Kier Harcourt came to his office every day. They were a dime a dozen, and he did not have the sensitivity to realize that in Kier he had found a man who had greatness written all over him. All Howard could see was a bright man, probably talented, but no more so than anyone else.

It was this sense of could-take-it-or-leave-it that Oriel tried to explain now, as Perez Prado came over the radio playing 'Cherry Pink and Apple Blossom White'.

But Kier understood just what she was saying. He'd gained the same impression himself and knew all about vicious circles. No studio wanted to take a chance on a new director who hadn't made a film before. Until someone was willing to take a chance on a new boy, there was no way in. Although they didn't actually say it out loud, neither Kier nor Oriel thought that Howard Shoesmith was the man to give a guy a break. Since arriving in the fabulous city, both had heard the horror stories, meeting men who had been in the city for years and were still only second- or third-string screenwriters, dogsbodies to established directors or little more than office clerks. Kier had been here two months, had sold no play, had been offered no apprenticeship or way in, and their money was running low. Sometimes it seemed impossible.

They pulled up in front of their boarding house on Maple Street, and he turned off the noisy engine. The house was white clapboard, with a white picket fence that needed repainting, and a broken swing hung from an old oak in one corner. It looked like it belonged on the set of a thirties movie, where cherry blossom fell in spring, and perfect children played in perfect gardens, and had perfect parents. The landlady was a Miss Tillson, a sprightly old thing who had Hollywood fever. Her idol was Cary Grant, and she leased her rooms only to film people. Oriel's looks and Kier's tales of Oxford plays had been used to talk their way into the two rooms on the second floor that were all they could afford.

They were quiet now as they walked up the path, but the ever-alert Miss Tillson was waiting for them.

'Hi, there. How did you get on? Tell me about the studio!' She had a moon face, grey hair tucked into a tight bun, and always wore flowered aprons. Oriel and Kier's eyes met, a fond smile coming on to both their faces as they joined her on the old-fashioned porch swing, telling her outrageous tales of bumping into Cary Grant and watching him shoot a robbery scene.

In turn, Miss Tillson told them the latest gossip. It mattered not at all to her that Juan Perón was hiding out in Paraguay, or that the Reds-under-the-beds hysteria was affecting the country, stirring up paranoia about communism to extreme heights. Miss Tillson didn't care that people 'used Modess . . . because', and she had never heard of the revolutionary roll-on deodorants and filter-tip cigarettes. Her talk was about important things. 'You know, of course, that the Yankie Clipper and Blonde Bombshell have decided to call it quits?'

Oriel, blinking at the old lady's determined use of Hollywood jargon, translated in her mind that she was talking about the marriage of Marilyn Monroe and Joe DiMaggio being on the rocks, and shrugged, looking across at Kier, confident of her love and marriage. Especially now.

'That'll never happen to us,' she whispered, and Kier reached across and held her hand, much to the thrilled delight of Miss Tillson, who loved romance in any shape or form. It would be just the kind of thing Cary Grant would do . . .

'Well, I must get on with the dinner,' Miss Tillson said, satisfied that she had gleaned the last drops of information about Cougar Studios from her favourite tenants, and picking up her copies of *Modern Screen, Movie Mirror* and *Photoplay*, she toddled off into the house, humming the theme tune of From *Here to Eternity*.

'I hear that everywhere,' Oriel commented idly, leaning back in the swing chair and closing her eyes, humming the tune softly, picking it up where their landlady had left off.

'Not surprising. That beach scene between Lancaster and Deborah Kerr is a classic. Believe me, that's going to be talked about for years to come.'

'You could have directed that picture,' she said seriously. It did not seem to her naive to tell her young husband that,

163

for she had no doubts at all that Kier would become one of the names in Hollywood, another Huston or Hughes. Even his surname began with the right letter.

Kier sat up, feeling depressed and discouraged, and began to pace the porch. 'I've got to make friends here. It's no good being the best damned director in the world if you don't know the right people in all the right places. I hate it — but it's a fact of life.'

'I know, honey. I really do.' She joined him at the wooden railing, warm from the sun's rays, and looped her arms around his waist, resting her chin against his back. Perhaps now was not the right time to tell him her own, very special news. Then again, perhaps it would cheer him up and give him the added motivation that he needed.

For two whole days she had hugged the knowledge to herself, and now she needed to share it. Now, when he was depressed; now, before things took off and started to happen. Now, while she still had every bit of him all to herself. 'Kier . . .'

'That picture he was talking about. *Night of the Invaders*. It's just up my alley,' he interrupted her, the energy that was such a major part of him beginning to churn again, unable to be repressed for long. 'What is it that audiences want from that sort of film?' He turned to her, his face lit up with that look that she knew all too well. His whole face was animated, his eyes narrowed and excited, and she swallowed back her own news, forcing herself to think as he thought, to get into the mood, to play along.

'Excitement,' she said thoughtfully. 'They want to be scared by the monsters.'

'Yes, yes, that. But they want to relate to the characters as well. Most of the people who watch movies are from small towns, girls who work in soda joints, boys who wait on tables. They want to believe that something extraordinary can actually happen in *their* town, that it can happen to them. Shoesmith was talking about setting the film in Los Angeles, but that's no good. Sure, it's got grandeur and it's local so it'll keep the budget down, but the layout's all wrong.'

Oriel felt a familiar excitement as she listened. It was when she heard him talk like this that she knew everything was going to work out.

'He's got the invaders coming in the opening scene,' Kier carried on, thinking out loud. 'That gives the audience all it wants right at the start. What it needs is a slower build-up, to hint at things being amiss. We can use the girl, Sally, to show the audience that people in her town are changing, to make it dawn on them slowly that something's terribly wrong. It'll force the audience to the edge of their seats and get them wondering just *what* the hell *is* happening. Don't you see? The audience needs to guess about the invasion too, to experience it through the characters, and not just be saturated in gory monsters right from the start.'

Oriel caught his mood — she always did — and, like Kier, could now almost see the finished picture in her head. She could see what he was getting at, grasping immediately what he meant, and knew that he was right. 'That way, when the audience finally see the monster, they'll be all the more keyed up,' she finished for him, and he hugged her absently, kissing her for her cleverness.

'Right. Hell, I've got to write this all down.'

'Then send it by messenger to Shoesmith. I know it's expensive, but it'll get to him tonight while our interview is still fresh in his mind.'

Kier kissed her again. 'What would I do without you?' he murmured throatily, then ran into the house. A minute later she heard their battered old typewriter begin to rat-a-tat. Slowly she sat down on the swing, her euphoria evaporating now that Kier was no longer beside her.

She felt suddenly alone. Alone and missing something. Kier had a dream — he had fire in his belly and visions in his head, but what did she have? She placed a hand on her stomach and smiled. She had a secret. She had another life in her body besides her own. And she had not told him. While she understood and applauded his ambition, while she would stand by him and move any mountain she could to see him

165

succeed, she had kept silent about the baby for the simple reason that when she told him about it she wanted it to be the most important thing in the world to him. For once, she didn't want to compete with a project, with the images in his head, with the fire in his eyes. For once, for just a moment, she wanted to be everything . . .

She felt a warm tickling on her cheeks, and raising her fingers to her skin, was surprised when they came away wet.

Suddenly, and without warning, she had a longing to speak to her mother. She was not sure why; the past two years had barely dimmed her anger at her for trying to buy off Kier.

And yet . . . she'd never been pregnant before. When the doctor told her, she'd been thrilled, of course, but also just a little bit frightened. She felt vulnerable and nervous, and just now her mother's voice would be so welcome, bringing back memories of Georgia, of her old nanny, now dead, of afternoons in the nursery rocking on old Dobbin, of fried chicken cooked only the way Cook knew how, of mint juleps without the alcohol, of moss-draped trees . . .

She found Miss Tillson immersed in her magazines and walked through the hall to the payphone, digging in her purse for a few coins. She would have liked to make the call collect but did not want her mother to know just how tight things really were financially. She might think she was calling for a handout and such a thought made her shudder. She dialled the numbers with a shaking finger and heard the phone ring all the way across the continent.

It was answered on the fifth ring by Willie, her mother's servant. 'Hello, Willie, it's me. Oriel.'

'Oh, Miss Oriel!' she heard the excited squeak and could almost see Willie's face split from ear to ear in a big, white-toothed grin. 'Oh, Miss Oriel, I ain't heard your voice in ages.'

'It's good to hear you, too, Willie,' Oriel said, meaning it, then bit her lip. 'Er . . . is my mother there?'

There was a small silence that spoke volumes.

'Please, Willie — just tell her I'm on the phone. Tell her it's important. Urgent, even.'

'OK, Miss Oriel — I'll do that. Hold on a minute.' A minute stretched to two, and she had to put in another coin. She felt her nerves begin to string out and was just about to hang up when she heard the phone being lifted, and then her mother's voice, crisp, clear and slightly anxious.

'Oriel? What's happened?' Her voice was sharp, but it was the kind of sharpness that came with anxiety and concern, and Oriel felt tears sting her eyes. In her heart of hearts she'd missed her mother and been hurt by the separation. Now, presented with evidence that her mother cared after all, she sniffed hard, wiping away the tears that were pouring down her face. 'Oriel! Are you crying? What's wrong, baby? What has he done to you?' Clarissa's angry voice buzzed in her ear, making her smile.

'No, Mama, I'm not crying. That is, I am, but because I'm happy. Oh, Mama, I wanted you to know. I'm gonna have a baby!'

For a long, long second there was total silence. Oriel's fingers curled nervously around the wire, and then her breath exploded out of her as she heard Clarissa's voice, choked now with tears of her own.

'Oh, Oriel . . . oh, my baby . . . I'm . . . I'm . . .' Oriel waited, praying for the reaction she needed, then burst into more tears as Clarissa said, '. . . so happy. I'm crying like a silly schoolgirl. Hold on a minute while I get a hankie.'

Oriel leaned against the wall, grinning and crying like a mad woman. She was glad Kier was typing upstairs and that Miss Tillson was poring over the latest gossip about Fernando Lamas and Arlene Dahl. She'd hate for anybody to see her like this!

'Honey, you still there?'

'I sure am, Mama. You really are pleased, aren't you?' she asked, and over the miles Clarissa could hear the trace of the little girl that had so unexpectedly come back into her daughter's voice. In that instant, all of Clarissa's anger and sense of betrayal vanished as she groped for a chair, and gave a wavering smile at the hovering Willie, who was grinning from ear to ear, as he'd overheard the good news.

'Oh, baby, of course I am . . . but I'm too young to be a grandmother!' Even as she said it she glanced anxiously into a mirror, relieved that it told her she was still a woman in her prime. She still had her period and could be a mother again if she wanted. And she still had Kyle.

Didn't she?

But she couldn't think of Kyle now. Or the terror that had been her constant companion since that day by the lake.

'Oh, darling, I'm so thrilled,' she said truthfully, forcing her mind back to Oriel and her startling, wonderful news. 'Just wait until I tell your father.'

'Where is Daddy?'

'In Germany. His committee are gathering evidence from that man Wolfgang Mueller's concentration camp. I tell you, your father has become obsessed by the Nazis,' Clarissa said, but without heat. To tell the truth, she was rather proud of Duncan's crusade, so much more so since Duncan had been personally unaffected by the war. But he knew evil when he saw it, and hated it, and was so gallantly determined to do something about it. If only more good men had his principles . . .

Oriel swallowed back more tears and took a deep breath. 'Mama. Will you come over . . . for a visit? I . . . I want you to be here when the baby comes. I'm a little bit scared, Mama,' she finally admitted breathlessly, her lovely Scarlett O'Hara voice wobbling just a little.

Clarissa swallowed hard. 'Of course I'll come, honey. Nothing could keep me away . . .' She paused, then straightened in her chair, but only Willie could see the wariness creep over her face. 'What does Kier think of all this? Did he agree?'

Oriel bit her lip, then shrugged. 'He will. I haven't . . .' She was about to say that she hadn't told him about the baby, but something stopped her. It would sound disloyal, she realized, and give Clarissa a false impression of their marriage. Instead she said, 'I haven't any doubt at all that he'll be glad to have you visit. It wasn't his intention to split us up, Mama. Kier loves me, and he'll do anything for me,' she stated confidently, sure that she spoke the truth.

Clarissa fiddled with a jade ornament and swallowed her pride. 'I'll come over as soon as I can arrange it. Maybe next Monday. Is that all right?'

'Oh, yes. But . . . you'll have to book into a hotel, I'm afraid.'

There was a short silence then Clarissa said expressionlessly, 'I see.'

As they said tearful goodbyes, the rift healed at last, Clarissa hung up thoughtfully. This changed everything, of course. She could not countenance her grandchildren growing up without her, and she simply refused to be strangers to her own kin. That meant finally accepting Kier as a son-in-law. There was no chance of a divorce now. And what if . . . what if Oriel really was happy? What if Kier Harcourt was the *man* for her? Such an outlandish thought had never crossed her mind before.

As she phoned her husband with the good news, Duncan agreeing to take time off to fly out with her, she was already thinking furiously. Clarissa had a practical streak that most people would have found surprising.

Clarissa wondered what kind of a dump Oriel was living in, if she felt too ashamed to have her mother stay with her. Probably in some squalid little backwater, filled with roaches and those dreadful film people. Well, if it must be Kier, then it must be Kier. She would have to do something to make him more acceptable. She simply couldn't have her daughter, or her grandchild, living in squalor.

She walked across the cool tiled hall of her mansion, ordering Willie to bring her tea. She reached for her address book, looking through the long list of names until she found the one she wanted. Lifting the phone she dialled the California code and number. 'Hello, Gloria? This is Clarissa. Yes, it's been simply ages, hasn't it. How are you?' Clarissa, like most women of her class and generation, kept in obsessively close contact with all her old schoolfriends, even though Gloria Finchely-Gallerton had located to the other side of the country when she married a Hollywood movie mogul.

After a few minutes of pleasantries, the two women got down to business. 'Look, Gloria, I had to call you and tell you the wonderful news. I'm about to become a grandmother. Can you believe it?' she squealed happily. 'Yes, me, can you imagine? Of course, my son-in-law lives in Hollywood as well, so you probably know him. Kier Harcourt? You'll have to invite him and Oriel over for dinner some time. Kier's a director, I believe. I think your Frank must have heard of him. Frank is still on the board at Paramount, isn't he . . . ?'

Gloria said of course they must have Oriel and her husband over. And Frank was still so very amenable . . .

Both women knew how the game was played. Gloria might need a favour of her own, one day.

Three days later, the rent was due, and Miss Tillson was listening enraptured to Oriel relating Kier's idea for Night of the *Invaders*, carefully not mentioning the fact that they had not heard back from Howard Shoesmith.

She had at last told Kier about the baby. He'd been overjoyed, acting just like a typically expectant father, and treating her like precious china. Now, the two women talked baby talk, Miss Tillson, of course, bringing the conversation around to the stars who'd had children that year, and wondering what on earth had happened to Shirley Temple.

Suddenly the Olds screeched to a halt outside the gate, and Oriel stood up, her heart leaping as Kier jumped the gate without bothering to open it, his heroics making Miss Tillson's heart flutter. He'd acted just like Errol Flynn would have done.

Kier's face was alight as he leapt onto the porch, reached down and plucked her from her chair and then swung her around in his strong arms, ignoring Miss Tillson's warning about not doing that in her condition. 'I got the film!' he yelled, waltzing her off her feet and onto the lawn. 'I got *Invaders*!'

Oriel squealed, and began to kiss his face all over, laughing with sheer delight.

'I just ran into the studio head at Cougar who told me to go down this afternoon and talk to Shoesmith. He loved the ideas I sent him about the film. He's willing to take a chance on me. Oh, baby, it's happening at last.'

'And so much quicker than we ever hoped,' she added, clasping his handsome, excited face between her hands. 'Ooohhhhheeeee!' she hollered, oblivious to neighbours, to passing cars, to children playing in the streets. Thus encouraged to abandon her ladylike ethics, Miss Tillson whooped louder than they did, and for a reward they took her out in the car to the drug store on Sunset Boulevard, where they had sodas and watched Miss Tillson's head swivelling in all directions as she counted the stars who came in for tubes of Ipana toothpaste and Tangee's Red Majesty lipstick.

The world was suddenly theirs. They had come, they had seen, and they had conquered. Kier's ideas, his brilliant ideas, his talent, his dream, his forceful character and personality, had won the day after all. They would soon have a baby, and he would soon have a career. Life was sweet, love was sweeter, and success was the sweetest of all.

'To us,' Kier toasted with strawberry soda, the three solemnly clinking glasses. Kier promised to take Miss Tillson to the studio one day to let her watch him making the movie. They talked about casting, about costume, about lighting, about everything, kissing openly, laughing at anything and everything, Kier even pulling the blushing Miss Tillson onto his lap and telling her he was going to introduce her to Bud Westmore, the famous makeup man to the stars who'd make her look thirty years younger again, and win her the heart of Cary Grant. That afternoon was the most golden of all their afternoons, knowing even then that *Invaders* was only the beginning — only the first step on the road to a sparkling career.

Over at Cougar Studios, Howard Shoesmith congratulated Clarissa Somerville warmly for investing so generously in *Night of the Invaders*.

Clarissa inclined her head and smiled. 'You must thank Mr Finchely-Gallerton for putting me in the know,' she dropped the name of the powerful man cleverly, and watched the ridiculous Mr Shoesmith preen. 'He's such a good friend,' she added, just to make sure he got the picture.

Howard Shoesmith gushed and showed her out. Who'd have thought the Harcourt kid had such good contacts? Still, the world was his oyster now. And Howard Shoesmith would ride the rising Harcourt star for all it was worth.

Outside, Clarissa took her hired car back to the hotel. Time to let Oriel know she was in town.

Back at the first class hotel, she walked tiredly to her bed, and pulled off her shoes. Then she glanced behind her at the empty bed, her lovely face slowly crumpling.

Kyle had refused to accompany her. And, for the first time ever, she'd been unable to force him.

CHAPTER 15

London

The Windsor Hotel, with four storeys of mellow sandstone, black wrought-iron terrace and good English cuisine had an ambiance that was priceless to its loyal clientele. It enjoyed a reputation for English breakfasts, English maids, English conservatism and, most of all, for English guests. Wayne chose it over and above its more famous rivals such as the Ritz, Connaught or the Savoy for just this reason. At the moment he had no use for more cosmopolitan surroundings since the rest of Europe was, for the moment, off limits.

He'd sold the Maserati in France, getting top money from a collector. Such was the popularity of the car that the waiting lists were huge, making second-hand cars in prime condition sell for an even higher price than the new models, simply because buyers had to wait anything up to six months to a year for delivery. Looking up a yachting acquaintance who was sailing to England saved him an air fare and allowed him to arrive in England with enough money to give the appearance of casual affluence.

The Windsor had been the next stop. Its fees were exorbitant, but Wayne fully expected it to be a wise investment.

He was practising hard to rid himself of his French accent and was quickly succeeding, except for when ladies were present. French was still, after all, the language of love and he badly needed either a rich wife or a sponsor.

He had been at the Windsor a week. His arrival had caused something of a stir among the hotel's regulars and permanent residents for a variety of reasons. To the women, of course, the advent of the huge, handsome Frenchman had caused shockwaves, even affecting the chambermaids, who quarrelled among themselves for the privilege of cleaning his room. One maid had confessed to her friends that she'd seen him topless, shaving in his antiquated but efficient bathroom, and had assured everyone he was not at all hairy and had muscles that you could see quite nicely, but not the horrible kind that bulged and looked ugly.

Matrons, with unattached daughters, bristled visibly whenever he came down to the high-ceilinged, darkly decorated dining room, but Wayne was too clever to isolate himself by flirting. Instead, after almost a week, his quiet good manners, his lack of adventurousness and his gentlemanly conversation had done much to rub the stiff English bristles back the right way. His Savile Row suit, Turnbull & Asser shirts and Bull Brothers shoes helped. A Frenchman who dressed like an Englishman was marginally more acceptable than some foreigner who *looked* like a foreigner. Luckily for Wayne, his skin was naturally fair and his suntan was fast fading. That didn't hurt either.

Among the men, also, his presence had been immediately felt. A man of his size was an immediate rival to their own masculinity. The talk whenever he walked into the bar turned to boxing at Eton, or rowing at Cambridge, all the men present talking about some sporting triumph or other. Wayne, naturally, listened and complimented, decrying his own schooling at the Sorbonne where the emphasis had been on academic achievement, not sportsmanship. Thus, being able only to shoot (which was, Wayne knew, a must in English society) but not having any sporting tale to tell, manly pride had been quickly and expertly re-established.

Now Wayne was readily accepted into the little clique that gathered in the bar for pre-dinner drinks with good humour and just a little condescension. He was, after all, still a foreigner. This evening, Wayne joined Stanley Wetherington at the bar, one of the Windsor's 'something-in-the-city' brigade.

'Good evening, Wetherington,' Wayne greeted him, having learned early on the English preference for surnames. He ordered drinks and asked for them to be put on his tab.

As Wetherington murmured, 'Jolly decent of you. I'll have a Scotch,' Wayne shook out a copy of *The Times* and turned to the business section. Wetherington, a part-time drunk, sipped his malt whisky with a true connoisseur's appreciation.

Dinner at the Windor was served at seven, never earlier, never later. It was not a restaurant and, if guests did not arrive on time, there was no second serving. Wayne found the English race both difficult to understand, and yet, in their own way, charming. The nation seemed to be cut in half — the aristocracy and the rest; and there was no intermingling, no overlapping, and definitely no room for manoeuvre. As a foreigner he avoided this particular trap, but it also precluded him from joining the aristocracy unless he could find a loophole. Turning to Wetherington, he asked casually, 'Ever been to Bordeaux?'

'Bordeaux? No, but I've drunk enough of it,' Stanley's eyes, red-rimmed and a cheerful hazel, twinkled pleasantly, and Wayne laughed dutifully.

'My family has a vineyard there — several, in fact.'

'And you left? Are you crazy, man?'

Wayne shrugged — an English kind — and shook his head. 'I don't have the vintner's nose or feel for grapes. Besides, I have several younger siblings who do have, so I've managed to shake off the old man.'

'Ah. Spot of good luck, that. That's why you've moved over to jolly old Angleterre, hmm?'

The man's pretentiousness never ceased to amaze Wayne, but he managed a grin and nodded. 'Absolutely. The thing is' — he leaned forward in a confidential manner, immediately rousing Stanley's interest — 'I'm not at all sure what I'm good at. Do you follow me?' Wayne was sure he would. For all his 'something-in-the-city' tag, Stanley was obviously one of life's drifters. As expected, his cow-like face took on a look of total sympathy.

'I know just what you mean, old bean. Bit of a bugger, isn't it?' Wayne agreed and waited. Naturally, when a chap confided in you, you did your best to help him, especially when he was buying the drinks. Stanley ordered another whisky and began to think. It was obviously a new and painful experience for him.

'Well, old chap . . . er . . . D'Arville, the question is . . . what *can* you do?'

Wayne shrugged. 'Speak French and English. I studied economics at the Sorbonne. I'm pretty good with my own share portfolio, too. I can drive a sportscar, sail a yacht, and can be pretty useful in a casino. And that's about it.'

It wasn't, but Wayne had chosen the list carefully and it did its job. 'Hmm . . . just like the rest of us, then, old chap.' Stanley laughed at his own joke, then became thoughtful. 'Hold on . . . I wonder?' He turned on his stool and searched the small anteroom, his hazel eyes coming to rest on one old man sitting in a corner, reading a heavy tome bound in ancient leather. 'Ahh, yes, he is. Come on. Follow me and let me do the talking.'

Wayne, curious but not especially hopeful, followed Wetherington to the old man's corner. Wayne had seen him before and knew him for a regular.

'Hello, Sir Mortimer. Head buried in the share index as per usual, eh?' The hearty greeting made Wayne wince, but the old man glanced up without a hint of surprise, looked Stanley over quickly with all-seeing, disapproving eyes, and then over his shoulder to Wayne. There the bird-sharp green eyes remained.

Wayne felt a stirring of his instincts, his nose telling him that at last he might be on to something. The eyes were watery but full of intelligence, and Wayne felt his back stiffening automatically. He had to be careful here — very careful.

'Sir Mortimer, this is a friend of mine — Wayne D'Arville. He's a bit French, I'm afraid, but a good chap for all that.'

Wayne smiled, unable to help it, and found Sir Mortimer Platt doing the same. 'So, you're the chap who has my chambermaid in a tiz-woz. She's always so damned anxious to get out of my room and into yours that she whizzes through it like a tornado.' The voice was crusty but humorous and Wayne shrugged, this time with exaggerated Frenchness.

'*Les femmes*,' he murmured, making Stanley look at him quickly, his eyes warning him not to go all foreign on them. Wayne apologized in a perfect English manner, and Sir Mortimer asked them to join him. He was drinking tea, Wayne saw at once, guessing accurately that he was probably teetotal. His suit was tweed, fifteen years old and perfect. His hair, white and wavy, had probably been cut in the same style all his life. He had false teeth, walked with a cane, and sported fierce, bushy eyebrows. Wayne understood him at once.

'D'Arville here is from France, just escaped from the family business.'

'Oh?'

'Wine,' Wayne said, sensing immediately the disapproval in the tone. 'In that business you have to have the nose. It is no good graduating from the Sorbonne with honours in economics and a way with shifting money about if you don't have the instinct for the vine. I don't. Nothing I can do about it but strike out on my own in a totally different direction and make something of myself.'

Wayne had noticed the strange, almost staccato way many of his fellow guests talked, and had set about adopting every English habit he could unearth. As expected, the disapproval that had shuttered Sir Mortimer's face now turned to complete approval.

'Oh, well, there was nothing else for it, then,' Sir Mortimer conceded, understanding at once that a fellow couldn't bang his head against a brick wall indefinitely. He liked a man who could see straight, make firm decisions and then stick to them. Took guts, too, to leave your own country. Of course, this D'Arville fellow showed taste and common sense in coming to England. If only Toby was cut from the same cloth . . .

'Thing is, Sir Mortimer,' Stanley chimed in, 'he needs a push in the right direction. And when he told me about studying economics, and being a whizz at shares and things, well . . . I immediately thought of Platt's.'

Something in Wayne's mind clicked. 'Platt's? The investment house?' he asked, genuine excitement in his tone.

Sir Mortimer nodded, flattered that a foreigner had heard of the English company. In England, of course, Platt's stood for tradition, centuries of trading and a reputation untouched by scandal, its very name synonymous with class and style. Platt's had provided financial advice to crowned heads, moguls and owners of diamond mines.

'Our people have access to the finest homes in England. Why, even the old king once consulted us about some . . . er . . . real estate purchases,' Sir Mortimer boasted.

Wayne nodded, not needing to feign his respect. 'At the Sorbonne library, practically every English book on modern economic policy devotes chapters to Platt's. Wasn't one of your founder members an ex-Chancellor of the Exchequer?'

'Dinner is served, ladies and gentlemen,' George, the head waiter for thirty years, dressed impeccably in Royal Navy serge, announced from the doorway, his voice not at all raised, yet somehow managing to carry to every corner of the room.

'I'm noshing with old Clinker Haycroft tonight,' Stanley apologized quickly. 'Sir Mortimer, could you take D'Arville here off my hands for this evening?'

'Of course?' He made it a question by raising one of those bushy eyebrows in the Frenchman's direction, and Wayne accepted readily.

George had an underling set another place at Sir Mortimer's table, and Wayne was left alone at last to begin a preliminary probe. The first course was game soup, brought down by train from Scotland where the Windsor had a sister hotel called the Highland. The soup, dark and rich, was pleasing to the palate, and Wayne found himself pleasantly surprised by the food. He had heard horrific tales of English cuisine from childhood and was almost disappointed at finding them to be so untrue.

'So, you went to the Sorbonne. Who took you for economics?' Sir Mortimer opened the gambit, and Wayne launched into a tale of the university, racking his brains for amusing incidents, inventing them where necessary and making the most of his accomplishments without seeming to, and finishing up with a good dose of humility.

'So you see, I find myself in England, very well qualified, but actually, qualified for nothing, as it were.'

'Hmm. Well, that's not quite true. Platt's, of course, is always trying to expand. And why not into Europe? It might be interesting to take on a johnny who knows how the French share market works. You have your own portfolio, you say?'

Wayne nodded. 'Oh, yes. Papa gave me a settlement when I finally persuaded him I had to leave the vineyards. Since then, with some careful buying, and watching blue-chip . . .'

For the next half an hour, Wayne talked competently about his non-existent portfolio.

'That sounds like some very careful dealing. Of course, at Platt's, you'd be doing much the same thing, only for select clients, and on a much grander scale. Fifty thousand pounds is the very least we take on. Most of our clients trust millions to us to invest, of course. If you had no objection to starting on the lesser commissions, would you be interested?'

The offer was made ultra-casually, but Wayne was not fooled, and he was too clever to snap at the bait like a novice.

'As an advisor? Well, that's very kind of you. And I'm sure it would be interesting . . . as a start. But I'm not looking for a job, *per se*. What I need is a . . . oh, I don't know. A career, of course, but also a . . . vocation, I suppose you could call it. I'd really be interested in seeing what your plans are to take Platt's into Europe. It might be useful to study more European law, also.'

Sir Mortimer nodded, his eyes narrowing on the handsome young man. What he meant, of course, was that he was not willing to be a paid clerk, not even one with a grandiose title. Sir Mortimer liked this man. Apart from his size and nationality, which were both unfortunate, he had intelligence, wit, tact and charm. He was careful, too. Was he *too* careful? Sir Mortimer, tucking into roast duck with orange sauce, realized with a surprised start that he had spent over an hour in this man's company and knew practically nothing about him. Oh, he knew the background, and he could see he dressed with understated style, which was excellent. There was nothing he despised more than a flashy dresser, and any outrageous flaunting of wealth was too vulgar to be endured. But what did he really know of the man's *character*?

Reading his mind, almost thought for thought, Wayne decided it was time to rectify the oversight. His instincts were now totally attuned and quivering, telling him that beyond doubt here was the mark, here was the sponsor he so desperately needed. But he had to secure his position fast.

'Of course, my younger brother will inherit the vineyards,' Wayne commented, sipping the wine, but not giving a run-down on its pedigree even though he could have ably done so. Showing off was definitely not on the agenda tonight. 'In France, the wine business is totally above the laws of common man.' He twisted his lips ruefully. 'And I don't envy Jean-Jacques the job. Wine tends to become the master of the man, instead of the other way around.'

Sir Mortimer nodded, his head movements as clear and precise as his speech. 'Hmm. A man who lets himself become a slave to anything is a fool.'

Wayne bit the inside of his cheek, knowing that pain always made him go pale. He looked down too quickly and deliberately took a bite out of his duck. Looking up at the alert eyes, he smiled bleakly. 'No. A man shouldn't. And especially not to a woman.'

'Ahh,' Sir Mortimer said, instantly relieved. There were worse things a man could be than a lady's man. As he knew only too well. If Toby had only— He cut his thoughts off abruptly. No good fretting about his son now. Instead, he glanced once more at the big Frenchman. So he'd had a sour love affair, hmm? Well, a man who looked like this was almost certainly destined to get his fingers burnt by the fairer sex sooner or later. Best by far to get it over with when you're young. And, in Sir Mortimer's opinion, it did a man no harm at all to acquire a few knocks in life.

He himself had, in his earlier years, fallen completely under the spell of one Maud Fitzsimmons, a flighty little thing who had promised to wait for him until after the war. But she hadn't. He'd come home with a VC and found her married to Freddie Carstairs, a farmer who had avoided the draft on medical grounds. Now he grunted, half in laughter, half in self-mockery. 'Women!'

'You're married, of course?' Wayne prompted, his bland eyes showing no ulterior motive, and for once Sir Mortimer's usually accurate ability to read character let him down.

'Hmm, for the second time.'

Now that, thought Wayne, was interesting, but instinct warned him not to push it any further. When the duck was cleared, there was a choice of puddings, and Sir Mortimer plumped for the apple pie, while Wayne selected the gooseberry tart.

'So. You're at a loose end?' Sir Mortimer brought the subject back to the matter in hand, pleased that Wayne had not done so. He hated to be hurried, and the more time he spent in this man's company, the more he found himself admiring and liking the man.

'For the moment,' Wayne said, his voice firm but polite. Meeting the Frenchman's unwavering blue eyes head on, Sir Mortimer nodded, his mind made up.

'Of course. Well, the job of junior advisor is, of course, only the first step on the ladder. There are several departments in Platt's — insurance, brokerage, real estate, et cetera — with heads who are, like me, getting on in life. Not that I plan to retire any time soon, of course,' Sir Mortimer added with such ferocity that Wayne blinked, then grinned.

'I don't blame you,' he said simply, the words more flattering and ingenious than fawning denials could ever have been.

'Humph,' Sir Mortimer grunted. 'You free tomorrow morning?'

'Yes.'

'Good — that's what I like to see in a man. No messing about. Can you find your way to my office, say . . . ten-thirty?'

'I'd be delighted.'

'Fine. That's settled, then. Ah, cheese and biscuits. I must confess to a weakness for water biscuits.'

Wayne leaned back and reached for a piece of cheddar, his eyes on Sir Mortimer level and full of good will.

But the internal smile that lurked behind the bland facade belonged to that of a crocodile. A hunting crocodile . . .

* * *

Platt House had its main offices on the oddly named Tubb Street, a small, select area, where Wayne found himself surrounded by internationally famous names.

It was five storeys of red brick, with elegant cornerstones and a semi-circular shallow flight of stone steps that led to two enormous double doors. Over the mantel there was a motto in Latin, which he translated to read 'Advisors to Kings' and the date of 1645. Inside, the hall was chilly, but Wayne was used to this by now. The English, for some obscure reason, liked to shiver. The tiles under his feet were a rich deep red, the panelling on the walls of a matching reddish wood that looked as if it might also be over three centuries old. Antiquated glass lamps were set in the walls, and the hall seemed to smell of book dust and ink, confidence and wealth.

He approached the reception desk, glad of his English clothes and the English haircut he had taken a chance on having the second day he was in England. 'I have an appointment with Sir Mortimer at ten-thirty,' he told the desk clerk, who didn't bother to check the old-fashioned ledger in front of him.

'Of course, sir. This way.' He led him to a lift, an old-fashioned concoction of sliding iron doors and pull-out buttons, and tugged on the one labelled '5'. Slowly the machine crawled to the top floor, the lift opening out on to a corridor that was carpeted with an ancient but hardy red weave. On the wall were prints of past famous clients and notable successes. Bridges that were built with investors from Platt's. A brand-new marina. Works of art, sold to museums, with the aid of a Platt's fine art expert. It was all comfortingly traditional and staidly impressive.

But everywhere he looked, Wayne could see only the potential for modernization, for profit, for different kinds of investments that appealed to a wider, less rarefied market.

'Mr D'Arville, Sir Mortimer,' the clerk announced him, leaving his secretary, a middle-aged woman with a pair of fiercely pointed glasses and a mannish haircut, to remain in her seat, industriously typing on an antiquated Imperial typewriter.

'Ah, D'Arville,' Sir Mortimer's hearty greeting didn't go unnoticed by the clerk, who had it all over the building by the end of the morning that some foreigner had invaded the establishment.

Sir Mortimer's office was like a study from a country house. Wood panelling gave way to flocked velvet walls, while a huge aspidistra plant stood in one corner and African violets and spider plants lined the window-sills. The desk was a huge Sheraton, intricately patterned and an obvious antique.

Wayne shook Sir Mortimer's hand in a firm and warm greeting. 'This place is overwhelming,' he said, making no attempt to stint the childish delight in his voice. 'It's like walking back in time. Outside, the city seems to be changing, with buildings going up like mushrooms, and then I stepped in here and it was like nothing I'd ever felt before. I half-expected to meet Dickens himself.'

Sir Mortimer beamed. He had fiercely resisted modernizing the office, only allowing the installation of the lift to save his workers' feet. Every other modern encroachment, though, had been determinedly resisted. And since Platt's was now privately owned, with Sir Mortimer holding 90 per cent of the shares, it had been easy enough for him to get his own way. He firmly believed that when people handed you their money to invest, they wanted to do so to a favourite uncle figure, not a modern, jumped-up spiv.

And after Toby's continual whingeing about how old-fashioned and out of date he was, it did his old heart good to find a young man who shared his belief that the firm shouldn't be ransacked by modern ways. 'Well, I'm glad you came. Please sit down. Tea?'

Wayne took tea. He hated tea, but he never mentioned it, instead letting his eyes feast on the room. Two of the walls were taken up with manuals, folders, brochures and portfolios from floor to ceiling, and he gravitated to these with an ease that looked natural, his eyes scanning the titles. For an hour, with Sir Mortimer at his side, they worked their way around the shelves. Wayne's obvious enthusiasm for handling other people's money did him no harm at all, and his seduction of Sir Mortimer became complete.

Retiring back to the desk and yet more tea, Sir Mortimer's lined face was flushed with pleasure. 'You obviously have the feel for the way money works, m'boy, if not for wine.'

Wayne smiled. 'It may be called "filthy lucre" but I like it!'

Sir Mortimer guffawed. 'Me too, lad. Me too. If only Toby—' He broke off suddenly and shook his head. Wayne didn't bother to ask, because his weasel-like cunning had already enabled him to guess. Toby, who must be a son, was patently unsatisfactory. Sir Mortimer was obviously in need of a surrogate son who *did* measure up . . . Silently he sipped his tea, almost enjoying it this time.

'Why don't we stop off at the Windsor for some lunch, and then, if you're free this afternoon, I'll show you round the London Stock Exchange? A bit of a madhouse, but it has a kind of frantic energy that you wouldn't believe. We'll have to get you licensed and all fixed up, of course, but I know a man who knows a man, as they say.'

Wayne laughed. 'I'd love to see it.'

'Splendid. I've got to see a man about a horse first. Why don't I meet you at the hotel later?'

Wayne rose and shook hands. 'The Windsor, then.' Sir Mortimer walked him to the door, Wayne nodding pleasantly to his secretary on the way out. Only then did he permit himself a wolfish smile. The lift came and he entered, surprised when it stopped at the fourth floor and a huddle of staff crammed themselves inside.

Suddenly he realized it was probably their lunch hour, and he sighed, glancing at his watch impatiently. As he did so, his eyes met those of a young woman, crammed up in the front corner right beside him. She was of average height, with short black hair and chocolate eyes. Her skin, though, was magnolia pale, her cheekbones high and exquisitely moulded, and as their eyes met Wayne felt jolt of electricity shoot through him. Vaguely, one part of his brain saw her eyes widen and her lips part on a small gasp, while another part of his brain began to sound delighted alarm bells.

She was wearing an ugly heavy skirt and a white blouse and clutched in front of her a huge black folder. She was obviously a secretary, Wayne realized, since Platt's would hardly employ women advisors, but the idea flashed only briefly across his mind.

The lift began its snail's-pace descent, and he half turned so that his back was presented to the rest of the crowd. They were jammed so tight that her elbow was in his stomach, her hip against his thigh, and he felt his body stir.

Her eyes, trapped helplessly in the blue magnetic pull of his, never left his face. Time seemed to hang still, the noise of the lift and the chattering of secretaries and clerks diminishing to an indistinct hum, like bees on a midsummer's day. They were both simultaneously aware that there was something primitive weaving a web around them, something that went beyond civilization, whipping past normal words or explanations.

In fact, Wayne didn't think he could speak at that moment if his life depended on it.

Veronica Coltrane could hear only the hammering of her heart, which was deafening her. Where the stranger touched her, her skin burned, and in his eyes she could feel herself drowning.

Nothing, but nothing, in her mundane, uneventful middle-class upbringing had prepared her for a moment like this. She had, up until the moment she'd first looked into the stranger's eyes, thought herself to be an ordinary girl, with good common sense and a fine head on her shoulders. Now, she knew herself to be nothing of the kind. Her bones felt liquefied, and as he continued to stare at her, hooked by the same magic that had her own mouth going as dry as a bone, she began to sway back against the lift wall.

She forced herself to drag in a ragged breath. What on earth was the matter with her?

Wayne moved an inch closer. Unbidden, he watched his hands reach up in front of him, reaching under the folder she clutched with white-knuckled intensity, and closing around her breast.

Veronica gasped, the tiny sound lost in the noise of the cramped lift. Oblivious to the fact that they might be seen, uncaring that she was letting a stranger touch her in a way that not even her steady boyfriend was permitted to do, her eyes widened, then half-closed. Her mouth, with the barest touch of lipstick, fell open.

Her mind put up the faintest murmur of warning, which was quickly drowned out by the thump-thump of her heart. Here was a dream come true. She had stepped into a lift, to find the most handsome man in the world staring at her as if he loved her more than the breath in his body. He was bold, like a knight from a fairy tale, touching her as if he had a right. She was mad. Utterly mad. But she couldn't seem to find the key to her usual sanity. Where was Veronica, the level-headed Veronica, the school bluestocking?

Wayne saw her lovely chocolate eyes feather closed, and for the first time in his life, literally felt himself becoming ensnared by a woman. He felt almost giddily relieved, and yet, at the same time, horrified.

Yet he couldn't pull away. Under his thumb, he felt her nipple harden, and as she arched her back in helpless instinctive reaction, her eyes came wide open again.

Veronica had meant to tell him to stop. That he mustn't . . . touch her so. But instead, when she opened her eyes, it was to see a strange, almost pleading look on his face that made her want to reach out and hold him instead.

So she was not the only one bowled over by a thunderclap? She felt her whole body tingling, as if she'd been struck by an invisible lightning strike.

Her vagina contracted, her knees weakened, and Wayne straightened stiffly as the lift doors slid open and the tiny cubicle began to empty. A hot wave of embarrassed colour belatedly flooded her cheeks, and Veronica dashed forward, hugging the folder to her chest as if her life depended on it.

She looked over her shoulder only once, to see the stranger all alone in the lift and watching her with those compelling blue eyes, then she dashed into the Ladies', her breasts heaving as she took deep, shuddering breaths. Shakily, she leant her burning forehead against the cool white tiles, wondering what on earth had just happened to her.

Wayne took a taxi back to the hotel, his mind a curiously shocked blank while he changed and awaited Sir Mortimer. He kept his mind diligently off the girl, telling himself it was nothing, nothing at all. Just a little risqué touch-up in a lift, that was all. Nothing to get so . . . unsettled about.

Sir Mortimer unwittingly helped him dismiss the incident from his mind as he proudly showed him around the London Stock Exchange an hour later. When Wayne finally left, it was with his ears still buzzing from the raucous male shouts and the strident ringing of telephones, and with a weekend invitation to visit Sir Mortimer's country residence in Berkshire.

Being without transport, he rode down on Friday afternoon with Sir Mortimer himself in a 1930s Bentley, an overnight case slung in the back boot.

The Platt residence turned out to be an eighteenth-century manor house of solid stone with neat rows of windows set in a squarish building. It had a yew-lined gravel drive, expansive lawns, two fountains, clipped box-hedging in formal rose gardens, and acres of landscaped grounds by Capability Brown. He was shown to the east wing by a blank-faced servant, where a four-poster bed and antique wooden wardrobes awaited him. He unpacked in record time, and stood outside his room, looking up and down the portrait-lined corridor with interested eyes. The place was a rabbit warren; as he hesitated, a young woman turned the corner. She was dressed in jodhpurs and a green velvet riding jacket with matching hat, and was obviously on her way to the stables.

'Hullo, you're a new face.'

Wayne introduced himself, noticing how the hazel eyes looked him over with brief, almost impersonal appreciation. 'I'm Amanda Platt, Morty's daughter-in-law.' They shook hands. 'You're here for the weekend bash, I take it? I suppose I'd better take you in hand, then, seeing as you're new,' she offered without preamble. 'First of all' — she set off down the corridor at a brisk pace — 'you'll have to avoid my husband, Toby,' she warned him, pausing long enough to eye him over, 'especially looking like you do. He goes for big boys — know what I mean?'

Wayne went cold, then hot, then smiled charmingly. 'I assure you, I shall avoid him as if he were leprous.'

Amanda shrugged uninterestedly. 'Next, don't eat the rhubarb. It'll have you on the loo for weeks. Then there's her ladyship, of course — the second Lady Platt. First gal died when she went over Old Man's Dyke but her horse didn't. Our Beatrice, a younger filly, was brought in by the old man to try and get another son or two, but it hasn't worked out. Poor old Morty's past it, you know, so she consoles herself with the groom.' They had reached the grand staircase by now and were rapidly descending the curved marble steps, and still Amanda was in full swing. 'Toby's sister, Cynthia, has three children, all of them terrors, I'm afraid. Oh, yes, and mind out for the Labrador. The bugger bites. Righty-ho, I think that'll do you. Welcome to England, Mr D'Arville.'

Wayne watched her go, not sure whether to laugh or not. Didn't she care a fig for what she said?

'Ahh, D'Arville.'

Wayne turned quickly at the sound of Sir Mortimer's voice. By his side was a handsome woman of well-preserved years, with short blonde hair, interesting grey eyes and a wide mouth. She was dressed in burgundy silk. 'Let me introduce you to my wife, Beatrice. Beatrice, this is the young man I was telling you about, and our latest acquisition for Platt's.'

As she approached, Wayne felt her eyes coolly assess him and felt an instant reaction of dislike tinged with desire. 'Mr D'Arville.' She inclined her head.

'Lady Platt,' he said, and took her hand, capturing it with a steely grip and then bringing it to his lips to kiss it with deliberate skill. Beatrice stiffened, her eyes beginning to spit flames even as she dragged a hissing breath between her perfectly painted lips. It was during this moment of mutual antipathy, unspoken challenge and heady sexual one-up-manship, that Sir Mortimer said, 'I don't think you've met one of our junior advisors from the Jewellery Acquisition Department, have you?'

Wayne turned, still holding on to the simmering Beatrice's hand, and found himself looking into the lovely face of the woman from the lift.

CHAPTER 16

The woman sitting by the window looked dead. Her hair was kept short by the nurses, and her lips had not uttered a word in five years. Sebastien kept checking that her chest was rising and falling just to reassure himself that she was actually still breathing. Her eyes never blinked, not even when a blackbird landed in a bush near the open window and began to sing.

'Sarah. Sarah, are you listening to me?'

The woman frowned fiercely and the sudden expression made Sebastien jump.

'Sarah. Can you hear that bird singing?'

The eyes, a neutral grey, not blue, not hazel, but a colour in limbo, began to flicker. That voice again — she'd heard it before, coming from the clouds. Was it God? It sounded nice, sort of warm and loving, like she thought God's voice would be. What was it asking?

'Sarah, listen to the bird singing.'

Bird? What was a bird? She seemed to remember something . . . Sarah Cashman couldn't remember a bird, but sounds, like a flute, began to roll in on the smoke that surrounded her. She could hear it . . . 'God's flute,' she said, then wondered if she'd said it right. Sometimes she only thought things, and assumed she'd said them. But the angels in white frocks never listened to her, so perhaps she never said them at all.

Sebastien turned to Harry Chamberlain, the chief of the psychiatric staff at St Edmund's, who was a tall, florid-faced man, a father of nine children and Winchester-educated, and asked, 'When was the last time she spoke?'

'Five years ago — after she murdered her daughter.'

Sebastien nodded, and turned back to the woman, whose skin was so pale it was almost translucent.

'Sarah, can you hear the bird?'

'Yes, God.'

The words came out in a croaking, rasping breath that was nevertheless the sweetest thing either man had ever heard. 'You've got through to her, Seb! By hell, you have!' Harry crowed as Sebastien moved closer. But not too close — Sarah had a habit of suddenly launching herself at people who came too close.

'Do you like the bird singing, Sarah?' Seb asked, praying that the blackbird would not move on just yet. Again a ferocious frown crouched on her face, which was pitifully thin and old before its time. Sarah was tired — she thought she hadn't slept in a hundred years.

'Tell me what you're thinking, Sarah,' the voice demanded, making her rub her ear against her shoulder as she thought. He had a lovely voice, this bird.

'Sing for Janey, bird,' she said, but the ugly sound that was her own voice made her clamp her teeth shut tight.

'She's biting on her tongue,' Sebastien said urgently and Harry moved forward to help him prise open her mouth and free her badly bleeding tongue. Summoning an orderly, one of the many large men with rubber-soled shoes, well-muscled bodies and discreet mouths that proliferated in the asylum, he ordered her to be taken to surgery where one of the medics would see to her. Sebastien watched her go, noting that her face was dead again.

Seeing his expression and understanding how tough the first few months always were, Harry clapped a hand on his

191

shoulder. 'Congratulations, Teale. You're the only one who's been able to get through to her since she became catatonic.'

Sebastien nodded but felt no self-congratulatory smugness. There was still so far to go. So much pain and struggle ahead, and even then . . . 'Lord, I'm tired,' he said, unknowingly echoing his patient's very sentiments. He had been working at the asylum for over five months now, so far just learning his way around and getting to know his colleagues. Sarah Cashman was only one of his patients, but hers was the first sign of progress he'd seen.

'You know, Sir Julius was telling me that he thought you had a flair for this kind of thing,' Harry Chamberlain said, his offhand language taking Sebastien by surprise for a moment, before he remembered that he was in England. The English had a way of bringing everything down to a proper size. When it was cold enough to make brass monkeys run for cover, the janitor in his apartment building would comment that it was 'a touch nippy'; when a ferocious pair of pint-size dogs yapped constantly in an empty flat below, the general complaint to the dogs' owners was that the 'little chaps do tend to make something of a racket'. This determination by the whole country to make everything sound manageable and reasonable took some getting used to. Even when they were talking about mental disease and human suffering, it was all couched in terms of mild understatement.

'Sir Julius, I'm fast learning, is a very capable judge of character, so I hope he's right,' Sebastien laughed, thinking back to his first meeting with Sir Julius Remus, the second day after his arrival at Heathrow.

It had been Sir Julius's secretary who had met him at the airport and showed him to the flat her employer had selected for him. Located just out of town, it was housed at the top of a three-storeyed Victorian house in a quiet residential street. His landlady had once been a patient of Sir Julius, was now completely cured of her mild paranoia, and was only too thrilled to have one of his 'young men' living in her house. She showed him to a bay-windowed room, pleasantly light and airy, that overlooked a flower-bedecked back garden. It had the added bonus of being very reasonably priced.

The following morning, he unashamedly played the tourist. From the elegant dome of St Paul's to the grandiose size of Buckingham Palace, from the chilly ancient rooms of the Tower of London with its ravens and Crown Jewels, to the Father of Parliaments, where Big Ben chimed the hour and where Tower Bridge raised its massive hinges to let through tall-masted vessels on the River Thames, Sebastien snapped away with his camera. Photography was his only hobby, and he was good at it.

But in spite of giving himself a good talking-to, he'd felt nervous when he finally took a taxi to Mayfair to dine with his tutor. He was shown in immediately by the cheerful, slender housekeeper Vivienne, and barely had time to draw breath before finding himself face to face with the famous man himself.

Sir Julius was a commanding figure. Six feet tall with thick white hair, he was dressed in a maroon smoking jacket and black creased trousers. He looked so English and venerable that for a second Sebastien felt totally out of place. Then his hand was taken in a firm grip, and he found himself meeting head on a pair of penetrating, all-seeing electric-blue eyes. It was an odd sensation; he could feel a probe going right through him, ferreting out every weakness, every dream, every secret he'd ever had.

'Sebastien — you don't look much like your father,' were the great man's first words to him.

'Thank you,' Sebastien had instantly replied, meaning it, and then blinked. Sir Julius had roared with laughter. It had broken whatever ice there was instantly and, despite the differences in age and culture, the two men quickly established themselves as equals.

'I wanted to thank you for smoothing the way to St Edmund's, Sir Julius,' Sebastien said the first opportunity he got, uncomfortably aware that he didn't feel happy about receiving any privileged treatment. Sir Julius told him to drop the 'Sir' and assured him that with his examination results, references, and experience with the shelter and his many other community projects, St Edmund's had been only too pleased to have him.

Over dinner, and at Sir Julius's request, Sebastien gave a clinical account of his own mental condition, Julius listening intently. He liked this boy immensely and could well imagine that everyone else did too. Years of experience told him that this boy had an indefinable but definite 'something extra' that would draw people to him, freeing them to confide, to trust him and believe in him. And that, as any good psychiatrist knew, was more than half the battle fought and won.

Now, following Harry Chamberlain into the staff canteen, Sebastien selected apple and cheese for a light lunch, knowing he would be having a good dinner tonight with Julius. Every Monday, Wednesday and Friday night he ate regularly at the Mayfair house where they would talk for hours, Sir Julius keeping notes for the obligatory records that would have to be approved by the medical commission before Sebastien was finally and legally qualified as a practising and licensed psychiatrist.

Sir Julius rang Sebastien's office a few days later to tell him that there was a small cocktail party being given by one of his friends that evening, and did he want to come? 'It's an anniversary party really, for a big financial advice firm. One of my oldest friends, the chairman, invited me. There'll be free champers and finger sandwiches, the whole kit and caboodle. It'll give you a chance to see the English upper classes in full swing, complete with snobs, the compulsory company drunk and nymphettes.'

Sebastien laughed. 'It sounds like just the sort of hotchpotch of neurosis and paranoia that a budding shrink shouldn't miss. What time?'

The party was being held in a private residence in Belgravia and, forewarned by Sir Julius, he rented a tuxedo, much to Mrs Glynn's approval. His landlady was not so old that she couldn't see immediately the startling and handsome effect the black and white outfit had on his auburn hair and amber eyes. He took a taxi to the address given him by Sir Julius and introduced himself at the door. In the foyer, festooned with enormous arrays of gladioli and roses, a butler took his handwritten, silver-edged invitation. He half-expected an official announcer to boom his name into the hall that was already crammed with a dazzling array of people and was mightily relieved when one didn't.

Sensing his unease, Julius bore down on him immediately. 'Bloody hell,' Sebastien practised the English phrase experimentally, 'there are more couture dresses here than in a Paris boutique.'

Julius laughed delightedly. He approved of the boy's no-nonsense sense of humour, and Sir Julius noted that the American's easy-going grin earned him several approving glances from many of the bejewelled women.

'Ah, there's a young lady I'd like you to meet,' Julius said, and led Sebastien through the throng to a woman who reached up to kiss Julius's cheek in obvious and genuine affection.

'Veronica, I want you to meet Sebastien Teale, a visitor from overseas, currently working out his slavery notice at St Edmund's. Sebastien, Veronica Coltrane, a long-time friend.'

Sebastien immediately liked the young woman who laughed up at him, with her exotic black hair and chocolate eyes, and her simple, pale blue velvet evening gown.

'Sebastien, nice to meet you. This is Wayne . . . Wayne . . . oh, there you are.' As she spoke, half turning to bring forward a man who had been waylaid by a white-haired patron of the arts, Sebastien found himself looking up into the most handsomely arresting face he'd ever seen. Heavy-lidded blue eyes sat widely spaced in a squarish, powerful face. But while the man's size was the first thing that struck most people about him, Sebastien found his breath being taken away by the aura of pain and anger that emanated from the giant stranger like a toxic cloud. There was such a feeling of silent suffering about the man that for a moment Sebastien found it hard to breathe.

'Dr Teale, nice to meet you. Sir Julius.'

During his few moments of shock, Veronica had introduced Julius as well, and the French accent took all but Veronica by surprise.

'Monsieur D'Arville has just joined Platt's to help us break into the European money markets,' Veronica explained, looking from Julius to Sebastien. She loved Julius like a second father, and she sensed his strong interest in the young man who was obviously something of a protégé. She turned sharp eyes on the American again, but it took her only a second to be reassured, immediately soothed by the kind, sherry-coloured eyes. Trust canny old Julius to pick a winner.

'So Platt's is trying out the waters in Europe?' Sir Julius said, eyeing the Frenchman with a wary eye. 'That's interesting.' He, too, was fond of Veronica, and there was something about the big Frenchman that made him uneasy.

Wayne hardly heard him and found it hard to respond to Sir Julius's intelligent questions with his usual care. Instead, he found his eyes again and again wandering to the young American, a strange feeling, almost of peace, coming over him whenever he met the steady, reassuring gaze. Yet at the same time, he felt uncomfortably exposed, and in the back of his head he felt a throbbing pressure begin to build.

'Sir Julius is a top man in his field, Wayne,' Veronica told him softly. 'He practically revolutionized psychiatric care in this country. We're all so proud of him. Don't say I never introduce you to anyone interesting.' She laughed, her eyes caressive and unknowingly expressive as she gazed up at him.

'Really? And are you too a . . . psychiatrist?' Wayne turned to Sebastien, already knowing and dreading the answer. Something screamed at him that this man was dangerous and to keep away, but something else, something deeper and stronger, urged him to get closer, to learn more, to find out what mysterious power lay behind those sherry-coloured eyes. There was a power about this man, and Wayne knew all about power. But there was something more . . .

'I'm only a beginner,' Sebastien said, his voice quiet and thoughtful.

'Don't you believe it,' Sir Julius snorted. 'He might not have the paperwork yet, but this boy's a genius with people. Only today, I heard he got through to a catatonic patient that nobody else had been able to reach in five years. Take my word for it — Sebastien is a healer,' he finished with typical theatricality.

Wayne stiffened almost imperceptibly at this news, but Sebastien noticed it instantly. And Wayne knew that he had. His jaw clenched and an expression of panic, pain, anger and, finally, of forced cynical amusement crossed his face, all of which Sebastien read accurately.

At that moment, Veronica saw a friend of hers, and Wayne made no objection to being led away. Sebastien watched them go, noting the Frenchman's stiff and tense shoulders and the way the blue eyes constantly flickered over the room.

'I think my little Veronica has fallen in love,' Sir Julius said, a trifle anxiously. 'I used to live next door to the Coltranes, years back. Used to dandle Veronica on my knee . . .'

Sebastien beckoned a waiter and took two glasses, but his eyes remained fixed on Wayne's broad back. At that moment Sir Julius looked up at him, noticing his intense expression, and nodded, somewhat relieved. Perhaps Sebastien would be able to save the big Frenchman from whatever demons were destroying his soul. He hoped so. For Veronica's sake.

* * *

The party wore on. Sir Julius introduced him to an old Cambridge chum, but Seb found himself again and again seeking out Wayne, who was currently dancing with Veronica. He held her too tightly, and his eyes were fixed on the floor. A casual observer might have been inclined to put the display down to passion, but Sebastien knew that

197

there was something else, something tormented that lurked deeper down in the Frenchman's psyche that had nothing to do with desire.

Sir Julius introduced him to his host, the oddly named Sir Mortimer Platt, a fierce seventy-year-old who was the personification of Old England. And still he observed the tall Frenchman, watching him drink and then eat without even a semblance of enjoyment. In a flash of intuitive realization, he wondered if Wayne D'Arville had ever actually enjoyed anything at all in his entire life.

Wayne nodded when Veronica breathlessly excused herself to go to the ladies' room. 'Don't be too long,' he told her, his words a command but also a plea. He felt ridiculously alone and vulnerable since meeting Sebastien Teale. Oddly, he felt himself to be in some kind of danger.

Veronica nodded quickly, her eyes as bright as coals that had been set alight, and promised huskily, 'I'll only be a moment.'

Since the weekend at Sir Mortimer's, Veronica spent as much time with Wayne as he'd allow. She knew he was wary of her, and suspected a bad love affair in his past, but she was determined to break down his barriers. She was already halfway in love with him.

Wayne watched her go, unaware that every nuance of expression on his face had been seen and noted. He looked around, wincing as a woman's diamond necklace caught the light and dazzled him. Suddenly the sound of music, 'The Blue Danube' by Strauss, sounded nauseatingly trite, and the smell of cucumber and celery made him want to heave. He turned and bumped into Sir Mortimer, who was looking for an old friend. 'Wayne. You haven't seen Henri, have you?'

For just a moment Wayne went white as he heard his dead brother's name for the first time since watching him drown, and he stared blankly at the old man's face. From a few yards away, Sebastien almost made a dash towards him, sure he was going to keel over. As it was, he had moved close enough to be able to hear Wayne's weak reply.

'Er . . . n-no. Can't s-say as I have,' the hated old stutter was back but, in Sir Mortimer's inebriated state, it went unnoticed. But Sebastien heard and understood. Almost shouldering his way outside, Wayne stepped out onto the balcony, dragging in lungfuls of air, his whole body shaking. It had been raining, and the breeze was cool and heavy. Automatically he plucked a flower from the tree that grew by the side of the stone balustrade and began to twirl it absently in his fingers. The terrace was lit only with candles, and in the cool darkness Wayne slowly felt his heartbeat returning to normal.

'Damn,' he said, his voice tormented. He'd thought he'd seen the last of those ugly moments, when the world felt as if it were about to crash in on him. He'd had these attacks regularly after Hans had drowned, but over the last year they had diminished to nothing. Why tonight, of all nights, did they have to return?

In the doorway, Sebastien watched him, listening, waiting.

Wayne's head hung low, as if it were too heavy for his head. In his treacherous mind, he could see again a picture of that young, hurtling body splashing into the sea. He rubbed a hand across his eyes, feeling the unexpected brush of flower petals against his face. It was a stem of lilac — Hans's favourite flower. Looking down at the bloom in his hand, Wayne hissed in a breath that was clearly audible to the man who stood watching him. Then, slowly and deliberately, Wayne held the flower over a candle flame and watched the simple flowers curl up, go brown and wither.

Wayne stared for a moment at the pathetic burnt corpse in his hand, then gave a strangled yelp that barely sounded human. Quickly, as if it was he and not the flower that had been burned, he dropped the mangled stem over the balustrade where it disappeared into the darkness of the lawn. He felt suddenly lost and totally without hope, almost wishing for death and the precious oblivion that meant the end of all pain. He didn't think it was possible to endure so much agony and confusion and just keep going. But he must. He had to.

Then he turned and found sherry-coloured eyes silently, steadily, offering him an alternative.

* * *

Thousands of miles away, Kyle snatched up the telephone, his head full of facts and figures. 'Yes?' he said absently. He was reading the specs for a new chain of garages he was thinking of opening in the Carolinas.

'Darling,' Clarissa's soft tone snaked into his ear, making him catch his breath. Carefully, he put down the papers and moved to the bed.

'Clarissa,' he said softly. 'How's Hollywood?'

'About like you'd expect.' Clarissa, from the other side of the country, gave a slightly nervous-sounding laugh. 'I wish you were here. We could do all those trashy things people are supposed to do. You know, walk down that sidewalk where all the stars have their own plaque on the ground. Visit the Chinese theatre. Picnic under the big Hollywood sign . . .' Her voice sounded wistful.

And scared.

For the first time, Kyle heard the fear in her voice as plain as day and wondered how he'd ever missed it before. 'I told you, I had work to do that just couldn't wait,' he said truthfully, his voice becoming gentler now. 'It really couldn't, Clarry,' he tried to explain to her, for what seemed like the hundredth time. 'I have managers, money-men, bankers to see. This new garage chain is really going to happen. I can't just take time off in the middle of it to accompany you to Hollywood.'

Clarissa sighed. 'I see,' she said, her voice tremulous. What he really meant was he had a good excuse, and now he could use it. Before that day at the lake, he wouldn't have dared. Now . . . now, she thought miserably, she no longer had a hold on him. And he was slipping away, just as she'd always known he would.

Kyle sighed heavily. 'I don't think you do, sweetheart,' he said gently. 'I think you're like I was once. Blind.'

Now, Kyle could look back over all their years together and see it in a totally different light. He no longer saw himself as the helpless victim, a man trapped by his own inexplicable longings and sexual desire. And Clarissa was no longer the Queen Bitch. The spider with a fly in her web.

In Hollywood, Clarissa tensed like an animal waiting for a rifle shot and noticed how her fingers had curled around the telephone cord. Her knuckles were white. When she glanced up and saw her reflection in the mirror, she was not surprised to see that her face was even whiter. For she knew what was coming. Kyle was going to dump her. At last, the nightmare that had plagued her ever since meeting him was upon her. The only man she'd ever loved was going to tell her goodbye . . .

'Clarissa? Are you still there?' Kyle asked sharply and, over the miles separating them, heard her catch her breath.

'Of course I am, darling, where would I be going?' she asked with her usual waspish sarcasm and heard him drag his breath in sharply.

'Don't!' Kyle said harshly.

Clarissa closed her eyes. Have pity, my darling, she thought silently, a tear trickling down her cheek. Didn't he realize she needed to build up all the pitiful defences she had?

'Don't what, sugar?' she purred.

Kyle picked up the phone and paced the room. He ran a hand across his forehead, his throat feeling suddenly dry. So much depended on what happened next, and he was unprepared for it. Ever since his startling discovery at the lake, he knew that this moment was coming. But he'd not expected to be doing it over the telephone, of all things. 'Don't come the southern bitch with me, Clarissa,' Kyle warned her, his voice harsher than he meant it to be. 'I won't fall for it. Not again. Not ever again. Do you hear me?' he demanded.

In her luxurious hotel room, Clarissa disguised her sob as a laugh. 'Why, darling, what else could I ever be?' she

201

asked, and felt her heart crack in her chest. She actually had to double over, to put her hand out on the bed, to keep herself upright. This was just too hard. She couldn't listen to her world collapse around her and not perish.

'You could be whatever you wanted to be,' Kyle's voice said in her ear, and Clarissa blinked, not trusting her own senses. Whatever she'd expected him to say, it had not been that.

'I don't . . .' she began, then stopped. Oh, what did it all matter? It was over and she just couldn't stand it. 'Kyle . . .' she said, 'don't leave me. Oh, Kyle, please,' she begged unashamedly and began to cry, her lovely southern voice breaking into ragged sobs. 'I'll die if you leave me.'

Kyle closed his eyes. A huge weight seemed to lift from his shoulders. He felt as if he could actually float around the room. 'I know,' he said softly. 'I know.'

He returned to the bed and sank down, his dark head lowering. 'Oh, Clarry,' he said. 'All those years wasted . . .'

In Hollywood, Clarissa drew in a deep ragged breath. He was not saying goodbye. Unbelievably, he wasn't. Or was he playing some game of his own? Did he want revenge now? 'I don't understand,' she said at last.

Kyle gave a derisive bark of laughter. 'Neither of us understood. That was the problem. We played a game, we set the rules, and it nearly destroyed both of us. But the game's over now. You love me. I love you. And we're going to do something about it,' he promised.

For a second, Clarissa was positive she hadn't heard what she thought she'd heard. She had wanted him to say those words for so long, she was half-convinced her disintegrating mind had conjured them up. Then, she swallowed hard.

'You love me?' she said numbly.

'Yes,' Kyle confirmed, almost aggressively. 'And I know you love me, so don't try to deny it,' he warned, his back straightening, his head lifting. 'And if you don't leave your husband, divorce him, and marry me . . . we're through.'

CHAPTER 17

Hollywood

The stars were out tonight. Limousines pulled up in front of the premiere cinema like taxi cabs pulled up on Rodeo Drive, and the gathering crowd jostled and shoved as every new car disgorged its glamorous occupant.

Gina Lollobrigida, with her famous waist the same size as that of her husband's neck, was dressed in black silk so crisp it looked like layers of fine metal, rising to stand in a high collar around her carefully coiffed head where diamonds sparked at her earlobes and around her throat. The Shah of Iran was in town, having sailed his yacht halfway around the world to visit the American West Coast, and Earl Wilson, the famous newspaper columnist, kept mental notes in his computer-like brain.

All of Hollywood's 'A' list had turned out for the premiere of *Night of the Invaders*, since the gossip concerning its stars and director had begun almost from the first week of shooting. Kirk Douglas was there, just to see if Cougar Studios, that veteran producer of B movies, actually could pull a first class box office smash out of its hat, as rumour insisted it had. Certainly the budget for *Invaders* had been astronomical, increasing the speculation tenfold. Not noted for such generosity, Howard Shoesmith's behaviour had been noted avidly. Louella Parsons teased him constantly in her column, hinting at a mid-life crisis. First he took on a brand new director, from Kansas no less, that nobody had ever heard of, and fresh from producing plays at Oxford University! Then he allotted a budget that would not have looked miserly for giants like Paramount, MGM and Universal. And how, Louella asked, had Howard Shoesmith and the most talked about director, Kier Harcourt, managed to persuade Bud Westmore to do the intricate makeup? How had they managed to get Bette Daniels, the rising star contracted to Universal, for the leading lady? Or Warren Wainwright, the hottest up-and-coming sex symbol in town, for the lead role? And as for importing English technicians for the special effects . . . Louella had a field day. Somebody, somewhere, was pulling some very special strings for Kier Harcourt.

The hype had been astronomical. Newspaper reporters had been wined and dined as they never had been before, and even television chat-show hosts had been dragged into the circus, calling a cease-fire between the film studios and their hated rivals, the TV networks. Yes, *Night of the Invaders* was breaking all the rules, and pulling in all the stars. The crowds jostled for Kim Novak, oohing at her daring low-cut lemon-yellow dress, the exact shade of her hair. They jostled even more for Robert Mitchum and Ava Gardner, and women practically swooned over the debonair good looks of James Mason.

A mile from the cinema, Kier sat in the back of the limousine, feeling uncomfortable in his tux. The collar felt as if it were strangling him, he had iron butterflies in his stomach, and he was sweating all over.

'Honey, leave your collar alone. See, you've messed up your bow tie.' Oriel leaned over to fix it, her eyes teasing and wry, making Kier grin.

'OK, OK. I admit it. I'm nervous.'

'Nervous?'

'OK. Scared witless. Does that make you feel better?'

'Of course not, darlin'. It's just nice to be reminded that you are only human after all, and not Superman. '

Kier looked across at her, his eyes taking in every detail, from the elegant chignon of her hair, interwoven with the family pearls her mother had brought from Georgia, to the peach satin dress's full skirt and V-shaped neck, where a single topaz hung from a slender gold chain. She didn't look as if she'd given birth to a daughter just eight months ago. 'Did I tell you you look ravishing?'

'No. You told me the projector had better not break down, and that the seating had better be right, and that the red carpet had better have arrived, and that the usherette uniforms had better be the ones you wanted and not the flash ones Howard wanted, and you told me . . .'

'Don't,' he groaned. 'I'm a monster. I know. But I'll make it up to you and Bethany now that the film's finally finished.'

'Bethany isn't yet a year old,' Oriel smiled, rubbing the back of her hand down his smooth cheek. 'She's clever as a button, though, and she loves her daddy no matter when she sees him, whether it's the middle of the night or in broad daylight.'

'I haven't been coming home that late!'

Oriel cocked one eyebrow up at him, saying nothing.

Kier gave her a sheepish look, then shrugged. 'OK. But you do look ravishing,' he added irreverently, then suddenly grabbed her. Oriel squealed. 'So I suppose it would be downright insulting of me not to ravish the lady,' Kier growled, and bent down to nibble on her ear, his hand slipping inside the V-shaped neckline to cup her left breast.

Oriel moaned, oblivious to the chauffeur who might or might not have been watching. 'Oh, darlin', you do pick the damnedest times!' Oriel sighed, thinking of the many nights she had spent over the last year, her body aching for him. There had been times when she had cursed the film, swearing over the perfection he demanded, bemoaning the constant rewrites he did to keep *Invaders* up to date and, most of all, different.

'I want to make a *different* kind of film,' he'd said to her a thousand times. 'A new kind, one that will change the way this damned town sees films. It's still in the thirties, in the days of Bette Davis and Ronald Colman! America's changed and changing every day. Jimmy Dean practically invented teenagers, and more and more . . .' On that occasion she'd managed to shut him up with a kiss on his throat and a well-placed hand on his thigh.

Now she moaned, her body reacting as it always did to the expertise of his touch.

'Kier, for pity's sake,' she gasped as he bent down, nuzzling aside the peach satin of her bodice to suckle on her pert nipple. Since Bethany had been born, her breasts had become bigger and sometimes, like now, he felt a trickle of sweet milk spill into his mouth. Urgently his fingers tightened on her waist. He'd been neglecting her this past year, he knew that. But by the time production had finally started she'd been eight and a half months pregnant, and he'd been in the middle of the space-craft landing scene when the call came from the hospital. And since that magical moment when he'd held his newborn daughter in his hands, looking so tiny, so red and wrinkled, and so incredibly beautiful, things had been pure chaos.

As director and screenwriter, he never stopped, and even after shooting had finished, he'd spent ten weeks with the editor, learning so much about that side of things that his name would appear on the screen three times — as director, screenwriter and assistant editor. Sometimes, watching his daughter become a toddler seemingly overnight, he wondered if it had all been worth it.

Oriel struggled to sit up. 'Kier, oh hell, we're there.' She struggled to tug her bodice back into place, her cheeks flushed with desire, her eyes sparkling gems. Kier took several deep breaths, willing the embarrassing hardness between his legs to subside. Glancing out of the smoke-glassed windows at the cinema lit up with rows of coloured lights, his eyes blinked at the dazzle of flashing camera bulbs. The media cameras and paparazzi were everywhere. And when he took in the sheer size of the avid crowd, Kier found the iron butterflies had come back with a vengeance.

'Hell, the zoo is out in force tonight,' he commented, making Oriel grin. The phenomena of 'film watchers' had been something new to him. For parts of the film he had actually shot on-location in a small town in Ohio, taking the cameras out into the streets. It had been daring, practically unheard of, and the whole town had been out in force to watch, which was, of course, the last thing he'd needed. Great crowds didn't usually congregate in small towns, and he'd been forced to make a barrier to keep them back so that the actors could work. But for the scene where the spaceship landed, he'd had the chief cameraman take shots of the crowd during the filming of a minor stunt, and the awed, avid faces of genuine people had been worth a whole cart-load of extras.

'Would you rather have the place deserted, darlin'?' Oriel asked mildly, and Kier shot her a quick look, then smiled.

'Did I ever tell you how glad I am that you married me?'

'Nope.'

'Aren't I a stinker?'

'Yep.'

The crowd surged forward again as their limo drew to a halt, and as they alighted there was a ripple of disappointment. No famous faces there. Then the whispers began — this was the director, the one they were all talking about. And wasn't he young, and handsome? Was that his wife, or a mistress, or what? And wasn't she beautiful? Kier felt the uncomfortable weight of hundreds of eyes boring into his back as they walked along the red carpet, shaking hands with the cinema manager to a sudden spurt of flashing of camera bulbs. Finally, after what seemed like an eternity, they walked inside, meeting Howard Shoesmith in the lobby.

'We got a good turnout, boy,' Howard said, a fat cigar in his mouth, a smug grin firmly in place on his face.

'And to think my stars actually enjoy that,' Kier laughed, and nodded to the crowd outside, just as a white stretch limo pulled up to disgorge the leading lady and man. That had been Kier's idea. Usually the leads showed up separately with separate dates, but Kier had thought it prudent to give the crowd something more to gossip about. Were they lovers in real life? He could almost read Hedda's or Louella's column tomorrow, word for word, alive with their usual innuendo and bitchy wit.

'Well, here we go,' Howard said, looking over Kier with an amused eye. 'Now we get to see if all the ballyhoo has been worth it.'

Kier smiled coldly, wondering if Howard wasn't actually hoping for the film to flop just for the satisfaction of seeing Kier fall flat on his face. Then he shrugged the thought off as unworthy. Dislike him though he might, Howard had given him the job and had lavished an amazing amount of money on the budget. He had given in to every demand Kier had made, from experimental lighting to the English special-effects crew, and revolutionary camera angles.

Kier had stuck his neck out, and he knew it. Inside, the critics would be already seated, along with the big brass. If the film flopped . . .

He felt a small hand slip into his, and squeeze. Looking down into blue eyes, still hot from remembered passion, he felt himself relax, even smile.

'Come on,' Oriel said softly, and together they walked into the dimly lit auditorium.

They were seated, at Kier's request, midway in the front section. He wanted to sit behind the critics and newspaper columnists, the better to watch their reactions. And he had no desire to sit with the 'stars'.

As they took their seats, they found themselves among the lucky Joe public, who'd queued for hours to buy the 100 tickets available.

The lights went down, and the opening credits rolled, presenting the audience straight away with something new.

Usually, films began with music and a straight roll of credits. Not so with *Night of the Invaders*. Kier had asked an old friend of Betty's from the Ruskin School of Art in Oxford to do the graphics for the opening credits, and one of Viv's musical friends had composed a score that was a weird mix of classical musical with a creepy undertone, overlaid with a haunting melody. With the arty, startling graphics that used animation to turn flying saucers, planets and robots into the leading names, the audience was hooked from the start.

Kier leaned back, beyond nerves now, feeling utterly calm. The film was either going to flop or take off like one of the flying saucers that was as far away from Flash Gordon's smoking rockets as it was possible to get. Kier had gone to NASA for ideas and had let the set designer run wild. And it showed. What also showed was the on-location shooting in Ohio. Instead of being presented with the mock-up studio idea of a town, the audience was presented with the real thing and he felt immediately a sense of rapport from the people around him, a rapport that was transferred to the actors as the leading man and lady got into their roles.

Every girl there knew what Sally was going through as she prepared for her date, the audience actually seeing the curlers come off, the tangles in her hair being brushed out and the makeup being applied, instead of just being presented with another Hollywood glamour model that was light years away from their own, mundane lives.

The camera angles were stunning, too. Kier shot from second-storey windows, looking down on the actors. He shot from the floor, looking up at them in the confrontation scene between Joe, the hero, and the local bully boys. Sound effects, too, had been changed. Out were the wild, overstated punches, crunches and explosions. In were more realistic sounds, and under his direction, the acting had the gritty bite of realism. When forty-five minutes had passed, the tension was high. The characters were real flesh-and-blood good ol' boys, and the sense of something being seriously wrong had transferred itself to the audience. Kier could feel the tension all around him when Sally finally stumbled onto the underground landing site. There she turned slowly, her eyes finding the creature that stood behind her. But Kier forced the audience to guess at what she saw, giving out clues only sparingly in the shape of its shadow, in the shuffling of its feet. As he'd always known it would, the ambiguity added to the terror.

Sally did not scream. Sally did not faint. *Night of the Invaders* was not playing by the set rules, and every critic there knew it. The hero Joe was also fallible, and his mistakes were all very human and very plausible. By the time the climax of the film had come around, the audience wasn't at all convinced that he'd actually arrive on time to save the girl, and the safety of the usual foregone conclusion that there would be a happy ending had been long since snatched away from the spellbound audience.

For long, long minutes, the audience warred with differing opinions — Sally was doomed. Then Joe was getting nearer — Sally would be saved. Then, and only then, was the monster at last revealed, full-faced, and here Bud Westmore had earned his exorbitant fee.

This was no Hollywood monster, a mere man dressed up in green gunge, his very human eyes clearly visible through the slits in the mask. This was a combination of makeup, animal, man, and other-worldly ugliness. Several girls in the audience screamed as, on screen, everything went silent. Joe and the monster faced off, the camera swivelling from one to the other, slowly at first, and then faster, until the audience could hardly tell what was happening.

And then the *coup de grace*. Joe took the home-made flame-thrower that the alien had already seen, but instead of just firing it off, he dove under the monster, firing up, the camera angle going with him. High-pitched, eerie squeals, which his dubbing editor had gleaned from dolphins and speeded up, filled the cinema, making the audience jump and then look around in surprise. Kier had had the wiring men place the speakers all around the room, so that the noise seemed to come from everywhere.

And then Sally crawled over to Joe and helped him up. Together, battered, human, shaking, crying, they stumbled out into the cool night air. A mile away, the small town was lit up and the audience could hear a barn hoe-down tune fill the air. As he'd expected, the return to normality was startling.

Then the final credits — this time the stars of the night sky forming the words, the moon shimmering into the name of the actors and the director. The lights went up and there was total silence. All around him people were blinking, dumbfounded, looking at their partners to see what they made of it.

A boy a few seats away from Kier said loud enough for everyone to hear, 'Gee whizz! I think I'll cancel the visit to Uncle Elmer's farm.'

And then everyone was laughing, the kind of laughter that came after tension, and Oriel started to clap. In a moment the room was awash with applause, whistles and stomping feet.

Kier got up, every head turning his way and for once ignoring the leading actors who also stood up. Slowly, Kier walked on stiff legs to the bottom of the screen to where his leading lady was beaming — as well she might. She'd just been made into a superstar, and she stretched up on tiptoe to kiss him. Kier turned to look at the critics, his eyes level. Now they could write what they damn well liked. He knew he'd done it. He knew he was there.

Clarissa looked across at Howard Shoesmith, then away again, her face blank. Howard stood up, but suddenly there was a crowd around his director, other leading men from the big studios and gossip columnists, all eager now to talk to the boy genius, as Hedda Hopper would call him the next day, which would be his nickname for the next twenty years.

Alone in her seat, Oriel watched him, tears running down her cheeks.

'Darling, are you all right?'

Hearing the soft southern drawl, she turned to her mother and nodded speechlessly, her eyes travelling on to those of her father. Duncan looked almost as proud as the day he'd first held his little granddaughter.

Finally Oriel said, 'Isn't he wonderful? Didn't I tell you?'

Duncan's face split into a wide grin. 'You sure did, honey. I think I've just gone and gotten myself a famous son-in-law.'

Oriel laughed and cried and hugged her mother and kissed her father and watched her husband being mobbed. After a while the whole circus decamped to the Beverly Hills Hotel. The Polo Lounge was ready for them, the elegant *porte-cochere* at the front of the hotel entrance quickly becoming blocked with stars, producers, directors, newspaper men, agents and models. With great aplomb, the *maître d'* moved them along, seating the most prominent in the curved banquette tables, the priority seating being quickly taken up with the film world's elite. Pride of place was left for Kier Harcourt and his lovely wife.

Clarissa looked around, satisfied that everything had been prepared correctly. Huge floral displays were everywhere and the menu she'd discussed with the hotel's French chefs had been strictly adhered to. Pâté de foie gras and beluga caviar littered silver trays, accompanied by Melba toast. Lobster souffle competed with Dover sole and shallots, turtle soup with sherry rubbed shoulders with salmon and capers. Roast lamb with mint, roulade of beef, and quenelles of pheasant tempted the appetites of the most ardent carnivores. Dessert trolleys overflowed, with baba au rhum, parfait, apricot snow, fruit soaked in kirsch and jellied consommés the order of the day. As well as the pink champagnes of Pommery and Grande, there was a selection of harder liquor, and of course, Mouton Rothschild and Pouilly-Fuissé by the crateload.

There had never been an *après*-film party like it. But then, Clarissa Somerville had never sojourned in Hollywood territory before.

A ten-piece world-famous band serenaded the guests with thirties' Glenn Miller classics and modern jive.

'Well, how are you feeling?' Oriel asked when the last of the emptied plates had been cleared away, and it seemed the endless hours of congratulations were at last winding down.

Kier leaned back in his chair, his bow tie long since having been discarded.

'I don't know . . .' He met her eyes and began to laugh. 'Yes, I do,' he said softly, then shouted, 'I feel bloody great!'

Several heads turned and teeth flashed in grins, the ambiance one of high good humour. Success was all that counted in this town, and when you made it, people were magnanimous. Stars who'd never spoken to him before congratulated him heartily, angling for roles.

Oriel licked her lips slowly, her hand gently going to her throat, where she began to trail a finger down her sternum. Abruptly Kier stopped laughing. 'You feel so great you're gonna stay here all night?' she asked huskily.

'Uh-uh.' Kier shook his head, rising to his feet as Oriel excused herself to go to the ladies' room and collect her coat. Watching her daughter leave, Clarissa slipped a little nervously into the chair her daughter had just vacated. With a sinking heart, she watched Kier's eyes become shuttered. Although she had stayed for two weeks when Bethany had been born, Clarissa had lacked the courage to try and reach out to her son-in-law. Now, the neutral state of their relationship was beginning to wear her down.

'Clarissa,' Kier said, his voice carefully bland, 'I hope you've enjoyed this evening?'

Since Clarissa's advent back into their lives, Kier had been determinedly polite. He had not failed to see that having her there for the birth of Bethany had meant a lot to Oriel, and he had to admit that, so far, Clarissa had kept her pretty nose out of their marriage and had graciously met Kier halfway, always polite and never descending on them without prior warning. And Kier was not a man to hold grudges.

'Indeed I have,' Clarissa agreed. How best to offer the olive branch? 'I'm really glad I was able to help,' she said, and smiled hopefully.

Kier stiffened. 'Help?'

Clarissa put a tentative hand on his arm. 'It was after Oriel rang me for the first time — to tell me she was going to have a baby. I . . . so wanted to do something . . . positive for you both.'

Kier felt a cold hard knot forming in his stomach. 'Oh?'

Clarissa looked at him warily. 'Didn't it occur to you that the budget for the movie was much higher than Howard usually allowed?' she began, trying to feel her way into it. She had always thought that, when she told him, he'd be grateful for all her help. So why was she beginning to feel so tense? 'I thought I should invest in your career. After all, I so wanted you to be successful.'

Kier paled but said only, 'You're a backer?'

'That's right,' she agreed, relieved at last that they were beginning to speak the same language. 'And I must say, you used my money so well. All those wonderful little gadgets and things. It really made the film *shine*. And, of course, I arranged this little shindig,' she added offhandedly, and looked vaguely around the room.

Kier took a deep, shaken breath. 'Clarissa, as long as I live, I'll never ask you for one damned thing. And neither shall Oriel.'

Clarissa's smile faltered. 'But! . . . I thought it would make things easier for you. I so wanted the film to be a success . . .' she began, dismayed.

'So that you could rub my nose in it?' Kier gritted. 'So that you could say I'd never have made it without my mother-in-law's money?'

Clarissa felt her jaw drop open. 'No! No, I swear. I . . . well, I will admit, when I came over, I was worried about Oriel living in such a poky little place. But I could see she was happy. I only wanted to *help*.'

Clarissa's fingers tightened on his arm. 'We got off to such a bad start, and then all those years we didn't even talk . . .' She felt her voice begin to wobble, and her eyes to water, and cursed softly. She reached into her handbag for a hanky, and so missed the astonished expression that crossed Kier's face.

'You really mean that, don't you?' he said, so surprised he couldn't think of anything else to say.

Clarissa glanced, saw his astonishment, and smiled rue-fully. 'I'm not *that* much of a bitch,' she said wryly. 'Can't we start all over again, you and I? And if you don't want me to back any more of your films, I won't.'

Kier laughed and reached across to her. 'It's a deal,' he said, and kissed her cheek. Oriel, watching them from the other side of the room, felt a lump rise in her throat and went to collect him. She noted her mother's happy eyes and smiled. 'See you tomorrow, Mama,' she said happily, and Clarissa nodded.

Then her mother's eyes picked out those of her husband, and a troubled expression crept into them. Oriel was about to ask her what was wrong, but Kier was already tugging on her elbow. He was anxious to finish what he'd started in the back of their limo!

On the way to the hall, Frank Lockwood from Paramount waylaid him. 'Well, m'boy, you certainly scored a hit tonight. Look, not to beat about the bush — I'd like to offer you a three-film contract, right now. You can choose the genre, you can even do the screenplay. *Carte blanche*, and a budget even better than this one. What do you say?'

Kier grinned. 'I say yes please, Frank!'

In the car, Oriel leaned her head on his shoulder, and sighed tiredly. 'I'm glad it's all over,' she admitted softly, turning to run a finger over his nose, across his chin, and then tracing his lips. 'And I'm so glad you and Mama have finally patched things up.'

Kier grinned. 'She's not such a dragon after all.'

Oriel thumped him playfully. 'I think tonight has been the third-best night of my life,' she sighed.

Their house, once owned by Bogart, was only a short drive away; as they alighted from the limo, Kier nodded a curt goodnight to the driver and took Oriel possessively by the elbow. Inside were twenty-five rooms, an indoor and outdoor pool, a conservatory, a gym, a games room, en-suite bathrooms and marble flooring. And now, with *Invaders* an unqualified success, he was going to be able to pay off the mortgage in one fell swoop. Wearily they trudged up the stairs, Kier shrugging off his jacket and shirt as he did so. In the bedroom the circular bed awaited, with its over-the-top white satin headboard, sheets and canopy. Quickly, Kier stripped himself of his clothes.

Standing in front of the vanity mirror, Oriel had just taken off her jewellery when his arms snaked around her, his hands slipping flat inside her gown and covering her breasts. Oriel sighed, leaning back against his naked body, her gown cool and soft against his skin. In the mirror she watched him free her hair, kiss the nape of her neck and then sweep hot avid kisses across her naked shoulders, making her spine tingle deliciously.

'Kier,' Oriel whispered his name softly as he drew down the zip at her back and the dress rustled to the floor in a silken whisper. She was wearing no bra, and he picked her up, laying her in the middle of the round bed and staring down into her eyes as he took off her silken stockings and panties. He kissed the instep of her foot, then the backs of her knees, working up her thighs, holding them apart with firm hands as he thrust his tongue deep inside her. Oriel jerked and cried out, her peach-painted nails digging into the pillows either side of her head. Above them they were reflected in a pink-tinted mirror. Her breasts were white, her nipples stiff and red, and she could see the top of his silky head between her thighs, his arms dark and hairy across her stomach as they held her still.

'Kier!' she moaned his name urgently, pulling him up, watching as his head hovered first over one breast and then the other as he tugged passionately on her nipples.

Finally, when his lips were against hers, he whispered, 'I love you, Mrs Harcourt.'

Oriel's eyes widened as he plunged into her, big and strong, deep and sure, her eyes fixed on the mirror above her. She looked small and white and almost crushed underneath the muscular frame of her husband, whose buttocks rose and fell as he plunged into her, over and over again. The erotic image began to waver as she felt the first sweet wave of ecstasy begin to build inside her with tense, unbearable pleasure.

'Oriel!' Kier shouted her name, his voice hoarse and breathless. And then, as her legs locked around him, her vagina contracting and caressing him into a frenzy, he added gruffly, 'Don't ever leave me. I'll die!' And they both moaned their ecstasy into each other's mouths as their bodies sweetly exploded.

* * *

In their room, Clarissa slowly slipped off her tight shoes and sighed in relief. By the dresser, taking off his cufflinks, Duncan smiled at her. 'Happy, m'dear?' he asked vaguely. Clarissa hesitated, then took a deep, deep breath.

'Not really, no.'

Duncan paused, one cufflink still in his hand, and turned to look at her thoughtfully. For a long moment, man and wife stared at one another, and then Duncan smiled slowly. It was a sad but oddly relieved sort of smile.

'You want to be free, don't you, Clarry?' he asked softly, and watched her nod miserably. She ducked her head, her eyes suspiciously bright.

'Am I the only one, Duncan?' she husked, and heard her husband sigh.

'No. Perhaps not. We both did what was expected of us, old thing.' Duncan wearily put down the cufflink and glanced at his reflection in the mirror. He looked old, suddenly. 'It just wasn't enough, that's all. You're going to marry him, aren't you?' he added quietly, and Clarissa's head shot up.

'Yes,' she said at last. 'Yes, I am. When Kyle first gave me the ultimatum, I thought I'd never be able to go through with it. Divorce you, turn my back on the old way of life. Ride the gauntlet of cruel gossip to marry a man so much younger than myself. But . . . the more I thought about it, the more I knew . . . Duncan, darling, I just can't live without him. I'm so sorry. I never meant to hurt you.'

'I'll see to the lawyers as soon as we get back.'

Clarissa nodded numbly. So that was that. The safety of her old life was gone. But . . . a new life with Kyle awaited her.

CHAPTER 18

Veronica Coltrane dove neatly into the pool, resurfaced and pushed the hair from her eyes. It was six thirty in the morning, and she doubted if even Sir Mortimer was up yet. She was once again spending a weekend in the country, and she loved staying at the big house. There was something deliciously hedonistic about swimming in an indoor heated swimming pool on a Sunday morning.

Especially on a Sunday morning when you awoke to find yourself in love. Ridiculous, she knew, to fall in love so quickly, but there it was.

She touched the side of the pool, flipped neatly and began the return journey, her muscles stretching nicely. The tiles beneath her were patterned into a peacock's tail, while above her a glass dome helped the greenhouse plants littering the side of the pool to thrive. As she swam, however, her mind remained on Wayne D'Arville.

When he had caressed her in the lift at Platt's, she'd felt thrilled and afraid, like a rabbit caught in headlights. She hadn't objected to his outrageous behaviour, simply because she hadn't been able to. She'd only been able to look up into his eyes and fall prey to a shattering excitement that gnawed at her still whenever she thought about him.

And just when she'd made up her mind to try and forget him, she'd found him again — here at Sir Mortimer's. The heart-stopping stranger would actually be a colleague. It was like a miracle, and she could only wonder why she had been so lucky. She was, after all, just plain Veronica Coltrane, who had lived in Canterbury with her parents for most of her life. She was averagely pretty and had an average job. But suddenly, without warning, something extraordinary had happened to her in the guise of a tall Frenchman with heavy-lidded azure eyes who had caressed her outrageously in a lift, turning her brain to mush and her body to quivering, responsive jelly.

She closed her eyes, a slight smile on her lips as she swam mechanically, remembering the dancing last night. She had felt dwarfed in his arms, the scent of his expensive aftershave tantalizing her nostrils. She was fascinated by his voice, by its timbre and tone, making the simplest and most ordinary of words something special.

He had not asked her, as an Englishman might, 'Would you care to dance?' but instead had walked straight up to her, taken her hand and said instead, 'You will dance with me. Now . . .'

And she had. The way he never took his eyes off her all night, looking at her openly and without shame or pretence, made her feel at first flustered, but then so painfully needy that, by the time the night was over, she craved the feel of his eyes on her like a drunk craved his bottle.

Veronica was not totally naive. Although twenty-one and still a virgin, she knew enough to understand what the smouldering looks in his eyes meant, and what the corresponding melting feeling deep inside her own body signified.

A loud splash had her thoughts jerking back to the present, and she looked around, the wake at the other end of the pool warning her she was no longer alone. Her mouth went dry as he resurfaced a few feet away, his copper head darkened by the water. As Wayne stood and waded towards her, water ran in rivulets off his deep, hairless chest. He was wearing short black trunks that did little to disguise his aroused condition, and she turned towards the steps, instinct urging her to run.

She wasn't ready for this, she knew that. She was far too unsure of the game of love to play it like a professional.

Wayne reached her as she had her foot on the first step, his hand around her waist pulling her back firmly but gently. As her back pressed against his chest, she felt her heart flip in her breast. 'Wayne, I . . .'

His lips on her neck drained the energy right out of her, and she felt her legs buckle beneath her. Wayne lifted her slightly, turning her around and holding her against the tiles that surrounded the pool, her head falling back.

'Wayne,' she whispered again, not sure of what she wanted any more, now that his eyes were burning into hers and his body heat was doing strange things to her skin. She felt her nipples tingle and harden against the clammy cloth of her one-piece swimsuit, and then gasped as she felt his fingers caress her there, tweaking her between his thumb and forefinger, making her jerk in helpless reaction. She drew in a harsh breath, the sound of it shocking her.

Wayne slowly pulled the straps past her shivering shoulders, freeing her breasts that were covered with gooseflesh, rosy nipples burgeoned and uptilting.

'Wayne, please . . . I can't.'

He bent his head to her right breast and pulled on the rosy bud that trembled there, aware of her knees jerking either side of his thighs. She raised her hands to his chest, her feeble strength barely making any impression as she tried half-heartedly to push him away. He responded by taking her hands and spreading her arms out along the poolside, the action lifting her body even further from the pool, allowing him even easier access to her body.

'Someone might see!' she implored, her voice sounding thick and strange to her own ears.

In reply, Wayne left her breasts and moved up her throat, kissing and nibbling his way to her ears, where the sound of his hot amplified breath made her heart pound even harder.

'No one's up yet,' he muttered, nipping her lobe and smiling at her small moan. Over the weeks he'd found his growing fascination with Veronica Coltrane startling. He'd watched her, listened to her, asked about her, but only when his mental file on her was complete did he feel safe enough to decide that he had to have her.

Even though she was a little nobody — a little Miss Average.

He pulled down his trunks, unable to stand the pressure on his groin any longer, but was careful to turn slightly to one side so that he didn't press directly against her and frighten her away.

Gently and so subtly she was hardly aware of it at first, he pulled her swimsuit down her stomach and past her thighs.

He kissed her hard and deeply, his tongue pushing past hers in an erotic sword-dance. She thrashed in the water, the sensation so overpowering that she found it sparking off other clamouring needs deep inside her. Dimly she was aware that she was being seduced, but his hands were on her legs now, pulling the swimsuit free and running his hands over her well-shaped, naked buttocks. She gasped, her eyes widening ever further as his clever fingers parted her thighs, dipping in between to find her clitoris.

'We sh-shouldn't,' she gulped, her voice hopelessly cracked. But his hands were between her thighs now, and no matter how hard she clasped them together, his fingers still rubbed her, spreading heat and flame throughout her entire body. After a few minutes she was delirious with pleasure, uncaring about anything as the water splashed around them in time to her undulating rhythm, which was in turn dictated by his diabolical rubbing. Just when she thought she would die of it, he suddenly stopped. She whimpered, looking up at him with wide, bruised eyes.

He was only inches away now, and she could see his pupils dilate. 'Open your legs for me, Veronica,' he demanded, and she found her legs falling open magically. Before she could even think, he was between them, his hands lifting her buttocks, forcing her to grab his shoulders for support and balance. It was then that she felt the heat and strength of his throbbing shaft between her legs. Her eyes opened wide in a fleeting moment of recognition, and then Wayne thrust deep inside her, filling her.

At first there was only sudden pain, but his lips on hers quickly cut off her cry of surprise. But then, slowly, the pain began to fade, and she felt a quivering surge of relief. Then her eyes flooded with total surprise and disbelief as the relief gave way to a mounting sensation of pleasure that rose ever higher, quickly becoming a gasp-inducing ecstasy.

She found her body responding to his invasion with eagerness, as if it had been pre-programmed in some primeval lesson that her consciousness had all but forgotten. A delicious tight tension began to build deep within her. Her mouth fell open as she began to convulse, caught totally off-guard by the violence of her first orgasm. Wayne hung on to her grimly, thrusting ever more quickly, ever more deeply into her tight, hot, sweet body as he fought past the peak of his own pleasure. He kept his lips on hers as her cries of pain became cries of pleasure and he shuddered against her as his seed exploded from him, jetting deeply into her body as he, too, cried out in the final moments.

He pulled out and away from her, and swam sluggishly to the side, climbing out on limbs that felt leaden. He walked, naked and silent, to the changing rooms, and never looked back.

Veronica lay gasping in the pool, her mind slowly collecting together its shattered fragments.

In his room Wayne began to pack, the urge to leave totally overwhelming. He didn't trust women — and he didn't trust his own reaction to Veronica Coltrane. Love was a foreign thing — a disease to be avoided. Besides, he couldn't afford to be distracted when he had other things to do.

Determinedly, he shrugged her from him, like a man shrugging off an unwanted coat, and reached for the telephone by his bedside, dialling a number in Soho he'd paid twenty pounds for. It rang five times, then a sharp, openly aggressive and suspicious voice barked, 'Yeah?'

'I want to speak to Ryan. Vince gave me this number.'

'Hold on a mo'.' A few seconds later another voice came on the line, and Wayne got quickly to the point. He wanted a man by the name of Toby Platt to be set up with a call boy. It wouldn't be difficult, he told the anonymous voice, his lips twisted into a sneer. Toby Platt was a known homosexual. Once that was arranged, the dirtiest, sleaziest rag in London was to send over a photographer to catch them in the act.

Ryan, as expected, agreed at once, and when Wayne promised an extra hundred pounds for quick action, was told it could be arranged for that very night.

Wayne hung up and fastened his suitcase.

At breakfast he barely glanced at Veronica, but she didn't mind. The breakfast table was too crowded anyway, and she wanted to avoid any potentially knowing, smirking eyes. Although Sir Mortimer liked to entertain his staff and friends at these cosy little weekends, Veronica had no desire to become the unofficial entertainment.

As the meal wore on, however, Veronica realized Lady Beatrice had taken a dislike to Wayne for some reason, and it was only Sir Mortimer himself who seemed unaware of the tenseness around the table.

'I hope you enjoyed your second weekend with us, Mr D'Arville,' Beatrice gritted, 'now that you've had a chance to settle down at Platt's.'

Wayne smiled at her pleasantly. 'Very much so. I look forward to coming again.'

Beatrice's eyes flashed, but she didn't speak fast enough to forestall her husband.

'Of course you will, m'boy,' he said pleasantly, smashing down his spoon on a boiled egg. 'You'll be needing a lift back to London, I suppose? I'll get Higgins to drive you.'

'Oh, that won't be necessary, Sir Mortimer,' Veronica said quickly, with what she hoped was a bland smile. 'I have to get back too. I can give Mr D'Arville a lift.'

Sir Mortimer looked from one to the other with a twinkle in his eye. 'Of course. You'll stay to lunch, though?'

'We'd love to,' Wayne said, angry at her for leaving him no way out. His glance slewed from Veronica's openly happy smile to Beatrice's smirking one, and his hand tightened ominously on his fork.

Veronica ate little. She was still too euphoric to have an appetite. She'd never before guessed how wonderful intimacy could be. And not just the physical side of it, either. As she looked at Wayne, she felt so close to him she wanted to cry. She knew that beneath his pristine shirt was a mole on his left shoulder, and she longed to kiss it. She could still feel the memory of him inside her, and she wanted to reach across and hold his hand. Simply that. Just hold his hand. She'd had no idea how remarkable love could be.

With breakfast at an end, Beatrice suggested Veronica show Wayne the garden, since he hadn't had a chance to see it when he'd first come down, stirring up trouble with real finesse and gloating openly as Wayne reluctantly followed Veronica out into the sunshine.

Once outside, Wayne remained so strangely quiet, however, that Veronica began to feel uncertain of herself. She led him silently to the boxed rose garden, glancing at him anxiously. 'I feel . . . awkward somehow,' she eventually said, her voice coming out in a nervous laugh. 'I feel like I know everything about you. We've been working at the same office for a while, and yet, at the same time, it's as if I don't know anything at all, really. Do you feel the same about me?'

He looked at her — at her wide innocent eyes, full now with anxiety — and remembered the feel of her silken limbs around him.

He frowned. So far in his life he'd been able to fit everyone into a category — they were either his enemies, like Hans and Wolfgang, or they were to be used, like Sir Mortimer. A brief vision of kind, sherry-coloured eyes flitted across his mind, but he quickly squashed it. The last time he'd seen Sebastien Teale, he'd all but shoved past the psychiatrist with the dangerously kind, knowing eyes to run back into the safety of the crowded room. Once there, he'd kept a safe distance, never letting the American shrink get near him again. Even now, weeks later, Sebastien Teale had the ability to terrify him.

Still getting no response from the stranger who was her lover, Veronica launched nervously into the story of her life — her home, her father and her job. Her voice was innocent, her motives honest as she laughed at herself a lot, further confusing him. It was only when she mentioned her book that he found his mind sharpening.

'What sort of book?'

Veronica shrugged in embarrassment. 'It's a theory, really. An economic forecast for the coming years. I see computers as really taking off . . .' Glad at last to have some kind of response from him, she gave him a blow-by-blow account of her work to date. And as she talked, Wayne's interest sharpened even more. Having studied economics, he knew genius when he heard it. Some of the points she made were naive, and would need work, and, of course, could be phrased in much more academic terms, but even he could see that Veronica had one of those brains to which money, and the way it worked, held no mysteries. More, Veronica had an original concept that sounded, to Wayne, little short of brilliant.

'And what does Sir Mortimer think of it?' he asked curiously. He knew Sir Mortimer was already ahead of the times in his thinking, having employed a woman in the first place. Obviously, Veronica more than earned her pay.

Veronica laughed. 'He doesn't know. I haven't told a soul. Practically everyone who works at Platt's is writing a book. We're all convinced we have the secret to economic fame and fortune.'

Wayne's eyes narrowed thoughtfully. 'So no one knows about it?' he asked, his voice strangely tense. 'What about your parents? A friend? You must have told somebody?'

Veronica shook her head. 'No. Only you,' she added, her heart in her eyes. 'I wanted you to know.'

Wayne looked down into her soft, trusting eyes, then smiled and kissed her tenderly.

He needn't have worried after all, he thought, relieved. Veronica Coltrane had just slotted herself neatly into her own pigeonhole. Victim. If this book of hers was as good as he thought, of course.

Gently he took her hand in his and held it as they walked around the grounds, stopping every now and then to kiss and smell the roses.

* * *

The scandal broke on Monday morning. Buying a scandal sheet for the first time in his life, Wayne read of Toby's disgrace over a glass of orange juice and a slice of toast.

The caption read: 'Platt Boy in Homosexual Love Tangle.'

Wayne ate heartily and went to work, where the company was abuzz. Office boys whispered together in huddles and executives went around as if there was a bad smell under their noses. His own immediate superior, Alfred Hawkes, spent the entire morning shaking his head, wondering what was to become of Platt's.

Wayne, of course, knew exactly what was to become of Platt's. He worked through his lunch hour, making sure Alfred was aware that he did so. Consequently, it was mid-afternoon before he saw Veronica again. She was working at her desk and looked up, love shining in her eyes as he whispered softly, '*Bonjour.*'

'Hello. How about this for a rotten day! Poor Toby!'

Wayne shrugged a very Gallic shrug. 'I came to ask if I could read your book. You know I did a degree in economics at the Sorbonne? I could give you an honest opinion on it before you try to submit it to a publishing company.'

'Would you?' Veronica half-smiled, half-frowned, and forced back a nagging feeling of unease that was suddenly and unaccountably eating away at the back of her mind.

'OK.' She glanced around a little self-consciously, unlocked the bottom drawer of her desk and took out a thick padded envelope, and handed it over.

Wayne took it but didn't even so much as glance inside. 'Don't worry—' he leaned over and kissed her quickly '—I shall be honest but gentle, hmm?'

Veronica smiled. 'OK.'

'Dinner tonight? Yes?'

Veronica nodded, so happy she thought she'd burst. 'Yes.'

Wayne nodded and left. If the book was good, it would be easy enough to convince her it was not. And if she proved bothersome . . . well, he could always have a discreet word with Sir Mortimer. He planned to have many discreet words with the old man, now that his son had turned out to be such a disappointing embarrassment . . .

Wayne left the office at six, and went straight to the Windsor, where he bathed and changed before settling down to give the book a speed-read. She didn't have a title yet, he noticed, and wondered if that was a bad omen. The first page gave him his answer. It was not.

The book was a winner, he could tell that five minutes into his reading. Her theories were well-rounded and sweeping, but different enough to be exciting. Her predictions on computers had his heart pounding. If she was right . . . there were fortunes to be made. And a book like this meant instant kudos and fame for its author. Her money-management schemes were revolutionary and fool-proof. He'd even re-invest his own pitiful pool of money, based on her ideas.

A few hours later he was on the last chapter when a knock came at the door. An angry glance at the clock told him it was still too early for Veronica, so he carefully put the book away out of sight, and walked to the door, yanking it open.

Sebastien watched the look of panic flood his eyes before the barriers came up and a cold smile gave way to carefully blank eyes.

'Hi,' Sebastien said softly. 'You remember me?' It was not a question, for they both knew that Wayne remembered.

Silently, without knowing really why, Wayne stood aside, and Sebastien entered, looking around curiously. He saw a hotel room — neat and impersonal. There was nothing of the man in here. No pictures on the dresser. No ornaments on the shelves. Sebastien knew from Sir Mortimer Platt that Wayne had lived at the hotel for over three months now. Time enough to add some individuality to the room. But there was nothing.

Wayne stood looking at the psychiatrist, feeling curiously numb. He knew this man was dangerous — he knew it with every fibre of his being, and yet another instinct, equally as strong, was urging him to keep the American near. There was something so wonderfully . . . warm . . . about him. He could feel ice, deep in his soul, threatening to melt. The urge to talk to the man, to bare his soul, to cry and rant and rave, was almost overwhelming. The floodgates that kept the secrets of his darkened soul wanted to crumble at his feet. But why? Why this man? His own father hadn't been strong enough to bring him to his knees. Why did this man, with just his mere presence, make him feel so vulnerable? Curiosity, not something he felt very often, began to nibble at him like vicious piranhas.

He felt giddy, and curiously light-headed.

'What can I do for you?' Wayne finally asked, aware that the psychiatrist was not going to be the first to speak. His own voice sounded dry and nervous. The man's power angered him slightly, even as it intrigued him.

Deep down, he knew this man, Sebastien Teale, was his match — his equal. Younger he might be. Softer he most definitely was. But still, in some odd, terrifying way that was oddly not terrifying at all, Sebastien had the power to destroy him.

Why then was he not already busily planning how to destroy him first?

Sebastien looked at Wayne, who was staring determinedly out of the window, and said nothing. Waiting patiently until Wayne finally met his gaze head on, then, and only then did he say softly, 'I think it's more a question of what I can do for you. Isn't it . . . Wayne?'

CHAPTER 19

Spain

Andalucía lay in the deep south, an area of Spain where tourists seldom ventured, and where electricity, gas and such twentieth-century conveniences as cars and radio had yet to leave any notable mark. The extraordinarily high and crumpled mountains clustered around sun-baked, half-green valleys, where tiny villages huddled up steep slopes with houses piled high around narrow alleys. Clothes fluttered on washing lines strung between houses, and everybody seemed to be somebody else's relative.

And everyone was equally poor.

Buzzards wheeled high overhead, their sharp cries the only birdsong the bleak mountains could tolerate. Here Spanish flowed in harsh, guttural, regional dialects, and women still congregated around the village wells while men still played an ancient form of checkers around the village taverns in the morning sun.

The region invariably struck its few visitors as desolate and remote. Few trees could grow in the poor soil and those that did were twisted by the harsh mountain winds. Only a few crippled olive groves and the occasional orange orchard defied the bleak landscape by frothing forth beautiful blossom and fruit.

The village of Guajar Frontera, a humble collection of stone and earth-baked dwellings, with a pitiful square complete with defunct fountain and one grandiose residence, lay high in the hills, unchanged since its beginnings centuries ago.

No cars came to the village, except the Don's, and even that car, hardy as it was, found the mountainous tracks strenuous and the narrow alleys hazardous to its pristine paintwork.

It wound its way through the village now, its windows glinting in the sun. Sitting in the back of the Italian model, imported only last year, was Don Luis de Silva Cortez.

Don Luis was a man extremely proud of his name, never letting any of his intermittent visitors forget that his ancestry could be traced back to *the* Cortez of Mexican fame and notoriety. He even had a family tree hung up in pride of place in his palatial villa's main salon, showing the tortuous route by which he could claim his illustrious ancestry. It was a beautiful piece of workmanship, the calligraphy written in natural-dyed black ink, the capitals enscrolled with real gold and silver, the parchment hundreds of years old, cracked and creamy now with age.

Only Don Luis knew it to be a fake. But what did it matter? None of the peons in the village were going to argue, and his occasional guests, picked for their fame or wealth, were too polite to mention it.

The car slowed down as it approached the village square, where two donkeys with loaded panniers of potatoes and turnips were slowly ambling up the village's one main street.

'Frederico, get him out of the way,' Don Luis imperiously ordered his driver, impatient as always with the locals who lived in his village all year round.

The Cortezes had owned Guajar Frontera for centuries, the peasants paying him a pitiful rent for the houses, while in return he paid them a pitiful wage for working in his olive groves, orchards, farms and quarries. He had been educated in Madrid, had seen the world, had courted Italian princesses and married a Spanish countess. His home in the hills did not please him, but it was his home.

His wife had provided him with two sons, and then very decently died, leaving him free to pursue his own pleasures. He had just returned from visiting his eldest son in Barcelona but bouncing his grandson on his knee had not improved his temper or patience and the sudden blast of the car horn frightened the donkeys, who brayed loudly, kicking out filthy back legs in panic, upsetting the panniers, and dumping vegetables into the street.

The young boy leading the donkeys began to sniffle, knowing his papa was certain to beat him when he got home for bruising the vegetables. Not only would he be late, but already young children were filing into the streets and stealing the produce, and he could not run, his stick held up and shouting threats, in four different directions at once.

Balefully, he stared at the car as it crawled by. Catching a brief glimpse of the silver-haired Don, with neatly trimmed moustache, grandee beard and small black eyes, like vicious jets, the boy shuddered and crossed himself.

Once the car was out of sight, he set about beating off the tenacious thieves, quietening the donkeys, and reloading the cart. Perhaps, if he told his papa it was Don Luis's car, he would be spared the beating. For, of one accord, all the villagers hated Don Luis de Silva Cortez.

There were rumours and tales about him that curdled the blood of even the village priest. The sudden and odd disappearance of one of the Don's serving maids, brought back from Seville, was still not forgotten, fifteen years after the fact, and Carlos Montoya swore he heard someone screaming up at his villa late at night.

The Villa Cortez was situated on the very outskirts of the village, its grand architecture and opulence set apart from the ramshackle, ugly group of houses, much to Don Luis's delight. It overlooked the valley, and had fruit orchards to its right, and a formal garden spread on the north, east and west borders. Here the fountains worked perfectly and modern technology thrived in the form of sprinklers, carefully timed, to give the Villa Cortez lush lawns and exotic blooms. A generator provided the villa with as much electricity as was needed to power the heated pool, the sauna, the private cinema screen, the kitchen with its vast ovens and the electric chandeliers hung in practically every room.

Don Luis alighted from the car and stepped onto the paved driveway, his white suit a little crumpled. He was a small man, no more than five feet five, and thin as a whippet. He walked with a silver-topped ebony cane, and as he approached the portico, the tap-tap of his stick could be heard echoing inside the villa where doors were left constantly open to catch the cooling mountain breeze. The heat, high in the unprotected mountains, was phenomenal.

Rosita Alvarez, one-time maid to the D'Arvilles of Monte Carlo, heard the cane and went as cold as ice. She was in the kitchen, preparing the prosciutto with figs for the first course for his midday meal. His leanness was misleading, as she had soon found out. He ate like a horse and demanded the best. Quickly she wiped her hands on the voluminous white apron she wore and glanced nervously at her little daughter, now nearly six years old, playing with a straw doll the gardener's boy had made for her. Thankfully, she looked nothing like her father, the devil called Wayne.

'Maria, *por favor*, go play outside,' Rosita said quickly.

Sometimes Rosita remembered to speak English to the little girl, sometimes not. Vaguely she had a half-formed idea, more of a hope than a plan, that her child would one day somehow escape from the village of her birth, with its rigid social strata that had placed her, as a hated bastard Americano, at the bottom of the heap.

Some way, Rosita and her daughter would make their way back to civilization.

Of Wayne D'Arville she had forced herself not to think at all. The harsh, ugly years had not been kind to Rosita.

233

Now, as Maria Alvarez glanced up from her straw doll, she saw not the beautiful woman Rosita had once been, but only her mama, with a streak of premature grey at her temples, and worried eyes surrounded by creases, her face tired and defeated.

'*Madre*, I don't want to play on the garden,' she wheedled in her imperfect English, jutting out her bottom lip and looking mutinous.

The tap-tapping of the cane came closer, and Rosita glanced fearfully across her shoulder, her anxiety rising to fever pitch.

'Maria, *rápidamente*. If you go, I will take you to the supermercado in Arcos de la Frontera tomorrow. *Sí*?' she begged, near to tears now.

The promise of a trip to the nearest town, with its brand-new supermarket, was enough to make Maria's eyes glow. 'You promises? And can we buy some pasta *de dientes*?'

'Yes, yes, you can have some toothpaste,' Rosita promised, not bothering to scold her daughter for her vanity.

Although she was still only a child, Maria nevertheless seemed aware of her extraordinarily delicate beauty that, even at such a tender age, set her apart from the rest of the earthy peasant children of the village.

Almost beside herself now that she heard the outer door to the kitchen swing open, Rosita hissed urgently, 'But only if you go now. Right this moment!'

Maria quickly scampered up, her long legs allowing her to run through the open door and out into the vegetable garden by the orchard just as Don Luis entered the kitchen, bringing with him the scent of Havana cigars and terror.

Briefly Maria heard his voice say in purring Spanish, 'Ah, there you are, my little harlot. I have been away too long from my house and my comforts, I think . . .'

Maria realized she'd left her doll behind, but she did not go back to the kitchen. She did not like Don Luis, although she always curtsied when he spoke to her, as her mother had told her to, and he sometimes gave her a sweet.

But she never felt safe around him, which was strange. All the other servants pinched her and tripped her up and called her horrid names. The Don never did such things, and yet she felt she would rather be with the spiteful village women who pulled her hair than sit on the Don's lap as he sometimes insisted she did.

She sighed now, a heavy sigh that shook her little body, making Juan, the gardener's boy busy tending radishes, glance her way and grin. 'Hey, *chiquita*. Why the long face, hmm?' he asked her, his voice thick with an accent that was missing from the cultured, smooth voice of Don Luis.

'Nothing, Juan,' Maria lied, coming closer to watch him wield the hoe in the dusty earth. But she followed it a moment later with, 'Why is *Madre* afraid of Don Luis, Juan?' She noticed immediately the way the candid brown eyes suddenly slewed nervously away.

Maria noticed many things. She was brighter than the other children, even though they went to school where the *padre* taught them the rudiments of reading and writing. They did not realize that Rosita taught her daughter privately, late at night, after stealing books from the Don's library, forcing the little girl to learn English as well. With a determination that bordered on obsession, Rosita taught her daughter not only the rudiments of a basic education, but much more.

As much as she was able, Rosita taught her daughter about the modern world, about cars, huge cities, people as different from the suspicious, hardened villagers as it was possible to be. Maria's eyes would widen as she listened to the stories of Monte Carlo, her imagination allowing her to see the palm trees, the lush gardens of hotels bigger than all of the village put together.

Maria hated the servants at the villa who called her *bastarda* and never let her play with their own precious sons and daughters. She cried herself to sleep every night, but the next day she would stick out her proud little chin at the villagers, who treated every stranger with suspicion and distrust, and threw stones at her whenever she walked down the streets.

'Nobody likes the patron,' Juan whispered now, looking around to make sure that not even his whisper could be overheard. 'But you must never say so. Without the Don, we would all starve,' he repeated the words hammered into him by his own parents since he was old enough to understand. The Don was all-powerful, and without him they would all perish. The Don owned the land, so he owned everything. Including the villagers.

Maria scowled, the answer insulting her simplistic, childish logic. If people could live in cities as big as the mountains, then people could live without Don Luis, surely? Maria sighed and shrugged, and looked back at the villa. The Don would have left the kitchen by now, wouldn't he?

Saying *adios* to the only friend she had at the villa, she walked back on tiptoe, peering cautiously into the kitchen which was now empty. Good. She sneaked in and picked up her doll, then suddenly jumped, her eyes widening, her heart hammering at the sound of her mother's muffled scream.

It came from their room — a small, box-like room, with a single mattress on the floor which they both shared, a crucifix on the wall, a single rickety chair and a chipped washstand.

Maria licked her lips nervously, but curiosity goaded her on. With typical childish craftiness, she took off her shoes and left them by the door, then walked silently down the cool passage, dodging the cook and one of the other maids to pause outside the door of their cell-like room.

Slowly and carefully, her little heart thumping, she turned the handle very slowly, barely a quarter of an inch at a time. She could hear muffled sounds coming from within; her mother's voice, begging for something, and Don Luis, laughing.

But she couldn't make out what her mother was asking for because she was sobbing so hard, the noise making Maria's own eyes fill with tears of sympathy and a nasty kind of creeping fear.

She pushed the door open a crack, her eyes widening at what she saw. Her mother was lying flat on her stomach on the mattress, her face buried in a pillow. She was stark naked, and kneeling above her, Don Luis was also naked. He was sweating like a pig, and his lips were pulled back over his teeth in a feral smile. But Maria's eyes barely glanced at his face, for she was too fascinated by the thing between his legs. It was long and thin and red, and he kept touching it. Then his hands parted Rosita's buttocks and the red thing was pushing down into her.

Rosita's body convulsed and she moaned in pain. Briefly Maria felt the urge to run into the room, to launch herself at the Don, to punch him and bite him and scratch him like she did the cook's daughters, who were always picking on her. Even though she was always punished for fighting back, Maria felt her hands clench into fists.

The pig was hurting her mummy. She wanted to kill him. If she had Juan's knife now, she would kill him! She would, would, *would*!

But even as she put one foot forward, she suddenly felt a strange sense of shame steal over her and could almost taste the disgust that her mother must be feeling. Without really knowing why, Maria was suddenly sure that her mother would hate it if she knew that Maria was there, that she had seen what was happening to her.

So instead of launching herself in fury at the Don, Maria silently closed the door on the ugly scene and ran out into the orchard, passing a startled Juan, who watched her hurtling body with interested eyes and then glanced back at the beautiful villa basking in the sun. All the servants knew how the Don used Rosita Alvarez, of course. But what could she expect? Coming back to the village of her birth in disgrace, with a bastard child, after her father had worked so hard to work passage to France? What chance had any of them had to escape?

Juan shrugged and got back to his hoeing.

Deep in the orchard, Maria leant against an orange tree, her arms around the trunk, her face pressed against the rough bark. She cried savagely, great howls of anguish that shuddered her whole frame, making her throat ache and her eyes and nose run.

Young though she was, she knew she had witnessed a forbidden scene, one that she must never, ever repeat to anyone. They would only blame her *madre*, anyway. Nobody ever blamed the Don for anything.

But she hated the Don now. The Don with his red thing and his ugly words, calling her mother a whore. She would never forget, or forgive. Never.

Never.

By one o'clock, the Don's five-course lunch was ready. Maria, dry-eyed now, went back to the kitchens where the cook had prepared the last tray, and was ordering her mother to scrub out the ovens. Maria hid until the cook had gone, her ample girth making her waddle like a duck, and then slowly walked into the room.

Rosita glanced up at her and smiled wanly. 'Hello, baby. Are you hungry?'

Maria nodded, although she could not look at her mother without remembering what she had just seen and feeling sick. Quickly Rosita cut open a crusty roll, adding to it a runny goat's cheese and sliced tomato. She handed it over, looking behind her to make sure no one was looking, and then cut a huge slice of banana cake and gave it to her daughter.

She was beyond caring that the cook would notice it missing and heap yet more abuse on her head.

'*Madre*, why have we to stay here?' Maria asked plaintively. Rosita corrected her grammar automatically, before shrugging. Once, a long time ago, she had promised herself that her job at the villa would only be until her baby was born, and then she would leave. Once, she had still believed she could make a decent life for herself and her daughter. But no more. Spain was not Monte Carlo.

'We have nowhere else to go, Maria. In this life it is money that matters. Only money. Not goodness, or being right, or being clever. If you have money, you can do anything, be anything you like and no one will stop you.'

Her eyes became harder than ever, her mouth thinning into such a bitter line that her lips almost disappeared. Maria hung her head, shuffling in her chair and then taking a desultory bite out of her roll.

Her mother had told her all this before, but she didn't understand the vehemence and hatred that crept into Rosita's usually kind and gentle voice whenever she mentioned leaving.

'*Madre*,' she said slowly, thinking that now was as good a time as any to ask a question that had been burning in her brain ever since Anita de Avalonso had told her that her father was an Americano dog, '*Madre*, won't my *padre* help us to leave?'

Rosita glanced at her daughter sharply, her lips twisting into an ugly sneer, the hatred so obvious on her once-pretty face that Maria took a quick, instinctive step backwards. 'Your *padre*,' Rosita spat, 'was the reason we were left to rot in this stinking hole in the first place. He doesn't care whether we live or die. He . . .'

They heard the cook returning, Maria already backing out of the room as Rosita fell to her knees to ferociously scrub the oven, her hands red and chapped and soon beginning to bleed against the wire wool and wood.

Maria took her booty out into the orchard where she ate the banana cake but left the roll. In her mind she linked Don Luis with her *padre*. Her *madre* hated them both the same and she would too.

She left the orchard after feeding her roll to the sparrows, and walked towards the tropical house, where Don Luis grew his orchids. Some were rare, so the cook said, and worth thousands of pesos.

Maria could hardly imagine such a thing. Who would pay so much just for flowers? You couldn't eat them.

The greenhouse was off limits, but today Maria didn't care. Walking to the glasshouse, she peered in, then gave a muffled scream as she came face to face with Don Luis, who had been bending down to water some seedlings.

Maria backed away slowly, not understanding, but instinctively shivering under the speculative gaze from the small black eyes as they ran over her body dressed in a faded pink smock.

As she turned and fled, she prayed piteously for somebody, anybody, to help her and her *madre* to escape the village. To escape the Don.

But deep inside, she already knew that nobody would.

CHAPTER 20

After three months, the scandal at Platt's was old news. Other events had taken place to fill in the countless hours of gossip, and clubs and restaurants now buzzed with hushed conversations on newer, juicier disasters. Only Toby and his long-suffering wife still suffered from the backlash. Sent to a family estate in the highlands of Scotland with strict instructions to lie low and keep their heads down, Toby's presence was now hardly missed in the London offices or the Berkshire mansion.

Wayne D'Arville pulled up to the front of the now familiar mansion in his second-hand Bentley, old enough to look a classic, new enough to be within his budget, and cut the engine. Since Toby's disgrace, he had motored down to the house practically every other weekend, much to Beatrice's distress. Sir Mortimer's wife was in a quandary about the man she both desired and feared, and had decided today was the day to do something about it.

Looking out of the library window, Beatrice watched him alight, her eyes narrowing as two distinct emotions assailed her — anger and pleasure. She had never seen a man more masculinely pleasing. Neither had she met one who rivalled herself in cunning, deceit, manipulation and downright ruthlessness. At first the game had been fun, the barbed comments, the sexual punch whenever their eyes met, the rivalry of cat and mouse. But that had been in the beginning, when she had thought herself the cat. Now things had changed. Alfred Hawkes, her husband's right-hand man at Platt's, had retired, and in his place Wayne D'Arville had somehow managed to reign supreme.

The scandal with Toby couldn't have come at a worse time; as she watched Wayne jog lightly up the steps, she was convinced he was behind the whole thing. And Mortimer, the idiot, was playing right into his hands. Long into the night, the two of them would sit in his study talking about this marvellous new book of Wayne's Mortimer was so keen on. She could picture them clearly: Mortimer sniffing into his brandy and bemoaning his son while the Frenchman, damn him, comforted, wheedled, and oh-so-carefully ingratiated himself. It was enough to make Beatrice want to spit.

Now Wayne was such a regular visitor that Mortimer would comment on it late on a Friday night if he hadn't appeared. His talk was full of the Frenchman — the good job he had done on the French connection, the new European department he was setting up, the damned book that was going to change the face of current economic thinking.

Beatrice let the lace curtain swing back into place, her eyes thoughtful. She had to do something. Fast. Wayne bloody D'Arville was making himself too indispensable, setting himself up too well as the ideal surrogate son. With Toby and Amanda languishing already forgotten in Scotland, there was no one but herself to tackle the interloper. And tackle him she would. She opened the French windows, her eyes scanning the stables for John. She was feeling in the mood for the groom, admitting to herself that it was the Frenchman's arrival that had prompted the desire to light up her body. Catching the groom's eye, she nodded to the upper floors and John, who knew the route to her room via the servants' back stairs as well as he knew the back of his own hand, nodded and held up both hands, indicating ten minutes.

From the study Wayne watched the by-play and smiled slowly.

'Hmm . . . good opening, I must admit,' Sir Mortimer said, making Wayne turn to look at him questioningly. The old man looked older than ever, his fingers gnarled and trembling as he turned over the pages of the manuscript. He had totally rewritten Veronica's manuscript, of course, making it sound more academically significant, and carefully writing, in his own hand, notes in the margin. He'd made sure it also sounded as if it had been written by a Frenchman. No one would now believe Veronica, if she were foolish enough to try and tell anyone the book was really her work.

'I'm glad you think so,' he smiled modestly.

'Language needs a bit of tightening up, though,' Sir Mortimer said. 'Make it less . . . foreign-sounding. Hope you don't mind if I put a good editor onto it?'

Wayne almost laughed out loud. 'Of course not.'

Sir Mortimer grunted. 'Always knew you had a good head on your shoulders. Nothing of the prima donna about you either, praise be!'

'Look, I'll leave you in peace to make any notes on it you want. Then, after dinner, perhaps you can give me a good idea of which publisher to approach?'

'I'll do that. And if this—' he tapped the manuscript '—has as much impact as I think it will, you might as well have a seat on the board while we're at it. Platt's could always use the kudos of having an economic genius at its board table.'

Wayne turned at the door, an astonished, then sheepishly gratified look on his face. 'I don't know what to say, Si— Mortimer. I certainly never expected it.'

'Well, well, it hasn't happened yet,' Sir Mortimer said gruffly, waving him away, but his old face was smiling and well pleased.

Wayne left, closing the door softly behind him, then beckoned the butler and told him to ask the groom, when he'd finished with his other duties, to give his car a wash and waxing. That done, he walked quickly up the stairs to the room where Lady Beatrice slept alone at night. How she had managed to wangle the separate sleeping arrangements he wasn't sure and didn't care. It was time he dealt with Lady Beatrice once and for all.

He opened the door, his eyes making a quick inventory of the room. The deep maroon velvet curtains were drawn, throwing the room into semi-darkness. Lady Beatrice lay in the middle of a four-poster bed, completely naked, wearing only a black velvet sleeping mask. Wayne slowly smiled and walked across the Savonnerie carpet, past the Venetian mirrors, the Louis XIV bergères, the Sheraton tables and beautiful matching armchairs, his eyes fixed on the woman on the bed. She had kept herself well, he saw at once, for her body was still slender and appealing.

She sighed, twisting on the bed, her mouth curling up into a smile. 'Hurry, John,' she whispered, patting the bed with her hands invitingly, and Wayne glanced at the bed, then at the door behind him, and then smiled, reaching for the buttons of his Savile Row jacket.

Beatrice heard the rustle of clothes being removed and smiled like a cat, stretching luxuriously, her body pleasantly tingled and trembling in anticipation. Wayne, naked now, sat on the side of the bed and reached for her calf, trailing a hand across the smooth expanse of shaved skin. He stared at the black mask across her eyes, his hardening body already burning with desire. He knew damned well she would never have slept with him willingly, knowing that withholding her body was practically the only weapon she had at her disposal. She had no real power over Sir Mortimer since failing to produce another heir, and they both knew it.

'Hmm . . . yes,' Beatrice murmured, her legs falling open as he knelt either side of them, his free hand coming to her other calf, slowly moving to the back of her knees and then further up her thighs. She was wet already, her triangle of corn-coloured hair moist and waiting. Watching her closely, he slipped two fingers between the glistening red lips and began to move them tantalizingly. Beatrice moaned and licked her lips, her heels digging into the white satin quilt as she shuddered in brief climax.

Quickly, Wayne delved his tongue into her navel and then travelled higher. He kissed every part of her breasts in slowly decreasing circles until his lips fastened over her nipples. When her hands lifted to caress his back he caught them quickly and pinned them either side of her head, so that she could not feel the lack of hair on his back, or the size of his shoulders. John was smaller and certainly more hirsute than himself.

'Hurry, hurry,' she urged him, her voice thick with desire, and Wayne smiled, opening her thighs with his own and pressing the tip of his penis against her. 'Yes, yes, hurry!' she moaned again, and Wayne grinned savagely.

'Anything you say, *cherie*,' he whispered in French. Beatrice stiffened, and behind the black velvet her eyes struggled to open. Her hands began to twist in his grip as she struggled to free herself.

'You French bast—' she began, but then his lips were on hers and he plunged deep inside her. Beatrice felt her body convulse at the invasion. Never had she felt a penis that big inside her before. Beatrice moaned under his lips, in frustration at first and then in helplessly growing passion. She could feel her muscles stretching to accommodate him, could feel him pushing up, up, up all the way into her womb. She wanted to scream, to curse him, to kill him for doing this to her, but already a shattering climax was upon her. She bucked and shuddered, and still Wayne kept up the erotic rhythm, watching her sweating face only an inch away with savage satisfaction. But it was not enough. Quickly he yanked off the mask. He wanted her to see who was mounting her, so that she would never forget. Her eyes snapped open, spitting hate, fire and passion in equal proportions.

'I'll kill you for this,' she panted, and Wayne laughed, increasing the rhythm to even faster, deeper thrusts, watching her face contort helplessly as she once again began to climax. Quickly he released his seed into her, his collapsing weight pinioning her to the bed.

Beatrice dragged in deep gulps of air, ripples of pleasure still seeping through her body minutes later. His breath back to normal, Wayne quickly got off her and pulled on his clothes.

'Thank you, Lady Platt. That was very nice,' he said, his voice painstakingly English now, even down to the upper-crust accent.

Beatrice watched him walk to the door, and gave a yowl of hatred, picking up a delicate Meissen vase worth easily a thousand pounds and lobbing it at his head. But Wayne was already out of the door, listening to the china shatter harmlessly on the other side. All he had to do now was wait until she was entertaining the real John again, and then find an excuse to send Sir Mortimer into the room. That would put paid to any poison she might try to whisper into the old man's ear about him. As he walked back to his room, he began to whistle.

* * *

In London, Veronica was dining with Sebastien and Sir Julius.

'Hmm, this is delicious,' Veronica complimented Sir Julius's cook on the beef Wellington, her mouth pleasantly full.

'Well, when I knew you were coming, I made enough for six,' Sir Julius teased her, watching her eyes widen at the insult, before she began to laugh, putting a hand to her mouth as she attempted to swallow the tender beef.

'You pig. Isn't he a pig, Sebastien?' Veronica appealed for support.

'He oinks when he walks,' Sebastien agreed, his face dead-pan as he reached for his glass that held a fruity red Bordeaux. Opposite him, Veronica began to choke on her food.

Sir Julius slapped her back heartily, then turned to Sebastien. 'You see? I can't take her anywhere,' he complained. 'Even as a little girl no higher than my kneecap, she ate like a gannet. Tell her something interesting — it's the only thing that stops her wolfing down her food.'

Veronica threw her napkin at Sir Julius, who fielded it neatly with his fork.

Sebastien grinned. 'We certainly can't let her choke, can we? That's not at all gallant. Let me see . . . Well, there have been some interesting psychological experiments done recently.'

'Oh, goodie,' Veronica enthused, batting her eyelashes extravagantly. 'Do tell!'

Sebastien blinked under the battery of eyes suddenly watching him and grinned. 'Well, one done in America last year had to do with measuring conformity.' Veronica stared at him blankly. 'What happens is that a volunteer is put into a room with three or four stooges,' Sebastien explained.

'Stooges?' Veronica looked puzzled.

'Hmm, assistants of the doctors — not genuine guinea pigs. The tester gives the stooges and the genuine testee a simple sum — say 15 plus 34 plus 58. Something like that.'

'A hundred and seven,' Sir Julius said promptly.

'I'll take your word for it,' Sebastien grinned. 'Anyway, the plants each give the answer as 106, say. Now the testee may have got the right answer, and he probably tallied it up again, and still came up with the right answer. But in some instances, he'll say 106 as well.'

'So that he doesn't stand out in the crowd,' Veronica said, understanding the reasons why most people would do the same.

'Huh,' Sir Julius snorted. 'I'd say 107, no matter what.'

'You would,' Sebastien said fondly, then leaned back as the housekeeper brought in the plates and a fresh coffee and walnut gateau.

'I hate you,' Veronica said, staring at the luscious dessert. 'You want me to get fat — admit it.'

'You don't want any, then?' Sir Julius asked, winking at Sebastien as he cut a fair-sized wedge and handed it over to him.

'Not fair!' Veronica wailed. 'I want a bigger piece.'

'Didn't I say she was gannet?' Sir Julius groaned, cutting the cake in half and lumping it onto a dish, setting it before his startled guest. Veronica shot Sir Julius a killer look, then reached for her spoon.

'How are things at Platt's nowadays?' Sebastien asked Veronica later, when they were all sitting on the settee, sipping coffee and trying to digest their huge meal.

'Oh, not so bad. Toby never really did much work anyway, and now that Wayne . . . well, he and Sir Mortimer are getting on really well. Wayne's set up a European department that's doing killer business. Everyone is going around with a big grin on their face. Especially the accounts department. The initial expenditure Sir Mortimer forked out is already showing signs of paying off.'

'So, it's back to normal, then,' Sebastien said softly, then added very casually, 'Are you and Wayne still seeing each other?'

Veronica flushed, then smiled, her face so open and happy that Sebastien felt a trickle of unease drip down his spine and land in the pit of his stomach. Beside him, he felt Sir Julius stiffen.

'Oh yes,' Veronica murmured, thinking of the nights they spent together making love. Her world couldn't be better. And yet . . . 'He's wonderful,' she said softly, and Sir Julius glanced at Seb.

For months now, ever since Sebastien had gone to Wayne's hotel room to ask him to let him help, he'd been seeing Wayne on a strictly casual basis.

Whenever he and Wayne met for lunch or the occasional trip to the theatre or musical concert, Sebastien would write up his meticulous and detailed notes, then pace about restlessly. But even though Sir Julius knew that he regarded Wayne as a patient, the old man was worried. Sebastien, of course, never discussed what the Frenchman's problems were, but Sir Julius was deeply concerned that Wayne D'Arville was much more seriously disturbed than Sebastien knew. For all his natural potential, Sebastien was still very young and inexperienced.

Now Sebastien said carefully to Veronica, 'Just be careful not to take things too fast. That isn't always good for a man, you know.'

'Oh, but Wayne's different,' Veronica said quickly. *Too* quickly. Her defence of him lacked conviction, and Sir Julius could hear the stress in her voice. 'He's a wonderful man, he really is. I . . .' She met Sebastien's devastatingly kind sherry-coloured eyes, so lacking in judgement and so knowing, and faltered to a halt. 'Sometimes,' she said, her voice less strident, more afraid, 'I get the feeling . . .'

'Yes?'

'I don't know how to explain it. I get the feeling he isn't always . . . well . . . aware of things. It's as if life is just something he gets through . . . He seems to see things in black and white, with no shades of grey . . . Oh, hell, I can't seem to put it into words.'

'It's all right,' Sebastien said soothingly. 'I understand. And I think he sees a lot more black than white.' He wondered, in fact, if Wayne saw any white at all. From what little he'd said about his childhood, Sebastien knew that he suffered from maternal deprivation for a start.

A long time ago, psychologist Seymour Levine had raised rats, half of which he petted and stroked daily, half of which he left totally alone. The petted ones opened their eyes sooner, showed less fear in strange situations and were less emotional. From such humble beginnings came the theory that maternal deprivation led to 'affectionless psychopathy'. And the more he saw of Wayne, the more convinced he became that the Frenchman felt nothing for people, but saw them only in distinct categories, as either threats, victims or allies. And that, Sebastien knew, was only the beginning of his problems. Sebastien had watched him carefully, noting how deeply he felt insults, always reacting way over what could safely be termed 'normal' to emotional stimuli. But how could he explain any of this to Veronica, who was so in love with the man it scared him? Nevertheless, he felt the need to warn her. But before he could speak, she turned to look at him intently.

'You know that Wayne is always talking about you, don't you? I don't think he has any other friends. He never talks about them, anyway, and I've never seen him with anyone. Even when he left the Windsor and moved into his new flat, he never invited anyone over for a housewarming party.'

Sebastien nodded, well aware of how Wayne regarded him — as a cross between a father confessor and a possible victim. After visiting him at the Windsor that night, Seb had been constantly aware of how dangerous the game was that he was playing with the Frenchman. It would have been all too easy for Wayne to have pigeon-holed him as yet another threat, and the fact that he hadn't — that over the months he had gradually allowed Sebastien to become his confidant and even his friend — was due solely to Sebastien's skill.

Of course, Wayne lied to him. He was sure that the family background Wayne had given him about the wine business back in France was totally false, but that, in itself, was irrelevant. Wayne, fascinated by Sebastien and their growing friendship, talked much more than he realized. Sebastien already knew that his mother had rarely shown him physical affection, that from an early age his parents had expected little from him, and there was strong evidence of psychopathic sibling rivalry. In particular, though, Sebastien was very worried about the way Wayne saw his father. Concerned with protecting Veronica and touched by her innocence and warmth, he found himself, very uncharacteristically, abandoning his usual tact. 'I think Wayne is deeply disturbed, Veronica,' he said gently. 'I think he is capable of doing almost anything . . .'

Veronica blinked, totally unprepared for Sebastien — kind, gentle Sebastien — to say something so cruel, and she reacted instinctively, quashing down a small voice in her brain that was already telling her that she was not surprised at all. 'That's not true,' she denied hotly. 'You just don't like

Wayne, do you?' she accused them. 'Neither of you do. Did you think I was too blind to see that?'

Sebastien reached for her quickly. 'No, it's not that. You don't understand . . .'

Veronica stood up stiffly. 'I understand that Wayne needs you. I think he needs a friend, and I had hoped you'd be good for him. But if you're going to put him down behind his back . . .'

She was halfway to the door and openly crying, with Sebastien close behind her when Sir Julius held him back. 'Let her go,' he advised softly. 'She's not in the mood to listen. I'll ring her up tomorrow and talk to her. I'll tell her, for what it's worth, that I agree with your diagnosis.'

Outside, Veronica felt ashamed of herself for the scene she'd just created. She sniffled and hailed a taxi, knowing full well the real reason behind her emotionalism.

She was pregnant.

* * *

The following Monday Veronica waited nervously for Wayne in his office, pushing Sebastien's warning to the back of her mind. She was sure Wayne would marry her and was equally sure he would be thrilled about the baby. After all, Frenchmen were notorious for delighting in big families, weren't they?

Five minutes later Wayne opened the door to his new office, his eyes narrowing on her for a moment before he smiled. 'Hello.' He shrugged off his coat, glad in a way to find her there. He had to tell her about the book some time.

'Wayne, I have something to . . .' she began nervously, licked her lips, fidgeted, then said in one quick breath, 'I'm pregnant. Isn't that marvellous?'

Wayne stared at her for a moment, then slowly sat down, visibly shocked. This was no Spanish maid about to produce a bastard offspring, but a respectable English girl. The thought of a son and heir was appealing for one brief moment, but then he shook his head. He could produce an heir any time, that was obvious, but the book and the chance of making some real money was different. He had to seize *that* opportunity now.

'I see,' he said, his cool, thoughtful words giving her a premonition of what was to come. Slowly she sank down onto a chair and swallowed hard. 'I have something to tell you as well. I took your manuscript to Berkshire with me. I've spent the last few weeks totally rewriting it. Tidying it up. It was rather naive in places.' He lifted his head and looked her straight in the eye. 'I told Sir Mortimer that I had written it.'

Veronica blinked. She'd been so focused on her own news that at first she couldn't take in what he'd said. 'What did he think of it?'

'He loved it. I'm going to publish it. Under my name, of course,' he added the last words with quiet finality, watching as the excitement faded from her face. He'd been getting far too fond of Veronica Coltrane recently. This was the perfect opportunity to cut her out of his life once and for all. The thought should have pleased him, but he was suddenly assailed by a feeling of bereft despair. He clenched his hands together tightly.

'Under your name. But . . . Wayne, you can't be serious. Having a book published is like a dream come true. I'm glad, really grateful to you for taking it to Sir Mortimer, but you can't really mean to publish it with your name on it . . .' Her voice trailed off, her mind refusing to believe what her heart already knew. 'You think it will sell better under a man's name, is that it? You're right of course. I could always use yours as a pseudonym.' She was babbling now and knew it. But her heart was breaking, her head was whirling, and she needed something, some single sane thought, to hold on to. He couldn't be betraying her like this. *He just couldn't.*

Wayne needed to be angry with her now. Very angry. No doubt she wanted to believe the best of his motives, and it was touching in a way. She probably even thought he was going to marry her because of the child she was carrying.

But how could she have been so careless as to get pregnant in the first place? Didn't she realize she was trying to ruin everything for him? She didn't love him. If she did, she'd stand by him, damn her.

'I told Sir Mortimer I wrote it, and as far as he's concerned, that's that,' he said flatly, his hands clenching and unclenching on the desk. 'I've already signed the deal with the publishers. Quite simply, I need the royalties, Veronica. The flat and the car and living at the Windsor all those months left me practically broke.'

Veronica slowly shook her head, her face pale, her eyes bruised dark pools in her face. 'Wayne, you can't . . .' she began, but suddenly Sebastien's words came flitting back into her mind. *He's capable of anything* . . . And he was right.

Suddenly, her pain fled, and in its place was a growing, healthy surge of anger.

'You won't get away with this,' she warned him, her voice hardening as she got up and slowly backed away. 'I won't let you.'

'Oh?' Wayne slowly raised an eyebrow, looking nonchalant and amused. 'And why not? Who knows you were even writing a book, *cherie*?' he asked, almost feeling sorry for her. It must be terrible to be so stupid. 'I already have the manuscript with my name on it' — he nodded towards the safe set in his new office wall — 'along with your pathetic original.'

Veronica's eyes followed the direction of his and froze. Suddenly she realized how vulnerable she was. There was only one copy of her original manuscript, and surely Wayne would destroy that now? At the same time, she suddenly remembered that, as an executive officer, she too had keys to her own office safe. And all the safes might open with the same key. They were designed to keep company papers safe from burglars, not to keep out other executives. If she came back tonight and took back her manuscript . . . Possession was nine-tenths of the law. She could take it to Sir Mortimer and explain. He'd listen to her. She'd worked at Platt's for over three years, after all.

'Sebastien was right about you,' she said at last, her voice full of contempt. She was also bitterly aware of the way he had suddenly come alive at the mention of the American's name. It hurt even now to realize that her love and her belief in him meant nothing.

'What did he say?' Wayne demanded sharply, always eager for news about Sebastien. Sebastien, the greatest danger in his life. Sebastien, his obsession.

But Veronica shook her head, too sick at heart to bear it another moment. She stumbled through the door, wounded to her soul. She felt sick but fought the urge to crawl into some dark corner and die. She would fight back. She was not her father's daughter for nothing.

Wayne leaned back in the chair and glanced at the safe. Slowly he shook his head in a mixture of pity and contempt. She was so transparent, she might as well have broadcast her thoughts aloud.

That night, when she came back to sneak into his offices and open the safe, the police were waiting for her.

* * *

Two weeks later, Sebastien and Sir Julius left a top criminal lawyer's office, having secured his services for Veronica's defence. Sir Julius had tried to talk Sir Mortimer out of prosecuting, but the old man had been adamant.

It was the principle of the thing, he had insisted. The betrayal of trust. And to accuse Wayne of the things she had . . . No, Sir Mortimer had been vindictive in his determination that Veronica Coltrane should stand trial.

Sebastien understood why, of course. Having been so disappointed in Toby, Sir Mortimer simply *couldn't* and *wouldn't* face the possibility that Wayne, too, might let him down. And, to be fair to him, the evidence in favour of Wayne, and against Veronica, was overwhelming.

Outside the lawyer's office, Sir Julius sighed deeply. 'Sir Mortimer needs his golden boy. If only Veronica had told somebody, *anybody*, about the book . . .'

Sebastien sighed deeply. He had been allowed to visit Veronica only briefly. She had still been in shock then, uncommunicative, dull-voiced and without hope. She told him about the baby and the book in flat tones, as if she was reciting a recipe. She seemed unaware of the grimness of her surroundings, unaware of the possibility of being found guilty of attempted burglary and serving time.

Listening to her, watching her, Sebastien felt more and more guilty. He should have foreseen it somehow. He should have followed her that night she'd left Sir Julius's flat, and explained . . . But how? He could not break Wayne's trust. To do so would be totally irresponsible and against all his training. Besides, he was well aware that one false move on his part could send Wayne plummeting into insanity. And he had seen too many drowning souls at St Edmund's to do that to anybody, regardless of what they had done.

He told the investigating officer about Veronica's claim to the book, but nobody believed Veronica's version. Literary experts called in by Platt's were unanimous in their verdict that the writer had been male, foreign — probably French — with a distinctly academic background, and nobody was going to go against Sir Mortimer's favourite.

'He didn't sound very optimistic,' Sir Julius said now as they left the offices of Jackson, Smythe and Cruickshank in Tate Square, thinking back over the interview with the sharp-eyed, no-nonsense barrister who had laid the cards straight on the table.

'No, he didn't,' Sebastien agreed, unaware that other eyes watched him as they got into Sir Julius's car and drove away. A few cars back in the line of traffic, Wayne followed them, feeling cold and empty.

He'd seen Sebastien only once since the arrest, and although he couldn't admit it, even to himself, he felt scared. The soft sherry-coloured eyes had been harder than he'd ever known them, the voice not quite so soothing. And now his hands trembled on the wheel.

'You think she's telling the truth, don't you?' Sir Julius said in the back of his Bentley as his driver stopped at a red light.

Sebastien nodded grimly. 'I'm sure of it.'

'What did Wayne say when you confronted him?'

Sebastien was silent for a long while, then said, 'He denied it, of course. What else?'

'And?'

He shook his head. 'I said I believed him, but that I'd also try and help Veronica at her trial.'

'And how did that go down?'

'Once he was reassured that I wasn't going to fight *him*, it didn't seem to matter to him whether I helped Veronica or not. It was amazing. I think he'd already forgotten her. She was dealt with. Gone. I think . . . I think he was becoming too involved with her. He's terrified of women, you know. Of falling in love. And Veronica came so close to . . . touching him.'

Sir Julius grunted angrily. 'Didn't he care about the possibility of his baby being born behind bars?'

'No,' Sebastien said tiredly. 'I tried to get him to see what he was doing, but I honestly don't think he's capable of seeing his own offspring as another human being. It's just an inconvenience to him and definitely Veronica's problem.'

At his home, Sir Julius opened the door, unaware that his voice carried across the quiet street to where another Bentley had just pulled in opposite.

'Sebastien, I want you to seriously consider the possibility of not seeing him anymore. He's dangerous — I know he is.'

Wayne's eyes narrowed, his fingers on the wheel tightening. His eyes shot to Sebastien, scrambling to read his expression, relieved beyond measure to see him shake his head. 'You know I can't do that, Sir Julius,' Sebastien said quietly, and Wayne almost wept with relief.

If Sebastien had agreed to drop him back into the bleak black hole where he had first found him . . . The thought made Wayne shudder. He'd have had to kill him. And to kill Sebastien would be like killing himself.

Inside the house, Sir Julius was still trying to convince Sebastien to stop seeing Wayne. 'It's Veronica who really needs you, not that bloody Frenchman.'

'You're wrong,' Sebastien said quietly. 'We've got the best lawyer for her, we'll testify for her, and we'll visit her as often as visiting times permit. We're doing all we can for Veronica, and in the end, even if the worst happens and she's found guilty, her jail sentence won't be too stiff and in the end she'll be free. She's strong and whole. But Wayne . . .' He shook his head, his expression pained. 'Wayne's been given a life sentence, and he's already served thirty years of it. And he's so brittle, one knock will shatter him like a cracked vase.'

'That doesn't change the fact that he set her up,' Sir Julius pointed out. For the first time in his life, he felt helpless, and he didn't like it.

'No, it doesn't,' Sebastien agreed quietly. 'And because of Veronica, I quite understand why it doesn't matter to you why he did it. But it matters to me. He's damaged, Julius. You, of all people, have to acknowledge that.' He took a sip of his drink and frowned down into his glass, unaware that his every expression was being monitored as Wayne watched them through the open window, eyes blazing dangerously as his acute hearing listened in to every word. 'He's in constant pain, I'm sure of that. He has a guilt complex, maybe more than one. Oh, hell . . . let me worry about Wayne.' He sounded so dejected and weary that Sir Julius immediately felt guilty for pushing him.

'All right, m'boy. If you really want to take him on . . .'

Sebastien smiled grimly. 'Julius, when I think of what he must have gone through to make him like he is I could . . . I could just damned well cry.'

Sir Julius nodded. His compassion was what made him so good. But, he thought with a shiver, it was his compassion that made him so damned vulnerable.

Outside, Wayne took deep, shaky breaths. For a moment he wanted to kill them both, but the thought of life without Sebastien made him want to cry out loud. Slowly he leaned back in his seat and shook his head. He could do nothing about Sebastien. Sebastien was the drug he needed to get through the day. His own human painkiller. He could only pray that Sebastien would never let him down. Because if he did . . .

CHAPTER 21

Hollywood

Oriel stepped carefully from the back of the chauffeur-driven limousine, gratefully taking the hand of her driver as he helped her out. She was seven months pregnant with twins, and she looked, even to her own eyes, huge.

She had chosen Chasen's to have lunch with Theresa Schwartz, who she sometimes thought was the only true friend she had in this crazy town. Since *Invaders* had smashed previous box-office records, things had become so hectic, and she saw Kier so seldom, she often found herself wishing she were back in Oxford, where she had Kier all to herself. Lovely Oxford, where there were no would-be agents, studio lackeys and the ever-present fans ready to mob them. And no would-be actresses on the make!

The sun bounced off the paving stones and onto her face as she left the car behind, and even with the dark glasses, the glare made her wince. She felt sweaty and sticky just from walking the short distance into the restaurant's cool interior, and found herself looking forward longingly to the birth, just for the sheer relief afterwards of not having to carry around so much weight.

'Ah, Madame Harcourt. We are delighted to see you again so soon.' Andre, the *maître d'*, was famous for using the royal 'we' and for being the greatest snob in all of Beverly Hills. And that was some feat. 'Your usual table, madame?'

Oriel shook her head, taking off her glasses and looking around. 'No, I'm meeting Mrs Schwartz . . . ah, there she is.' She nodded towards a very tall woman with short curly hair, who had just stood up and was waving frantically. Andre's eyes swivelled to the table in a definitely second-rate area, tucked into one corner on the side nearest the kitchen. He sniffed disdainfully. If only he'd known the dreadful English woman was dining with Oriel Harcourt, he would have placed her in the priority-seating section. Still, the damage was done now. 'Very good, madame,' he murmured, escorting her himself to the humble table.

Oriel, in her designer maternity dress of purest cotton, so pale a blue it was almost white, bit back the smile of amusement she felt at the great honour and nodded to several people who turned to look at her. It was midweek, and the place was quiet, boasting only a few television stars, the odd chat-show host, and an Italian producer who was causing a bit of a stir because of his wealth and title of 'Prince' something-or-other.

'Hi, Tease,' Oriel greeted Theresa with her pet name, and collapsed into the chair Andre held out with more relief than grace. Andre magnanimously decided to let it pass. The woman, after all, was very *enceinte*, and could be excused the social gaffe. 'Boy, I tell you,' Oriel said, 'I feel like I'm carrying a sack of coal around with me!' She poured some iced mineral water that was kept on every table into a long-fluted glass and gulped thirstily.

'Just think of all the muscles you're building up in your back and legs,' Tease advised her, her round, amber-flecked eyes sympathetic.

Oriel was glad she had found Tease. The English wife of an American television producer, Tease had only recently come to Hollywood and was, consequently, still free from the

Hollywood disease that she called the 'get-ahead syndrome.' It could, she had grumpily told Kier one morning (when he had not left for the studio at the usual crack of dawn), mean either the obvious, or refer to Tinseltown's distressing habit of taking scalps in order to push your own personal star higher into the ascendant. She had known women sell their best friend's secret to the gossip magazines in order to discredit her if they were up for the same bit part in a movie. She had known agents lie, steal and cheat their own clients to accommodate one of the studios who were having casting difficulties. Nothing but nothing was sacred in a town where betrayal was a way of life.

'What are you having?' Tease asked, perusing the menu with a jaundiced eye. She was not totally convinced, yet, that she liked American food.

'Just a salad,' Oriel said quickly. 'I can't face much else these days.'

Tease joined her in a Caesar salad, followed by fresh fruit, Tease selecting a dry white wine to wash it down while Oriel stuck it out with water.

'So, how's the new film coming? Rumour has it that it's nearly in the can, as you lot say, and that Wiseman is walking around on razor blades.' Tease got characteristically straight to the point, her curiosity open and in no way the furtive, ugly kind that Oriel was getting used to.

She shrugged, speared a piece of pineapple, chewed and said thoughtfully, 'I think Kier has just begun the editing. You know him — he isn't happy with just directing — he's got to do it all. I'm surprised he doesn't work the cameras and set up the lights as well.'

Tease gave a sympathetic grunt. 'Men,' she said suc-cinctly. 'I suppose you've been pumped over *Sacred Hearts* more than anyone else?'

Oriel smiled grimly. 'You got that right. Everyone's waiting to see what Kier will do with his own picture. He wanted to do a completely independent film first, just to see how hard it was. I ask you! But he was right. He's had much more creative freedom than he ever did on *Invaders*. He wrote the script for *Sacred Hearts*, he got Wiseman to back it, and he rented out part of Finegal Studios in order to shoot it. I swear, the fuss that caused, you'd think this town had been dealt an earthquake warning.'

Tease laughed, throwing back her head and making no effort to disguise the volume or pitch of her raucous hoot of derision. Several heads turned their way, failed to recognize Tease, lingered on Oriel, and then got back to their steaks and French Chablis. 'I'll bet,' Tease said. 'An upstart director actually having the gall to lease a studio. I'll bet the bigwigs at Paramount and MGM had seven different kinds of fits all at once.'

'They did. They all tried to talk Jason Finegal out of it. Kier even thinks someone at Colombia tried to sue him. But Jase knew a good thing when he was on to it. When *Hearts* comes out, it'll have the Finegal trademark.'

'Do you think it's going to be a hit?' Tease asked, more thoughtful than avid. She had the English openness that Oriel sorely missed in the town of tinsel, make-believe and perpetual gossip.

'I think everyone will go to see it just to see what all the fuss is about,' Oriel said, her lips ruefully twisted as she added, 'Rumours can have a great effect on the public pocket.'

'Hmm. Old Hedda's certainly straining a gasket. How did that blow about Grace Kelly affect Kier?'

'Not at all. He asked Grace if she wanted the part of Maureen, she said no. That was that. She's too busy with her Monaco prince anyway.'

'Hmm . . . Is it really as risqué as the gossip has it? Come on, give me all the hot and readies.'

'Hot and readies?' Oriel echoed and began to grin. 'Don't ask me. Kier's the genius. Now that some of the censorship's been lifted, I know he's taking advantage of it. But that's all. Besides, hints of sexy scenes never hurt a movie that I know of.'

'And he actually shot some of the footage in Ireland?'

262

'Yep.'

'That must have cost Wiseman a pretty penny.'

'Yep. He didn't like it none, but Kier won't be stopped. Honestly, Tease, you should see him. He's like a . . . a . . .'

'Steamroller?' Tease offered helpfully, and Oriel nodded, chasing a cherry around her dish with a silver-handled spoon.

'Ever since Mama stuck her oar in over *Invaders*, he's got this bee in his bonnet about being his own boss on *Hearts*. And that's only the beginning. He's got feelers out already about his next film, and this one's not even in the bag.'

Tease grunted, her long thin nose quivering at the vehemence with which she sniffed. 'It's this damned town. I tell you, it's nothing like I expected. To start with, LA airport is so damned pot-bellied-pig ugly.'

Oriel loved the way Tease talked. The second daughter of a minor baronet, her voice was that of a perfect lady, but her words were more like those of a weird and wonderful eccentric the English race habitually threw out. Tease was like a juicy bone tossed from a nation of dog-lovers.

Kier had been responsible for the two of them meeting over five months ago at a small party that was strictly non-prestigious. No 'A' list for Herman Schwartz. Just a barbecue, a small pool, a few real friends in informal clothes, and a wife who said exactly what she pleased. And from the moment Oriel had looked into the six-foot-tall woman's open amber eyes, she'd felt better. She had been lonely, high up in her Beverly Hills mansion while Kier worked all the hours God sent and then some. Her mother was an infrequent visitor now that the divorce from her father was going through, and she didn't count her hairdresser, manicurist, masseuse, chauffeur or pool man as bosom buddies. Occasionally Betty came over, with her slimmed-down figure and her racehorse-owner fiancé, but when her old finishing-school buddy and Oxford cohort left, her loneliness was only that much more acute.

Naturally, the unexpected news of her pregnancy had been greeted with total joy by the Harcourt household, even little Bethany becoming affected by the excitement in the air. Oriel had insisted that Bethany have a tutor at the age of two, and she'd been right. Already her daughter was reading anything and everything given to her, and had grasped the basics of mathematics.

'We've got a little genius here,' Kier would say, lifting his flaxen-haired, placid daughter onto his lap, watching her build toy houses with her building bricks, the structures square on all sides, with windows and doors catered for. But the pregnancy was hardly enough to keep Oriel occupied, nor was playing with Bethany, although their afternoons together were the highlight of her day.

Yes, there was no doubt about it, Tease had been a godsend.

The very first thing she'd ever said to her was, 'You look as bored as I feel. Is this rinky-dink town real?' From then on their friendship was inevitable, and they spent at least every other day together. 'No use going to that Rodeo Dive place,' Tease would dismiss Rodeo Drive with its glamorous boutiques and 'in' salons with a wave of her blunt-fingered hands. 'Nothing would fit me there. Don't you have any jumble sales in this place?'

Oriel was hard-pressed to find jumble sales, but they did tour flea markets, venturing deep into LA where the Hollywood bug didn't bite quite so hard, and where Tease remarked that at least there were some 'real people' around.

'So, what did you expect from Hollywood?' Oriel asked now, watching her friend with a lifted eyebrow. Tease wasn't wearing make-up but didn't consider that as particularly brave. She had confided to Oriel long ago that she hated putting 'gunge' on her face.

'I don't know. I suppose I expected it to be Bette Davis transferred to brick and stone. You know — elegance, glamour, quirky fun. I thought Katharine Hepburn would have given the place some sort of *savoir-faire*.'

'You poor, misguided, naive child,' Oriel commiserated, fluttering her eyelashes and drawling in her best Scarlett O'Hara voice. 'And what did you find?'

Tease grimaced, her face contorting into a marvellous mask. 'Ugh. Where do I begin? First of all, everything's instant. Instant food, instant sex. Did I tell you when I called for a pool man, this six-foot-two gorgeous hunk arrived, expecting a roll in the hay?'

Oriel gagged on her mineral water. 'Oh dear.'

'Oh dear's right. I told him to get clearing the bloody pool before I tossed him in and held him under with the rake. Bloody cheek. Then there's the lack of class! I mean, I don't care about being ignored as a humble wife of a humble producer, but the first thing everyone wanted to know was how much money we had! I mean, hell's bells and buckets of blood, in England we do our best to hide our wealth. Out here, if you don't have money, then . . .' She waved her square, mannish hand in the air, and sneered off to a speechless halt.

'Ain't Hollywood grand?' Oriel piped in, her voice as sweet as maple syrup, and again that loud, messy laugh of her friend's filled the restaurant.

'Thank cotton-picking bluebells I've got you, miss wife of the hot-shot tightrope-walking director. Otherwise I think I might just pack my bags and swan off back to Kent and let poor old Herman sink or swim on his own.'

'Yeah, sure,' Oriel said, knowing that wild horses wouldn't drag Tease away from her easy-going husband.

'You know, I had no idea when I married him that he was so rich? He said he inherited the family business from his father. How was I to know that it was a bloody great steelworks in Lucerne? Or that he'd get stars in his eyes and yearn for Hollywood? Men!' she snorted again, mashing an innocent grape against her dish.

'Don't worry,' Oriel said, deadpan, 'Herm's only worth a million or so. In this town, that's considered being down on your luck.'

Tease grunted, then ordered a second fruit salad from the scandalized Andre, who secretly complied while thinking dire thoughts about women with appetites like horses. 'I think if I hear one more person say, "Have you heard the latest gossip this week?" I'll stop doing whatever it is I am doing and scream my bloody head off. Honest, I mean it,' Tease threatened, attacking her replenished dish of fruit, picking out all the strawberries first.

'Well, just give me a bell and I'll come over and join you,' Oriel promised, pushing her plate away and ordering coffee. 'I get the feeling everyone's just waiting around to watch my marriage disintegrate.'

Tease looked at her shrewdly, then shook her head. 'You and Kier haven't got any worries there. Kier's a class act. If anyone's going to lure him away from you, it would have to be a *femme fatale* in Garbo's class. Nowadays there are so many young girls just giving it away, sex has become boring. Besides, your husband loves you. Even if he hasn't been around much just lately.'

'I know it,' Oriel said with smug satisfaction. 'And I don't mind him slogging away so hard. He's got a point to prove at the moment, that's all. Once he's done it, things will settle a bit.'

'Then you can go around chanting "yah-yah yah-yah-yah" and thumb your noses up at all this lot,' Tease nodded her head vigorously, giving the general inhabitants of the restaurant a ferocious scowl.

Oriel grinned, then glanced at her watch. 'Look, I can't stay long. Bethany's having her first piano lesson today, and I want to be there.'

'Oh, don't mind me,' Tease said, chewing a pert raspberry. 'Just bugger off any time you like.' A passing waiter, who was the epitome of servile elegance, heard the remark, paused in mid-stride, then carried on, his face expressionless. Oriel watched him, laughing helplessly, and then struggled to her feet.

'Take it easy. And don't go taking any chances,' Tease warned, noticing the difficulty with which her friend moved. She really was *very* pregnant.

'Huh, tell that to Kier,' Oriel commented. 'He's already got the cinemas booked for the previews, and he has to have the film cut by Friday if he's gonna keep to the schedule.'

'Rather him than me,' Tease said with feeling, and watched her friend go with warm, speculative eyes. She hoped *Hearts* made it. If not, Kier Harcourt was washed up in this town. The old guard wouldn't allow a youngster who took so many risks and sailed so close to the wind to survive if the film fell flat. Then Tease wondered if perhaps being exiled from this ugly, backstabbing town would be such a bad thing after all.

* * *

Nearly a month later, *Sacred Hearts* opened at the Wilshire Palladium cinema. After Grace had turned him down, Kier had cast an unknown for Maureen, the heroine of his turn-of-the-century love story set in Ireland, choosing an Irish immigrant actress for the part. He'd had to fight the American union of actors all the way, and that was only the beginning of his troubles. It was common knowledge that the film had gone way over budget, and that Wiseman had consulted his lawyers. No papers had been served yet, but every critic, guest and paying member of the public knew, as they sat in their seats, that they would be if the film flopped.

Oriel, dressed in raw Singapore silk the colour of jade, had a weird feeling of *déjà vu* as they sat in their chairs, the lights dimming around them, Kier's hand holding hers tightly as the hum of conversation slowly died. But this time there was no Howard Shoesmith and no Clarissa Somerville. Her mother was too busy happily planning her wedding to Kyle.

The opening credits began to roll across a colour scene of Irish moors, purple with heather and yellow with gorse. There was a grey stormy sky, and no music played as the credits rolled. Instead, a howling wind and a lone curlew were the only sounds, together with the roaring of the sea as below the craggy cliffs, white water broke over the cruel black rocks. As 'Directed by Kier Harcourt' disappeared from the screen, the camera picked out a seagull, then the scene suddenly swept up into the air, the camera angle lifting high above the hills. The audience gasped.

For this shot, Kier had hired a glider (silence being a necessity) and the audience strained forward as a small figure, at first no more than a white speck between the rolling hills of gorse and heather came into view, the figure getting bigger and bigger as the camera swooped lower. Kier had used a crane for the next shot, swinging the camera around and around Colleen McGyver, the unknown actress he'd discovered working in a laundry in downtown LA. The shot almost made the audience feel giddy.

Maureen was dressed in a rough black woollen dress and wide white apron. A white cloth cap covered her tumble of auburn curls, but her face was flushed and pretty, her green eyes sparkling with the joy of life, and Oriel felt every man in the audience react to her screen presence.

She let loose a long, low breath, and turned to Kier, who was watching her. He looked tired, but already jubilant, and slowly she began to smile.

The story was a love story, beautiful in its simplicity. Maureen, a simple Irish girl who works in a big Irish house, falls in love with an English soldier, stationed in Ireland during the peace talks. She has to weather the hatred of her own family as they slowly turn against her, while Aubrey, the English hero, played by the current flavour-of-the-month actor, faces the scorn of his own regiment and the disapproval of his commanding officer.

But *Sacred Hearts* did not run as the audience expected it to. There was no tragic ending, with Maureen dying, or Aubrey getting killed in the uprising of the Irish peasants. Nor was there a happy ending, with Maureen sailing off into the sunset with her lover. Throughout, the film firmly kept hold of gritty reality. There were no mock-ups of cosy Irish cottages, but interior shots of the real thing — dark, damp, small. Maureen hardly wore any make-up, relying on Colleen's own pure skin and natural beauty to give the illusion of a simple country lass. The love scenes were long, tender, but passionate, a chemical reaction between the two leading actors so obvious that rumours about a real-life romance were now inevitable.

But it was the dialogue, more than anything else, that lifted the film from the usual run-of-the-mill Hollywood glamour into a classic. The accents were right, the mood was one of hopelessness, and the situation was fraught. The film had only one possible ending under the circumstances, with the two lovers being forced to bow to the peer pressure of their differing class and status, and agreeing to part. Aubrey went back home to his fiancée, the daughter of a rich farmer and landowner, and Maureen married her simple Irish crofter, who had stood by her through thick and thin.

When the lights went up the audience was forced reluctantly back to modern-day America, left with the feeling of a real tragedy — of two people, so right for each other, being forced apart by prejudice. Women were openly crying, and some of the men looked suspiciously bright-eyed, too. As the applause started, Kier and Oriel had one last quiet moment together, Kier raising her hand to his lips for a gentle kiss, before the circus began all over again.

Outside in the foyer, the pressmen had first pickings.

'Mr Harcourt, the audience reaction to this first showing of *Sacred Hearts* has been phenomenal.' A big radio mic was stuck under Kier's nose, bearing the logo of a television network. 'How do you feel right at this moment?'

Kier looked the young, eager-faced reporter straight in the face and smiled grimly. 'Wonderful. And I'm sure Mr Wiseman also feels wonderful, even if his lawyers don't share the joyousness of this occasion.' Not after losing their prospects of a big fat fee, he thought, the same thought obviously shared by the others as a ripple of genuine laughter spread among the spectators. Next came the woman who was Hedda Hopper's main rival in the gossip stakes, nudging her way closer, ruthlessly elbowing out younger novices.

'Mr Harcourt, do you think the rest of the country's cinemas are going to take to heart *Sacred Hearts* as readily as our Hollywood audiences have done?'

Kier glanced across the sea of eager faces and found Oriel's loving, proud eyes. 'I hope so,' he said smoothly, 'but if not, I feel confident we'll have better luck at Cannes.'

The bombshell exploded quietly, then there was a great torrent of noise. Kier held up his hands, eventually the hubbub dying down. 'I've been invited to show my film at Cannes next week when the film festival opens. And yes, I'm definitely doing so.'

'Mr Harcourt, that's quite an honour. And only your second film, too. Do you expect to win an award?' He couldn't see the face behind the voice, but it hardly mattered.

'Yes, I do.'

The answer, so candid and so without the usual show of false modesty, momentarily stunned the crowd. Kier took advantage of it to make an announcement of his own. 'My wife and I will be flying to Paris tomorrow for a short holiday before going on to Cannes. I think she deserves it, and I know I do.' He grinned feelingly into the television cameras, and all across the county feminine hearts melted at the handsome, boyish grin.

The interview went on for ten more minutes, then Kier wrapped it up. Oriel, in deference to her condition, had long since been escorted to the limo, and she looked up as Kier opened the door and climbed in amid a sea of flashlights. The car quickly moved away. Kier muttered a heartfelt 'Never again,' and closed his eyes, letting rip with a deep, heavy sigh.

'Thanks for letting me know about Paris in such good time,' she said drily, then patted her rounded stomach. 'We appreciate it no end.'

Kier grinned at her, then yanked off his bow tie. This year his tuxedo was white, and just one of a whole wardrobe of expensive clothes. This year, there was nobody to take the limelight away from him. This year, there was Cannes.

He felt like singing and shouting and sleeping for a whole week. Oriel ankled off one sensible flat shoe and then slowly ran her foot up his calf. He looked across at her, his lids lazily half-closing as her toes nudged the bend in his knee and then moved even higher, her dress riding up her thighs and showing off her still exquisitely shaped long legs. 'If you weren't so pregnant, Scarlett, I would come across there and make the chauffeur blush.'

'If I weren't pregnant, you wouldn't get the chance. I'd already be ravishing *you*!' Oriel shot back, her stockinged foot slipping higher up his white-clad thigh. 'But there's more than one way to skin a cat, as Tease told me only the other day.'

Wriggling into a more comfortable position and ignoring the niggling pain in her back, Oriel slipped her foot between his thighs, which obligingly fell open, her big toe nudging the hardening bulge it found there, then slowly beginning to rub it. A red tide of colour began to ebb high on Kier's cheekbones, and he leaned back, his breathing becoming ragged.

'If you don't stop,' he warned, 'my tux is going to be ruined.'

'So? It's not a rented one this time,' she said, grinning widely as he began to gnaw on his bottom lip.

'This is your revenge, isn't it?' he accused her, swallowing hard. 'You're getting back at me for all these weeks of neglect.'

'True,' Oriel said, wriggling her other foot between his thighs, her feet massaging him now in earnest. His hands dug into the cream leather of the upholstery, the material squeaking under his clawing fingers. He stared at her, his nostrils flaring as she stared openly back at him, her eyes dancing with mischief.

'Have you ever been to Paris?' he gritted, and Oriel shook her head, her eyes wide and innocent.

'Nope. I think I'll like it though.'

'Hmm, I hope so. It's s-supposed to be quite r-romantic . . . oh, hell!' He shuddered briefly, letting out a long, harsh gasp, and then slowly opened his eyes. 'Just you wait until those kids are born,' he warned, his mouth soft and vulnerable now as he smiled, making Oriel laugh. 'I'll make you regret your feet were ever out of their shoes.'

Oriel raised one eyebrow, trying to look scared. 'Oh? Well now, I have four weeks until they are born. If I'm lucky you'll have gotten over your pique by then.'

* * *

They flew to Paris the next day, booking into the Paris Plaza where they occupied the whole of the top floor. They ate in their room, the flight having exhausted Oriel, but strangely enough she couldn't sleep. A niggling pain in her back was beginning to make her wonder if coming to Paris had been such a good idea after all.

Nevertheless, the next morning she kept quiet and packed him off to a business lunch with some of Cannes' representatives, and settled down to a couple of boiled eggs and forty winks.

When Kier came back two hours later, an overwrought desk clerk pounced on him, telling him his wife had called down for an ambulance to take her to hospital just an hour ago. It was hard to tell which of the two men panicked more, but eventually the desk clerk managed to hail him a taxi and explain to the driver in rapid and excited French what was going on.

Inside the battered Citroën, Kier was rolled about in the back seat like a football as the driver careered around the streets of Paris, paying scant heed to the policemen directing traffic, and paying even less heed to his fellow drivers. Watching his pale passenger intently in his mirror, gesturing and gabbling on in unintelligible French, the taxi driver delivered the expectant father to the maternity hospital in record time. Kier stumbled out, surprised to still be alive, and handed over a huge bundle of money, not bothering to wait for change, and running up the stone steps with the Frenchman's words of good luck and congratulations still ringing in his ears.

Inside, he found a receptionist who spoke broken English, and after five nerve-wracking minutes was shown into a small, white-washed room. He expected Oriel to still be in labour, and he skidded comically to a halt at the sight of his wife, pale and sweating, but beaming happily, with a tiny baby in each arm.

'That was quick,' Kier said the first thing that came into his head, and Oriel grinned, then shrugged.

'Well, why hang about, that's what I always say,' she shot back. The nurse, looking slightly puzzled, backed out, wondering about the strange behaviour of Americans. Now a Frenchman presented with newborn twins would already be kissing his wife and babies, and blubbing his eyes out.

'Well, what have we got?' Kier asked after a short, emotional silence, walking nervously to the bed, as if afraid any of its three occupants might jump up and bite him.

'Well, this one,' Oriel nodded to her left 'is a boy. And this one is a girl.'

'One of each, then?' His mouth was dry as he stared at his babies, both dark-haired, both red and wrinkled and so tiny. 'Well, that's handy, at any rate. They're . . . a little early, aren't they?'

Oriel nodded. 'A little. But they're both all right. The doctors said so. We always have strong, healthy babies. You know that,' she said softly.

'We wouldn't dare do otherwise,' Kier swallowed hard, and sounded jaunty.

Oriel wasn't fooled for a minute. There were tears in her eyes as she said, 'I thought I'd name this one . . .' she nudged her son's forehead tenderly with her lips '. . . and leave you to do the honours for this one.'

'Sounds fair to me,' Kier agreed, taking a deep shaky breath. Then he reached down and gingerly picked up his minutes-old daughter, holding her in his hands as if he were holding the Crown Jewels.

He glanced down at Oriel, then back at the tiny bundle of life in his hands. 'What are you going to call him?' he asked suspiciously.

Oriel looked a little shamefaced for a moment and then blurted out defiantly, 'I'm calling him Paris — after the city where he was born. And because he's going to be handsome enough to win his own Helen of Troy one day.'

Kier grinned, then looked down at their daughter as Oriel countered softly, 'What are you calling her?'

Kier watched as his daughter opened her deep brown eyes and frowned, punching a tiny fist in the air. 'Oh-oh,' he said softly. 'We're going to have trouble with this one.'

After a thoughtful few moments he said quietly, 'Gemma,' then looked down at his wife with eyes that were bright with tears.

'Why Gemma?' Oriel asked curiously, swallowing hard, feeling impossibly full.

Kier laughed. 'Because she's going to be a little gem, of course.'

Oriel smiled. 'Of course. And we're going to be so happy.'

Kier glanced at her, a little surprised. 'Did you ever doubt it?'

'What? That we'd be married, have three precious babies, and that you'd be the best and most famous director and filmmaker in Hollywood?' she asked.

Kier nodded.

Oriel threw her head back and laughed. 'I never doubted it for a second. Not from the moment I first set eyes on you, and you called me "Scarlett" in that damned sarcastic way of yours and tried to have me thrown out of your precious play.'

Kier bent and kissed his daughter's head. She responded by yowling at him angrily.

'I never had a single doubt either . . . Scarlett.'

CHAPTER 22

Veronica had not been granted bail after the preliminary hearing. Sir Mortimer's old school tie was one of the best, and although her father had been prepared to sell his house and everything else of value to free his daughter until the trial began, he was never given the opportunity. Sir Mortimer was dedicated in his defence of Wayne — his new, unofficial son and heir.

Consequently, Veronica arrived at the Nottinghamshire Open Prison for Women on a bleak November morning, with one small suitcase and the judge's words still echoing in her brain.

The prison itself was — oddly — pleasant enough, with tall brick buildings full of windows, square courtyards and car parks, but the place had an institutional flavour that curtained windows and flowerboxes couldn't quite dispel.

She was now four months' pregnant, still prone to morning sickness, and had at last shaken off the shock that had been a constant companion. But she was paying the price. Her palms sweated and her heart hammered as she was escorted to the warden's office by a tall but pleasant-faced female guard.

The warden was a middle-aged woman with bobbed blonde hair, kind hazel eyes and a firm voice. The name plate on her office door proclaimed her to be Mrs H.A. Gardner, Governor. Veronica was shown quickly into the office, which was small, white-washed and full of pot plants. Old green filing cabinets lined the walls, while under her feet a dusty beige carpet softened the sound of her footsteps. Faded curtains hung at the windows, keeping out a cold draught.

Mrs Gardner looked up from behind her desk, eyes quickly taking inventory of her latest acquisition. Her file recorded that Miss Coltrane was pregnant, but as yet the slender, dark-haired woman showed no signs of it. She had wide, nervous eyes, a pale pinched face, and looked too vulnerable to survive the prison system for long. Honor Gardner sighed, then stood up, forcing a smile onto her round, pleasant face. 'Miss Coltrane. Welcome to Nottingham.'

Veronica blinked, then quickly took the outstretched hand and shook it. During the journey to this place, sitting in the back of a swaying security van, she had not quite known what to expect. Scenes from old movies kept coming back to haunt her, bringing nightmare visions of damp, dark cells and vicious, mentally unbalanced bullying guards. To come to this inconspicuous office and meet this totally normal woman of the same type that she saw in the shops and on the streets every day of her life made Veronica feel oddly off-balance.

'Please, sit down, Veronica. I always like to have a little talk with all my new girls, especially the ones still awaiting trial.'

Veronica sank down gratefully onto a firmly padded wooden-backed chair, and took several deep, calming breaths.

'It is important that you understand the rules, of course,' Honor Gardner said, promptly reciting a bewildering list of statutory prison rules. 'If you can't remember them all, don't worry. There's a set of them taped up in every room.'

'I see.' They were the first words Veronica had spoken since arriving, and she was glad (but a little surprised) to find that her voice came out both firm and polite. Mrs Gardner nodded and, looking deeper into the brown eyes, was relieved to find a good deal of steady strength growing in them. Honor was glad. This beautiful young girl was going to need all the strength she had for some time to come.

'It's important that you understand the difference in status between yourself, who has yet to stand trial, and the prisoners here who are actually serving out their sentences. In effect, and to put it simply, you are not yet guilty of anything. That is to say, you are not a convicted criminal. As such, you have much more liberty than most of the women here.'

Veronica nodded grimly. She was not guilty, but she was still locked up. She glanced down at her hands twisting in her lap, and quickly unfolded them.

'Mrs Gardner—' She took a deep breath, needing an answer to the question that had been gnawing at her innards like a cancer. 'Can you tell me . . . I was wondering . . . is it possible for me to . . . have my b-baby here, instead of . . . in a real prison?' She now had no doubts about Wayne's ruthlessness or his thoroughness. Although she told herself she was being stupidly pessimistic, in her heart, she didn't believe she would be found innocent at her trial.

'You're four months' pregnant?'

'Yes.'

'Then I think it's highly probable that the judge will order a delay until after the birth.'

'Oh, thank God for that.'

Honor opened her mouth and then quickly shut it again. It would serve no purpose to tell this naive young girl that judges knew that juries, when faced with pregnant women, were often inclined to bring in a not-guilty verdict. In all probability, Sir Mortimer's prosecuting lawyer himself had already argued that Veronica should have her child before standing trial.

'Well, I think that's all for the moment,' Mrs Gardner stood up slowly. Veronica did the same and was led to the door. 'I think you'll find the food here is passable, and the prison doctor will monitor your pregnancy as closely and as professionally as any other doctor. Ah, Adams. Escort Miss Coltrane to room 113, will you?'

Adams, a tall, cheery-faced woman wearing a navy-blue prison officer's uniform, nodded and then smiled at Veronica, making no attempt to take her arm or touch her in any way. Again Veronica felt foolish for her dire imaginings about the hellish quality of prison life. The woman called Adams even made small talk as they walked down stairs and corridors, where the sound of music came from individual rooms, and chattering voices made the place seem more like a girls' school than a prison. They passed several common rooms, where women sat reading, drinking coffee, playing board games and even watching television.

'Here we are.' Adams opened the door marked 113 on the second floor. A young girl, no more than sixteen, with lank yellow hair, a spotty face and big blue eyes, lay sprawled on a single bed. She sat up as Veronica walked in and put her case by the second bed, which had two folded sheets and several blankets placed on the mattress, ready to be made up.

'Well, I'll leave you to unpack. Lunch is from twelve-thirty to one-fifteen, in the dining room. Mary will show you around.' Adams nodded and left. Veronica looked at the younger girl awkwardly, and then wandered to the window. It overlooked a lawn and flower border where two women were busy weeding.

'That's the gardening brigade,' Mary said, coming to stand beside her, her voice childishly clear and shockingly young. 'Old Gardy — that's the big chief — works out gardening details every month. We do all the other stuff as well. Laundry, ironing, even cooking. She says it saves money on auxiliary staff, stops us getting idle and gives us exercise too. Ginny Fuller, she's the dumps mole, says that the rest of the open prison lot might follow suit. She's a real trendsetter, is Gardy.'

'Dump mole?'

'Hmm — this place is the dump and Ginny works in the office — she can type, you see, so she sneaks a look at the memos and stuff. She's a whizz at reading upside down.'

'Oh.' Veronica felt an absurd desire to laugh. This morning she had left the holding cells convinced she was heading for some Dickensian horror prison, and here she was, in a pleasant if small room, listening to a little cockney sparrow of a girl chatter on about dump moles.

''Ere, why don't you unpack your stuff? This half of the wardrobe's yours, and I moved my clobber from the bottom two drawers.' She pointed to the cheap but functional furniture against one wall and then bounced back onto her bed, watching with avid, all-seeing eyes as Veronica unpacked her few clothes. Shaking out the maternity dresses, she saw the girl's eyes widen, and prepared herself for what was coming.

'You up the duff, then?'

'Yes.' She managed a shaky smile. Now that she was here, she felt a deep and dangerous desire to just collapse on her unmade bed and cry her eyes out.

'Married? Nah, course you ain't. Some man got you in here, didn't he? What did he do? Leave some stolen stuff in your flat?'

Veronica shook her head but didn't volunteer any information. She couldn't even think about Wayne without a whole wave of emotional bitterness bogging her down. And somewhere in the back of her mind she already knew that she was going to have to fight it fiercely if she didn't want to end up a nervous, twisted wreck of a human being.

Mary shrugged, not concerned about her new roommate's lack of chatter. She'd start talking soon enough. They always did, once they settled down.

'I'm in here for shoplifting,' she said, studying her nails, which were chewed to the quick. 'I knew this little girl in the home where I used to live who was wild about pop music. Crazy about it. So I thought I'd get her this little radio from Woolies and, well . . . got nicked. Damned store detectives. Thought I knew all their tricks. Oh well, just goes to show—' the girl gave a huge grin that bore no grudge '—you live and learn. That's what my old matron used to say.'

Veronica nodded grimly. 'You certainly do.'

'When you go to court, then?'

'I'm not sure. After the baby's born, I hope.'

'Sure to,' Mary nodded sagely, knowing the ropes as well as Honor Gardner. 'Who you got to take care of the sprog?'

'My father. He said he'll hire a nurse.'

'Oh, la-de-dah,' Mary said, then leapt up as a bell buzzed loudly outside, making Veronica jump. 'Don't panic,' Mary grinned, tucking a wad of greasy hair behind one ear. 'The dump ain't on fire. That's the dinner bell. Coming?'

Veronica wasn't hungry but she forced herself to go, following her chirpy little roommate down a flight of stairs and into a long, warm room where about eight or nine long tables were set with plastic place mats and cutlery.

Veronica found herself running the gauntlet of what seemed like a thousand eyes, and unknowingly moved closer to her roommate as they stood in line by a long, heated counter, where other women, with equally interested eyes, dished out steak and kidney pudding and string beans.

'Don't worry about this lot,' Mary said loudly, looking around her. 'You won't be new for long; then they won't even know you're here.'

And strangely, out of all the words that had been thrown at her over the past month, from solicitors, doctors, prison guards, Sebastien Teale, friends and fellow inmates, those simple words were the ones that would stick with her for the rest of her life. She found them echoing in her head, even as she sat down on a long bench and picked at her food. 'You won't be new for long; then they won't even know you're here.' Did Wayne, she wondered, prodding her cooling dinner, even remember that she was here?

* * *

Wayne didn't. Sir Mortimer Platt had had a slight stroke, throwing everyone into a panic, and especially Beatrice, who had been the cause of it. Sir Mortimer had found his wife in bed with his groom and had not been amused. He had done nothing so dramatic as collapse on the spot, but instead had walked stiff-legged from the room where a red-faced John was yanking on his trousers, and made his way into the study. A pain in his chest and a trembling weakness in his left arm had been enough to make Wayne send for his doctor, who had then diagnosed the stroke.

Sir Mortimer, pale-faced and looking a hundred years old, now met the Frenchman's concerned blue eyes over the head of the doctor knelt by his chair, a stethoscope placed on Sir Mortimer's withered chest, and said grimly, 'See to that damned woman, will you, dear boy?' His words were slurred and tired, and he looked more defeated than disgusted.

Wayne dealt with Beatrice with extreme pleasure. She was forced to bear the humiliation of watching the servants pack all her bags, and then as insult added to injury, had to ask their chauffeur to drive her to the train station in his own little jalopy, as Wayne gave orders for all the family cars to be locked in the garage.

The stroke, the doctor told them, was a mild one, but should be treated as a warning. 'You must take things easy, Sir Mortimer. No more working, no more board meetings. And no more cigars. You can keep off the brandy, too.'

Sir Mortimer grunted, then listened gravely to the doctor as he prescribed pills and gentle exercise. Wayne saw the man out, then went back to the study. The first thing Sir Mortimer said was, 'Pass me the cigar box, will you, m'boy?'

Wayne smiled and handed over the teak and mahogany box. Sir Mortimer's hands shook as he took one out but his gnarled fingers were unable to hold it. Wayne gently took it from him, clipped and lighted it, then handed it back.

'Thanks,' he said, taking a deep puff, then glanced at Wayne sharply. 'You knew about Beatrice, didn't you?' he said, both his words and knowing eyes catching Wayne off-guard. 'Don't look so surprised,' Sir Mortimer grunted, his voice almost fond. 'I don't think there's much your eyes miss. Not like mine.'

'I'm sorry,' Wayne said. 'I suppose I should have told you.'

Sir Mortimer shrugged his painfully thin shoulders, took a deep drag on his cigar, coughed, and then licked his lips. Wordlessly, Wayne poured him a brandy. 'I don't suppose I shall last long now,' Sir Mortimer mused meditatively. 'People don't, you know, when the old ticker starts to grumble.'

Wayne opened his mouth, then closed it again. He had to be careful now. Very careful. One wrong word, one missed opportunity, and he could ruin it all. 'That's not always the case,' he said, helping himself to a brandy, suddenly needing it. He had not expected to feel so . . . sorry for the old man. Briefly the absurd thought flashed across his brain with deep and soul-cutting clarity: *If only you had been my father.* Then, when he found the old man staring at him, he went white, looking genuinely appalled when he realized he'd blurted it out loud.

'Forget I said that,' Wayne said quickly, then took a deep gulp of brandy, the liquid settling his stomach. 'I think your damned stroke has addled my brain.'

Sir Mortimer laughed, then stared into the fire in the grate. 'What am I going to do about Platt's, Wayne?' he asked, the question more rhetorical than anything else, but it gave Wayne the opening he needed.

'Leave it to your grandchildren, of course,' he said, sounding surprised that there could be any doubt.

Mortimer snorted. 'How the hell do I do that? The kids have years yet until they come of age. And Toby will have control, for all intents and purposes. He'll run the company into the ground.'

'So appoint a trustee.'

'You?' Sir Mortimer said, looking at him closely.

Wayne jerked his gaze away from his own contemplation of the fire and looked at the old man with rounded eyes. 'Me? Why me? Surely you have people on the board you can trust? The very first thing that struck me about Platt's was its family atmosphere. I kept bumping into people who told me what the firm was like before the war. The first one, I mean!'

Sir Mortimer smiled crookedly. 'Just my point. They're all as old as I am. I need a younger man to take over the reins. The world is changing . . . yes, it is,' Sir Mortimer said quickly as Wayne looked about to argue. 'I'm glad I shan't live to see it, but if Platt's is to survive, then I need a man not only with a feeling for tradition, but also able to compete in a modern market. A man like you. You know your book is due out in four months, don't you?'

Wayne shook his head. 'As soon as that?'

'Yes. And it'll sell. That's what we need at Platt's. A man who knows how to rewrite economic history. A man who knows how money works. That's what Platt's needs.'

'Toby is bound to contest the will if you nominate me as trustee. I'm a foreigner, don't forget, and still relatively new to the firm. And I don't see how an English court would ever go against him.' Wayne watched him closely as he spoke, and only when he saw the anger gradually creep over Sir Mortimer's face did he relax. If there was one thing the old man hated, it was being defied. He had become used to having his own way, and the thought of his last wishes being denied when he was dead and unable to do anything about it made him as mad as Wayne had guessed and hoped it would.

'I won't have my will contested,' Sir Mortimer said, banging his hand against the armrest of his chair like a spoiled, petulant child. 'I won't!'

'There might be a way . . .' Wayne began gingerly, then shook his head. 'No. No, that isn't—'

'What?' Sir Mortimer said testily. 'Out with it, boy.'

'Well . . . I was thinking . . . you could write out a new will, naming me as the sole beneficiary. Then I go to Toby, telling him what you've done, and asking him to come down and make you change your mind. After all, I'm rich enough in my own right; I don't need your money. Naturally, Toby will come down to talk you out of it.'

Sir Mortimer snorted. 'You bet your sweet Fanny Adams he will. That boy was always a sponger . . .'

'Yes, but the point is, if he thinks he's going to lose everything, then you're in a good bargaining position. You can tell him you'll change the will so that the grandchildren inherit, but only on the condition that I'm appointed as the trustee. Surely your lawyers can draft an agreement whereby he agrees not to contest the will under such circumstances? That way I can steer the firm and teach the children how to run Platt's at the same time.'

He held his breath, letting it out only when the old man began to grin mischievously. Sir Mortimer began to cackle as he thought about the look on his son's face when he heard the shattering news. 'I'll do it! And while I'm at it, I'll cut Beatrice off without a damned penny to boot.' He began to cackle again, and Wayne sat back in his chair, laughing with him, swirling the Napoleon brandy in his glass, his eyes glittering like blue diamonds.

* * *

Two months later Sir Mortimer's will was rewritten, in the presence of three lawyers, and signed by five servants as witnesses. Sir Mortimer lay in bed, the victim of a second stroke that had paralyzed the whole of his left side. The side of his mouth was pulled down, as was his left eyelid, but he'd had several doctors confirm that his mind was still as sound as a bell.

As he signed the document, he looked up at Wayne dressed sombrely in black, then gave a gasping chuckle as Wayne winked at him. It was a good idea of Wayne's to have the doctors sign official documents testifying to his solid state of mind. He was quite right in saying that his weasel of a son might contest the will on the grounds of mental incompetency.

As the servants left with the two other lawyers, Wayne watched Sir Mortimer's official solicitor fold away the will. Graham Hines had been Sir Mortimer's oldest and closest friend for years. He was a small man, bent and white-haired, but button-sharp. He glanced now at the tall Frenchman, then at his friend, lying like a pitiful wreck of his former self in the big four-poster bed. 'Mortimer, are you sure you want to do this? I know Toby made a damned mess of things a while back, but . . .'

'Don't w-worry, Graham. I know ex-exactly what I'm doing.'

Graham didn't like it. And he most definitely didn't like the giant of a Frenchman, who was never far away. He had tried and failed on numerous occasions to get Sir Mortimer on his own, but always the Frenchman showed up. Every instinct in his body cried out against this new will, but Mortimer was adamant. So Graham decided to try a different tack. Turning to Wayne, he folded the airtight legal will into his briefcase, and said coldly, 'I hear from friends at Platt's that there are big changes afoot?'

Wayne, who knew just what the interfering old bastard was up to, nodded and smiled easily. 'Yes, I suppose most people would think so. Having a new man in Mortimer's office sent cold shivers running down many spines. Mine included!' Both men turned as a dry wheezy laugh came from the direction of the bed.

'Get that will f-filed or r-registered, or whatever you do with it,' Sir Mortimer said, nodding to the briefcase. 'I know I've been r-riding you to have it w-watertight, and I've seen the suspicious looks you've been c-casting our f-friend over there.' Sir Mortimer nodded to Wayne, who smiled briefly. 'B-but we have our r-reasons. Don't we, boy?'

Wayne nodded again, and said softly, 'Yes, we do.' Graham, who knew when he was beaten, left a few minutes later, a very unhappy man. 'W-well, that's part "A" over with,' Sir Mortimer said, closing his eyes for a few moments as a fresh wave of weakness washed over him. Lord, he felt tired.

'Don't worry about part "B",' Wayne reassured him. 'I've already booked a ticket to Edinburgh from Paddington. I'm travelling up to see Toby this weekend. I shall be suitably distressed and assure him that I had no idea what you were up to.'

Sir Mortimer wheezed another laugh. 'G-good. Oh — by the way, I have s-something for you. Here, in the top drawer.' He pointed awkwardly to his bedside nightstand. Wayne walked over and opened the drawer. Lying inside was a hardback book in pale blue. On the cover was a picture of a stock market, in full, hectic swing. The title read *Computers and the New Economic Wave* by Wayne D'Arville.

'The first copy. The rest come out in two months' time. I thought you might like the very first one off the presses,' the dry-as-old-leaves voice informed him.

Wayne picked up the book, stroked it, turned the first page and read the first line that Veronica had written. Then he turned away from the man lying as still as death on the bed and walked to the window, so that he couldn't see the satisfied smile on his face.

* * *

On the same day that the first of the books were finally delivered to the London shops, Veronica Coltrane gave birth to a six-pound, ten-ounce baby boy in the Nottinghamshire prison. She named her son Travis, and a few hours after the birth she had her first visitor.

Geoffrey Coltrane held his grandson in his hands, unspeakably relieved that his hair at least was dark, like that of his mother. Yet in the baby's face he could already see a squareness, with his father's nose and mouth, but Geoffrey cuddled him lovingly as he looked down at his pale, hollow-eyed daughter, feeling totally useless and frustrated.

'Daddy, I want you to tell . . . *him* . . . that the baby died. That it was stillborn. He won't bother to check up on it. He won't care.' Her voice was dull and lifeless.

Geoffrey nodded. He wasn't sure that he could face the Frenchman without killing him, though, so he compromised. 'I'll telephone him.'

Veronica nodded, then turned her head away as Geoffrey went to hand Travis back. 'No,' she cried wretchedly. 'I daren't hold him.' Her eyes screwed tightly closed. 'Tell the nurse to take him away now.'

'But, darling, he needs to be fed.'

'I can't. Don't you understand, I can't?' she screamed. 'How can I nurse him, feed him and then . . . watch him being taken away? For pity's sake, do it now.' The nurse, who'd been sitting in one corner, rose at the first sign of Veronica's distress and took the baby wordlessly from Geoffrey, who then walked out of his daughter's room on unsteady legs, unable to bear the sound of her sobs.

'When can I collect him?' he asked the nurse when they were safely outside, watching the chubby, sympathetic woman cradle the sleeping baby in her arms.

'In about ten days, when we're sure there are no problems with the little mite.'

'Ten days?' Geoffrey echoed. 'My daughter's trial starts in ten days.'

* * *

True to his word, Geoffrey called the Frenchman at his office the next day. He kept it very brief, saying only that Veronica had given birth to a stillborn boy, before hanging up. Wayne put down the phone and slowly leaned back in a black leather swivel armchair. For a few moments he stared blindly around his big new office, with all the wealth and power it represented, his eyes finally resting on the copper nameplate that sat squarely on his desk: 'Wayne D'Arville — President.'

He reached for a decanter of expensive brandy and poured a full glass. His limbs felt stiff and disjointed, and he emptied the glass in one swift toss of his head. So — the baby was dead. It was probably just as well. And since he could do nothing about it, why think about it? It was not as if he didn't have other things to do.

He left the office quickly and drove his brand-new Italian Ferrari downtown, toward his new Belgravia apartment. He wound the window down, letting the cold air attack his face. He didn't fancy going back to the office that afternoon, so instead he headed north to Charrington Private Hospital, where Sir Mortimer had lain for the past four days in the intensive care unit.

Wayne hated the smell of the antiseptic and the uniform whiteness of the rooms, but he visited the old man every day, giving the nursing staff strict instructions that no one else was to visit. And since he was paying the medical bills, no one argued with him. Sir Mortimer's last and certainly fatal attack had arrived just in time. The old man had begun to ask questions about Toby's conspicuous and continuing absence. Why wasn't the boy battering down the doors, demanding that the will be torn up, like they'd always planned?

Of course, Wayne had never informed Toby Mortimer about the new will. He had never intended to.

As he stood at the foot of the old man's bed, machines bleeping out the frail heartbeat, the old man's eyes fluttered open. A question that he could no longer physically speak was obvious in his eyes.

Wayne smiled gently. 'Don't worry, Sir Mortimer.' He took the old man's hand and squeezed it. 'It's all sorted out. It's all gone just as I planned . . .'

* * *

Three days later, Sir Mortimer Platt died, his last will and testament unaltered. The day after that, Veronica Coltrane was found guilty of attempted burglary, and sentenced to three years' imprisonment. As she had served six months already, and as it was a first offence, the judge abbreviated the sentence to one year, with the possibility of parole in six months.

Wayne hadn't needed to testify, and now only her father sat in the public gallery to hear her being sentenced.

As she felt a firm hand on her elbow pulling her away from the dock and down into the holding cells, she wondered where Wayne was, and what he was doing. Then she made a vow.

She would never think about Wayne again. She would never allow even the image of him to cross her mind.

She gave a final glance around the courtroom, and smiled bravely at Sebastien Teale, who'd always been there for her, helping her through it. He'd been her lifeline after Travis was born, getting her to talk, helping her to control and understand the guilt she felt at being forced to abandon her baby, listening sympathetically as she offloaded much of her anger and bitterness. His kindness, constancy and warmth had been the only things that had kept her sane the last few months.

But she knew that she wouldn't be seeing Sebastien again. Sebastien was on a crusade to help Wayne. And Wayne . . . Wayne no longer existed.

As she climbed into the police van and heard the cell door slam shut behind her, she told herself that, in future, she wouldn't trust anybody.

She would certainly never trust a man again as long as she lived.

CHAPTER 23

One fine day in June, so many things were happening to so many people.

In Atlanta, the 'ageing belle' Clarissa married her 'dirty, low-born' Kyle, amid much gossip and malicious glee. All her friends cattily agreed that the marriage wouldn't last, that the excitement would fizzle out now that they were legitimate.

Only Clarissa and Kyle knew better.

As she walked down the aisle with her young, handsome new husband on her arm, Clarissa smiled at her daughter, her daughter's husband, and their beautiful children.

Life was wonderful.

* * *

A few miles away, Duncan Somerville was reading a startling new document on Wolfgang Mueller, the hated commandant of a notorious concentration camp.

If the evidence was true, then Wolfgang Mueller was alive and well and living in Monte Carlo.

And Duncan Somerville was going to get him.

Life was exciting.

* * *

In Spain, a little girl played in a garden, careful to keep out of sight of the Don, who watched her with such an odd, greedy look in his eyes.

But Maria had a secret. She and her mother were running away to a big city that very night.

And much later, when she was all grown up, Maria was going to find her papa and make him pay for what he had done to them. Maria Alvarez would not cry herself to sleep at night like her poor mama did.

Maria had a mission in life now.

Life was full of possibilities.

* * *

In Holloway prison, Veronica Coltrane began to plan her future. She didn't want to stay in England — she wanted to take her son and just go. Somewhere, anywhere, far away from where she was.

Life was dark.

* * *

In his little semi-detached home in Reading, Geoffrey Coltrane nursed his grandson. Travis was a handsome, loving baby, and Geoff had no doubts that he'd grow to be a fine young man. A man that any father would be proud to call his own . . .

* * *

Walking down the ward of a psychiatric hospital, Sebastien Teale thought about his patient, Wayne D'Arville. As he soothed a woman convinced she was being eaten alive by snails, only he knew how close Wayne was to a similar insanity.

And he also knew, deep in his heart, that it was up to him to save him.

Life was frightening.

* * *

In his office, Wayne D'Arville signed some papers that would make him another eighty-eight thousand pounds. His personal fortune was now massive. His career as head of Platt's was unchallenged.

He was riding high.

But that only meant he had a long way to fall . . .

PART II: RESOLUTIONS

CHAPTER 24

New York, 1965

Veronica Coltrane paused outside Ohrbach's to study the fascinating window display before hurrying on to Nibbits Department Store on 68th and West.

It was a freezing January morning, and as she waited by the crossing for the 'Walk' sign she blew into her hands to try and warm them. Without much success. She had thought her native home of England could get cold in winter, but this was new to her.

Not that she regretted coming to America, of course. No, she would never, *never* feel regret. She had needed to escape from England, and all the hideous memories it still held for her, with a passion that she knew was not healthy. The knowledge of her own vulnerability, even after all this time, still lurked uneasily at the back of her mind.

She still had so much to do. And keeping her job was, at the moment, top of her list. Travis was relying on her. But on a cold January morning her responsibilities seemed to lay all the more heavily on her shoulders. It sometimes felt as if she was carrying around her own personal iceberg. It made life so cold sometimes.

And so many people, kind, good people, had had to pull so many strings just to get her an entry visa and work permit for this new country that she simply *had* to make a go of it. She couldn't let them down. Not when they'd taken such chances for her. And she knew, more than anyone, how hard it must have been for them to trust her. Considering . . .

The 'Walk' sign flashed on, and her unhappy thoughts were suddenly jostled out of her. She found herself abruptly carried along by a human tide as thirty people made a mad dash across the road. Once on the other side, she glanced at her inexpensive watch and gave a sigh of relief. She was not as late as she'd thought.

Travis had been scared to start school at first, poor mite. She'd had to walk him to school and introduce him to his teachers, just to settle him down. His English accent initially let him in for a lot of teasing by his fellow classmates, but Veronica was confident he'd soon make friends, and he did. Her son was a very open and lovable five-year-old, even if she did say so herself. Everyone said he was full of fun and a charming kind of cheek. Everybody commented on his warm and generous nature.

If only they knew who his father was . . .

No! Veronica quickly cut the thought off. She would not think of . . . *him*. Never again would she let that man so much as cross her thoughts. He'd been told that his son had died at birth and had not even bothered to check it out. No doubt he'd been only too happy to believe it was true. The shame of having a son born in . . . such a place . . . had probably curled Wayne D'Arville's fastidious lip. The thought was enough to make her want to scream or burst into tears. Quickly, she thrust the past away from her.

Instead, Veronica conjured up the sight of her son as he'd been on the plane coming over — cherub-cheeked and dark-haired, with big blue eyes that had stared out at their new home. America.

Running part of the way saved her more time, and as she pushed open the swing doors of the gigantic shopping precinct it was just coming up to 9 a.m.

She had worked at Nibbits for the past two months, and she quickly made her way across the grey-flecked carpet that lined the vast acreages of floorspace. Her own little niche in the giant store was on the cosmetics/pharmacy floor, and as she approached the colourful counter, lined with exquisite crystal perfume bottles, she pulled off her warm brown serge coat. She'd found it at a rummage sale just two days after arriving in New York, and although it was old it was of an elegant cut and just about passed muster on the Nibbits dress code for employees. And it was just as well — the thought of the expense of a new coat was enough to push her heart into her boots. She was managing her budget on a precarious shoestring as it was.

'You're cutting it fine, aren't you?' Julie Preston, her ever-cheerful fellow worker, said with a knowing wink as Veronica lifted the wooden bar on the counter and closed it behind her.

'I know. I was up all night; Travis had a restless night. I only hope he behaves himself at school today. The last thing I need is a phone call asking me to come and pick him up. Old man Howard would have a fit if I had to have so much as an hour off.'

Julie gave a sympathetic shrug, then groaned as the two-minute warning bell sounded. Soon they'd be inundated with matrons looking for something 'different', teenage girls trying to sneak samples of Joy perfume, and the inevitable light-fingered professional shoplifter or two. 'You have to have eyes in the back of your head to work in this place,' Julie had told her the first day she'd started, and Veronica had soon understood what she meant.

Now, Veronica quickly turned to one of the large mirrors that Nibbits supplied for its customers and checked her appearance.

The rather elegant and capable-looking Veronica Coltrane reflected back at her was very different from the defeated woman who had served six months at Nottinghamshire Open Prison for Women and a further six months at Holloway.

Had it really been five years ago? It seemed as if it were only yesterday . . .

She could still hear the bell ringing at six o'clock in the morning, and the muttering sounds of discontented voices. In her dreams, the sound of keys turning in endless locks chased her through restless nights. She could still remember queueing to 'slop out'. And queueing for breakfast. And queueing in work lines. Her whole world had consisted of queueing in a relentless place that existed in shades of grey.

It was not surprising that she had lost weight so drastically in prison after giving birth to Travis.

She'd suffered badly from post-natal depression and had quickly slipped down to a dangerous six stone. Even though she had regained a few pounds during the five years she'd lived with her father in their Reading semi, her figure was still pencil-slim. But her breasts were well-rounded, no doubt as a legacy of breast-feeding her son.

Veronica felt guilty at lying to the recruiting officer at Nibbits, but she knew she'd never be hired if she was honest about her past. And she didn't think the store had been the loser by it. She was now the top saleswoman on the floor.

Anxiously, she turned to a side view in the mirror. The dress she wore was also second-hand, for money was perpetually tight, but it was simple, black, and suited her.

Her cap of sleek black hair gave her a distinctly Parisian elegance, always handy when selling trifles to rich women, and her small, piquant face needed the barest amount of make-up, which was just as well. Veronica had spent the last of her woefully pitiful savings on getting to New York, and now only her wages at Nibbits kept herself and her son from poverty's door.

Sebastien, being Sebastien, had offered to lend her a substantial amount, of course, but she had firmly refused. He'd done quite enough for her already in managing to get her into America at all. With a criminal record, she was still not sure how he had managed to secure her a work permit and visa, but she knew better than anyone that Sebastien Teale could move mountains when he wanted to.

Besides, as ungrateful as she knew it was, she didn't want to have anything to do with anyone who was friends with . . . *him*. Not that Sebastien was Wayne's friend, exactly. Were psychiatrists allowed to be friends with their patients? She wasn't sure and cared even less.

When she'd asked him how he'd managed to get her the necessary documentation, he'd just smiled at her with that devastating smile of his. 'Let's just say I've got friends over there,' he'd murmured, his eyes crinkling at the corners as he smiled, his boyish grin flashing his usual gentle charm.

Sebastien had written to her the day after her trial had ended, telling her he believed in her innocence and always would. It had been the only ray of sunshine in a world turned unbearably bleak, and she had immediately written back. A long and life-saving correspondence had resulted, with every two days of her sentence seeing her receive a long, cheerful and chatty letter. Those letters had enabled her to keep a grip on reality in that grim and awful place.

Regular visits from her father and Sebastien had also kept her sane, but even so, after her time was up, she had left a changed woman.

Trust was completely gone. You learned not to trust anyone in that place. Her things were stolen with almost monotonous regularity — stupid things like her toothpaste, the emery board with which she used to shape her fingernails, her hair grips. She had not realized how precious freedom was until it was taken away from her.

You could wear no make-up or perfume. You could have only one letter a day, and those were read, both incoming and outgoing. Any parcels sent in by friends or relatives were searched, and no food parcels were allowed. Looking back, Veronica wondered how she had survived it all.

'Excuse me, young woman, how much is this?'

Veronica blinked, shaking off the memories, and focused on the woman in front of her. She was one of what Julie called the 'blue-rinse brigade', for her hair was silver-blue and her face, aged and lined, pinched in perpetual ill-humour.

Veronica checked the pot of moisturizer, and said, 'That is four dollars sixty-seven, madam.'

'What? For this tiny thing? Preposterous! What else do you have?'

Veronica reached behind her for the wooden box of creams, catching Julie rolling her eyes at her. She grinned, quickly wiped off the smile, turned and began to explain the uses and prices of the creams. After half an hour the woman left, a small tube of cream costing sixty cents clutched triumphantly in her gloved hand.

The woman's white silk gloves alone, Veronica thought grimly, would have paid her rent at Mrs Williams's boarding house for a whole month.

Life was so screamingly unfair sometimes that it still managed to catch Veronica on the raw. And because she knew how quickly bitterness could destroy a person, she forced herself to think of something good.

She had been so lucky to find Mrs Williams, her landlady, for instance. Mrs Williams was a sixty-six-year-old widow who took boarders more for company than for the money. All her tenants were women, for the thought of a man in the house filled the tiny four-foot-eight woman with quivering trepidation.

Veronica had spent three miserable days trying to find a place that she could afford that also allowed young children. It had just been getting dark when her last attempt at finding a room had failed, forcing her to contemplate paying for yet another night at the YWCA.

But the porter of the modern apartment block she had just tried had taken pity on her and given her Mrs Williams's name and address. It was raining hard by the time she got there, and Travis, snug and dry in his padded anorak, was chatting happily to a stray cat, who was sniffing his chubby hands in search of titbits.

She walked up the broken steps of the once elegant house opposite Central Park, hardly paying attention to the scrubby plot of land that was supposed to be a garden, too tired, weary and despondent to care about the flaking paint or the haphazard roof. Looking back on that interview, Veronica supposed that it was her too-slender appearance and the dull, hopeless expression in her eyes that had been the deciding factor in making Mrs Williams abandon her strict 'no children' policy.

That, and the fact that, when the old woman looked down at him, Travis had, with miraculous timing, decided to bestow on the old lady one of his dazzling, happy smiles.

Since then, Mrs Williams and Travis had developed a bond that had allowed Veronica to leave him in the landlady's care without having to pay the cost of a childminder.

That alone had probably kept her from starving.

It was approaching lunchtime and Veronica and Julie were swamped. The January sales were just winding down, and last-minute panic-buying had brought out the housewives in hordes.

Her feet were killing her, her face ached from wearing its customer-smile, and the counter was a mess.

''Allo. I'm lookin' for a perfume, luv. What ya got?'

The voice was loud, male, and easily rose above the rest of the babbling female crowd. And its broad cockney accent had Veronica swinging around in amazement, her eyes picking out the voice's owner in an instant.

He was six feet or so, with brown, longish hair, deep-set cheerful brown eyes and a narrow, boyish face that was as full of cheek as his voice.

Veronica, aware that she was staring, pulled herself together with a snap. 'Certainly, sir. What price range did you have in mind?'

The man's face broke into a huge grin. 'Luv a duck,' he said outrageously, his accent deliberately exaggerated. 'A bloody Englisher, as I live an' breave. What ya doing over 'ere?'

Veronica's smile suddenly changed from her customer variety to a very different kind. 'Working. Hard. And you're holding up the traffic,' she all but growled. She had been a virgin when she had met Wayne D'Arville, a young and foolish woman who didn't know enough to get out of the kitchen when it caught fire. The result was a severe burning, and she was not about to get burned again. Every instinct in her screamed at her to get rid of this . . . this . . . outrageous stranger.

The stranger in question glanced around him, noting the shoving feminine crowd as if for the first time. 'Don't worry about them. I promise I'm gonna buy somefink expensive.' He paused just long enough to rub his fingers and thumbs together in an expressive gesture. 'Money talks, luv.'

He noted her flashing dark eyes, with just a tiny tigerish glint deep in their depths, and grinned widely. 'Just fink of your commission.'

Veronica looked him up and down with quick, jaundiced eyes. His jeans were faded at the knees and frayed at the ankles, and the shirt he wore had its buttons done up in the wrong order, so that the white cotton sat on his thin frame at an awkward ankle. On top of that, he wore a fur coat of dubious pedigree. It even . . .

She leaned forward slowly and gave a delicate sniff, her prettily shaped nostrils flaring as she did so.

Yes. Just as she thought. It actually *smelled*.

She met his eyes, which were by now twinkling with laughter, and slowly shook her head.

'I am the genuine article, luv, 'onest. You'll be getting a humungous commission from me. I'm after the biggest and most expensive bottle of smelly stuff yer got.'

'Uh-huh,' she said without the merest hint of expression of any kind. Keeping her feet firmly on the ground, both physically and metaphorically, she turned at the waist to reach for a gigantic bottle of the most expensive perfume available, in a real silver and crystal flacon.

The stranger's eyes nearly popped out of his head. Rapidly he ran his eyes over her slender curves, his eyes lingering at the angle of her shoulders, the teasing thrust of her breasts, and the very shapely length of her legs.

As her fingers fastened around the bottle, and she prayed that old man Howard wouldn't choose that moment to come on the floor to see her humouring a tramp, she caught a rapid movement out of the corner of her eye. Quickly, she turned her head to look at Julie, who was waving her hands frantically about below the level of the counter and mouthing something at her that she couldn't quite lip-read. She had no idea that her unusual pose had made the stranger's appreciative smile turn oddly intense.

The man began to positively stare at her profile. With her body twisted one way, and her head another, she should have looked awkward, ridiculous even. But she didn't. She looked . . .

'Gorgeous,' he muttered.

Veronica, still wearing a puzzled frown, turned back to the cockney who reminded her so much of a Victorian barrow boy for looks and cheek. She smiled stiffly. 'Did you say something, sir?' she gritted through her teeth.

'I said you look gorgeous,' the stranger confirmed helpfully.

Veronica attempted to freeze her eyes. She did it remarkably well. In fact her whole face seemed to change, without really changing at all. It was a trick very few women could manage, as the stranger knew only too well.

He could feel his whole body begin to tremble. She was perfect.

'This is a thousand dollars, sir. But it's guaranteed to make the lady smile.' Veronica held out the bottle. Let's see how quickly *that* took the wind out of his arrogant sails!

'I'll bet. But is it guaranteed to make her forgive me?' The brown eyes widened in mute appeal, but the grin he gave her was strictly dastardly.

'That depends,' Veronica snapped. She was aware that she was enjoying herself enormously, and the feeling was more frightening than reassuring. She didn't want a man, any man, to make her feel anything. Not ever again. And certainly not a dirty, scruffy, too-cheeky-for-words cockney!

She turned her smile to one of plastic. It was her best I-have-to-serve-you-whether-I-feel-like-it-or-not smile that was designed to make even princes feel abashed.

The stranger's grin widened. 'Magnificent,' he muttered.

Veronica sighed. Hard. It made her breasts rise and fall, and she was not surprised to see the stranger's eyes fall to that area of her anatomy.

Men. They were so predictable.

She had to get rid of this clown, and now. She felt guilty at leaving Julie to cope with all the backlog he was causing.

'It depends on what, me luvverly?' the stranger responded to her taunt at last, and she just managed to stop herself from crowning him with the bottle. It would have been such a waste of good perfume to smash it over his ugly head.

'On what you've done, sir.' She smiled ever so sweetly.

'Oh. I've done just about everyfink,' he admitted, shaking his head sadly.

'In that case, sir,' she said, reaching under the counter to bring out a beautiful cosmetics case, 'perhaps the perfume *and* this would be in order.'

The box was of cream leather with an enamelled top in jade, turquoise and rose pink. She opened it out to reveal an interior of tiers lined in rose-pink silk that housed everything from blusher to eyeliner, from moisturizer cream to the latest shade of nail varnish. 'This model is four hundred and seventy-nine dollars ninety-nine, sir.'

'You don't say? I'll take it. And the perfume. In fact . . .' he paused and thought about it for a moment '. . . I'd better take two of each. I somehow double-dated meself into one 'ell of a nasty pickle last night. So I've got two sets of ruffled feathers to smooth down.'

'Two of each?' she echoed stupidly. Did this idiot not know when enough was enough? Then she all but groaned as she saw Mrs Fitzpatrick, the floor manager, bearing down on them from a great height, no doubt attracted by the large queue. She was an extremely tall redheaded woman, with imperious eyes and a voice to match. 'Oh, no!' Veronica

303

muttered, her face dropping to such a crestfallen low that her pain-in-the-neck customer turned his head curiously to follow her line of vision.

He gave a long, low whistle from between his teeth.

'Oh-oh,' he said. 'The dragon lady approacheth.'

Veronica closed her eyes briefly then opened them again, stiffening her backbone and so missing the expression in the brown eyes that watched her like a hawk.

The kid looked really scared. Did she really need this dead-hole job so much? A kid who looked like *she* did? Never. The stranger knew she could get a job anywhere. Doing anything . . .

As Mrs Fitzpatrick approached, her eyes fell at once on the disreputable-looking man hogging the counter, and Veronica tensed, just waiting for the disdainful look to plaster itself across her supercilious face.

Instead, to her utter astonishment, the dragon lady beamed a smile of almost fawning adulation across the remaining few yards. Her hands came out in a supplication of toadying welcome.

Veronica felt her jaw drop. Literally.

'Ahh, Mr Copeland.' The floor manager all but sang the name. 'I can't *tell* you how honoured Nibbits is to have you.' Her white teeth flashed into a perfect public-relations smile.

Veronica had noticed before that the supervisor tended to refer to the shop as if it were a person, not a pile of bricks. It was always 'Nibbits prefers its employees to wear heeled shoes' or 'Nibbits is very good to its employees if they work hard.'

Now Veronica stood and gaped as she watched several of the women who had been queueing impatiently suddenly begin to whisper among themselves. Like one animal, all their eyes swivelled to watch the tall, beaming man. Lashes fluttered.

Incredible! Veronica thought. One minute they were elbowing and muttering about queue-hogs, the next, even the oldest of them were blushing like schoolgirls.

What the hell was going on?

'Well, now, I can only say I'm right sorry I never came before.' Was it her imagination, or had the cockney accent broadened again? 'I can only say that if I knew you always employed such helpful and pretty staff...' he turned to blow the still open-mouthed Veronica a hearty kiss '... I'd've come before, so I would, and that's the 'onest truth.'

Mrs Fitzpatrick blushed as if the compliment were directed at her personally.

Veronica looked from the scruffy man in front of her to her beaming boss, feeling like someone who'd come in during the middle of a play. She knew she was the only one who was not in on the plot, and it worried her.

'Catchin' flies, luv?'

Veronica turned her head once more to her customer, like a spectator at a tennis match, and then, when the meaning behind his words finally filtered into her befuddled brain, she snapped her teeth shut with an audible click.

'Can I be of help, Mr Copeland?' Mrs Fitzpatrick asked, and Veronica nearly fainted. Mrs Fitzpatrick, offering to serve, to actually manually serve, a customer? Veronica wished she could sit down. Her legs had gone quite watery.

'Ah, that's a luvverly thought, but this young lady was just showing me all this marvellous stuff. I only came in to buy a tube of toothpaste. I must say, you certainly know how to pick your salesladies.'

Veronica opened her mouth to deny the outrageous lie, then quickly snapped it shut again.

His eyes met hers and twinkled. Damn him.

'I tell yer what,' he said cheerfully. 'I'll have three of these...' he tapped the flacon of perfume '... and three of these.' He indicated the cosmetics case.

Veronica's mind began to spin as she thought of the commission, and without another word, and not giving him so much as half a second in which to change his mind, she practically flew to the till and rang up the purchases while she still had witnesses to back her claim.

'Would you like them gift-wrapped, sir?' she asked, her voice now very Nibbits'-best-customer in tone.

'Only two sets of 'em,' he said. 'This and this . . .' he pushed forward one box of cosmetics and one bottle of perfume '. . . are for you, luv.'

Veronica stared at him, blinked, then looked to Mrs Fitzpatrick for help. The dragon lady, however, couldn't make up her mind whether to smile graciously at Mr Whoever-the-hell-he-was or scowl at her.

'I'm not sure if I can accept, sir,' she eventually said, and smiled through her gritted teeth so sweetly that she was sure her face would crack.

'Oh? Well, now, if you don't, I won't pay yer a penny. Eh, ladies? Ain't that right?' He suddenly turned and appealed to the avid audience, who began to titter and nod their heads as he folded his arms stubbornly across his narrow chest.

Veronica glanced at her boss helplessly and shrugged. 'Very well . . . sir . . . er . . . thank you very much.' She forced the words out with a great deal of effort. He noticed her hesitation over the polite 'sir' and grinned even more widely.

'My name is Valentine Copeland,' he said. And gave a bow. 'Use it, why don't ya, luv?'

'Certainly, Mr Copeland. What colour paper would you prefer? We have pink, silver-green or navy blue with gold poppies.'

For the first time he looked genuinely disconcerted. 'Er — the pink's fine,' he said, and then he began to smile in earnest as he watched her professionally gift wrap the four purchases. 'Ta ever so,' he said, took the parcels from her, and turned and kissed Mrs Fitzpatrick's cheek.

The woman blushed scarlet.

From his pocket he produced a small white square of paper and presented it to the flustered woman. 'A ticket for my show. You will come, won't ya, luv?'

'Oh, indeed, Mr Copeland. Indeed. Thank you so much. Nibbits is honoured.'

The man kissed her cheek again, but as his lips touched the perfumed skin of the delighted redhead, his eyes slewed over to Veronica and he dropped one eyelid in a slow, audacious wink.

Then he turned, and, whistling loudly and excruciatingly out of tune, sauntered off.

Veronica let out a long, slow breath. Mrs Fitzpatrick, clutching her ticket as if it were gold, floated away. 'Bloody hell,' Veronica said softly, but had a chance to say no more as the female deluge, after craning their necks for the last glimpse of the apparently famous Mr Copeland, once more besieged the desk.

CHAPTER 25

It wasn't until the store closed at five-thirty that Julie at last had a chance to speak to her.

Veronica had noticed that her friend had been straining at the bit ever since the incident with the cockney had happened, and she sank down wearily on to a stool and slipped off her shoes, preparing herself for an explanation of the morning's extraordinary events.

'Well, you're a bright spark and no mistake,' was Julie's opening gambit, her blonde hair tumbling around her shoulders as she pulled it free from the chignon she habitually wore. 'Did you see his face when you pretended not to recognize his name?'

'I wasn't pretending,' Veronica said drolly. 'Just who *is* he?' She couldn't deny, even to herself, that the man had thoroughly bamboozled her. He acted the tramp but was obviously nothing of the sort. He made her want to thump him, at the same time as she wanted to laugh at him.

And, worst of all, he was so damned attractive. And Veronica knew all about the devastation attractive men could cause. Which meant she would have nothing to do with him again.

Even so, she was naturally curious. 'I've no idea what all the fuss is about,' she added crossly, and wondered, with a lance of panic, just who she was trying to kid.

This time it was Julie's turn to gape at her, then she began to laugh helplessly. 'Oh, Ver, honestly. He's only the hottest hot-shot fashion designer of them all. Nobody's more "in". Everyone's wearing Valentine.'

'A dressmaker?' Veronica squeaked. 'Him?'

It was not only the raggedness of his own clothes that made his profession surprising, but the character of the man himself. There was something raw about him, something so openly virile and masculine and . . . sexy . . . that she just couldn't picture him creating women's clothes.

Julie gave her a quick run-down on the meteoric rise of the Valentine fashion comet, and repeatedly wished aloud that she could own just one, *just one* of his creations.

At last she wound down about how fabulous Valentine was and muttered more incomprehensible grumbles about the floor manager as they prepared to leave. Collecting coats and bags — and in Veronica's case her unexpected presents — they walked wearily on sore feet through the mall to the outer door.

'Oh, hell,' Julie moaned, looking out. 'It's pouring. Doesn't that just beat all?'

It was indeed raining as if it meant it — a cold January downpour. The two girls shrugged and glanced at each other in silent resignation. 'Oh, well,' Veronica said, and then they each made a dash for it in opposite directions.

But Veronica had only gone a yard or so in the direction of the subway when a nifty little black sports car, an E-type Jag no less, with wired wheels and a silver racing stripe, suddenly pulled up at the kerb, and the door was thrust open.

'Get in, luvverly lady. I wanta talk to you.'

Veronica knew the voice instantly. Could there be any forgetting it?

She hesitated, nearly got her eye poked out by an umbrella, and then shrugged. She quickly dipped into the

309

small and cramped interior and slammed the door shut behind her.

'Hello again,' she said, a little nervously, smoothing down her dress over her knees and rearranging herself more decorously in the bucket seat.

Valentine Copeland watched her with avid brown eyes.

'You can forget that for a start,' she snapped, and he blinked.

'What?'

Veronica didn't bother to reply but gave him a speaking glance instead. He grinned and gunned the engine. She gave him her address and then sat back and sighed, utterly exhausted. What a day!

His next words, however, had her eyes snapping open with a vengeance. 'How d'ya fancy bein' a model?'

'What?'

'I said,' he repeated patiently, 'that you should be a model. I mean, just look at yah. Biggish boobs, slender as a whippet everywhere else, and with that 'airdo — you look like a fancy French trollop already.'

'Gee, thanks.'

'Don't mention it. With a little work, you could look real decent. Do I turn here?'

'Next left.'

He pulled into the narrow street, stared up at the decrepit building, and sorrowfully shook his head.

'Thanks for the lift, Mr Copeland,' she said crisply. Bloody nerve! Did he really think she would tumble into his bed just because he spun her some old chestnut about getting her into showbusiness, or the fashion-world equivalent? Hah! She wasn't born yesterday. She had been naive once, but now she was a thousand years old. Way too wise for one of his clumsy attempts, at any rate.

The man was a rank beginner. She'd been taught about male perfidy by the best. For an instant, a look of such bleakness crossed her face that Valentine Copeland felt his heart do a funny kind of lurch in his chest.

Then she was opening the door, without so much as a goodbye, and making a mad dash up the steps. She fumbled in her bag for the key, the wet rain managing to drip, as cold rain always did, down the back of her collar. She shuddered, opened the door and turned.

'Oomph,' she grunted as he cannoned straight into her.

'Shut the door, for Pete's sake. It's bleedin' perishin' out there.'

She snapped the door shut and glowered at him in the dingy hall. She opened her mouth, about to enjoy the experience of chucking him out on his ear, when her anticipated pleasures were interrupted.

'Is that you, Veronica? Ah . . . oh, I didn't realize you had a young man with you.' Mrs Williams's gentle voice took on a flustered tone.

Veronica opened her mouth again but was too late.

Valentine spun on his heel, looked way down into the wide watery blue eyes of the silver-haired Mrs Williams and grinned. He bent, took her withered hand gently in his, and kissed it.

Actually *kissed* it?

Just who does he think he is now? Veronica fumed. Don bloody Juan?

Veronica closed her eyes, groaned silently, counted up to a hundred and listened in disgusted silence as he charmed the little lace knickers off her landlady.

'Oh, but you must stay for dinner, Mr Copeland,' she heard her landlady twitter a few minutes later. 'I've never entertained a famous gentleman before,' the old woman went on, making Veronica blink. Good grief. He really was famous if even Mrs Williams knew all about him.

Giving her an I-told-you-so look, mixed with the clear message 'it's pointless to resist', he followed the gushing woman into her cosy little kitchen.

Mrs Williams didn't often cook for her guests, and as she began to lay the table Veronica was worried that they were putting her out. She watched Valentine shrug himself out of the tatty coat, revealing a long and skinny chest, and then felt a small tug of something dangerous pull at her stomach as he rolled up his sleeves and said, 'You'll need some extra spuds done. Where they at, luv?'

To her surprise, Mrs Williams didn't demur, but pointed under the sink. She watched, totally nonplussed, as he poured water into a bowl, hunted about for a knife and then began to peel potatoes as if he'd done it every day of his life.

Veronica, knowing when she was beaten, shrugged and left them to it, going to her room to change and let Travis know she was home. As she expected, he was full of school, and what they'd done in art class, and all about his new best friend, Ira, who was a Jew, and what was a Jew anyway?

Veronica patiently explained about Judaism and gave him a thorough lecture on the evils of antisemitism, and then stood, looking at her son thoughtfully.

A slow smile spread over her face.

It was time to launch a counter-offensive against the cocky Mr Valentine Copeland. It was time, she thought, taking her son by the hand, to bring on her secret weapon.

Valentine glanced up from the sink as she paused dramatically in the doorway, his eyes going straight to the dark-haired boy she was holding a little awkwardly on one hip.

Travis was getting a little old to carry around like a baby, but she was anxious to create the right effect.

Across the top of the boy's head, her eyes met his, and she smiled grimly.

Now what are you going to do about *this*, Mr Fashion Guru?

Travis looked around him keenly, spotting the stranger instantly, of course, his blue eyes widening warily. He turned his head shyly into his mother's shoulder. Then he chanced another peep. Men were rare in his life. His grandpapa had stayed behind in England.

Having a man in the kitchen was something new.

Valentine met the boy's curious gaze and gave him a jaunty grin, which was instantly returned by the toddler, and looked back at his mother. His eyes dropped to her left hand. Seeing no ring there, he gave her an even jauntier grin and turned back to shelling some peas. Then his loud, timeless whistle once more filled the kitchen.

Veronica felt oddly unnerved. It was not the reaction she had expected. Or been hoping for. There was supposed to have been a look of horror across his face, quickly followed by some sort of sickly grin and an excuse to leave.

No man wanted a woman with a child. A single, unmarried woman with a child . . . So why the hell couldn't he act true to form with the rest of the male kind? she wondered furiously.

Nervously she guided Travis to the table. It was as if a whirlwind had come into her life, turning it upside down. And it scared her. She'd had enough of whirlwinds; the last one had almost killed her.

They sat down to eat an hour later. Valentine had wolfed down almost half of the pile on his plate by the time Veronica had unfolded her napkin, put it on her lap and poured a glass of orange juice. She gave him a vicious 'you pig' look and speared a piece of lamb.

Mrs Williams looked from one to the other, her blue eyes twinkling. She suddenly felt years younger.

Turning to the old woman, Valentine said, 'Don't you think Veronica—' he said her name for the first time, savouring it as if it were an exquisite wine '—would make a good model for my spring collection next week, Mrs Williams?'

'Oh, yes!' The old face lit up like a Christmas tree. 'Yes, I thought the first moment I laid eyes on her what a pretty little thing she was,' Mrs Williams admitted, the two of them quite happily talking about her as if she weren't there.

'Stop it,' Veronica hissed at him. 'Mrs Williams, he's just teasing you. I couldn't possibly be a model. I don't even know how to walk.'

'You just put one foot in front of the other, darlin'.'

'Shut up!'

'See how she treats me, Mrs Williams?' he whined. 'An' all I wanta do is make her a star!'

The old lady tut-tutted, and then broke out the best cream sherry for an after-dinner nightcap. Veronica glanced pointedly at her watch, and then went upstairs to put her son to bed.

But for once Travis was reluctant to leave the company of adults. Several times he looked over his shoulder at the stranger as they left the room, and each time Valentine winked at him.

Travis had said suspiciously very little at the table, but Veronica suspected it was only shyness. Now, as he more or less co-operated with getting into his pyjamas, he looked at her with a curiously adult look.

'I like that man, Mummy,' he said sleepily.

She winced and kissed his newly washed face. 'Do you, puss?' She pushed his hair off his face and straightened, her face thoughtful and just a little scared. She knew a boy needed a father, but . . . she couldn't let a man into her life again.

She just couldn't risk it. Love was too dangerous. Love could betray you. Love could leave you in prison, pregnant and in despair. Love was a killer.

She lingered for ten minutes in her son's room, just to make sure he was asleep, but when she came back down she was not at all surprised to see that Valentine was still sitting in the same chintzy armchair looking as if he were set for the night.

'It's getting late, Mr Copeland,' she said, smiling calmly and glancing at the old lady, who was trying valiantly not to nod off in her own armchair.

'So it is. I'll pick y'up tomorrow about ten and show you round the House of Valentine. After all, my star model must know about the ins and outs of the trade.'

Veronica sighed sharply. 'I've told you. I'm not taking the bait.'

Val glanced at her. She was nervous, no doubt about it. It wasn't hard to see why. A single lady with a son had to have had a few knocks in life.

So she was wary. That was all right with him.

He settled back and folded his arms across his chest. 'I ain't movin' till you agree to come and be my new Venus.'

'I have to work tomorrow,' she lied, and then wanted to scream in frustration as he slowly shook his head.

'Oh, what porky pies you do tell,' he said sorrowfully. 'It's your day off tomorrow — I checked.' He used the cockney rhyming slang for 'lies' on purpose, she was sure. In fact, she wouldn't have been surprised to learn that he actually came from upper-crust Cheltenham or some other such place.

'Oh, all right,' she snapped ungraciously. She was obviously not going to get rid of him unless she placated him. 'Ten o'clock, you say? But I'm only going to look around the place, mind.'

By nine-fifteen the next morning she'd taken Travis to school and returned. She was just putting on her coat to go out again. After sleeping on the matter, she'd awoken that morning with a screaming determination to be out when Mr Valentine Copeland called. A trip to the park, then the zoo was called for, so that when the pest called in she'd be long gone.

She simply couldn't risk it. She knew it was cowardly, but there was something about Valentine that scared her. He was so different from Wayne D'Arville, for one thing.

She must remember that threats came in all shapes and sizes.

She said goodbye to Mrs Williams, opened the door, slipped her handbag over her arm and, keeping a wary eye on the wet and slippery steps, walked down the path, straight into his waiting arms.

'Oh, I do like a lady who's always punctual,' he said, bundling her into his waiting car before she could draw breath. He was wearing the exact same outfit as yesterday, and she wouldn't have put it past him to have slept in it, either.

'You're early,' she accused, then met his knowing eyes for a brief second before he started the car. A tingle started

315

deep in her stomach and she swallowed hard. 'Why, you dirty, no-good, sneaky . . .'

He pulled away from the kerb, her insults loud in his ear. When he pulled up outside a large warehouse looking over a dirty, sluggish stretch of the East River, she was still at it.

'. . . low-down, uncouth, arrogant, pig-headed . . .'

The warehouse was huge, warm and full of fabric, people, chatter and girls in underwear.

'This is the manufacturing floor,' Valentine said, taking a huge and unmistakably heavy roll of white silk under one arm and carrying it as if it were a suitcase.

Veronica practically had to run to keep up with him. 'These magnificent ladies with their sewing machines—' with his free hand he swept a gesture through the air that encompassed at least ten women, all busily sewing, hand-stitching or cutting fabric '—are the backbone of the House of Valentine.'

'Too right,' somebody's harassed voice piped up from the back, causing a wave of laughter to ripple across the floor.

'Girls, this is our new model for next week. Since Darlene left in spitting fury and vowing never to come back, I had to work fast. Do you think she'll do?'

Veronica blushed red as she suddenly became the focus of all eyes. She wished she'd put on a different coat, then shrugged angrily. What did it matter? She wasn't really going to model in his damned show!

'I'll take that resounding silence for a yes,' Valentine said, and juggled the enormous roll of silk more firmly under his armpit, before setting off once more.

'Now, you've got to grasp some basics of fashion styles,' he said, then stopped abruptly to look closely at her. 'You do have a fairly good brain, don't yah?'

'Yes, I have. A damned good brain, in fact!' she snapped back. 'I wrote a book on—' she began, then stopped so abruptly he gave her a quick glance. But she had gone so pale that he knew better than to push it.

316

There was something nasty lurking in this girl's brain, he thought grimly. And it had no place being in there. He'd have to hoick it out.

'Good. In that case,' he began, 'take a gander at this.'

An hour later her brain was awash with new facts, figures and jargon. She knew now that fasteners came in all sorts besides zips and buttons — there were press studs, button-down tabs, lacing, Velcro, braces and snap-fasteners, not to mention rouleau fastenings. She also knew that collars were not merely collars — they were either funnel, bertha, Gladstone, Quaker, poet, sailor, Eton, Pierrot or mandarin. And dresses, according to Valentine, were not dresses at all unless they were appliqued, riddled with bias-cuts, draped, embroidered, gathered or smocked. And that was not to mention the insertions, jabots, shirring or quilting.

They were back among the sewing machines again when he seemed to run out of steam. Veronica watched a woman with a big press putting pleats into a dress. 'That's a bonded silk organza sprayed fabric with a cutwork edge. She's putting box pleats into it,' he explained, catching the direction of her look.

'I know,' she lied. 'There are at least four sorts of pleats, right?'

Valentine tut-tutted, then finally put down the silk roll. In the same spot where he had picked it up.

He put both hands on his narrow hips and looked at her, shaking his head. 'Coltrane, Coltrane, Coltrane,' he said sadly. 'There are knife pleats . . .' he ticked them off on his fingers '. . . impressed pleats, inverted, accordion and anchored knife pleats. Then there are crystal pleats and—'

'If you don't shut up,' Veronica screamed, totally at the end of her tether, 'I'm going to murder you!'

The silence was complete for a few seconds, then the same harassed voice of over an hour ago said tiredly, 'You're going to fit right on in, I can see. Welcome to the wonderful House of Valentine.' This time the laughter came louder, while Valentine grinned and Veronica glowered.

'Well, now you know summat about how they make the stuff you're gonna wear, let's get one of the gals to sort you out for the actual catwalk. By the way, I've always thought they named the catwalk very well. Put in your claws and behave yourself. Here, Chrissie, luv, will you show Veronica the ropes? You've got a week to get her right.'

'A week!' The skinny blonde woman who approached, covered in pins, tape measures and ribbons, looked almost dead on her feet, but the sharp hazel eyes she turned on Veronica were as alert as a bird's. 'Walk over there,' she said, pointing imperiously to a far-flung table.

Veronica, caught on the hop, did so, then stopped and stalked back. 'Look here, I'm not . . .'

'She walks well enough already. She's got natural style,' the tired blonde said, both of them ignoring Veronica completely. 'She just needs to sway her hips more. I'll give her some exercises to do. She's had a kid?' she suddenly asked.

Veronica began to look like a thundercloud. Valentine nodded complacently. 'Yep. You can tell, yeah?'

The washed-out blonde nodded. 'Babies do good things for the hips, funnily enough.'

Veronica stamped her foot, but the blonde had already been called away to deal with a recalcitrant bra strap giving a tall, big-breasted brunette some trouble, and nobody else paid the slightest attention to her tantrum.

'Look, once and for all, I'm not doing this damned show. I have to work, for a start,' she yelled, feeling as if she was being steamrollered by an out-of-control maniac.

'Nah, yah don't.' Valentine shook his craggy head, his longish hair flying about all over the place. 'I called them up today and handed in yer notice. They was none too pleased, until I told them what you were doin' instead, and then they rubbed their hands in glee. Great publicity for them, you see. "Valentine model found in Nibbits".' He held his hands up as if at an imaginary billboard. 'Good headline, that, don't yah think?'

Veronica stared at him, opened her mouth, closed it, then opened it again.

'I hate you,' she finally muttered.

'Oh, good. Beats indifference every time. Anyway, I 'ear it's usual for married couples to 'ate each other.'

Veronica sat down abruptly, Valentine only just managing to yank a chair under her in time to save her from falling flat on her behind.

'You're mad,' she said at last.

Was it only yesterday that she'd been crossing the road in the rain, pursued by the demons of her past, determined never to have anything to do with another man again?

Where was that angry, bitter girl now when she needed her, dammit?

'You don't know anything about me,' she said at last.

'Not yet, nah,' he admitted cheerfully. 'But I dare say it'll be fun learnin'.'

She looked into those deep, dark eyes of his and swallowed hard. She had to stop it. She had to. This was madness. She was falling, and they both knew it.

For a long moment their eyes met, his for once totally serious and determined. Then she said the one thing that she knew would save her.

'I've been in prison,' she said, her voice flat.

'Really?' Valentine said, fascinated. 'So 've I. What were you in for?'

CHAPTER 26

Two years later

Duncan Somerville turned and glanced from the window of the descending plane and surreptitiously watched the man beside him. Ben Levi, the Israeli Mossad agent, looked perfectly at ease, but Duncan knew, from having read his file, that Ben had lost both his parents and an older sister at a concentration camp that he himself had barely survived.

Duncan smiled at a passing stewardess, who nodded and smiled back automatically. Duncan was always a favourite of stewardesses wherever he flew.

It was not his looks, nor the fact that he had money. It was his manners that made him the darling of everybody, but especially those in public service. For he was that rare commodity that was becoming more and more extinct with every passing year.

Duncan Somerville was a gentleman.

Somewhere in his sixties, he looked like everybody's idea of a favourite uncle. His suit was impeccable but not showy. His only jewellery was a pair of plain gold cufflinks. He had ordered only one whisky and soda on the flight, and had glanced angrily at the young couple across the way who had been determined to get drunk — and succeeded.

And when he spoke, feminine hearts began to flutter. He might be slightly portly, slightly balding and just a little florid of face. But his voice was pure syrup. Southern syrup.

Having been raised in Atlanta all his life, on a plantation that could have been used in a *Gone with the Wind* remake, his whole demeanour screamed gentle southern class.

The stewardess would have been astounded to know that Duncan Somerville was a first class Nazi-hunter.

He'd been in the Diplomatic Service during the war, stationed in Switzerland. He'd had a beautiful wife, who had left him for a younger man, but not before giving him a beautiful daughter. That daughter was now married to a world-famous Hollywood director and had made him a grandpa three times over. There was nothing about him that would have made anyone guess at his lifelong quest.

But since the war he, and a small group of people like him, had been responsible for bringing no less than five top-ranking Nazis to trial in Israel.

'Is your seatbelt secure, Mr Somerville?' the stewardess asked him, and her eyes fell to the belt in question, her eyes crinkling in a near-maternal smile.

The Israeli agent beside him hid a smile. He too understood the effect his gentrified friend had on people. When he had first met Somerville, over twenty years ago now, he had been expecting a loud-mouthed, know-it-all American. But he'd been prepared to put up with it, just because Duncan Somerville had proved himself a dedicated man.

Instead, the Mossad agent had been introduced to a man who could have played Santa Claus at a Christmas pantomime and not been out of place. It had taken him a long time to figure out a very simple truth.

Duncan had lost no relatives to the concentration camps, for he and his whole family for generations had been Anglo-Protestants. He had lost no money in Germany. He had, in fact, no reason at all to be so dedicated in the pursuit of Nazis. Except for one thing. Duncan Somerville was a passionate believer in what was *right*. Oh, he was also a profoundly compassionate man, who had been horrified right to the core of his soul when he'd first learned of the atrocities that had been perpetrated in Nazi Germany. And he also had this fear that some rich men had, of being useless in life. But it was his sense of justice that kept him on the track of Nazi criminals when most others had given up.

It had been his sheer dogged persistence that was bringing them now to France.

Wolfgang Mueller had been a commandant for two years, towards the end of the war, in a particularly obscure camp on the borders of Poland. For years Duncan had been sure that Mueller now lived in Monte Carlo, under the name of D'Arville. Through Duncan's meticulous research, which was his great speciality, he had learned all about Mueller/D'Arville.

The man had suddenly appeared in Monte Carlo after the war, with a wife and two sons, claiming to be second-generation American/French.

And, indeed, Duncan had been able to find paper traces of the D'Arville family in Kentucky. Too much paper. But nobody he'd questioned over the years in Kentucky could actually *remember* the D'Arvilles.

Patience had always been one of Duncan's strongest virtues. For years he had collated a dossier on D'Arville that was now complete enough to convince the Israelis that D'Arville was Mueller. When he had escaped Germany during the dying days of the war, one of his lieutenants had disappeared. Duncan suspected that Mueller had intended to use the lieutenant as a scapegoat. Many fleeing Nazis had killed aides, put their papers on them and then defaced the corpse in some way, thus leading the Allies to believe that many more Nazis had perished than really had. The fact that neither the lieutenant nor the supposed 'body' of Commandant Mueller had ever shown up had convinced Duncan that the lieutenant had got wise and left before Mueller could complete his plans. If they could find him, they would have iron proof of Mueller's identity.

The plane landed smoothly in the bright French sunlight, and Duncan checked his briefcase, then glanced at his friend. 'What if Mueller's already gone?'

His drawling southern accent, as ever, had the power to make his companion smile before he shrugged his massive shoulders. At six feet two, Duncan noticed, Ben had a great zest for life: he laughed a lot, ate a lot, and had a riveting habit of running his fingers through his bushy brown beard. Now, as he turned, snapping brown eyes on him, Duncan was once again flustered to see that they were full of good humour. 'He's already under surveillance. We owe you and the committee a great vote of thanks, Duncan.'

Ben found his eyes running over the smaller man, taking in every detail of his friend's appearance. It was a habit of his that he had no intention of breaking. In Duncan's case, his observations were hardly surprising, for he knew his friend well. Duncan's nails were manicured, and Ben's sensitive nose picked up the scent of his Dior cologne. The briefcase he was now clasping nervously to his English-made suit was of the finest hand-tooled Italian leather.

But inside it were documents that would make your hair stand on end.

Duncan's dossier on D'Arville made for interesting reading. He was the owner of the Droit de Seigneur casino and had been for many years. His wife, Marlene, who now called herself Mary, was a very discreet drunk.

His younger son, Hans, whose name had been changed to Henry, had died in a tragic diving accident when he was only a boy. Apparently he had dived off some cliffs, hit the water at a bad angle, and drowned.

His elder son, Helmut, who had taken on the very un-German name of Wayne, was a very different kettle of fish, however.

He had lived and prospered, although Duncan was convinced that there had been a massive rift between father and son at some point in their past. In his teens, Wayne had worked at the casino, when he was not earning a first class degree in economics at the Sorbonne. But suddenly Wayne D'Arville had left Monte Carlo and moved to England.

There, Duncan had been interested to learn, he had joined the ultra-conservative, ultra-reputable financial firm of Platts. Platts, headed by the late Sir Mortimer Platt, gave financial advice to the British aristocracy. The richer you were, the more you employed the agents of Platts. But on Sir Mortimer's death the private company did not come into the hands of Toby Platt, Sir Mortimer's only son, but into those of one Wayne D'Arville.

It probably wasn't as surprising as it sounded. Toby had caused a scandal in the past and was out of his father's favour. And Wayne D'Arville had written a book on modern economics that was still, years after its publication, *the* book to read. It was a work of undoubted genius and had changed money management not only at Platts but on a worldwide scale.

All of which meant that Wayne D'Arville, son of a Nazi, was now one of the wealthiest and most socially powerful men in England. Not that Duncan was interested in Wayne. He was not a vindictive man and did not believe the sins of the fathers should be visited on the sons. Wayne had been a boy of four or so when the war had started. What possible guilt could be attached to him? Children could not choose their parents but had to make the best of what they were given.

If anything, Duncan felt sorry for the man.

But what had really captured Duncan's interest was what had happened just before Wayne left Monte Carlo.

In another document, this time a medical file, it detailed the extraordinary fact that Wolfgang Mueller was now blind. And, try as he might, Duncan had been unable to find a doctor who could tell him why or *how* Mueller had been blinded.

The plane slowly began to disembark, leaving only Duncan, Ben and three others seated. To Duncan's mind at least, the rest of their team were an odd assortment.

One was tall, slim and dark and so movie-star handsome that he reminded the Georgian of an Italian playboy prince. Only the glint of steel in the dark, melting eyes warned him that the illusion was dangerous. The second of the team, by contrast, looked like a ruffled salesman, with short frizzy hair and a tendency to sweat that left dark patches under his armpits. He ate toffees as if they were going out of fashion and kept a blue duffel bag cradled possessively on his lap. The third man Duncan had difficulty remembering, simply because, wherever he went, he seemed to fade into the wallpaper.

Medium height, medium weight, medium hair colour and medium everything else; Duncan had trouble realizing he was even there.

But all were dedicated men. All had lost relatives to the camps. All were devoted to Israel. It was a good team to have on your side when you were fighting evil.

And Mueller was evil.

'Right — let's get going.' Ben's hearty voice was the signal for all of them to leave at intervals, mingling with the crowds in the airport and making their individual ways to the hotel that was their rendezvous point. They took no chances. Ever.

Duncan took a taxi, and he noticed the handsome member of their team take a bus. The others he didn't spot at all.

The hotel was in Cannes, in the old part of town the locals called Le Suquet. On the road to Mandelieu, only five minutes' walk from the port, it was a small, family-run hotel, situated above a restaurant.

Duncan checked in, nose twitching to the scent of food. His room was square, airy and possessed a single bed, wash-basin and wardrobe. He didn't bother to unpack but walked instead to the window and looked out to sea, where a ferry was steaming across the Iles de Lerins, Saint Honorat and Sainte Marguerite.

He sighed, aware he was deliberately letting his mind wander to avoid facing the question they were all here to answer. Namely — if Marcus D'Arville really was Wolfgang Mueller, how would they get him out of France and to Israel to stand trial? He knew Ben was as convinced of D'Arville's true identity as he was, but Duncan was still afraid. Oh, not afraid of being too close to a man who had been responsible for the death of hundreds, but that he *might* have made a mistake. That he was stalking an innocent quarry — and a blind man to boot. It was Duncan's only recurring nightmare: that he might be responsible for the trial and execution of an innocent man.

A discreet tap on the door had him quickly crossing the room. Over the next fifteen minutes all four men arrived at his small, inconspicuous room, the cloak-and-dagger aspect of it never failing to give Duncan a schoolboyish thrill.

Ben and the others watched in bland silence as Duncan dialled the combination on his suitcase and extracted the papers from within. Spreading them out on the bed, the four men inspected them in silence. The pictures were of a stoop-shouldered, blind old man, taken mainly in front of his casino.

'Did you have any luck finding out how he came to be blind?' Duncan asked, knowing that the Mossad had also been intrigued by the man's disability. After all, if it was due to some kind of hereditary disease, there was no way he could be Mueller, for extensive research had showed that no such genetic disorder was prevalent in the Mueller medical history. But D'Arville had not been blind when he had first arrived in Monte Carlo, that much had been easy to ascertain.

'No,' Ben admitted shortly. 'We found the doctor who treated him, but neither money nor threats could open his mouth.' Ben smiled at the American's wince of distaste, and winked at the scruffiest member of the team, who winked back.

'And that's what makes it so interesting,' he added slowly. As expected, Duncan's sharp eyes glanced questioningly up at him.

'How so? I thought doctors were supposed to be discreet?'

Ben smiled, showing massive white teeth. The southern gentleman's naivety and innate goodness went a long way to soothing his battered soul, and he clasped a large hand on Duncan's shoulder, squeezing gently. 'It means, my friend, that the doctor is more afraid of D'Arville than of us. Now why should he be afraid of a mere blind casino owner?'

'Oh,' Duncan said, feeling stupid.

Ben squeezed his shoulder a little harder, then let him go, and, picking up a folder, began to read in concentrated earnest. The family history was vague — too vague. By the time he'd read through the newest findings, he was even more sure that D'Arville was their man. Eye contact with the rest of his companions confirmed that it was unanimous.

'What now?' Duncan asked.

'We go to Monaco, of course. You have rented a villa?'

Duncan nodded and handed over a set of keys.

'Good. And you, my friend . . .' Ben slapped Duncan's back with his meaty paw . . . will have the time of your life in D'Arville's casino. Who knows, you might even win another fortune to go with the one you already have!'

* * *

The Corniche Road to Monte Carlo was notorious. Its serpentine coastal route was full of hairpin bends and skirted towering cliffs that looked down on wave-washed, jagged rocks. Duncan was glad to sit sandwiched between rock-solid Ben and the handsome playboy, who, Duncan noticed nervously, never kept his eyes in one place for more than a moment.

* * *

Two miles from the Monaco border, a black French Citroën stood parked on a grassy knoll opposite a cliff. With tinted black windows that reflected the sun, Wolfgang Mueller waited in anonymous impatience.

His hands were gnarled with rheumatism and constantly ached, but he hardly noticed the pain anymore. Through the sunroof he could hear the screaming of the gulls and the hollow, echoing boom of the waves below. He could smell the sea air and beside him he could hear the slow, regular breathing of Gustave Landro, a Frenchman who had been a collaborator during the war and had made a living as an expensive 'odd-job' man ever since.

'When did Waldo say they left the hotel?' he barked, his voice making the man by his side jump.

'They'll be here soon, Monsieur D'Arville. Try to relax.'

'I am relaxed,' Wolfgang lied, keeping his temper with an ease that spoke of long practice. For Wolfgang Mueller had changed in recent years. Ever since he'd been blinded, in fact.

He had lain on the floor of his study for what had seemed like hours after his bastard son had left, his head on fire with pain, his hands cupped in silent horror over his mutilated, useless eyes. Then the doctor had come, and a needle sliding into his arm had brought temporary relief. But the next morning he had awoken to the same hideous darkness as before.

For months afterwards he had stayed in his luxurious villa, utterly depressed. Not even the call he'd made to his son's would-be father-in-law, a rich and aristocratic vineyard owner, had helped ease his rage. Oh, Wayne's precious little fiancée had chucked him instantly, but Mueller knew that would not be much of a set-back for his poisonous offspring for long. Nor had it. The devil-spawn had quickly moved to England, and out of his father's reach.

Now his frustrated desire for revenge was instilled in him like a festering thorn. Marlene, his own wife, had been relegated to only a voice. After a while he could not even remember what she had once looked like.

But, eventually, and with an immense effort of will, he had forced himself up and out of the mire of his living death, and over the ensuing years found his remaining senses sharpening acutely. He heard things others did not, could interpret scent in a way that others found impossible. Food was now his main sensory pleasure, and three chefs worked in his kitchens.

'There! Jacques has given the signal.' The sudden excited words of his companion dragged Wolfgang from his thoughts, and he stiffened in his seat, a smile of satisfaction pulling at his thin and bloodless lips.

Mossad. Did they really think that they and their American lackey could dig into his past without him knowing? Fools! They were still all fools. The Fatherland knew how to produce men who would always rise to the top, like the cream of the human crop they truly were.

He heard the sound of a heavier motor starting just behind his car, and he let out his breath in a slow, satisfied whoosh. 'You are sure the lorry driver is legitimate?' he asked for the second time.

'Positive. Jean was hailed as a hero of the Resistance. No one will suspect either him or the genuine tragedy of the accident.'

Wolfgang grunted. 'He'd better be a saint. They'll investigate him until Doomsday. The lorry is just as I ordered?' he added sharply.

'Yes, sir. We had to search fifty transport firms before finding one with just the right amount of metal fatigue. The brake failure will be perfectly genuine — and if you could see the rust-bucket Jean is driving . . .' Wolfgang felt him give a lift of his shoulders '. . . you wouldn't worry. There is no one who can equal Jean in this kind of thing.'

The lorry rumbled away. Wolfgang nodded, and slowly leant back in his seat. So be it. The die was cast now. And he trusted his luck to hold . . .

* * *

'Wind the window down, Ben,' Duncan said. 'It's getting hot in here.'

Ben did as he was asked, then breathed in gustily. 'Ah, God knew what he was doing when he created the earth. Just smell that air!'

The rumpled salesman was driving, the duffel bag still on his lap, and Duncan smiled as he leaned forward, eager to catch his first glimpse of Monte Carlo, and only wishing that the circumstances were different. 'What's the first thing we do when—?' he began, then broke off in surprise as the driver began to shout something in high-pitched Yiddish.

He felt Ben stiffen beside him, and then his own eyes widened in terror as a lorry lurched around the bend in front of them, its overbalanced load of fruit already beginning to topple the vehicle on to its side. The salesman tugged frantically on the wheel, desperately trying to steer the car clear, but it was already too late.

Duncan felt his throat close tight in fear, his stomach and heart rising up to choke him as the squealing sound of the brakes and the scent of burning rubber filled the air.

He cried out as the car hit the solid rock that skirted one side of the road, and then gripped Ben's knee in mute terror as the car was catapulted back over the opposite side of the road, to where a flimsy crash barrier awaited them. Beside him, he heard the handsome member of the team begin to chant a Hebrew prayer as the car mounted the barrier, paused like an ungainly eagle for a split second, and then began to plummet down the hundreds-of-feet drop on the other side.

Duncan was not spared the obscene sensation of falling, and he closed his eyes on a terrified groan. Just before the car hit the bottom, he felt Ben's huge hand curl around his own, warm and human and strangely comforting.

Wolfgang Mueller listened to the sounds, cataloguing them in his mind: the squeal of brakes, the crunch of metal, the sudden silence, and the final groan of the dying car and the dying men.

Slowly he nodded. 'Well done. We said a hundred thousand francs, I believe?'

* * *

Far away, in a psychiatric hospital in England, Dr Sebastien Teale looked up as his last patient of the day was brought in.

The girl was so pitifully young. She looked no more than fifteen but was in fact in her twenties. Years of anorexia had reduced her to skin and bone. As she sat down, she fiddled with her long, mousy-coloured hair with hands missing several fingers. She also had a long history of self-mutilation.

Sebastien smiled at her. The girl smiled back. 'Hello, Dr Teale,' she said nervously, but happily. Although she usually hated talking to the doctors, she loved Sebastien. He was her greatest friend in all the world.

Sebastien stood, slowly walking forward and sitting on the edge of the desk. He kept his sherry-coloured eyes alert for any signs of distress at his proximity and was relieved to see none. That was a good sign. People with Selena's problems usually saw any physical closeness as a threat.

'Now, Selena. What's all this I hear about you not eating your vegetables?'

The girl looked up at him pitifully, and Sebastien felt his heart crack just a little more, deep inside him. He'd been working in psychiatric hospitals and asylums for the criminally insane for all of his career. He had only one 'private' patient. If Wayne could be called that.

For a man still only in his late thirties, Sebastien's reputation was second to none. His late mentor, Sir Julius, had been a lion in British psychiatry, and although Sebastien Teale was an American, he'd never felt the desire to return to his native land.

His life was here now. With his patients.

Patients who were slowly, unknowingly, breaking his heart.

An hour later, Sebastien left the hospital, trudged across the full car park and climbed wearily into his car. He didn't notice two nurses watching him with eyes filled with a mixture of admiration, respect and desire.

Every nurse in the hospital knew that Sebastien Teale was the best. And not because of the books he had written, or the lectures that he gave regularly at Oxford and Cambridge either. Sebastien Teale was, quite simply, the nearest thing to a saint that any of them had ever seen. He was of medium height, but had hair the colour of conkers, which caught any stray gleam of light going. His eyes, too, were warm and sherry-coloured, and so kind that they could break down the hardiest barriers with just one look. His voice could soothe the most terrified of patients into healing sleep.

And there was something so . . . so . . . *human* about him that made him the favourite of every patient in the place. Nurses had caught him rocking a terrified seventy-year-old man in his arms. They had seen him stroke a patient in a straitjacket into a calm, nearly lucid human being. He was not detached, as all the other doctors were. And he paid the price for it.

Every single nurse, and some married ones too, longed to take him as a lover. And not only because of his looks. Or his innocence, as appealing as both were.

No, they knew that Sebastien Teale was a prize any woman would want. He would never patronize them. Never cheat on them. And would always understand a woman's point of view. Men like that were like gold.

But so far, no woman had been noted in the great man's life, and many jealous female eyes kept a sharp lookout. It was the nurses' sad but respectful conclusion that the man was just too dedicated. But now, as he climbed into his car, his face was drawn, pale and exhausted. The job was killing him.

He drove carefully through the rush-hour traffic and pulled up at his flat, feeling like a washed-out dishrag. He let himself in, yanked off his tie and slumped down on the sofa in utter exhaustion. A movement caught his eye and he looked across the short expanse of his living room, not at all surprised to see a six-foot-four Frenchman seated in the chair opposite him. The man was one of the richest in the country. He was handsome, powerful and quite, quite insane.

'Sebastien,' Wayne D'Arville said, his voice soft and chiding. 'You look like death warmed up. I wish you'd leave

332

that place. You could go into private practice and make a fortune. Besides, I need you more than they do.'

Sebastien leaned back, and breathed slowly and deeply. He knew how dangerous this man was. He knew what he had done to Veronica Coltrane, although she was safe enough in America now, and he doubted if Wayne even gave her a thought.

He also knew that he was the only chance Wayne had.

He said softly, 'Why don't you tell me what kind of day you've had?'

CHAPTER 27

France

In the Chateau de Montigny in southern France, a single gunshot shattered the peaceful autumnal air. Gardeners ran in from the rose gardens, and outside the study door three maids hovered, none of them daring to go in. It fell to Jules, the sixty-seven-year-old major-domo, to knock timidly on the door.

'Monsieur le Due? Can you hear me?' A Louis XIV carriage clock chimed the hour of four, making everyone in the hall jump.

Jules knocked and called again. When he received no answer for the second time he pushed down on the gilt-handled door, surprised to find it opening silently and obediently beneath his hand, and looked inside.

The study was a classic of its kind. French tomes lined ancient wooden shelves, while the scent of dusty books, cigars, fine old leather and Napoleon brandy wafted around on the meagre air currents. Sitting behind a fine seventeenth-century writing bureau was the slumped figure of the Due de Montigny. Jules and the others could plainly see the shining dome of the Due's head reflected in the sunlight filtering in through the open French windows. The door of the cabinet that housed his set of ancient duelling pistols hung open, and a fine eighteenth-century pistol hand-tooled in heavy silver was missing from its place.

Slowly, feeling suddenly much older than his years, Jules walked across the Savonnerie carpet to approach his master. Jules's family had worked here since before the days of Bonaparte, and he felt tears begin to burn in the back of his gentle grey eyes. The silver pistol lay a scant inch from the Due's limp left hand, and he slowly dragged his eyes away from the functional but beautiful instrument of death. A deep, dark red hole in the Due's temple had him shuddering, and he half turned, glancing behind him to his pale-faced staff. 'Call the police,' he instructed no one in particular, hardly aware when one of the gardeners turned away to do his bidding.

The desk was empty except for the Due's usual items. Stiff cream paper of premier quality, bearing the Montigny crest and printed address, was stacked in a neat pile on the left, together with a silver rack of matching envelopes. Fine gold-plated pens with old-fashioned nibs stood in ebony and ivory holders, ready to be used. Jules's eyes scanned the desk, but could see no suicide note, only a single typewritten sheet. Unable to withstand his curiosity, Jules picked it up and read it, holding it gingerly by the very topmost corners.

His old, sad face barely altered in expression as he read to the end. It was just as he had feared. The vineyards had had a bad four years. Early frosts and heavy rainfall had ruined the last two harvests, and their back up supply of grapes was sadly depleted. The Due had borrowed heavily from the banks last year, and this year there had been a rumour circulating in the town that they had insisted on the Montigny castle being mortgaged for collateral before giving a second, massive loan.

As he read the words, Jules frowned, recalling the name of Wayne D'Arville. Wasn't that the upstart of a casino owner's son, who had once, many years ago, been set to marry the Due's only daughter and heir?

Of course, the Due had put a stop to that. If Jules remembered correctly, the casino owner had disowned his son, and told the Due so. Fortunately, the Due's daughter was a sensible girl who knew her duty well. She had jilted this D'Arville character, and had since married into an old and respected aristocratic family from the north.

Now why, Jules wondered, did Wayne D'Arville buy the options for the vineyard and castle from the bank? Surely it could only be for revenge. And after all these years . . .

He shook his head sadly and put the paper back. Whatever the reasons, this man had called in the loan, knowing the Due could not possibly pay it. And so he had taken the only way out left to a beaten old man who had only his proud name left to call his own.

Jules turned away and walked slowly back to the door where the women were sniffing quietly into their aprons. He didn't have the heart to tell them that the castle was no longer owned by a Montigny. The news would spread soon enough.

Poor Monsieur le Due. To lose the family home, business *and* honour had been more than he could stand. As he closed the door on the dead man, Jules wondered what the Englishman would do with the castle now.

He would probably sell it. After all, it had not been the business he'd been after. Jules shuddered at the thought of a man who could hold such a grievous grudge, and for so long.

His soul must be as black as midnight.

* * *

Wayne received official notice of the Due's death two days later, via the bank. The chateau, so he was informed, was now all his. The Due's daughter had been informed but had not taken it well. Her husband's family was rich in social status, heritage and history, but not much else. Both families had been relying on the Montigny estates to provide for their future.

Wayne intended to sell the vineyards to the highest bidder, which would undoubtedly be the house of Villiers,

Montigny's oldest rivals. The chateau had already been promised to a hotelier of Wayne's acquaintance, who was anxious to turn the family home into a showpiece hotel for the rich and famous.

Wayne had forgotten about the Due and his poverty-stricken daughter by the following Friday. After spending a few days in France sorting out the paperwork, he was strangely glad to get back to England. He was very much aware that his father, Wolfgang Mueller, still lived in Monte Carlo. And, although it galled him to admit it, he didn't feel totally safe in France.

Once home, he drove his Ferrari to Platts with quick and efficient skill, pulling into the underground car park he'd had installed, his own space indicated by a huge placard that read 'President: Wayne D'Arville'. Since inheriting Platts, Wayne had made sure his own name appeared often throughout the firm. The stationery bore his name, the boardroom door bore it, his own office, the advertising literature and even the financial statements to their myriad clients played host to it.

He wanted no one to forget who was boss here.

He walked into a building that bore no resemblance to the old Platts. Gone were the dark, antique rooms, the old-world ambience, the cosy, cheerful family atmosphere that had so reassured the firm's older, more stick-in-the-mud clientele. Instead he walked into a foyer where huge windows let light flood over the muted grey carpet, functional furniture and modern switchboard and reception desk. The receptionist was young, pretty and up-to-date, and smiled at him with wide wanting eyes and big white teeth. Wayne walked past her to the express lift with electronically operated doors, not even noticing that she was alive.

The offices that he walked past were doorless; the days of individual, cosy little rooms had totally gone. Wayne kept a sharp eye on his employees. In their place stood open-plan offices, full of light, modern typewriters and messenger systems. Most of the old directors were gone and in their place were new men, only a few of them from Oxford or

Cambridge. The movers and shakers that Wayne employed were of the new schools: economists, forecasters with an eye for the flashy, the trendy, the money deal that sold.

Over the past few years, Wayne had become rich. Not wealthy, not well-off, but rich, and mainly because Platts was totally his and he could do what he liked without consulting shareholders, directors or board members. Toby Platt, Sir Mortimer's disinherited son, and his wife Amanda had filed a lawsuit against him, contesting Sir Mortimer's will and claiming undue influence. Their case had been thrown out almost at once, but they were doggedly filing an appeal.

Wayne routinely received correspondence threatening more legal action, as well as a regular influx of hate mail from Toby's friends and some of Platts' ex-directors. It all went into the bin. Now, as he stepped into his office that was unrecognizable as Sir Mortimer Platt's, he worked solidly for two hours, clearing his desk of messages and returning phone calls.

At last, he pressed the button on his newly installed intercom, and his young, attractive secretary quickly responded.

'Miss Forsythe, call a meeting of the research division, will you? Monday morning, ten o'clock.'

'Yes, Mr D'Arville,' Judith Forsythe said, pencilling in the appointment, and then typing out the memo. So, the rumours about the research division being phased out were true. She was not surprised. It was the least profitable of all. That meant more redundancies. Judith sighed as she typed, glad that she was not a researcher. But Platts was a non-union shop, and she glanced at the closed door and shivered. Like all the female staff, she found Wayne D'Arville a fascinating mix; she couldn't stop herself from wanting him, while being simultaneously terrified of him. And although she wore her blouses with the top two buttons undone and her skirts to just above her knees, she knew deep down that he hardly noticed her presence.

But Wayne D'Arville was six foot four, with copper-coloured hair, a lantern-jawed face and the most beautiful blue eyes she'd ever seen, so she was not about to give up trying to attract his notice. Especially as he was still, unbelievably, single.

Unaware of his secretary's aspirations, Wayne folded away his papers and drew out the blueprints of a planned new office complex but found he could not concentrate.

He'd have to start looking around for a wife soon.

An Englishwoman, with a hereditary title. One as unlike that bitch De Montigny as he could find.

He frowned, then rubbed his hand tiredly across his forehead. He felt restless and in need of his regular 'fix'. Lifting the telephone receiver, he dialled a five-figure number.

'Hello?'

Wayne took a deep breath, the familiar voice immediately affecting him. Slowly he leaned back in his chair, the nasty taste of France and Platts and everything else leaving him for a few wonderful minutes.

'Hello, Seb. It's me.' Ever since meeting the American psychiatrist, several years ago now, Wayne had felt himself being pulled inexorably closer into the man's orbit. It was where he yearned to be, and yet he fought against the magnetism furiously.

'Oh, hi. When did you get back from France?'

'Yesterday. I was wondering if you're free for dinner tonight.'

Sebastien twirled the telephone wire in his fingers and sighed. He just couldn't face Wayne tonight. He said quietly, 'No, I can't make it this time.'

Wayne sat up straight abruptly, the rotten taste of the world once more flooding into his mouth. 'Why not?'

Sebastien felt the man's need bite into him. It was no use — he just couldn't deny somebody who was in so much pain. He swallowed hard and ran his hand through his hair. 'Look, why don't I come to your place for lunch tomorrow?' he said softly, his voice soothing, even over a telephone line.

Wayne smiled, unutterably relieved, and leaned back in his chair. 'That's even better. I'll order in from Le Grille.'

'Don't bother, I'll cook. I'll bring some groceries with me.'

'OK. I'll give you a hand.'

'Fine. See you tomorrow, then.' Sebastien hung up, putting the phone back on its hook slowly, then took a deep breath and straightened his shoulders.

* * *

Sebastien left just after ten o'clock, driving the small Mini he had purchased second-hand just a month ago, and headed for the open-air market. Money meant little to him, hence his refusal to go private. And, in truth, he never envied his more wealthy colleagues, a fact that had not gone unnoticed.

At the market he bought fresh fruit and vegetables, a crusty loaf, beef and some crabmeat.

Wayne had moved into a house in Belgravia six months ago. It was a two-storey yellow-stone building with black railings surrounding the square gardens at the front and rear. Sebastien was let in by Wayne himself, who took the groceries from him then followed him through elegant rooms, decorated by the latest interior designer, to the kitchen. Wayne always dismissed his servants whenever Sebastien was due. Wayne wanted nothing and no one to spoil these precious times.

Sebastien didn't comment on the rooms decorated in the minimalist style. He knew Wayne barely registered the house in which he lived, which was why the place had a curiously unlived-in feel to it. There was not an ornament out of place or one personal item to interrupt the harmonious colour scheme. He thought of his own flat, with its untidy bookshelves crammed with all sorts of titles, the throw cushions that clashed with the curtains, and felt so utterly sorry for the tall Frenchman. To an outsider he seemed to have everything anybody could ever want, but Sebastien knew he had, in reality, nothing at all.

Over the years, he had carefully picked his way across the minefield that was Wayne D'Arville's tortured mind, picking up the barest scraps of information. It was a strange game they played, Sebastien trying to find clues to the man's paranoia and pain, while Wayne erected barriers to deny him. Half-truths, evasions, downright lies. Sebastien saw through them all. Wayne was both terrified of the psychiatrist and utterly dependent on him. Sebastien was the only friend he had ever had. Sebastien was the only man he trusted not to betray him. Sebastien was so dangerous, Wayne always came out in a cold sweat whenever he was around.

And yet, without him, Wayne knew he would perish.

Yes, it was a very strange game they played. But Wayne could not stop it, and Sebastien wouldn't.

And so it went on.

In the kitchen, Wayne put on the kettle, and heaped coffee into the percolator.

'How's work nowadays?' Sebastien asked, checking the man for any overt signs of disintegration since their last 'session' but unable to find any. He knew Wayne had been excited over his 'business deal' in France. Too excited for it to be mere business. But Sebastien knew he would have to tread carefully.

'I didn't know you were interested in wine,' he said mildly.

Wayne stiffened. He always knew when Sebastien was on a hunting mission.

'I'm not. I'm selling the vineyard business.'

Sebastien looked at the tense, wide shoulders thoughtfully. 'Perhaps you've just always wanted to own a castle?' he mused quietly.

Wayne shrugged. He didn't know what kind of a mental 'symbol' a castle represented. And with Sebastien it didn't pay to take any chances.

'That's not it,' he said easily, turning to give him a careful smile. 'I've already got plans to sell it to a hotelier.'

Sebastien nodded. He knew how hard it was to get any kind of clues from a man as tightly controlled as Wayne. But even so, over the years, he'd learned an awful lot about the

Frenchman. He knew he harboured intense guilt over the death of his younger brother, and Sebastien suspected he had been present at the diving accident. He knew he loathed his father, but not why. In fact, if Wayne had an inkling of just how much Sebastien had garnered on him, the psychiatrist might have been in much more danger than he already was.

'I'm glad business is doing so well,' Sebastien changed tack. 'Power means a lot to you, doesn't it?'

Wayne smiled. 'It means a lot to everyone. Except you, of course,' he added softly. Sebastien's uniqueness was just one of the many things that added to Wayne's fascination for the soft-voiced, soft-hearted American.

Wayne quickly began to tell him all about the plans for the new office block. That was safer. The routine was familiar, and he talked unguardedly. 'I should have another ten million by the time I'm fifty,' he concluded with such grim satisfaction that the psychiatrist's antennae were immediately set twitching.

Sebastien put down the knife he'd been using to chop meat and wiped his hands on a towel. 'You need it for something, don't you?'

Wayne looked across the table, silently cursing, telling himself for the thousandth time that he was a fool to keep up this friendship, but knowing that he could not stop now. Sebastien was the friend he'd needed all his life, the friend he'd craved so badly during those dark days after the hideous fight with his father had pushed him over the edge.

Quite simply, Sebastien kept the pain at bay for a few glorious hours and was the only man Wayne could ever hope to regard as an equal. Even though, of course, he could destroy Sebastien whenever he wanted . . . He shrugged idly and bundled some tomatoes into a dish. 'Who doesn't need money?' he asked glibly.

'I don't,' Sebastien said softly. 'Money isn't everything.'

'Oh, I know that,' Wayne said grimly, watching with only half an eye as Sebastien crumbled a meat stock cube into some water. He began pouring it over the dish of meat and vegetables, then abruptly stopped as he caught the look on Wayne's face.

'What's wrong?' Sebastien asked quietly, keeping the urgency out of his voice. 'You know you can tell me.'

'Nothing,' Wayne said quickly, trying to fight off the urge to confess everything without much success. 'I just . . . I think, you know, it's time I got married. I want a family.'

'Ahh. You miss your brother, don't you?'

'Yes,' Wayne said before he had time to think, and then glanced at Sebastien quickly. For a moment his blue eyes blazed in anger, then he managed to smile. Talking to Sebastien was like taking a narcotic. Exciting, dangerous, soothing, wonderful but potentially lethal . . .

Sebastien put the casserole in the oven, scraped some potatoes and prepared the French beans. He was wearing plain jeans and a simple cheap white shirt. His hair was brushed casually back from his forehead and shone with the exact colour of conkers that littered the English countryside at this time of year, and Wayne felt a familiar peacefulness settle over his shoulders like a mantle. It was always like this when Sebastien was around. That was what made him so addictive.

'OK,' Sebastien said with satisfaction. 'Now all we have to do is wait two hours.'

'Fine. Come and have a drink.'

In the living room, with its pink, grey and cream colour-coded elegance, Sebastien watched him pour two Scotches. He took his but didn't bother to drink it, instead sinking down into a chair. There he watched the Frenchman drink mechanically and without any evidence of pleasure.

Slowly Sebastien put his drink down on to the cream leather armrest of his padded chair. 'So, tell me about your new vineyards. What do they look like at this time of year?'

Wayne shrugged and yawned. 'I don't know. I never looked. I just signed the papers over to the vintners who bought them.'

'What about the chateau? Are French castles as romantic as popular fiction would have us believe?'

Again Wayne shrugged. 'I stayed in a hotel at Nouvion. What?' he added, catching the sherry eyes on him with their usual mix of pity and strength.

Sebastien shrugged helplessly. 'Doesn't it seem odd to you that you went to France but didn't even look at what you own? That you didn't take time out to enjoy the sights, even?'

Wayne smiled grimly. 'I looked at the grave,' he said, then snarled in anger at himself and tossed back the last of his drink.

'Whose grave?' The questioning, as usual, was gentle but persistent. Like the exquisite probing of a needle, after a thorn in the thumb. Wayne got up and refilled his glass. When he came back to his chair, he crossed his legs at the ankles and looked the young American straight in the eye.

'You know, in your own way, you're almost as ruthless as I am.'

Sebastien nodded, not at all confounded. 'I guess I am,' he acknowledged simply. 'So, whose grave did you visit? Your brother's?'

'No!' Wayne said sharply, then slowly shook his head. Pleasure and pain, that was Sebastien. 'I should get rid of you,' he said softly.

'But you won't.'

'No. I won't. I don't think I can now. But you already know that, don't you? You always knew that. Right from the beginning. Didn't you?' Wayne pressed, his desire to punish himself so obvious that Sebastien wondered how the man himself could be so unaware of it.

'Yes. I knew. So, whose grave was it?'

Wayne smiled a brief hard smile, a mere acknowledgement of his adversary's persistence, and took another gulp of liquor. 'The Due de Montigny. Once I was engaged to his daughter.'

'Oh? Tell me about her.'

Wayne shook his head. 'You're barking up the wrong tree. The old man didn't want me to marry his daughter when I . . . So I waited until I was rich enough to buy the notice papers from the bank. He committed suicide,' he added defiantly.

Sebastien reached for his drink and took a slow sip, taking time to make sense of the disjointed sentences. The fact that Wayne felt no remorse for driving a man to suicide was the strongest indication yet of his true mental condition.

But Sebastien knew he did not have enough yet to enable him to have Wayne committed. Wayne was a rich and powerful man. An influential man. To have a man committed, you had to go through certain channels, and be very sure of your diagnosis. Sebastien knew his word as a psychiatrist would be hard to shake, but he also had no illusions as to what Wayne would do if he got to hear of any moves against him before the committal papers were signed. Sebastien wasn't so much afraid for himself as he was for others. Wayne had all but destroyed Veronica Coltrane, one of life's innocents. Who knew what damage he could do if he, Sebastien, tried to have him committed, and failed?

Sebastien knew it was imperative, if he was to save Wayne, to learn more about what drove him. So he swallowed his own sense of outrage and forced himself to concentrate on the problem at hand. 'So he was punished for going against you?' He kept his voice deliberately expressionless. 'How did Mortimer Platt go against you?' He knew that Wayne's takeover of Platts had been a hostile one.

Wayne shook his head. 'He didn't. He just had something I needed.'

Sebastien knew what that was without being told. 'So, now you have money, and your revenge on the Due. What next?'

Wayne smiled so savagely that for a moment Sebastien felt a cold shiver shudder its way up his spine.

'Oh, I still have things to do,' Wayne assured him softly.

'I'm sure you have. Tell me about your father.'

Wayne shifted on his chair and took another gulp of Scotch. He was dressed in pressed white cotton trousers and a turquoise shirt. He looked cool and elegant, in perfect harmony with the room, and yet Sebastien knew that there lurked beneath the handsome exterior a personality so laby-rinthine, so tortured, and so full of self-directed hate that he wondered how Wayne had survived it.

'I've already told you about him.'

'No, you haven't. You've told me lies.'

Wayne looked from the rich amber colour of the liquid in the glass to the man opposite him, his eyes narrowing. 'I could crush you,' he said softly. 'Ruin everything you have.'

Sebastien smiled, totally unafraid. 'I know. So it won't matter if you tell me the truth about your father, will it?'

Wayne smiled, almost glad that Sebastien was not afraid, that he was not like all the others. He knew, in a sudden, shocking flash of self-knowledge, that he'd die if Sebastien turned out to be like all the others. He looked Sebastien in the eye for a long, long second, not sure whether to be glad or sorry when Sebastien refused to back down, then sneered, 'OK. You asked for it. Here it is. He was a Nazi. For a time he was the chief officer at a concentration camp. He killed and tortured people for a living.'

Sebastien paled, but had no doubt at all that, this time, he was telling the truth. 'And your brother? The one who drowned? Tell me about him.'

'I killed him.'

'You said he drowned.'

'He did. I was on the beach when his dive went wrong. I could have swum out and saved him, but I didn't.' Wayne was proud of his voice. It was level and strong. He might have been discussing the weather.

Sebastien heard only the pain. The so obvious pain. He knew that later, much later, he would think about a drown-ing boy who need not have died. He knew he would probably even shed tears over him. But he would not sit in judgement of Wayne. He could not help a boy who had been dead for years. He *could* help a man whose life was a living hell. 'He was your father's favourite, wasn't he?' he said, knowing he was on the right track even before asking the question.

Wayne blinked, then shook his head, shaking off the numb feeling of apathy that had allowed him to blurt it all out the way he had. 'You know,' he said, 'I've often wondered how easy it would be to lie to shrinks like you. Now I know. My father is a French winemaker. That's all. Now, hadn't we better fix some dessert?'

Sebastien nodded, knowing Wayne had had enough for one day. But they'd made some giant leaps. It was enough. Together the two men walked into the kitchen.

CHAPTER 28

New York, ten years later

Veronica Copeland nodded to Francis, the dour doorman, who grinned back and gave a cheerful wave. It said a lot about her long-time standing in the thirty-storey luxury apartment complex that she even received acknowledgement from the man, let alone such a conspicuously friendly greeting.

At nearly sixty, Francis had been in the building since its completion twelve years ago. The place, full of luxury, designer flair and every modern convenience known to man, simply would not be the same without the grumpy, sour face of the doorman, who did his job well but with such a totally grudging reluctance that his fame had spread throughout the whole quarter. Once, Veronica knew, several tenants with no sense of class had tried to have him fired. When Francis, looking even more glum than usual, had told anybody and everybody who lived in the building that he was being sacked, there had been uproar.

Now Veronica winked back at him as she walked to one of the sets of lifts, all of which were carpeted, with pot plants in two corners and awash with pleasant music, and pushed the button for the thirteenth floor. As she did so, she had to smile. Trust Val to select an apartment on the thirteenth floor. It was totally typical of him, and as usual he was right. Thirteen might be unlucky for some, but it hadn't done either of them any harm over the years.

As the quiet elevator whizzed her up, she checked in her handbag for the keys. Their apartment was at the end of the corridor, and, like all those similarly situated, was one of the largest in the building. Suites ranged from two-roomed large expanses for the modern bachelor to the twelve-roomed apartments like hers.

There was no doubt about it. Valentine Inc. had done well over the years. Very well. Valentine designed, and Veronica invested. It was a match that had made them both very rich, and very happy.

Against all of Veronica's gloomy predictions!

She opened the door and stepped inside, looking around at the wide expanse of living room, noting with familiar appreciation the muted and elegant peach-tinted walls, lightly stuccoed brilliant white ceiling, and peachy/beige expanse of carpet that seemed to stretch as far as the eye could see. The furniture was dark walnut, the couches and sofas a mixture of black and white leather. A few Picassos hung on the walls, and every alcove was festooned with greenery from towering pot plants.

Veronica walked briefly to a smoked-glass coffee table and slung down her handbag, kicked off her shoes and went to the space-age kitchen. Done out in steel grey, royal blue, silver and white, it was sparse, functional and strangely elegant. There she put on the coffee percolator, then walked into the bathroom, slipping off her tailored three-piece navy-blue suit as she did so.

The bathroom was a gothic mixture of black, gold and red, with one wall entirely lined with mirrored tiles. She watched herself as she stripped, trying to gauge her face and figure with unprejudiced eyes. She was nearly forty but didn't think she looked it. Her black hair was still lush and thick, the lines at the corners of her eyes were very fine and not visible under a light dusting of make-up, and her skin looked as youthful as ever.

Her slender body, slowly being revealed as she pulled off the expensive suit to reveal a lacy teddy and pure silk stockings, looked as firm and curvaceous as ever. Val loved her to wear sexy lingerie, and although she had felt a little self-conscious about it at first, now she was quite at home in the pieces her husband still liked to design.

She sighed contentedly, turned away from her reflection and stepped into the shower, turning on the gold taps and murmuring in pleasure as the warm water cascaded on to her head and over her shoulders.

She had come a long way since that first fashion show of Val's. How he had ever managed to bully her into it, she still didn't know. She felt her lips curve into a smile of remembrance as she let the years slip back . . .

* * *

The venue was the Plaza hotel. The huge conference room had been transformed into a lush harem with cleverly draped red velvet and layers and layers of gauze. The theme was Turkish, from the ornate drinking vessels that served guests with the finest of champagnes to the menu.

Val had refused to serve them an actual meal, stating with his usual combination of brash arrogance and faultless logic that they had come to see a fashion show — *his* fashion show — and not to stuff their faces.

But the entrees and titbits served with the finest of Turkish coffees were sensational. Imported Turkish delight and traditional nibbles from that country had been flown in the day before on a specially chartered plane, and looked good on ornate beaten silver dishes, served with finger-bowls in which floated a single blossom. The whole layout was set on banquet tables festooned with tropical fruit and set against a mural backcloth that depicted belly dancers and lounging sultans.

'If they want to nosh, they should go to a soddin' restaurant,' Val had muttered around a mouthful of pins as he readjusted a double-breasted jacket (sticking her with the pins more often than not) as they worked together in the warehouse just two days before the showing.

'Stand still, for gawd's sake,' he'd gone on to snap as she jiggled and tried to dodge the pins, and she'd glowered at him, hating every lovely hair on his head.

Right up until that very morning, when he'd called to take her to the venue, she was still denying that she was going to walk out on that catwalk with all the others.

'Don't worry so much,' Val told her, dressed in ragged jeans and a loose shirt. 'The other girls are the stars — Patrice and Jasmine. Everyone will be looking at them, not at your recalcitrant mug. You're just in there to fill in for some second-rater who threw a wobbly. Relax.'

Veronica, not at all sure whether she should feel reassured or insulted, glared at him, crossed her arms savagely over her breasts and sulked all the way to the Plaza. Once there, however, she began to sweat in earnest.

The famous hotel was as impressive as she'd always suspected it might be. And so was the guest list. Senators, TV stars, even pop stars were filing through the famous doors, flashing golden invitation cards and causing a backlog of black stretch limos, pink Rolls-Royces and nifty Italian sports cars.

In contrast to the splendour of the hotel, the changing room that Val breezed into, oblivious to naked female bodies, reminded Veronica of a cramped rabbit hutch. Hung up beside the mirrors that lined one wall were costume jewellery, garters, stockings, even newspaper clippings. The room was chaos — the wardrobe girls each had their own model to look after, and everyone was talking at once. Hairdressers added last-minute changes to glossy curls, toenails were being painted, and make-up girls fixed faces on the run as models dashed from one costume to another, arguing, groaning, grinning.

Veronica took one look, turned around, and almost made it to the door. Almost.

Valentine's strong hand on her arm swung her about in mid-stride and he firmly frogmarched her back to an empty chair, set beside a washbasin. She felt his strong hands on her shoulders forcing her down, and as her knees already felt weak as water it didn't take much pressure to make her buckle.

Her face in the mirror looked white, scared and angry. Her dark eyes were huge, and as she met his smiling face in the mirror she could cheerfully have committed murder.

'Here's Carrie,' he said as a harassed-looking brunette, fifty if she was a day, swooped down on her. 'See if you can make this sow's ear into a silk purse, luvvie, eh?' He gave the unimpressed and hardly listening Carrie a peck on the cheek and then sauntered off, his sharp eyes on the lookout for badly hanging skirts.

Veronica stared after him then jumped as the touch of a make-up brush slid across her cheek. 'I've gone mad,' she said forlornly. 'I think I've gone totally out of my mind.'

'It does help, duckie,' Carrie said, her droll, tired voice sparking off a memory inside Veronica's head. Then she grinned. Carrie was none other than the droll voice that had so amused everybody on her first visit to the warehouse. She had an immediately calming effect, as he must have known she would. Bless Valentine for assigning Carrie to her.

The rotten dirty bastard.

'I don't have any idea what I'm doing,' Veronica wailed, watching Carrie's lined and bored-looking face carefully for signs of her own unease. After all, what Val was doing — assigning a complete unknown a place on his prestigious show — must have caused a few shockwaves. But washed-out blue eyes met hers calmly in the mirror and the older face smiled, suddenly looking lovely. 'Don't let that worry you too much. There's a first time for everything, duckie, just remember that. Now, do you remember the order of costume change?'

Veronica nodded. 'Val's done nothing but drum it into me until it's coming out of my ears.'

'Good. But it'll probably be changed anyway. The girl who goes on before you will suddenly find a zipper gets stuck, or there's a run in her stockings and she'll have to change, and you'll have to go on instead. By the time the show's over the schedule will be in pieces. Just don't worry about it. I don't.' Veronica stared at her, swallowed hard, and then, when Carrie ordered her, raised her arms above her head and let herself be stripped down to the skin. Literally.

Nobody took the slightest bit of notice.

The other girls, whose names she'd now learned — Jasmine, Debbie, Gayle, Patrice, Grace, Connie — were all like obedient dolls, letting the hairdressers, make-up girls, wardrobe mistresses and other assorted personnel daub, paint, brush and work on them as if they were marble statues instead of flesh and blood.

Veronica glanced around, her hands hovering modestly and nervously over her breasts. Her gaze quickly found Valentine, who was on his knees, his head stuck up Gayle's skirt.

Veronica gaped.

Then he crawled backwards and emerged, a trifle flushed, his mouth still full of pins, around which he angrily shouted, 'Who the hell did the tambour beading on your underskirt?'

Veronica looked away. 'I'll kill him,' she said, making Carrie glance at her, and then shrug with a knowing twist of her lips. 'I will. I'll bloody well kill him.'

Her first costume was a tiered skirt and lace blouse, the picot-edged organdie frills a bright scarlet, while the rest of the costume was brilliant white. When the make-up girl had finished with her, she turned to the mirror and gasped.

What she saw was somebody else, some glamorous model strayed from the front pages of *Vogue*, with her chic Vidal Sassoon short cap of black hair and huge dark eyes. Whenever she moved, the rippled tiers of the skirt seemed to shimmer and move like waves around her knees and slim calves, and the stark contrast of white, scarlet and black fairly dazzled her.

'Oh, my giddy aunt,' she said, her voice little more than a rasp, and behind her Valentine's face appeared, reflected in the mirror. His eyes were thoughtful as they ran over her. Today his look was almost mechanical, and so unlike his usual hot, lazy, threatening gaze that she actually shivered.

She felt so cold suddenly. As if he'd turned off the sun. It was not her first taste of his professionalism, but it was the first time she'd realized for herself how very 'great' the 'great Valentine' really was.

'You'll do, luv. Just don't tip arse over tit down the catwalk, and I think we'll get away with springing you on 'em.'

All of Veronica's new-found respect for the man took a nose-dive. She dragged in a harsh, growling breath. 'You slimy, miserable, low-down . . .'

Val had already turned away by the time she'd run out of names and was busy adjusting a lacy camisole top that barely covered Debbie's large breasts. The sight made Veronica turn away with a gasp that some would have sworn was a mixture of pain and jealousy.

Outside she could hear the soft wail of thick-bodied flutes and the shimmer of tambourines. The level of human chatter slowly ceased.

Veronica felt her insides turn to jelly. Panic attacked her, and she quickly looked around for Val, who was gone. Damn him! The girls clustered around the door, which one of them pulled ajar, and, straining her ears, she could just hear Val's deep cockney voice welcoming the audience to his show.

It was real! It was happening. Now! She was the fourth one on . . .

The first three girls walked quickly out of the door with no trace of panic, their perfectly made-up faces calm and blank.

Calm and blank, she thought as she stood shivering just inside the door, then forced herself to step nervously out into a small alcove waiting for Connie to finish her turn. The model was wearing a slinky blue turquoise wrap-over day dress with a rakish turban to match. She walked like an undulating snake, every curve of her oozing sex.

I can't do *that*, Veronica thought, feeling suddenly wobbly on her three-inch scarlet heels. Her throat was so dry that she rattled as she breathed. I'm an economist. I'm supposed to work in an office, for crying out loud, with a calculator and a secretary! If I go out there I'll fall flat on my face. I know I will. I'll freeze, I'll forget everything . . .

'And now we have Veronica, in a romantic day ensemble . . .' She heard his words, but from where she was behind the corner she couldn't see his face. Suddenly she grinned. Wouldn't it serve him right, she thought with panicky bravado, if I just didn't show up? Wouldn't he look a right Charlie?

She ought to have known he would think of such a contingency. And that Carrie was as devoted to Val as anybody.

Suddenly she felt Carrie give a firm push in the middle of her back, just enough to make her stagger into view, and then she had no choice.

Her legs moved automatically as the flashlights suddenly blazed, dazzling her for a moment. She walked on to the catwalk totally blind, her brain buzzing. Suddenly her vision cleared. A cool voice, oddly cockney in accent, began coaching her in the back of her mind.

Walk to the end slowly, turning left and right in slow circles. Turn three times, holding out the skirt, spinning to show the way it flies into the air. Then walk straight back. Smile. Always smile. Her face felt stiff, as if all the make-up on it would crack like fine plaster. She twirled, feeling dizzy. She was going to faint. She *was*.

The sea of faces became one blur. The hum of appreciation was like a faint droning in her ears. She found herself at the end, turning, her hands on her skirt. Then she found herself walking back.

As she passed the rostrum where Val stood, still in his baggy shirt and jeans, she threw him a speaking look. If looks could kill, he'd be dead in an instant, burned to a cinder.

He winked at her and launched into the next description as Jasmine sashayed past her in a dress of tie-dyed rough-looking sacking that nevertheless managed to look unbelievably sexy. She got past the curtain and collapsed into her chair, then had to stand up again as Carrie hissed at her to get out of the dress and into the next one.

'You mean I have to do all that again?' she wailed, as Carrie shot her a funny look.

'Weren't you listening?' she asked, reaching for a sequinned evening gown of glittering ruby brilliance. 'I thought all you models had the ear.'

In Carrie's mind there was now no doubt. Veronica Coltrane was a model.

Veronica, however, missed the sudden change in Carrie's attitude. Instead she cocked a puzzled head on to one side. 'The ear?'

'Yeah, the ear,' Carrie muttered, using moisturizer on Veronica's eyelids and repainting them a deep maroon eyeshadow. 'Every girl who goes out there has her ears tuned to the audience reaction. And you got a big one.'

'It was the outfit,' she mumbled. Even though she hated — literally detested — to admit it, Val had produced some stunning designs.

'That as well,' Carrie corrected, 'but the fuss was about you. You have to understand . . .' Carrie paused as she began some delicate work on Veronica's lashes, then carried on when she'd finished '. . . this is a small business. Every model is known, every face keenly inspected. New faces have an advantage over the old ones to begin with, but still . . .' she daubed on some deep ruby lipstick over Veronica's quivering lips '. . . every girl who goes out there listens for the gasps. And boy, did you get some! Val was right about you,' she added with satisfaction.

This time Veronica didn't miss the awe in the woman's voice and her eyes snapped open.

'Watch the mascara. It isn't dry yet!' Carrie wailed.

'Sod the mascara,' Veronica bit back inelegantly, erupting on to her feet. Really, being around Val so much was having an atrocious effect on her manners. 'Just what did Val say?' she added more politely.

'That you were a winner, of course. Why else would you be in his show? Now sit down.'

'He put me in to fill in for that other girl,' Veronica said, then saw the flash of irony in the blue eyes and felt suddenly foolish and way out of her depth. 'Well, that's what he said.'

'You think Val would put just any girl in his show?' Carrie asked, obviously not taking Veronica's stunned look seriously. 'They loved you out there. You'll see — tomorrow you'll be inundated with offers from Ford and every other modelling agency. You'll have mags fawning all over you.'

This time Veronica did sit down. Hard.

'I thought he only wanted—' She stopped abruptly, going red, but Carrie laughed, her world-weary eyes missing nothing.

'You thought he just wanted to get you into the sack, hmm?' she finished the thought for her with a twinkling eye and slightly bawdy laugh. 'Hell, I know he does. But Val is *the* Valentine. He wouldn't risk his show no matter how hot he was for a girl. Oh, grow up, for heaven's sake,' Carrie snapped as Veronica continued to stare at her dumbly.

'But I didn't want to do this!' she wailed, then promptly shut up as Carrie grunted in total disbelief.

'Sure — whatever you say. Now — slide into this.'

Veronica did indeed have to 'slide' into the gown, which was so tight it fitted her like a second skin. Any imperfection in her body would be instantly visible, Carrie knew, and she studied Veronica with minute precision until she was finally satisfied.

'OK. You're on.'

Veronica walked stiffly to the curtains and then stepped on to the catwalk, this time listening properly. She went hot, then cold, as she realized Carrie was right. The hum of voices and the flash of bulbs were far greater for herself than for any of the others. She walked down the catwalk, this time without turning, forgetting completely about the half-turns and teasing movements for the photographers, she was so stunned.

Watching her, Val realized that her apparently haughty unconcern for the photographers was egging them on, building her prestige and mystique more fully than any of the other models' usual flirting tricks could ever have done.

When she walked past him, looking perfectly calm and cool, he grinned. He felt his loins harden in sudden animal reaction and was glad that part of his anatomy was hidden behind the stand.

As she passed him she turned eyes on him that were deadly. For a second his slick commentary faltered, and then he smoothly picked it up again. What a woman! A tigress had nothing on her! She was going to kill him in bed, he just knew it.

The thought was not unpleasing.

The rest of the show was faultless, but Veronica hardly noticed. She felt utterly depressed and couldn't understand why. When it was all over, the models had to change into their after-show party dresses and mingle with the guests and photographers.

Veronica's own outfit was a deep emerald dress with a V neck that plunged to her navel, and a similar plunge at the back that reached to the bottom of the spine. The other girls changed quickly, but she was aware of a shift in the atmosphere. She was no longer a rank amateur, a fancy of Val's to be petted or ignored.

Now she was a threat, a success, the girl who had stolen the show. She could feel the hate all around her.

The make-up girls, wardrobe mistresses and other personnel were busy packing away the scattered clothes. Accessories alone would fill several trunks — all the handbags, hats, gloves, costume jewellery, umbrellas and parasols, shoes, fans, shawls, scarves and stoles.

Still dressed in her last costume, she was told smartly to take it off, which she did, sitting back down again, totally exhausted and dressed only in a fine silk half-slip. Her last costume had not allowed her to wear a bra, but such was the atmosphere of the room that she sat bare-breasted without feeling the slightest bit of embarrassment.

She was aware of the noise in the other room rising continuously as the champagne flowed more fully and the celebratory party got into full swing. For there was no doubt about it. Valentine had pulled off another success.

Slowly she leaned her arms on the cold table top and leaned her forehead on her wrists. She felt tears, warm and hot, slide down her cheeks on to her skin, and took a deep, shaking breath. With only half an ear she heard the door open, and then Val's voice ordering the backstage women out.

Val stared down at her shaking shoulders and listened in an awkward silence for a few minutes as she sobbed with a quiet desperation that scared him.

Eventually he shuffled up to her, put a gentle hand on her naked back and said softly, 'You OK, darlin'?'

Veronica's head snapped up, her mascara-streaked face glaring at him in the mirror. 'Of course I'm not OK, you bastard,' she snapped, unaware that her pert, rose-tipped breasts quivered with every harsh breath she took, and of the effect they were having on Val. 'I wish I had a gun so I could shoot you straight between your lying eyes.'

Val grinned. 'That's better. I can't stand to see a grown woman cry.'

'You knew what would happen out there, didn't you?' she squawked, standing up and spinning around, arms akimbo, oblivious to the fact that she was naked except for the half-slip, lacy briefs, garter and white stockings. Her expression was tight and furious.

Val leaned back against the Formica surround and nodded. 'Course I did. I told you from the start you should be a model. You were sensational, sen-bloody-sational.' He threw his arms wide and gave a shout of triumph.

Part of her knew that it was just the usual end-of-show euphoria. He had spent months working on his designs, and the critics out there could have destroyed him, his reputation and his company with just a few vitriolic sentences. But he had wowed them again, and the relief must have been enormous. Part of her knew and understood that.

Another part of her screamed out for blood.

His!

Veronica stared at him for one long moment, then picked up the nearest hairbrush and slapped it at his face. It hit the side of his cheekbone with a dull thud that made her hand tingle.

'Owww!' he yelped loudly, standing up to put a hand to his stinging face. 'That hurt, you rotten bitch.'

'It was meant to!' she screamed back.

Val stared at her, his eyes changing and going as hard as black coal. She flinched when he snatched the brush from her hand, and for a moment she thought he was going to hit her back with it. Then he threw it away and grabbed her, hauling her into him so hard than she felt the breath slam from her body.

Then, before she could drag more air into her depleted lungs, his mouth was on hers, hard and hurting.

She struggled briefly, aware of her head pounding and funny lights flashing before her eyes. Just as her knees began to buckle he suddenly snapped his head back. She had time to see an ugly red bruise beginning to form on his cheek, and then the room spun as he pushed her back on to the centre table, scattering ribbons, lace and pins in all directions.

'Val,' she groaned, then said no more as his head dipped and his lips began to savage her neck, her throat, her ears, her sternum and then her breasts.

His hands, so nimble with garments, had her naked in moments. It had been so long, so very, very long since a man had touched her this way.

And for a moment she forgot who that man had been.

Then she remembered. The visage of Wayne D'Arville flitted across her mind. So tall and broad, not at all like Val's wiry body. His hair was copper and sleek, not the unruly brown mop that was Val's. His eyes had been piercing and blue. Val's were warm and brown.

And, slowly, the image of the handsome Frenchman was defeated. His face was pushed back, swamped and superseded by Val's.

She gasped as his hands splayed across her flat stomach. Instead of remembering a soft, purring French accent, she heard only harsh, guttural cockney words.

'It's about time you learned you can't go waving 'airbrushes about without some retaliation, my gal,' Val warned her, but his voice was thick and heavy, and shook with too many short, panting breaths.

And suddenly she knew.

She was free? The past, Wayne, the bleak months in prison — it was all gone.

She had a future once more.

And with this man.

She laughed, almost giddy with delight, and stretched back on the hard cold table, her head falling over the side to hang loosely as he knelt above her, his hands pushing aside her thighs.

She jerked and moaned, the room at an upside-down angle pulsing in time to her heartbeats that pumped blood to her head as he began to suck and nibble on the pulsing button of flesh he found there.

She felt herself began to jerk in spasms of reaction and closed her eyes.

'Yes,' she said. 'Yes, Val, yes!'

This was what she'd always wanted. From the moment he'd stepped into her life and turned it upside down. She'd wanted a champion, a knight in shining armour to rescue her.

Thus encouraged, he stepped back on the floor and pulled down his jeans, his manhood springing proudly to attention. His hands reached for her knees, pulling her back more squarely on to the table, and when he moved between her parted legs and slid fully into her, her eyes watched him, every bit as hot and eager as his own.

This was where he belonged, and they both knew it.

Val's brown eyes seemed to melt and darken.

She moaned, her fingers clutching his shoulders, which were still covered by his shabby shirt.

Eagerly she thrust it from him and ran her hands across his collarbone. Her legs twitched and jerked over the edge of the table as he began to slide in and out of her, faster, harder, almost savage, almost brutal, and yet never actually hurting her.

His power and passion were so far removed from Wayne's more practised love-making that she was catapulted into ecstasy almost at once. Veronica held nothing back. It was too noisy outside for anyone to hear her, and she moaned and cried out with every thrust of his hard, hot member inside her.

Val winced and gasped as her strong muscles clenched him, and when finally his hot seed gushed forth into her, he yelled triumphantly and collapsed on top of her, his weight pinning her firmly to the table.

For long, long minutes their ragged breathing shuddered into the untidy room, and then, slowly, Val straightened up, his legs feeling like water beneath him as he stared down at her, so much love in his eyes that Veronica felt drunk with it.

Her body was bathed in sweat, her face, mascara-streaked, flushed and sweating, her hair soaked.

'So when will yer make an 'onest man of me an' marry me?' he asked, zipping up his trousers but never taking his eyes from her.

'How about tomorrow?'

CHAPTER 29

Veronica was still smiling at her memories as she turned off the shower. It had all been so long ago, and yet it seemed like only yesterday.

Since then, of course, a lot had happened . . .

She had been his top model for only two years, at her own insistence. She was well aware of the reputations being established by Twiggy and Jean 'the Shrimp' Shrimpton, who had come to the States on a huge tide of English sixties fever.

'But you can compete with them. All that's needed is a change of image, that's all,' Val had reassured her, and although she knew he was right, she still shook her head.

'No. I've had enough. Besides . . .'

'Besides?'

From all those years ago, the words of her young cellmate had come back to her, and she'd repeated them with soft irony. 'You won't be new for long, then they won't know you're here.'

They were in Val's warehouse conversion (where they had lived after their marriage) lying in bed at the time, at about five o'clock in the morning. Val sat up and turned on a light. 'That sounds suspiciously like a quote to me,' he commented, curiously.

Although they had been husband and wife for just over two years, he still knew very little about her background. He had not liked to pry, sensing her reticence on the subject.

'It was,' she admitted, and turned on to her pillow to face him and smile whimsically. 'Come on, Val. The seventies are coming. You want new faces for it. Don't forget, this is an English wave, and you'll be riding it high, being from the Smoke yourself.'

'Ahh, good ol' London,' he said sentimentally. 'But don't change the subject. Are you tryin' to back out on me?'

'I'm trying to save you the embarrassment of having to sack your old lady. Besides, I have . . . something else I want to do.'

'Oh?' He turned to look at her curiously. Veronica watched him in silence for several minutes, almost hearing the wheels turning in his head.

'OK,' he finally said, as if *he* were doing *her* a favour. 'You don't have to do any more modelling. So what is it you have in mind now that you won't be on half the magazine covers in the good ol' US of A?'

Veronica smiled, and lay on her back, staring at the ceiling pensively. 'Did I ever tell you about a book I once wrote?' she asked softly, and by her side she felt him tense.

Val sensed that the time had come for confessions, and although he knew he would never stop loving her no matter what, he was only human.

'Nah,' he said softly. 'I can't say as you ever did. What kind of book was it?'

'It was a book about money,' she said finally. 'How to make it, how to move it around, how to invest it, and, most importantly of all, how to make it grow. It also predicted that computers would change the world, and that the smart money would make full use of them. It was a . . . brilliant book.'

She waited, expecting a shocked laugh, a grinning, teasing reaction, but instead Val continued to watch her carefully.

'OK.'

Just that. Nothing more.

She turned to look at him, surprised at his bland reaction. Then she saw it was not blandness but trust in her that kept him so calm, and she felt tears prick her eyes.

'I wrote it when I worked for a company called Platts.'

'I've 'eard of that place,' Val said. 'Go on.'

'I was only a junior member. I wrote the book as an exercise really. I didn't tell anybody. It was so ambitious I thought they'd laugh at me. But a . . . man . . . at the company read it. He must have known how good it was . . .' she laughed hollowly '. . . because he stole it. Put his name on it and told Sir Mortimer Platt that he had written it. There was only one copy, in the company safe, and when I found out what . . . this man . . . had done, I tried to get the book back.'

Val felt his muscles stiffen and forced himself to relax.

'And you were caught, I suppose?' he said softly.

Veronica gasped. 'How did you know?'

'I remembered you told me once you'd been to prison. I didn't think it was for armed robbery, luv.'

Veronica, unbelievably, found herself smiling. She had thought bringing the past back to life would be much more painful. Trust Val to be able to deaden even that pain.

'I thought you didn't believe me,' she said at last. 'About being in prison.'

'Well, I did,' he said. 'Like I told you — I'd been in the clink too. Well, Borstal actually. My mate picked me up from school once in a car — a nicked motor, as it turned out.'

'Oh, poor baby,' Veronica crooned. 'Aren't we a hard-done-by pair?'

'Too right,' Val grinned, then sobered. 'This . . . man . . .' he echoed her own hesitation over the words. 'He's Trav's biological father, ain't he?'

Veronica nodded.

Val whistled. 'I'm glad I didn't know all about this when we first met,' he said, then saw her go white and cast a stricken glance his way.

'Nah,' he said, quickly taking her into his arms. 'I didn't mean *that*. It's just that when we met, I knew some bloke

365

had given you a hard time, and I was determined to give his memory a good kick in the old goolies. But at the time, I thought it was just the usual story. You know, the stupid sod had found someone else. If I'd known you were so prickly because of all this book and prison business goin' down, I wouldn't have been so cocky about winning you over to me.'

Veronica almost wilted in relief. 'Oh,' she said, then laughed. 'But you wouldn't have hesitated, even if you had known,' she predicted. 'You'd still have come traipsing into my life with your clod-hopping boots and walked all over me.'

'True,' Val said. 'Now, about this book. It was good, huh?'

'A bestseller,' Veronica said, a touch bitterly. She hadn't had the heart to buy a copy for many years, but she could hardly live in England and not know that the book had been a smash. 'Which brings me to my not-so-new career,' she said, running a finger beguilingly around his nipple.

'Oh, ye-eah?' Val said, knowing when he was being set up for something.

'Val,' she coaxed, nipping his nipple between thumb and finger and hearing him gasp with pleasure. 'How do you feel about giving all your money to me and letting me play with it?'

* * *

Veronica's thoughts suddenly snapped back to the present as she heard the apartment door open, and she hastily pulled on a white cashmere sweater and black trousers and opened the bathroom door. 'That you, Val?'

'Nope, it's me,' a younger voice called back. 'How did it go this afternoon?'

As she closed the door behind her, she glanced across the room at her son, and smiled. Travis, her son, was now, unbelievably, seventeen years old. He was a tall teenager, at six feet, with dark hair, wide blue eyes and a handsome square face that made him a natural target for all girls.

'It went fine. Valentine Inc. now owns a new range of boutiques. I'm signing the papers next month.'

For Val, of course, had agreed to hand over to his wife whatever she wanted providing she went on tweaking his nipples, and over the years she had turned a one-man fashion show into a multinational corporation.

Travis grinned, showing wide white teeth. 'That's great!' He was dressed in a baggy T-shirt and oil-stained jeans, having learned his careless dress sense from Val. 'Where is Dad, anyhow?' he asked, uncannily echoing her thoughts of only a moment ago.

'I'm not sure. Probably still caught up with his French friends.'

'He's determined to hold a show in Paris, then?'

'Totally. And you know your dad once he's made up his mind.'

Travis grinned and launched himself on to the settee, where he bounced a few times and then came to rest, his head buried in a paper. 'How was school?' she asked, walking to the kitchen and pouring them both a cup of coffee.

'Great. I've been made editor of the college rag. Voted in, sixteen to two. It was probably Smith and Cann who voted against me. Neither of them knows a good rag from the *Inquirer*.'

'That's slander,' she said, handing him the cup. 'You have to watch out for libel and that sort of thing in the newspaper business.'

Ever since he was ten, when Travis had informed them oh so seriously that he wanted to be a 'newspaper man', he had worked steadily towards this goal. Now, neither Val nor Veronica doubted he would one day realize his dream to own his own newspaper.

'Publish and be damned,' Travis drawled in response to his mother's teasing, his eyes twinkling as they rested on her. 'I've got a summer job on the *NY Sentinel*. Nothing flash, just a gofer, but it'll be great experience for me. That OK with you?'

'So long as your schoolwork doesn't suffer.'

'It won't. I need the grades to get into a good journalism school.'

Veronica nodded. His determination was awesome. When he'd told his father — both Travis and Veronica considered Val as such — that he wasn't going to go into the 'frock' business, neither of them had dreamed of trying to change his mind.

They were behind him one hundred per cent in whatever he wanted to do.

Veronica was ecstatic to admit that Val was a wonderful father. From the very start, after they were married in a civil ceremony two days after the fashion show, he'd taken on the role of father with an ease that was, nevertheless, serious. He had given Travis his first 'birds and bees' talk. He'd taken him to baseball and football games. Together they went to PTA meetings, and together they disciplined him, although Val had only given their son's backside a well-deserved tanning on one occasion. Travis, at the age of nine, had been goaded into taking a swipe at a girl at school who insisted on tormenting him. Val had very promptly told him that no man ever hit a woman. It was the lowest of the low.

Now, at seventeen, Travis was showing every sign of turning out wonderfully, much to Veronica's immense relief. He was not on drugs, didn't drink anything stronger than beer, had not, so far, got any girl into trouble, and always let her know if he was going to be late. He showed none of his natural father's ruthlessness.

Veronica knew she had good reason to be so well pleased with her life.

Val had teased her unmercifully about her success with money, demanding that she pay to take them on a world cruise when she'd made them their first million. They had compromised on a tour of the Caribbean, and since then she'd made them three more million.

Val had been able to expand his fashion houses, which now encompassed New York, Milan and London. He would soon add Paris to its collection.

As she watched her son read every single word on all twenty national and local newspapers, she felt relaxed, contented, happy and sure that her world would always be as perfect as it was at that moment.

She was wrong, of course.

* * *

Thousands of miles away, Sebastien Teale closed the dossier he had been keeping on Wayne D'Arville and leaned slowly back in his chair.

He was still living in the same modest apartment. He still worked at the same psychiatric institutions, although he was now head of the hospital's governing body.

But the passing years had done more than merely elevate his career. His deep russet head now had just a few touches of grey at the temples that, as so often happened with men, only made him look more handsome than ever.

He'd taken to 'working out' over the years, and his simple but effective exercise regimen had toned his body into a lean, lightly muscled machine that made him move with eye-catching grace.

His face was thinner too, though it showed little trace of the intervening years of heart-breaking work. A few crow's feet had appeared at the corners of his sherry-coloured eyes, which crinkled attractively whenever he smiled, and his cheeks were more gaunt, but that was all.

He was still single.

Now, as he put the dossier aside and pulled on his jogging shoes, he tried to thrust all thoughts of his most elusive patient away. Jogging to Hyde Park, he let his mind roam freely, but it always came stubbornly back to the big Frenchman.

Since learning of Wayne's horrific past, he'd at last begun to make some progress with him, giving him mental exercises to do in times of stress and helping him control his more destructive impulses, but it was slow and hard work.

Now, with the sun shining and the birds singing, he was suddenly made aware that spring was once more rampant in England. He found himself admiring the daffodils as he jogged past, and he breathed deeply as the strain slowly began to ease out of his shoulders.

With his head down, he was just breaking into a more energetic run when, from out of the blue, a black and brown furry body suddenly wrapped itself around his ankles.

The little dog yapped, enjoying the fun, as Sebastien faltered, desperately trying not to step on the animal. It was hopeless, of course, and with a sense of the inevitable he felt the dog's tail under his foot as he began to fall.

The dog let out a blood-curdling yelp.

Sebastien felt instant guilt hit him, even as his knees hit the grass. He put out a hand to try and save himself, saw in dismay that the little dog was right underneath him and would be crushed, and heard a wailing female voice, somewhere over his right ear, cry out, all in the same instant.

'Jackson, you stupid little mutt. Get *out* of there!'

The stupid little mutt, Sebastien thought with a sudden flash of humour, didn't stand a chance. Time seemed to coalesce into a long-drawn-out sigh. Reaching for the small furry body, Sebastien lifted it high up into the air, at the same time twisting his body. Consequently, his ribs hit the floor with a breath-robbing crack.

His other hand, still holding the wriggling dog, shot out comically and catapulted the dog safely out of the way.

Sebastien's head hit the dirt with a star-making thud.

'Ooomph,' he grunted, and closed his eyes.

Jackson, of course, promptly showed his gratitude by standing at his head and yapping ear-piercingly into his face.

'You shouldn't be telling him off, you ungrateful cur,' the same female voice suddenly said, and Sebastien opened his eyes in time to see a strong pair of pink-nailed hands reach down and snatch the dog up. 'He was saving your hide, you ingrate! Honestly. Dogs!'

The ungrateful Jack Russell was set down, and suddenly a face appeared in Sebastien's view. Since he was lying sprawled flat out on the grass, he blinked in surprise.

A woman was on her hands and knees in front of him. Sparkling green eyes dropped on to a level with his as the woman dipped down to him, so close that their noses were almost touching. He could feel her breath, sweet and cool, on his cheek, and felt something flutter in his chest.

'Are you all right?' she asked, then laughed at her own stupidity. 'Sorry, of course you're not all right. You were brought down in mid-run by a Jack Russell. Let me rephrase that. Do you think your ribs are still intact?'

Sebastien was feeling dazed, but he wasn't sure it had anything to do with his fall. He blinked his eyes, and focused them on a mane of thick, sable hair.

'Huh.' He forced himself to his elbow. 'It's not my ribs that worry me,' he finally managed to mumble, and rubbed the back of his smarting head ruefully.

'Oh no!' The woman scrambled around him. It was an amazing sight — she was dressed in a very expensive cream leather coat, which was now badly grass-stained. Gentle hands went to the back of his head.

Sebastien winced.

'You've got a bump there the size of a quail's egg,' the woman said, reluctant laughter in her voice. 'Sorry I couldn't be more dramatic and say it was the size of a duck's egg. Or an ostrich egg, to get into the realms of melodrama!'

Sebastien was about to say that a quail's-egg-sized bump was quite enough to be going on with when he felt warm, strong hands on his shoulders, pulling him back.

He let out a startled gasp, all his muscles instinctively clenching, but found himself being drawn back on to a cradling lap. Where he'd never felt safer. His head touched soft thighs, and his body began to tremble.

It was not, he knew, due to delayed shock.

He looked up into the most arresting face he'd ever seen.

The woman was not as young as he'd first thought. Her face was sharp and angular, like a cat's. Her skin had a series of fine lines that put her age on a par with his own, but Sebastien found those very lines so attractive. They gave her face character that younger women didn't have.

Her eyes were like emeralds, and right now they were laughing down at him. Her hair was so long it brushed his face. He could smell a delicious peachy smell coming from it. The desire to run his hand through it was so strong that he reached up for it.

Mistaking his intention, and thinking it was annoying him, the woman brushed it back. 'Sorry about that. I keep threatening to have it cut, but my ex threatened to stop my alimony cheques if I did.'

Sebastien felt his heart trip. So she was married — no. Divorced!

He smiled, then realized how ridiculous they must look. He struggled to sit up and the woman, with some signs of reluctance, helped him.

'Think you can get to your feet?' she asked, with that mixture of concern and humour that soon had him laughing too.

Sebastien struggled to his feet, chuckling and a little embarrassed. 'I hope your dog's all right,' he said at last, wondering where all his powers of urbane and clever speech had gone. Talking to people had never been a problem for Sebastien Teale. Now, as he looked at this stranger with the cat's face and cat's eyes, he found himself, for the first time ever, tongue-tied.

'Oh, it's not mine,' the woman said. 'I'm looking after him for a friend while she's on holiday. I'm Lilas Glendower, by the way,' she said, and thrust out a hand.

Sebastien blinked at her for a moment, and then jumped, aware that she was raising one eyebrow slowly as her hand remained, untouched, thrust out between them.

'Oh, er . . . Sebastien Teale,' he said, for a moment having trouble remembering his own name.

It must be the bump on his head, he thought ruefully. Then, as his hand closed around hers and he felt a current of electricity shoot up his arm to his heart, he knew that it was nothing of the kind.

Lilas Glendower watched the most handsome man she'd ever seen blush like a beetroot and smiled.

It had suddenly turned into a very good day.

'Right, Mr Teale, I think I owe you a drink. Don't you?'

CHAPTER 30

Hollywood

Bethany Harcourt turned the last page on the Kafka novel she had been reading, her pale oval face creased in concentration until the very last word had been read. With a soft sigh she snapped shut the leather-bound book and rolled on to her back, luxuriating in the expanse of the huge Queen Anne bed.

Outside she heard the 'pop, pop' of tennis balls hitting a pair of racquets, and got off the bed, stretching luxuriously as she did so before walking to the wide double windows that led to her balcony. She was dressed casually in blue cotton shorts and white blouse, the outfit showing off her long, sun-tanned legs and arms.

The Harcourt mansion was sixty acres of luxury, but to Bethany's pale blue eyes it was simply home. She knew every fountain, and had traced the stories behind every statue and sculpture that sprinkled water in the vast gardens. At only six she had read the Greek and Roman mythology that explained the fountain of Eros, near the white wooden pagoda on the east boundary of the estate. At seven she had read the English story of Beowulf, which had sparked in her fertile brain a lifelong interest in ancient English history, and at eight she had made a catalogue of all the art treasures lovingly collected by her mother over the years.

The Harcourt residence, set in the most exclusive tract of Bel Air real estate, boasted six tennis courts, two outdoor pools and one indoor one, sculpted landscaped gardens, rockeries, two greenhouses where tropical flowers were grown all year round to decorate the twenty-foot-long dining table whenever they were entertaining, numerous fountains, gazebos, summer-houses and a two-acre lake where huge fish swam unimpeded among flowering lilies and trailing river weeds.

It was not surprising. Kier Harcourt, her father, was the most successful movie director of his generation. He had yet to make a film that was not a solid-gold hit. Her mother, Oriel, had once been a Somerville of Atlanta. She had been raised in luxury, although her marriage to Kier had brought about a temporary rift between Oriel and her mother, Clarissa.

Bethany liked her grandmother, even if she had caused a scandal all those years ago by divorcing her first husband, Duncan Somerville, and marrying a mere garage mechanic many years her junior.

Her grandfather, Duncan, had been killed some years ago in a traffic accident in the south of France. Bethany wished she had been able to have him around for much longer. She admired and respected her grandfather, who had spent the latter years of his life in a dedicated pursuit of war criminals. A pity that such a good man had had to die so comparatively young.

Bethany forced the sad thoughts away and smiled in contentment as she let her gaze roam across the landscaped grounds and beautiful gardens — her mother's pride and joy. But Bethany's true domain was the Harcourt library, which she had all but taken over at the age of twelve. Gemma, her younger sister by two years, made an almost daily habit of moaning about the size of Bethany's allowance compared to her own, her stubborn mind rejecting as irrelevant the argument that Bethany spent the money on improving the family library.

'Who the hell cares about three-hundred-year-old books of poetry, for crying out loud?' she'd snapped on more than one occasion, her ferocious scowl smoothing out to reluctant laughter, as it always did, on interpreting the amused look that passed between her parents.

Nobody doubted that if Gemma were let loose with such a generous amount of money there wouldn't be a boutique, beauty parlour, jewellery shop or car showroom safe in all of Beverly Hills!

Bethany leaned on the black wrought-iron railing that surrounded the second floor of the three-storeyed white edifice in which she lived, her eyes narrowing against the sun as she watched her little sister on the number one tennis court.

Bethany smiled wryly. Number one. Would Gemma ever play on anything else?

From where she stood the figures were small but unmistakable. Gemma, five feet six, with short but carefully styled dark brown hair, was dressed in a white tennis skirt that barely covered her thighs, and her top was little more than a white bikini bra exposing her midriff and a generous cleavage.

Bethany looked to the man on the opposite side of the net, her mind grappling to come up with the name of the tennis coach but failing. She shrugged and turned, walking barefoot across the thick-pile blue carpet and retrieving a huge, floppy straw hat from off the hat-stand in one corner.

Hats were Bethany's one extravagance. She seldom wore make-up, much to Gemma's amazement, didn't give a hoot about what she wore by way of clothes and could take or leave perfume and jewellery. But hats were different. Their shade from the hot California sun was the reason why her narrow and thoughtful face was always so pale. In a state full of tanned people, it set Bethany Harcourt apart, but other things accomplished that as well. In a town of frantic paranoia, she had an inner peace and harmony that drew people to her, people from all walks of life who found relief in her intelligent, kind and quiet company.

The number of female friends she had was the one thing her sister truly envied her. Gemma, who needed to be liked by everyone, found it much easier to relate to men.

Bethany skipped down the wide, semi-circular marble staircase, her bare feet slapping noisily against the cold black and white tiled hall as she walked past a Louis XIV *bergère*, on which resided a huge floral display of gladioli. She barely noticed the high-ceilinged elegance of the rooms she walked through before she found herself on the patio. There the warm flagstones heated the soles of her feet before she moved across to the grass, heading for the tennis courts. Once there, she slipped on to one of the sun-loungers that lined the court, glancing at her dozing brother, Gemma's twin, who was bare-chested and wearing only a brief pair of black swimming trunks.

'Who's winning?' she asked idly, and Paris, named after the city where he and Gemma were born, opened one brown eye and looked lazily across the court.

'From the look on her face it must be Carl,' he said, his voice already deep and rich and highly amused. At eighteen, Paris was almost as tall as his father. Like Kier, he had rich earthy brown hair and eyes, a tanned, handsome face, a wide mouth that was always curled into an easy-going smile, and his obsession with swimming was shaping up his body nicely.

The Harcourt family had it all — success, money, fame, looks and a tight-knit family unit. On that warm summer's afternoon, none of them could have known that the entire family would soon be thrust into the midst of a battle with a man they'd never even heard of before. A battle that was as deadly and dangerous as any fought in a war.

But the dark presence of Wayne D'Arville was still hidden from them in the mists of the future, and when Bethany looked at her sister's scowling face as Gemma whacked a ball back with more viciousness than precision, she grinned in happy ignorance.

'As usual, Paris, you're right,' she murmured.

'Out,' the tennis pro called the shot.

'What? No way. I saw the chalk dust fly into the air. It was in!' Gemma stood, arms akimbo, her flashing eyes fixed aggressively on the six-foot-tall man with the mop of blond hair, deeply tanned face and piercing grey eyes.

'Oh-oh,' Paris drawled, still with his eyes shut. 'I think that was the cue for Armageddon.'

Bethany leaned back on the cheerful sun-lounger and pulled the huge straw hat over her face.

'Come on, Gem. I was here, and I've got eyes in my head. The ball was out. Now serve again,' the pro coaxed reasonably.

'Bad move,' Paris tut-tutted, *sotto voce*, from the sidelines.

'Like hell it was,' Gemma's voice raised an octave and sounded even more as if it belonged to a querulous child.

Carl Foreman watched as his pupil walked closer, her small but well-shaped breasts jiggling up and down as she trotted angrily to the net. He felt his body stir in an all-too-familiar way, and inwardly groaned.

'What's the big deal?' Carl forced himself to ask in his usual laconic drawl. Gemma Harcourt was not the kind of girl you should show weakness to; she'd eat you alive. 'It's not as if it's a double fault or anything.'

'Obviously he doesn't know her very well yet,' Bethany muttered to her sibling, who yawned audibly.

'Apparently not. He must still be fairly new.'

'What happened to her old coach?' Bethany asked, lazily scratching her leg.

Paris shrugged. 'Perhaps she ate him.'

'That's not the point,' Gemma grated, pointedly ignoring the commentary from her laid-back audience. Her voice dropped to a dangerous octave. 'It was not, NOT, not out.' She stamped her foot for good measure, then abruptly felt foolish.

Carl tapped the base of his tennis shoes with his racket and looked down into the furious face of his pupil. Gemma had huge brown eyes, like velvet pansies, that were fringed with ridiculously long, black lashes. Her face was heart-shaped, her chin pointed and as cute as a button. The same description could also fit her slightly uptilted, three-freckled little nose.

Carl gave another silent mental groan, and moved his racket in front of his loose white shorts. 'OK, OK, it was in. We'll play a let,' he sighed, backing away.

Gemma smiled — not so much because she had won the argument, for she'd never had any doubt about that, but because she'd seen the reaction she'd had on Carl's body. Good. If she could affect Carl in that way, then surely she could successfully seduce the man she loved?

She was getting tired of being a virgin. Every girlfriend she had had lost her innocence *years* ago. Gemma hated being the oldest virgin around. It was time she did something about it.

As she walked back to the baseline, she smiled with great satisfaction.

She served the ball again, this time well in, and for long minutes a baseline volley sent regular 'pops' into the air.

'Looking forward to Oxford?' Paris asked, seeing that the fun was over for the time being, and turning over to give his back a roasting.

'Mm, I am. I can't wait to get there. Mum and Dad both loved it so.' They had, in fact, met and fallen in love there. 'I wonder if it's changed much since they were up?'

Paris snorted. 'I doubt it. Those sorts of places stay the same for centuries, don't they?'

'I hope so,' Bethany said with a beatific smile. 'I can't wait to get my hands on all that culture.'

'Ugh,' Paris said, and gave a long theatrical shudder.

'Speaking of "ugh",' Bethany riposted, 'have you thought about what college you're going to go to? Always provided you can graduate from our local high, of course.'

Paris groaned again, this time for real. 'Oh, Beth, do I have to? You know I'm no student. Couldn't you wheedle your way around Dad? You know he always listens to you.'

'He always listens to me because I always make sense,' Bethany said, with just a trace of grimness in her tone that her brother, luckily, failed to pick up. 'And you have to get some sort of degree. What do you want to do — bum around doing nothing for the rest of your life?'

'Sounds just great to me,' Paris grinned, then slowly sat up. He looked across the court at his twin's yell of triumph as she shot an ace straight past Carl's tall, swaying figure.

Bethany too sat up. 'I've had enough sun. Fancy a swim?'

Paris always fancied a swim. As they walked across the lawns towards the shaded pool in a stand of lemon trees in the south quarter that was Paris's favourite, they held hands, swinging their arms in time as they walked.

'Really, Beth,' Paris said as he eyed the water eagerly, 'I don't know what I'm going to do. Dad's some role model to measure up to. He's got his own studio, and nine — count them — Oscars for his films. He works like mad for six months then relaxes for three, then he's off again. And he and Mum are as much in love now as ever. You'd think this town and all those groupies would have tempted him, but not Dad. No wonder I feel inadequate.'

Paris executed a perfect dive and proceeded to swim ten laps, so fast that Bethany could only stand and watch in genuine admiration.

'And then there's the rest of you,' Paris added, coming to a rest, and treading water below her. 'You've got a brain the size of Texas. You're off to Oxford in the fall, and you know just what you're going to do with the rest of your life. A BA, then a PhD. Then what — a professorial position at Berkeley?'

'Am I that dull?'

This time Paris did catch the undertone in her usually placid voice. 'Hell, no. You're missing the point. You're great — everyone loves you. I just meant that all the rest of my family know just what they're doing and where they're going. Mother's already the greatest fundraiser of all time, and I don't just mean another Hollywood charity matron. She gets things done — look at last summer when she went to Sudan. She's really doing something — actually saving lives. You're going to be the academic genius, Dad is and always will be the brightest director in town, and Gemma's going to be a human tornado, break millions of hearts and take the world by the throat. But Paris? What about Paris?'

With that forlorn ending he grinned, realizing how self-pitying he sounded, and so did another twenty laps at breakneck speed. Less enthusiastically, Bethany stripped down to a modest blue bikini and waded into the shallow end. Paris might have finished off his monologue with his usual sod-it-all grin, but she sensed a quiet desperation behind those easy-going brown eyes of his.

She began a slow breaststroke, her shoulder-length blonde hair trailing behind her as she gave it some thought. What exactly could Paris do? He had no favourite subject at school, no hobby save swimming . . . Suddenly, as her brother powered past her, she stopped swimming and stood upright, her face wearing what her father called her 'brain-wave' look.

'Hey,' she called, watching as Paris lifted his head from the water, and then obligingly butterflied over to her. 'Why don't you start training seriously?' she asked, her voice all at once excited.

'Huh?'

'Swimming, dummy. For the Olympics, the world games, the state championships or whatever it is swimmers go in for these days?'

Paris stared at her and then threw back his head and laughed. 'Oh, Beth, you take the biscuit. You think you become an Olympic swimmer just like that? Come on. I'm eighteen already. Most kids start at four.'

'You did start swimming at four,' she said stubbornly. 'You're already super-fit and fast. You've been training all your life, in everything but name. All you need is a coach. You've got rich parents to back you and nothing else to distract you. Why don't you give it a try?'

Paris stared at her, frowned, laughed, then went strangely silent. 'You mean it, don't you?' he finally said, his voice barely above a whisper.

'Sure I do. Why not?' Her eyes flashed in that determined way that was all Bethany.

'Because chances are I won't make it, that's why,' he snapped back, not sure why he was feeling so angry with her.

'Scared?'

Paris opened his mouth, then closed it again.

'Come on — what have you got to lose? You must know an official swimming coach — you're a member of every club there is on the west coast. What would it hurt just to have someone in the know clock your times for you? If you're not fast enough, they'll tell you and that'll be that.'

Paris trod water thoughtfully, an unfamiliar feeling of excitement beginning to knot in his belly. 'I don't know . . .'

'Of course not. For the first time in your sybaritic life you've been presented with a challenge. The question is — what are you going to do about it?'

Paris met the wide pale blue eyes of his eldest sister, and felt the knot deepen. 'Oh, hell,' he said. She watched him swim to the side and climb out. 'Oh, hell,' he said again, pushing the wet hair off his forehead and shaking out his arms and legs, droplets of water flying everywhere.

Bethany watched him, aware of the tenseness of her own limbs. She raised a challenging eyebrow as Paris turned and pointed an accusing finger at her. 'You're too damned smart for your own good. You know that?'

Bethany grinned. 'Good luck with the stopwatch,' she called gaily, and turned away to finish off her laborious length of breaststroke. When she'd reached the other end, her brother had gone. She pulled herself out, dressed and walked back to the house. Passing the tennis courts, she noticed vaguely that they were now empty.

Inside she sat on the third step up in the hall and began to gnaw on her lower lip again. Had she done the right thing? Suppose he wasn't quick enough? There was a world of difference between being a hot-shot swimmer in the eyes of family and friends and impressing a professional, world-weary coach. And what did she know about swimming anyway? Was Paris a sprint swimmer or a long-distance one?

If he came back crushed and humiliated, he'd be even worse off than before. Bethany sighed heavily, then jumped as her father's voice came from her right, where he had been in his study. 'That sounded ominous. What's up?'

She turned and smiled half-heartedly. 'Paris. I think I may have just done him an injury,' she admitted. Standing up she walked towards him, her eyes troubled.

'Oh?' Kier shoved his hands deep into his pockets as he watched his eldest child rub her damp hair with a fluffy white hand towel. 'Do tell.'

Bethany grinned and did so, Kier listening intently. He had changed little over the years. The hair at his temples was now flecked with grey, the crow's feet at his eyes a little more pronounced, but other than that the years had been kind. Money and success had mellowed him. Bethany knew that her father had come from a very poor farming family. She hoped it didn't still haunt him. She loved her father more than anyone else in the world.

'Hmm. I can't say that I would have thought of swimming as a career,' Kier said, thinking over her words. 'But then, Paris has always been a water baby, right from the word go. I think he could swim before he could walk. Frightened your mother to death!'

'But you've noticed lately how restless he's been, haven't you?' Bethany pressed, needing to be reassured that she'd done the right thing.

'Of course I have,' Kier agreed with a sigh, his eyes looking troubled. 'To tell the truth, I've been feeling damned useless, being able to do nothing for him. When I was his age I had burning ambition to guide me. But Paris . . .' He trailed off helplessly, leaving his daughter to pick up the slack.

'Is like a rudderless ship?' she said, half teasing, half serious. Kier gave her a strong hug.

'Exactly. And you've just given him a rudder. What a princess.' He punched her jaw playfully, and she flushed softly with pleasure.

Gemma paused halfway down the stairs, her heart-shaped face tightening at the happy scene, a harsh stab of pain lancing through her. She had changed into a simple yellow dress that did little to hide the fact that she was wearing no underwear at all beneath it. Her white sandals slapped softly against the steps as she practically ran across the hall, pulled open the doors and then slammed them shut behind her, breathing hard. Bethany had always been her father's favourite.

Her eyes scanned the driveway restlessly, then settled in delight on Simon's broad back as he washed the Rolls. The chauffeur was dark and gorgeous, and the love of her life. Craftily, she sneaked up behind him. Let Bethany be the goody two-shoes. She, Gemma, would have the man she loved.

'Simon,' she purred, and playfully slapped his rump. Simon jumped as if he'd been scalded, and turned around, his grey eyes wary.

'Hello, Gemma.'

Gemma walked two fingers up his chest, as she'd seen an actress do once, in one of her father's films. Simon's grey eyes took on a panic-stricken look. Like everyone else in Hollywood, Simon was a would-be actor. He had taken the job as Kier Harcourt's chauffeur just to be near the great man. But his daughter was smitten with him, and he himself was too young to know how to handle the situation.

'Let's go to lunch. My treat,' she said. 'I've got accounts at Ciro's, Chasen's, the Polo Lounge — you name it. Come on, Simon, you know you've got to be seen in all the right places.'

Simon felt torn. She was right — it did pay to be seen at the 'in' places. But . . .

Sensing his hesitation, Gemma wanted to kiss him.

He was so sweet. And so unbelievably good-looking. No wonder it had been love at first sight — for both of them.

'Come on — I'm famished,' she purred, and Simon, knowing when he was beaten, held open the back door of the Rolls for her.

'Oh, let's take the Caddy,' she said, and walked towards the garages. Simon's stomach churned and his brain told him he was a fool to do it. Gemma Harcourt was trouble — with a capital 'T'! Nevertheless, he walked obediently towards the gleaming white Cadillac with black windows and five thousand dollars' worth of extras and pulled it up beside the waiting girl.

In the back, Gemma was immediately conscious of the smell of expensive leather. As they pulled out on to the country roads — Kier had demanded a home set well away from the Hollywood circus — she pushed a button in the side of her door and slowly a bar swung out in front of her.

'Pull over here for a minute, Simon, and come back here. I want you to have a drink with me.'

Simon reluctantly pulled over on the deserted road, and climbed into the back, his heart pounding. With a sense of the inevitable he saw her press a button, and a tinted partition of black glass cut them off from the front seats. They were now totally hidden from the view of any passer-by.

'That's better. Much more private, don't you think?' Gemma purred and looked at him from under her lashes. It was now or never. Simon was too much of a gentleman to make the first move.

Simon gasped as she reached across and slipped her hand under the leg of his loose shorts, her fingertips just grazing across his hardening shaft. He jumped again, as if scalded.

'Er, Gemma . . . Miss Harcourt . . . how old did you say you were?'

Gemma laughed. 'Don't worry. I've had plenty of lovers,' she lied airily, then, as if to prove her point, pulled suddenly down on his white shorts, yanking the garment under his buttocks and letting it fall to his feet. Gemma looped her finger under the tighter elastic of his male briefs and wriggled her hand down. Simon gave a weird and wonderful groan, then gritted his teeth. 'I knew . . .' he said, then closed his eyes on another helpless groan as her small hand curled around him.

'You knew what, Simon?' Gemma asked, her heart pounding.

Simon shook his head. All rational thought seemed to desert him, but when she pulled at his briefs he managed to lift his thighs from the seat long enough for her to free him.

Gemma stared down at his beautiful body, her throat clogged with emotion. At last — she had dreamed of Simon for so long. Seeing him every day, and now . . . at last . . .

Before she could get cold feet, she knelt before him and pushed his thighs further apart. She'd heard Cindy Blake telling her best friend all about how to do this properly.

Simon's lips thinned as she began to roll his member between her two hands and she watched, fascinated and hot-eyed, as the sweat began to break out on his forehead. Tenderly, she reached out to smooth the damp, dark hair off his forehead. Then, without warning, she swung herself across his lap, and lifted her dress up to her waist. Then she let the yellow material settle around them again as she slowly sank back down.

As his eyes flew open she impaled herself on him with a small gasp of pain.

Simon's eyes widened. 'Gemma!' he croaked, his voice shocked.

'Shut up,' she said tightly, and gingerly began to rub herself against him, up and down, slowly at first, cautiously, giving the pain time to fade away. 'Hmmm,' she said, a few minutes later, her breath coming in short jerky pants. 'This is beginning to get . . . interesting.'

Simon's fists clenched and unclenched on the seat beside him as he battled to control himself. He felt a heel because the kid had only been putting on a sophisticated act after all. He swallowed hard, then moaned as she discovered muscles in her body that she'd never even guessed existed before. Her wide red mouth pulled up into an almost feral grin as she watched him begin to thrash his head from side to side against the cream leather backrest. She jerked up and down harder, faster, feeling a tight, relentless tide of tension begin to build deep in her womb. She let her head fall back and began to moan herself as she experienced her first sexual climax, giddy with pleasure at her own audacity, glad to be a woman now, and not a girl any longer. She'd bet everything she owned that Bethany was still a virgin.

Simon watched her face, smiling with satisfaction at the almost animalistic pleasure that contorted her features as she shuddered and shook her way to climax, then collapsed into a still, warm heap on his lap. Then, because he was still hard and strong inside her, he put his hands on her waist and began to move her up and down once more.

Gemma straightened up and smiled ruefully. 'Sorry, lover, I'm still learning,' she apologized. Her knees clamped hard either side of his thighs, her stomach muscles, so young and untried, gaining in strength as she took over the rhythm. Simon's eyes widened as he stared into hers, and for a second he was almost scared of her, scared of the youthful intentness of her expression, scared of the burning determination glowing deep in her dark eyes.

Then, like two children, they began to grin at each other until a second climax overtook them both and she fell on to his chest, her head resting on his shoulder as they dragged in great gulps of air.

Yes, Gemma thought, listening to the sound of Simon's moans and ragged breathing. Let Bethany be the goody two-shoes. Gemma had found a much better way of getting male attention.

Now they'd see who proved to be the more popular Harcourt daughter . . .

CHAPTER 31

Kent, England

Lady Sylvia looked up at the sound of a softly purring car as it turned into the gravel-lined driveway and swept to a halt in front of her thirty-roomed stately mansion. Her long, slender hand tightened on the gold pen she held, and it began to shake over the half-finished letter to her aunt. Nervously she licked her lips and then slowly rose to her feet, her legs shaking precariously underneath her as she walked to the large bay windows and pulled aside the green velvet curtains.

Stepping from a large black Rolls-Royce, her husband straightened his impressive form and slammed the door, the pale but brilliant blue eyes turning to scan the house with brief approval. Sylvia felt her stomach flip and then heard the familiar pounding of her own heart as it thumped faster. She walked quickly across the oriental rugs to the carved ash door and pulled it open, walking into a light and airy hall where Gainsborough portraits clung to the walls and Venetian mirrors reflected ancient Ming vases and eighteenth-century carriage clocks from all over the world. All were legacies of her seafaring merchant ancestors.

Sylvia paused in front of the nearest mirror and checked her reflection with a mixture of despair and self-directed anger. What looked back at her was the picture of a forty-year-old woman with short, permed brown hair, wide grey eyes, a rather big nose, generous mouth and too-round face. Her skin was clear and flawless, her lashes long and generous, but she was no beauty — passably handsome, as her father had once told her with his usual blunt honesty. She jumped as she heard the sound of the door opening behind her and something flashed deep in the back of her grey eyes. Fear? Excitement? Hope? Love? Yes, all those and something more. Something that kept her chained to her husband of the last ten years when any other woman would have left him and filed for divorce long ago. It was not that she hadn't thought about it. The first time the idea of divorce had crossed her mind was on her honeymoon. And yet . . .

'Sylvia.'

The sound of his voice sent an icy shaft slicing down her spine, which burned even as it froze, and she spun around. A sickly smile was already on her face as she began to walk towards the tall, towering figure. 'Wayne, this is a surprise. I thought you were going on to London from Paris?'

Wayne D'Arville watched his wife walk up to him, his nose picking up the scent of her Nina Ricci perfume as he bent down to kiss her. The gesture was automatic rather than affectionate, but as his lips brushed hers he felt her shudder. 'I was, but then I doubted that there'd be anyone around over the weekend, and I wouldn't be able to get anything done, so decided I might as well come home.'

Sylvia felt pain slice through her heart, and bit her lip, calling herself all kinds of a fool as she half turned away.

'Why don't you come into the drawing room? We'll have some coffee and you can tell me about the trip.' She realized she was sounding trite, like some awful character from a bad play, but as usual she felt tongue-tied. Wayne came home so seldom that when he did deign to show up she felt as if she were entertaining a stranger. She walked to the concealed bell-pull that hung by the side of the Turner seascape and pulled it briefly three times.

Wayne, watching her, tugged off his tie and dropped his crocodile-skin briefcase by the side of his armchair, then walked restlessly to the big bay windows that looked out over the acres of landscaped grounds. Nothing changed here, he thought, wondering why he felt so depressed. The fountains always bubbled, the koi carp always swam among the flowering lilies. The flowers bloomed in strict adherence to the army of gardeners' wishes, and even the birds seemed to sing on cue. Greenway Manor, the ancient stone house set deep in the Kent countryside, looked exactly the same now as it had on the first day he'd set eyes on it, when old man Greenway had invited him down for the weekend, ostensibly to play some golf, in reality to try and sound him out about Platts' threatened takeover bid of his company.

Lord Greenway had not taken the Frenchman's moves seriously. After all, Platts had never been a corporate raider before. When he'd finally realized the danger, his obvious adoption of the old adage, 'Keep your friends close, but your enemies closer,' had amused Wayne. So too had Sylvia Greenway, his only child. Plain, virginal, shy, and smitten with him. It was only after he had added Greenway's to his already enormous empire that Wayne had begun to realize that little Sylvia Greenway was everything he needed in a wife.

Even now, as he watched her motion the maid to set down the silver tray, he realized that she had class stamped all over her. It was a strange thing, class — and nobody had more of it than the British. For years Wayne had tried to pinpoint it but couldn't. It was not style, that was for sure. Sylvia was a country bird through and through, plain and dowdy. She wore baggy dresses, wellingtons, bulky anoraks, and tramped the countryside looking like a female scarecrow. Yet still she wore that aura of 'quality' about her that was instantly recognizable. It was not beauty either — Sylvia was built like a stick with bumps and had the face of a moonstruck cow. Nor was it intelligence. Although his wife had attended Roedean and Girton, she owed her minimal academic success to a good memory and ability to retain facts rather than to any ability to think for herself.

And yet she was still, and always, Lady Sylvia Greenway. Never Mrs D'Arville. That at first had angered him, then amused him. As the gold-edged wedding invitations had gone out, offering the local gentry the opportunity to attend the wedding in St Paul's of Lady Sylvia Greenway to Wayne D'Arville, he had begun to see the way the English mind worked. Sylvia would always be both a Greenway and a lady. And since there was nothing he could do about that, he'd decided to let it work to his advantage. In the world of finance he was still an upstart foreigner who had gained Platts by nefarious means. The continued and unsuccessful campaign by Sir Mortimer's grandchildren to regain the company had left him with a stigma that was hard to shake. But with a wife called Lady Sylvia, of good English country stock, stately manor and fine guest list, he was better equipped. Yes, in all ways but one, Sylvia was the perfect wife. Docile, obedient, well-connected.

If only the bitch weren't barren.

Wayne longed for a child of his own. It was the only area where his father still managed to beat him. Wolfgang had managed to sire two sons. So far, Wayne was childless, and it galled him considerably. He had married primarily to produce his own heir. But after ten years — nothing.

'Milk, no sugar, right?' Sylvia asked, then flushed as his lips curled into a sneering smile.

'Well done, darling. You got it right — for once.'

Sylvia's hand shook just a little as she poured the coffee from the silver Spanish coffee urn into the delicate Royal Worcester cups, but she never spilt a drop. 'So. How was Paris?' she asked, leaning back against the Sheraton sofa and taking a deep breath as she did so, uncomfortably aware of the tightening sensations in her breasts. Was she always doomed to be like this? To turn into a quivering, useless mess of . . . of

. . . *want* whenever he was near? But in all fairness to herself, nothing in her sheltered life had prepared her for Wayne. Her mother had died when she was only seven, leaving her to be brought up by a succession of nannies who looked after her every need. No great beauty, and tucked away in the country-side, Sylvia had seen the tall Frenchman as a tiger in a genteel chicken house. She had not stood a chance. Now she took a deep sip from her cup, uncaring that the hot liquid scorched her tender mouth and made her eyes water. How many mistresses did he have tucked away in London? She knew of at least two, but there were probably more.

'Paris is always the same,' he said crisply, but his eyes, resting on a jade table lamp, seemed far away and there was a tenseness in his body that she was only just beginning to notice. He was excited about something, but what?

'It must be nice to be so blasé,' she said, her voice sharper than she'd intended, and she looked down quickly, her breath coming in rapid jerks as a mixture of fear and tense excitement knotted her stomach. Wayne looked at her, a flash of genuine surprise in his eyes. She was usually such a mouse that her show of spirit was intriguing. But only for a moment. One glance at her feverish eyes and the way she plucked at her skirt soon provided him with the answer.

'You're feeling neglected, I see,' he said laconically, rising to his feet and shrugging off his jacket to reveal a wide expanse of chest covered by a white silk shirt, the trappings of civilization doing nothing to disguise the emanation of raw masculine virility that oozed from him like hot honey.

Sylvia felt her heart stop and then begin to pound. 'No!' she cried desperately, standing up and looking around her like a trapped rabbit. 'I didn't mean . . .'

Wayne began to unbutton the shirt, his eyes never leaving her face. She was staring at his hands as if fascinated. The years had been kind to Wayne, that much she was at least experienced enough to know. Most men of his immense size ran to fat, the bulk of their body becoming flabby, but Wayne exercised regularly and had zealously avoided this trap. His hair as yet showed no signs of greying, but when it did she knew that the contrast of copper and silver would be spectacular. Her lips parted in a soft gasp as he pulled the shirt from his shoulders, revealing lightly tanned skin. She glanced at the door. Wayne wondered idly if she was seriously thinking of running, or was only worried that a servant might come in. She closed her eyes and gave a soft, despairing moan. Why had she been born so weak? And unlucky? If Wayne had not come along she'd be safely married now to some chinless wonder who came home every weekend to make love to her in the dark, in bed, at night.

Instead . . . instead . . . Wayne barely smiled as he reached for her, lifting her cleanly off the floor. She was wearing a summer dress that was at least five years old and of a faded blue colour, dotted with similarly faded red poppies. For a moment, as she was lifted to his chest height, their eyes met, hers a yearning, hating, desperate grey, his a bored, merciless blue, and Sylvia felt her soul shudder deep inside her. Then the moment was past, and she was laid on the floor in front of the empty fireplace. She turned her face away from that of her husband and stared at the large bowl of flowers resting in the recess. Roses, of course, yellow and white, tinged with peach. And there was love-in-a-mist, with its dreamy blue and tiny green fronds. And Ginny had mixed them with columbines. What a strange mixture. She sighed and then stretched.

Wayne splayed his hands across her small breasts and felt the nipples like tiny pebbles under his fingers. Sylvia's eyes fluttered shut, the long lashes lying across her flawless cheeks like dead insects. Wayne shook his head, aware of the stirrings of his body that seemed totally remote from his brain. He didn't kiss her. He realized the dress unzipped at the back and couldn't be bothered to turn her over. Instead he simply took the dress at the neck in both hands and tore it down.

Sylvia flinched and cried out, the sound quickly strangling in her throat as she began to shiver. Wayne looked down at her body, then dipped his head to take her left nipple into his mouth. Quickly he pulled down her plain Marks and Spencer white pants, at the same time undoing his zip and wriggling out of his clothes. He spread her legs with hands that he pressed imperiously against her thighs.

Sylvia shuddered as she felt her legs opening, and her eyes shot open as he pushed his massive organ inside her. His eyes met hers briefly. They were mocking, still bored, and as hard as cold diamonds, an erotic contrast to his hot member inside her, which quickly began to stroke in a diabolical way that always totally defeated her. She closed her eyes helplessly, her hands coming to cup his hard, muscular shoulders, her fingers digging into him as she began to thrash beneath his large body. The unyielding hard floor made his penetration of her that much deeper, and she wondered grimly if he thought he could make a baby more easily if his sperm had less far to travel.

She smiled suddenly, a triumphant smile that changed into a contortion of ecstasy as the first orgasm hit her. She cried out, then bit down on her own lip in case the servants heard. Wayne glanced over her head at the cool elegance of a Chippendale cabinet as he kept up the smooth, deep rhythm, his body moving like an automaton. Sylvia was sweating hard by the time he finally climaxed, and as she felt his hot rush of semen flood into her belly, a second, crowing smile flickered across her face. This time he saw it. Briefly his eyes narrowed, then he rose quickly, zipped up his trousers, and walked barechested across the room and through the hall. Sylvia turned her red and wet face just in time to see him almost run up the stairs. She waited a few seconds and then heard the faint sound of the shower running.

She lay still for several minutes, waiting for her breathing to return to normal, and then slowly, painfully sat up, her body aching pleasurably, and pulled the ruined dress over her as best she could. Then she walked unsteadily to the door and looked to her left and right. The house was quiet. Quickly she went to the semi-circular white marble staircase and climbed the stairs, going into the bedroom that adjoined his and using her own shower. When she had towelled herself dry, she moved to her built-in wardrobe and reached for the first thing that came to hand. It was another summer dress, just as old as the last one, that had once been a bright, buttercup yellow, but had now faded to a deep cream. She pulled it over her slender body and slipped on a fresh pair of Marks and Spencer pants. She glanced at the door that separated them and then looked away, instead lying on the bed and burying her round face into the pillow. As she did everything else, she cried quietly.

Gradually the sounds of movement in the other room faded away, and at four o'clock she felt sufficiently recovered to go downstairs for tea. Mercifully, Wayne was nowhere in sight. She nibbled her digestives with vague hunger and then brushed the crumbs into her hand and deposited them into a copper wastebin. The afternoon was warm and sunny and she eagerly stepped out into the garden, which always made her feel better. The smell of the earth and flowers, the sight of bees disappearing up foxglove trumpets, the sights of colourful borders and the sounds of birds and water trickling over stones always soothed her. She felt weary but almost content as she walked towards the lily pond, where she watched the lazy, flickering fins of the gold koi carp as they swam in the cool water. Her favourite black wrought-iron bench was beneath a honeysuckle bower and she sat down and leaned back, feeling the dappled sunlight warm her skin. 'Oh, Wayne,' she said softly, then more sharply, 'Wayne!'

* * *

In the study, redolent of leather, books and fine brandy, Wayne unlocked a black leather folder and studied the contents. His father's casino was practically his. All he was waiting for was the final report from his private investigator.

Over the years the documentation he kept on his father, Wolfgang Mueller, had built up into a vast horde that filled two filing cabinets. No less than four private detectives monitored Wolfgang's every move, reporting on his every action. Two more PIs were digging into his past, both in Monte Carlo and Germany. But it was his father's precarious financial situation that was the most fascinating of all. Now, at long last, the Droit de Seigneur was almost his.

Wolfgang had overreached himself. Not content with the casino as it was, he'd made plans to extend and upgrade it, but costs had risen astronomically since he'd first purchased the Seigneur. Consequently, Wolfgang was heavily in debt to the banks and had taken on two partners to help finance his work. One partner had already secretly sold out to him, and Wayne had just finished negotiations with the second. All that was left were the banks — and with his contacts, and the ageing, sightless Wolfgang looking less and less like a wise investment, the Droit de Seigneur would soon be his. Then he could go back, proudly and openly as the conqueror, not the banished, unwanted son. Wayne closed his eyes briefly, feeling the bittersweet pleasure bite deep into his innards.

Over the years he'd prayed constantly that Wolfgang would not die, as had his mother. Her official death certificate read 'heart attack', but his detectives had discovered it was really liver and kidney failure. Poor Marlene had literally drunk herself to death, but Wolfgang was made of sterner stuff. Wayne didn't know what he'd do if his father died before he could have his final and ultimate victory over him. Wayne hated his father so much, it was a physical pain.

He glanced at his watch and stared at the phone. Pierre Arnot was due to phone at four-thirty and report on this mysterious lead he said he had. Wayne drummed his fingers on the tabletop, and then reached for the phone. Whatever this lead was, it could hardly be that important. And besides — he needed his fix. The line burred on and off about three times, and then the calm and pleasant tones of Sebastien Teale were at last in his ear.

'Hi. Where are you?'

'Home,' Wayne said, then added, 'Kent. Are you free for Sunday dinner?'

'Love to. What time?'

'Whenever you feel like it. Why don't you come down today, then you can spend the night? We can do some fishing tomorrow.'

'That sounds wonderful!' Sebastien laughed, the sound making Wayne smile. He seemed happy for some reason. 'But not the salmon farm this time. Let's try our luck in the local river.'

'Whatever you like,' Wayne said easily, feeling the muscles in his body begin to unwind at the thought of a quiet day's fishing and talking. 'See you tonight. We'll hold dinner.'

'OK. How's Sylvie?'

'Sylvia? Oh, she's OK. How are things your end?'

'As grim as usual.'

Wayne sighed. He hated the leeches who made such demands on him. Why Sebastien insisted on slogging his guts out for the losers in the hospital he just couldn't understand. 'You shouldn't push yourself so hard. People take advantage of you.'

There was a brief pause at the other end, the quality of silence making Wayne shift on his chair and quickly backtrack. 'When will you be down?'

'Eight OK?'

'Fine. See you then.'

Sebastien slowly hung up and stared for a long while at the receiver before replacing it. Through the open door, Lilas Glendower watched him swinging thoughtfully in his chair. She sensed his tension and was intrigued.

After the incident in the park, she had taken him to a little pub she knew and insisted on buying him a brandy. There, she had quickly found out that Sebastien Teale really *was* as good a find as she had suspected the moment she'd held his head in her lap.

She'd wangled a dinner invitation from him, and over the candlelit meal had learned all about him, from the disapproval of his parents, who had all but exiled him from his native San Francisco, to his dedicated work at the psychiatric hospital. And, unlike Wayne, Lilas had admired him for not taking the easy and more profitable route into private practice. A little delicate probing had yielded other diamonds — he'd never been married but wasn't gay. His social life was a big fat zero.

Eventually, Sebastien had caught on, and he'd leaned back in his chair, his eyes twinkling but a little surprised. 'If I didn't know better, I'd say I'd just been given the third degree by an expert,' he'd mused, his voice just a shade worried.

Lilas smiled. 'It makes a change, though, doesn't it?' she'd said softly, understanding him at once. 'Talking to someone about yourself instead of listening to others.' Her eyes had held his, her gaze level and unthreatening.

And when she'd seen his eyes widen in shock as he realized just how unusual it was for him to relax around someone else, she'd known, in that instant, that she had to save this man. Save him from himself. He was far too precious to be allowed to self-destruct. Besides, she wanted him too much.

After her divorce, Lilas hadn't thought that having a man in her life was an option anymore. Now, after just one look from those eyes of his, she knew differently. The thought was an exciting one. A warm and pleasing one. Lilas was too worldly wise to be afraid. Besides, it was Sebastien who had to look out!

Now, she was at home in his apartment, having all but invited herself back there after that first date, and visiting it regularly since. She'd taken him boating on the Thames, and given him his first ride in a hot-air balloon — one of her favourite pastimes. They'd spent a lot of time together in just a few short weeks, Lilas making it obvious, in every way she knew, that she didn't need a shrink. She had no problems. She was single, with a good job and her own place. Her life was one long bed of roses. Sebastien Teale, psychiatrist, was not needed. Sebastien Teale, potential lover, life partner and soulmate, however, was definitely on the agenda.

And she was sure that she was succeeding in getting just that message across.

'Who was that on the phone?' she asked now, having sensed something different about him, and — as usual — feeling curious. She saw him stiffen — a sure sign of unease.

'No one. Just a . . .' Sebastien shrugged '. . . private patient.'

'I didn't know you had any.'

Sebastien smiled. It was a strange, weary smile. 'I don't. Wayne is . . . different.'

Lilas, for some reason she didn't then understand, felt a cold shiver travel up her spine. But with her usual common sense she shrugged it off and walked slowly towards him, noting with pleasure how his eyes warmed at the sight of her. 'Why don't we . . . play chess?' she asked, and quickly whipped out Seb's old board from the cabinet.

Sebastien burst out laughing. Lilas was . . . well . . . Lilas. He hadn't been able to figure her out. He knew enough to know when a woman was hunting him. And he had no objection to being hunted. But so far she'd made no move to take him to her bed, and he was far too unsure of himself to try to take her to his. Besides . . . he was intrigued. Lilas was so strongminded, independent and spontaneous. She was just what he needed.

And he knew it.

She knew it too.

* * *

Wayne changed for dinner. It was a habit he'd picked up from Sylvia, who was herself dressed in a navy-blue shapeless gown, and as he sat opposite her he sipped his brandy with quick, uninterested sips. She nervously crossed her legs and checked her watch. She'd be glad when Sebastien arrived, for he was the only person Sylvia knew who had the ability to make her feel totally at ease. He'd also been Wayne's best man and his only guest at their wedding.

She'd seen Wayne's cold nature from the start, of course. Her own father had fallen victim to it, and there

399

were those who thought her marriage to him was the ultimate in bad taste. Especially when her father had died so soon after losing his business. But how could she possibly explain to her peers the power of his dark fascination? How could she say, in polite society, that he totally overwhelmed her? Made her ache to please him, made her burn just at the thought of it?

But Sebastien, she'd felt instinctively, did not judge her, and now she looked forward to his visits every bit as much as Wayne himself, although she had to be careful. Wayne was almost pathologically jealous of his friend, and she'd soon learned to hide her affection for Sebastien, knowing instinctively that if her husband guessed at it, then Sebastien would never come down to Greenway Manor again. She knew that he and Wayne dined often together in London and wondered from time to time if Sebastien wasn't secretly analysing Wayne. They seemed to talk in intense earnestness, walking in the garden, heads close together, deep in conversation.

Then she smiled. Sebastien probably analysed her as well. It hadn't taken long before she found herself pouring out her life story into the gentle American's receptive ears. There was something about his soft voice, his instinctive understanding and soothing gentleness that broke down all her English barriers which decreed that troubles should be kept strictly to oneself.

She was even ready to believe that Sebastien knew more about the true state of her marriage than she did.

'What are we having for dinner?' Wayne asked, feeling more restless than usual. The phone call from Arnot after he'd spoken to Sebastien had been something of a surprise. Wolfgang had personally overseen the assassination of a Nazi war crimes investigation squad, led by Duncan Somerville, ten years ago. That, in itself, was interesting. Although everyone was convinced the car accident was genuine, Wolfgang must still worry about it. What if he dropped a few hints in all the right places that another team was on its way? How would his dear father react to that?

Sylvia watched the vicious smile curl his lips and looked away, murmuring something about roast duck. 'What time did Sebastien say he'd be here?' she added quietly.

'Eightish. Why?' he added sharply. 'Not pining for him, I hope? Sebastien wouldn't look twice at you. No man in his right mind would.'

'Oh? That says a lot about you, then, doesn't it?' she flashed back. 'And it makes me wonder why your best friend is a shrink.'

Wayne felt a brief stab of anger that quickly faded, leaving him only curious. She was very brave all of a sudden. Why? 'You obviously have something to say, darling,' he drawled the last word sardonically. 'Why don't you just come out with it?'

Sylvia's eyes flickered then slid away. 'It doesn't matter,' she mumbled, and nervously sipped her own glass of dry sherry.

But her thoughts winged their way upstairs, to where the precious slip of paper, which had arrived from the hospital only today, rested underneath her blouses and skirts.

Again she smiled secretly. For the first time she could ever remember, she held the upper hand. If only she dared to use it . . .

CHAPTER 32

Unobserved, Wayne watched his wife in the mirror, curious rather than interested. She'd been acting strange for days now, and he was certain it was not just his imagination that she'd suddenly found some spunk.

He shrugged the thought away and turned to more pleasant topics. He could start a two-pronged attack on his father any time he wanted. The casino was practically his already and all that was left was to let the old man know it. And then there was the Mossad. The documents his excellent detectives had uncovered about the lorry driver who had murdered their team were bound to convince them of his father's guilt. The thought of Wolfgang being forcibly extradited or kidnapped and standing trial in Israel was so wonderful that it almost gave him a sexual kick, yet he knew he couldn't do it. The newshounds would have him traced as the son of a Nazi within days, and then his own business empire would be in dire jeopardy.

His eyes sharpened as Sylvia paused in front of her dressing table and stopped humming, her face taking on an expression he'd never seen before. Excitement, certainly, tinged with satisfaction and a touch of sadness. In the doorway he stiffened, instinct alerting him to possible danger. He watched as she opened the second drawer and took out a long white envelope. His first thought was that she had taken a lover, and he smiled savagely.

'I hope that isn't some secret rendezvous you have there, Sylvie.' He used Sebastien's version of her name deliberately, and smiled with satisfaction as she jumped and turned around, looking white and almost ill. She stood paralyzed as he walked towards her and then wordlessly took the envelope from her stiff fingers. He pulled out the sheet, seeing at once that this was no love note. It was typewritten and headed 'Hortland Hospital'. His eyes flickered briefly back to her. Was she ill?

Sylvia almost managed to smile, but not quite. She didn't have the heart, nor the cruelty for it. Instead she nibbled on the inside of her lip and turned away to stare blindly out of the window as Wayne read the words, his eyes widening in incredulity.

When he'd finished, he read it again, just to make sure. Sylvia had undergone every test in the book to see whether or not she could conceive and had passed every one. Wayne licked his lips, forcing his stunned brain to think. All these years he had assumed it was *her* fault they were childless, since he'd had ample proof of his own virility. Veronica Coltrane had been impregnated by him, though the child was still-born. He'd also given his father's Spanish maid . . . what was her name? . . . a child, too.

But now. Ten years. Ten years they'd been trying for a child, and nothing. And it was not her fault. Wayne slowly folded the paper back into the envelope, glanced once at his wife's stiff back, then threw the paper carelessly on to the top of her dressing table. Without a word he turned and walked away, his legs feeling stiff as he walked down the stairs, across the impressive hall and headed for the garage. He ignored the Bentley and other classic cars and took instead the key for the E-type Jaguar he'd bought new and kept in immaculate condition.

Upstairs Sylvia watched the bottle-green shining car spin out of the garage and accelerate up the drive, spewing gravel chips from under its wired silver wheels. Sighing, she wondered when she'd next see him. She doubted he'd be in a hurry to return, and boy was she glad of it . . .

* * *

Wayne drove to London with automatic skill and too much speed. He was stopped once by a traffic cop but sweet-talked his way out of it and arrived at his doctor's office in Harley Street just as they were leaving for the day.

Sir Roger Davenport took one look at the Frenchman's hard face, waved away his receptionist-cum-nurse, and showed him into his plush office. Briefly Wayne told him the facts, keeping his voice curt and making it very clear he didn't want sympathy, platitudes or bullshit. The doctor had him booked into a top clinic the next day for morning and afternoon tests, the results of which came through within two days.

Sir Roger phoned him at his office and asked him to come back to the clinic for a talk, already giving Wayne the answer he'd been dreading. Somehow, somewhere along the way, he'd become impotent. Useless. Incapable of fathering a child. There would never be a legitimate heir, one that he could raise, mould and use to further the glory of his name.

When he arrived at the Harley Street clinic on a wet Wednesday afternoon, he listened without apparent emotion as the doctor explained the problem. It was so simple. So utterly ordinary. The bout of mumps he'd caught just before his marriage to Sylvia had been the culprit. He'd thought at the time that it was a mere infection of his glands; had not even considered the possibility of a grown man catching such a childish ailment. Sir Roger had to admit there was nothing to be done. He launched into a medical explanation of it, but Wayne was hardly listening. As he stared at the oak-panelled wall behind the doctor's Brylcreemed head, his thoughts were turning savagely to a way out.

He had children — or at least, a child, somewhere in the world. Rosita Alvarez — he had since remembered the

Spanish maid's name — must have been Roman Catholic and therefore unlikely to abort her bastard. And a bastard child was better than no child at all.

Sir Roger had stopped speaking for some time before Wayne finally focused his hard blue eyes on him and managed to pull his lips into a semblance of a smile. He rose, shook hands, murmured something adequate, and left, his mind buzzing. He took a taxi to his Mayfair flat, then telephoned the airport. Before it was answered he hung up again, realizing he didn't have the faintest idea where the Alvarez woman was.

Instead he called the detective agency that was handling all his Monte Carlo work and set them on the trail of his father's one-time maid. He offered an extra five thousand pounds for a quick result and was then forced to wait.

He slept only a few hours a night, aware of a pressure building in the back of his head, hearing in the darkest hours a silent scream that seemed trapped in the caves of his brain. He tossed and turned and drank too much, in the vain hope that it would ease the frustration. He neglected his work and forgot to shave.

Even Sebastien, when he called, was put off. The flat became a prison that he could not leave in case he was out when the phone call came. His executives at Platts had a field day, tasting the unusual, sweet flavour of delegated power. Wayne had always thought he had so much time and so many opportunities to raise a worthy heir. Now he was obsessed, driven by the need to find his child, a human being that had sprung from his seed.

Eventually, five days after his first phone call to the agency, he received a special delivery parcel. Inside was a folder that contained all the information he needed. Feverishly he began to read. Rosita Alvarez had given birth to a baby girl in a Roman Catholic charity home for fallen women in Madrid and had then gone on to Andalusia where one of the staff had found a job for her with the local grandee of a small peasant village.

Wayne paused and shook his head, the first sentence slowly filtering through. He screwed his eyes up tightly and then covered them with his knuckles. A girl. A *girl*. The insult, the catastrophic injustice of it made a scream rise to his throat, and he had to grit his teeth to stop it from actually escaping. Sweat broke out on his forehead. He knew that if he started screaming, he'd never be able to stop. He had a sudden hideous vision of himself in a straitjacket, screaming whenever someone took off his gag. Sebastien was there, with his kind, gentle hands and kinder eyes, but this time not even he could stop the screaming. Wayne groaned, took a deep breath, opened his eyes, and then suddenly felt perfectly calm as a cooling wave of certainty washed over him.

Leaving the folder on the cluttered desk, he walked into his kitchen and brewed some coffee, then went into the bathroom to shower and shave. When he came back he was wearing a fresh beige cotton suit and cream shirt. He poured the coffee, picked up the folder and read it through to the end. Rosita Alvarez was dead and had been for five years. Her death, the detective hinted, was rather mysterious. He'd taken the liberty of investigating the grandee, Don Luis, and discovered that no less than six maids, without family and of bad reputation, had worked for him and died within a matter of years. Although unable to get confirmation, there were rumours hinting at sadism, unusual and unlawful sexual practices. But no one had followed it up.

Wayne skipped through this, barely interested, his attention sharpening on the report of his daughter. Rosita had named her Maria, but the detectives had no photographs of her. Her mother had obviously been too poor to have such a thing as a camera, and all her possessions had been burned by the Don. The young woman, in her late teens when her mother had died, had run away. Neither the detective nor Wayne were surprised. Here the trail had become more difficult. The girl could obviously speak English and French, but all her education must have come from her mother, since there was no record of her attending even the local school. Wayne turned the final page and finished his coffee.

Maria Alvarez had been found in Barcelona, working in a sweat shop that churned out cheap T-shirts for the tourist trade. Her hours were 6 a.m. to 9 p.m., with a half-hour lunch break. She lived in a tenement in the slums in the northern part of the city and rode to work on a bicycle, probably stolen.

Slowly Wayne shut the folder and walked to the telephone, where he booked a ticket on the earliest possible flight, the 7 a.m. to Madrid.

* * *

Spain, in the height of the tourist season, was as awful as he'd expected. The pavements were crowded with red and peeling English holidaymakers wearing straw hats . The Japanese contingent was also in full swing, cameras hanging around their skinny necks, patrolling the bullrings and architecturally interesting sites like squads of schoolchildren. The heat was unbearable.

As he boarded the express train to Barcelona, Wayne squinted in the sun and felt the sweat trickle down his back. The train did nothing to improve his humour, being cramped and stinking of human sweat and stale food. Everywhere he looked, swarthy-skinned and dark-eyed men and women stared at him, his height and colouring attracting attention even to a people grown used to summertime invaders.

Wayne found a first class carriage and sat down. Even here Spanish businessmen, puffing on nauseating cigars, watched him with interest, and he pulled down the shade to keep the hot sun off him. Over the years, Wayne had become more English than he realized. He'd grown acclimatized to the moderate and wet weather, and had even adopted the reticent nature that made the garrulous Spanish people seem an annoying and intrusive race, better left to themselves.

The journey was tediously long, so monotonous that Wayne felt once again that silent scream migrating dangerously to his throat. He ordered coffee from the lazy steward and was then unable to drink the lukewarm brew he was given half an hour later.

At Barcelona he checked into the top hotel, took a cold bath, shaved once again and ate a respectable meal. It was seven-thirty, the sun was endurable, and yet he felt strangely reluctant to leave the hotel. Everything about the country nauseated him: the language, the heat, the insects, the people, the dirt, the gaudy lack of order and class. And his daughter had been raised in all this chaos, by a semi-literate Spanish whore who had done who-knew-what with a perverted old man with delusions of grandeur. He sighed deeply, then made his way outside. He was unable to find a taxi and was forced to go back in and ask the concierge to telephone for one. He then had to wait half an hour before a battered yellow and grey vehicle of indiscriminate pedigree showed up. He climbed gingerly into the back seat, his nostrils picking up the faint smell of vomit and beer and gave the address of the sweat shop in terse, clipped Spanish. The driver stared at him in the mirror, noting the thousand-dollar suit and gold cufflinks, the perfectly cut hair and handsome face. What would an English *turista* who looked like this want in that part of town?

'Wouldn't you rather go to a nightclub, *señor*? I know all the best—'

'Do as you're told,' Wayne snapped back, his hands itching to grab the greasy man's neck and strangle him. The tension was getting the better of him and he was aware of a blind desire to lash out. Without a word the taxi was slammed into first gear and roared away, belching smoke from its dodgy exhaust.

Wayne ignored the furtive looks the driver kept giving him in the rear-view mirror and watched instead the passing scenery. In this day and age the centre of any big city looked very much the same, whether it was Cairo, London or Istanbul. It was only in the suburbs that a country's true

408

character showed through. And whereas in Cairo or Istanbul there was a certain flavour of dignity or ancient culture, in this part of Barcelona there was only filth and decay. Wayne felt the desperation of the place seep under his skin like a cancer, and he shuffled in his uncomfortable seat. The buildings became pathetic hutches, with tiny windows and crumbling walls. Clothes-lines hung across the narrow streets, getting dusty as the traffic began to trundle over pot-holed roads. Gangs of youths hung out on street corners, looking mean and dangerous, and in doorways to small bars and dirty inns, half-naked women with dead eyes and switchblades touted for business.

The sweat shop he was taken to was five storeys high, with most of its windows boarded up; it looked like a big box turned upside down. Wayne got out slowly, looking around at the dustbins being rifled by starving cats, at the interest he was attracting from the women in the streets and at the small children who gathered around him and began to beg.

'That'll be five hundred pesos, *señor*.'

'Wait,' Wayne said crisply. The driver opened his mouth, then thought better of it. '*Si, señor*,' he muttered instead, then cuffed one small boy around the ear as he poked at a rusty wing mirror that was half hanging off.

Ploughing his way through the gang of children, Wayne walked towards the large red double doors that led to the sweat shop. A broken-down link fence guarded the grounds, and he noticed that none of the children followed him past the perimeter. No doubt the owners of the building had been more generous with guard dogs than they had with workers' wages. The red doors were rusted and hard to open, but once inside the heat and airlessness hit him like a physical force. He gasped, the smell of cloth, dust and human sweat almost making him retch. The room was lit with bare bulbs that pumped out only forty watts at a time, and the clatter of noise came from armies of sewing machines.

As he became accustomed to the light, heat and noise, his eyes scanned the room, taking in every detail. Large wooden benches lined the room, crammed into the minimum of space needed to allow a person to squeeze between them. Shoulder to shoulder in front of ancient sewing machines was an army of women. Wayne moved closer, still unobserved. The women were practically uniform. All wore sweat-soaked white blouses and long, thin skirts. All wore bandanas that hid their hair, which were also sweat-soaked. The eyes were all black and fixed on the white cottons and coloured silks that were flowing under the hammering needles. Some were old, some middle-aged, some looked like only children, but all wore the same expression of hopelessness.

As he moved closer he realized none of them were talking. At first he thought it could only be because no one could be heard above the rattle of machines, but then he noticed several men walking around the perimeter of the benches close to the windowless walls. The women's eyes flicked nervously towards them whenever they passed, and Wayne slowly nodded.

Suddenly one of the men noticed him. The sweat-slicked face turned his way, the black eyes briefly flashing in surprise before he came towards him. As he approached he put his hands on his hips and thrust forward his chin in as threatening a gesture as he could make to a man who was so obviously his physical superior. He said something in harsh, guttural Spanish.

'I want to talk to Maria Alvarez.'

The man did not understand English, but the name was familiar. Julio Corsecia had picked out Maria Alvarez for his own. All the overseers chose girls, for it was the overseers who could protect them, put forward their name for transfers and even bargain for a few more measly pesos. But so far Maria Alvarez was proving difficult, and Julio's eyes narrowed on the handsome stranger. Was this her lover? Was this why she was playing so hard to get? She was by far the most beautiful woman he'd seen, and also the most intelligent.

Then he realized that this *gringo* couldn't possibly be her lover — he was wearing thousands of pesos in jewellery alone. He could afford to keep Maria in downtown luxury if he chose.

Wayne reached into his pocket to withdraw a bunch of notes. He pointed to the women and said again, 'Maria Alvarez.'

Julio took the money quickly and nodded to the fifth bench from the right, then pointed his finger six along. Wayne stepped closer, his eyes searching for the girl in the dim light. She was sandwiched between two other women, and he strained his eyes, hoping to see something different about her, something that would mark her as his. But her head was bowed and all he could see were wisps of black hair on her forehead. At that moment she leaned back slightly, and he could see that her face was sweating and streaked with grease that must have come from her machine, which looked so dilapidated he was surprised it even worked. Her face was pinched and paler than the others', but the eyes were black.

Wayne felt himself recoil, as if he'd just confronted a snake. There was nothing about her that he wanted. Nothing he could salvage. A sweating peasant, with bovine eyes and a dull brain. What else was she doing here? Suddenly he wished she'd never been born, never been allowed to raise his hopes. The bitch. Trust Rosita to produce this . . . *creature*.

He sneered a smile. He could just imagine springing this peasant on London society as his wrong-side-of-the-blanket daughter. She'd probably go around barefoot and get fat on chocolates. Wayne glanced at the openly curious Julio, nodded curtly, turned and left.

Maria Alvarez did not look up.

Wayne found the taxi driver waiting for him and ordered him back to the hotel. There he repacked his overnight case and called the airport, every action savagely controlled. He was in luck. An eleven o'clock plane had just had two cancellations.

* * *

411

Maria heard the buzzer and almost cried in relief. As if by magic the machines stopped, whether or not a garment was only half done, and the sudden silence almost hurt her ears. Then the gabble of female voices began, along with a general exodus towards the doors, where the usual bottleneck formed. She remained seated. After fifteen hours of being lodged between two sweating bodies, she didn't need another ten minutes of it at the door.

She leaned forward and tugged off the bandana, allowing her wet but lush hair to tumble free over her shoulders. Leaning her elbows on the table, she took deep gulps of stale air. At first, when she'd begun to work here she'd been sure she was going to suffocate. She'd fainted regularly, as did all the newcomers, until she got used to it. The guards and fellow workmates had totally ignored her. She'd been working six months now and it felt like sixty years.

She had to get out. She had to. Even if it meant starving. Even if it meant working the streets. Anything had to be better than this.

'Waiting for me again, I see.' The words were leering and uttered in the thick local dialect. Inwardly, Maria moaned.

'I'm waiting to leave, Julio,' she corrected him wearily. Every night she had to fight him off, and it was getting more and more difficult.

'Aw, come on, Maria. Why don't you come back to my place? I have some wine in the fridge — nice and cold. And if you were more friendly I could get you transferred upstairs.'

'Great,' she sneered. 'They actually have hundred-watt bulbs up there, don't they?' Standing up she found herself trapped against the bench as he pushed against her.

'Ah, you are so ungrateful, little Maria,' Julio chided her. 'They make beautiful dresses up there. Silk and lace. Mmm,' he put his fingers to his lips in a silent kiss, and Maria almost laughed. Almost. This Lothario thought he was God's gift to women because he was not fat and because he earned two hundred pesos more than the women. It was pathetic and strangely sad.

'I must go now,' she said, shoving against him fearlessly, and walking towards the door. Since running away from the Don's villa before her mother's body was even cold, she'd learned quickly how to take care of herself. She'd needed to.

'I hope you don't expect to meet your tall lover boy,' Julio spat after her, his masculine pride severely knocked. 'Where did you tell him you worked? In some boutique for the *turistas*, huh? Well, I'm afraid, *chiquita*, he's found you out.'

Maria turned around and stared at him. 'What are you gabbling on about, you imbecile?'

Julio laughed spitefully. 'I'm talking about the tall Englishman who came here asking for you, my little *cucaracha*. I suppose I could have let you have a few minutes off, but . . .' He shrugged his shoulders graphically, rejoicing in putting the haughty bitch in her place for once.

'Tall Englishman?' Maria echoed, her heart suddenly diving in her chest. On her deathbed, and in a highly feverish state as she died of untreated syphilis, Rosita had mumbled about her father. About his copper hair and blue eyes. Maria had even learned his name.

'What did he look like?' Maria asked sharply, trying to keep her voice neutral. If he guessed how important it was, Julio was likely to clam up.

'Ahh, he thought he was something, because he had the blue eyes and gold hair. But he was nothing,' Julio said, shrugging his shoulders and laughing. 'Not like me. Not even that much taller.'

Her father was French, but Maria doubted if Julio would know the difference. And if it *had* been her father come to find her . . . She glanced at the benches and could easily imagine a rich man's shock and disgust at what he'd seen. A girl, sweating, dirty, a mere peasant . . . Oh, *madre mia* . . .

Maria began to run. She ran to the back, where her buckled and tired bicycle was kept, and pedalled furiously up the road a few hundred yards to the nearest phone. There she used up precious pesos phoning all the best hotels. In her fever,

Rosita had muttered the name D'Arville over and over again, and as she asked after any guest by that name, using her best and most cultured accent, she could feel her heart hammering in her chest. He had come for her. It had to be that. Who else in the whole stinking world knew or cared where she was? The fifth hotel she phoned, one of the most luxurious in town, confirmed that they had had an Englishman called D'Arville staying, but that he had just checked out.

'Where? Where did he go?' she all but screamed, and then calmed down, spinning them a tale about finding his wallet. The desk clerk assumed he had gone to the airport and told her so. Maria hung up and almost cried. The small local airport was so far away. She could not possibly bike it. She stashed her battered only means of transport behind a derelict building and ran to the main thoroughfare, where she hailed a taxi. It took up her last pitiful amount of cash.

At the airport she ran into the departure lounge, headed for the nearest free departure desk, and asked if Wayne D'Arville had left yet. The clerk, a middle-aged woman dressed in a red and blue uniform, with perfect make-up, hair and grooming, sniffed politely that they couldn't give out that kind of passenger information. For a second Maria stared at her, wanting to rip her eyes out. What did confidentiality mean when her whole life had just been flushed down the toilet?

Then she turned away, her shoulders slumped, totally defeated. What did it matter? She already knew, deep in her heart, the answer.

He had come at last to find her, and then decided he did not want her. No doubt she was not good enough for him. No doubt the rich man didn't need a nobody for a daughter. If she'd been beautiful and worked as a shop girl in some fancy jewellery store . . . If only she'd looked different, he would have taken her. All the years of working for a pittance and dodging men who wanted her body had been made bearable only by the thought of being rescued one day. By someone. By anyone.

And although Rosita had taught her to hate the man who had deserted them, leaving them to a life of misery and poverty, the little girl in her, raised fatherless, had nevertheless secretly yearned for her father to come and claim her. To assure her it had all been a terrible mistake. But now, Maria shared her mother's hatred of the man. Wayne D'Arville. What kind of man was he? Knowing that he'd seen her and the kind of life she'd been forced to lead, knowing that he had stood only yards away as she'd sweated and toiled in that awful place, and then just calmly abandoned her for a second time, made the hatred burn, searing down into the very depths of her being.

She stumbled out into the warm night air and dodged the conductor on the airport train back into town. Walking the streets back to the factory, she found that her bicycle was gone. Somebody had stolen it, as she had stolen it in the first place. Slowly she leaned against the wall and began to cry, helpless, hopeless tears of anger, rage, frustration and pain.

Suddenly she heard voices, Julio's and one of the other guards, and watched dully as they began to load the beautiful dresses from the second floor on to vans. Slowly her tears stilled and a hard, cold knot took their place. When they both went inside for the second batch, Maria found herself running. She crouched low, waited for them to reappear, load the next batch and then re-enter the building. Still crouching, she sidled up to the van and looked inside. Quickly sorting through the racks of dresses, she lifted down an evening gown of deep red silk that shimmered in the pale moonlight, the outer covering of plastic crinkling as she folded it over her arm and ran back into the night.

It didn't matter if they found out who had stolen the gown — she already knew that she would never go back to the workshop. She was through with just surviving. She was through with being a good girl, trying to make for herself a decent and honest life.

One thing her father's visit had taught her was that she could rely on no one but herself. From now on, she thought, stumbling through the dark streets with a stolen dress and about ten dollars' worth of pesos to her name, things would be different. She would travel north, to Madrid, where all the rich men were. She'd steal some make-up, do her hair differently, steal some shoes. With her lovely dress she would find a rich man. She would demand jewellery, cars and furs, then sell them for cash.

Then, and only then, would she be ready to find her father.

For leaving her in that awful place, for finding her unworthy to be his daughter, she would destroy him.

She would destroy him if it was the last thing she ever did . . .

CHAPTER 33

Hollywood

Kier frowned as the telephone shrilled loudly and glanced up from the screenplay he was reading to see if anyone else was about to answer it. Apparently nobody was, and after the seventh ring he lifted the receiver and leaned back in his large leather chair. 'Yes?'

'Is this Mr Harcourt?'

'Yes.'

'You are the husband of Oriel Somerville, the daughter of the late Duncan Somerville?'

Kier frowned and sat up straighter. 'Yes.'

'Ah. My name will probably mean nothing to you, but I am Daniel Bernstein. I was a good friend of Duncan Somerville's for many years.'

Kier relaxed again and smiled. 'Yes, I remember Duncan talking of you. You were on the committee in Switzerland, weren't you?'

He rubbed his forehead tiredly, the typed lines of the second-rate screenplay dancing before his bleary eyes. It was three months since he'd finished work on his last film, due out at Christmas, and he was anxious to find another project.

He was never easy with his almost mandatory three-month vacation after every film. Hollywood changed constantly and new kids appeared on the block every day, anxious to take his crown of 'top director' away from him. Sometimes he felt like a hamster in one of those wheels where he had to run harder and faster just to stay in the same place.

'Indeed I was,' the voice on the other end confirmed, warming considerably. 'I was due to go with him on the Monte Carlo expedition but a family crisis at the last minute made it impossible.'

'Then I'm glad you didn't go.'

'Yes. Yes.' The voice hesitated, then coughed. 'Ahem. Mr Harcourt, I am in Los Angeles at the moment. Would it be possible to come over and speak to you?'

'Now?' Kier asked, surprised.

'Yes, if it isn't too much of an inconvenience. I . . . have some news that can't be given out over the telephone.'

'All right.' Kier glanced at his watch. 'I'll expect you in half an hour. Do you know the way?'

'I imagine every taxi driver in town knows your address.' The voice laughed warmly, and then, without another word, hung up. For several seconds Kier stared at the receiver, then shrugged and put the phone down, telling himself there was no need to feel so uneasy — Duncan had been dead almost eleven years. Yet he was unable to settle back down to reading the so-called thriller that sat in front of him, and instead he poured himself a weak Scotch and soda, wandering with it into the living room.

The house was deserted. Paris was at the swimming baths, where he seemed to live nowadays, training for the California State Championships next month. Bethany was at a college lecture on the Oxbridge university system, and he never knew where Gemma was. For weeks he'd been meaning to have it out with her, nightmare visions of drug addiction or worse disturbing his dreams, but Oriel was against it.

'If you lay down the law now you'll only make it worse — drive her out even more. Believe me, I know,' Oriel had said, then smiled and took his hand. 'I'll see to it. In my own way. Trust me?'

Of course Kier trusted her. He glanced at his watch and wondered if she'd be back in time from the fundraiser for African Famine Relief to meet their mysterious visitor.

He stretched out on the settee in the main lounge and flipped through the TV channels. Some of his earlier films had been bought by the top channels, and it would be interesting to see them with the distance of time. But just then he heard sounds in the hall and looked through in time to see his wife slip off her shoes. Her hair was shoulder-length now and bobbed into a neat curl but dyed to hide the approach of grey. Her figure, however, was as slender as ever and her face had matured from being girlishly pretty to being womanly beautiful.

'Kier?' she called, the sound of her clear, sweet voice making his heart glow, as it had always done.

'In here, sweetheart.'

She turned at the sound of his voice and walked in, smiling as she snuggled up against him on the couch, her back pressing against his chest, her hands reaching for his and resting them on her waist. He smelt the fresh rose scent of her hair and leaned forward to kiss her neck.

'Not working?' she asked, pinching his drink and taking a small sip.

He told her about the phone call, and she leaned her head right back to give him a worried, upside-down look. 'Is that all he said?'

'Uh-huh.'

'I wonder what he wants?'

'We'll soon find out. Unless I'm mistaken, that's a car now.' A few moments later the doorbell rang and Margery, their housekeeper-cum-cook, opened it.

Kier rose as their visitor was shown in.

He was a small man, about five feet six, with short grey hair, a neat moustache and smiling brown eyes. Dressed in a rumpled blue suit, minus a tie, he walked briskly, like a pedigree dog. 'Mr Harcourt.'

'Mr Bernstein. This is my wife.'

The man turned, and, seeing Oriel for the first time, beamed a smile. Walking over to her, he took her hand and bowed over it in touching old-fashioned courtesy.

'Ah, Mrs Harcourt. Your father often spoke of his beautiful daughter, but I must confess I thought that it was a father's exaggeration. I can see now I did Duncan an injustice.'

Oriel almost blushed, then nodded him to a seat. 'Please sit down. What would you like to drink?'

'Oh, a dry sherry if you have it, please.' He took a seat opposite the couch, looking nervous and out of place as Oriel handed him a drink and then once again joined Kier on the couch. The old man took a sip, smiled, sighed and then came straight to the point.

'I imagine my telephone call came rather out of the blue, and you're wondering what all this is about?'

Oriel looked at Kier, who read the silent message in her eyes, and slowly leaned forward to dangle his arms across his knees. 'We are curious, yes. It has something to do with Duncan and his work?'

'Yes. Yes, it does. It has, actually, more to do with his death, and the man in Monte Carlo we suspected of being Wolfgang Mueller. I . . . are you conversant with all the facts?'

'Yes,' Oriel said sharply, feeling a cold chill suddenly snake down her spine. 'You must have learned something else, Mr Bernstein, or else why come here?'

Daniel Bernstein nodded thoughtfully. 'Yes, Mrs Harcourt, we have. The Mossad, or rather only a division of it that is attached to the War Crimes Committee, have found several death camp survivors who are willing to testify that D'Arville is in fact Mueller. We are also investigating the possibility that Mueller's lieutenant at the time may have absconded with valuable and irrefutable documentary evidence. Naturally we are searching for that lieutenant now.'

Kier leaned forward and frowned. 'All this has taken rather a long time, hasn't it?'

Daniel Bernstein smiled sadly. 'It always does. If you had seen the chaos, the shock . . .' He shrugged, and as he did so the ill-fitting blue suit rode up his shoulders, and with a cold shock Kier saw the tattooed numbers in faint blue ink on the man's wrist.

'I'm sorry,' he said, knowing that it was totally inadequate but not knowing what else to say. Daniel Bernstein smiled that sad smile again and shook his head.

'We are dedicated to bringing the Nazis to justice, despite the help they receive from the US and Britain, and the other countries as well.'

'The US shelters war criminals?' Oriel echoed, her voice raised several octaves in genuine horror, and watched as again the old man gave that fatalistic shrug.

'To be sure. But that is not why I am here. There has come to light some new evidence about . . . the car crash that killed your father, and all my other good friends. It seems that a . . . friend of mine, living in Monte Carlo, had a tip-off about a private detective investigating Mueller. Naturally, my . . . friend . . . er . . . bribed the man concerned, who then handed over copies of his findings. There is some discrepancy about the legitimate nature of the lorry driver, and other factors that lead us to believe —'

'Daddy was murdered,' Oriel interrupted flatly, but her voice was appalled and deadened with shock, and Daniel Bernstein spread his hands helplessly.

'Yes, madam. I'm here to ask you if you know of any of your father's papers that may help us reopen the Mueller case.'

Oriel, pale-faced but composed, shook her head. 'No, I . . . no. My mother probably took care of all that. She's the one you should ask.'

Kier reached across and squeezed her hand, and Oriel closed her eyes briefly. She could see a perfect replica of her father's laughing face on her closed lids. He had been so kind, so gentle. And to be murdered by some Nazi . . . It was almost unbelievable. And yet, here was this little man, with his tattoo and his nightmare memories, drinking dry sherry in her lounge in Bel Air, telling her just that.

'I thought that would be the case. Actually I tried to find a Mrs Somerville in Atlanta but couldn't. I was hoping that you could give me her address?'

Oriel nodded. 'Yes, of course. She remarried several years ago.'

'Ahh, I see.' Daniel waited as Oriel left and rummaged in her handbag for a piece of paper and quickly wrote down the address where her mother and Kyle had lived for the last eight years.

Oriel had long since overcome her immature attitude towards Kyle. Now they had dinner regularly at Thanksgiving and Christmas, and Kyle was even a favourite with her children, especially Paris, who loved him like an older brother.

In a way, Oriel could even admire her mother for marrying her long-time lover. She had certainly run the gauntlet of Atlanta gossip for marrying a man several years her junior, and a poor one at that. She walked back with the piece of paper, her hand trembling as she handed it over. Daniel rose as he took it, obviously in a hurry to leave. Kier looped his arm comfortingly around her shivering shoulders as they walked the old man to the door.

'You will keep us informed about things, won't you?' Kier prompted, and, assuring them that he would, Daniel Bernstein left.

* * *

Thousands of miles away, Wayne D'Arville disembarked at Honolulu airport, where he was given the mandatory *lei* of frangipani flowers. He took a taxi the four miles or so down the strip into Honolulu centre. Everywhere he looked he saw lush tropical flowers, towering white hotels, blue pools and bubbling fountains. Even the trees that lined Tantalus Drive and other famous avenues such as Pali Highway and the beach-fronted Kalakau Avenue were the owners of such exotic names as hau and milo, pandanus and ohia. He vaguely took note of the shower trees, in full colourful bloom as the taxi headed for the famous Pink Palace, or Royal Hawaiian hotel, where film stars and royalty regularly stayed.

The taxi driver obviously had ambitions to be a tour guide, and gave him an unwanted commentary on the city, the Aloha Tower and volcano bowls, going on to wax lyrical about the Hawaiian gods. Wayne would have given him an extra-large tip just to shut up, but he was exhausted from the flight and wanted only to rest before seeking out the man he had travelled more than half the world to find.

The streets sped past, packed with gaudily dressed holidaymakers. In that respect the city reminded him of Spain, and he shuddered as he remembered it. He wished he'd never gone.

'Here we are — the Pink Palace.'

A bellboy grabbed Wayne's luggage straight out of the back of the taxi and led him up to the main lobby, through the lush gardens rife with palm trees and fountains. In the high-ceilinged hall, he checked in, ignoring the fountain in the middle of the room and the small, tropical fish that swam in the white marble bowl amongst the flowering water lilies.

'Would you like to dine downstairs, Mr D'Arville, or would you prefer to be sent up a tray?' the bellboy asked as Wayne walked through the four-roomed suite on the top floor and stepped out on to the balcony. His room overlooked the azure expanse of the ocean, and below him men and women stretched out beside one of the pools, reminding him of fish grilling on a skillet.

'On a tray. Fetch me a menu, will you?'

The bellboy nodded, beaming at the tip Wayne gave him, and hurried away. A maid entered and began to unpack for him, but he didn't turn around. The hotel was set in a sea of tropical colour — rhododendrons, bougainvillaea, hibiscus and bird-of-paradise flowers. Huge banks of lilies and orchids seemed to grow like weeds, yet Wayne was blind to their beauty, as he was to the sight of that white beach, the most famous in the world — Waikiki.

He turned as the bellboy returned and handed over a heavy leather-bound menu and glanced at it, almost too tired to feel hungry, barely noting that the menu was as exotic as his surroundings: lomi-lomi salmon, kalua pig, saimin and loco moco. He ordered the macadamia-crusted chicken and *haupia*, the popular coconut pudding, and a bottle of white wine, saying only that he wanted the best vintage. He couldn't be bothered with a wine list that was probably as long as his arm.

The meal was delivered quickly, and he ate it just as quickly, collapsing on to the bed as soon as his spoon was down. When he woke, it was the following afternoon. Evidently he'd remembered to put out the 'Do Not Disturb' notice. He was doing more and more things lately without remembering them later. It was . . . odd. He was also feeling more and more tired. He'd have to ask Sebastien about it. He would know. Sebastien would look after him.

He showered and changed, walking into the main restaurant and ordering coffee and a salad before he saw to hiring a car. For his money he got a chauffeur-driven limousine and a driver who knew the city inside out. The driver was guaranteed to be discreet. Which was just as well.

Reading the address from a notebook the PI agency had sent him, he smiled for the first time that day. He looked around with more interest as he was driven northeast out of the city towards Kaneohe Bay, where Lt Friedrich Heinlich now lived a life of mild luxury as Billy Hawker, a retired beer baron from Yugoslavia.

Beer baron. Wayne smiled again as his thoughts winged back all those years to that clandestine boat ride across Lake Constance when he and his father, mother and little brother had fled Germany. Heinlich had also been on board, but only Wayne had spotted him. And had kept quiet about it, knowing that his father would have given anything to get his hands on Heinlich. Would the man who had cowered under the tarpaulin, convinced the son of Wolfgang Mueller was about to give him away, remember him?

The car cruised along Route 83, hugging the spectacular coastline, and then turned off, a few minutes later pulling in at a low, large bungalow that boasted a kidney-shaped pool, carefully tended gardens and two guard dogs. Wayne nodded to the chauffeur to stay seated and let himself out.

Heinlich was seated by the pool, a flabby old man. He watched the stranger alight from the impressive car with thoughtful but unworried eyes and slowly sat up as his tall visitor drew to a halt in front of him. As a rich widower, Heinlich was used to being visited by strangers, most of whom came bearing invitations to some social function or another, but this tall individual was obviously nobody's errand boy. He found himself stiffening and straightening even before the man opened his mouth. There was something strangely familiar about him, and something, from a long way off, tugged at his memory.

'Yes? What can I do for you?' he asked, more abruptly than was characteristic of him, and Wayne raised an eyebrow, a little surprised by the broad American accent. Of course, Heinlich had lived on the island for decades. No doubt financed by blackmail in all the right places. He wondered where his father's cronies had all come to rest, and how much they had paid this balding, unattractive individual to keep his mouth shut. With the files he had stolen on them, he had been set for life.

'I'm so glad you asked . . . Herr Heinlich.'

Billy Hawker, as he'd been known for more years than he cared to count, went as white as a shark's tooth. '*Mein Gott* . . .' he muttered, rising shakily to his feet and staring up into Wayne's blue eyes. 'Come inside,' he said stiffly.

Wayne followed the ex-Nazi into the interior of the impressive bungalow. Inside it was all cool tiling and plain white alcoved walls, each alcove housing original Hawaiian masks. Native instruments, such as guitars and ukuleles, flutes, ipu drums and uli'ulis stood tall and proud in a dark showcase in one corner. Wayne walked past lush plants climbing rattan screening and down into an ultra-modern room of black smoky glass, chrome and white leather.

'You live well, Herr Heinlich. Much better than a humble lieutenant would, I think,' he commented, selecting a chair and making himself comfortable.

Heinlich took several deep breaths, poured out two neat Scotches, and handed one over. 'Who are you? And what are you doing here?'

For a moment he had visions of kidnapping Israelis or revenge-mad concentration camp survivors, but the man's lack of a weapon and his relative youth calmed him. Heinlich walked stiffly to a chair but did not sit down.

'Not a very original opening,' Wayne chided, and took a slow sip of his drink. 'Actually I'm very hurt you don't remember me. After all, I did save your life once.'

Heinlich jerked around at that and stared at Wayne. 'Not in the war,' he stated firmly. 'You're too young.'

Wayne smiled and took another sip. 'I was only a boy, I admit. Stood on a boat. Lake Constance . . . ah, now I see it's all coming back.'

Heinlich sank on to the white leather chair, his mouth falling comically open. The English turn of phrase 'like a stunned mullet' had never seemed more appropriate. 'Mueller's son!' he breathed, and Wayne nodded, enjoying himself.

'None other. I've come to collect. For keeping my mouth shut all those years ago.'

Heinlich drained his glass but didn't feel strong enough to get up and pour himself another, although he badly needed one. All these years he'd felt safe, and now . . . 'What exactly do you want?'

'Your documents on my dear father, of course. What else?'

'Ahh. I see. I had heard that the Mossad . . . never mind. Forget it. I never said it.'

Wayne smiled, took another sip of his drink, and then crossed his legs at the knee, one black leather shoe swinging absently. 'Well?'

'I don't have them here,' Heinlich said, swallowing nervously, his prominent Adam's apple bobbing up and down on his liver-spotted throat. An old man, Wayne thought, just like his father. And once they were called the master race! He half-laughed, and then shook his head. Hell, what a joke that was.

'Then we'll go and get them, shall we? My car's out front.' He stood up and walked to the old man, who tried to shrink back into the chair. Slipping a hand underneath his arm, he all but dragged him to his feet.

'Why now?' Heinlich whinged as they walked out into the hot afternoon sunshine and headed for the black limo. 'Why not before? If you could find me any time . . . It doesn't make sense. Why didn't you turn me over to your father all those years ago?'

'You don't have to understand,' Wayne said softly. 'Just obey.' He looked down into the old, red-rimmed eyes and said with the softness of a snake, 'You were wise enough, all those years ago, to keep out of my father's way. You'd be equally wise to obey me now. Believe me, my father is a weak, helpless old fool, and is nothing, *nothing*, compared to me.'

Heinlich listened to the hissed words, his old eyes fixed in fascinated terror at the tight, hate-filled face of the man once known as Helmut Mueller, and believed him. His lips were as dry as paper as he crawled across the back seat of the limo.

The driver glanced blandly in the mirror. 'Where to, sir?'

Wayne looked at Heinlich, who swallowed hard. 'First Hawaiian Bank.'

Wayne smiled. 'That's a good boy, Lieutenant. And don't forget, I want all the copies. Yes?' He tweaked the old man's white-whiskered chin and felt him quake. 'No keeping back any photocopies for yourself. If the Mossad do track you down,' his voice fell to a tormenting whisper, 'and you spill your guts to save your own neck, and they come for my dear, dear papa before I'm finished with him, I'm going to be most put out. *Most* put out,' he echoed softly, making the blood freeze in the old man's veins.

'I understand,' he said, his voice nothing more than a hoarse rasp. 'Anything you say.'

Wayne laughed. 'It always has been so,' he murmured softly. 'Anything I say, and it's done. You see, I really am one of the master race.'

It was then that Heinlich knew the Mueller whelp was insane.

* * *

Sebastien looked straight down, hundreds of feet, across the beautiful Berkshire countryside. He jumped as a loud 'whoosh' sounded just above his head and instinctively looked up. Above him, the flame from the burner gusted into the huge, billowing canopy of the red balloon. Like magic, he felt himself lifted even higher into the air.

'Great, isn't it?' Lilas said, reading the altimeter out of the corner of her eye. It was the first time she'd taken Sebastien up alone. But she'd had a good reason for wanting privacy.

Sebastien looked out at the rolling green hills way below him and nodded. He sighed deeply, feeling utterly relaxed. It was a new sensation for him. 'It's breathtaking,' he murmured.

There was hardly any wind, just what Lilas had hoped for. She'd planned this day, and this location, carefully. They were too low for planes or gliders to be a problem, too high to worry about electric pylons or cables. And this area of the downs was wild and empty.

'Come here,' she said softly, and Sebastien slowly turned his head. She was wearing a plain white dress that did wonders for her black hair and green eyes. His eyes fell to her beckoning arms. So inviting. . .

His eyes seemed to melt as they looked at her, and Lilas felt her breath catch in her throat. 'Come here,' she said again, soft and imperious.

Sebastien smiled and went to her. How could he not?

She snaked her arms around his neck. 'Now, kiss me,' Lilas said.

Sebastien kissed her. Her mouth was warm and mobile under his lips, and he felt his whole body shudder in reaction as her tongue darted out to duel with his.

He drew in a deep, shaky breath. Her hands moved from his neck to his shoulders, which were free of their usual tension.

She had started a campaign to take the pressure off of Sebastien Teale, and so far it was working. Now, it was time she gave herself — and him — a little reward!

Her hands dropped to his lower back, then down, to cup his delightful derriere under her palms.

Sebastien gasped. Their kiss deepened.

'Better,' Lilas murmured. 'Much better. Now kiss me again.' She smiled against his lips and pressed herself harder against him.

Sebastien shuddered. It had been so long since he'd held a woman in his arms. So long since he'd taken something from someone, instead of giving. It was heady stuff.

Lilas felt her nipples tingle against the hard press of his chest. 'Touch me,' she moaned, and gasped as his hands moved between them. His fingers were feather-light on her abdomen, and she threw her head back in joy.

Sebastien kissed her exposed throat as a flock of lapwings broke formation to fly around them. Their wings whirred as they passed by, and Sebastien's hands moved to her breasts, tenderly cupping them in his hands.

Lilas moaned again and feverishly reached for the zip at the back of her dress. With one brief movement, the garment slithered to her feet.

'Lilas!' Sebastien groaned, a little shocked, and totally delighted. For she was naked underneath it. Tenderly, she clasped his head in her hands and lowered him to her breast.

Sebastien felt the nub of her nipple harden against his tongue, and felt his knees weaken. His hands on her bare skin were infinitely gentle as they ran from her breasts to her ribcage, to her waist, and down over her thighs.

With a quick glance around, making sure the altimeter was still registering a good height, and taking a last check that there were no obstacles for miles around, Lilas gave a low growl, and pushed Sebastien back.

He landed in the bottom of the five-foot-tall basket, his face slack with surprise, and looked up at her as she dropped lightly on top of him.

'We can't,' he said, half laughing, half feverish with desire.

For an answer, Lilas's hand went to his trousers and she quickly unzipped them, slipping her hand inside and rubbing hard against him.

Sebastien's head thrashed back, his hips rising off the floor of the basket in instinctive reaction. A low moan groaned from his throat.

Lilas smiled and pushed his shirt from his chest. She had waited for this moment for so long. Slowly, savouring every moment, she lowered her head to nip one of his hard male nipples. He gasped and shuddered, just as she'd always imagined him doing. Slowly, she ran her hands over him, delighting in each gasping sigh.

Then, business-like, she stripped him naked, but her eyes were glowing like jade as he turned his head to look at her. His own sherry-coloured eyes were aflame with desire.

Eagerly, she lowered herself on to him, her head thrown back in wild abandon as she felt him push deeply inside her. His hands came up to her waist to steady her, his touch still that firm, gentle one that made Lilas want to sing for joy.

She began to ride him, like some fearless bucking bronco. Her face was tight with passion, her eyes continuing to glow like green fire. Sebastien watched her, his body singing her song, his heart so full of gratitude, love and admiration that it felt as if it would outgrow his body and burst out of him.

'Lilas!' he called her name out as the sun began to slowly set, turning the red silk balloon above him into a glowing ball. 'Lilas!' he said again, as she moaned and thrashed above him, her strong thighs holding him a willing prisoner beneath her.

They both cried out together, high above the Berkshire hills, as pleasure overcame them both.

Sebastien lay, naked, satiated and gasping on the basket floor as Lilas rose unsteadily to her feet. Totally and unashamedly naked, she reached up and turned up the burner again.

Like an obedient slave, the hot-air balloon rose on the thermals. Sebastien watched her, loving the long white lines of her body, the slender arms, loving without any conditions the generous, independent spirit that they housed.

'You're magnificent,' Sebastien said softly.

Lilas looked down at him and smiled sleepily. 'I know.'

CHAPTER 34

Spain

The Villa Fortunata gleamed like a white imperial palace in the noonday sun. Its red-tiled roofs, black wrought-iron balconies, shaded courtyards with bubbling fountains and imported genuine Greek statues all sat on the crest of a hill overlooking the ancient city of Seville. The whole house, all seventy-three rooms, was eerily quiet, as if the building itself, as well as the army of servants that attended it, was busy enjoying a siesta.

Inside, lying on a king-sized bed, the pink satin sheets cool to her back, Maria Alvarez stared at the sculpted ceiling. A small Venetian chandelier hung from the exact centre of the ceiling, supported by white plaster cherubs and winged dragons. She looked into the dead plaster eyes and slowly stuck out her tongue.

She could hear, very faintly, the hum of the air-conditioning, and the cool air on her all but naked body made her shiver; but it was a delicious shiver.

The first thing she'd noticed about Carlos's lifestyle was the cool air in which he travelled. It was with him in his big white limousine, with him in his offices downtown, with him here, in his private home. Cool, fresh, breathable air. Maria slowly lowered her feet to the genuine Roman mosaic flooring, the tiny coloured pieces forming flowering patterns in reds and greens. This colour scheme echoed green curtains and red cushions that were scattered liberally over the Gothic Spanish furniture.

She walked slowly to the balcony and stepped out into the sun, looking down on the cobbled courtyard below. Far over to the right, well out of smelling range, were the stables where some of the finest horses in the country were kept. They were all white. When Carlos had first shown them to her she had felt no special interest, and it was only when he talked for hours about dressage, gait, rhythm and breeding that she realized how important they were to him. She was beginning to appreciate the horses a little more, seeing the absurdity of their prancing more in the light of the equestrian ballet that Carlos always saw. She could look at the cups and trophies the Severantes horses had won without thinking, 'So what?'

Now she had Carlos's measure much more fully.

The Villa Fortunata was gabled, like a Gothic piece of history, with belltowers that still rang out the matins, and ancient fish pools where monks from the sixteenth century had once kept their trout stock. The cellars, deep underground, boasted one of the finest wine collections in the country, and more often than not the luxurious, impeccably appointed rooms received weekend visits from top statesmen, up-and-coming businessmen, the odd movie queen and a smattering of literary or musical giants.

Maria loved talking to them all. She loved exploring the exotic foods these people ate. Once, bored out of her skull when Carlos had invited over another horse owner, she had wandered down to the kitchens — vast cavernous places — where an army of cooks and helpers prepared sixteen-course meals. The trouble they had gone to! Some of the dishes that only took a moment to eat, a mere nibble from a delicate silver tray, had taken days to prepare. Meat was beaten and pulped for hours. Fruits were slowly simmered and boiled for a whole day. Whole larders were filled with herbs and spices that she had never even heard of.

Carlos, of course, had been miffed when the servants had told him where she'd been. 'My dear girl,' he'd told her patiently, his moustache lifting and falling as his small, somewhat feminine mouth formed the words, 'it's just not the thing to be done. Leave the kitchen to the servants, hmm? All you have to do, that is to say, your part of the job, if you like, is merely to eat the delicacies and smile. Yes?'

Maria turned away from the balcony and shut the windows, feeling the air around her became cool again. She loved the cold. Perhaps she could persuade Carlos to take her to Switzerland, or some other place where there was snow. She needed to be able to ski. She'd overheard a television presenter from Madrid, a stunning and overpoweringly groomed woman, say that skiing was as much of a social skill nowadays as speaking good French.

Maria was now taking French lessons. In fact she was also taking English lessons, for although she spoke the language she did not quite have the diction that Carlos required of a first-rate mistress. At first she hadn't understood why it was so important, but now she did. Now she was learning words like 'requisite', 'Bloomsbury', 'neo-classical' and other tongue-twisters that she spent hours practising before nervously joining one of Carlos's famous weekends. She had an instructor in art, an instructor in music who was teaching her the piano, an instructor in fashion, and, of course, an instructor in riding. But still she felt uncomfortable astride a horse, scared either that she would fall or that she would injure the horse. Not that Carlos allowed her to ride any of his prize greys, of course. She could still remember the way he had rocked with laughter when she asked him why he called the horses 'greys' when all of them, without fail, were a brilliant white. How naive she must have seemed to him then. How pathetic.

Now that she knew the names of the real fashion giants — Dior, Chanel, Saint Laurent — she wondered why Carlos had bothered with her at all, dressed in her stolen, cheap little red dress.

She did not hear the door open behind her and did not turn around.

Carlos Severantes closed the door softly behind him and watched her. The curve of her back was delicate and fine, as was the creamy skin that covered her exquisitely shaped calves and shoulders. Her long black hair was lying loose down her back and all she wore was a white silk slip with delicate spaghetti straps and a lace ruffle that just covered her thighs. He smiled slowly, a fond look in his small black eyes.

Carlos was the latest in a long line of Spanish grandees, but, unlike most of his contemporaries who had foundered and sunk in the modern world where peasants could make millions and no one regarded a title seriously, he had had the foresight and ability to survive. He had converted his many thousands of acres into lucrative tourist sites, buying up land on the coast and selling it for a vast profit to the hotel consortiums. A flair for stocks and bonds coupled with wise investments had quadrupled his fortune until now he was rich enough to do anything he wanted. Anything at all.

The horses had been his last salute to the old world. Their grace and pedigree was ageless. The enormous cost of their upkeep was a mere pittance to his pocket and their beauty made him want to cry.

During his forty-one years, he'd also sponsored a Formula One racing car and driver, a local from Seville with enough talent to make a name for himself, and, by association, for Carlos as well. He had gambled in Las Vegas and won, he had bought a yacht and sailed it around the world. He had bought his own radio station which played only good, classical Spanish music, which had earned him the title of Patron of the Arts. And this girl, this little enigma, was the latest in a long line of experiments.

Carlos had married his father's choice for him at the age of eighteen, the girl dying only two years later, leaving Carlos with an infant son and sudden, unwanted freedom. His son,

435

affectionately known by one and all as Pedro, was currently at the Sorbonne. Carlos had insisted he have a European education, and had in mind Cambridge and then a tour of the United States before Pedro finally came home and got down to the serious business of being a worthwhile Spanish playboy.

Already he could play polo like a prince, and Carlos had a polo pony all lined up. It was still only a foal but Carlos knew a winner when he saw one. It was the same instinct that was the reason why, much to all his friends' amusement and horror, he had taken on the woman who had so openly tried to pick him up one night in a Madrid nightclub.

Carlos's small mouth curled into a wider smile as Maria sighed and stretched, remembering the first time he'd met her . . .

The Flamenco Club was a four-hundred-year-old establishment set deep in the Old Quarter that had a reputation for being ultra-selective. It had taken Carlos all of a month to be granted membership, and even then the cheeky club had asked him for references. Amused rather than insulted by this, and finding himself in Madrid one night on business, he decided to visit the club of which he had been, officially at least, a member for the last six years. It was more or less what he'd expected. The timber itself breathed history, whispering of past Inquisitions, political scandal, and grand love affairs that ended in the public suicides of rich society women and impoverished waiters and *picadors*. The food and wine were horrendously good but priced beyond description. The singer, an international star just returned from a mediocre tour of France, had a husky, suggestive voice that bored him, and he had spent the entire evening blinking back the Havana cigar smoke from his eyes as his companions, a merchant banker and the son of a prominent minister, had become seriously drunk.

Carlos noticed the girl at once, mostly because she was dodging the men who guarded the front door, but also because of the way she moved. Even in the dim lighting he could see that the dress she wore was tawdry and dotted with too many sequins, but as he watched the silent chase through the oblivious crowd he felt his senses begin to stir.

The girl was lovely, he saw that immediately as she stepped in the path of a beam of light from one of the small jade wall-lamps. With one man closing in on her left, the other coming from her right in a pincer movement, the girl had swivelled surprisingly light brown eyes in all directions, reminding Carlos of a panicked filly trying to find a way out of a too-small corral. Perhaps because he was sober, or perhaps because some of his curiosity and sympathy showed in his eyes, the girl selected him, and quickly headed for his table. His two companions rose drunkenly to their feet, their experienced eyes taking in the girl and pigeonholing her in two seconds flat. She had just enough time to say, 'Please, *señor*,' when one of the bouncers grabbed her arm, jerking her upright like a marionette. 'Let go of me, you pig,' she hissed in gutter-perfect Spanish, making Juan, the minister's son, giggle like a girl and wave an admonishing finger at her. 'Can't you see I am with these gentlemen?' The girl nodded her head with imperious arrogance at Carlos, who found his lips curling in silent applause at her bravado.

In spite of her dress, in spite of the way she'd caked make-up on her face, and in spite of her Andalusian accent mixed with ghetto phrases, Carlos noted the fine planes of her cheekbones and the sensitive way her nostrils flared. He also saw in a glance her mixed parentage. Her body was too slender, her skin too light, her eyes too cool to be totally Hispanic. But more than all of these things, Carlos could feel what he always called 'the tingle'.

The tingle had told him which stocks to buy. The tingle had told him which ungainly foal was going to grow to be a champion. And the tingle now told him this girl was something special.

'That is so, gentlemen,' Carlos said, and rose slowly to his feet. At only five foot seven himself, their eyes were almost level. Almost, but since she was wearing atrocious four-inch heels, he found himself at just a slight disadvantage. The two men looked at one another nervously, then bowed out. At Flamenco the customer was always right. But as they left, their eyes mocking him, Carlos thought that he wouldn't be at all surprised to find himself soon the recipient of a polite letter informing him that his membership had been cancelled. The Flamenco had turned snobbery into a fine art.

The girl, a comic mixture of satisfaction at besting her pursuers and total incredulity at pulling it off, gave him a huge grin that did nothing for her face. The very first thing, Carlos thought as he pulled out a chair for her and graciously seated her, would be to teach her to smile properly. Carlos had a soul that cringed at anything that was ugly. His two companions watched them with amused, drunken interest.

'What would you like to drink, Miss . . . ?'

'Alvarez. Maria Alvarez.'

Carlos was sure that was her real name, for there was something forthright and direct about the way she looked him in the eye as she said it. He had rather expected some exotic *alias* and was glad that she had resisted the urge. It boded well for her ability to learn.

'I'd like . . . chardonnay, please.'

Carlos nodded approval at her choice. Soon she'd learn about vintage, vineyards, what was 'in' and what was appropriate. But not a bad choice — simple and safe.

The rest of the evening turned into a subtle game of cat and mouse, with Carlos ferreting out bits of information on her, and Maria probing for some hint about his intentions. She made it clear, much too bluntly, that she was not a one-night stand. He winced at some of her more crude overtures even though his body reacted predictably to the caress of her stockinged foot on his crotch.

'Subtlety, my dear,' he murmured to her on their way out, where his white limousine awaited. 'You must learn subtlety.' The companions they left had passed out at the table. Maria liked the word 'subtlety'. It sounded good.

She half-expected him to take her to a hotel. She was, after all, resigned to sacrificing her virginity. More than anything else, she was a realist. But instead, after about ten minutes, they pulled up outside a small but luxurious villa on the outskirts of the city that was very obviously a private home. As the car pulled up the cobbled driveway Maria felt the first shiver of apprehension slide up her spine. It was one thing to contemplate bedding a man — but quite another to be so close to having to do it.

Carlos felt the fine tremble with mild concern but much relief. It meant that she was not quite the streetwise, hard-boiled character she was projecting.

'This is nice,' she said, nervously looking around the interior. She was reminded of the Don's villa back in Andalusia, and she shuddered again. She had got away from him just in time. But what was the point if she'd only swapped one dirty old man for another? She glanced at Carlos out of the corner of her eye and smiled weakly. He was small, like the Don, and dressed in the same expensive clothes, yet he was different. Of that much she was sure. As he took her on a brief tour of what he called his town house, she tried to discover where the difference lay. Just then, he turned to hand her a glass of mineral water with a twist of lime, and she caught his eye. In an instant she knew what it was. There was no menace in those coal-black depths. Just . . . what? Amusement. Curiosity. Desire? She wasn't sure.

She drank thirstily, surprised at its non-alcoholic content, and nervously paced the room. What if tonight they . . . did it . . . and then tomorrow he had a servant throw her out? That would hardly fit in with her plans.

As if reading her thoughts, Carlos rose, yawned ostentatiously, and told her he was going to bed. Halfway out in the hall he turned back, and as an afterthought told her that the spare bedroom was the second on the left. Maria watched him go, her mouth hanging open, totally at a loss. She spent ten minutes just wandering about, feeling strangely anticlimactic, then, as her stomach rumbled, found her way to the kitchen and attacked the contents of the refrigerator. It had been three days since she'd last eaten, and as she demolished olives and ham, alternating her mouthfuls with lush tomatoes and a thick chunk of bread smothered in butter, she began to calm down.

Watching her wolfing down the food, for he'd been too curious to stay upstairs and not see what she would do, Carlos shook his head. The second thing he must do was teach her table etiquette.

They had flown back to Seville the next day, and that same afternoon the shopping began. Maria would never forget that day if she lived to be a hundred. They were driven by a chauffeur to the finest stores, where Carlos oversaw the purchases. 'These are just to tide you over, you understand, until we find a designer for you. But you need a few things while we acquire a proper wardrobe for you,' Carlos had explained. The things that 'tided her over' were enough to make her want to yelp and dance in the streets. Dresses of silk, satin, velvet and lace were purchased by the suitcase-full; shoes from Italy and handbags to match were followed by belts, scarves and accessories. Carlos even took her to the finest lingerie boutique in the city, showing no embarrassment whatsoever as he sorted through the lacy underthings that included white silk negligees and see-through baby-doll nighties. The lack of embarrassment was shared by the manageress, who saw only money, vast stacks of it. Next came cosmetics, then scent. The day seemed to go on forever. Carlos paid by cheque and gave his address as the spot to where it should all be delivered. Maria, who had never even dreamt of such sophistication, wondered how they could be sure that he had the money to pay for it all.

That night, at his permanent home, a villa that made the Don's villa back in Andalusia look like a garden shed, she waited once more for Carlos to come to her bed and once again she was disappointed. If that was the right word. The next day had been punctuated by a visit to the finest hair salon in all of Spain, and lessons from a beautician who would then come every morning and every evening to do her 'look'. The following days were taken up with elocution lessons, visits to the museum and galleries, whilst the evenings were spent at the opera, ballet or theatre. Maria was delighted. It was what she had always dreamed of. With every day that passed, the peasant girl disappeared and a sophisticated European was taking her place.

It was only after almost five weeks that Carlos finally came to her room. Looking back now, Maria could see why he had not come before. After five weeks her new persona had been firmly enough in place for Carlos's fastidious taste.

Her accent was now pure Seville. Her slender body wore the finest designs as if created for it after the deportment and 'walking' lessons of one Señor Jose Curralas. Her hands were manicured, her feet pedicured, her make-up, which she had learned to apply herself, understated and perfect, as was the cut of her long, heavy hair. Only now was she worthy of Carlos's king-sized bed.

The first night had, inevitably, been awkward. But Maria had grown fond of him over the weeks, and Carlos was as willing to teach her the manners and techniques of love-making as he had everything else. He had a dry sense of humour and an old-world courtesy that she'd never before encountered. The old books she was now reading, with their poetry that talked of honour and family pride, suddenly became reality as Carlos talked of his illustrious ancestors. She found herself listening to him because she liked to hear him talk, rather than because she wanted to hoard away knowledge for herself. But most of all, she was hideously grateful to him for introducing her to the world she'd always craved to meet. Now she was getting used to the aeroplane journeys to Florence and Paris. Now she was getting used to ordering food in the best restaurants and discussing *Carmen* with the country's leading mezzo-soprano. Carlos became brother, father, teacher and friend. And then, as a most natural progression, he became her lover.

In her room, Maria suddenly turned, aware of his presence behind her at last. Carlos smiled. 'Not enjoying the siesta?'

Maria shrugged and turned fully around, watching without embarrassment as his small eyes ran over her breasts. She smiled and held out her hand, nodding to the bed questioningly. Carlos smiled but shook his head.

He had no self-delusions and knew himself to be a slightly undersexed man. He felt the need for sex only rarely. He had, however, been touched by her gift of innocence, and it had paved the way to her excessive, compulsive buying of jewellery. Carlos knew that the jewellery was her way of providing for the day she would leave him, but he did not begrudge it, just as she had not begrudged giving him her virginity. In the back of his mind he knew that she would be leaving soon. Already she had learned such a shocking amount. She was like a sponge, learning rapidly everything from French verbs to a witty repartee that would stand her in good stead for any jet-set party anywhere in the world.

'No, not now,' he said smoothly. 'We have a surprise guest. Vincent Marchetti has just arrived. Can you get dressed and come down?'

'Of course,' Maria agreed at once. She was scrupulously honest about keeping up her end of their unspoken bargain. If Carlos wanted her to entertain, she'd entertain. Sometimes, on occasions like this, she almost felt like an employee. 'Who is Vincent Marchetti?'

'He's the man I told you about from the Centre for Paranormal Research. Dr Gottenburg's star pupil. You remember I was talking of him last week?'

Maria smiled. 'I see.' At first she had been shocked that a man of Carlos's education and experience could be fooled by the occult. Silly people looking into crystal balls to cheat people out of their money. How could he fall for it? But then he'd brought her some books on the subject, serious scientific research by eminent professors, that had changed her thinking. The tests in ESP in particular had fascinated her, but she'd never quite managed to push away her suspicion about charlatans and fakers. And Vincent Marchetti sounded extremely dubious.

Reading her look, he laughed. 'You'll have that doubting attitude wiped away, my dear, I'm warning you.' Blowing her a kiss, he left her to dress in private. That was Carlos. Sometimes his thoughtfulness brought tears to her eyes. That, and the way he always treated her like a lady. Maria had never felt anything like it before in her life. The doors being opened for her, the chair being pulled out and pushed in for her at dinner and a hundred other little things that Carlos did that made her feel like a real *somebody*.

There was no doubt she would miss Carlos.

She showered quickly and donned a simple white sun-dress by Valentine. She added only a touch of Chanel behind her ears and the lightest dusting of make-up. Adding a garnet bracelet to her wrist and matching red sandals to her feet, she looked spectacular, and knew it.

In the hall, she followed the sound of voices to the main salon and found herself brought up short by the sight of Vincent Marchetti. She had expected some oily, matinee-idol type, oozing charm and false, trite phrases. Instead she was confronted by the smallest, ugliest little gnome of a man she had ever seen. He was about five foot three, balding, squat, and wearing pebble glasses so thick that his eyes looked huge. In turn, the Italian stared at her, equally entranced for totally the opposite reason. Suddenly, Vincent knew why he had felt the psychic urge to drop in on his old friend Carlos Severantes.

Maria forced herself to stop staring. Never commit a social gaffe, that was Carlos's golden rule. She quickly forced a smile to her face and walked forward, swaying with uncon-scious grace. Once she had walked, book on head, for hours to perfect her movements, which had now become automatic.

Vincent swallowed hard, his little Adam's apple bobbing obscenely in his throat. Carlos, eyes twinkling, introduced them and handed round a fine Madeira.

'Mr Marchetti. I've heard a lot about you from Carlos. And about the institute, of course. Tell me, what exactly do you do there?'

Polite curiosity was the mainspring of conversation, Carlos had told her. Even if you were bored out of your skull, you must never show it. Vincent nervously launched into a description of telekinesis, precognitive perception and poltergeist phenomena. He was uncomfortably aware of the closeness of her bare knee against his leg, and he stumbled several times over his words. Maria nodded encouragingly, only vaguely interested, her mind on the dossier she kept upstairs. She had needed to ask for Carlos's help in compiling it, although she had not wanted to do so. But how else could she find out about Wayne D'Arville without Carlos's help?

Typically, he'd asked no questions, but had put the best detectives on to it. Consequently, she now knew every detail of her father's life. The early years in America before he moved to Monte Carlo, her grandfather's casino and the fact that they were estranged. His years at the Sorbonne, his aborted engagement, and then his career in England. She had studied the book he wrote, grudgingly admitting it to be a work of genius. She had pored eagerly over the pictures of his wife, Lady Sylvia, and had been rather surprised at her father's choice. But by now she was reading between the dry typewritten lines and gaining a good impression of the way her father's mind worked. His acquisition of Platts had been almost diabolically clever and manipulative. In the light of his social climbing and ambition, Lady Sylvia made more sense than some outrageously lovely but socially unacceptable beauty. Oh yes, she was beginning to know her father very well. She knew about his upcoming takeover bid of his own father's casino, and felt, instinctively, that this was his most vulnerable spot.

It was rather ironic. He was going after *his* father, whilst he himself was being hunted by *her*. Perhaps it was a family trait. But knowing all about him and finding a way to defeat him were two different things, and she knew she couldn't involve Carlos in this. For one thing she was not stupid and knew that his Professor Higgins to her Eliza Doolittle act was, and always had been, the main attraction for him; now that he had all but succeeded, she sensed a waning of his interest.

Besides, she was too fond of Carlos and owed him too much to get him involved with a monster like her father. He would gobble Carlos up for breakfast as he had Sir Mortimer Platt.

'Perhaps Maria needs a demonstration to make a believer of her, Vincent,' Carlos said softly, snapping Maria back to the present. She forced herself to watch, contemptuously amused, as the little man fairly leapt up, his ugly round face alight with excitement.

'Yes, indeed. Yes, yes, a demonstration,' he said, looking at Carlos like a beseeching puppy as his host searched out a pack of playing cards.

Maria watched indulgently as the man removed the cards, and then obeyed as the little gnome asked her to shuffle. She did so, and then raised her eyebrow questioningly. 'Place the pack face-down on the table, please . . . Maria,' he added her name shyly, the blush creeping up from his cheeks to cover the bald head. Maria smiled. Really, the man was sweet, in a dorky kind of way.

'The first card is . . . the six of spades,' Vincent said. Maria turned the top card over. It was the six of spades. Her eyes sharpened on the little man with genuine interest now, and he fairly bristled in pleasure, sensing that he had at last commanded her whole attention. With a fast-beating heart she turned the next card over, which was, as Vincent had predicted, the jack of hearts. On and on they went, right through the pack, going faster and faster, and when the last card had been turned over, Vincent had got only three wrong. It was amazing. Stupendous. Fantastic . . . Wonderful.

Maria moved closer to the little man, her eyes alight. Carlos watched her, somewhat sadly. So, he'd lost her at last. Well, it was inevitable, he supposed. But why to Vincent? What use could she possibly have for him? If he knew Maria — and he did — he had no doubt at all that she must have something in mind.

Maria did.

Just like the man in the song, she was going to break the bank at Monte Carlo.

CHAPTER 35

New York

Wayne looked out of the window, the world-famous panorama of the Big Apple slowly slipping by beneath him as the plane continued on to the airport. Unlike most of New York's visitors, he found nothing exciting and certainly nothing beautiful in the city. He'd never had to come to the States before, and as he hailed a taxi, giving the gum-chewing driver the name of the Plaza Hotel, he looked out of the window with sharp eyes.

It was just approaching the rush hour, and traffic lined the roads to make one long caterpillar that stretched for miles. The driver took the scenic route, passing Régine's and CBGB, giving him a slow tour past Bloomingdale's and Maud Frizon, the famous shoe shop. Wayne glanced at the ticking meter with a bare twist of his lips but made no demur. He didn't mind the extra time which allowed him to school his thoughts and calm the rough pounding of his heart. The noise of the city was immense, and in a different kind of man the towering skyscrapers might have produced the cloying anxiety of claustrophobia; but Wayne barely glanced up at the huge monoliths of chrome, glass and steel.

Big Apple or not, he was used to taking bites out of what he wanted. On the streets, pedestrians lined the sidewalks as thickly and with as much congestion as traffic lined the roads. There was the usual mix — winos and drunks begging for dollars, women in Russian lynx jackets carrying Elsa Peretti designed evening purses, no doubt on their way to an early dinner with some up-and-coming lover. Men and women with tired faces and simple suits poured out of offices and headed for the subway trains, buses and taxis. Wayne could smell above the carbon monoxide the scent of frying onions from a street vendor, reminding him of his own hunger.

'Where can I get a decent meal in this city?'

'Huh? What kinda money you got?' The accent was broad and drawling, and although Wayne didn't know the difference between downtown Manhattan and the Bronx, he instinctively placed the man's origins as being firmly from the latter.

'Plenty,' he said shortly.

The driver snorted. 'There's three places in here for you lot.' He offered the knowledge grudgingly. 'There's Delmonico's, the Carlyle and Le Grenouille.' Wayne winced over the pronunciation of the names, and then nodded. The cab smelt of vomit and cheap vinyl. He would be glad to get to the hotel but the tour seemed interminable, up Fifth Avenue, on to Park Avenue, then Madison Avenue, giving him a wonderful tourist-style look at Central Park, Times Square and Broadway. The driver certainly knew how to push his luck. Eventually, when the meter seemed in danger of running out of clicks, they pulled up at the Plaza, and he paid the cab fare in exact money.

'Hey, what about a tip?'

'Forget it.'

He followed the bellboy into the hotel's interior, oblivious to the colourful language coming from the taxi behind him. He checked into the best suite available, took a quick shower and changed into a white suit with a blue shirt that matched exactly the colour of his eyes. He combed his hair, added a gold Cartier watch to his wrist, and slipped his croc-odile wallet, thick with credit cards, into his inner jacket pocket. He needed, for a reason he couldn't quite identify, to look his very best. When he re-entered the lobby, every pair of feminine eyes watched him leave. The desk clerk looked down and memorized the name — Wayne D'Arville. Sure enough, five minutes later the first woman came and asked after him: Mrs De Winter, the steel tycoon's widow from Alabama. The desk clerk elegantly accepted the hundred-dol-lar bill and gave out the man's name and room number, knowing others would soon follow.

* * *

Veronica was curled up on the settee, reading a chatty let-ter from an old friend, when the doorbell rang. It surprised her, for usually the doorman screened all visitors and always buzzed through before allowing anyone up. She uncurled her legs and walked barefoot to the door. She was wearing a long turquoise kaftan of cool cotton with embroidered pea-cocks that curled exotic feathers over her thighs and across her back. As she walked to the door and opened it, there was no warning sensation to prepare her for the shock that was to come. Her first impression was of something solid, massive and white, and then, as she looked up into the blue eyes, her face drained slowly of all colour. Her mouth went dry as sand, and she gasped as her breathing abruptly stopped, trapping air in her lungs. Aware of a fine trembling breaking out in every part of her body, she took an involuntary step backwards.

'Hello, Veronica.'

She blinked. The voice was different. Every other thing about him seemed the same — the overpowering height, the gut-wrenching good looks, the aura of power, of tight, danger-ous energy. But the voice was definitely different. It took her a second or two to realize that he had lost the French accent.

Wayne moved forward and she was too slow to stop him. Shock held her immobilized for the few seconds he needed to step around her and into the room, and immediately the place felt violated.

'What are you doing here?' she finally managed to croak, her voice sounding pitifully weak and ineffectual even to her own ears. Wayne, who was looking around the apartment with assessing eyes, turned back and glanced at her.

'You might as well shut the door. I'm not leaving until I've got what I came for. And while I personally couldn't care less if it's advertised to all your neighbours, unless you've changed radically in the last seventeen or so years, you will.'

Veronica felt her fingers release the door before her brain had even given the orders. Dimly she heard the door click shut over the roaring of the blood in her ears. 'Of course I've changed,' she managed to say, her voice coming out hard now, almost sneering. 'I went to prison because of you, or had you forgotten?'

Wayne shrugged, unmoved. 'I had, as it happens. You were never particularly memorable, Veronica.'

She dragged in a harsh breath, hate and venom rising from out of nowhere. 'You filthy bastard. You stole my book, you stole two years of my life! How could you forget something like that?'

Wayne moved towards a picture, studying the brilliance of a Dali with an experienced eye. 'That's good,' he said, his attention captivated by the melting clocks. 'Melting time,' he murmured. 'Have you ever noticed how true that is?'

Veronica blinked nervously as some of the protecting numbness began to wear off. 'If you don't leave,' she said, every word coming out crisply and clearly, 'I'm going to kill you. I've got a gun — hell, every New Yorker has a gun.'

Wayne turned, looking her over without fear. Her hair was shorter than he remembered, and she had a patina of sophistication that had been missing before.

'Oh, come now.' He shook his head mockingly, feeling almost pleasantly content at the confrontation. 'You should really thank me for what I did.' As her mouth fell open in stupefaction, he suddenly smiled, and Veronica felt a gut

449

reaction deep inside her that made her want to vomit. 'If it hadn't been for me, you would never have come to this fine city and then you'd never have been a world-famous model, and never have overseen such a large business empire. Just think.' He moved to a low white leather couch and sat down with all the lithe grace she remembered so well. 'You'd be a bored English spinster by now, writing cookery books in Cheltenham, if it weren't for me. Now, be honest. You wouldn't have had the guts for all this otherwise, would you? Hmm?' The soft encouraging voice was a parody of gentleness as he waved a hand to encompass her flat with its view of the huge city, and she felt bile rise to her throat.

'You're sick,' she hissed, her hands clenching and unclenching by her sides. 'You have no idea what you did to me, have you? *Have you?*' she all but screamed, her breaths coming in short, sharp gasps. She walked unsteadily to the drinks tray and poured herself a brandy with hands that shook so much she nearly dropped the decanter.

'I don't care what I did to you,' Wayne said bluntly, sounding suddenly bored.

Veronica took a deep gulp of the Napoleon brandy, feeling it erupt hotly in her stomach before spreading out in a slow burn, deep in her veins. The hatred must have been inside her all along, maturing like the brandy. It gave her a sense of strength at last, and drove out all fear, all self-doubt. When she turned to face him, her mouth was smiling, but Wayne saw that her eyes were like jets: hard, brilliant and sharp. He leaned back, resting his arms straight out along the back of the sofa, and crossed his legs elegantly at the ankle.

'You don't, hmm?' she repeated mockingly. 'For a man who couldn't care less, it seems to me that you're pretty up to date on all my comings and goings,' she pointed out, gently swirling the amber liquid in its huge bulbous glass. 'I'll bet you've got a dossier on me this thick.' She held out her thumb and finger about two inches apart. 'That doesn't sound like a disinterested man to me.'

450

Wayne slowly grinned. 'Oh, I have. You and your Valentine.' He saw her stiffen at the mention of her husband's name, and slowly smiled. 'I even bought one or two of his designs for my wife,' he lied, watching her eyes narrow, and anticipated her next words.

'So, you actually found someone stupid enough to marry you, did you?'

'Oh, yes. There are plenty of women around, just like you. This one, however, happened to have a title and an estate the size of this city.'

She blanched at the mention of how she too had once yearned to marry him and looked down into her glass. She felt a familiar sense of helplessness begin to impinge on her hatred and grimly tried to fight it off.

'That was a long time ago. A lot has happened since. I've found a real man, for a start.'

Wayne leaned back his head, blue eyes watching her closely. 'A lot *has* happened,' he agreed, his voice losing its mocking edge, and she glanced at him sharply, scenting danger. Suddenly she asked the question that should have been asked immediately, if she hadn't allowed shock, anger and fear to get the better of her.

'What do you want, Wayne? Why are you here?'

Wayne smiled a smile that made her blood freeze. 'I'm here for my son, of course. What else?'

For a second, a wild, wild second, the room seemed to angle away from her. Then it rushed back, making her head spin, and without conscious effort she found herself beginning to laugh. 'Your son?' Her voice was hoarse and ugly before she turned her laugh into a broad grin. 'Your files must be out of date, Wayne. The only son I have is Travis — Valentine's son. In fact, he's with him now.' Wayne didn't move but he was aware of a shifting of power — in her favour.

'Is he?' He kept his voice neutral, aware that they had come to the crux of the whole matter much faster than he'd intended.

Veronica forced herself to stare at him, hoping she was a good enough actress to bring it off. 'Didn't my father tell you? Our baby died. I asked him to inform you.'

'Naturally he told me. But just because I get a phone call telling me my child died at birth, you don't seriously expect me to believe it, do you?'

Veronica prayed her shock looked real, then forced a slow, bittersweet smile to her lips. 'He told you that, did he?' she asked flatly, watching for his reaction out of the corner of her eye.

Wayne's heart did a quick flip, but only his blue eyes wavered for the merest moment. 'Are you admitting it isn't true?' he asked eventually.

'Of course it isn't,' Veronica said. 'I had your child aborted. Scraped out of me, like the unwanted . . . thing! . . .' she hissed the word with all the disgust and venom she could muster '. . . it was. Trust Daddy to lie that way. He's hopelessly old-fashioned.'

Wayne stared at her, feeling as if he'd wandered on to quicksand. 'My people didn't find any record of an abortion,' he said suspiciously, and Veronica felt a moment of panic. Fool, she cursed herself. Why did you tell him something that could so easily be checked out? But in the next instant she was rallying.

'Were they looking for it?' she challenged.

Wayne slowly uncrossed his legs and leaned forward. No, they hadn't been. He'd had them looking for a death certificate for Veronica Coltrane's baby. They hadn't found it, and although they hadn't found a birth certificate either, it had been enough to have him on the next plane to New York, convinced that his baby lived, the birth covered up by his bitch of a mother. The fact they hadn't found a birth certificate in the name of either Coltrane or Copeland had him even more convinced of the cover-up, that the Spanish whore who was his daughter was not the only child he had fathered. But now . . . Wayne felt a deep, dark hand clutch his guts. He had been so sure of victory. So sure of the outcome. He felt a horrifying wave of defeat slowly creep up his throat, strangling his vocal cords, filling his head like gas filling a balloon. No — it was not possible. It wasn't. Travis *must* be his. He *must*!

Veronica sensed the silent desperation behind the blue eyes and relaxed for the briefest moment before an overwhelming urge to twist the knife made her smile. At last, after all these years, she had her revenge. Unexpected, unasked for revenge. It was like having champagne injected straight into her veins. 'What's the matter, Wayne?' she asked softly, allowing a hateful parody of concern to soften her voice. 'Why this sudden urge for a son? Is your lady wife incapable? Or is it you . . . ?' She broke off with a small cry as Wayne suddenly lunged to his feet, and in spite of herself she quickly backed away. Violence filled the room like a tangible force, and for one moment, one truly terrifying moment, she was certain he was going to kill her.

Wayne thought he was too. He took a step towards her, and then stopped, his brain throwing the cold water of logic into his consciousness just in time to prevent him pouncing on her. He had no alibi if he killed her now. Besides, she was not important — she was a nothing that had just managed to hit him on a raw spot, that was all. Slowly he relaxed, even managed to smile.

'How old is Travis, Veronica?'

'He's fifteen,' she lied. Just as Wayne knew she would, but he figured it was worth a try.

'Hmm . . . You said he's with Valentine at the moment. At the — let me see — Warehouse 15, I suppose?'

Veronica released a long sigh of relief, then managed a cool shrug and was amazed when her voice was just as cool. 'I expect so. Why?'

Wayne didn't bother to reply, but instead walked quickly to the door and opened it. He had to see the boy. He had to see his face. He would know if Travis was his or not. He would just know.

Veronica followed him silently at a safe distance, and the moment he was gone she threw herself against the door and locked it. Her hands were shaking so much that it took her almost a minute to perform the simple task, and then she slowly leaned back against the wall and hugged her arms around her waist. 'Oh, God,' she whispered, over and over again, tears squeezing past her closed lashes as reaction began to set in.

A dull but persistent question prodded at her, denying her desire to just collapse on to the bed and crawl under the blankets and forget the whole nightmare had ever happened. She stumbled into the living room, spotted her still half-full glass of brandy and reached for it, gulping it down in one go. As the alcohol exploded in her belly, the truth exploded in her brain. He was going to the warehouse. To see Travis. Blue-eyed, square-faced Travis!

She ran to the phone, in her panic misdialling the number. She slammed the receiver down and forced herself to breathe deeply. It would take Wayne at least half an hour to get to the warehouse. She dialled again, this time correctly, and got through to Stan, the security guard, and asked for Val.

'Come on, come on. Oh, Val, come *on*!' She took the phone to the settee in front of the coffee table and collapsed back against the orange cushions.

'Yeah?' The voice sounded preoccupied but so fantastically dear that for a few moments she could say nothing but his name.

'Val! Oh, Val!'

Ten miles away, Val frowned, his skin beginning to prickle. 'Veronica? You OK? What's up?'

Veronica took a deep, shaky breath, clearly audible to her now thoroughly worried husband, and launched into speech. 'Listen. There's a man on his way over, right now. You've got to get Travis away. Hide him somewhere. Anywhere. Do it now.'

'Hey, hold on, luv. What man are yer talking about?'

Veronica groaned. 'Don't argue with me! For pity's sake, just trust me. Val, please!' She was screaming now, her voice coming out in a tangle of sobs and squeaking, panicky demands.

Val glanced over his shoulder. The workers had gone home half an hour ago, leaving only a few lights burning. Vast benches of half-finished garments cluttered the acres of floor, and Travis, walking around with a clipboard, was taking stock. Val's eyes narrowed on the boy who would always be his son and looked back at the blank brick wall on which the telephone was hung.

'This man,' he said quietly. 'It's Travis's . . . other father, ain't it?' He couldn't bring himself to say 'real father', and something strong in his quiet, composed tone got through to her and calmed her down as nothing else could.

'Yes,' she said dully. 'Yes, it is. And he's dangerous.'

'Dangerous?' Val ran his hand through his overlong hair and sighed. The day had been a normal one up to now.

He was silent for a long, long moment, and then began to think quickly as Veronica's voice, panicking again, said urgently, 'Val. Val, are you still there?'

'Course I am. Where d'ya think I'd got to?'

Veronica sighed with fond impatience, then said once again, 'Val, you've got to hide Travis. Quickly. He'll be there in a few minutes.'

'Wait a minute. Just wait. You think he's coming here to take Travis?'

'Yes. Maybe. Oh, you just don't understand. You're not dealing with a normal man. He's warped, twisted. He's power-hungry. Valentine, he's a . . . monster! I told him I had an abortion, but when he sees Travis he's going to know. His eyes, the shape of his face . . . He'll know I was lying.'

'If I hide Travis we'll never get rid of him,' Val pointed out with cold logic. 'We've got to convince him, now, that Travis is mine.'

He turned, suddenly aware that Travis, made curious by the sound of his own name, was stood right behind him. Val glanced at his son, meeting the concerned, puzzled blue eyes, and reached out his hand to his shoulder and squeezed tightly.

'What do you mean?' Veronica asked, but already she was beginning to understand what he was getting at. All the paraphernalia of his last fashion show was stored at the warehouse, and since Valentine Inc. had gone unisex there would be men's wigs and make-up there as well.

'Leave it to me,' Val said abruptly, and rung off, leaving Veronica to wait through the worst hour of her life.

'What's going on, Dad?' Travis asked, looking troubled.

'Listen, Trav . . .' Val put his other hand on the boy's other shoulder and leaned forward so that their faces were barely inches apart. 'We never thought we'd have to tell you this . . .' He paused, searching for the right words but coming up with only blank air.

'Tell me what?' Travis prompted.

Aware of time ticking away, Val shook his head, then looked Travis straight in the eye. 'We don't have any time,' he said, his voice regretful. 'You're gonna have to take it straight. Veronica had you before she met me. You're not mine . . . hell, that's not right. You *are* mine . . . just . . . not physically mine. You understand?'

Travis managed a weak grin. 'Hell, is that all? I thought something terrible had happened. I was old enough to remember you at the start, actually. I was five when we first met, remember?'

Val stared at him, and then began to laugh. Abruptly, however, he sobered. 'Your . . . biological father is on his way here now. From what your mother said, I think he's gonna try and take you away.'

'What?' Travis yelped. 'Dad, I'm hardly a kid anymore. I'll soon be voting.'

Valentine grinned. 'I know. But your mum's in one lulu of a flap. From what your mum's told me in the past, he's rich as Midas, as powerful as a Kennedy, and has the mentality of Attila the Hun. And she should know.'

Travis shook his head, grappling to come to terms with it all. 'So what are we going to do?'

Val smiled grimly. 'Trust me,' he said, and, grabbing him by the arm, led him to the changing rooms. 'I have no idea what he looks like,' Val muttered, searching out a wig

456

that was the exact shade of his own hair, 'but the idea is to make you look as much like me as possible.' He fitted the wig over Travis's natural hair, who grinned at his reflection in the mirror. Val then selected a tiny box. Travis watched, fascinated, as the lid was lifted to reveal sets of coloured contact lenses. 'Sometimes,' Val muttered, selecting a brown pair and reaching for the cleaning fluid, 'I need a model to have eyes to match the dress . . .'

Travis tensed, his eyes doing strange gymnastics as Val put them in, and then blinked rapidly. 'Hell, they feel funny,' he complained, and then blinked some more as he stared at his image in the glass. It felt distinctly weird to meet brown eyes instead of the blue ones that had always been his.

'At least there isn't anything you can do to change the shape of my face.'

'Oh, ye innocent,' Val muttered, and reached for some cotton wool padding. 'Open up.'

Travis had just enough time to moan, then gagged on cotton wool that seemed to fill his cheeks. 'I feel like a chipmunk,' he mumbled, swallowing hard, and fighting the urge to retch.

'Shut up,' Val muttered, reaching for the make-up case. Travis groaned again and closed his eyes.

Outside, Wayne told the taxi driver to wait and walked around the building, finding a side door open that creaked loudly.

Inside Travis and Wayne glanced at each other at the sound, and quickly left the dressing room. Wayne walked into the interior of the huge building, his footsteps echoing on the concrete floor with a hollow, reverberating sound. He looked around vaguely then turned to the right and began to walk past the racks and racks of plastic-wrapped clothes, following the sound of human voices.

'Silk?' The man who asked the question was tall, very slender, and was dressed in scruffy jeans and a loose wool cardigan that fitted about as well as a sack would fit a parking meter. It could only be Valentine Copeland, fashion guru.

'Sixteen tonnes.'

Wayne's head shot around, seeking out the owner of that young voice. It took him a second or two to locate the boy by a far wall.

'Hello. Can I 'elp yer?'

Wayne turned, the cockney voice taking him slightly by surprise, and found Valentine approaching him. Instinctively Wayne felt the hackles rise on his back. It was a strange sensation, one he hadn't experienced before, and it unnerved him.

Val approached the man responsible for Veronica's imprisonment and felt the intense urge to thump the bastard in the stomach, just for the pleasure of seeing his huge frame double over. As he got closer the blue eyes came as something of a shock. They were Travis's eyes, but deep-frozen. He sensed no warmth, not even anything remotely human, in their depths. He could almost have been a robot — a well-dressed, too-handsome robot. Valentine hated him on sight.

'I'm looking for Travis Coltrane,' Wayne said. Val had no doubts now that this man was all that Veronica had said he was and more.

'Nobody here by that name, Sonny Jim,' Val said with painful bonhomie. 'Only my lad over there — Trav Copeland. Trav, come over 'ere a minute, will ya?'

Travis ventured closer, feeling his limbs move stiffly. He left the darkness reluctantly and stepped into the circle of light, forcing his lips open. 'Yeah?' He half turned towards Val, not intending even to glance at the tall stranger who was supposed to be his real father. But, before he knew what was happening, he was looking full-face at the stranger. He saw his own blue eyes staring back, and felt a sudden, terrible fear. He could not explain it, and had never felt anything like it before, but it made him almost faint.

Val stepped closer so that Wayne could compare them. Exact same shade of hair, exact same shade of eyes. Even Travis's naturally pale skin had been darkened to Val's own more swarthy shade by the make-up he had applied.

Wayne stared at the boy and felt suddenly cold. He glanced briefly back at Val, feeling again an almost animalistic surge of violence, but pulled his lips into a snarl that was supposed to pass for a smile. 'My mistake,' he said simply.

Val nodded and gave his best cockney grin. 'We all make 'em, mate.'

Wayne nodded, turned and walked away. He did not look back.

Travis waited until he was gone and then said quietly, 'I think I'm going to be sick.'

'Well, do it in the lav,' Val said, not unkindly, giving him a gentle push. 'I have to phone your mum. Was she ever right about that bloke.'

Travis *was* sick. That . . . that . . . creature with the snake-like eyes and unmoving face was his father?

* * *

Back at the hotel, Wayne walked to the window and stared out at the bright lights of New York. Another dead end. Another defeat. But she would pay. The bitch Coltrane would pay. And her husband. He walked to the phone, dialled a number, and waited for it to be answered. 'Sutter? It's me. I want you to dig around and find out the date of an abortion. Yeah, that's right, the Coltrane woman. It would have been done in the prison hospital, I imagine. I want to know the time, as well, if you can.' He listened for a few seconds and then hung up.

Slowly he walked back to the window. She had robbed him of his heir, but she would pay.

Once he knew when the abortion had taken place he would make his plans. At exactly the same time, on exactly the same date that she had killed his baby, Veronica Coltrane herself would die.

CHAPTER 36

Sebastien depressed the switch on the tape recorder and leaned back in his chair. 'Wednesday 25th. Wayne D'Arville. Personal case, continuing notes. I have recently become concerned at this subject's NUC during our sessions. His recent trip to New York has agitated him considerably, and I am more and more convinced that secondary crisis oscillation has occurred. Concurrently, I believe his achievement motivation has been severely disrupted, and will attempt to carry out a thematic apperception test on the subject at the first opportunity.'

Sebastien paused for a moment. He thought he'd heard the door open, but there was no other sound. He shrugged and continued. 'I am more than ever convinced that there was sustained physical abuse by the father during the patient's infancy, as well as maternal deprivation. The combination, mixed with the obsessive compulsion to succeed shown continually by the patient, is, I believe . . .'

In the hall, Lilas listened to his tones, a happy smile on her face. She hadn't intended to eavesdrop, but she'd been surprised by the sound of his voice. At first, she'd thought he had a visitor, but . . .

She jumped as someone knocked on the outside door. Feeling suddenly guilty — she knew how fierce Seb was about confidentiality — she quickly nipped into a closet, stifling a giggle. Really, a middle-aged woman should have outgrown this kind of thing!

Sebastien put the small recorder into the top drawer of his desk and walked to the door. Wayne pushed past him without waiting for an invitation, and through the crack in the closet Lilas felt every hair on her body quiver. A cold hand seemed to catch her heart. She knew instantly who the man was — Wayne D'Arville. Seb's only 'private' patient. She couldn't have said why, but she knew he was dangerous. Or, to be more specific, a danger to Sebastien.

Sebastien led him to the living room, alarms going off in his head. 'Hi. Sit down. Want any coffee?'

Wayne shook his head, then, unusually, changed his mind. 'Yes, OK. Black.'

Sebastien made it quickly, all the time watching his guest. He looked fit and healthy, but there was a tightness to his face that Sebastien had never seen before, and his eyes, always a bright, brilliant blue, seemed to be actually glowing.

Wayne glanced at him, his lips tight. In the hall, Lilas very carefully crept from the closet and hovered, torn with indecision, by the closed door.

Inside, Wayne reached for his cup, Sebastien noticing how the fine shaking of his hand made the black liquid shimmer.

'I'm going to Monte Carlo on Friday,' Wayne said abruptly, his loud voice carrying clearly to the woman outside.

'Oh. You're not a secret gambler, I hope?' Seb teased.

It was a joke, but not funny enough to warrant the great burst of laughter that made the tall Frenchman nearly double over. Outside, Lilas jumped in alarm. The man was coming unravelled! It was the kind of situation where she knew Sebastien excelled. And normally she didn't worry about her lover — didn't give his rather depressing and potentially dangerous job a thought. After all, Seb had been working in hospitals for the insane long before she met him. And doing very nicely, too. But something about this man . . . Lilas just *knew* there was something about this man . . . She wanted to march in there and put her arms defensively around Sebastien, and tell Wayne D'Arville that he was hers and she'd guard him to the death! Ridiculous, she knew. So she just hovered, unsure of what to do. It was not very Lilas-like.

Inside, oblivious to her plight, Sebastien watched Wayne in silent alarm, making sure that his eyes were carefully neutral when Wayne looked his way.

'In a way, it is a gambling expedition,' he admitted softly. Then, like a tap being turned off, all expression left his face. Sebastien had seen this phenomenon in him before, but never to such an extent as this. 'I have business there,' Wayne said, his voice as flat as the top of Sebastien's desk. Only the glow in the back of his eyes, a demented and, to Sebastien, tormented glow, begged for help and understanding.

'It has to do with bad debts,' Wayne corrected himself, his lips twisting briefly. He finished his coffee and slowly stood up. Staring down at Sebastien, his eyes seemed to focus on him properly for the first time. He opened his mouth, closed it again, and gave a brief nod. 'I thought I'd drop in and tell you I wouldn't be here for dinner on Saturday.'

'OK. Thanks.'

Sebastien watched him walk to the door, unaware that outside Lilas was just darting back into the closet. Seb gave a brief smile as the copper-coloured head turned to glance at him, then stared thoughtfully at the door as Wayne closed it behind him.

He reached for the phone and dialled the home number of Clive Jamison, the chairman of a conference team due to fly out to Monte Carlo in the morning for a three-day conference on the causes of socio-psychological voting patterns. He'd just secured himself a place on it when the door opened.

But it was Lilas who entered. 'Hello,' she said cheerfully. 'Who was the big guy who just left?'

Seb glanced at her sharply. 'No one,' he said. 'No one for you to worry about, that is,' he added, aware that he had surprised her. He hoped Wayne wouldn't find out about

Lilas. If Wayne became aware that he, Sebastien, had a lover . . . well, Wayne was capable of anything.

Lilas nodded. Just as she'd thought. Seb was well aware of how dangerous the man was but was trying to help him all the same. Typical of him, of course. It was one of the reasons she loved him so much. Well, she was not about to just sit back and let Sebastien fall prey to his own goodness. No way!

* * *

Two days later, Wayne stepped out on to the balcony of a Monte Carlo hotel and glanced across the harbour. He reached for the *Nice-Matin* and unfolded the paper, ignoring the croissants that cooled on his breakfast tray. The news was full of a *monte-en-l'air*, a daring cat burglar currently prowling the ripe villas and relieving inhabitants of jewels and fine art. The Marine Cup de Monaco was due to start next week, and the sports section was full of news of the speedboat trials. The event fought for supremacy with the Monaco Grand Prix, but Wayne ignored both, turning to the financial pages instead with steady hands but a heart that was doing strange gymnastics in his chest.

It was there in black and white, sensational news only to those interested in the financial life of the principality — which was practically everybody. Marcus D'Arville had lost the Droit de Seigneur to an unknown company called Helm Enterprises. The paper speculated on the ethics of the take-over, and a final editorial asked for news of the mysterious Helm Enterprises, making veiled and empty threats against the corporation that had so scurrilously attacked one of the country's finest citizens, a tragically blinded American emigre. Slowly, Wayne returned to the bedroom where a maid, ostensibly retrieving damp towels and replacing them with dry fresh ones, glanced his way, and smiled shyly.

She was small, with a cap of dark hair and huge dark eyes. Her eyes flitted from his bare legs to the deep V of chest visible under the robe. 'Is there anything else I can do for you, sir?' she asked in perfect French. Wayne smiled and nodded.

'As a matter of fact, there is,' he said and the dark eyes lit up. Wayne walked to his suitcase and extracted a hefty envelope, which contained copies of all of Lt Heinlich's documents. 'I want you to post these — post them, mind, not send a messenger — to Marcus D'Arville, at his home address. Not his office. Can you do that?'

As he turned around, the girl managed a disappointed smile, but nodded as he approached with the envelope in his hand. 'Of course, sir. Anything else?'

Wayne handed over the envelope and then slowly raised his hand to rest under the girl's chin. He could feel a pulse hammer at the base of her neck and heard the soft catch of her breath as she gasped. 'Yes,' he murmured. 'You can come back again.' Slowly, curious to see if she would react, he lowered his hand across the prim black dress that she wore and splayed his long fingers around her right breast. 'I think you can do much more for me than post a letter. What's your name?'

'Odette,' the girl said on a slowly exhaled breath.

'Odette. Will you come back?'

'Yes, sir.'

Wayne watched her leave, his eyes on the envelope. Wolfgang would get it later today. Following the blow of losing the casino, it might even finish him off.

Wayne wandered around the room feeling strangely lost. He had enough money to do anything, but he couldn't think of a single thing he wanted to do. It was like being in the eye of a hurricane, waiting for the storm to hit. Restlessly he wandered to the balcony once more. Below was the usual pool, the usual topless bathers, the usual mobile bar dispensing cocktails at an absurdly high price. Wayne was about to turn back when the sight of a familiar face stopped him. Even though he was five floors up, he knew he couldn't mistake that certain turn of the head, coloured a deep chestnut.

His heart lurched and then settled down. *Sebastien.* Sebastien was here. He felt a moment of uncontrolled joy and relief, then almost cried aloud as it fizzled and burst. Wayne's first instinct was to go down and demand to know what he was doing. But he wasn't sure he could withstand those sherry-coloured eyes just yet.

A few minutes later, the maid returned. As she walked towards him she began to strip. Wayne watched her, unimpressed but able to admit that she had a good body, young and slim, and tanned a light golden brown. She was quickly out of her clothes and entirely naked when she reached his position just inside the balcony. Wayne glanced back over his shoulder. Sebastien was still there, waiting for him. It felt good.

He turned as a small hand curled against his chest, the fingers tugging at his left nipple. The girl murmured something in French, something seductive and suggestive, and Wayne closed his eyes. 'Shut up,' he said in English, and kissed her hard. The girl reacted eagerly, clutching his shoulders and swinging her legs around him to lock behind his waist. Wayne gasped, then laughed as they staggered towards the bed. He threw her down, falling with her as her legs clung to him tenaciously. He was naked beneath his robe, and it had fallen open enough to allow his member to rear up, strong and hard, through the navy silk. The girl, feeling the hot shaft touch her thigh, released her leglock, but Wayne shook his head as she wriggled under him. The girl frowned, then gave a gasp of surprise as Wayne flipped her over, his impressive strength easily turning her. The girl gasped as she found her face stuffed into the pillow, and then moaned in desire as Wayne's hands slipped around her stomach and lifted her half off the bed. He closed his eyes as he parted her thighs and pushed deeply into her.

* * *

Sebastien ordered a Coke with ice and waited under the shade of the sun umbrella. He would wait all day if he had to.

* * *

The postal service in Monaco was excellent. With the principality being so small, there was no reason why it shouldn't be, and within five hours of the letter being posted it was delivered to Wolfgang Mueller's home. His secretary, Vince Perroit, glanced at it curiously, but did not interrupt his employer's lunch. Actually, Wolfgang was not eating. He knew the meal was there, for he had heard it being delivered and could smell the scent of herbs and the appetizing aroma of cooked meat, but the news that had arrived yesterday was still robbing him of any appetite.

Vince, as usual, had shared the breakfast table with him, reading the morning's correspondence over the toast and coffee. The first inkling Wolfgang had had of impending disaster was when the voice of his secretary faltered and then stopped. He had been reading a letter from a company called Helm Enterprises, one that Wolfgang had never heard of. Vince had got as far as, 'Dear sir, this is to inform you that the casino known as the Droit de Signeur is . . .' and then had choked to a stop.

'Vince?' He remembered he had been impatient, his blinded eyes imagining the little man to have stopped for a drink of coffee or bite of toast, and he'd been annoyed at the man's impertinence. But it had not been hunger but stunned surprise that had stayed the secretary's voice. Shakily he'd read the letter through, a letter that informed Wolfgang that he was no longer owner of the casino, and then glanced at the blind old man, his anxious green eyes taking in the sudden pallor, noting the way the old man's body went rigid in shock. The same shock that was only now just beginning to fade. Wolfgang reached forward, his fingers 'reading' the table, and pushed the plate of food away. He rose slowly to his feet and picked up the cane that went everywhere with him, and tapped his way into the foyer. 'Perroit. Perroit, where the devil are you?'

He swung to his right, towards the sound of the man's reply. 'I'm here, sir. The mail has just arrived.'

Wolfgang grunted, and Vince tensed. He had always been in awe of his employer. He was not so stupid as to underestimate the old man, as so many did. To their cost.

Wolfgang made his way to his favourite chair and sat down. He was used to relying on Vince to be his eyes. Wolfgang trusted him implicitly because he knew that he could destroy him if ever the need arose. 'Has Ariche come up with anything more yet on Helm's identity?'

Ariche, one of Wolfgang's lawyers, had been assigned immediately to check the claim from Helm Enterprises that the casino was now legally theirs. Five hours after being given the assignment, the confirmation had come. Helm had done all that Helm had claimed. It did indeed have the banks and two of his partners in the corporate back pocket.

Wolfgang shuddered now as he remembered the frustration that had hit him and kept him awake all night. How could the faceless Helm have done it? How? Wolfgang was sure he'd been so careful. Hell, he *knew* he'd been careful. Who knew him this well? Who had betrayed him?

'I haven't heard from Ariche yet, sir, but he must have arrived in Geneva by now.' Helm Enterprises had been registered in Switzerland.

'This smacks of Swiss expertise, all right,' Wolfgang murmured. 'But why the Droit de Seigneur? It doesn't make sense.' Wolfgang cursed silently, feeling like a rat in a maze. Someone had taken away the cheese, and he could not even see who, or why, or when. The helpless sensation of having been successfully stalked was a new one, and one that he hated.

The phone rang half an hour later. Vince had read through the other mail, consisting mainly of invitations from friends and the odd letter from disgruntled casino punters. He left the large envelope till last, some instinct making him avoid it. Its padded bulkiness gave Vince a strange feeling of *déjà vu*.

The secretary lifted the phone, spoke briefly, and then took Wolfgang's hand and placed the receiver carefully into it. 'It's Ariche.'

Wolfgang lifted the receiver, banging it against his ear. Normally his co-ordination was good, but his nerves had been impossibly strained over the last twenty-four hours. 'Yes, Philippe. What have you got?'

'Nothing,' Philippe Ariche said, his voice clipped and angry. 'The offices here are nothing but a rented shell. There's one girl who sits behind an impressive desk and does nothing but read romances all day long. She knows nothing, not even the name of her employer. She gets a regular pay cheque from the bank. It's just a front.'

'Shit!' Wolfgang said, then let loose a long list of expletives in German, making Vince glance at him in puzzled surprise. 'The bank?' Wolfgang asked briefly.

'As close-mouthed as a duck's arse.'

Wolfgang almost cried. He felt the absurd desire to stamp his feet and scream, and he swallowed it back. 'Any ideas?' he asked, but without hope.

'No. Not at the moment. But . . . there was a message waiting for me.'

'Message? What do you mean?'

'A letter. The girl gave it to me. She said that she'd been told someone would come and that she was to give it to whoever it was.'

'And?'

'And it says that you're to clear out your desk. Today.'

'Like hell I will!' Wolfgang shouted, getting to his feet. 'They can't insist. Can they?' he added, his voice suddenly sounding small and old in the vast recesses of the enormous and empty villa. Ariche confirmed his worst fears. Wolfgang listened, slowly slumping back down into his chair. Ariche promised to keep digging, but they both knew there was little promise in it. Wolfgang hung up a few minutes later, and Vince nervously smoothed the big envelope that rested on his knees, still unopened. 'I have to go to the casino,' Wolfgang said, his voice flat. 'Have Finalle bring the car round.'

'Yes, sir. There's one more letter we haven't dealt with.'

'Leave it.'

'It's a bulky one, sir. It looks . . . important.'

'Then bring it. You can read it to me in the car.'

* * *

Miles away, Wayne stared at the ceiling, a sheet hanging loosely across his loins, even though the girl had been gone for hours. He watched the patterns of light on the ceiling, letting no particular thought stay in his mind for longer than the briefest second. The buzz of the phone made him frown, but its persistence made him leave the bed and pad naked to the *bergère* on which it rested. 'Yes?' he barked, then stiffened, listening to the voice on the other end, a slow smile crawling across his face.

'Good. I'll be right there. And, Ariche . . . you'll be getting a nice fat bonus.'

Wayne walked to the shower and turned it on to the cold setting before standing beneath it. Five minutes later, as he left the hotel and hailed a cab, he forgot, or would later suppose he did, that Sebastien Teale had been waiting for him.

* * *

Wolfgang's car, a large black American Cadillac, pulled to a halt in front of the casino. Raymond Galvalais, the manager, watched it and waited, but to his surprise the old man did not immediately emerge. Everyone had read the papers, of course, but still everyone hoped the takeover was just rumour. The papers had been wrong before.

When Marcus D'Arville finally emerged, he looked . . . ancient. But Raymond's hazel eyes were not the only ones that watched the old man's approach. Wayne had arrived at the casino five minutes earlier, having driven like a madman. It had felt strange to walk into the crimson and gold cocoon of the casino again. He had felt oddly nervous, as if expecting someone to stop him, someone to point at him and shout, 'There he is. There's the old man's son. He blinded his own father. Get him!'

But no one had, of course. Everyone was too busy staring at the roulette wheels spinning the magical white ball that could either bankrupt them or award them a fortune.

It was as if he had never existed. This strange sensation of being a non-person was still with him when he saw his father again for the first time in almost twenty years. He had moved to the doorway, his breath trapped in his lungs, his big body shaking so much that he felt, for a moment or two, as if he was going to pass out.

Sebastien had followed him, and now his eyes narrowed on Wayne sharply, as he too moved to a side door, curious to see what had prompted the reaction. But, looking out, he saw only an old man carrying a white stick, and a tall, thin young man, obviously an employee of some kind. He turned and watched Wayne again. His face was still; too still. Only his eyes burned. Sebastien could feel an awful, creeping, dark hatred filter into the room, the sensation becoming overpowering as the old man with the stooped shoulders and black glasses entered. He watched Wayne follow them like a stalking hunter, walking parallel with them as they moved through the gaming rooms, through the smoke and rolling dice.

Wayne saw the man with his father shift something to his other hand and stared at the envelope. It was open, and slowly he smiled. So, his father had had his present. He glanced at the thin white face of the secretary and wondered how he had taken the news that his employer was actually a Nazi criminal, responsible for the death of thousands.

Not well, apparently.

Wolfgang paused. He felt terribly cold. His blind eyes swivelled uselessly, trying to pinpoint the location of something that instinct told him was in the room. He could smell it. It was a familiar smell. The smell of an old enemy.

'Is there anyone not playing the tables, Vince?' Wolfgang hissed, almost sniffing the air.

'Only a man in the corner. Over six feet tall, with reddish-blond hair, and . . . blue eyes,' Vince said, his voice wavering. He felt badly rattled. The contents of the envelope were obviously forgeries, designed to smear Marcus D'Arville's name, but even so . . .

Wolfgang shook his head. He was sure he could feel danger . . . It felt, in some way, familiar. He dismissed Vince, who protested mildly. 'I can find my own way to the office,' barked Wolfgang, but the energy it took to be angry was too expensive and he finished in a quieter tone, 'I want to be alone for a while.' Relieved, Vince backed away, anxious now to go.

Wayne watched the old man push aside the heavy velvet curtains and disappear. Quickly, he followed. He walked to the end office and slowly pushed open the door, careful to be quiet. Even so, Wolfgang's sensitive ears heard the faint noise, but he felt, more than heard, the presence of another man. And not just another man. The enemy.

'Who are you?' His voice sounded loud in the room, and for a moment he wondered if anyone would answer him. He flinched when someone did.

'I own Helm Enterprises.' The voice was English.

Wolfgang's lips twisted into a bitter smile. 'Just making sure that I cleared my desk, eh? Scared I might refuse to leave?'

'No. You'll leave,' the voice said confidently. 'If you have to be dragged out kicking and screaming. The sight might make your customers look up from their cards for a second, but only for a second. Then you'll be forgotten.'

Wolfgang snarled, showing yellowed teeth. 'You think so?'

'I know so.'

Wolfgang frowned. It was not the words, which he knew to be perfectly accurate, but the voice itself that troubled him. 'I know your voice,' Wolfgang said, then stiffened. He thought he heard someone else in the corridor.

'I imagine you do. You've heard it often enough in the past.'

Wolfgang slowly shook his head. He shifted, aware of a pain in his chest, but not giving it a second thought. Indigestion from eating still-warm croissants hardly seemed important at this moment. 'I don't . . . remember,' Wolfgang said. The coldness was back with a vengeance, and he could hear the ticking of an ormulu clock not five feet away. 'Who are you?' Wolfgang demanded finally, his fingers tightening around the top of his cane.

'I told you. I'm Helm Enterprises. I'm also the one who sent you that little parcel your secretary was holding just now. Read it to you, has he?'

Wolfgang felt an explosion of rage detonate inside him. 'Where did you get those documents?' For a split second all the old authority was back, the voice, the anger, the familiar demand that he bend to his will, and Wayne was a small boy again, crying in the dark. Then his father stumbled against the table, and the moment was gone. Wayne relaxed, unaware that Sebastien, standing just behind him, had seen him tense in terrified reaction.

'From your old friend, Lieutenant Heinlich, of course,' Wayne said. 'What's the matter, Herr Mueller? Did you really think your days as Commandant of a death camp were forgotten?'

Sebastien shuddered but made not a sound. 'Who are you?' Wolfgang asked again, but his voice was nothing more than a whisper now.

'Doesn't the name Helm mean anything to you?' the English voice goaded, sounding almost amused. 'It should. It's short for Helmut.'

'Helmut?' muttered Wolfgang, then shook his head, totally dazed. 'Helmut?'

'You remember Helmut, surely?' the voice mocked. 'Your firstborn. The best of them all?'

'Helmut,' Wolfgang said, and sat down abruptly into the chair. The indigestion was worse now, spreading to his left arm, making breathing difficult, but he barely noticed. 'You,' he finally said, without heat. There was no strength in the word, just a defeated, helpless acknowledgement.

'Of course it's me, Father. Who else?' Wayne moved closer, close enough to lean his knuckles on the table top.

Wolfgang reared back in his chair. 'You killed your own brother,' Wolfgang said, uncaring that he was crying, beyond caring if he looked foolish. 'Hans. Hans.'

Sebastien stifled a gasp. Was that true? He'd had his suspicions over the years he'd been treating Wayne, but to hear them confirmed made him feel sick to his stomach.

'You killed me first,' Wayne replied. 'Or have you forgotten the whippings and the beatings?'

'You blinded me,' Wolfgang accused, and Sebastien felt the floor tilt underneath him. Was that possible? Was Wayne capable of that too?

'You were trying to strangle me at the time, if you remember — and you'd stabbed me,' said Wayne airily, sounding as if he were discussing old times with a schoolfriend.

Suddenly Wolfgang launched himself forward, taking both Sebastien and Wayne by complete surprise. The old clawing fingers were on his throat for the second time in his life, but this time he dragged his father's weak fingers away easily before stepping back and testing his neck for bruises. Wolfgang fell across the desk, his breath rasping horribly. He felt his face pull into a grimace, his left cheek and eye seeming to fall from his face. The pain in his chest tightened into a screaming agony.

Above it all, he heard the voice again. 'I told you I was the best, but you wouldn't listen. Now you have to. Now I have your precious bloody casino. Now I have the evidence that'll send you to Israel, to die for what you did . . .'

They were the last words Wolfgang Mueller ever heard.

Slowly he slid sideways, falling off the side of the desk and on to the floor with a heavy thud. Wayne stared at him, then looked blankly as Sebastien appeared and knelt by the old man's body, turning him over, checking his heartbeat. Slowly, from his kneeling position he looked up, his expression unreadable. 'He's dead,' Sebastien said.

Wayne didn't look back at the old man's body. Instead his eyes remained locked on Sebastien. He could feel insanity open its jaws and yawn around him. He could feel himself falling and was terrified. He swallowed hard, unaware that he was as white as snow and trembling uncontrollably.

'Sebastien!' he said. Just that, but it was enough. He fell forward slowly on to his knees, but Sebastien was there to catch him. He buried his face against the white cotton shirt, feeling Sebastien's skin warm his cold cheek. Slowly he closed his eyes, aware of fingers gently brushing the hair from his temple, aware of a voice, soothing, warm and kind, washing over him in anaesthetizing waves. Then he said the words Sebastien had been waiting for years to hear.

'Sebastien. Help me. Please.'

CHAPTER 37

Sebastien watched from the windows of what had once been Wolfgang Mueller's villa as Wayne began to stir on the lounger. Putting down his half-full coffee cup, he opened the French windows and stepped out on to the patio. It was just after seven, and the day had that mild feeling of approaching evening. A blackbird sang sweetly amidst the branches of a magnificent magnolia tree as the sun began a slow descent out at sea. He could hear the drone of bees in the honeysuckle bowers as he sat down on the lounger's matching chair. Wayne opened his eyes, aware of his presence. 'Hello.'

'Hi.'

'What time is it?'

'Just after seven. You've been asleep for a few hours.'

Wayne nodded and slowly sat up. His face was gaunt and pale, and he pulled a green and white robe further across his chest. He sat forward, putting his hands over his eyes, and took a deep breath. 'Is everything sorted out?' he finally asked. Sebastien said nothing, forcing him to take his hands away and look at him. Only when he did so did he answer.

'Yes. The body's in the morgue. There's going to be an autopsy, but that's nothing to fear. He almost certainly died of a heart attack.'

Wayne glanced at the psychiatrist, his gaze skidding off the familiar face and across to the gardens. 'What happened . . . just after? I can't quite seem to piece it all together.'

Sebastien felt totally exhausted himself, his body aching dully. He wanted Lilas, and the thought, coming from nowhere, made him frown, then smile. But he quickly turned his thoughts to the matter in hand. 'I fetched the manager. I told him I'd heard a sound from behind the curtain. When I looked, I found the old man dead, and you, an old friend, in a state of shock. He called the ambulance and police. I gave my statement, insisted as a doctor that you were in no fit shape to be questioned until morning, and had your father's chauffeur bring us here. I thought it was better than a hotel. More private.' In fact Sebastien had wanted to bring Wayne back to what had once been his home in the hope of triggering off more memories, striking while he was still vulnerable. Sebastien felt the coldblooded ruthlessness of it and hated it; yet at the same time he wasn't going to let it stop him. He was not sure how much those final words of Wayne actually meant. The cry for help in times of stress was not always a reliable indicator.

'You'll have to talk to the police tomorrow, but by then they'll be sure it's natural causes. They'll probably only want to know the details.'

Wayne tried to smile but found his stiff face uncooperative. 'It won't matter. I'll just say the shock of meeting his long-lost son was too much for him. It's no more than the truth, after all.' This time he did manage a twisted travesty of a smile, but still couldn't look the American in the eye.

Sebastien shifted on the chair, sensing the approaching crisis. If he could get him to talk now — freely and without lies before giving his damned barrier a chance to get back in place — he might stand a chance. 'You've spent a long time planning this, haven't you?' he asked quietly.

Wayne stared down at the patio tiles beneath his feet. 'I suppose. Since I was four.'

'Four?'

476

'Yes. Four. It was in Berlin, and he'd just come back from a party. One of those Nazi parties — he was full of talk of Goebbels, I remember. I heard him out of the window — he'd locked me in my room. I wasn't supposed to listen out the window . . .' Once the words came he found them unstoppable, like a dam that had burst with an unending supply of dirty water. He went on to relate the fiasco with Heinlich on the boat, still not knowing, after all those years, the motivation and instinct behind that defiant gesture. Sebastien listened, appalled and yet elated. So many things began to explain themselves. The need for revenge, his strange, ambiguous nature with women. No wonder he treated them, and everyone else, as no more than pawns in a game.

'Tell me about Hans,' he urged softly when Wayne's voice began to falter and fade away.

Wayne ran his hand through his hair and turned to face the sea. 'I don't . . . I can't.'

'Did he hate you? Is that why you killed him?'

'No!' Wayne turned to him, his eyes blazing. 'He loved me, the poor little bastard. He only did the dive to try and show me . . .' He got to his feet in a quick, jerking movement and walked several paces across the well-tended lawn, knowing that Sebastien was only a step behind him. He was always just a step behind him, like a bloodhound. A very subtle, very clever bloodhound, pinching little drops of his blood here and there, over weeks that turned to months, that turned to years. Like a parasite, like a leech. A leech that he needed. A leech that gave his whole stinking life some kind of relief. 'You're a ruthless bastard, Sebastien Teale,' he said, not sure how he wanted his voice to sound. It came out flat and hopeless.

Sebastien smiled gently. 'I know. With you, how could I be anything else?'

Wayne felt a kick of reaction in his gut and took a deep breath. 'What do I have to do to make you give up?'

'Tell me about Hans.'

Wayne gave a harsh bark of laughter. 'That will only make you dig into me more.'

'I know,' Sebastien said simply, his eyes level and facing the blue glare head on. Slowly, the pale lips tugged up at the corners.

'I could still destroy you, Sebastien.'

'Tell me about Hans.'

Wayne looked out to the flat blue line of the sea, his shoulders suddenly relaxing. 'He was . . .'

'Mr D'Arville, sir. Telephone.'

Sebastien turned abruptly, glaring at the poor servant in a moment of blind frustration. He could cheerfully have throttled the inconspicuous little man at that point. By his side he heard Wayne heave a great sigh. Was it anger, despair or relief?

'All right.' Wayne did not look at Sebastien as he turned and followed the man into the house. Once there, he picked up the phone. 'Yes?'

'Johnson, sir.'

Craig Johnson was one of Wayne's army. Over the years he'd acquired men at regular intervals, poaching them from security firms, police forces, even catching some of them from the fallout of the armed services. For three years now he'd had a team on his father, another team on the Platt off-spring, still trying to make trouble all these years later, and another team to look after his private security. Johnson was on the Mueller team.

'Yes?'

'Trouble, sir. The family of Duncan Somerville, the man your father . . . entertained . . . a few years ago?'

'I remember.'

'His family, that is, his daughter and her husband, are on their way to Monaco tomorrow. They were recently visited by our old friend Daniel Bernstein.'

'Bernstein,' Wayne repeated slowly, having difficulty dragging his mind back to reality. Those few wonderful minutes talking to Sebastien had been a catharsis, hurting like hell but feeling wonderful. Now reality was back, and with it, all of life's landmines just waiting for him to step on one. 'They could be trouble,' Wayne said grimly, speaking his thoughts aloud, giving himself a few more seconds to get his brain back to proper working order. 'If they have information, they could expose me.'

'Yes, sir.'

Wayne knew that no mention had yet been made of Wolfgang's death to the press. Damn, why couldn't they have waited a few more days? He hung up and turned around just as Sebastien stepped into the doorway.

Sebastien took one look at Wayne's face and knew that the barriers were back. Wayne smiled slowly. 'It seems that "saved by the bell" isn't just a cliche after all.'

Sebastien leaned against the doorjamb, feeling ready to lie down and die. 'You weren't saved, Wayne,' he said tiredly, but his voice held the ring of defeat. For a long, long second the two men just stared at one another. Wayne swallowed hard. He had a strong, almost overwhelming desire to walk across the few feet separating them and . . .

He turned away quickly, but not before Sebastien had time to see the overpowering look of pain and desperation that flitted across his face. Wordlessly, Sebastien watched him walk away.

He wanted Lilas.

As a Louis XIV clock began to strike the half-hour, he suddenly shuddered. He didn't believe in prophecies, but for a wild, ugly moment he had the unshakeable feeling that it was all too late.

Too late for Wayne, and too late for himself.

* * *

It was approaching four o'clock in the afternoon when the plane that had stopped over at New York touched down at Nice. 'It looks hot out there,' Kier said, and lifted Oriel's hand to kiss it. She was wearing a yellow summer dress by

Valentine and her hair hung loose across her shoulders. She smiled and squeezed his hand in reply, but her face wore a pinched, tight look.

'It's Nice, isn't it? If it had been raining I'd have asked the pilot to turn around and go back!'

Kier grinned. That was his Oriel. His one constant rock in a sea of Hollywood junk. Slowly he stretched then stood up to retrieve his jacket from the overhead rack. Oriel took a deep breath and slowly rose to her feet. Her legs felt shaky, and it was not just because of the long flight they'd made. They were to meet an associate of Dan Bernstein's at the airport, and although Dan hadn't been very forthcoming on the phone she knew that to ask them to come to Monte Carlo he must have something very definite.

For the thousandth time she found herself remembering her father, his voice, his smile. Duncan had been so supportive.

'Come on.' Kier gently took her hand and together they followed the queue of passengers off the plane and out through the concrete and glass tunnel to Customs, where their luggage awaited them. As Kier lifted the heaviest suitcase, Oriel took the smaller one, both their minds on the forthcoming interview and the consequences for them both of trying to prosecute Duncan's killer.

'I'm feeling really dry,' Oriel said wryly. 'Let's stop off and have a cup of coffee.'

Kier smiled. 'You must be feeling really parched if you want airport coffee!' But he was already leading the way to the functional coffee lounge. Once there, he queued up for the usual brew and took them back to their table. Oriel took a sip and sighed. Her eyes roamed over the coffee table in front of her, where she noticed a copy of a recent *Nice-Matin*. Suddenly a picture of half a face caught her attention, and she leaned forward and opened it up.

'Kier!' she gasped, looking up as her husband leaned over her. 'Isn't that . . . ?'

'Mueller,' he said with conviction. The man was older, but they both remembered seeing his pictures in Duncan's files, when they'd gone over his things after his death. The headline confirmed the name.

'*Marcus D'Arville Mort*,' Oriel read aloud. 'He's dead, Kier!' She slowly shook her head. 'This doesn't make sense. We've come all this way only to find . . .'

Kier frowned. 'It does seem rather . . . convenient, doesn't it?' he murmured.

Oriel looked at him. 'You think something . . . funny's going on?'

Kier shrugged. 'I think, now that we're here, we should have a nose around. What could it hurt?'

* * *

Back at the Harcourt mansion, Gemma was reading *Nice-Matin*. She'd ordered it, ever since her parents had sat down and told their children what was going on, and why they were flying to France. It was thrilling, in a way, to have a grandfather who might have been murdered by Nazis. Sad too. She'd noticed how pale and angry her mother had looked.

Now, the notice of Mueller's death was splashed across the front pages! Damn! She'd just been in the middle of planning a wild party, with Paris's grinning help, and now this.

'What are you scowling at,' Paris said, wandering in after doing his usual two hours' practice in the pool.

'He's dead,' Gemma said succinctly.

Paris gave a double take. 'Who's dead?' he demanded.

'Mueller. Here, have some breakfast.' Gemma pushed a plate of toast his way. She could see her wild party disappearing in smoke. And she'd told Matty Haines it was definitely on!

'Well, if Mueller's dead, I expect Mum and Dad will be back soon.'

Gemma sighed petulantly. But, no sooner was the sigh echoing around the room when the phone rang. 'Well, that's our party gone down the tubes,' she muttered as she lifted the receiver. 'Hello? Oh, hi, Mum . . .'

Paris listened to her giving a lot of 'uh-huh's and 'oh?'s before she hung up. When she turned back, she was wearing a very strange expression.

'Mum and Dad are staying on in France for a while,' she said slowly, and Paris threw a cushion at her. She fielded it expertly.

'So, let's party on!' he yelled exuberantly, then settled down as he realized that Gemma was hardly enthusiastic. 'What's up?'

'They think there's something odd about Mueller's death,' she mused, her eyes taking on a bright gleam that had Paris instantly alert. He knew that look. It meant trouble.

'Gem?'

'What if it was murder?' she breathed, her face taking on an excited look. 'Mum and Dad could be mixed up in this great Nazi murder mystery, and we're stuck over here in boring LA.'

'Gem!' Paris groaned, but he could already see where she was heading. And, in spite of himself, he could feel himself becoming intrigued. 'Perhaps it was his son,' Paris mused, and, finding his sister's glowing eyes fixed on him, quickly grabbed one of his sporting magazines and began to hunt through the pages.

'What are you talking about, rodent-breath?' Gemma asked, craning her head to look over her brother's shoulder as he found the page he was looking for.

'Here,' Paris handed it over. 'Wayne D'Arville. I thought I knew that name. Some English financial firm that he owns is sponsoring the open golf classic at Gleneagles next year.'

'The son!' Gemma breathed. 'Daddy said something a long time ago about Mueller having a family.'

'It makes sense,' Paris said, turning the page to be con-fronted by a full-page colour picture of a smiling, redheaded man. 'He can't want the whole world finding out his father was a Nazi.'

Gemma squealed and grabbed the magazine. 'What a hunk!'

Paris watched her with smiling eyes. 'First he's a killer, now he's a hunk.'

But Gemma wasn't listening. She turned the magazine so that the picture of Wayne D'Arville stared straight at her, the blue eyes seeming to bore deep into her head, making her blink. She felt her breath flutter in her throat as her breasts tingled and her nipples tightened into hard nubs. Slowly she began to read the article.

'The imposing figure of the six-foot-four entrepreneur with the copper hair and sky-blue eyes has set more hearts fluttering than any other man of his generation, but for widely differing reasons. Though the ladies have fallen in droves for the man with the looks of a movie star, their husbands react to his shark-like presence on the stock exchange with deep shivers of foreboding. So far in his impressive career . . .'

When she'd finished the article — written by a woman, she noticed — her eyes were glowing. 'So that's the son of the man who murdered Grandad,' she said quietly, but her voice was excited rather than disgusted, and Paris, in the act of buttering his toast, glanced at her worriedly.

'You know, Paris,' she said, reaching forward to filch the toast from his hand, 'I don't think he should get away with this. Why should Mum and Dad have all the fun? Bethany's off in Oxford, living it up. Why shouldn't we see Europe too?'

'Huh?' Paris said, around a mouthful of toast. Slowly she stood up and stared down at the magazine. The blue eyes seemed to laugh at her, mocking her, challenging her . . . 'I think it's about time he was taught a lesson.'

Paris, his voice doubtful, asked nervously, 'What are you going to do?'

Gemma looked at him. Her eyes were bright, her face flushed, and her red-painted, beautiful mouth was forming a cocky grin. She was wearing a pair of cyclamen-pink shorts and a white lace top, and with her short cap of dark hair she reminded him of an all-too-beautiful, mischievous pixie.

'Fly to Monte Carlo, of course,' she said. 'Mum and Dad need never know we're there.'

'Gemma!' Paris wailed. 'You can't just . . .' He waved a hand vaguely in the air, feeling his stomach turn over. 'Gem, you can't be serious.'

'Why not?' She looked incredibly young, incredibly stubborn, and Paris was suddenly terrified for her.

'He's the son of a Nazi, for Pete's sake,' he yelped. 'He moves money around as if . . . He probably has an army of men . . .'

Gemma let him splutter and flounder, still wearing that aggravatingly confident smile. 'He's used to dealing with the most powerful men in the world!' Paris finally exploded.

'He hasn't dealt with me before,' Gemma pointed out softly, with the supreme confidence of youth, and the utter certainty that only the truly spoiled could generate. She simply could not conceive of not getting what she wanted.

'Look, Gem, I know about you . . . I have friends at school too, you know. I'm not deaf. You've got a reputation that would curdle Mum's blood if she ever heard about it, but this is different. He . . .' he tapped the photo of Wayne D'Arville with a jabbing finger '. . . is not some high school kid or college jock that you can just wrap around your little finger. He's bloody dangerous. And what do you even expect to gain from it?!'

Paris got to his feet as he realized he was not getting through to her, looking alternately angry and alarmed. 'Gem, you can't!'

Gemma looked up at him, put her hands on her hips, cocked her elfin face to one side and smiled beguilingly. 'If you're so worried about me, big brother,' she purred, 'why don't you come with me?'

CHAPTER 38

Wayne stared at the photographs in front of him, as unmoving as a chameleon. Reluctantly he dragged his eyes from those of a blue-eyed boy and reread the report from his team investigating Veronica Copeland, which had come in only half an hour ago. 'The subject's birth certificate was registered under the grandmother's name, not that of Coltrane. This is what led to the initial delay in double-checking the certificate.' Wayne gave a brief snarl and skipped the page. He wasn't interested in why Veronica had registered the birth under her mother's maiden name. No doubt she wanted all traces of the child being born in prison to a jailbird mother covered up. Perhaps, even then, she'd subconsciously been afraid he would take the child away. Again his eyes wandered to the photographs. Immediately on finding the birth certificate that had 'Father Unknown' written in the appropriate section, and a suspiciously timely date of birth, the team had staked out the Copeland boy. The resulting pictures bore hardly any resemblance at all to the boy he'd seen in the warehouse that night in New York. The photographs, hundreds of them, had been taken over a series of days, and caught the boy in every daily ritual possible: leaving for his summer job, on the bus, carrying trays of coffee to the newspaper journalists he worked for, talking to a pretty blonde-haired girl, and eating a hamburger. And always the same face stared back at him.

His hair was as dark as Veronica's, not the mousy brown hair of that bastard Valentine. That had been the first thing that had struck him. As Wayne had turned over the photographs for the first time, a full-face shot had had his heart stopping in his chest. The boy's eyes were blue — as blue as his own. The face, too, looked different from the one he remembered. The colour shots were of the highest quality, and Wayne found himself looking down at skin as fair as his own. And the shape of the face . . . How the hell had Valentine managed to change the boy's face? It had taken only seconds for Wayne to piece it all together. The bitch had phoned her husband the moment he was out of the door. He should have realized that the dressmaker was a make-up artist too.

Wayne glanced at his watch. He had another four hours before his commercial flight was due and made a mental note to purchase a private jet at the first opportunity. He paced the villa, now legally his, unable to stay still. 'Travis,' he said his son's name, over and over again. The boy was just seventeen. Wayne could remember well what it was to be seventeen.

'Travis,' he said again, savouring the two syllables. 'You're going to love Monte Carlo.'

He put in a call to his man in Monaco. 'Fletcher? I want you to buy an oceangoing yacht. I'll have the bank transfer the funds. No, I'm going to New York. Hire a crew and have the boat meet me there. What? I don't care about that, or the paperwork. Just rush it through, will you? And Fletcher — I want a discreet crew. Find as many of your men with seagoing experience as possible. I want it there within the fortnight. And Fletcher — I want the boat named the *Travis Helm*.' If he was going to kidnap his own son — and he was — he could hardly take the boy bound and gagged on to a jumbo jet.

* * *

486

Travis was up to his neck in files. Jake Conran, the features editor, had asked him to research a series of murders several years ago of five drug pushers. Jake was sure that the death of a pusher downtown was the work of the same killer. 'The MO, boy.' He had tapped his nose. 'Always look-out for the MO.' Travis had spent four hours going through old editions, ferreting out the relevant stuff from all the dross. Now he glanced at his watch. It was getting late; he'd have to call home and tell them not to hold dinner.

'Hey, kid, how's it going?' Travis turned to see the sweating, grinning face of Andy McCall, the baseball and associated sportswriter, blocking the doorway.

'How does it look like it's coming?' he shot back, grinning as the man began to wheeze in laugher.

'Welcome to Grub Street, kid.' And with that cryptic comment the big man lumbered off, leaving Travis grinning. He turned, and glanced at the towering piles of old editions and files stacked around him.

'Hell, I love this job,' he said softly as, high in the air, a Boeing jet from Nice began its descent to New York airport.

* * *

'Get the phone, Val,' Veronica called, lifting one sud-covered leg as she lay back in the bath. She had the Mancini buyout to oversee tomorrow. The thought of dealing with all those accountants was enough to send her barmy. 'Aaarrghhhh,' she groaned, as Val stuck his head around the door.

'Dying?' he asked, going down on to his knees beside the bathtub.

'At least,' she sighed. 'It's a rare disease called Chronic Accountant Dyspepsia.'

'Sounds painful,' Val said, and slipped a hand into the bath, uncaring that the hot soapy water drenched his sleeve.

'Hmmm,' she sighed as his hand curled around one calf and began to stroke higher. 'Who was that on the phone?'

'Travis. He'll be late. He's researching a gory story for the feature creature.'

'You're a poet and you don't know it.'

'I do my best. You do the rest.'

'I think you're a . . . oh, Val!' Water sloshed over the side of the bathtub, but neither of them noticed for quite some time. Fully dressed, he joined her in the tub, his jeans soaking into a darker blue as he lay between her parted legs.

* * *

Downtown, Wayne listened to Cyril Francis and Frank Parton as they brought him up to date. Cyril, an ex-Marine who'd been dishonourably discharged, was a tall man, with a mean face that would have sent a Hollywood director into fits of rapture; dark, saturnine features were offset by a vivid white scar on his cheek. In direct contrast, Frank Parton looked like the ex-FBI man that he was. He wore a powder-blue suit, which offset the careful cut of his pale hair and watery blue eyes. Frank was the electronics and surveillance expert, Cyril the strategic brain and muscle.

'You have his school records?'

Frank handed them over and watched as his employer read through the ten years' worth of essay reports and exam results. Frank was openly intrigued by his employer. Cyril's eyes were unreadable as the tall man paced and read. But then Cyril's eyes were always unreadable.

'What else?' Wayne demanded, spending the next few hours going through the bulk of material that had not been included in the preliminary report. By the time dawn pushed away the night's darkness, Wayne had read every medical report on the boy, read details of every place the boy had ever lived, every school, every teacher, every friend. Frank wondered how he'd been so careless as to misplace a son in the first place.

'Where's the boy now?'

Frank lifted a small box to his mouth and spoke quietly into it. Wayne heard a crackle of static and a tinny voice answering.

'The boy's home, sir. The complex on . . .'

'I know where it is. Has there been any unusual activity since my last visit?'

'No, sir. The boy is still working at the paper. He worked late last night. School's out for summer, but I've got prior notification of his results. He graduated third in his class.'

Wayne nodded. 'College?'

'He has a place at the local uni, sir. He could have gone to one of the top places, with his result and financial backing from his . . . mother. Obviously he wants to stay local.'

Wayne walked to the window and looked out over the city. It never stopped. He thought of all the racial unrest, the drug pushers, the street gangs, and shuddered. What a place to live. Travis could have been killed by this place. Or had that been Veronica's intention? The bitch. And Valentine. An image of the cockney man grinning at him suddenly superimposed itself over the city landscape, and Wayne felt that familiar hot spear of antagonism. All these years, that . . . that . . . dressmaking nancy-pancy bastard had been raising his son. Who knew what harm he'd done? What if . . . ?

Wayne turned so suddenly that both men tensed. 'Girlfriends?' Wayne snapped out, almost wilting in relief as Frank Parton began to read a list of names. He finished up with Gayle Granger, the blonde girl in the set of photographs Wayne had left behind in Monaco.

Wayne said softly, 'I want them dead.'

The two men remained silent. Slowly he turned around, expecting them to look shocked, or at least uneasy. Neither did. Frank Parton merely wanted clarification. 'The Copelands, sir?'

'Yes.'

'Both?' It was Cyril who spoke, for the first time since Wayne had entered the room.

'Yes,' Wayne said again, his voice firm.

'You want it to look like an accident?' Parton again.

'Of course.'

'Car crash?'

Wayne looked down into the street below. 'No. They might not die. I want to be sure they're dead. I want them . . .' He paused, then enunciated the next word with grim relish. 'Eradicated. I want them . . .' He blinked as the sun emerged between two high-rise towers, throwing a deep orange light into his eyes. Slowly Wayne began to smile. 'I want them burned.'

'Burned?' Frank repeated, puzzled. He thought they'd already established that he wanted them dead.

'A warehouse fire happens nearly every day in this city,' Cyril mused, having caught on at once. His voice was surprisingly soft coming from a face like his.

'Oh. You mean *burned*,' Frank repeated. 'That warehouse is full of flammable material. Solvent, too. And all that make-up. Did you know almost ninety-nine per cent of make-up is based on flammable substances?' Frank asked of nobody in particular.

Slowly Wayne turned back from the window and stared at him. Something in the quality of those blue eyes made Frank go cold. Cyril smiled. 'I want it done now,' Wayne said, successfully wiping the smile off the older man's face.

'You mean this week?'

'I mean this day. Now. This afternoon.'

'But Mr D'Arville! These things take planning. They take time. We have to be careful . . .' Frank began, his voice rising an octave.

'Are you saying you can't do it?' Wayne asked, mildly enough, but again Frank felt a cold chill climb up his spine.

'We'll do it,' Cyril said, his eyes meeting those of his partner, a silent message passing between them.

Wayne nodded. 'Good. I'm going to get some sleep. Wake me when it's all set up. I want to watch.'

Both men were silent as he kicked off his shoes and walked towards the bed. Equally silent, they then left. Frank closed the door after him, and turned to his partner. 'I don't know about you,' he said, as he pressed the button for the elevator, 'but I think we're working for a nut.'

'A clever nut,' Cyril corrected with what seemed pedantic nit-picking.

'Yeah,' Frank agreed heavily. 'They're the worst kind.'

* * *

Val was just about to take a Budweiser from the fridge when the phone rang. He glanced through the alcove to where Veronica lay on the settee, poring over her latest business scoop. She got up and walked to the old-fashioned white and gold telephone. 'Hello.'

'Is that Mrs Copeland?'

'Yes.'

'Oh, thank heavens. This is Phelps here — I'm the watchman at Warehouse 15.'

'Yes?' Her voice sharpened. The man sounded distinctly panicky.

'A few minutes ago your son came in. He said he had to check something to do with the shipment of Bruges lace that came in last night.'

'What? Travis? But he's at the paper.'

'No, ma'am. That's what I'm trying to tell you: he's here. And there's been an accident, ma'am.'

'Accident?' She heard her voice yelp out the word, and glanced up as Val sprinted closer and jammed his ear against the outside of the phone. 'What do you mean? What's happened?' Her voice was sharp with anxiety, and to Val she mouthed the word, 'Travis.'

'Well, ma'am, somehow one of the stacks of bales came loose. I ain't sure how it happened. I heard him call out, and when I found him his legs were pinned under the bales. It's the Thai silk shipment, I think.' Quickly Val snatched the phone away from her.

'Have you called the ambulance, man? Good. Can you get the bales off him?' Veronica waited, scanning her husband's face for any expression. 'OK. We'll be right there.'

Val drove to the warehouse with grim speed. Veronica could feel a tremor in the pit of her stomach, making her

491

breathe in small gasps. What if his legs were crushed? What if he could never walk again? When they arrived, the warehouse looked deserted.

'Why aren't the ambulances here yet?' Veronica asked, getting out of the car without bothering to lock it.

'I dunno,' Val admitted, looking around. 'Where's the watchman?'

'He must be with Travis,' Veronica said, her voice wobbling as tears filled her eyes. 'Val, he must be so damned scared!'

Val took her hand, pulling her inside. 'Come on.'

The place was deserted. 'The silks are over here,' Val said, and set off deep into the heart of the warehouse. Veronica looked around her at towering bales of beige sacking. They both jumped as a hollow 'clang' echoed through the building. 'Well, somebody's about,' Val said. 'That was the outer door.'

By now Veronica was hopelessly lost. Since giving up modelling she hardly ever came to the warehouses any more. 'Travis?' she called, making Val jump. Nobody answered.

'Perhaps they've already got him out,' Val whispered, and for a few seconds they ran through the maze of bales, eyes swivelling. Suddenly Val slowed down to a stop, staring straight ahead, then began looking around, his face puzzled.

'What is it?' Veronica whispered.

'This is the place,' Val answered, waving a vague hand around at the bales clearly labelled as Thai silk. 'But there's nothing here.'

'I don't get it,' Veronica said. 'Where's Travis?'

Val began to speak, then stopped as a sound came from behind them. It was an odd sound — a sort of small *whump* that echoed in the big room.

'What was that?' Veronica demanded, her voice strangled.

'I don't know. It sounded like—' He broke off as Veronica clutched his arm.

'Look!' She pointed to the top of a pile of satin from Vienna where a plume of smoke curled high into the air.

For a second they both stood and stared, then Val grabbed her arm, his voice terse as he ordered gruffly, 'Come on.'

They began running in the opposite direction, Val sure of the layout. They ran a few yards, turned down an aisle stretching to the right, and skidded to a halt. A wall of flame blocked their exit a few yards away.

'But the fire's back there,' Veronica panted, jerking her head in the direction behind them and beginning to panic for the first time. She looked sideways and up at Val, and saw his jaw clenched so tight that the whole bottom half of his face was white. 'Val?' she said in a small voice, like that of a terrified child. Val looked down, opened his mouth, shook his head, and dragged her back. They ran to the left, but again, only a few yards away, there was a third fire. Veronica felt tears on her cheeks which were dried in seconds by the hot air surrounding them. 'We've got to find Travis,' she cried. 'He'll burn to death!'

'I don't think Travis was ever here!' Val had to shout now to be heard over the rising roar of the fire. The materials were burning much too fast — they had to be covered with petrol or something like it. Quickly he looked around. The windows were situated almost at the roof, a good thirty feet above them. 'Quick. Help me stack these bales.'

Veronica began to cough and choke as the smoke attacked her lungs, and behind her she could feel the hot lick of air that was becoming super-heated by the flames. She could feel the oxygen being burnt off, and her lungs were already beginning to labour.

Within five minutes they had built a rickety stairway of bales, but she could hardly see it as her eyes began to water from the smoke. She could feel death all around her and clung grimly to Val's hand as he began to climb. 'Watch where I put my feet and . . .'

'What?' she screamed. All around was a loud roar of crackling flames. Val pointed at his feet, then the bales. Veronica nodded. Outside they could hear the wail of sirens.

'Oh, thank God,' Veronica said, but Val didn't hear her. They were already four bales up, and the whole structure began to wobble precariously. He looked down ten feet or so and saw the flames slowly creeping towards the bottom of their makeshift ladder.

Veronica took off her shoes, but forgot that she was wearing stockings, which were hardly designed for traction. Above him Val could see the thin line of windows. They had to be wide enough to allow them out. They *had* to be. He glanced down and saw the top of Veronica's dark head.

'I've got to let go of your hand for the next bale, OK?' He choked on the smoke, but Veronica nodded and let go of his hand, clinging to the next bale with two white-knuckled hands. Her heart was thumping so loud in her chest that she thought it was going to burst. She just couldn't get enough air into her lungs. She could feel herself begin to pass out. She wanted to be sick and scream and cry, all at the same time.

The bales wobbled as Val pulled himself up to the next one and she clung on grimly. Below her she could not even see the ground, only the orangey-yellow flames that glowed beneath the thick black smoke. She looked up and saw Val beckoning her. Taking a deep breath, she choked and retched, then reached up. Her hands grasped the red string that bound the bales together and, feeling with her feet, she found a foothold. Hoisting herself up, she balanced precariously between the two bales, like a fly on a wall.

Suddenly and without warning her foot slipped and she fell forward, banging her chin on the bale and biting her tongue, filling her mouth with the iron taste of her own blood. She lost traction and scrabbled desperately with her hands. She glanced up just in time to see Val lunge forward, desperately trying to grab her hand. For a second it looked as if she must fall. For a second, a horrible second in time, she seemed to hang suspended in mid-air, and then she screamed.

But Val, with a superhuman effort, just managed to grab her. Her weight threatened to pull him down, and he rocked precariously on the bale. But he did not let her go. If she died, he was going to die with her.

He grunted as he pulled her up. She hung limp in his arms, and he realized she'd finally succumbed to the smoke.

'Veronica!' he screamed her name, and began to haul her up to him, calling on every ounce of his strength. Once there, he held her in his arms, gasping and choking himself. He looked up at the window. It seemed so far away.

* * *

In the newsroom, Travis had just placed a cup of coffee on the desk of Owen Twinsmith, one of the top 'hot-shot' boys, when the desk phone rang. Travis would have moved on except that the mention of Rineway Street caught his attention. Sharply his eyes focused on the young reporter who was busy scribbling down in shorthand. 'Is it worth covering? Really? Shit! Have they saved the other buildings yet? OK.' He hung up and grabbed his jacket.

'Hey what's going on?' Travis called after him.

'Fire at the warehouses,' Owen mumbled, already running and shouting for his photographer and back-up man. Travis stared after him, an ugly feeling uncoiling itself in the pit of his stomach. There had to be hundreds of warehouses on Rineway Street. Even so . . . He reached for the phone, punching out his own numbers.

'Hello. Valentine's,' said the chirpy voice of their cleaning lady.

'Glenny? It's Travis. Listen, is Dad there?'

'Nope. He and your ma left for the warehouses about half an hour ago.'

Travis hung up and left at a dead run. It took him only ten minutes to get to the site, but he had to abandon his taxi at the top of the street and run the rest of the way, as fire trucks and police blocked the road. He dodged a policeman keeping away spectators, his eyes fixed on the sky ahead where black smoke choked the air. He was gasping and totally out of breath when he reached the first engine, his agonized gaze confirming what his heart already knew. Warehouse 15 was just a wall of orange flame. Travis pushed past the people who had also got around the cordon, uncaring of the disgruntled yelps coming his way.

'Is anyone in there?' he yelled, grabbing the first fireman he found.

The heavy-set man with a sweat-soaked, soot-blackened face shook him off angrily. 'Outta the way,' he snapped.

Travis let him go and walked to the nearest engine where a driver sat in the front, controlling the pressure gauge on the hoses. 'Is anyone in there?' he yelled through the window. The man didn't take his eyes off the instruments. 'Please! My father owns the warehouse. For God's sake . . .'

The man glanced up at him. 'They got two people out about ten minutes ago.'

Travis stared at him. 'Alive?' he croaked the word, barely managing to get it past his tight throat.

The fireman shrugged. 'The ambulance took off fast, so I guess so. But . . .'

'But what?' Travis all but screamed.

The fireman looked at him with sympathy. 'They were in there a long time, by all accounts.'

Travis turned to the burning building, his face a sickly white. 'You mean . . . they got burned?'

The fireman sighed. He felt sorry for the kid. But it was best to know the worst. You had time to prepare that way. 'It's not just the flames, kid,' he said gruffly. 'It's the smoke. Smoke burns off the oxygen, see? And if your brain is robbed of oxygen for any amount of time . . .' He trailed off.

Travis stared at him blankly for a few seconds, then swallowed. 'What hospital will they have taken them to?'

But at that moment, a part of the warehouse started to collapse, and the fire chief ordered his men back. Travis stumbled away, his head reeling.

A fire crew rushed past him, knocking him to the ground. He barely felt it. But, just as Travis straightened, the sight of a copper-coloured head, standing head and shoulders above the rest of the crowd, caught his eye.

Travis went cold. Since Wayne D'Arville's last visit, Val and Veronica had researched the man thoroughly, coming up with some startling and ugly facts that had made them all feel sick. Now Travis froze as the head turned his way. He expected the blue gaze to keep moving, not expecting to be recognized as the same boy he had seen just over a month ago, but instead the blue eyes sharpened and remained fixed on him.

Travis began to shake. As he looked deep into those blue eyes, he suddenly knew. He'd started the fire. He glanced at the burning building, then looked back to the space where Wayne D'Arville had stood, only to find his biological father bearing down on him, shouldering his way through the crowd with arrogant ease. Travis looked once more into that face, then turned and fled.

He knew the district well, and dodged down the narrow, twisting alleys at random, pausing every now and then to look over his shoulder. Having set off at a run, he then walked for miles, in no particular direction, feeling dazed and totally disorientated. Val and Veronica might both be dead — or worse — but his other father, the man called Wayne D'Arville, was very much alive, and coming after him.

Travis stumbled into a café and ordered a coffee. His legs felt like rubber. He tried to lift the cup to his mouth, but it shook so hard that the coffee fell to the table top.

'Hey, you! Junkie. Get outta here.' The man who served him the coffee was scowling at him. Travis blinked then he looked blankly down at the coffee cup. 'Bloody junkie. Do the world a favour, kid, and go top yourself.'

Travis stumbled to his feet and lurched out the door. He looked left and right, not sure where he was. He had to go home. He had to get safe. He found himself at a bus stop. Swaying on the bus, he felt curiously light-headed. He knew it was shock and got off at the nearest stop to his apartment building. He staggered to the nearest wall and leant his hand against the solid concrete. The few minutes it took him to walk a block and a half seemed to take forever. But eventually he found himself staring at the blue and white awning that was the entrance to his building.

Through his misery, Travis felt a slow prickling start low down on the back of his neck. Quickly he swung around. A few yards away a man was walking towards him wearing a fancy blue suit, his blond hair neatly trimmed. He was smiling. Travis stared at him for less than a second, and then inexplicably found himself running. He was not sure why, but at the corner he half turned, and almost cried out loud. The man was almost on top of him. He dodged, cannoning into a man in a brown suit. He was tall and lean, and as Travis looked up to apologise, he saw a vivid white scar slashed across the man's right cheek.

The blue eyes of the frightened boy in old jeans and windcheater met the steely brown eyes of the man in the brown suit, and a silent message that Travis understood only instinctively passed between them.

There was no point trying to run.

CHAPTER 39

Monte Carlo

The moment Maria stepped out of the taxi, she felt a great wave of happiness wash over her. Facing her was the Beach Plaza Tower, built in front of a small, curving beach of white sand. Once this whole scenario would have overwhelmed her: the white city that was Monte Carlo, the plethora of yachts, the smell of money. She could almost have wished she had come straight to this place from Andalusia, just for the thrill of the total contrast. Then Vincent was by her side, his head just reaching her shoulder, and she forced a smile to her face. 'Well, this is it. What do you think?' she asked gaily.

Vincent Marchetti glanced up at the building and shrugged. 'It is all right. Let's get out of the sun.' Maria watched him walk ahead, a small smile on her painted lips. She watched the bellboys collect her mountain of luggage, for she had taken everything with her from Carlos's villa. The jewellery she had halved, keeping the very finest pieces to wear and selling the rest. Now her bank balance practically dazzled her with all the zeros.

The hotel room boasted air-conditioning, a queen-sized bed, private bathroom, colour television, minibar and telephone, but the first thing she did was check that her adjoining room with Vincent Marchetti was locked. It was, and the key was on her side. Not that he was in any way threatening, and she knew she had to keep him sweet. So far she had succeeded in bringing him to Monte Carlo, but already he was making noises about rejoining the institute and continuing with his proper scientific work.

But she was confident she could handle him, without having to go as far as sleeping with him. After all, who really cared about science when there was life to be lived, and all the treasures it held to be explored? Treasures like parties, new places, love. And revenge. Oh, yes, she was looking forward to revenge.

A sea breeze feathered across her skin, cooling her arms and making her shiver. Somewhere in that jungle of white-painted buildings, hotels, casinos, shopping malls and royal palaces was the lair of Wayne D'Arville, her not-so-beloved father.

Ironically enough, she had arrived in Monte Carlo almost five weeks to the day after her grandfather's funeral. She wondered what he had been like as she walked to her cases and began to unpack. She had worked hard for all those magic labels — Valentine, Dior, Saint Laurent, even a few classics from Balmain and Chanel — and she didn't want some maid creasing them. She had just put away the last of her things and was holding her jewellery case in her hand, ready to take it down to the hotel safe, when a soft knock came on the door connecting the two rooms. She walked towards it but made no move to turn the key. 'Yes?'

'You hungry?' The voice was muffled but she was relieved to notice he made no move to turn the door handle. In his own way, Vincent was a sweetie.

'Starving,' she admitted. 'Meet me in the restaurant in ten minutes.' She changed quickly into a summer dress of dramatic ruby-red, which was practically nothing more than a poncho that flowed and rippled whenever she moved, leaving a long length of leg bare. Watching with eagle eyes as they put her jewels into the safe, she asked for directions to the restaurant, which turned out to be practically empty. They ordered *poulet sauté aux olives de Provence*, followed by raspberries in a rich cream, enjoying the meal after the short flight. Maria drank sparingly of the white wine. She had to remain clear and level-headed. Later on tonight, she would face her father not as a filthy peasant working in a sweatshop but as a wealthy, beautiful woman who was taking his money.

'Shall we take a walk on the beach?' Vincent asked, his voice hesitant and containing his usual hopeful squeak.

Briefly she shook her head. 'No. I want to check out the equipment.'

Vincent's face fell, but he rose obediently when she did, leaving his dessert unfinished to follow her to the lifts. Upstairs, Maria unlocked a black leather briefcase from which she extracted a small box. Inside was a small oddly shaped disc, designed to fit snugly into her ear. She carefully inserted the pink plastic mould into her right ear then walked to the mirror to check it was invisible under her dark curtain of hair. It was. 'OK. Try your end. No — not here,' she murmured as Vincent retrieved a small microphone from the same briefcase and held it up to his hand. 'Go outside — by the pool — and then try it. If it'll work from that distance we'll have no trouble at the casino.'

Vincent flushed with anticipatory pleasure. He was looking forward to tonight, too, though for different reasons of course. Maria smiled indulgently. She was getting fond of little Vincent. 'And, *querido*, try practising a little more discretion, yes? My . . . Mr D'Arville will have security men scattered all around the place on the lookout for cheaters with angles. You can't just lift up your hand and talk into it. Pretend to be scratching your cheek or something. You can do that for me, can't you, darling?'

'Of course. I'll practise in front of the mirror tonight. Before we leave.' His face wreathed in a smile. He was having more fun in one day than a whole year at the institute!

Maria wandered around the room restlessly, occasionally touching her ear to make sure the disc had not fallen out. It felt strange at first, but the plastic had been moulded especially for the purpose of fitting snugly into a human ear, and she suspected that after several nights of wearing it she would hardly notice its existence. How or where Carlos had found such state-of-the-art listening and transmitting devices she didn't know or care. Even the microphone of Vincent's was barely bigger than a thimble.

She jumped, then smiled broadly as she heard a small, tinny but unmistakable voice deep in her ear. 'Maria. Can you hear me? I hope so. I'm by the pool now. I'm coming back. We'll talk in a minute, OK?'

Vincent felt as if he'd just stepped into a James Bond movie. He only hoped he wouldn't let her down, but he wasn't really worried about his 'gift' failing him. He had a ninety-nine per cent success rate that sent the professors and occasional visiting experts from other countries into fits of rapture.

He returned to Maria's room and knocked timidly. He knew he was making a fool of himself with her, but she was so lovely, how could he deny her? The door was flung open and he saw instantly that her face was glowing; her eyes were shining like stars, and her cherry-red mouth was wide and laughing. 'It worked, Vincent! It worked.' She reached out and pulled him inside, dancing with him around the room.

Eventually she danced to a halt, and then impatiently tugged out the pink plastic from her ear. 'Come on. Let's tour this little city of his and see some sights!'

Vincent wanted badly to ask exactly who Wayne D'Arville was and why she wanted so desperately to take his money, but he was scared of spoiling her mood. So they rented an English Jaguar and got lost in the maze of streets that bore exotic names like the Boulevard des Moulins, Avenue de la Costa, Rue Princesse Florestine and Boulevard Albert-Premier. They drove to the Port de Fontvieille and watched the yachts as the sun slowly set, then drove past the cathedral, the high arched windows aglow with colour. As night slowly approached, the lights came on — thousands, millions of twinkling lights. She could feel the pulse of the city begin to stir and hum, like blood in invisible veins.

'Let's get back. I want to change,' she said, her voice suddenly lower and colder. She had work to do.

Back in her room, Maria stared at her wardrobe carefully. She wanted this first meeting to be something special — something he would never forget. She thought of white first, for dramatic contrast with her hair and eyes, but then decided against it. White was the colour of a victim, and tonight it was Wayne D'Arville who was going to bleed. Red, then. She pulled out a sequined gown by Halston, then shook her head. Too bold — she was not a whore, but a sophisticated woman. Her eye ran along the rails of clothes and stopped at a deep orange velvet gown, cut with a narrow but plunging V at both neck and back. Thoughtfully she pulled it on and checked her reflection in the mirror. The orange velvet, as rich and luxurious as any material could be, glowed softly against her creamily tanned skin, turning her hair into a midnight-black and making her light brown eyes look intriguingly tawny. Slowly she smiled. After adding a golden-brown shadow to her eyelids and burnt orange lipstick to her mouth, she donned a tiger's eye necklace that consisted of a single stone on a delicate gold chain, the gem nestling between the braless valley of her breasts, drawing all eyes to that point. To complete the outfit she stepped into three-inch-high gold shoes that glittered as she walked and took out a matching clutch purse.

She slipped in her earplug and brushed out her hair, as a final touch spraying gold glitter sparingly over her ebony locks. She walked a few steps, turned her head, and saw how the glittery drops flashed in the light as she moved. Perfect. She knocked on the adjoining door, rechecked her appearance and turned as the door opened and Vincent walked in.

He was dressed in a dinner jacket. 'Vincent, darling, you look very debonair,' she said, trying to be kind.

Vincent said nothing — his mouth was open, his eyes almost standing out on stalks. 'Maria,' he said hoarsely.

503

'You're . . . beautiful isn't enough. There must be a better word. You're . . . everything!' He shrugged helplessly. Maria felt tears come to her eyes and she swallowed hard. Vincent went hot, then cold as she ran a few steps towards him then leaned down to kiss his cheek, but when she straightened up again, her eyes and voice were hard.

'Right. Are you ready?'

* * *

At the Droit de Seigneur, Paris stood behind the roulette wheel. His mother and father, he'd managed to find out, were following up a lead on Hans Mueller, the son who had drowned, and had travelled up the coast to interview the fisherman who had pulled the young lad from the water all those years ago.

Unlike Vincent, Paris's tuxedo fitted him perfectly, accenting his lean, tall body, deepening his brown hair and eyes and giving him an added maturity that belied his tender years. At the moment his gaze was fixed on the small white ball bouncing around like a thing demented before settling into the red sixteen spot. He groaned silently and looked across at his sister.

Gemma was wearing shimmering black in a four-teen-tiered dress that glittered with her slightest movement. Her short cap of hair had been teased by a top hairdresser to curl to a point at each cheek and in the middle of her fore-head. Her make-up was dramatic, all deep red lips and heavy dark eyes. She looked young, and at the moment impossibly alive. Paris felt a stab of panic as she eagerly thrust out a stack of chips on to the black two spot. Don't get the bug, sis, he prayed silently. Dad'll kill me!

They had arrived yesterday and checked into the best hotel, Paris learning only an hour later that they were relying on one of Gemma's credit cards. He himself had all but emp-tied his bank account and had a fistful of traveller's cheques, but he hoped that their money would run out soon and force them to leave. Monaco, and the casino in particular, made him nervous.

At first it had been intriguing. They'd toured the harbour on one of the tourist trips, tried out French croissants and coffee, listened with wide eyes to the gabble of languages around them — French, Portuguese, German and Italian — and dressed up for gourmet meals at the best and priciest place in town. Used to the Hollywood syndrome, where everybody was involved in 'the business' to some degree, as producer, agent, starlet or whatever, Paris found the cosmopolitan sophistication of Monte Carlo an eye-opener. In fact, with all the water-skiing, powerboat-racing and topless beaches, Paris might never have wanted to leave.

Except that tonight they had come to D'Arville's casino.

Paris had not known quite what to suspect. Certainly there was no sign of the man himself. Gemma had insisted they go to the bar first, where she'd ordered a Bloody Mary. He himself ordered a beer, both of them turning to look around. The sight of the world's wealthiest people, all competing to lose their money faster than anybody else, was an awesome sight, but Gemma's head had swivelled ceaselessly. 'I don't see him,' she'd hissed after ten minutes, and Paris, bored and nervous, had shrugged and turned to pump the barman. 'Hey, who owns this place?'

The barman obliged, not only with the owner's name, but also with the information that Monsieur D'Arville was in New York. Whilst Gemma fumed, Paris had to bite back the laughter. They'd travelled the ocean to come here, even stopping off in New York, and found they needn't have bothered. It was hilarious. Gemma, however, didn't appreciate the irony, and to prevent the evening becoming an entire waste had promptly stalked to the nearest roulette table, with Paris following more cautiously.

At first she had won — almost ten thousand dollars — and her youthful delight had even made the world-weary oil sheikhs and professional gamblers raise a smile. But then came the losing streak. The ten thousand dwindled and went, and she was back to using her own money. As the total of losses mounted up, Paris began to fidget, at one point even shouldering his way around the table, leaning over her shoulder and whispering in her ear that perhaps it was time to quit.

For his brotherly concern and trouble she had given him a vicious fulminating stare that had sent him away, smiling ruefully. 'OK. But you're the one who's gonna have to face Dad,' he'd warned her. Now, ten minutes later, she had lost another two thousand dollars.

Paris sighed and moved away. Hell, he didn't have to watch! Suddenly he stopped, jerking like a marionette whose strings had just been pulled. Not ten feet away, dressed in flame orange, was the most beautiful woman in the world. Paris swallowed hard, ridiculously unable to move. The girl turned and pulled off a gold lace shawl and handed it to a small, ugly man by her side. The contrast between the two was comical. Paris found himself moving towards her but was not aware of his feet supporting his weight.

Sensing a tall presence moving in on her, Maria Alvarez spun around, expecting her father. Her mouth opened ready to spit venom, then, as her head completed the ninety-degree turn, her eyes froze in shock as they met those of the handsome young boy who was staring at her with an absorbed, almost stunned expression. For a long, long moment, Paris Harcourt and Maria Alvarez did nothing but stare at one another. Then Paris managed a smile, nothing more than a bare movement of his lips. 'Hello,' he whispered.

Maria blinked, her mind grappling for a hold on reality. Something had happened. She was sure of it. But what? 'Hello,' she whispered back.

Vincent turned and looked up at the handsome face, frowning deeply. His small pudgy hand tugged at her dress as a child might tug on his mother's apron strings.

Maria looked down, focusing her eyes on Vincent with some difficulty. But the sight of his jealous face snapped her back to reality. She had a job to do, and she needed Vincent.

'*Señor.*' She nodded coolly at Paris, smiled brilliantly down at Vincent and then moved away, as regal as a queen.

Paris turned and stared after her, his eyes wide and pained, his thoughts chaotic. As he watched, her ugly companion condescendingly patted her hand, and he saw her smile at him vaguely, the meaning seemingly unmistakable.

Just another beautiful woman with another rich but ugly man.

Paris's young face suddenly tightened, and the eyes that followed her progress around the room were suddenly those of an adult. In a city like Monte Carlo, there were probably many such sights. It meant nothing. It was just a chance meeting — a little unpleasant, certainly disappointing, but nothing to get het up about.

He should just forget her. He knew that.

But he also knew that he wouldn't be able to.

CHAPTER 40

'Sir, I think you should see this.'

Wayne looked up from the ledgers in front of him, meeting the worried eyes of Antoine Dorlhac, the newest manager of the Droit de Seigneur. He was a small man with snapping brown eyes and a voice to match. At the moment he was hopping nervously from foot to foot. 'What is it?'

'A winner. A big winner. Every night for a week now.'

'Claude?'

Antoine Dorlhac shrugged. 'He says he cannot see how they are cheating.'

'What are they playing?'

'*Vingt-et-un.*'

Wayne shut the ledger with a snap. His mind was not really on the work anyway, but on the boy safely tucked away in his newly purchased residence at La Turbie. Since it appeared his son was determined to be difficult, his father's old villa had not been nearly secure enough, and the events of the last week were never far from Wayne's mind.

He wished Sebastien was there to help, and then was glad he wasn't. His manager said that Sebastien had received a call from a woman and had returned to London. Probably a secretary at one of the psychiatric hospitals. It was for the best. He couldn't explain it, but Wayne was sure that if Sebastien ever turned against him, it would mean the end.

Almost a week ago to the day, a team of doctors had been waiting for them on board the *Travis Helm*.

Shortly after, Wayne had gone to the radio room and ordered his team in Monaco to find him a house high in the hills with an outstanding security system. What kept people out would keep people in.

Wayne had had to pay almost double what the Villa du Soleil was worth but didn't care. His team had done wonders in the three days they had been allotted before Wayne took up residence, putting new, electrified gates into the twenty-five-foot wall and chopping down any trees that grew too near the walls and might be used in an escape bid. Wayne had approved the extra security cameras and doubled the guards patrolling the house.

Travis, wrapped in a quilt and seated in the back of the black limousine with his father, had watched the sliding electronic gates open in silence, his eyes seeking out and finding the cameras, the Dobermann dogs, the polite but armed guards. Wayne had expected him to say something sarcastic, but the boy had merely leaned back against the seat and closed his eyes. Wayne hoped the defeat that it signified was real, but he was not counting on it. He had the strongest feeling that Travis was only waiting to rebuild his strength before trying once again to escape him.

The boy couldn't seem to understand that he was *his*, Wayne's; that he had been stolen from him, his *true* father, by a lying bitch and her male whore. He had spent hours trying to tell him he wanted only the best for him, and was interested only in improving the standard of his life, but the boy was stubbornly silent, refusing even to talk except for a few truculent syllables . . .

'We're down twenty thousand and still losing,' Antoine Dorlhac said now as he followed the towering figure down the white-washed corridor, dragging Wayne's impatient thoughts back to the present. 'How long has it been going on?'

'An hour. Maybe a few minutes more.'

'What's the average size of his bet?'

'*Her* bet,' Antoine corrected grimly. 'A hundred to two hundred francs. Petty stuff. If she wasn't winning so consistently I'd swear she was an amateur. She doesn't have the confidence or the familiarity with the chips and cards of a true professional.' The little man shrugged. 'I cannot figure it out.'

'Her accomplice?'

Antoine snorted. 'Must be seen to be believed.' The low hum of voices, the clacking of dice and the whine of roulette wheels that percolated through the casino twenty-four hours a day became louder as Wayne stepped behind the curtain. 'Room four,' Antoine murmured, glancing around to make sure everything was in perfect order. It was. Managing the Droit de Seigneur was Antoine's biggest break to date, and he was determined not to blow it. Besides, there was something about his good-looking employer that scared him witless.

Wayne moved quickly but with unconscious grace through the rooms, his eyes scanning and taking in every detail around him. He saw but paid no particular attention to a fresh-faced young man, obviously an American, nor the girl with him, though she was startlingly pretty, with an elfin face, wide dark eyes and clinging silver dress.

Gemma nudged Paris in the ribs, making him spill his drink, but her eyes never left the man making his way through the room, stopping to chat here and there to a particularly favoured customer. His progression through the room made her think of a king and a receiving line. 'There he is,' she hissed unnecessarily, for his towering figure and copper hair were hardly inconspicuous. Paris looked at the hooded blue eyes and saw the cold ruthlessness.

Gemma looked and saw something she wanted. His height, the way he moved and wore the expensive white Saint Laurent suit as if born to it, made her palms itch. The blue eyes, meeting hers briefly and then moving on with just a flicker of sexual interest, was a challenge that made her mouth water. Even his age, the experience she knew he'd have, stirred her. She wondered what he looked like stripped, imagining him walking towards her, slowly removing the jacket, the shirt, bearing down on her . . . Gemma took a deep, shaky breath.

Meanwhile, Paris shivered. Suddenly he felt scared. Before, when D'Arville had been safely in New York, it had all seemed like a game. An exciting but hardly dangerous game. Now Paris felt outmatched, outclassed and outrageously nervous. 'Gem, let's go home, huh? Or let Mum and Dad know we're in town.'

'You can go home if you like,' Gemma said scornfully, giving him a long, level look. 'But I'm staying right here. I wonder where he's going.'

Paris watched her as she moved away, following in the wake of that leonine head. The silver lamé dress she wore was cut low at the back, and he could see her young spine swaying subtly as she moved. Paris sighed, and quickly followed her, his interest quickly veering away from that of his sister's impetuosity the moment he spied the woman at the blackjack table.

Paris felt the breath being squeezed out of him as he moved closer. There was quite a crowd around the table now, but Paris elbowed his way in without a qualm. He could hear the excited whispers around him only vaguely and guessed there must be a big winner at the table but couldn't have cared less about the gambling that lured so many people into a life of debt and ruin.

Instead his eyes were on her. She wore green tonight, a deep jade green that made her hair look as blue-green and glossy as a raven's wing. Green shadowed her lids, and picked up the tints in the emerald and diamond necklace she wore like a spider's web around her creamy throat. She looked up barely a moment later, her eyes finding his in the crowd, and he saw a flicker of expression shimmer in the tawny brown irises, making his spirits soar. He had not been imagining it! That tight sensation of awareness was the same as the night he had first seen her, over a week ago.

He'd been in a state of moody despair for days, convinced he'd never see her again. Gemma had given up on him in disgust, exploring the town on her own, getting invited to an inordinate number of parties. Some feat, since she was still a stranger in town.

Maria Alvarez felt her stomach begin to quiver as the boy called Paris Harcourt continued to stare at her; she'd found out his name and where he was staying the very next day after their first meeting. She'd been ready to scream in sheer frustration that first night on learning that her father was not even in the country, and she'd needed to do something to stop herself going mad. At least, that was the excuse she had given herself to justify her sleuthing spree.

She had even found out something about Paris's background. His father was a big-time hot-shot in Hollywood; she was sure she had even seen one of his films once. The girl by his side was beautiful, and if she had not known that she was his twin sister, Maria knew that jealousy would be eating into her even now.

'The next card's a two. Take it. We'll try for a five-card trick.'

The tiny voice in her ear snapped her thoughts back to the table, and reluctantly, feeling it to be an almost physical wrench, she tore her eyes away from the handsome face and indicated to the croupier to turn her another card over.

'Two of diamonds to *mademoiselle*, possible five-card trick. Dealer stands.' The two players on the right folded; an old colonel-type man opposite her took an eight and busted. 'The next card's a five. Take it,' Vincent's voice hissed in her ear. She took it and completed her trick. A small murmur of delight and admiration for her luck and daring rippled around the gathered crowd.

Her nails, painted a pearly pink, stacked her growing pile of chips. Paris stared at them, then looked back at her, realizing she was the one drawing the crowd.

Beauty and luck too. He felt a powerful punch of sexual awareness deep in his loins and took a steadying breath. He had lost his virginity at fourteen to his mother's masseuse, a tall Swedish girl with kind eyes and knowing hands. Since then he'd had a few steady girlfriends, but nothing had prepared him for this.

Maria glanced up, feeling his eyes burning into her, and her hands trembled in front of her on the green baize.

'There he is — behind the tall brunette with the fake pearls. See him?' Antoine whispered in Wayne's ear, and Wayne found himself looking at a tiny, ugly man with quick nervous eyes and an immobile expression that only came with intense concentration.

'What signal are they using?' he asked.

'We can't tell. Hand signals certainly — see how he keeps scratching his cheek? But no one can get near enough to him. Watch.' Antoine signalled René, one of the casino's 'watchers', dressed in a waiter's suit and carrying an empty tray. As he moved around, working his way behind the small man, Wayne saw the ugly creature spot him and slowly move around the table. René followed, a silent game of chase being played out in front of the unsuspecting crowd until Antoine ordered René off with the merest lift of his eyebrow.

'Interesting,' Wayne said, feeling the first stirrings of anger in his gut.

'It is more than that, Monsieur D'Arville. It is dangerous. I — none of us — can see how it is being done.'

Wayne moved closer, still standing at the back, watching the dwarfish man in his overlarge tuxedo. He'd already made up his mind the girl was just the mule, doing the work whilst the man was the brains behind it. Concentrating on the little man, trying to figure out how the scratching fingers conveyed to the girl whether to pass or not, it took a few seconds for the warning alarms to sound in his head, but slowly his skin began to crawl, telling him that he was being watched. Wayne let his eyes wander around the room. All eyes were on the game, except for those of the young American girl, whose dark eyes met his boldly. Wayne's eyes narrowed on her, then passed on, recognizing the hot look, but also knowing it was not the one making his spine shiver.

Gemma's heart began to thump with a painful, wonderful power.

Finally Wayne looked to the table, confident that no one in the audience was giving him the trouble. Maria Alvarez felt the exact moment the eyes dropped on to her face, like vampirish worms burrowing into her soul, and she forced herself not to shiver. This man, this . . . monster was her father. The thought was so repellent that it made her feel nauseous, and her chin came up as she stared him down. Wayne was mildly surprised by the force of the venom in the eyes, but Maria was aware that there was not even a flicker of recognition in the assessing gaze he gave her.

'Monsieur?' Antoine prompted.

'Give Jean-Luc the nod.'

Antoine smiled happily and met the eyes of the croupier, not even needing to move his head. Jean-Luc, sociology student by day, croupier and ladies' man by night, palmed the cards expertly. Maria saw the queen of hearts that Vincent promised her turn into a five of diamonds and frowned. In her ear, she heard Vincent swear. 'It was the queen. I know it was.'

She lost the hand, and three thousand francs. She lost the next hand too, but by then she knew what was going on. Her eyes shot daggers at the handsome croupier, who gazed back at her with placid, innocent eyes.

Slowly she rose to her feet, collected her chips and turned away, ignoring the disappointed murmurs all around her, not feeling sufficiently in charge of her emotions to meet her father's no doubt crowing and triumphant gaze. She made her way slowly to the grille, where she exchanged her chips for cash.

'I don't understand what went wrong,' Vincent's whining voice complained in her ear, and she turned, looking around to find him. He was standing behind a huge umbrella plant, and she moved slowly past it, not looking at him but murmuring loud enough for him to hear her.

'I do. He ordered the damned croupier to deal from the bottom of the pack.'

Vincent watched her walk away towards the cloakroom with sad eyes. He had done his best. He could not be expected to deal with cheats, after all. They never cheated at the institute. Suddenly Vincent felt very homesick. He turned away sadly, knowing they would meet back at the hotel and discuss strategy. But Vincent, much as he admired and feared her determination and intelligence, could not see how even she could do anything about this.

Maria didn't see how she could either. As she handed over her ticket and waited impatiently for her stole, she fought against the urge to go back, march into his office and claw his eyes out. The bastard had not even recognized her — his own daughter. She would make him pay. Oh, he would squirm . . .

'You're not thinking of going out alone with all that cash, I hope?'

She spun around at the sound of the voice, looking up into caressing dark eyes, for the first time in her young life knowing what it was to actually *want* a man. Not need a man. Not be grateful to a man. But *want* a man. Panicking just a little, she managed a cool shrug. 'I can take a taxi.'

'So can I. Why don't we share one?' Paris smoothly took the mink stole from the checkout woman, who nodded and turned discreetly away. He settled it lovingly across her shoulders with hands that shook, not sure what he'd do if she said no.

Maria did not say no.

In the taxi she sat nervously pleating her dress with her fingers, aware of their arms pressed together, their mutual body heat warming them, speaking all the words they could not say themselves.

At the hotel Paris watched her hand over the cash to go in the safe and then turned and walked with her to the lift. Maria did not know what to say. For the first time ever, she was not with a man for what she could get out of it.

At the door, Paris took the key from her unresisting fingers and followed her inside the dark room, locking the door behind him. She made no move to put on the light, but after a few moments their eyes became accustomed to the dark.

'What's your name?' Paris whispered.

'Maria. Maria Alvarez.'

Paris reached for her, drawing her into his arms where she fitted snugly against him. 'I love you, Maria Alvarez,' he murmured, then lowered his head to kiss her. It should have sounded ridiculous, of course — he was a young man, and, since they'd hardly met, the line was corny.

But it was not ridiculous, because Paris meant it.

And Maria knew he meant it.

Her lips were like padded, perfumed velvet under his mouth, and his arms tightened compulsively around her. Maria forgot the frustration of the night and determinedly pushed aside thoughts of what she was going to do next. She felt herself moving backwards and gasped as Paris lowered his head and sucked her nipple through the green silk of her dress. Her knees threatened to buckle and she gulped in a great gasp of air.

Paris lifted her, moving to the bed and falling across it with Maria beneath him, taking his weight on his elbows. Maria arched her back, feeling the strong pressure of his thighs against hers, her thoughts becoming hazy. So this was desire. Real, honest desire.

Paris began to undress her, clumsy in his urgency, but Maria did not care, not even when she heard the expensive gown tear as the zip got stuck. Paris kissed her exposed neck, throat, shoulders and ears, working his way down her sternum to her bare breasts, where the rosy nipples stood straining to attention, eagerly awaiting his smooth, warm, wet tongue. Maria buried her hands in his clean, silky hair, her neck falling back, her eyes staring at the blank ceiling. Only her occasional gasp or moan and Paris's muffled words of encouragement and adoration filled the room with sound.

516

Her legs jerked in helpless reaction as his fingers curled around her calves before pulling off her shoes and panties. Impatiently he shrugged out of the tuxedo, letting the expensive clothes lie where they fell.

Maria felt the soft hairs on his chest scrape across her belly as he moved lower down her body, dipping his tongue into her navel, making her knees jack-knife in reaction. Her arms came above her head and grasped the antique wooden headpiece as he firmly pushed her thighs apart and nibbled on her engorged clitoris.

Carlos had never done anything remotely like this to her. His caresses had been practised, carried out expertly under the covers, and were always over in minutes.

Already she felt as if this slow, painstaking exploration of her body had been going on for tormenting hours. She jerked and thrashed on the bed as the first climax of her life hit her, rippling waves through her belly, turning her knees, her arms, her brain to water. She was gasping, almost sobbing as Paris moved gently to lie atop her, taking her chin in his hand and kissing her deeply.

As his tongue delved deep into her mouth, so he thrust deeply inside her, feeling her body convulse around him. Maria almost screamed. Carlos had felt nothing like this inside her. Paris seemed to reach all the way to her womb, his hot velvet shaft spearing deep into her, thrusting, plunging, making her want to buck off the bed. Instead she wrapped her legs around his hips, her heels digging into the whiter flesh of his buttocks, her actions allowing him an even deeper penetration into her body. He took advantage of it immediately, of course, their young, sweating bodies beginning to strain and buck in a wild, seemingly uncoordinated rhythm that brought ecstasy crashing through their veins minutes later, flashing light across their vision, their fused mouths filling with the silent crescendo of each other's cries.

Beyond a sensation of almost tormenting ecstasy, Maria was aware of his collapsing weight pinning her to the bed with satisfactory heaviness, and above the sound of her own laboured breathing and happy sobs she heard him moan. It was a long, long time later that they began to talk.

'You were doing well at the casino tonight,' Paris complimented her, feeling a little shy now, and choosing what he thought was a neutral subject. 'Are you always that lucky?' He was lying beside her, running his finger lightly over her forehead, down her nose and then outlining the shape of her lips.

'I wish!' she sighed, her eyelids fluttering closed as his fingers travelled on past her neck and began to turn in ever decreasing circles around her breasts until they were gently nipping her nipples. 'Vincent was telling me what to do.'

'Vincent?'

'Mm. The little man I was with. He's a psychic. You know? He could tell which cards were going to come out before the croupier turned them over.'

Paris stopped his caresses and stared at her. 'Are you kidding me?'

Maria smiled. 'No. How else do you think I won?'

'What went wrong towards the end?' he asked, not sure yet whether he believed the outrageous story. Briefly Maria told him her theories and Paris shrugged. 'That's easily solved. Just go to another casino.'

'Uh-uh.' She shook her head so hard that her hair splayed across his cheek, and a firm scowl settled across her satiated, softened face. 'It has to be the Droit de Seigneur. I want to break *him*, not the casino.'

'Him?'

'Wayne D'Arville.'

Paris looked away quickly, his eyes thoughtful. His voice was almost a whisper when he said, 'What do you have against him?'

Maria slowly expelled her breath, fighting a brief battle inside herself. On the one hand it was crazy to give away her plans to a stranger. But on the other hand, with the afterglow of her climax still rippling in her body, the comfort and closeness of lying in his arms gave her a nagging urge to tell him everything.

Trust won out over cynicism. 'He's my father,' she said simply, and turned to find the dark, caressing eyes looking at her oddly. Surprisingly they were not accusatory, just puzzled and questioning.

'What did he do to you?'

It took her an hour to relate her life history, and she found it both therapeutic and cleansing to talk, glorying at the intimacy possible only between lovers. She had a man of her own now — a real lover to talk to in the early-morning hours, to love and lie beside for the rest of her life. The thought made her glow deep inside.

When she had finished he was silent for a long while. Finally, she turned to him and said, a question in her voice, 'You don't seem surprised.'

Paris took only a few minutes to explain the reason they were there. Maria gasped as she heard about her grandfather — a concentration camp *commandant*. It left her feeling oddly disorientated. She hadn't thought *anybody* could be worse than Wayne. Now she knew where her father had inherited his treachery and cruelty.

It was four o'clock in the morning before they were talked out, both knowing every intimate detail their partner could think of about childhood, home life, country, customs, personal favourites and ideals. Knowing her favourite colour was pink, his orange, they were free to discuss other topics. Such as what Maria could do about her plan now.

She sighed dejectedly in the darkness. 'I don't see what we can do. Vince can't help if they change the cards at the last second.'

Paris looked up at the ceiling, a thought formulating in his brain, and he slowly began to smile. 'You're wrong, you know,' he said softly. 'There *is* something we can do. Or rather, something the Gambling Commission can do.'

* * *

The next night they were back. Antoine called in Wayne immediately. The scene was almost an exact repeat of the night before, with the same crowd clustering around the same table. Except that now there was an extra spectator at the forefront, dressed inconspicuously in a dark suit. Only Antoine and the croupiers noticed him, and it was Antoine's dubious privilege to point him out to Wayne and explain the trouble the man's presence was causing them.

Wayne listened in tight-lipped frustration to Antoine's words, then glanced at the Gambling Commission agent and frowned. The girl was winning heavily, and there was not a damned thing he could do about it. Any misdeal by the croupier would be spotted immediately by the Gambling Commission expert, resulting in a heavy fine, maybe even a revoked licence.

Monte Carlo was proud of its 'honest' games. It gave Wayne no satisfaction at all to realize that the Commission's man could no more make out how the girl was winning than he could. 'When she's finished, have her come to my office. Keep closing the tables, and limit the bets to a hundred francs,' he ordered, leaving abruptly.

Antoine bowed and watched the tall Frenchman leave. He didn't blame him. It was a painful thing to watch.

* * *

By one-thirty Maria was willing to call it a night. She knew it would take her another week at least to break the casino, but so long as the Commission agent stayed with her she was safe from Wayne's cheating. She knew the tall pock-marked man was itching to find out how she was doing it and knew that that alone would have him coming back tomorrow, allowing her to win another six hundred thousand dollars, unimpeded by her father's cheating dealers.

She walked to the barred grille to cash in her chips, stiffening as two men materialized either side of her. Paris, waiting by the door, quickly walked forward, but Maria herself waved him away. He watched, feeling cold and scared, as she disappeared behind a curtain that led to the offices.

Wayne looked up at the knock, nodded to the two security men to leave, and waved a hand at a chair. 'Sit down, Miss . . . ?'

Maria sat. She was wearing burgundy tonight, shot through with silver. Platinum and diamonds sparkled at her wrists and throat. Wayne looked her over, a disinterested part of his brain telling him that she was truly beautiful, while another part wondered how much he'd have to pay her off.

'Cigarette?'

She shook her head, her eyes glittering with satisfaction as he leaned back in his chair. She had him! She had him now! The glory of it made her want to leap up and dance around the room.

Wayne saw the glow banked deep in the eyes and slowly straightened. This was personal. Suddenly he knew it, though he couldn't see how, and on top of that thought came another realization. He had seen her before. He knew he had. He frowned, scraping through his memory without success. 'Tell me, Miss . . .' Again Maria remained stubbornly mute. 'Just how much is it going to cost me to have you go elsewhere?'

He reached into his desk where he withdrew a small strongbox. He opened it up with quick, precise movements, and turned it around, so that she could see the notes stacked inside.

Maria slowly leaned back and allowed herself a brief, ironic laugh. 'There's not enough money in this world that'll make me back off,' she warned him, slowly straightening her spine so that she was ramrod-straight in the chair, her face pinched into a tight, vengeful mask. Even so, she realized that he looked more amused and curious than worried.

'I intend to come back . . .' she said softly '. . . night after night . . .' she enunciated each word clearly '. . . until I've broken this bank . . .' she slowly stood up '. . . this casino . . .' she leaned across the desk, her breasts rising and falling with every panting breath she took '. . . and you . . . *Father.*'

Wayne's face froze into immobility at that last word. In a tidal wave, memory returned. 'Maria,' he said softly.

Maria tossed back her waving mane of black hair and walked to the door where she paused with her hand on the door handle, staring at the handsome man as still as a statue behind the imposing desk.

'See you tomorrow night for another half-million, Daddy dearest!'

CHAPTER 41

Gemma checked her appearance as she passed the seven-foot mirror that graced the reception hall of the Chemin de Fer, the hottest restaurant in town. Then she glanced into the dimly lit interior, where candles and ornate silver wall-lamps were the only providers of light. She ignored the elegant man standing behind a podium, checking her reservation. Instead her eyes turned again to the huge mirror, just to make sure she looked perfect. Tonight was the night — she could feel it in her bones. She'd dined at the restaurant three times so far, knowing that sooner or later he'd come. Everyone came to the Chemin de Fer eventually.

Her reflection reassured her that she did indeed look perfect. The dress was sleeveless, strapless, backless and almost frontless. Only two scarlet diagonal swathes cut across her breasts, revealing the sides of two perfect white orbs before meeting in a diamond cut at her tiny waist. From there, accordion pleats fell to the ground with seemingly out-of-place modesty, the cleverness of the design only becoming apparent when she walked, for then side splits at both thighs revealed practically all of her legs. The dress came with matching scarlet panties and was one of Valentine's latest designs. She hoped the man recovered soon — no one could design drop-dead-gorgeous gowns like Valentine. The last she'd heard, he and his wife were 'improving' in hospital, so it looked hopeful. To do the gown justice, she wore three-inch-high silver shoes, and rubies glittered in her ears and in a silver choker at her throat. Silver eyeshadow and evening bag completed the look, along with deep ruby-red lips and dark, penetrating eyes. Yes. Tonight had to be the night.

'You have your . . . usual table, *mademoiselle*.' The concierge finally condescended to admit her, and Gemma almost laughed aloud, so obvious was his disapproval of a lady dining alone. Well, to hell with him, and to all the rest of the sheep. She was her own woman, and if she wanted to eat alone she would. Besides, Paris was too busy with his latest little pet to accompany her. Gemma frowned as she walked into the room. There was something about this Spanish girl that was different. She could sense it when she saw them together. Paris had introduced her yesterday morning, and Gemma detected a nervousness in the girl that was unexpected. She was overly anxious to be friendly, needing too much for Gemma to like her. And as for Paris . . . he looked as if he'd been hit by an express train. Could it be love?

Her thoughts suddenly jerked to a halt, her body almost following suit. There, at the best table of the house, Wayne D'Arville was reading a menu. Her eyes made a quick inventory of the woman sitting next to him. Tall, blonde, slender. Gemma smiled. The hair was bleached, the nails and breasts were false and the body was like a beanpole. No match for her.

'*Mademoiselle?*' the waiter prompted her. Gemma gave him a short, sharp look, then left the man open-mouthed as she moved away from her paltry table tucked into a dark corner near the kitchen, and headed for the centre table stood on a small dais. Wayne caught a glimpse of dazzling scarlet out of the corner of his eye and looked around. Gemma felt the blue irises contract slightly and shivered as he watched her approach. His hair, in the candle and lamplight, gleamed like copper, and the dark shadows deepened his cheeks and the planes of his face. His eyes glittered.

'Mr D'Arville,' Gemma said, ignoring the blonde completely and holding out her hand. Wayne rose, Gemma's head falling back and back until he'd reached his full height. Wayne took her hand, kissing it continental-style. Gemma's lips parted to allow her to hiss in a harsh breath. Wayne felt her hand tremble and, still bending over her fingers, lifted his eyes to hers. He was amused by her boldness, intrigued by her dark, youthful beauty, and knew she'd probably had the restaurant staked out for weeks. 'Enchanted, Miss . . . ?'

'Harcourt,' Gemma said, her left eyebrow raising in a challenging stare. 'Gemma Harcourt.'

Wayne recognized the name immediately, of course, as she knew he would, and his own eyes became less bland and much, much more interested. Gemma saw his lips twitch with something that could have been amusement or annoyance, she couldn't decide which.

'Ah,' he said softly, straightening again, not taking his eyes off her for a moment. 'I see.'

Gemma gave a delicious shudder. 'Aren't you going to invite me to join you for dinner?'

Wayne glanced at the blonde . . . what was her name . . . Frida, Frederika? She was glowering like a bad actress and Wayne gave a Gallic shrug and turned back to Gemma. 'Alas, as you can see, I am already entertaining.'

Gemma turned to glance at the blonde woman dressed in powder-blue. Insipid. Unimportant. The words were in her eyes as she turned back to Wayne, who had to agree with her. This firebrand of an American was distracting, if nothing else. 'Tell her to go,' Gemma said simply.

Wayne slowly smiled, turned to the blonde and said, 'Frida. Would you like to go?' The blonde blushed an ugly red, picked up her silk evening purse and stalked off without another word.

'Well?' Gemma prompted.

Wayne held out the chair for her, giving the waiter a brief, dismissive nod. Gemma held the menu in front of her face and took several deep gulps. She stared at the white card

525

for a long, long while, making him wait, and only when she sensed a waiter's renewed presence did she lower it. 'I'll have the *carre d'agneau de Sisteron.*'

The waiter inclined his head and glanced at Wayne. 'I'll have the same.'

The waiter left. 'We're being stared at,' Gemma said.

'I'm not surprised,' he agreed mildly, his face deadpan. Gemma began to laugh, slowly at first, and then threw her head back and laughed in earnest. Wayne watched her, his eyes hooded. How young. How beautiful. How naive. How sure of herself. How stupid.

Wayne said nothing as the food approached, his eyes glancing towards the clock. It was nearly ten. It should be happening any minute now. He turned his eyes back towards Gemma Harcourt, the irony of the situation amusing him enormously. That he should be sitting here, pursued by one Harcourt twin, while, miles away, his long arm was reaching out for her brother . . .

As Gemma flirted and tantalized, he began to smile.

* * *

Paris was whistling as he made his way to the exit of his hotel. He had wanted to move to the Beach Plaza Tower to be nearer to her, but Maria was against it. She was touchingly old-fashioned in many of her ways. He'd promised her faithfully that he'd introduce her to his parents the very next day after Wayne D'Arville disappeared down the drain of bankruptcy.

His daydreams were so pleasant, he didn't realize he was being watched.

Outside two men waited in a car, a third beside the hotel door. Seeing Paris in the foyer walking towards the swing doors, the third man nodded briefly at the parked car. The driver remained where he was, but the passenger, a big, heavy-set man with hooded grey eyes and hands like melons, left the car and began to stagger towards the door. He was singing something in French. Paris stepped on to the pavement and looked around for a cab, grinning as a drunk stumbled against the kerb. He couldn't understand the words of the song, but the jaunty tune and some of the man's hand gestures made guessing easy. The drunk tripped over his own feet and lurched towards Paris, who caught him, more to save himself from being knocked down than anything else. 'Hey, buddy. Take more water with it next time, huh?'

The big man gazed up at him, bleary-eyed. Just then a car pulled in across the street, and the driver leaned out, calling out, 'Claude,' and waving his hand. Paris glanced at the car and shook his head.

'Come on, buddy. Over here. I hope your friend's in a better state to drive than you are.'

Behind him the third man left the shadows and walked up behind Paris. The driver opened the backseat door, still gabbling in French and wearing a helpless grin. Paris manoeuvred the drunk with surprising ease, considering his weight and state. Suddenly, just as he was pushing the man on to the back seat, he felt a shove in the middle of his own back. He grunted, falling forward into the car, where the drunk suddenly straightened, clamping a firm hand over Paris's startled face, cutting off his shout of surprise. Off balance and off-guard, Paris found himself falling over the man's lap. Behind him a third man got in, shoved his legs aside and slammed the door as the car accelerated away with a squeal of tyres.

* * *

Gemma felt her tongue and cheeks turn icy cold as the lemon sorbet she had ordered numbed her face. It was delicious — tangy, freezing and refreshing. Wayne poured her a fourth glass of wine. 'Brandy?' he asked, and Gemma leaned back in her chair, twirling her long-stemmed black champagne glass.

'I'd love some.' She waited until he'd imperiously flicked his hand for a waiter and then added, 'At your place.'

He smiled and rose. 'Whatever you say.' He didn't bother to pay the bill. He had an accountant who paid his bar and restaurant bills at the end of every month, including generous tips. Gemma gave him her hand, which he held with ironic patience as she stepped down off the dais. She could hear the whispers behind her as every table they passed began to hum with yet another discussion of the spectacle.

Gemma felt as if she were walking on air. Outside, the bus boy drove up in Wayne's Ferrari, which was midnight-blue. Wayne seated her in the bucket seat of cream leather and tipped the boy. His own seat had been modified to accommodate his height, she noticed. The engine started with a powerful roar and then softened to an idle, almost contemptuous purr. Wayne glanced at her, then at his watch. 'I have to make a stop at the casino. If I give you ten thousand pounds' worth of chips, do you think you could entertain yourself for a few minutes?'

Gemma gave him a sharp glance. 'Oh, I can do a lot of things by myself,' she assured him. 'But it's more fun with two.' This time she had succeeded in shocking him, she realized with a great wave of delight as he turned his head quickly towards her, the blue eyes wide and surprised. Then it was his turn to throw back his head and laugh.

* * *

At the casino, Maria looked around, even as she played her hand and won another four thousand. Where was he? Paris was supposed to meet her before they began playing. Only Vincent, anxious to get on with it, had insisted they start without him. 'The lady wins. *Mesdames, messieurs, faites vos jeux.*' Maria glanced at the Commission man, who was wearing his usual puzzled, frustrated frown, and then at her watch. Paris was over an hour late. It was not like him. She stiffened as she saw her father walk in. Her eyes flew to Gemma by his side, her eyes questioning. Was Paris's sister pursuing some private idea for revenge on her own? Perhaps she was out to avenge her grandfather, Duncan Somerville. Perhaps Paris was helping *her* tonight? Yes, that must be it. Maria slowly relaxed, only to stiffen again as she found her father making his way purposefully towards her. Gemma watched, only vaguely interested, and placed her first bet. Wayne leaned forward and whispered into Maria's ear. She glanced at him, then gave a short nod to the Commission man and left the table.

Vincent, from his position behind a Grecian column, hopped nervously from foot to foot.

'Make it quick, Daddy dearest,' Maria said a few moments later, leaning against the door to his office, watching warily as he walked across the room to sit behind his desk and lift the phone. Quickly he punched out the numbers.

'Is it done?' he asked. He listened for a brief moment, then hung up. Slowly he leaned back in his chair and looked at her. She was dressed in white tonight, and the contrast with her long dark hair and red lips was stunning. 'I made a mistake about you,' Wayne murmured thoughtfully. 'When I saw you in that sweat shop, I thought . . .'

Maria smiled grimly. 'I know what you thought,' she spat out, the old familiar pain of rejection making her eyes glitter with tears.

'Not that it matters,' he carried on, his tone still conversational. 'But how did you manage the transformation?'

'I thought you had something important to say,' she snapped. She was in no mood for a trip down Memory Lane. 'I wish you'd hurry. I still have a hundred and fifty thousand more francs to win before calling it a night.'

Wayne leaned further back in his chair and folded his hands behind his head. 'That's what we need to talk about. You've done well, Maria, I'll grant you that. I'm impressed, and I apologize for not seeing your potential before. And if you want to, you can stay on in Monte Carlo and we can get to know one another better. But the time has come for you to take your little man and whatever extraordinary system you have, and inflict it on someone else.'

Maria sneered out a laugh. 'Save your phony apologies,' she scoffed. 'You think I'm going to let you off the hook just because you're suddenly so magnanimous? Hah!' She tossed her head, standing with her hands on her hips. 'I'm staying, and I'm bleeding you dry.'

Wayne watched her, almost smiling. She was magnificent. A pity her mother had not had more of the same spirit. Yes, things were looking up. Not only did he have a worthy son, but also a daughter worth acknowledging.

'I'm going to destroy you, Father,' Maria said, her hand on the door handle.

'I don't think so, Maria,' Wayne said softly, almost regretfully.

'Nothing will make me stop,' she warned him, but her voice did not hold quite the same conviction as it had before.

'Won't it?' he queried softly. 'Not even the life of Paris Harcourt, Maria. Won't that stop you?'

Maria went white, her eyes rounding into dark pools of pain. She sagged against the door as Wayne slowly walked towards her. She began to shake her head. 'No. No.'

Wayne slowly reached out and brushed a few strands of raven-black hair from her face, his voice still the same gentle, regretful tone as before. 'I have your American lover,' he said softly, looking down into her dazed brown eyes. 'I'll kill him, Maria,' he continued, sounding almost friendly now. Maria moaned, and turned her face into the door, her bare shoulders shaking uncontrollably. Satisfied, Wayne turned and walked back to his desk.

'Send your little man packing,' he ordered, his voice crisp and business-like now. Maria slowly turned around and stared at him, defeat in the slump of her shoulders. 'And return all the money you've won to me. Will you be broke then?' Numbly she shook her head. 'It wouldn't matter if you were. I'll buy you a villa here in town — or would you prefer an apartment? Never mind.' He jotted something down on a notepad as Maria continued to stare at him speechlessly. Wayne glanced up, and slowly smiled. When would his children ever learn that they couldn't fight him and win? Travis was still being difficult. Only last night he'd tried to escape the villa by hiding in the back of a laundry truck.

'Get to it, Maria,' he prompted softly. 'I want the little man gone by tomorrow — daughter dearest.' He saw her back stiffen at his final parting shot, but she didn't turn around. Instead she walked stiffly out of the door like a disjointed doll and closed it quietly behind her.

Gemma looked up from the bouncing white ball, on which rode the last of her chips, and promptly forgot about the roulette wheel. Maria looked awful — dazed even. She left the table and intercepted the Spanish girl, who let herself be led to a quiet corner. 'What's wrong? You look like death warmed up.' Gemma stared at her. She was shaking and breathing in short, sharp jerks. 'You're not going to faint, are you?'

Maria shook her head. 'No. No . . . I . . . have things to do. Oh, God, he wouldn't really kill Paris, would he?'

Gemma's mouth fell open. 'Kill Paris? Who? What are you talking about?' Her voice was sharp, and she had to resist the urge to shake the Spanish girl by the shoulders.

'My father,' Maria said listlessly. 'He says he has Paris. And I believe him. I have to stop winning or he says he'll kill him.'

Gemma frowned. 'Who's your father? And what has your winning streak got to do with anything?'

Maria slowly raised her head and looked at Gemma with hopeless eyes, crammed with terror. 'He—' she tossed her head in the direction of the offices '—is my father. I came here to deliberately break the bank. Oh, it's too complicated to explain now. Paris was helping me. My father says he's got Paris. He'll kill him if I don't stop. I must stop. I must find Vincent and tell him to leave. Excuse me.'

Gemma watched the girl get up and walk across to where an ugly little man awaited her approach nervously. They talked for several minutes, but Gemma was already on her way to the payphone, where she rang the hotel. The clerk told her Paris had left two hours ago for the casino. Gemma hung up and looked around, but already knew that her brother wasn't there. She quickly marched towards the offices. A man moved to block her path, took one look at her face, grinned and let her pass. He had noticed his boss enter the room with her earlier, and as he heard her clacking heels recede down the corridor, he vaguely wondered what was eating her.

Wayne looked up as the door was flung open, then smiled as she slammed the door behind her. 'Where's my brother, you bastard!'

Wayne spread his hands as he got up. 'I assure you I'm not a bastard. My parents were legally married.'

'If you don't tell me right now,' she gritted, her cheeks high with furious colour, 'I'm going to call the cops.'

'And tell them what? That I . . .' he spread his hands with innocent shock '. . . a wealthy and respected businessman, have kidnapped some upstart little American?' He laughed and shook his head. 'I don't think so, do you? Now . . .' His face changed in a shocking instant from laughing mockery to savage coldness. 'How about that brandy you wanted?'

'Brandy?' Gemma echoed, then gave a brief cry as he suddenly lunged for her. She staggered backwards, falling on to the huge, overstuffed black settee behind her. Her eyes were wide and disbelieving as he stood over her, his hands already shrugging off his jacket and undoing the buttons of his shirt.

'No!' she screamed, struggling to sit up, but with one hand on her sternum he easily pushed her back, his hand fumbling now with the zip to his trousers. His eyes were like blue diamonds — hard and without feeling — and Gemma felt the first waves of numbing shock begin to wash over her. This wasn't true. It couldn't be happening. Not to her! 'I'll scream,' she whispered as he knelt over her, but he only shrugged, fumbling to free himself from the trousers.

'Scream all you like,' he offered carelessly. 'No one will hear you out there. And no one will be allowed to interfere with us even if they do.'

Gemma rammed her hand upwards, trying to hit his face, but her reach was too short. She gasped, and then began to struggle furiously as his hands pulled down the scarlet silk of her panties. 'No. *No!*' She felt her legs being pulled apart, and struck out wildly, her clenched fists glancing a harmless blow off the solid muscle of his shoulder. He leaned over her, yanking her hands together and holding them in a tight, numbing grip. She was going to be raped! The thought hit her like a cold tidal wave of drowning water. The fear, the revulsion, was something she had never felt before.

With a cry of utter panic, she raised her knee. Luck was on her side. Her timing turned out to be perfect.

Wayne grunted and turned red in the face as her knee connected with his groin. Still panicking, Gemma shoved him aside, but he was too big to move. Scrabbling frantically, she wriggled under him, biting his hand hard as he reached for her.

Then she was sprinting for the door, pulling her panties back up into place. She rushed from the casino, uncaring of the spectacle she must have made. She hailed the first taxi she could find, and only then, in the back seat, did the numbing fear begin to recede. But she knew the memory of it would stay with her forever.

Back in the casino, Wayne slowly recovered and straightened his own clothing. So the bitch had been lucky. He shrugged. He had more important things to think about. He wanted to get back to Travis. They were going to reach an understanding sooner or later, even if it killed them both.

* * *

Safe in her hotel room, Gemma nevertheless checked the lock. She had to think. Paris was in danger. No matter about her; she was all right. She'd nearly been raped, but she was alive. It was Paris who needed her. She went straight for the phone, asking for the number of the hotel where she'd discovered her parents were staying and asked to be put through to their room.

'Hello?'

'Daddy.'

'Gemma?'

'Daddy.' She was crying uncontrollably now, the sound of his voice breaking down her precarious calm.

'Gemma! Gemma, what is it? What's going on?' He was shouting now. Suddenly her mother's voice came over the line. The sound of the soft, drawling southern accent, so soothing and familiar, calmed her once more.

'Gemma, honey,' Oriel coaxed. 'What is it? Tell us, sweetheart.'

'P-P-Paris,' she stammered, wiping her eyes furiously with her fingers. 'Paris,' she said again. 'Something t-terrible's happened.'

'Oh, God.' That was her father's voice again. 'There's been an accident? Swimming, or something else?' For a moment Gemma was totally confused, and then remembered that her parents still thought they were at home.

'No. We're here in M-Monte Carlo.'

'What?! What are you doing here? No, never mind. Just tell us what's happened to Paris.' Kier sounded grim and angry, and Gemma began to shake.

'He's g-gone.'

'Gone?' The word came from her mother, whispered in a tone of such utter despair that Gemma realized immediately that Oriel had misunderstood.

'No, not d-dead,' she almost screamed. 'Gone. Kidnapped. By Wayne D'Arville.' Haltingly, she managed to get out the whole story and give them the name of their hotel.

'Gemma, honey, listen to me.' Her mother's voice came back a few moments later and she knew that her parents had been discussing strategy away from the phone. 'I want you to stay where you are. We'll come over to you. Understand?'

'Yes.'

'Good. Lock yourself in. Your father and I will be there as soon as we can. We're leaving now, right now. Do you understand me, Gem?'

'Yes,' Gemma said again and hung up abruptly. She must have a bath. She felt so dirty.

CHAPTER 42

Sebastien looked up, his eyes softening as Lilas walked towards him, wrapped only in a very see-through white peignoir. 'Here you go.' She put down a cup of steaming coffee in front of him. 'Don't say I don't know how to treat you right first thing in the morning.' She winked at him as she turned and headed for the bathroom. Seb laughed softly and sipped his coffee, his eye straying to the big brown envelope that had arrived with the morning post. He opened his other correspondence first. He knew what was in the big envelope and felt oddly reluctant to open it. His other mail consisted of two invitations to speak at functions, one an offer to become chairman of a fund-raising committee to finance a new wing of a psychiatric hospital. There was a sad letter from an ex-patient, a few hate letters threatening to kill him in any number of ways, a letter from his mother and the telephone bill.

He stacked them in order and finished his coffee. Only then did he finally reach for the hefty envelope and slit it open, pulling out week-old copies of New York papers, ignoring all but the reports on the Valentine story.

What he read did not make sense.

He had never met Valentine Copeland in person, but Veronica had written every now and then, and through those letters Sebastien felt he knew nearly as much about Valentine Copeland as he would if he'd actually been treating the man in person.

The story about attempted arson in order to defraud the insurance companies had finally been dropped due to lack of evidence. Valentine Inc. had no financial worries — it was, in fact, a very profitable company. Which meant someone else had to have set the fires — since the fire department was sure that the fire *had* been deliberately set.

Sebastien began to frown, and search through the papers more rapidly. They made absolutely no mention of Travis. How was he coping with all this? Why had the boy not replied to his letters, offering help? Sebastien had even suggested Travis come to London and stay with him for a few weeks or months, until things had settled down. It was possible, he supposed, that the boy had gone into hiding to escape the press, but surely someone would have forwarded his letters to him?

Sebastien sighed and leaned back in his chair. Something was wrong. He could feel it. And as usual he knew its source. Sebastien ran his hand across his forehead, feeling suddenly tired. He was not yet forty-five, but he felt ancient. In the doorway, Lilas stopped, her cheery words drying on her lips.

She saw the newspapers, and knew they had something to do with Wayne D'Arville. Whenever Seb got that strange, suffering look, it had to do with D'Arville.

Her lips thinned.

Sebastien knew that over the years he had helped many people, perhaps more than most psychiatrists had managed, but it was not enough. Not enough to stop feeling guilty for all the ones that got away. And all his failures in his never-ending battle against pain and suffering seemed to personify into one man — Wayne D'Arville.

His recent failure in Monte Carlo, which had so nearly been the triumphant breakthrough he'd been waiting for all these years, had only added to the growing feeling of hopelessness.

And now this. The fire. Travis missing. Veronica — that lovely, loving, warm woman, still in hospital, along with her husband. They were out of intensive care now, but still not up to receiving the press or any other visitors. And he knew who was responsible.

'Wayne,' Sebastien said, the word a cry of pain, of pity, of anger. 'Wayne, what have you done?'

In the doorway, Lilas made a sound, and he looked up. He forced a smile to his face. 'Hi, darling. Just in time to make me some toast,' he teased.

Lilas nodded. 'Sure thing, honey bunch.' And after she'd made his toast, she was going to arrange a flight to Monte Carlo. It was time she had a word with the man who was making her lover's life a misery.

* * *

It was a long day. Sebastien knew he had to go back to Monte Carlo; he could sense that things were coming to a head. But he had a crisis in the afternoon with one of his paranoid schizophrenics threatening imminent suicide, and he was not sure he would make the airport on time. He did so, but with only minutes to spare.

The girl at the BA flight desk was annoyed, but only for a few seconds. His totally sincere apology, gentle smile and sherry eyes crinkled at the corners had her practically escorting him on to the plane.

Sebastien shook his head to the stewardess's offer of a meal, but accepted a tiny bottle of Scotch, which he sipped neat. Something was troubling him, and for a while he couldn't pin it down. All around him were chattering and excited holidaymakers or bored businessmen. The aircraft was soon descending again. His ears popped, the Scotch warmed him but he had a strange feeling of displacement. If he'd believed in that sort of thing, he might think that he was having a premonition of doom. He felt cold, but he knew it was not a physical thing — he wasn't catching a chill. He just knew, in his gut, that something awful was going to happen. And he was scared. He was also almost asleep. Fear and sleep didn't mix. Or it shouldn't.

Sebastien shook his head. He was in trouble. Wayne was in trouble. And the closer he got to Monaco, the more uneasy he felt.

'We're landing, sir. Please do up your seatbelt.'

Sebastien glanced at the stewardess and realized he'd missed the announcement. 'Sorry. Sleeping,' he mumbled, and did up the belt with a smile. The girl passed on, checking for other slackers. The huge jet touched down safely at Nice, and he was through Customs quickly. He took a bus to Monte Carlo and tried without success to settle his nerves. But it was hard, much harder than he was used to, and when he stepped off the bus into a town coloured red by a sinking sun he stood on the pavement for long, long minutes before getting his bearings and heading for the casino.

He was still carrying his suitcase when he walked through the door of the Droit de Seigneur. He had not had time to change, and his beige jacket and trousers were crumpled, his white shirt a little travel grubby. Slowly he looked around.

Sebastien had been reluctant to leave Monaco before, but Wayne had reverted to his hard-eyed, locked-in self. To be locked in with constant pain was something Sebastien feared more than anything else. If he was tired after years of seeing other people's pain, then how much more tired must Wayne be after an entire lifetime of living with it?

'Can I help you, sir?'

Sebastien turned to see a small, dapper man dressed in a dinner jacket looking at him with polite curiosity, tinged with contempt. This was not the same manager he'd dealt with over a month ago, and the new man no doubt thought he was panting to lose his money — so much so that he had not even bothered to check into a hotel. Sebastien grinned, in spite of it all.

'Yes. I'd like to see Wayne. Mr D'Arville. Is he here, or at home?'

The man's eyes flickered, and Sebastien could almost hear the wheels turning. No doubt others had tried to bluff their way into the inner sanctum. 'Tell him Sebastien is here to see him. I think you'll find he'll want to see me.'

Antoine Dorlhac nodded. The man seemed very sure of himself, and there was something particularly unthreatening about him. 'Very well, Mr . . . ?'

'Teale.'

'Mr Teale. If you'll wait here a moment . . .' He left the sentence to hang in mid-air as he left the room, nodding to one of the security men to keep an eye on him.

Sebastien looked slowly around the room. At one table, a beautiful young girl with black hair had attracted a crowd. At first he thought it meant she was winning, but as he moved closer he could see that that was not the case. She was losing quite spectacularly, thousands of francs at a time.

Antoine knocked on the office door and walked in. 'I'm sorry to disturb you, sir, but there is a man here to see you.'

'A loser?'

'No, sir. I haven't seen him in here before. He arrived with a suitcase.'

Wayne looked up from the documents in front of him. 'Is Maria still losing?'

'Yes, sir.' Antoine smiled, the first genuine smile Wayne had ever seen him give. Wayne had insisted that Maria pay back the money in the same way that she had won it. It pleased him and re-emphasized the change in their positions. When she was humbled enough, Wayne would pick her up, brush her down and think of some use for her. He was currently chasing a Brazilian lumber lord for the paper rights to his timber, but he was proving to be difficult. The man was unmarried and had a weakness for beautiful women, as Wayne knew from the dossier he'd had compiled on him. And in Brazil, as in old Spain, arranged marriages were still more or less the norm.

'What shall I do about the man, sir?' Antoine prompted him from his thoughts.

'Did he give a name?' Wayne asked, sounding as bored as he looked.

'Sebastien Teale, sir.'

'Seb?' Wayne stood up, his eyes and face lighting up so obviously that Antoine felt his mouth drop open. 'Well, bring him in,' Wayne snapped, suddenly angry. 'At once. And in future, don't ever keep Dr Teale waiting again. Is that clear?'

'Yes, sir. Of course.' Antoine backed hastily out of the room and all but ran down the corridor. Only as he approached the gaming rooms did he slow down to a more dignified walk before he stepped through the curtains. 'Mr — I mean Dr Teale. Won't you please come this way? Guy!' He snapped his fingers at a man lounging by the cashier's window. 'Guy will take care of your suitcase, sir.'

'Thanks,' Sebastien said, but was already moving towards the offices. He remembered its location easily enough. He still had nightmares about it. He hadn't even reached the office when the door opened and Wayne's tall figure filled the opening.

'Seb! What on earth are you doing here?'

Sebastien reached forward to take the hand, the familiar handshake doing nothing to calm his nerves. As he was ushered inside he shrugged his shoulders. 'I just needed a break, that's all. And I thought of sun and sand, and Monte Carlo.'

'And me,' Wayne said softly.

'And you.' Sebastien sat down in the chair facing the huge desk, Wayne moving quickly to its other side. As he did so, Sebastien stared at him, hard. There was something different . . . something had changed since he last saw him. 'You look . . . contented,' Sebastien offered the opening gambit, and Wayne grinned.

'Why not? I've just gained a child. The casino is mine. My father is no longer around to haunt me and I'm finally free.'

'A child?' Sebastien said, his voice sharper than he meant it to be. Could it be that he knew about Travis? Sebastien's mouth went dry when he thought of another, more sinister explanation behind Travis's disappearance. Wayne watched him intently.

'That's right. You must have seen her outside?'

Sebastien blinked. 'Her?'

'Mmm.' Wayne grinned. 'In my younger days, there was a maid at my father's villa . . .' Wayne broke off with a grin and a shrug. 'She left the same summer and I never even guessed she was pregnant. Then, a few weeks ago' — he spread his hands wide — 'in she walked — Maria, her daughter. *My daughter.*'

Sebastien felt his whole body wilt in relief. Wayne's blue eyes crinkled at the corners as he watched it. Wonderful Sebastien. He never changed. 'Isn't she beautiful?'

'I'm not sure I—'

'The last I heard,' Wayne interrupted, 'she was losing quite a lot of my money. Luckily for me, this is my casino, so I get it all back again!'

'Oh — oh, yes. Yes, you're right. She is lovely. You must be proud of her.' Sebastien smiled, bringing the girl's face into mind.

'Oh, I am,' Wayne nodded, a strange smile on his face. 'Yes, I really am.'

'What does Sylvie think of her?' Sebastien asked curiously.

'Sylvie?' For a second there was a totally blank expression on his face and Seb felt a sudden tension tighten his insides. Incredible as it seemed, he knew that this man had forgotten he had a wife. 'Oh, Sylvia. They haven't met yet.' Wayne leaned back in his chair, just glad to be alive again. Sometimes it was easier to forget that only Sebastien could accomplish this. 'I'm glad you're here, Seb,' he said softly. 'I need you.'

Sebastien's eyes sharpened, as Wayne had known they would. 'Oh?'

'Relax. I didn't mean . . . that.' Wayne picked up a pen and fiddled with it. Sebastien knew it meant that he would get nothing more productive out of him that night. Unless he could catch him unawares . . .

'Did you hear about the fire in New York?' he asked abruptly. Wayne froze for a fraction of a second and then threw down the pen and looked up. Sebastien looked pale, on edge, and for a second Wayne was swamped with a feeling approaching painful tenderness. Then he shrugged.

'New York? I don't think I've ever been there.'

'Veronica and her husband were nearly killed in a fire there a few weeks back,' he said, watching Wayne's face for any tiny clue to emotion.

Wayne shook his head slowly. 'That's a pity.' He'd assumed they'd perished. Oh, well. He could live with them being just badly burned. Unless they tried to get Travis back. Then he'd have to make sure that his people did the job properly.

Sebastien nodded thoughtfully. 'Funny, isn't it, that you can forget you have a wife, but remember immediately the name of a lover from nearly twenty years ago?'

The voice was soft and speculative, but Wayne was not fooled. Clever Sebastien. Clever, clever Sebastien. Slowly he lifted his eyes from the top of the desk and looked the American straight in the eye. 'Memory's forever playing tricks like that,' he agreed softly.

Sebastien decided to take a chance. 'Apparently their son is still missing.'

Wayne slowly stood up. 'You haven't booked into a hotel yet, I trust?'

Sebastien rose in response, but more stiffly, feeling the weariness deep in his bones. 'No. I was hoping . . .'

'You didn't have to hope, Sebastien. You know damned well you'll be staying with me.'

'You still have the old villa?'

'Still?' He inclined his head with familiar mockery.

'I'm surprised you haven't sold it. Surely it has bad memories for you?'

'It has good ones too. I conceived a daughter there, remember?' They were in the outer corridor now, and as

Wayne pushed aside the curtain Sebastien found himself searching out the beautiful brunette, who was just rising from the table. Out of the corner of his eye he saw Wayne beckon her. The girl paused and then turned reluctantly. She was wearing a pale lilac that did wonders for her raven hair and creamy skin, but there were dark smudges beneath her eyes.

'She is lovely, Wayne,' Sebastien said softly as Maria walked towards them. He searched her face carefully, noting instantly the tight, pinched mouth, but it was the girl's eyes that fascinated him the most. They looked at her father and then away again in a confusing battery of emotions. Hate, fear, despair. Sebastien almost cried out loud. He looked at Wayne sharply, just one thought clearly ringing in his mind, and so well did they know each other that he might just as well have spoken it out loud. Wayne, what have you done now?

Wayne smiled, feeling deep in his soul the unique power that he had over this man alone, and yet also aware of the equally exquisite pain of being dependent on him. 'Sebastien Teale, this is my daughter, Maria Alvarez. Maria, Sebastien.'

Maria glanced at the man by her father's side. Any friend of his was her enemy. Her eyes were black and scornful, spitting hate and contempt. 'Señor Teale.' She made his name sound like a poison.

'Sebastien is a doctor, Maria. I want you to be nice to him. In fact, I insist on it,' Wayne said softly, but with an edge to his voice. Sebastien glanced quickly between Wayne and the highly strung girl in front of him, sensing a hidden message in those few bland, ordinary words.

Maria's lips pulled up into a fiasco of a smile as she tried once again. 'Dr Teale. I'm so pleased to meet you.'

Sebastien reached out his hand, taking hers in a firm grip when she would have pulled away. 'Hello, Maria,' he said softly, feeling the exact moment when the girl looked at him properly. He smiled. 'I look forward to getting to know you better. You're staying at the villa?'

'*Si.*'

'Wonderful. So am I. Perhaps we can have breakfast tomorrow?'

'You should be careful of talking too much in front of Sebastien, Maria,' Wayne said with a warning smile. 'He's a psychiatrist.'

Maria Alvarez looked once more into those warm, sherry-coloured eyes, and Sebastien saw a flash of understanding followed by desperate hope suddenly flood her eyes. 'I look forward to it, *señor*,' she said, her voice husky now.

Sebastien squeezed her hand, passing on to her his own hidden message to bear up, and then released her. Beside him Wayne said restlessly, 'Shall we go?'

Sebastien saw the silent plea in the Spanish girl's eyes and thought quickly. 'If you don't mind, I'd like to stay here for a few minutes. For all the times I've been in Monte Carlo, I don't think I've actually placed a bet.'

Wayne smiled, not fooled, but feeling too magnanimous to spoil their fun. 'Why not? How much money have you got?'

Sebastien laughed. 'Precious little.' He reached into his pocket and extracted all the notes he had — not quite thirty pounds. Wayne slowly reached forward and took them out of his hand.

As he did so, Maria noticed a strange, long, level look pass between them, and her heart began to pound. There was something . . . odd going on. It was almost as if . . . 'Excuse me a moment, please,' she murmured, making up her mind with an impetuosity that was second nature to her, and headed for the ladies' room, where she quickly used the phone.

'Gemma? It's me. Listen, something's happened. There's a man here, a friend of my father's called Sebastien Teale. I'm not sure, but I think he could be helpful. He's . . . I don't know. I can't explain it. He's a head-doctor . . . you know . . . what's the word? A shrink! Yes, a shrink, so he obviously knows all about Father.' She paused and listened for a few seconds, then shrugged. 'I don't know exactly. I want you to talk to him. I'll separate them somehow. Gemma, you must come here and talk to this man . . . I know.' Her voice lowered to a sympathetic murmur. 'You're so brave. So very brave. Good. Give me half an hour to think of something, then come. You can't mistake him. He's American, I think, like you. Not too tall, nice hair — like caramel, and eyes like sherry. Oh, you won't be able to miss him. There's something . . . oh, I don't know. Something . . . kind about him. Yes. All right. Your parents arrived all right? Oh. But I don't think the police will be much help. My father's such a powerful man, but perhaps it's worth a try. OK. I'll see you later. And try not to worry,' she added foolishly. She hung up, took a deep breath, and went to the craps table, where Sebastien was rolling the dice.

His eyes met hers briefly, and she smiled. He threw a neat seven. Maria glanced at her watch, then watched her father's face. He, in turn, was watching Sebastien with all the concentration of a cat at a mousehole. It made her shiver. Twenty minutes later, Sebastien's thirty pounds had become two hundred and twenty.

'Are these dice loaded?' Sebastien asked quietly as he straightened up and jiggled the dice in his hand. Wayne looked down at him, leaned a heavy hand on the younger man's shoulder and smiled grimly.

'The dice are always loaded, Sebastien,' he said.

Maria put her hand to her head and sighed. It was Sebastien who noticed. 'You all right?'

'Just a headache. Daddy, could we go home now?'

'Sure.'

'Oh, please, Dr Teale, you don't have to come as well,' Maria said, catching Sebastien's sleeve in an excruciatingly tight grip. Startled, Sebastien nevertheless caught on quickly.

Before Wayne could object, he turned and rattled the dice once more and rolled them. 'OK. Thanks.'

Wayne hesitated for a long moment and Maria moved closer, almost bumping into him. 'See you in the morning, Dr Teale,' she murmured, and Sebastien nodded. Only when they'd gone did he slowly straighten up, a small frown tugging at his brows. He cashed in the chips, pocketed the notes and wandered to the bar, settling down to wait.

He fully expected Maria to come back. He was drinking his third soda when he became aware of a young girl hovering nervously a few feet away. He turned but knew at once that he'd never seen her before in his life. She was young, no more than eighteen, he guessed, despite the sophisticated, high-necked navy-blue gown she wore. She smiled nervously. Sebastien smiled back. Maria was right, Gemma thought, her raw nerves reacting immediately to the gentle eyes. He does look kind. It had taken a great deal for her to leave her room, after her parents had told her to stay put. They had arrived late last night, and she had told them the whole story. Oriel had slept with her daughter in her arms, and this morning her father had been making phone calls to everyone he knew, calling in favours, and getting the names of the top men in Monaco. When they had left just a few hours ago to try and persuade the police to act, they'd told her to wait for them, and not to leave the hotel room under any circumstances. But now she was glad that she had. She sensed this man could help. 'Dr Teale?' she asked nervously.

Sebastien, surprised by her American accent, half turned. 'Yes?'

'I'm Gemma Harcourt. You don't know me. Maria sent me. She seems to think you might be able to help us.'

Sebastien left his drink at the bar. 'Is there anywhere we can talk in private?'

Gemma went white, her whole body tensing. Automatically she took a step away. Sebastien froze for a second, then said softly, 'Some café somewhere, where we can find a quiet corner, away from prying eyes?'

Gemma nearly wilted in relief. 'Of course. There's one just over the road.' Sebastien followed her in silence, noting the way she looked around nervously. It was not until they were out in the street and crossing the busy road that she relaxed. The café was quiet, only a few couples holding hands and slowly dancing by the juke box.

Sebastien steered them to a dark corner and purchased two coffees at the counter. He watched her add sugar and milk to hers, then said softly, 'How long ago was it that you were raped, Gemma?'

Gemma's spoon clattered in her cup, and she gnawed on her lower lip, taking several deep breaths before she could speak. 'I d-don't . . .' She lowered her head, unable to meet his eyes. 'I wish my father were here,' she said, irrelevantly.

Sebastien said nothing for a moment, but deliberately stirred his coffee. Watching the spoon go around and around, Gemma sighed and slowly relaxed. Then she reached for her own cup, taking it to her lips with shaking hands.

'It was recently, wasn't it?' Sebastien tried again.

The quiet words, soft, like raw silk on an open wound, made her wince. 'Please,' she said.

'You can tell me, Gemma.'

'You're his friend!' she suddenly hissed, her pale cheeks flooding with colour. 'How can I tell you?'

Sebastien stared at her, then closed his eyes briefly. 'Oh, God. It was Wayne, wasn't it?'

Gemma looked away. 'It was last night. But he didn't actually . . . I got away, just in time,' she mumbled. 'He did it because . . . Look, it's not important. It's my brother who's in danger. It's him we have to save.'

Sebastien looked up at her quickly, his expression stunned. 'Your brother?'

'Paris. Wayne's kidnapped him. Yes, I know.' She laughed harshly as he reared back. 'It sounds ridiculously dramatic, doesn't it? But it's true.'

Sebastien briefly rubbed his tired eyes with his fingers, then said softly, 'I want you to tell me everything. Right from the beginning.'

Half an hour later, Gemma had done so. She felt talked out, washed out, wrung out. She was beyond tears now, almost beyond feeling at all. 'So when Maria phoned, she just had this hunch that you would help,' she finished the story, and looked at him, her dull voice trailing away. 'You look like I feel,' she said with another harsh laugh.

Sebastien, who sat with his head in his hands, slowly straightened up to stare for a moment out of the window. 'I knew something was wrong,' he said. 'But not this. I never suspected this.'

'It's a mess, isn't it?' Gemma said, watching as the older man nodded his head. 'He's an absolute monster. He's crushing all the life and spirit out of Maria, just because she dared to defy him. He seems to enjoy . . .' Gemma grappled for the words that would help her understand '. . . actually *need* to hurt those who are nearest to him. I'm only surprised he hasn't done the same to you. Can you help us?'

Sebastien thought of all the years of his life boiling down to this one moment. Alone, sick to his soul, in a café in a town he didn't know, with a girl who was just one more victim of the man he'd tried to call a friend.

And Lilas — the one good thing in his life. His one chance of love and happiness, so far away. But he mustn't think of her now.

He didn't know that, at that moment, Lilas was flying across the Channel to join him.

He had to concentrate on one thing only. It had gone too far now. He would have to have Wayne committed and take the chance that he'd succeed first time. But he was in Monaco — Wayne's home territory. He'd have to be careful . . .

'Yes,' he said finally, his voice no more than a whisper, but nevertheless containing something hard. 'I can help.'

CHAPTER 43

Kier Harcourt looked across at Max Dupont and said crisply, 'Well?'

Max Dupont, now sixty-five, had at one time been a hero of the French Resistance. He was a big man, heavy-set, with iron-grey hair and big bushy eyebrows. 'Getting into D'Arville's villa without getting spotted is, as I see it, the greatest problem. Once inside, my men can take out the security guards. How sure are you of your intelligence?'

Kier smiled grimly. 'Sure enough. D'Arville's daughter herself has been compiling the information for us.' Kier, who'd never had much faith in the police, had quickly formed a back-up plan. It was a desperate plan — but he and Oriel were equally desperate.

'Ah, here's Pierre.' In the small, discreet hotel room, both men looked around as a tall lanky youth with bad teeth and a wide smile walked into the room, an envelope in his hand. 'Anything?' Max asked with a short grunt.

Pierre spilled the photographs on to the table. Kier slowly spread them, picking out one of a pale-faced but wonderfully alive boy looking pensively out of a top-floor window. 'That's him,' Kier said softly, wilting in relief. 'That's Paris.'

Max took the photograph and looked across at the American speculatively. Max had met Duncan Somerville only twice, but he was an ardent admirer of the Somerville Commission. So when he had been woken at one o'clock this morning, and found himself confronted by this man and his pale-faced but enraged wife, he had reacted immediately to Oriel Harcourt's maiden name. For three hours he had sat in the chilly bam of his kitchen, brewing innumerable cups of coffee and listening tight-lipped to their story.

He had agreed to help at once, and the speed in which he had everything organized took Kier's breath away. 'I'm just going to go and show these to Oriel,' Kier said, taking the photos. Max didn't bother looking up as the American rose and walked to a connecting door.

Oriel was standing at the window, looking out at the beaches of Sainte Maxime. Silently Kier walked beside her and handed over the photos. 'He's alive. That was taken just a few hours ago.'

Oriel took the photographs with shaking hands, tears flooding her eyes. 'Oh, thank God,' she whispered.

Kier looked across to the second single bed and glanced at his daughter's sleeping face. 'How is she?'

Oriel continued to stare at the photos of her son. 'She's not too good.'

Kier sighed. But he knew he could count on Oriel to look after Gemma. At first she had insisted on coming to the villa with them, but Kier had made her see that she would only be a hindrance, and therefore a liability to Paris. Now she was resigned to staying behind.

'What does Max say?' she asked quietly.

'Nothing yet.'

Oriel turned into Kier's arms, burying her face into his hard, comforting chest. Kier hugged her briefly, silently, then went back to the other room.

Max had the photographs separated into piles. There were four more shots of Paris, a whole pile of the grounds and every room of the villa, and three more of an unknown boy, about Paris's age. He too was dark-haired, but his eyes were blue. 'Do you know him?' Max asked, nodding his head at the pictures.

Kier lifted one and stared at it. 'No.'

'Pierre got the impression that he's also a prisoner at the villa. Apparently they're together quite a lot, and whenever they walk in the grounds, the guards follow both of them.'

Kier sat down heavily on the edge of the bed. 'I don't . . . want to sound hard-hearted,' he began, his voice as strained as his face. 'But . . .'

'But you want your son rescued come what may, and we'll worry about this other boy second, hmm?'

Kier grimaced. 'Life's strange,' he said quietly. 'Until a few days ago, I thought I knew myself pretty well . . .' He broke off the train of thought and stared thoughtfully at the unknown boy's face. 'You know, he looks a lot like D'Arville. The eyes, especially. And the shape of the face.'

Max nodded. 'You noticed that too, huh? Well, we won't have time to find out anything more concrete. We move tonight.'

Kier's head reared up. 'Tonight?'

* * *

Just a few miles away, Travis glanced at Paris nervously. 'Are you ready?'

Paris managed a half-laugh, half-shrug. 'No. Are you?'

Travis grinned back. 'Nope.' He glanced over the side of the balcony that seemed to hang over a sheer thirty-foot drop.

'You know, don't you, if those creeper cords don't hold, we'll probably break our necks?' Paris said, almost conversationally, as Travis leaned down and pulled on a fibrous, twisted cord of a green-leafed creeper no thicker than his thumb. Travis slowly straightened and looked out over the grounds. They were beautiful — full of lily-choked ponds and fish, iron and white marble gazebos, lawns mowed in criss-cross patterns, flower borders, rose arbours, honeysuckle bowers, fruit trees, even a bridged stream. How he hated it. He hated the house too, with its priceless *objets d'art*, Regency furniture, oriental carpets, modern stereo and entertainment centres and indoor swimming pool.

'Yeah,' Travis said heavily. 'I know. But personally I think I'd rather have a broken neck than stay here another day with that maniac. He's mad, you know. Not screaming, lock-me-up mad, but . . . twisted.'

Paris glanced across at the boy who, in only twenty-four hours, had become the greatest friend of his life. 'He looked down the vertical wall, and his thoughts drifted back. He had not known what to say in the car on his way to this place two nights ago. He had looked first at the drunk who was not a drunk, at the back of the driver's head and finally at the tight-lipped man who had sneaked up behind him. He knew he was not being mugged, unless the French had a very strange way of going about it. His heart had pounded uncomfortably, but he firmly kept his fear under control. He was damned if he'd panic and make an ass of himself. He kept telling himself over and over that so far they had not even hurt him. For all of that long, long drive, he'd kept up a wait-and-see policy that had allowed him to walk with dignity from the car when it was parked in front of the impressive villa, and not disgrace himself.

Paris had not expected the villa, which had the white-washed beauty of a truly luxurious residence. The driver left in the car, leaving the two others to 'escort' him upstairs. There, a large room that could have looked like a luxurious guest room except for the bars over the windows, awaited him. Without a word the two men had turned and left. Paris had tried the door, of course. It was locked. Then he'd walked to the windows. After making sure the bars were solid, he'd noted that they were newly installed. By then, of course, he had figured out that D'Arville was behind it all. Who else could it have been?

That first night he'd waited for hours, finally rushing to the window at the sound of a car arriving. There, in the light from the vestibule, he saw Wayne D'Arville get out and nod to the chauffeur. His height and the colour of his hair were unmistakable. It was almost unbelievable. Why had he done something so stupid? Surely not even Wayne D'Arville thought he could get away with kidnapping? And why? Why? He'd been nervous and uptight waiting for D'Arville to come to him, but as the hours passed, and it slowly dawned on him that he would have no visitors that night, he paced the room, ignoring the comfortable Queen Anne bed with white satin sheets, and forced his over-active mind and imagination to calm down and start thinking logically. When he'd done so, the answer was obvious, and came to him easily. He'd been snatched to put a halt to Maria's 'lucky' streak. For just a single fleeting moment, Paris wondered what would happen if Maria refused to comply. A little demon, twisting deep in his brain, reminded him of how obsessed she was with revenge. Then he shook his head. Maria would not let her desire for revenge outweigh the thing they had going between them. No way.

'You ready?'

Paris blinked, Travis's words bringing him back to the present. He managed a cocky grin. 'After you.'

Travis grinned back. 'Thanks a bunch.' It was a game between them, of course, all this grinning, all this wry laughter. It was supposed to cover up the fear and keep their spirits up. To a certain extent it worked. Only at times like this did the fear become a solid reality, sitting like a rock in the middle of their stomachs.

Paris had finally given in to mild shock that first night and lain fully clothed on the bed. About eight thirty the next morning, he'd been woken by the door opening, his disorientated mind snapping to attention at the sight of the tall, redheaded Frenchman. Wayne had been mercifully brief and straight to the point. Even now, as Paris swung his body over the stone balustrade, the dizzying pull of gravity making him grapple for vines and stone ledges, he could remember Wayne's words verbatim.

'Maria has agreed to give back the money, you'll be pleased to hear. It will take her a few nights to lose it all at the tables, however.' Seeing his surprised look, Wayne had smiled. 'I insisted she lose it the same way she won it. Once that's done, you'll be released.' Paris must have given himself away then, because the handsome face had looked more amused than ever. 'You think I'm going to kill you? You fool; I have no reason to. If you went to the police and told them I'd held you here, they'd laugh in your face.' Wayne had become impatient then, flicking his hand in a typical Gallic gesture. 'Think it through yourself,' he finished shortly. 'I have things to do.'

Paris had never been so relieved in all his life before.

'You OK?' a voice said now.

Paris looked across and down to Travis, who was ramming his instep tightly against a knotted branch. 'So far. Hell, the ground seems a long way down.'

'Don't it, though?' Travis muttered grimly.

The two boys only took a minute or so to reach the paved patio. Nervously they looked around. They had spent a day watching the guards patrolling the grounds and worked out their timetable. Now, they could see the elongated shadows of the evening across the lawns, and by their reckoning the fifth guard, whose sector this was, wasn't due for another ten minutes. Paris gave Travis a victorious punch to the top of his arm, and together they ran at a low crouch towards the trees. Once out of sight of the main house, they followed the line of trees to their end, and then crouched down behind the last trunks. Ahead of them stretched the open ground of the kitchen garden. Rows of radishes, lettuces and carrots competed with beans and peas climbing up wigwam-shaped sticks. 'Great,' Paris muttered angrily. Beyond them was the huge wall. 'There has to be a gap in that bloody thing,' he muttered, but Travis was already shaking his head.

'There isn't. I've been here longer than you have, remember?' He shook his head again. 'Believe me, it just goes on and on and on.'

Paris wiped his sweating forehead with his sleeve. 'What now?'

Both boys stared gloomily at the high red-brick wall with its topping of barbed wire. 'You gotta hand it to my old man,' Travis said, with a sarcasm made bitter by the taste of defeat. 'He sure knows how to build a prison.'

Paris looked back at the wall, his mind winging back to yesterday morning, when they'd first encountered each other in the grounds. Initially, both boys had suspected some kind of trick. Travis wasn't sure that Paris was not some lackey of his father's, sent in to try and win his confidence and spy on him. Paris had similar thoughts about Travis, but a few minutes of crisp, suspicious questioning on both sides had gradually given way to a growing trust.

'Can we use those sticks in any way?' Travis asked with a hopeless kind of desperation as he pointed at the thin bean-poles, and Paris shook his head.

'I doubt it. Unless you want to try and pole-vault that thing!'

Travis half turned, another grin on his face. Paris tensed as his blue eyes slewed over his shoulder. Paris felt his own shoulder blades tighten, and slowly looked around. A few feet away, two uniformed and armed guards watched them. Paris glanced back at Travis, who slowly stood up. Wordlessly both boys followed the guards back to the house. There was nothing else to be done.

Walking around the side of the house, they both saw the midnight-blue Ferrari parked out front. Now they knew how they had been found missing so quickly — Wayne was home.

The room they were taken to was hexagonal, the floor tiled in black and white patterns. It was obviously a music room. Sitting at a piano, picking out a tune, Wayne looked up at them. The energy in his blue eyes made Paris take a quick, involuntary step backwards. Travis, who'd had more practice at withstanding the icy blast than his friend, held his ground.

Slowly Wayne rose to his full height and approached them, but it was to Travis that he walked. When he was only a few inches away, father and son stared at one another, and Paris knew that this confrontational scene had been played out before. The room was deathly silent. 'Where did you get out?' Wayne asked. Paris was surprised at the soft tone.

Travis, who was not at all surprised, said nothing. Wayne turned and nodded at one of the guards. Paris had just enough time to yelp as the guard behind him grabbed his arms and then the other guard punched him solidly in the stomach. Paris had never felt anything like it before. Dimly he was aware of Travis shouting something and guessed that he was telling Wayne what he wanted to know. Pain radiated from the explosion in his stomach, making him feel viciously sick. He bent double but was prevented from falling on to the floor by the guard still holding him. He gasped, and gasped again, his eyes watering.

Travis watched him helplessly. Unseen by either of them, a third guard had been in the room, and was now hold-ing Travis in a similar but more gentle stranglehold. Slowly, painfully, Paris straightened up. Travis saw the beads of sweat pop out on his forehead, but his eyes, looking at Wayne, were dark with hate.

'That's better,' Wayne said. 'Now.' He turned once more to Travis. 'You checked out the patrol times of the guards?'

'No. We just took pot luck,' Paris said, one part of his brain telling him he was an idiot to goad him, while another part told him that if he let fear of pain rule him, he'd never be much of a man.

The guard in front of Paris swung his fist again, this time into Paris's face. His head exploded in pain, bright lights flashing across his closed lids. He felt something on his lip, and when he grunted in pain he felt the taste of his own blood in his mouth.

'Where were you planning on going, if you got out?' Wayne asked, once again looking to his struggling son. Travis was twisting and turning, desperate to free himself, wanting only to launch himself at his father and tear out his heart. 'Save your strength, Travis,' Wayne advised softly. 'Where were you going to go?'

'Don't tell him,' Paris found the words came out of his mouth in a lisp because of a loose tooth.

Travis looked at him with agonized eyes. '*No!*' he screamed, but too late.

This time Paris blacked out for a few moments. When he opened his eyes he realized he was lying on the floor. He tried to sit up and moaned before he could stop the sound escaping his lips. The guard had punched him viciously in the back, and his kidneys felt like aching rocks in his body.

'The American embassy,' Travis screamed. 'Stop it! All right? Just stop it! I'll tell you whatever you want to know but leave him alone!'

* * *

It was dark outside now, and as a catering truck approached the city limits, Kier Harcourt felt his heart pounding inside his chest like a jack-hammer out of control.

'We're nearly there,' Max said, watching as the American stiffened. But he was confident about Harcourt. Then he turned and looked at the other American, a frown of unease appearing between his bushy, iron-grey caterpillar eyebrows. Max wasn't so sure what to make of Sebastien Teale.

When Maria Alvarez had brought the American to them just an hour before the assault would begin, Max had been adamant that he was not to come along. He found the psychiatrist's innate gentleness worrisome. Kier, too, had been against it. He didn't know Teale, and didn't trust Teale, and didn't want the plan put in any kind of danger.

It was Sebastien himself who had argued both of them around, with a logic that was infallible. 'If things go wrong — and they might — you're going to need someone there who knows how to deal with D'Arville,' he'd pointed out simply. 'And if you don't take me, I'll simply call a cab and go in on my own.'

Still Kier had not liked it. Sebastien had looked at him steadily. 'What do you do if Wayne gets a knife to Paris's throat? What do you say when one wrong word or expression could mean death for your son? This man has no sense of right or wrong — none. He has no friends, no loyalties, no allegiances, only different grades of enemy. Right now, I'm the least of his enemies. He already hates you.' He turned to Max. 'And will have only contempt for you. Remember, this man was raised by Wolfgang Mueller.'

Finally, with time becoming pressing, both men had been forced to concede that Sebastien might come in handy.

'Teale comes,' Kier had finally said, his voice brooking no argument.

Now, as the van approached La Turbie, Sebastien, much to Max's relief, showed no signs of cracking up. Rather, he was grimly quiet, with a determination that Max recognized from the old days before a raid against the occupying Germans. It made him feel better about having the shrink along.

* * *

In a taxi, barely a mile behind them, Lilas Glendower stared resolutely ahead. It hadn't been hard to track down Wayne D'Arville's villa. Now, all she had to do was rehearse what she'd say to him when she got there.   .

* * *

Max glanced at his watch, then looked around at the six silent men, all blacked up and swaying easily in motion with the van. All were the sons of ex-Resistance fighters. All had been in the army. Max Dupont was still enough of a national hero to assemble such a team at short notice.

The van pulled up in a narrow lane, several hundred yards from the only entrance to the villa. 'Here we go,' Max said, and checked his gun. Sebastien had no weapon and had declined Max's offer to provide him with one.

The night was cloudy and moonless. Sebastien and Kier took up the rear, watching in silent admiration as two of Max's men efficiently cut the wires to the alarm system and knocked out the video cameras. One man fiddled at the gateposts. It seemed like hours, but was in reality only a few minutes, before the gates slid silently open.

Everyone knew the plan down to the last detail.

* * *

Paris was almost sleeping, aware of a dull continual pain all over his body. His face was stiff with caked blood. He had not been allowed to wash after a guard had carried him to his room, nor had he seen Travis for several hours.

Dimly he heard a scraping noise coming from behind him but couldn't be bothered to look around. The scraping persisted, and Paris frowned. But he was too sore to get up and investigate.

Outside, the first two bars had been removed. Kier was already halfway up the ladder. The one called Jacques, who had been removing the bars with acid and a lever, was the first one in, moving so silently that Paris was not aware of another presence in his room. Kier, however, was not quite so silent. Paris turned slowly on the bed, careful to keep his cut and misshapen lips firmly shut.

He would not moan again. If D'Arville had come for him again, then . . . A flashlight dazzled him, making him blink. Then he heard his name, spoken in a voice he knew so well that, for a second, he could not believe his ears.

'Paris. Is that you? God, son, what have they done to you?' Kier's face was barely visible in the dark, but Paris somehow managed to launch himself towards it. Kier, coming to kneel on the side of the bed, caught him, hearing the harsh breath of pain Paris gave at being held. 'Easy, son, easy,' Kier murmured, brushing back the sweat-damp hair from his face. Outside, they could clearly hear the sound of a car.

In the taxi, Lilas got out and paid the driver. She was surprised to see the gates standing open, but shrugged, straightened her shoulders, and walked determinedly up the path to the front door.

Upstairs, Kier lowered his son back on to the bed, staring grimly at the boy's bruises. Jacques whispered in French into his walkie-talkie, informing Max that they'd located the boy, and giving a run-down on his injuries.

Downstairs, Max had picked the lock of the front door and waved Sebastien inside. He too had heard a car out on the road, but doubted it was coming here. The rest of his men waited in the garden to deal with any guards. Wordlessly he motioned Sebastien upstairs, himself on the alert for individual internal alarms.

'Paris, listen,' Kier whispered. 'We're going to get you out of here now. These are friends. OK?'

Paris glanced briefly at the faces around him. 'OK. But we have to get Travis as well.'

'Travis?' Kier glanced up as Max joined them.

Behind him, Sebastien Teale said softly, 'Travis Coltrane. He's Wayne's son.'

Kier looked down as he felt his hand being held tightly. Paris's one good eye gleamed brightly. 'You have to get him out, Dad. I won't go without him. I mean it!'

Kier nodded. 'We'll get him. But you're leaving now.' As they'd talked, two of Max's men had tied a sheet into a hammock, and one of them put a gentle but firm hand over Paris's mouth as they lifted him. Paris's moan of pain as they moved him was a barely muffled sob. They walked with him out into the corridor. There Kier watched at the top of the stairs as the men silently carried his son out of the hall and into the dark night air. Back to the van, where he'd be safe.

They missed bumping into Lilas by moments.

'Pierre said the other one was kept in the room next to D'Arville himself,' Max whispered. 'This way.'

Wayne had just put the finishing touches to his letter to the Brazilian timber man, and enclosed a stunning, full-length photograph of Maria in a clinging silver lamé evening gown. He sealed the envelope, addressed it, and stood up, stretching hard. Suddenly he froze. From Travis's room he heard a small sound. Instinct had the hairs on the back of his neck standing on end. He turned, glanced at the connecting door, took two quick steps towards it, then stopped. He walked the rest of the way quietly and put his ear to the door.

Inside, Max Dupont had his hand firmly over Travis's mouth, and was looking down into the wide, startled blue eyes, which shifted to Kier as he came into view.

'Don't be afraid.' It was Kier who spoke, in no more than a whisper. 'I'm Paris's father. We've got him out, and he asked us to come for you. Do you want to leave?'

Under his hand, Max felt the boy's lips try to curve into a smile, and slowly withdrew his huge palm from the boy's face. 'God, yes!' Travis breathed, swinging his legs to the side of the bed, trying not to let the mattress squeak. He was wearing only his jeans.

Sebastien moved to the window to check that all was well outside. Travis and Kier were nearly at the door when the lights suddenly blazed on. Only Max responded immediately, spinning and crouching, his gun-hand coming up, whilst Kier, Sebastien and Travis blinked in the sudden brightness, disorientated and confused.

Below, Lilas saw a light go on upstairs. She stared at the open door, feeling suddenly afraid. But she had come this far, and for Sebastien's sake she would do almost anything. Grimly, she walked into the hall.

Upstairs, Sebastien jumped and went ice-cold as a small, silent 'pop' sounded in the room, and Max staggered back through the open door. His hand on his shoulder was red with blood. Even so, Max reacted quickly and ducked out of the door in the dimness of the corridor beyond.

In the hall, Lilas heard the sound and began to mount the stairs. Max disappeared into Paris's bedroom and made for the ladder. He had to get the rest of his men back in here, fast!

'Shut the door,' Wayne ordered grimly, looking at Kier. Kier glanced down at the level, deadly gun in the German's hand, and did as he asked.

'Dad, give it up.' It was Travis who was the first of them to speak. Sebastien knew that Wayne had not yet seen him. Long velvet draperies half covered him, and all of Wayne's attention was focused on the door area. In profile, Wayne's face looked tense and white, but for once Sebastien knew that others needed him more.

On the landing, Lilas moved cautiously towards the sound of voices. She hesitated outside the door, her hand going slowly to the handle.

On the other side of the door, Sebastien's thoughts were racing. He knew that Wayne would kill Kier Harcourt without a moment's hesitation, but Travis, he knew, was perfectly safe. Wayne would never kill his own son. He gauged the distance between Wayne and himself and realized that he could never cross it without being seen. The question was — would Wayne kill him also? Would he?

Sebastien tried to think it through like an analyst but found he couldn't. This was personal. This was so very, very personal.

'Father, please,' Travis said, taking a few steps forward, deliberately putting his own body between the gun and Kier Harcourt. Kier knew what he was doing, and hesitated, unsure what to do next.

Nobody heard the door open silently. The first person Lilas saw was Sebastien. She was about to push the door open and call his name happily. Although she was surprised to see him, she was also glad. She'd been feeling rather scared and out of her depth. Then, just in time, she noticed something strange. Sebastien was moving, very very slowly, away from the window. He was almost tiptoeing. What . . . ?

'Travis, move out of the way,' Wayne said, his voice cold and imperious. Lilas froze.

'No!' Travis gritted back. 'Kier, get out now. Quick!'

'Don't move!' Wayne's voice rapped out harshly, but it held no confidence. Travis's body blocked that of Kier's, and he moved a pace to the right. Travis immediately followed suit. It took them all further from the door, and

Lilas, her breath locked in her throat, slowly pushed it open. Thankfully, everybody was too engrossed to notice.

Kier didn't move. 'I'm not leaving . . .'

'Go!' Travis hissed. 'He won't shoot me!'

'He won't shoot me, either,' Sebastien finally spoke for the first time. In the doorway, Lilas watched as Wayne's body seemed to jerk like a puppet whose strings had just been cut. He spun around, his incredulous eyes searching out the source of that voice he knew so well, his brain, which a moment before had been so crisp and clear, suddenly turning into a confused maze of emotion and confusion.

'Sebastien!' The name leapt from his mouth, even as he lowered his hand. Wayne stared at him, the shocked, confused blue eyes finally coming to rest in the two sherry pools of Sebastien's own eyes. Sebastien took a few steps towards him, taking him closer to the open French windows, and the small balcony beyond. 'Keep back!' Wayne said sharply, his voice high and unnatural, the gun levelling once more to point squarely at Sebastien's heart.

Lilas moved quickly into the room. She had no idea what tragedy was being played out here, but she knew a maniac was pointing a gun at Sebastien. And that was all she needed to know.

Sebastien never stopped in his slow, deliberate approach across the room, and Wayne retreated further back, out on to the concrete balcony.

Travis glanced over his shoulder at Kier, who had moved up behind him. Then, out of nowhere, a woman was in the room. A woman neither of them had ever seen before. She silently crept up behind Sebastien.

Kier grabbed Travis, who made an instinctive movement to stop her. Neither Sebastien nor Wayne noticed the newcomer. They were too intent on each other.

Before their very eyes, the tall, powerful figure of Wayne D'Arville seemed to crumble, as the gentle, humane man whose voice and eyes were as soft as that of a deer seemed to grow in size and stature.

'Take my hand, Wayne,' Sebastien said softly, reaching out to him. 'You know I'm the only one who can help you.'

Behind him, Lilas wanted to sob out loud. Even now, with his life in peril, he was trying to help the maniac! She crept closer, keeping her slight figure hidden from view behind Sebastien's own body. She was close enough now to touch him. She didn't have the faintest idea what she was going to do. She only knew, somehow, that she must save him.

'Sebastien!' Wayne said again, his voice a strangled plea as he shook his handsome head from side to side. 'Don't make me kill you. Please!'

Sebastien shook his head, a gentle smile on his face. 'It's time, Wayne,' he said softly. 'Time to let go of all the pain. I'll help you. I promise you.' Overhead, the balcony light illuminated the two men, locked in their own private world. 'You have to choose. Now, Wayne. Now. I won't wait for you any longer.'

'I *can't* . . .' Wayne screamed, the words torn out of him like thorns that had been buried in his flesh.

Sebastien slowly reached forward, his hand coming out to take the gun.

Travis felt Kier's hand digging hard into his shoulder. They both breathed a massive sigh of relief as the psychiatrist took the gun from Wayne's limp fingers and tossed it harmlessly back into the room. It nearly hit Lilas, who was standing so close behind him. She saw the gun land on the carpet, and nearly melted with relief. She started to straighten up from her crouch as Kier leaned over to pick the gun up.

The movement distracted Wayne. Seeing the American with the gun, a sudden image flashed through his mind — an image of a media circus, crucifying him, branding him the criminal son of a Nazi. Looking into Kier Harcourt's eyes, he saw a prison sentence, exile, disgrace. He snarled, his arm pushing against Sebastien's chest as he tried to launch himself across the room. But Sebastien was too quick. Without thinking, he grabbed Wayne's arm, the sudden jolt making him stagger back. Sebastien felt his legs hit the back of the balustrade, and he gave a brief cry. Wayne was swung around by the unexpected force of the backlash and felt himself begin to topple forward.

'No!' Wayne and Lilas screamed together. Lilas flung herself forward, and just managed to catch one of Sebastien's windmilling arms in a fierce grip. But the sudden movement, and Wayne's sheer size, worked against him.

Sebastien's eyes met his for just a second. He tightened his own hold on Wayne's arm, but already the huge Frenchman was falling over the balustrade. 'Wayne!' he screamed helplessly, as the man's weight dragged him nearer the edge.

Lilas hung on to Sebastien for dear life. She knew only one thing. If Sebastien was going over, then so was she.

Wayne's blue eyes widened on Sebastien's for just a moment. He knew Sebastien would not let him go. He also knew that, unless he did, Sebastien too would plummet to his death.

With a sudden yank, Wayne tore his grip loose and fell into the darkness below. The last thing he heard was Sebastien's agonized voice, screaming his name.

When Travis and Kier ran to the balcony and looked down, Wayne was sprawled across the rock garden like a broken doll.

On the balcony, Sebastien fell to his knees and stared at Lilas. He didn't know how she had come to be there. It seemed like a miracle. One moment he was about to die, the next she was holding on to him, her grip as strong and sure as her love.

He stared at her, speechless with gratitude. Then, as if drawn by a magnet, he glanced down at the body sprawled below. 'He let go of me,' Sebastien said shakily. 'He knew he was going to die — that we were both going to die and he . . . let go . . . He wasn't all bad, Lilas,' he said urgently, turning back to her, taking her cold, shaking hands in his own. His eyes beseeched her. He wanted to tell her how much he loved her. Needed her. He also wanted her to understand. About Wayne.

Lilas already understood. She held him tightly. 'No,' she agreed softly, looking down at the body below. 'He wasn't *all* bad.'

CHAPTER 44

One week later, Travis walked into the hospital and caught his mother throwing a pillow at Val.

'Ow!' Val hollered. 'That 'urt!'

'Baby!' Veronica poked her tongue out at him, then caught sight of her son. 'Travis! About time too. I was beginning to get a craving for more grapes.'

Travis laughed and put the bag of mixed fruit on the side of the table. Val promptly leaned across and nicked the grapes.

'Hey!' Veronica yelled.

Travis laughed again, and silently thought what a good thing it was that his parents were in a private room, far away from the other patients. Now that they were almost fully recovered, and tests had proved there was no brain damage to either of them, they were becoming a handful.

'Now behave,' Travis scolded. 'Dad, give Mum her grapes back.'

Val scowled. 'She hit me. With a blunt instrument.'

'He called me baldy!' Veronica retorted.

Indeed, Veronica still had little hair on her head — but then neither had Val. The fire had singed it so badly, the hospital staff had shaved both their heads for them. Now, though, Veronica's skull was covered with downy-soft dark tufts, and it would soon grow back into its usual raven-dark cap.

Travis was only relieved that they hadn't suffered any serious burns. Just a few to the hands; Val's in particular were still bandaged. He'd burnt them trying to open the windows — the steel had been red-hot.

He'd learned, over the past week, how Val had carried Veronica, unconscious, from the flames. And he couldn't have asked for a better tonic, after all he'd been through, than to find his parents back to their usual, squabbling, loving selves.

But he wouldn't dwell on the past. Nor would he think of Wayne D'Arville. He'd told Val and Veronica everything, of course, but since that first visit they had never mentioned it again.

Now he pulled a large, square envelope from his breast pocket, like a magician producing a rabbit from a hat.

'What yer got there?' Val asked, munching a grape with a hearty appetite.

'A wedding invitation,' Travis said. 'To Sebastien and Lilas's wedding.'

Veronica squealed in delight. 'Give it to me!' She scanned the details of the invitation and sighed. 'April in England. How wonderful. I'm looking forward to meeting this Lilas. She'd better be good enough for Sebastien! Val, you'll have to design me an outfit especially for the occasion.'

Val groaned around a grape. 'Slave driver.'

'And,' Travis pulled out another square envelope, 'we also have a second invitation. To Paris and Maria's wedding. Don't worry — it's not till June. We can make it to both.'

Veronica, her eyes sparkling, turned to Val.

Val tossed the bunch of grapes disgustedly her way, and she caught them neatly. 'I know, don't tell me,' he grumbled. 'You'll want *another* outfit for that do.'

'Well, it will be a big Hollywood society wedding,' Veronica said, selecting a juicy berry. 'And you know what they're like.'

Val groaned and ducked his head under the sheet. 'Wake me up next Christmas.'

Travis grinned at him, then reached across and took his mother's hand and squeezed it in sheer happiness.

Veronica looked at him steadily. 'So, how's Gemma?' she asked quietly.

Travis shrugged nonchalantly, looked at her as she rather comically raised one burned eyebrow high on her forehead, and laughed. 'She's fine.'

Veronica nodded and squeezed her son's hand. 'You like her, don't you?'

Travis grinned. 'Yep. And in a few years . . . who knows? You might even get an invite to *my* wedding.'

Val gave a disbelieving snort from beneath the sheet.

Travis grinned, leaned back against his mother's headboard and pinched one of her grapes.

THE END

ALSO BY FAITH MARTIN

DI HILLARY GREENE SERIES

JENNY STARLING MYSTERIES

MONICA NOBLE MYSTERIES

Thank you for reading this book.

If you enjoyed it please leave feedback on Amazon or Goodreads, and if there is anything we missed or you have a question about, then please get in touch. We appreciate you choosing our book.

Founded in 2014 in Shoreditch, London, we at Joffe Books pride ourselves on our history of innovative publishing. We were thrilled to be shortlisted for Independent Publisher of the Year at the British Book Awards.

www.joffebooks.com

We're very grateful to eagle-eyed readers who take the time to contact us. Please send any errors you find to corrections@joffebooks.com. We'll get them fixed ASAP.